Praise for *Miss Mac...*

M000215376

"A work of stunning magnitude and beauty. . . . The book's mysterious readability is effected through enchantment and hypnosis. Its force is cumulative; its method is amassment, as in the great styles of Joyce or Hermann Broch or Melville or Faulkner . . . one of the most arresting literary achievements in our last 20 years. . . . It is a masterwork."
—William Goyen, *New York Times Book Review*

"Marguerite Young is unquestionably a genius."—Kurt Vonnegut

"*Miss Macintosh, My Darling* stands out in my mind as the most significant innovative novel since *Ulysses* and *The Waves*. Marguerite Young has added epic grandeur to the philosophical novel. Every page gleams with the poetry of existence."—Nona Balakian

"An extraordinary book by a woman possessed of a breathtaking verbal virtuosity. . . . There are times when her pages surge and beat on the heart and imagination like great music; other times when it shimmers motionless like an ancient Hindu painting."
—Lillian Smith, *Chicago Times*

"Marguerite Young's eloquence has no parallel among the novelists of our time. It comes in rivers and whirlwinds and carries on its back, along with bits of unidentifiable matter, masses of rich and surprising life."—Mark Van Doren

"The most important work in American literature since Herman Melville's *Moby-Dick*. . . . The beauty of the book is final and imposing because it is simply there, like some awesome, heroic rock that will never know decay."—Howell Pearre, *Nashville Banner*

"A novel of massive achievement."—Jerzy Kosinski

"The key to the enjoyment of this amazing book is to abandon one's self to the detours, wanderings, elliptical and tangential journeys, accepting in return miraculous surprises. This is a search for reality through a maze of illusions and fantasy and dreams, ultimately asserting in the words of Calderon: 'Life is a dream.'"—Anaïs Nin

"A captivating book. . . . Here we have something more than just a bash at the Great American Novel. . . . What strikes one about Miss Young's wonderfully unboring book is its quietude, a kind of passionate calm, something oceanic."—Norman Shrapnel, *The Guardian*

"A brave and often beautifully written book. . . . A masterpiece, the Great American Novel at last."—*The Spectator*

"Its lyric beauty, its symbolic urgency, its symphonic structure . . . come miraculously to life. . . . An unusual and creative imagination."—Angus Wilson, *The Observer*

Books by Marguerite Young

POETRY
Prismatic Ground (1937)
Moderate Fable (1944)

NONFICTION
Angel in the Forest (1945)
Harp Song for a Radical: The Life & Times of Eugene Victor Debs (1999)

FICTION
Miss MacIntosh, My Darling (1965)

FICTION & CRITICISM
Inviting the Muses (1994)

Miss MacIntosh, My Darling

VOLUME ONE

Marguerite Young

DALKEY ARCHIVE PRESS

Copyright © 1965, 1993 by Marguerite Young
First Dalkey Archive edition, 1993
Second edition, 1999

Library of Congress Cataloging-in-Publication Data:

Young, Marguerite, 1909-95
        Miss MacIntosh, my darling / Marguerite Young
        I. Title.
PS3547-O49M5   1993
813'.52—dc20   92-12145
ISBN 1-56478-013-9 (vol. 1)
ISBN 1-56478-014-7 (vol. 2)

Partially funded by grants from the National Endowment for the Arts, a federal agency, and the
Illinois Arts Council, a state agency.

Dalkey Archive Press
Illinois State University
Campus Box 4241
Normal, IL 61790-4241

visit our website: www.dalkeyarchive.com

Printed on permanent/durable acid-free paper and bound in the United States of America.

For all dead loves and all remembered things.
I have travelled through many seas.

CHAPTER 1

THE bus-driver was whistling, perhaps in anticipation of his wife, who would be a woman with ample breasts, those of a realized maturity. It would be impossible that he did not have, from my point of view, a wife and children, indeed, a happiness such as I could not imagine to be real, even like some legend out of the golden ages. He had spoken numerous times during our journey of his old woman waiting, and he was going home.

As if he were a Jehovah's Witness or a member of some other peculiar religious sect, his bushy hair grew almost to his shoulders. A Witness would not perhaps drive a Grey Goose bus, even in this far country, this interior America, but his head was large, bulging, an old, archaic dome of curled sculpture, and his eyes shone with gleamings of intensified, personal vision. He drove, in fact, erratically, perhaps because of the heavy mist which all but blotted out the asphalt road, the limitation, and more than once, with the bus's sudden lurching, I had feared that we might veer off into a ditch, that himself and his three passengers would be killed, our dismembered heads rolling in a corn field of withered corn stalks. He had whistled with each new escape, had turned and smiled back over his shoulder with a kind of serene triumph, even when the bus had brushed against the sides of a lumbering moving van with furniture piled up almost to the low sky, an upright piano, a rocking chair, a clothes' horse, a woman's feathered hat bobbing at the top in the grey mist like some accompanying bird.

Was he, after all, a bachelor, perhaps even some mad Don Quixote chasing windmills, a virgin spirit, nobody—and his family life, an emanation of my over-active imagination, really, my desire for established human relationships? All along the way, he had been drinking from a whiskey bottle, quite openly, yet with many calls upon God, the angels, the archangels, angel Gabriel. All along the way, he had been singing, whistling, talking to himself, guessing what the old woman would say when she saw him, that she would certainly take his head off.

There were a sleeping couple, a pair of lovers, boy and girl, the only other passengers. They had gotten on at a dust-colored pottery town in the burning sunlight and, shading their eyes, had tried to sleep through langorous, creaking miles of a too familiar landscape.

The girl, thin and faded, perhaps prematurely old, was pregnant— yet resisted, as if it were a deformity, her situation of growth, there being nothing langorous in her appearance, nothing which should give itself up to nature. Her tiny face was covered with an artificial complexion like a mask too heavy, streaked with grey, and her colorless eyes had the cold and transparent look of being not satisfied, of being not filled with the light which comes from love. She was obviously dressed in what must have been her most wonderful finery, though her ensemble was an acci- dental confusion, a chaos to the eyes of the bewildered beholder, she being too tightly laced and that protuberance under her heart standing out as if it were a disease she wished to cover over with all these discur- sive details which should not focus attention, yet drew attention to her. There were rings on her fingers, cheap cameos of an enormous size and pieces of colored glass, many brass and wooden bracelets on her arms, a gold chain with a heart on her gauze-shrouded ankle, straw flowers piled upon the snub toes of her velvet slippers spiked with glass heels which should not carry her far, velvet butterflies like pansies hovering upon the moth-eaten fox fur collar of her green cloth coat which would not close and was too tight and did not cover her, coming only to her hips, and was of an old-fashioned style with pointed sleeves and pointed cuffs and scalloped edges and many velvet-covered buttons or marks where the buttons had been, small, tinkling bells moving when, in her sleep, she moved from side to side, yet not yielding to the powers of sleep which she resisted as if they were the powers of oblivion and of death, and cascades of oblong ten cent store pearls were dripping from her coral-colored ears, and her eyelids were painted with blue shadows, her eyebrows plucked to an invisible line, giving to her the look of a plucked and naked bird, and her lips were enlarged to an angular squareness by the purple lipstick she might have put on in a rigorous dream. She wore, among all her heavy rings, no wedding ring, and her hands were pale yellow taloned by long red nails, her fingers continually scratching the worn surface of an old- fashioned patent leather vanity case she carried in her lap. Her dress of sleazy silk was bright burned orange painted with black sail-boats sailing over purple trees and red football players playing over steeples and white skiers skiing over sail-boats cascading to the hem and locked acrobats, the entire field of outdoor sports, it seemed, being on her body, for her scarf was painted with spidery tennis players and tennis nets and ice- skaters skating on silver ponds and red polo riders riding red horses, and there were little footballs hanging from her charm bracelets, tennis rack- ets and ice-skates and golf clubs and numerous other trophies, some of field and stream, satin fishes running around the hem of her chiffon petticoat edged with yellow lace, butterflies embroidered upon the knees of her thin silk stockings, and her skirts came up high above her knees, higher when she moved, showing her yellow satin garters and pairs of stuffed red valentine hearts dangling from ribbons and faces which were painted powder puffs, and the coat seemed shrunken or a size too small like something she might have worn in a remote youth. Her head was big on a narrow stem, her bleached yellow hair spirally built upward to a skein crowned with a spangled net and a hat which was a woven nest of dark and dusty funeral blossoms and ivory twigs with a pink enameled branch on which was perched, precariously at that high altitude in the cold air current, one stuffed yellow canary with a moth-eaten wing, a glassy eye.

Her stiff hand jogged in the aisle, a transparency through which one saw the knotted veins. She slept, narrow and turreted head stiff, upright, her eyes suddenly opening, seeming like insect eyes of many-faceted but cruel vision, her avid mouth in that small face opening to complain, with sudden rushes of metallic speech or with wild and hollow whispers, against her neighbors, against her mother, her father, the other girl, the way she had been caught, the growth of another life inside of her, this dark valley from which she might never return.

The boy seemed, by contrast, all blissful stolidity and broad-faced innocence, his chestnut-colored hair tousled like a pony's on his low forehead, his skin burned to a dark, brick-colored red as by some immensely blowing heat not of the sunlight. He wore a faded football sweater, the letter C across its front, red-stained, rain-washed dungarees, moccasins embroidered with white beads. Sleeping the miles away, his cheek against the cold bus-window, his long-lashed eyelids closed, never opened, his lips placidly smiling.

Now as the bus-driver whistled, imitating the calls of birds to their mates, the bluebird's trill, the woodpecker's pecking, the murmur of quail, a baby's cry he had heard in the winter grass, the bright redness of the sky's reflection on the glazed bus-window was disappearing, and with that redness, the distinct, dismal lurching of old Coca-Cola and aspirin signboards, tattered as tramps, which had accompanied our journey to the depths of southern Indiana, a state as yet unknown to me. The sky was drained and bloodless above the darkness of ethereal fields as if it had suffered, in one slow moment, the ultimate transfusion, as if the veins were shriveled to nothingness. There was hardly a drop of red where lately the red had swarmed and buzzed like thousands of wild honey bees. It was spring, but it might have been winter still, another planet, the face of the dead moon. The earth was bare and cold and the thorn trees without flower. The bus-windows had turned to a cold, steaming greyness as if only the ghost of the world were crying outside, as if the known world of familiar associations had disappeared, and that which remained must seem but the conspiracy of memories and dreams floating without purpose, without limitation.

We had passed, on this journey, many curious pieces of rural architecture, an enormous coffee urn with its lid opened against the sky, a wigwam nightclub where, under a denuded oak, a melancholy buffalo was tethered, incongruous as the faded washing on the line. We had passed a windmill, a leaning tower, Noah's Ark, the old woman who lived in the shoe, but these were miles back, and there were now no buildings but those of the amorphous distance, little, low-roofed houses, small as ruined birds' nests, a child's face at some near window, the individuality blotted out by the watery greyness of the Middle West, the train as small as a toy train crossing a toy bridge.

There was an endless greyness engulfing the bus which moaned, the road before us no longer seeming to bisect space, the low, shaven fields, both low and whitish, the cattle humps of vague, distant, treeless, mole-colored hills. The scene was increasingly enlarged like that which might have been the first creation when only the spirit of God had moved upon the deep. It was the face of the ambiguous waters, of no boundary line, no shore. The scene, in fact, to one who was accustomed to a great body of water, was oceanic, dotted by pale pools in the vapors of mist, and I should not have been surprised to see, drifting over these empty, unmarked meadows of the first creation, something of the last, a cloud of pearl-breasted seagulls, all crying with angelic voices, or moored at some far, receding horizon, a lost ship which would never reach port. We had passed, far back on the road, the last harbor, a lighthouse, a shipwreck. Frozen lights appeared now like flares of crystal warning in the mist-shrouded, dark plain as if all the houses from which they emitted were travelling with us into an unknown distance from which no man returns alive. Far away, like smoke, there were plumed trees drifting, bent by the actions of no winds, and no stars were visible. In the beam of our an-archic head lights which barely cut through mist and darkness, there stood, by the side of the road, a tall man with a child perched on his lean shoulders, a double-headed man, staring at nothingness or beyond it. We were the intruders upon this plain of silence, and he shook his fist, listlessly, perhaps figuring the danger of walking on this road which now, suddenly turning, seemed to go back the way it had gone before. There was now no landscape.

There was now no landscape but the soul's, and that is the inexactitude, the ever shifting and the distant. I would never know the man's name, the organization of this fleeting image, what were his hopes, what were his disappointments. Yet he would remain forever engraved on memory's whirling disc, that double-headed shape in curdled mist, as tantalizing as my ignorance of life. All my life I had been reaching for the tangible, and it had evaded me, much like the myth of Tantalus, much as if the tangible itself were an illusion. My life had been made up of just these disrelated, delusive images hovering only for a moment at the margin of consciousness, then passing like ships in the night, even ships manned by dead helmsmen, by ghostly crews, by one's own soul at large.

What was the organization of illusion, of memory? Who knew even his own divided heart? Who knew all hearts as his own? Among beings strange to each other, those divided by the long roarings of time, of space, those who have never met or, when they meet, have not recognized as their own the other heart and that heart's weaknesses, have turned stonily away, would there not be, in the vision of some omniscient eye, a web of spidery logic establishing the most secret relationships, deep calling to deep, illuminations of the eternal darkness, recognitions in the night world of voyager dreams, all barriers dissolving, all souls as one and united? Every heart is the other heart. Every soul is the other soul. Every face is the other face. The individual is the one illusion.

I had walked alone, searching, seeing only, though I sought for an ultimate harmony, the fleeting image, the disrelation, the chaos begetting the chaos, the truth as but another illusion, that which must perish, the rose which must fade, the heart which must stop. Nothing I had touched but that it had faded like a dream, there being no dream that would not fail, no life which would not cease, no soul which answered mine like deep calling to deep. I had walked alone, the seeker through mazes of sorrow, and none had answered me. That background of illusion from which I always fled like a drowning man who clutches at a straw, it was always that background of illusion confronting me again, even as the foreground, and there seemed no truth but what the erroneous mind provided, another dream which had nor purpose nor bearing. There were always the dead seagulls in the whirlwind, the brown leaves falling, an empty, resonant house of broken mirrors reflecting the light of the sea, my mother dead among her dreams, many others dead with her who had dreamed her life away and who still might be dreaming, for death might still be her life, and she had been already so much a part of the ethereal and of the abstract, of the things intangible, of the things unknown. I had peered into all faces, seeing none, only those who were already gone, only those who could not answer. My illness had been great, dead souls like the autumn leaves stirring where I walked, and could I have believed in that ultimate harmony, I could have been among them, but there had been only, in my narrow experience, the dream of chaos repeating chaos, so what I looked for always in the streets of those great harbor cities, was it not merely another illusion, that of the peace which should not be realized in heaven or on earth? Where should I go? Where should I turn? I had been too long half sleeping, cut off from communication with others, asking no more reasonable questions than a patient asks under the ether mask which seems like a train riding among the trackless stars or where there are no stars, no signposts any longer, and no one has ever seen the other person. All the other passengers, Negroes with white roosters crowing in their laps, beings unseen, merely sensed, each with his own dark and private heart, the darkness everlasting, their questions like my own, and no answer heard, for God is the loneliest of all, and there is perhaps no God but what we dreamed, and there is no train.

Long nights, searching for one who was dead, I, Vera Cartwheel, I, the imploring daughter of a mother under the sway of opium, a mother more beautiful than angels of light, I, Vera Cartwheel, had wandered through the streets of great, mysterious harbor cities, those which, at night, seemed all like each other, there where were the spectral faces appearing like foam, disappearing, faces as lost as mine, voices crying under water, seaweed locked in the hair of the drowned swimmer. I had slept in shelters for lost souls, those no one should miss, searching for one who was lost, forever outside, alone, the one person not dreaming and yet who had seemed, with the passage of years since her disappearance from my life, the central heart, the heart of all hearts, the face of all faces, the dead steersman, Miss MacIntosh, my darling, an old, red-headed nursemaid with her face uplifted toward the watery sky. I had walked through the desolate waterfront streets of those dark and intricate harbor cities, the neighborhoods of warehouses casting their shadows, shelters for old sailors, for lost souls, darkened lighthouses, had turned down the unlighted alleys where the starved cats prowl among refuse, gleaming fish, the drunken mariner lurches, the prostitute screams, had looked into every muffled doorway, under every dimmed, leering lamp, had searched for her among faceless old beggar women huddled in empty parks, the ragged men who sleep on fly-specked sidewalks, their mouths foaming with homeless dreams, had searched for her in old-fashioned saloons and bowling alleys and billiard parlors and under the falling leaves, had walked in whirling crowds that I might find her, had stopped at all corners where street preachers preached of the golden tides of the future world and harvests of dragons' teeth and reaping the whirlwind, had gone to baseball games in those packed stadiums, watching the pitchers pitch the moons, the suns, the stars, had visited a planetarium and an aquarium and a museum, had drifted with no purpose but this, had followed everywhere, searching for her, one so clear, thinking that, some day, just when I lost my way in the absolute darkness or crossed a traffic-roaring avenue of obliterating head lights, screeching whistles, screaming stars, I should surely find her, Miss MacIntosh, my darling, only a step beyond, her whaler's hat dripping with water, her plaid, faded waterproof flapping in the wind, her bent black umbrella uplifted like some enormous, dark, scudding bird against the clouded sky, the always overcast.

Long years, drifting without other purpose, I had searched for that hale companion of my lost childhood, no one but a fusty, busty old nursemaid, very simple-minded, very simple, the salt of common sense, her red hair gleaming to show that quick temper she always had, that impatience with which she would dismiss all shades and phantoms, even herself should she become one, for self-pity was not her meat, not her drink. Long years, my heart a dry, imploring emptiness, my eyes fixed on that one steady purpose, I had drifted from employment to employment, from hotel to hotel, searching relentlessly and everywhere for that old, plain darling who was lost, she who had cherished no illusions of noble grandeur, she who had rejected an aura, a crown of gold, she whose daily life had been unpresuming and hard, one not beloved then so much as now in memory, the dead steersman, her whaler's hat dripping with water, her boundless face concealed by fog and wind, her heart the weakness of all hearts, the strength. Where should I not find her again? Where should I ever find her? The years of her death had added to her stature, making her seem almost vague.

That she had only disappeared, I had always said, for hers had been the face of every face, the heart of every heart, and she had been the truest person ever I had seen, no one but a poor old nursemaid walking along the seashore, taking her constitutional, the salt crystals bearding her cheeks and her pointed chin, nothing amazing her, no phantom accompanying her in her morning or evening walks. She had no prince charming, and she was a spinster, married not even to the dream. We were always alone. We would sit under the storm lamp in the evening, an old nursemaid and a child playing at dominoes, two sentient beings alone in that great house of shades and monsters, my mother's citadel of dreams and visions and imaginary pretenders to vanished thrones, there where my mother dreamed, when the sea blew high, that fifty wild white horses had been struck dead by lightning in a ruined garden or that persons long drowned had walked out of the sea, their locks dripping. There was no one, however, and nothing had happened, Miss MacIntosh used to say, her knitting needles of ivory bone clicking like her false teeth, that no one must dream of what was not, of what would never be, that surely when I grew up, I must leave this realm of shades, this old New England house with its privileges of the past, those things which had been inherited, those which had been stolen from the dead, that I must strike out on my own, that I must lead a useful life and see America first, the broad interior, the spacious Middle West, that life which required no medium of the evil imagination to stand between one's self and the clear reality of simple things, for reality was very good and could be found by those who lived, could be seen even with the naked eye. Common sense is the finest sense, she had always said, that the soul should not dream of those things far distant and not to be realized, for the way was very plain, quite direct. It was a granite road and not the sea road taken by the ships falling beyond a far horizon. But when no longer under the dimmed storm lamp in the long evenings we played at dominoes or Chinese puzzles, Miss MacIntosh and I, two living beings alone in that great, enchanted house which knew no time, when I was left alone, screaming and wild, then I had dreamed of her, my red-cheeked darling, for there had been no one else so true, so good, and, even in her unkindness, so kind.

Who now would recognize that background of illusion from which I had fled, so many years ago, seeking for her in all those places where she was not, where she might never be—that background from which I still was fleeing? After her disappearance or death, the sudden, terrible shock of that great loss which had divided my heart against my heart, there had been no one to turn to, no other sentient being of stable consciousness, and my mother, believing herself dead, that she had died long ago, had tried to kill me in order that I should be free of the influence of reality, had offered to me that poisonous compromise, my death pulsing rosily in the midst of my life, the world of dreams which would kill the dreamer and leave only the dream, the memories floating without purpose. Long ago, however, and by great effort, I had escaped my mother's darkened and secluded house that I might find the life which needed no dream of death, that life Miss MacIntosh had spoken of in no uncertain terms, and I had wandered from darkened harbor to darkened harbor and from employment to employment, always with one clear purpose in mind, the search for a lost companion who was, for all I knew, already dead, swept up upon the other shore. I had lived in ducal suites, in tenements like rabbit warrens—wearing my rags, had slept in fine hotels in the beds of dead emperors and false princes and banished dukes—wearing my regal jewels and ermine cape and long white gown, had slept in the beds of the poor, even where the subway roared, for I had been indifferent to my environment, and I had not always remembered where I was, and I had known no one. I had drifted from place to place, holding such little jobs as I could concentrate on and yet continue my dreams, beginning to study architecture, then giving it up because I could not plan a house if there was one soul which could not live in it, and finally, having tried all else, had been a poor fumbling typist in an insurance agency, typing mortality rates through a blur of tears, the frequency or numbers of deaths in ratio to population, age, sex, color, employment, position in life.

No longer searching for her, the dead steersman, no longer dreaming, I was following now, at last, her advice, for I had come to this far place. No longer, by some momentary quiver of the dreaming eyelid, should I find reality itself the banished, that surface phantoms had displaced it, that the world had fled, that this was only its ghost blowing at the bus-window.

What motive in this quest but the search for life, for love, for truth that does not fail? I had come because of my own heart's need for an answer. I had come because of the searchings of other souls, the dead, the lost, because of a chance remark overheard on the city streets, because of the encompassing darkness, because of my mind which had been filled with nothing but the imaginary speakers, the endless dialogues of self with self, because I must find my way from the darkness to the ultimate light. I had come because of a dead girl's love letters scattered on the floor of her empty bedroom, the palm leaves crossed above the marble mantel piece, her rosary hanging on a brass bedpost, because of her suicide, because of a deaf musician, because of a drunkard's celestial dream of childhood, because of the answers not heard, because of a blind man's groping for his coffee cup at an all-night quick-lunch stand on the fog-shrouded waterfront of that great harbor city as he had asked of his companion—When shall the light, Peter, enter my soul? His eyes had been withered in their sockets—the bare light bulb glaring only three livid inches away from those burned-out hollows as he had groped for a thick white coffee cup, asking his plaintive, remorseless question—When shall the light, Peter, enter my soul again? Should he never again be as he had been in the old days, the world's greatest juggler, performing for the Lord's sake and glory, keeping six coffee cups mid-air simultaneously as he skipped a rope or rode on a bicycle, a sleight-of-hand artist who could pluck the playing cards off any man's sleeve, produce a rabbit out of any man's hat, make the invisible world visible as if an angel should be revealed?

Now as the bus groaned, each mile more laggard, the world stretching out to an unseen horizon, the world flat, I heard once more his question like my own—when shall the light enter my soul—and when should the deprivation cease, and when should the body be restored, and when should the heart beat again? Travel-stained, my cheek against the cold bus-window, my head roaring with the memory of space, how should I ever know the land I passed through, the deep calling to the deep, the answer, for I was cut off, alone, seeing the fleeting image, the fragment beyond realization, the memory? I had come by many means of passage, by train and plane, by evening comet plane, that from where one could see the earth's abstract curvature in space, the dark mantle, the snowy dome lighted by starlight, no human faces, by the morning star from where one saw the dreaming roof-tops, by day train which had jogged among steep hills of slag and burning eyes and coal-mining villages of bare-ribbed skeleton houses with their doors opened to the wind, the dust-colored rain, people blackened by coal dust, sweat, and sorrow, those who had gone down into the womb of mother earth, and now by this erratic bus which, plowing nowhere, suggested no landscape but the clouds, flight of angels drifting past the misted windows, no goal but something outside of time, some world more true than any that had been known, the beauty which would not be an aspect of the lie, the flesh and blood as organized, as complete, the hair, the lips, the eyes, the body organized, the human heart still beating.

And my search for this life was because of one already dead, she who had passed beyond, she who had been the moral guide, the unswerving, the true, her heart as stout as hickory or oak, her mind so sensible that she could not be deceived by any illusion or enchantment, she who was forever alone, outside, not taken in by all the sycophant luxuries of that opium paradise, a poor servant with patches on her best black cotton gloves, a fishnet reticule and rimless eye-glasses and no make-up, not even a touch of lip rouge, her face its natural color, her old black canvas umbrella lifted against the rain or sunlight as she had used to walk along the seashore, preferring that marginal estate to my mother's house where, though the roarings of the surf like the roarings of lions should fill it, the sea itself was but another dream and far away as if it were intangible. The great, sea-blackened house with golden spires and cornices and towers peeled by the salt air, dark allees, hidden interiors, the empty drawing rooms where the hostess had not set foot for many years, as many drawing rooms as tideless years, the rooms too many for mortal use, chambers within chambers, the gilded, mirroring ballrooms where no one danced, the hangings of scaly gold and rain-stained velvet, the heathen monsters everywhere, the painted, clouded ceilings illuminated by partial apparitions of the gods, the silken, padded walls, the ropes of rusted bells, the angels and the cherubim and the immortal rose, the dream of heaven, the lily-breasted virgins sporting in fields of asphodel, the water-gurgling gargoyles or those coated by dust, the interior and exterior fountains, the broken marble statues in ruined gardens sloping towards the sea, the disc throwers, the fat cupids, the thin psyches with flowing curls, the mute Apollo Belvedere, the king's horsemen, the life-sized chessmen seeming to move against the moving clouds that moved above the moving waters, the sea light lighting their wooden eyes, the seagulls perched like drifts of snow upon their heads.

What could Miss MacIntosh, a simple woman with a broken nose, find to admire in any broken marble statue, that which had been sculptured by man dreaming that he was other than he was or that he was man? Her religion was truth to nature, nothing else, as she would always say with a severity of good humor inviting no argument, no sad or meandering response. She disapproved quite heartily and firmly of all these unholy influences, these self-aggrandizements at the expense of common life which was the merest flesh and blood, her whole sensorium being repelled by the very dream of imagination which rejects reality, which flees from its bare face, for was she not sensible, the last person who would ever be taken in by what existed nowhere but in the dreaming mind, a plain, old-fashioned nursemaid, a red-headed and practical Middle Westerner, stoutly girded by her whale-boned corset, plainly clothed, visible to all, one who had kept her head above the waters in Chicago and elsewhere, one who had rejected an aura which should distinguish her from others, one who, with her way clearly set and her heart not foolish, would submit to no luxurious temptation of this old crazy house on a desolate stretch of the primitive New England coast, there where, though all the ghosts of the universe wandered, shrieking like winds, like tides, like daft sea birds, she had seen nothing but what was plain, the desolation which was enough for her?

CHAPTER 2

⋊⋉

My MOTHER was oblivious to the realities of flesh and blood, those creatures of chance, apparently even to Miss MacIntosh, loud-mouthed though she was, unimaginative, no possible rival in the world of invisible dreams, the prosaic, fusty, busty old nursemaid with reddening cheeks, her red, marcelled hair gleaming like the sand streaked with sunset when the sandpipers wade in the glassy surf as the last light fades, her footsteps always certain, the last person who would ever disappear, the moral guide to the pale, rejected child whose eyes had not craved reality. My mother trusted no one, nor was she ever to be surprised, it seemed, by unusual transformations or transports, shiftings of form, by anything that might ever transpire, by anything protean, for the opium dreams surrounding her had provided no pillars of strength, no rose which did not eventually fade, no voice which did not fail. She presumed always that things were not what they seemed, that all forms must change their shapes, that all characters must bear, even to those most familiar with them, an element of cold surprise, even of horror, that her life was this play of illusion, that there should be nothing certain but uncertainty, no pavement more secure than the glassy surface of the evening tide and the far wash of waves. All her days were her nights, and all her nights were her days, and there was an eternal twilight, an obfuscation of faces, a crucial bewilderment. If servants were known as she was known, would not their lives appear more monstrous than hers and terribly extra-human? So she would ask, talking half in her enchanted sleep, often when there was no one present but the dream of who was not.

Heavily laden with jewels as a Greek corpse, my mother, she who had retired from the brutal world, whose eyes were shielded against the vulgar sunlight, slept for tideless years which were her vast excitement, surrounding herself with a world of dreams, visions, phantoms, her bedroom as filled with visitors as the Grand Central Station, some from the shores of Hades, voices of the dead, faded movie stars of the silent flicker films, imaginary telephone operators plugging in at imaginary switchboards, spirits like long-nosed bird dogs, drowned pearl-divers, old kings, old queens, figures older than Oedipus or Troy, New England spinsters with faces checkered like chessboards, jockeys riding the skeletons of dead horses, angelic birds. Her sleep was a form of watchful, wide-eyed wakefulness. Her wakefulness was a form of sleep. Nothing would have amazed her so much as nothing, the complete deprivation, the absence of being, for that was something, too, and always present in her eyes, as familiar to her as human frailty. She hovered for years between life and suspended death, enjoying both, her eyes refulgently shining, her eyes opened at times when she profoundly slept, one cheek always toward the shadow, her dark hair arranged in such a way that this cheek was always concealed. It was because of this shadowed cheek that she had gone to bed in the first place, so many years ago, because of a blemish, a stain, a birthmark which was invisible to others and which, besides, was always covered with fine white rice powder, shadowed even then, she standing in only that position where, when her guests came, or even when they were absent, the shadow fell. Now she was always apparently in the bloom of some strange extension of health, though she was yet the eternal invalid, the horizontal person, one whose heart, as she believed, was not centralized but scattered through every nerve cell, shining like sourceless starlight. Lying still in a sumptuous bed carved with faceless dolphins and cherubim and kingly faces and heraldic devices, a box of sweets always within her reach, numberless pearls running through her ivory-colored fingers, a white satin coverlet covering her to the waist, her shoulders swathed in gauze and velvet and delicate cascades of ancient lace, she believed that she had died in her youth and was yet alive, that there were two selves, the dead, the living, that though she lay still, this beautiful corpse or effigy upon a marble sarcophagus, this was the living being, this with the bright, luminous eyes, the distracting visions, the endless stream of imaginary company, of fawns crowned with flowers, men who were birds, women whose heads were turrets, that the one who was dead was walking, walking by the sea, or riding a white horse through endless surf.

Thus she was peaceful. She had been frothing at the mouth once in her lunar hysteria, at least had been in great danger of losing her mind, but her madness had been averted through this means of slumberous life, had been regulated by the needle pits in her arm, the opium dosages, the sedatives, the dreams which went almost according to schedule, a moment extended, revolving like another planet, the enormity of space, and one familiar with her routines could almost have predicted, moment to moment, as by the readings of the barometer, the flickerings of the stars, her ghostly visitors, the lost constellations, the dead queens, the dead kings, the seasons, the years, the vanished tides, the life-sized chessmen moving in the garden, two sister ravens who had created the universe, the dead creation. She was ever the unchanging, changing only her mind, her body remaining always the same, that of the beautiful corpse who had peopled a void, she seeming hypothetical herself even to those one or two who knew her best, she seeming abstract, out of this world, surrounded by conscious cherubim, ethereal, drifting above the clouds, her eyes shining with tender or brilliant dreams, her dark hair as black as midnight, her neck and shoulders gleaming with snow-white satins and laces and the shadows of sable plumes, the velvet counterpane strewn over with white flowers as if it had been the coffin lid, the curious bed carved with fantastic figures seeming mobile, lutes, angels, arabesques, her face shadowed, powdered to conceal the invisible blemish, her life so seductive in its enchanted suspension that there were many who had not questioned her choice, who had only envied it, that extension of existence in isolation from the brutal facts, that death breathing in the midst of heightened sensitivity, her atmosphere of thought, her bedroom crowded with distinguished callers, some with golden feathers, some with crowns, some who had walked out of their graves. She was always radiant, charmed to greet each shade, for her dreams needed carry no credentials other than that they were her dreams, and her questions were ambivalently answered.

Why, as that birthmark was invisible, had she gone to bed in the first place, she who had been the most vivid of hostesses, even when there was no one, she who had been a rider with the hunt, even when there was no fox? Her own answers were many, varying with her stormy moods, her dazzling whims. She had gone to bed because of the invisible birthmark, the stain on her left cheek, because of the coldness of the snow, because of the wealth of her inheritance, that great wealth of burnished jewels and watery estates which had burdened her and made her different from others, because of the advice of tender, abstruse physicians who had foreseen, perhaps mistakenly, that if she walked, she would lose her mind, be mad like the others, because all those she loved had abandoned her and left her to the ravens in deserts, because of her social humiliations in Boston, because she had been refused admission to a fine hotel. She had gone to bed because her husband, a professional ne'er-do-well, a sportsman who had sported everywhere but in his bed, had left her with the unwanted child born of their fugitive marriage, with the immense sense of a meaningless woe expressed by flesh and blood, because he had abandoned her, leaving her unprotected and alone, the prey to strangers. She had married, as she sometimes recalled, the poorest man she knew, one she had hardly known but whose intense pity for the poor and whose desire to level the rich she had so greatly admired, little dreaming that he would become, in a single night, the richest man she knew, that he would emerge as only another of the international nightclub play boys, an irresponsible character running up long distance telephone calls to various ladies, those he never visited, keeping great kennels of dogs he never saw, polo ponies he never rode, yachts he never travelled in, sail-boats he could not rig, both tall ketches and long-winged sloops, a man whose great and only pleasure was to walk in a high wind on a waxed rope between two peaks above the Alpine clouds or where those diffused bodies of visible vapors floated against his face, blinding his eyes, a man whose dream had been always of the heights, the depths, the shifting shapes, who had already tried to scale her immaterial heights and had lost footing. Scaling the Jungfrau or Matterhorn, one of those perilous peaks, for she was always nebulous as to which, it making little difference to her, he had fallen head first, disappearing under a bank of snow and granite, and was never found, not even by the thrifty Swiss, but if he had been found, would have been still the uncorrupted dandy, preserved like herself in some fairy grotto of rock crystal chandeliers and musical stalactites, and had been wearing a white rose on his coat lapel when last seen, so should be easily recognized, and had always carried his cane, his calling card. Sometimes she thought he had disappeared in a spring snowslide in the Dolomites, a roof-top of snow falling, palpable as veil clouds, softer than cherry blossoms upon his head. She was sufficiently vague. He had been only her ex-husband, moreover, for she had already separated from him and paid him a fortune to go as far away as he could, to disappear, never to return again with her other callers. She had gone to bed for no reason at all, only that she had found the so-called real world unsatisfactory, that life had failed her, that her sensations had been numbed, that she had missed the contiguous impressions which might have been hers, that she had always been confined. Her body had failed her.

Her own mind had been all that was left to provide for her a better world, cities, mountains, dead faces, vague, clouded longings, and she could not tell where the divide was between what was real and what was unreal, for the unreal things were real to her, an exile on this subjective star, and the real were unreal. The dreams begot the only realities, and the dreams had begotten her, and she was their creation. She had not created the dreams, for they had created her, making her all she was and more than even she could realize. The opium enchantment was bountiful, expanding her soul to a far, enlarged horizon, making the impossible not only possible but plausible in her bright eyes which saw too much or yet too little. There had been, to keep her alive and everlastingly fascinated, her own irrational soul dilated and at large, as she realized, its wandering, illusive magnificence, its many shapes and forms, the lives of the inanimate objects to whom she endowed her speculative consciousness, the harps, the golden chairs, the plates of gold, the frozen chandeliers, the bellropes, the candle flames reflected in dark mirrors, the things enlarged out of proportion or reduced to infinitesimal size, the ghostly golf courses, the vague tennis courts, the plop-plopping of balls, the beclouded archery range and the magnified chessmen, all the empty, echoing, shadow-shrouded rooms, all her surroundings being nothing but the externalizations of her dreams, memories, impressions, floating and fragmentary, all the furnitures of earth and choirs of obsessed angels being also only an idea in the mind of God, and God was dead or sleeping as she was. Everything for her, the animated, bejeweled corpse, was complete, even the incompletion, the sense of palpable loss. She turned her face away from what she could not admit. She saw only what she wanted to see.

Then, according to one or two who knew her, she had gone to bed to escape from the domination of her father who had died before her marriage and who had been a wealthy manufacturer upon a mass scale, fabulously successful, a self-made man outdistancing all his disorganized rivals, his factories having been conducted like clockwork, wheels within wheels, and who had also been a man of severe personal disciplines, of orthodox faith of his own manufacture, himself controlled by the most fantastic rituals each hour of day or night, his house being conducted like a church although perhaps he was its only member, and a place set at his table for the wanderer angel, a salt shaker, a crystal goblet, a plate of gold, a spoon, a knife, an oyster fork, a napkin, a napkin ring, and he would turn no beggar away from his door for fear it might be an angel in disguise. He was always looking for an angel who had come from Tarsus or some far place. She had denied her father's domination, even Our Heavenly Father Who, perhaps a greater manufacturer than her father, had set the stars in motion and had divided the waters from the earth and had created great whales, but the table was still laid for the dead, and there were the empty chairs, the twelve goblets for the twelve hours in their places, the dull silver shining, white roses at the centerpiece. She was the agnostic, but the angels surrounded her in her opium paradise, their fleecy wings outspreading, shadowing her cheek, and the harpers harped, and the seas were turned to glass. She was ever the luminous, a mind which could leave the body.

She would imagine, in some slow moment of awakening, that the chandelier was Mr. Chandelier, her companion, not always faithful. There was also Mr. Res Tacamah, the drug bottle with ears to hear her ravings, her commands. She would imagine herself as living not at the edge of the sea but at the edge of the desert, that a bearded burro was her saintly companion, that there were chameleons crawling on her bed, her gold and ivory empire dressing table with its shadowed mirror, all the colors of an absent rainbow which was ever in her own mind. She would imagine that the house was crowded with the most amazing callers, their calling cards dropping from the ceiling, that the spacious rooms echoed with the voices of the dead and not with the sea, that she was surrounded by proud Bostonians, Platonists of the period of the intellectual flowering of Athens, drowned sailors, gold-turbaned Egyptians, centaurs with lilies in their mouths, cherubim spouting fountains, great frogs with jewels in their foreheads, men who had walked out of their watery graves, some who were living in another country. The air was filled with the strangest music. No one else could hear it.

She did not always realize her lack of communication with others, the living, their depths, for it was the ghost of love she loved the most, and that was always present. There was never an empty moment—or if so, never an acknowledged one. Phantoms buzzing around her like wild honey bees, like bottle flies, like gnats, pearl-divers diving above her swollen head, bubbles of light emitting from their mouths, the void filled with disoriented stars, leaden bells, golden echoes, acoustic errors, reverberations without cause or source, angelic intuitions. There were twelve grand pianos in the house, and no one ever played them.

She was downright rude at times, in fact, to her one faithful caller in the world of the sentient living, he whose presence could always be relied on, punctual as the evanescent evening light, the paste-colored, flabby Mr. Spitzer whom she had known since her girlhood but whom she addressed formally by his last name as if he still occupied, in her mind, the status of a dubious stranger. He bored her almost to extinction, for he was less illuminated, more dense than the angels, even as he knew. Though he had not been well for years, though the responsibility had been almost too great for him, though he had barely kept his secret life, he had been more faithful than she realized or cared to acknowledge. It was a long, puffing walk for him, but he came in the evenings down the ribboned sea road for that unwelcomed visit which his own sense of honor or habit had imposed, the feeling that he was her guardian. This feeling, she openly resented, saying that no one had asked him to come. What else, however, could he have done, he being, as he hoped, the man he was? He did not believe in Fate but in self-determination—yet Fate had assigned this peculiar role to him, and he could not resist it. He came alone each evening, walking a long way, exercising himself beyond his physical means, accompanied only by his shadow, that of his high silk hat, his cape, his cane, and punctually, as if he were welcome or had been expected, presented himself in her shrouded bedroom, always unaccompanied, so far as he could see, by anybody else. With him, however, she sometimes counted in, much to his interstellar confusion and possibly to hers, the spirit of his dead twin brother who had departed this mortal life so many years ago, it must have been shortly before her retirement to the bed of her heavenly dreams, a bed she imagined as a swan boat wafted by soft, perfumed winds. She would always say, of course, that it was only after the brother's untimely death that she had retired from the possible world to the impossible—would not admit, though there were many arguments to prove otherwise, that it was before, that she had already made her choice, or that her choice had chosen her.

Mr. Spitzer was patient, having known her in her earlier years, that she had never changed, that she had been constantly inconstant, having known her perhaps longer than she had known him and having always loved her in his hopeless way, as she would sometimes remind him, that his love had not been returned, that it had bored her to the last degree of extinction or beyond it. As for himself, he was a semi-retired lawyer, one who had seemed to have, in his own sad youth, great promise of a brilliant legal career which, however, only for a short period had seemed to hover upon the margin of realization, having faded like his imagination, his gifts of ethereal musical composition, so many other things, for truly, his life had been broken by his brother's sudden and unexpected death, and he had thus practiced law in only the most desultory fashion, often without fee, preferring the lost causes, and he had written only silent music, that which, for many years now, no one else had ever heard. His stupidity was now become, in fact, his only unusual gift, almost sublime, having increased with the years like his waistline, his paunchiness, his conflicted, clouded factual-mindedness. He was almost safely familiar with the lucid ravings of the charming invalid. He was not easily thrown off his guard. He could not be easily persuaded, he believed, even by the intoxicating, contagious madness of an angelic, lawless woman he had always compassionately, profoundly loved, one for whom he would have sacrificed his life, his being, his own best interests, having loved her just as much as his dead brother had hated her, scorning impatiently her love, not returning it, even making light of it in a most high-handed manner, even saying she had only pretended to be insane. Perhaps Mr. Spitzer loved her even more than his brother had hated her. His brother had been insolent, a gambler, a spender of borrowed money, a quick suicide, a four-flusher with a quick come-back, a ready apology or the banal dismissal of the need for apology, very different from cautious Mr. Spitzer who claimed never to have placed a bet on even that which he had been most certain of. His brother had been worldly, but Mr. Spitzer had always been, if he might sometimes say so, unworldly and abstruse.

Though she tormented Mr. Spitzer endlessly, sometimes implying that he did not exist, it was perhaps because, after all, in spite of the fact that she could be committed to no one, her imagination floating through unknown amplitudes, she had become grudgingly fond of him, this one faithful caller, he at least providing her a rare amusement. She was always making light of his seriousness, his offended, defenseless moods, his permanently aggrieved air. She was always seeking to confuse and confound him, to throw him off his mental balance, to make him think twice as he most certainly did. By her wandering, abstracted remarks, she would imply that there were others present besides himself in her shadowed bedroom, crippled Mr. Alexander Pope, for example, he who had been scorned by Lady Mary Wortley Montagu, Lord Byron with his club foot, Shelley's bright hair like a comet in the wind, blind Milton dictating Paradise Lost to those indifferent daughters, lost constellations, meteor flashes, colloquies of angels, that her faithful caller had certainly come to a place different from any he had supposed, the Boston South Station crowded with submarine musicians, watery apparitions dripping with worlds like pearls, mad sextons who had buried the wrong people, themselves, ski trains of the vanished skiers, snow upon their peaked faces, a social gathering, a maze, a garden party, the unwindings of time in one long instant. In fact, her devices for the confusion of Mr. Spitzer were endless if repetitive like her dreams and visions which floated in the air, homeless as if there were no earth. Mr. Spitzer, however, was not easily moved, could note that there were apparently no invisible presences, that this was not a public street corner as she sometimes implied, not a bar-room, that there was no bloody face staring through a window, that everything was as it had been before in a place of elegant desolation, that the stars no doubt continued in their courses, that the threads of reality had not been unwound and wound around different spindles from those he had presumed. He would only sigh, yawn, look vacant, try to change the subject, ignore the question. Had he met his brother as he was climbing the second marble stairway or the great rock? Had he seen himself recently? Had he met her in the seventh crystal drawing room? Why had he given her none of his time but the last dance, the silent music, the stupidity, the silence of man? Why had he been so selfish and self-centered?

Mr. Spitzer, she would ask of a now defunct attorney, he with his colorless face half slumberous, his high silk hat in his lap, his hands folded listlessly over his ivory-headed cane, tell me, is there or is there not an invisible elephant in the corridor leading to this bedroom? But the burden of proof, Mr. Spitzer had always hesitantly maintained, smoothing his grey velvet cuffs, his mouth yawning, his eyes dimmed, rested not on him but on my mother who had seen the invisible. And why should an elephant rest on her, she would want to know, such a huge elephant, a composition of sultry light beams, and with such a long memory, it could remember everything, and much more besides, even himself, Mr. Spitzer who was obliterated by time, even his dead twin brother, even the decapitated, bleeding head of John the Baptist and John the Baptist's memories most personal? Besides, if there was no elephant, then what was an elephant doing in the house?

Mr. Spitzer, an increasingly careful man who was always protective of his failing health, moderate of his tastes, whose habits were as punctual as his almost perfect watch allowed, and that was a jeweled watch which marked the hours, the minutes, the seconds, the days, the nights, the years, the revolutions of the planets around the sun, their relative distance and magnitudes, a starry wheel, would lean forward to cover my mother's dimpled foot with a purple drapery, never touching her foot, of course, as he was too polite to engage in fleshly proximity, and she had long ago rejected him with a finality leaving no doubt in his mind.

Her foot, she continually complained, threatened to get out of bed and walk by itself. Her foot was but the monument in a desert, treeless campagna. Her foot, fat, ivory-colored, flushed with rose, pulsing as if it might have a separate life, vaguely shocked him, perhaps stirring old, dusty memories, those which almost no one else could share with him except herself who had known him in his young manhood before his career was broken or practically stopped by his brother's death in an almost forgotten year. She had made her choice of retirement from the world long ago, and now in her advanced years, as he realized, even if she had wished to do so, even if she had always been sane, could not have walked again without endangering her life, what remained of it, to say nothing of her immortal beauty, the unstained beauty which must have made her quite famous in circles of the dead. He did not hold with those who thought she could walk if she wanted to, that her illness was an illusion, nor with others who were almost convinced that she walked when they were sleeping. He dismissed as mere superstition the fears of some of the servants that she must certainly walk at night, for they had seen the evidence of her nocturnal journeys, a bare footprint on a marble stair, the streak of her long white nightgown in the dust, the imprint of a medallion, and how else could she know so much? If she did not walk secretly at night, her dark hair drifting like a cloud, how could she have suffered, through all these years, no deterioration, and how could she have known so much, the servants fearfully reasoned, that the cook was feeding a secret husband whom no one had ever seen, that a dead seagull had been blown into a living room, unnoticed by anyone, that rooms which had been closed for years seemingly had been occupied, that there was crystal dust gathering on a distant windowsill, that someone had left the icebox open, that the second butler was drunk in the wine cellar, sleeping it off, dreaming of snakes and headless horsemen and maelstroms and mermaids with hooves, that an Irish maid had said a prayer for her brother's soul because of the burning of unbaptized babes and of green leaves in Purgatory, a temporary state forever in transition? Was she omniscient, following everywhere, her jeweled fingers reaching like mist, even Mr. Spitzer wondered, for seemingly, there was no lost perception which was not hers, no cough in a dark street she had not heard, no whisper which had not roared in her ears?

She would swear, often even to Mr. Spitzer's genuine confusion, that she was already walking and dead, that she had followed him at times he had not realized. She knew where he had been even when he had not told her of his latest journey, his crossing great chasms. He would knit his heavy brow in thought as if she were describing something lawless, as if, much against his will and better judgment, he might find himself involved in an illegal adventure, a game of chance, a number's racket, a baseball game of which the score was already known as if the future were the past. He would try his best to hold himself together, not to betray his anxiety. He would pull at his feathery and colorless mustache, scarcely at times visible in the dark air, consult his almost perfect watch, sigh in relief when he saw what time it was, what time it was not, protest gently that, after all, it was not possible, that she could not have followed him to those great, teeming cities which she had not seen for years, where she had not been seen. All his protestations, however, were not convincing to her, perhaps not even to him. She would catch him short, almost breathless, startling him by her exact knowledge of inexactitude, some recent event already lost in his clouded, unperceptive memory on which he seemed to pride himself, something so trivial that, at the time, he might hardly have noticed it, might not have noticed it at all, a head light going out, dark wings across the blood-red moon, a stranger whose sleeve had brushed against his, a voice speaking his name. Suddenly, however, he would remember what he had not seen or heard, his face turning cold with the awful realization.

Why, she would wish to know, was he increasingly absent-minded, always at a loss when it came to the real world, she having to remind him of these important things, that he had waded through a cloud-burst bright as a star, had read an old newspaper in a darkened room, had missed an evening train? She would tell him in great detail where he had most recently been—the persons he had seen whom he had not seen for years previously or those who had seen him, what he had said to them, what they had said to him or had not said, and sometimes, as he had no memory of person or place, the chance meetings he had forgotten or moments of eclipse. Much to his mild, always increasing astonishment, she would bring back to life for him the things he had supposed were dead, the old, dusty memories, and she would stir in him an anxious feeling, one which would arouse another to infinity, an increasing whirlpool. He would gaze with concentrated attention into the empty air, his hands scarcely moving above his ivory-headed walking stick, his brother's blue-stoned ring gleaming on his finger like a milky moon in the crepuscular darkness streaked with clouds as she described where he had most recently walked, what he had done or thought, what he had never thought of. Had she not seen Mr. Spitzer in the Boston Public Garden where, as she recalled for him, he having forgotten so recent an incident, he had ridden in a swan boat on the pale waters with a woman all in white, her face shrouded by a white umbrella, a white motor veil, a cloud, her white dress billowing like a great balloon with many streamers, her shoes like white boats, her face unseen at the time and yet visible in memory, one whom he had not recognized then but whom he now remembered from his cloudy youth? Perhaps the woman was the swan. Again, had he not been stopped at the top of a rusted ferris wheel for an hour, watching the slow stars glide by, their reflections in a still but undulating sea, the shadow of no one but his enormous self in that abandoned amusement park at the water's edge, the tents being all empty, the merry-go-round horses not running, the music boxes not playing, just as, he would ponderously admit, tapping the floor with his cane as the blue stone gleamed and flashed on his finger, his feet tapping the floor lighted only by the moonlight, had been his sad plight, for that was one of those impossible evenings when, as a lawyer handling old estates already closed or perhaps never to be closed, he had been tracing a lost heir through all the realms of earth and high heaven? It had been his legal business, however, and nothing else, of course, nothing to stop the traffic. Mr. Spitzer, even in spite of himself, would always have to consider anew the impossibility that she had really seen him in such an abstracted state, one he had hardly known. He would brush off the rim of his hat with the side of his hand. He would suddenly remember that he had talked to an old popcorn vender or sword swallower. She could not surely have followed Mr. Spitzer's labyrinthine ways, however, his many turnings, quick or slow, the adagio of the brown leaves falling on a distant horizon, a falling, cyclonic star, his clutching at his hat in a high gale, a sudden shift of fortune, his being caught bewildered between two streams of musical traffic, the horns honking like wild geese as he stepped forward or back, undecided which way to turn, unable to stand still.

He would also have to consider, in each instance, the possibility, the fact that she might have out-witted him, a man for whom there was nothing but the indefiniteness of forms, flowing, void memories, each merging into the other, forgetfulness of self, a man for whom there was only the senseless, the commonplace, so that all details were lost, extraneous, and not final in a scheme of truth, for he could not differentiate easily between person and person, place and place, due to, as he recognized, his tendency toward oblivion. Oblivion was his brother. In fact, he was often absent-minded, just as she said, and wrapped in other thoughts. When she seemed, lying on her frothy pillow, her eyes glazed with brilliant dreams, yet too sharply aware of his definite movements, those which had been indefinite to him, sudden sensations of doubt would disturb his mental and physical equipoise, his love of an ultimate, unbaffled harmony, the silent music, he feeling within all kinds of collisions, concussions, discords, the snappings of nerves, nerve cells going out like subjective star points, new irresolutions taking the place of the old, so that he would be almost visibly agitated by his coldly dawning suspicion that perhaps, after all, he had been traced by her, that she knew his present movements or the movements of his past.

She was perfectly correct in what she said, at least correct as far as he might know in any of numerous changing instances. It was perhaps just as she said, that she had hired a secret detective to trace him, a shadow, a private eye, a gumshoe, that there were at her immediate disposal the most minute-by-minute reports on Mr. Spitzer's lost or present movements, his turnings, his hesitations, his vague intuitions which were not expressed by actions, a complete, detailed description of his life, of where he had been, of what he had seen, of what he had done, of what persons he had talked to, their conversations, even their breathings, their whisperings, their sighs, yet though they were dead. After all, as she was shrewd and feminine and clever, as her financial resources were apparently limitless like her imagination, might not this have been, Mr. Spitzer would slowly reason, the immemorial possibility, else how would she have known all these irrelevant details, some so fleeting that he naturally had not noticed them, the wind lifting an old newspaper, a cough in an empty street, the shadow of a tall building, a cat's eyes, a cat's tail? He could not, in fact, but be genuinely amazed by her almost accurate accounts of his most unimportant movements, to all of which she seemed to attribute a great, fabulous importance which both dismayed and flattered him. Occasionally, too, she would trip him up with something terrifyingly specific, straight to the point, cruelly certain, at least to a man of his cautious, reserved temperament—as when he had told her he was going to Boston, yet had gone on to New York, having changed his mind only at the last moment, of course, so that she could not have known in advance of this change of mind, this extended journey. She would seem to be aware of each change of mind, each shade of thought, of many things which had passed, necessarily, beyond his notice. She would accuse him of trying to hold some things back, that he had not told her all the places he had visited, the world above, the underworld, all his changes of mind, all his needless errands. Why, she would ask, had he not told her he had tried to flag an ancient taxi cab but had attracted the attention of no driver, due to a driving thunder storm, that he had had, due to his obesity, difficulties in a subway turnstile or in a revolving door, that he had picked up an old woman's lean and empty purse of moleskin and handed it back to her, first adding several coins, that he had been lost on his way to meet a man who was supposed to be standing on any number of identical street corners, that with his usual absentmindedness, he had stopped a blind beggar to ask the direction to the place where he already was? The fact that, though he was only tracing a lost heir of certain immovables, lands, houses, lighting fixtures, furnitures, lakes, though it had not been his legal business, he had gone prowling about in the lower districts, looking into gilt-edged saloons which reminded him of his past, that he had surreptitiously entered a waterfront dive where games of chance were the order of the day, the night, where he himself had placed a wager upon which boxer would triumph, the black or the white, that he had laid his bet on the black man and on the black horse and on the black rooster in the black night, that his bet had been lost, for suddenly the golden feathers of light had streamed through the window, that he had looked over hunched shoulders of inscrutable card players in the grey dawn, that though he hated loud music and raucous voices, he had put a lead nickel into an old-time player piano carved with the heads of billiard hall angels and cupids and horses, one no doubt playing an entire orchestra as Mr. Spitzer conceded, that under a green lampshade in an empty poolroom, the cue stick in his unaccustomed hand, he had hesitantly shoved one billiard ball against another, his face smiling as his eyelids fluttered? Or if he had told her, he had told her only when she was fast asleep.

Also, why had he not told her that he carried a small whiskey flask inside the sphere of his ivory-headed cane, that on his way here along the long sea road in the cold night wind, he would sometimes stop to take a nip like some old Pan among the silver reeds? He swore, of course, that this was not true—that he carried inside his cane a tiny parchment with a message in his own spidery handwriting that in case of his death, J.S. should be informed.

She would seem to know his every move, his every step, though undoubtedly he must allow for her tendency to exaggerate in order just to fill these empty hours, her attributing to him, at such times, a more colorful life than he enjoyed. Pondering morosely over my mother's knowledge of these sensual, temporal, meaningless events, those he had himself forgotten or dismissed, he would consider, in each instance, first the impossibility, then the possibility, but finally, restored to serenity, his reason controlling him like his almost perfect jeweled watch which he would sometimes forget to wind, was assured of his own conservative habits and peace of spirit, his punctual-mindedness, the fact that he had not been late to the important appointment, that her mind was merely wandering, that she had described nothing which was destructive to him, nothing personal, nothing which should make him lose his self-control, that some of those things which had disturbed and distressed him were only certain universal phenomenon which might pertain, in the widest sense, to anyone, such as the falling stars, the falling leaves, the mere chaos. Or otherwise, as he would ponderously reason, continuing, after the problem was settled, the problem in his mind, why should she have drawn into her unframed picture of his walk through the city streets those things which were distant, the excrescences, the disfigurations, the altering illusions, the vain remorses, the bent profile of an old tramp searching a gutter, the fatuous smile of an old and toothless woman, all those adventitious, disconnected images which would be unperceived by the usual detective unless they were related to the case, such as a sky-scraper banked by purple clouds or the reflected skyscraper, such as a dusty sparrow falling?

Part of my mother was always in motion, turning like a spindle. Part of my mother was always still. The horizontal person, she lay still, her breasts like smooth and ivory-colored hills, her limbs like some far promontory, and she dreamed, as she would say, this perpendicular world of motion, that of her absent lovers whom she feared as she feared seduction, an act of ghostly rape. It was as if she had never married, so brief, so fleeting, so unreal had been her marriage night, and she was always virginal, scarcely aware of a physical act, the touching of hands. She simply had forgotten that she had ever given birth to a child. She was not sure of her own shadowed and dented face in a dark hand mirror wreathed with golden, budding cherubim, some which had lost their faces, her dark, glossy hair drifting over her snow-colored shoulders, her eyes too bright even in that ambiguous depth. Who was she? Did anybody know her? Had Mr. Spitzer's brother ever known her?

Mr. Spitzer might well have remained calm, peacefully confused, perfectly possessed, for how could she be sure that he even existed, he with his restrained affability, his lack of any real sense of humor or honor, his trust in law of which he knew no jot, his apprehensive feelings, his oblivion to faces, directions, differences, his failure in the realm of sense?

She was not even sure that she herself existed, that it was not all a stupendous joke played upon her, this seeming passage of life, this needless expansion of the firmament, that she had not been artfully tricked into believing that she lived when she was already dead, an evanescence never to be traced. The world was this deception played upon her, and it included Mr. Spitzer with his high silk hat, his intricately carved and gilded ivory-headed cane, a great dome, his grey velvet cuffs, his cape with its soft folds, the sand grains like diamond sparkles upon his double chin, his vapid concentrations which seemed to her to be the wandering mind, the thoughts sporadic as butterflies swarming before her eyes, as these delusive images. How did she know that they were not both dead, both she and Mr. Spitzer, that old lover of her untouched youth, he whom she had scarcely ever thought of? Could Mr. Spitzer determine whether she had ever lived at all, whether the world had not always been this vast, supernatural joke played upon her or someone, poor, euchred humanity which was the only world and was imaginary? She doubted that Mr. Spitzer, with his clouded uncertainties, was in a position to do so, as he was also egregiously deceived, presuming he held the two ace cards he did not hold, and he had always been out-witted by the other player. He was blind, and he did not live, she would accuse Mr. Spitzer, that it was not his life he lived, that his was but a secondary existence and depended upon her imagination only, that he was ephemeral as the Dog star which disappeared when she closed her eyes. That she had always been dead, this beautiful corpse, she would vivaciously insist, that there were the most amazing things going on which Mr. Spitzer could not see, he being prejudiced by the thought that he was alive, that there were these great balloon fishes trailing their negligee streamers in the enclosed atmosphere, these drowned Medusas, these giant crabs like monks, these old apostles walking around the town clock and striking a bell. How

place for everything, had dusted the dark mirror before she looked into it, the pale depths reflecting her silver eyes and hair, had detected the crystal dust on a distant windowsill, that a carriage needed painting, that a driveway lamp was broken, that a lace curtain was torn, that a pillow was faded, and had spoken frequently and increasingly of the appearances, the visions, the beautiful world of light, the formations of the clouds, the stripes of the tiger lily, the spotted wing of the butterfly, the speckled bird's egg, the sunrise, the sunset, the glow-worm shining, and had caused her husband to feel that, when she died, he could not see without her? He had begun to wear a dark eyeshade, perhaps to bring him nearer to his dead wife. He had felt that his eyes were gone, that his body was turning into starlight. When he was blind, he had gotten a Seeing Eye dog who had led him, old and stooped, through the garden. For a long while before anyone recognized this, and he himself had never known it, the old Seeing Eye dog was blind, yet never lost his path or brushed against an obstacle as he led his old, blind master upon his rounds. Thus did my mother's father spend his last years in the darkness waiting for the angel of light to come for him. He had walked in the evening in the garden he had planted for his blind wife, following those neat and circling paths where was no obstacle, no marble statue or bench. He had closed his eyes, reaching out to touch, to pluck those intangible flowers he might recognize only by their textures and their odors different from each other. In a long, chilling winter, he had died. The old Seeing Eye dog had died, too, and was laid at his feet. But they had both already known the darkness.

My mother slept for years, her eyes protected from the vulgar sunlight because already her visions were too many, the mirages, the maelstroms, the whirlwinds, her mind being that which could be oriented only through disorientation, through being forever lost. Sometimes, her eyes enlarged, shining in darkness, she saw, over her swollen head, red-tinged balloon fishes with all their streamers streaming, and she was the drowned swimmer caught among these negligee ribbons, borne forever downward. Peering stonily at her through miles of opaque, sunless water, there might be gargoyle faces, gods with their bulging heads, livid mouths, foaming curls. Sometimes, she floated dead upon the surface, her sightless face shadowed by clouds and seagulls, and thus she stayed for hours, staring at a dark and watery sky. She had stayed under water for longer than anyone knew, never for once losing her consciousness, her awareness of events, far ripplings, movings, stirrings, shadows. She had been everywhere in the world of water. A herd of barking seals would sometimes swim into her sheltered bedroom, the Eskimo hunter pursuing with his spear. Sometimes it was a drawing room with great chandeliers of ice, frozen fountains, cascades reaching from the sky. She had stayed under earth for six months at a time, frozen as crystal, had wandered through the world of the underground, had plucked, in that dark abode of shades, the golden apples of Hesperides, those which had turned to dust in her mouth, had climbed Jacob's ladder to heaven or some more distant place which was nowhere but in theory. She had been herself only as she had been projected upon the consciousness of others, fragments, a spirit easily broken, a flickering light that had gone out in minds less responsible and less responsive than hers.

There was no bare, empty moment, none which might not be filled with a vast, splendid excitement. Lying in bed always and seldom visited by any real person, for most real persons had forgotten her, she might think she was always elsewhere, that perhaps she was someone she had never met. She might always be the spectator, in memory, of some vanished regatta of ghostly sail-boats, their wings as pale as moths, or she might always attend, in memory, a dazzling ball where she had danced with many partners, or she might participate again in those old, vague archery tournaments where, with her hat profusely veiled, she had lifted her veils and scarves only long enough to take aim at a wavering target. To fill those moments which otherwise might have been bare and empty and dark, she might always return to the past as it had not been lived, that theme of affirmation which she had always known, remember forever one lingering instant as of that day when, twirling her white umbrella in the cold, moon-washed Roman sunlight, she had refused, gently and finally, as she had hoped, in a marble drawing room furnished with the sarcophagi of angelic cardinals and children dead in infancy, the young Mr. Spitzer's proffered hand, his offer of marriage due to his eager assurance that both of them should henceforth lead retired lives, that they should withdraw at an early date from the bitter world of this material chaos, he to write his beautiful and elegiac music which all ears should hear, she to dream, providing those endless, rapturous visions like bubbles of light breaking on some far shore, memories ineffable as an angel's wings, intuitions, moods, harmonies temporal which he might encompass with the harmony divine, the omniscience of love, how she had answered only that, heavily and with hesitant heart, she must prefer his brother to him, for if it had been a question of things physical, there could have been no difference in her eyes, but her preference was always his brother's wild, worldly, mercurial spirit, not his. And his brother had still been alive, the better on horses, which horse would come in first, the one no one else had thought would win. So there had seemed to be a chance she might win his brother. She would remember, for hours on end, Mr. Spitzer's withdrawing face, so like his brother's, his turning gradually away into the dusk, her feeling chagrin that there should be these great bodily resemblances beclouding dissimilars, a world of difference, that the Mr. Spitzer who loved her and had offered her his hand was not the Mr. Spitzer she loved and whose hand she might conceivably have accepted if ever it had been offered to her, even in a moment outside of time. Propped up on her lace-frilled pillows, her cheeks heavily powdered, her head roaring with dreams, she might also live through all those old romances which had never taken place, or she would ride in a carrozza with a dead prince through narrow midnight streets past palaces like great warehouses, or she would visit the house of some old friend whom she had never known in life. Before five minutes had passed, she would have established the sympathies of a life time. They would have discovered mutual acquaintances—no matter what era it was.

To fill those moments which otherwise might have been void, empty and dark, timeless and without excitement, she might also always go out riding with James still at the wheel, though she surely knew that the ex-chauffeur had left her employment long years ago, absconding with her old-fashioned automobile and its passenger when he might so well have taken her priceless pearls, driving perhaps as far as Alaska and a world of snow, perhaps even farther, evading the police and every mortal trace. That James was absent made him always present, still at the steering wheel, just as he had been before, an ex-convict who, while in her services and upon parole to Mr. Spitzer whose brother's friend he had been, had preferred to keep his head shaven, as his employment with her had seemed to him only the extension of his prison sentence. There was still no freedom in this life. He had yearned for the open spaces, for his untrammeled freedom, to get away from civilization, to shoot a moose and see the tears of the dying moose which takes a long time dying, and he had been always taciturn and unexpressive. She could only complain that she had not seen his face for years. He was always still at the wheel, his eyes steely with purpose, his shaven head as familiar to her as if he had not long ago disappeared, and he was still driving to Alaska, still evading, of course, the stupid police. The mileage had increased beyond even that perilous and endless distance, however, for she was always riding with him, talking through an imaginary horn, her commands as imperious as they had ever been, as helpless as ever, he being insolent, silent, never answering her least remark. Her lips were so frozen she could hardly speak, her limbs so cold she could hardly move, her life unprotected, she being at the pity of this monster, her countless pearls running through her thin fingers, as many pearls as hailstones driving against the windshield. Why had she come so thinly dressed, she would often ask, if they were going to Alaska, that cold place?

Obviously, she should have been appropriately dressed for a journey into the freezing ether, that which caused her pearls and her opals to crack and broke her mirror into fragments. She would call for her white ermine stole, a pair of elbow-length lace gloves, her fan, her motor veil, her white garden hat, the things to keep her from the cold, her white umbrella or several white umbrellas, her smelling salts, her camphor, her lace handkerchief, for she was on her way to Alaska, a place of extreme coldness where the snow creeps down the mountains, where the animals put on thicker coats, where the snow dogs mush ahead of the sleds, where only a few Eskimos should be seen. A handkerchief dropping should cause a great hole in the ice, an avalanche of icebergs, a ghostly regatta. There would be great snowbirds with red bills and only a few patches of purple grass, and then there would be nothing. They had started out definitely for Alaska, she and James, several years ago, he at the wheel, she would reason, so she simply could not understand, to save her life, why they had never reached Alaska, its mountains cloaked with snow and ice, its corrugated lakes of silver stillness, why, after all this mileage, all this gasoline, they were still pursuing the long, pale, monotonous street of an endless city, something mercantile, as she would say, why they must pass the same tortured houses again and again or buildings only slightly different from each other, piano-tuning factories which had been closed for years although their signs were keyboards, furriers' lofts, dental supply establishments with signs advertising false teeth, the blue, bulbous, rain-washed dome of an old Greek church in a neighborhood of extreme poverty, the ferris wheel rusted against the sky, wheel which might be only a circle of sea birds, why they were always crossing Brooklyn Bridge in that frozen, unholy atmosphere where the smoke of the ship's chimney was congealed in some terrifying shape, where the sound of the traffic whistle came always two seconds late, where the human voice was not heard until an hour or years after it had spoken.

Home, James, she would say, helplessly, for where is home? Home, James, for is there no turning? If we cannot get off this street, how did we get on it? Why this same barber pole always again? Why these great stone turtles? There is a stop light, James, but go through the stop light, for it will make no difference. Stop at the green light, James. Go through the red light. Pay no attention to the other drivers with cars and horses. James, do you hear my voice? James, why have you not answered me through all these years?

The beauty, the fascination of James was that he, an innocent man who had been falsely accused of rape by his last mistress, the ugly old woman, and who had served an unjust sentence breaking rocks for a state highway, the ex-convict whom my mother had employed at Mr. Spitzer's suggestion and with full knowledge of his aggrieved history and of his desire for revenge against human society, an excellent shot who had practiced for years while in her service and could not miss the seagull on the wing, was plotting to kill her when they reached Alaska, an expanse of frozen waters between two ranges of ice-bound capes or crystal headlands, there where would be no one to hear her crying out, no one to follow her bloody tracks across the mesa of snow, but that his first intention, however, was to first kill her father, the old ritualist who was already dead, the old gentleman with the long white hair and the burro's beard and star-lighted eyes, sometimes moving like Mr. Chandelier across the sky, sometimes part of the immovable starlight, there where the stars would be brightest and incorruptible. James would shoot at the starlight or at the shooting stars or anything which moved. The nights might last forever, or there would be only the most fugitive nights, night separated from night by only a moment, the sun dipping below the horizon and immediately arising again. Knowing full well James' unswerving intention, that he was absolutely ruthless and determined and would stop at nothing, yet she was unable to call out for help, as she would say, for who would ever hear her in that frozen land where the bell-clappers were broken? Her hands shivered with cold, and there were ice-packs on her head, and she was eating ice cream, and she was driving forever in Brooklyn or some such foreign place in order to reach the hallucinatory goal, Alaska, that which she could not reach. The smell of magnolias made heavy the summer air. There were purple trees like puffs of smoke. The numberless pearls ran through her stiffening fingers.

It had not been her chauffeur upon whom her life depended, however. There had been many dead selves, and there had been one, and there had been none, she would complain. Her only faithful companion had been nothing human, only a plain little bird, only a yellow canary with a glassy eye and ruffled wing, and on this, her life and everything else depended. This little yellow canary, sleeping in a gilded cage at her elbow, delicate as a puff of opium-colored smoke, its smooth head tucked under its wing, was all that had ever stood between her and tides of death, as she would used to say, and so long as this bird lived, she could not die. If ever this little bird went, then she must go, too, searching through all the realms of death with an empty bird cage and a package of bird seed in her hands. This little yellow canary, however, sleeping its life away, hardly ever moving, had been drugged by the poisonous atmosphere itself, perhaps by the opium in her gilded coffee cup where it would perch for a moment after its bath, and it was as changeable as her own dead selves, for it had died already many times without her knowledge. She did not seem to know this, and if ever this little yellow canary departed from her as the others had, she would complain, if ever it went, taking her heart away as had her human companions, the fickle, the changeable, then she must go, too, calling its name, and she should be seen no more. Perhaps, however, it might live forever, she thought, sleeping with its delicate head turned to one side like hers, dreaming its little canary dreams of moths and bumble bees and snails and flowers, of other canaries. Perhaps if it lived long enough, it would be an octogenarian canary, and she, when she was old, as preserved as she had been when she was young and beautiful, no cruel ravagement of time ever to show upon her blissful features, so that was why she was always very careful not to disturb the little bird brain and its dreams and its tender visions, gentle and calm like hers, why the little yellow canary must have everything arranged for its convenience, vases of minuscular flowers, a silken bed with a canopy and a soft pillow edged by lace, a dressing table with three gold-edged mirrors for the phantom birds, a marble bath, many objects for its pleasures, many swings, yet though it nearly always slept, and she was very careful that it should not be awakened by anyone but her. It never sang. Because of its long existence and the tedium of the days, the endless nights, she gave to her little yellow canary many names, depending on her moods and her position in space, depending on where she was or might be when she was voyaging between two stars—Juniper, Tulip, Cellini, Solomon, Methuselah, Marco Polo, Admiral Peary, Shackleton, Dante. Her canary, always the same canary and bubble of light, travelled with her through the ether and across the snow and across the waves. As she did not seem to realize, however, as she never guessed, as even with her heightened sensibilities she did not dream, her little yellow canary had deserved many names and more than she had given, for there had been many little yellow canaries in this cage, she but presuming the continued existence of one, an unbroken continuity of one small life and its dreams, this bundle of wilted feathers and this glassy eye as transient as flowers in a world of everlasting snow. She would notice only perhaps a slight difference in the shade of the bird, in the bird renewed and sleeping at her elbow, its head tucked under its pale wing, and thus the illusions were sustained, even by precarious subterfuge. When one bird died, always when she was unconscious, too heavily freighted with dreams to move or stir or breathe her last, another was stealthily put into its place in order that, upon her regaining consciousness, she might not notice this loss of so small a factor in the external reality, that on which reality had depended, and thus she seemed to live.

It was Mr. Spitzer who had arranged, in fact, that there should always be this secret change, this substitution of the living for the dead, another canary always in the house, a spare, or several canaries twittering in a housemaid's shadowed bedroom, for nothing pleased him but to humor her, to keep her alive, and he was always warning the frightened servants that she must not see the dreadful transaction, the plain deceit, the canary's funeral in the wave-washed garden under the dripping trees, or something worse might happen. The whole universe might topple with its sun-streaked clouds, the golden cities fade, or the servants might lose their jobs and have no recommendation from anyone. She must not even know the bird was drugged, he urging the utmost secretiveness so that there might be, as he believed, continuing forever in her mind, the scheduled madness, a continuity of these lost or phantasmagoric events and no change as between one day and another, day and night, at least no perceptible change. When one day, however, she saw with her own eyes Marco Polo flying out through an open transom into a wildly blowing thunder storm, green and yellow and rose-tinged like himself, a suddenly awakened bird, she was quite calm, resigned hopelessly to the fact that now she must certainly live, of course, forever, for who could locate one lost canary in a hurricane blowing off the Canary Islands, sweeping all continents, even the buried, sweeping all desolate islands, even the undiscovered? She would still hear, at times seeming very near her, a lost canary's far twitterings. But she thought it was only another dream, an optical illusion.

CHAPTER 3

Confusions, confusions innumerable, my mother's life, that opium paradise from which I had escaped, for all those adults were like the shadows of grotesque puppets dancing on a wall, and none was responsible. The puppeteer they dreamed of did not exist although he moved the strings.

There was only then, after all, to lead the bewildered child with her own dark problems of that childhood which groped toward light, one who could be trusted not to change her mind or her moral principles, one guide who seemed quite sure of herself if of no other being and no other body, Miss MacIntosh, my darling, truer than the North star, the plain, old-fashioned nursemaid Mr. Spitzer had employed, alive, certain of her likes, her dislikes which she was more quick to express than her likes which were apparently few, allowing no nonsense, no luxury of an endless moment, not even a game of chess as chess was the game of kings, an aristocratic pastime employing kings, queens, pawns upon the board checkered by shadows, all being not equal as they should be in her eyes if the game were to be democratic, her marcelled red hair fitting close like a helmet and lighting the dark days like a second sun or moon and flashing with sparks to show that quick temper with which she would do away with bodiless phantoms and monsters, with imaginary nightingales or turrets of ivory or turrets of gold or turrets of brass, her cheeks as pink as frosty apples in a wintry sunlight seeming almost as pale as moonlight, her character so commonplace that only in such an exaggerated, unhealthy, brooding environment and poisonous atmosphere and miasmic mists could it have seemed, by contrast, strange. It was more peculiar than flower-crowned satyrs and moon-eyed minotaurs among the rustling silken shadows, than giant periwinkle shells filled with mystic roarings, than moonstone faces gleaming from a darkened sea wall, for there was nothing about her which should not be obvious, so it would always seem. She was different from everybody else, from the first and second butlers, only the first being real, from the first and second and third housemaids, from the imaginary moose eating the bulbs of Arctic tulips, for she was under no influence of that hallucinatory atmosphere in which she lived, and she had never seen these phantoms thickening in the air around us, filling the air with the roarings of surf or of almighty wings, the old coach-painters who were the coaches they painted, the old piano-tuners tuning themselves, tapping their ears with their forks, the old long-toed kings sleeping in their long ivory beds, the court goldsmiths of the third century, some who were covered with the dust of pollen gold, the second gardener who thought he was a cosmic praying mantis reaching through miles of starlight, and all was plain to her, a woman keeping her own unamazed mind.

She was hale, hearty, sensible, dreaming no dreams like the others, entertaining no illusions as to herself or even as to them. She could always think of some way to obtrude upon the dreams I dreamed, the hidden thoughts which rarely came to the surface. We raced along the shore, a long-legged old woman and a long-legged child, or we tossed a red ball back and forth at the edge of the waves streaked with rays of the fading sunlight, for the sun had already dropped beyond the distant waves where a red light burned like a light burning at a distant window, or she would suggest that we should shell bean pods for a beach supper we might never cook, or we should gather up sea shells and throw them back into the tide, sweep the beach with brooms made of brambles, sweep away our footprints from the sand, or we should find some other task to keep the cobwebs out of our brains, to keep the birds from nesting in our hair, much though she admired the leisurely pace of the slow-flying sea-gulls and the stilt cranes, the kingfishers flying over the golden discs in the evening clouds, the pearl-catchers diving over distant oyster beds, the fishing birds flapping their fish-silver wings when the grey sky was like a sea filled with fish-colored clouds and silver fins of light like the wings of moths and scarcely distinguishable from the darkening waters.

The sunlight was her meat, her drink, the source of her strength, that which kept her so robust, so ready for any emergency, her clenched hand uplifted, her common sense invulnerable to any sudden attack of foolishness or weakness, and she was as honest as the day was long, it would always seem, and she did not believe in things invisible or in promising that which could never be realized by poorest mortals here below, perhaps not even by God Who had God's limitations, Who had not created everything. He had left many things uncreated. Her promises were few or none, never false as to important matters, her expectations as to a remote life being no more than her realizations had been in the immediate past, she living only for this present moment which faded in her grasp. She was cheerful in the face of adversity. We should not attribute importance to trivialities—indeed, we should learn to ignore them. She was always in the harness, as she might say when questioned as to her present life, that God had been her harness-maker, that He had hung her harness with tinkling bells so that it might always be known where she was, even when she was in the shadows or walking along the beach with her black umbrella like a cloud over her in the cold starlight, that labor was man's lot upon this earth, for he was made to pull the plow or the old carriage as God had made the furrows on the sea and the great waters to uphold little ships, and ours was not the problem of questioning or understanding God's remotest mysteries or things which were not our concern. We should do very well to take care of each new day as it came. We should be grateful for every new day we had gotten through, for every sunset, for that was our only success in this world of failure, the fact that we had lived through another day. If at night I heard the wings of time like angelic wings roaring faster and faster over the long grey reaches of the water, if I imagined that time itself was a dream, that there was no time, then I was only dreaming, and the sleep of the innocent should be deep and dreamless, and our days should leave us no time for the troubled dreams of the night. When we closed our eyes, we should see nothing, dream nothing, and we should not turn and toss in our sleep or cry out in the darkness. Each day's business should be finished and left behind us. We should fold our clothes each evening as carefully as if we never expected to put them on again. Death when it came would come so entirely that it would be a dreamless sleep unbroken by the sounds of the waves or the slow-honking water birds or the memories of faces, voices, shadows, for in heaven none should know his own face, and there was no heaven, and so we swept our footprints away from the sands before the waters crept over the crystal shiftings of those dunes which kept no real impression of us or of the wandering clouds.

Her hair brick red, perfectly in order, almost Tyrian purple in certain lights, yet seeming to give off sparks like the waves of the sea in the burning sunlight or like a glowing furnace fire with livid sparks, her ruddy cheeks often blowing out as when a dolphin breathes and turning pale only toward evening or when her strength was almost exhausted, her greyish, greenish eyes gleaming with severe good humor behind her shining or misted eye-glasses empearled with two pools of light, she was always busy at some useful task, and her only relaxation from her labor was a form of physical exercise, knocking down ninepins and the old kingpin who should be leveled like the old king of Bulgaria, throwing horseshoes, skipping a rope, chasing a red ball, the sport which she recommended for the sake of one's circulation and bony structure and eyesight and perhaps for the sake of one's immediate survival when one should be no more, our seeing a bright tomorrow with the pale sunlight streaking the wave-marked purple sand or the purple sunlight streaking the pale sand like the robes of a phantom king, and she could endure nothing that took its time, no snail wrapped in a dreaming castle, no moribund thing, no hawk's-wing sea shell with a broken wing or broken great keyhole limpet or star sea shell dragging its broken foot, no one who was preparing himself for exit from this world. She was bare-faced and clear of vision and could not endure a bare-faced lie or even the equivocal statement hovering between two truths and settling upon neither perhaps like this forever hovering tide with its wandering spume. If some questions were unanswerable, then she would not answer them, not venturing to do what the wisest man had failed to do, and I should not ask for an explanation of that which never was, perhaps might never be on earth. Instead, I should help her build something. I should make a useful contribution to human society, which was composed of simple people. She was always busy, always finding another task to employ her busy hands, hammering an old board in a rotted fence wandering in a scalloped pattern at the edge of the moving dunes, hammering together the boards of a broken raft, cleaning off barnacles and seaweed, mending an old sail, mending a hole in an old coat, her idea of heaven being that no man should have a hole in his coat here on earth, that all should have enough to eat and yet not wallow in these unusual luxuries which tempted no honest face and had never once deceived her. She knew, and she was not deceived by the speckled light, by the rose pulsings of the dead. She knew the difference between those who were sleeping and those who were dead. She also knew her own inadequacies, the ways in which she had fallen short.

She was brusque and rough and ready, perhaps sometimes more like an old sailor than an old nursemaid with the salt water stinging her eyes and causing her eyes to water, streaking her face with silver lights, her high-boned cheeks which quivered in the wind. Her face changed from rose to blue to green to gold to silver, seeming to reflect the changing colors of the atmosphere, for her skin was sensitive to light as were her eyes so that perhaps the small things were invisible to her as were those phantoms painted on the air. She was like a strong head wind, strong in all her movements even when the wind blurred the atmosphere with the demoniac whirlings of crystal sands so that often the days seemed lighted only by the lights of the invisible stars as in the nights when the stars were like pin-heads lost in the pin-cushions of the clouds, or this planet itself might be the invisible star, the minuscular particle, the star not visible to others, and she was vigorous and plain of courage, clear in her common sense, no matter if the sky was murky, the winds blowing most heavily where she walked, it would seem, and she liked to walk in the heavy winds, often in the eye of the wind, the teeth of the wind, never amazed by the wind's furies, just keeping her head well covered, yet wading through waters coming up to her knees, wading through the long whispers of the many-tongued surf or the salt pools left by the receding tides and still whirling, never protecting herself from the honest elements, the sudden sunlight breaking through pearl-colored fog and the blowing surf suddenly splashing as if with the wings of birds and the wind making the far waters glint with reflected lights, or protecting herself only so far as would be necessary, for man had dwelled too far away from nature and these immediate things, sunlight and surf and wind, and the best tonic she knew was physical exercise that the natural blood might flow into one's cheek, that one might breathe the heady and the stinging air, that one might sleep without the necessity of a drug or an illusion between her and the world or even the guardian angels who had certainly never guarded her, Miss MacIntosh, my darling.

She could not endure to be shut away under any narrow roof where she would be in close proximity with others. Even my mother's sea-blackened house, vast and almost empty, with many rooms which had not been visited for years and many roofs broken by skylights of many-colored glass and many glass towers radiant with light after the sunset had departed and many darkened towers, was probably too small for her.

She was always out of doors as much as possible, being in favor of exposing one's self to the natural climate which might be very different from the climate of my mother's house, the spiritual climate, the great snow storms blowing, the hailstones falling in a candle-lighted room where the lace curtains were drifting in the summer breeze, Miss MacIntosh preferring the blows of the winds which asked no questions of man, the blows of the exhausted waves, the fogs coming in or the burning sunlight, for she was no hothouse flower, certainly, and no one who required a roof, not even a roof which she had built, not even a roof of the clouds, no empty dreamer who would sleep in her narrow coffin and yet dream that she was walking. If she dreamed, she would dream that she was running. Even in her dream life, she would certainly be an active woman, but she was too busy to dream, it was a fact. She was always running along the beach, chasing a red ball. Sometimes the ball would chase her. Sometimes she would throw a pebble or a stick into the departing tide as if she were trying to placate it for something.

She was always walking out of doors, even in the inclement weather when others might seek shelter, when tramps crept into doorways, when the rain-soaked sea birds sought shelter under the overhanging rocks in the sea-swept garden or under the hulls of stranded ships with the moss growing over their prows or under the palings of rotted beach walks or old wharves, even through the rain pouring like a deluge shot with gleamings of burning fire or through furious snow storms whitening the sand with white patches though never the darkening waters, taking her constitutional, the best thing that one might ever take in this brief life, it was her candid opinion, and nothing about her should amaze these angels of death or cause them to lose their feathers or their minds, nor should she be amazed by them, her stout black umbrella uplifted above her well-protected head in the fine weather when the sunlight danced like prisms on the waters or rolling pea-souper or sudden squalls of rain making a music on its roof, bugling roof, her umbrella folded only in the heaviest winds blowing her athwart or darkest rains which, forever falling, made another sea of earth, and then her umbrella was her sword though it had been her shield against these adversaries she could not see, her black umbrella billowing before her eyes and blotting out visibility as she moved like a shadow through silver-lighted rains and fogs, her perfectly marcelled hair protected by a waterproof hat pinned under her chin or numerous oilskin wrappings or even a shroud of canvas, her large feet protected by coarse-ribbed woolen stockings and faded plaid golf socks and flapping sea boots which made a soughing sound like oars and might sometimes be water-logged as, wearing her salt-streaked mackintosh of almost faded plaids buttoned only at her chin, she waded through wading surf where the seagulls waded, seeming to know her, the surf blowing against her red cheeks as the sunset streaked the waters with a path of gold, her body bent by many winds to be this angularity, and sometimes she would seem to be searching through the waves at the shore's edge, searching for something she had not lost and had not found.

In the last of the evening light under the great cloud puffs fading, in the last of the evening light as the seagulls settled like snowdrifts upon the rocks or upon the life-sized wooden chessmen, upon the broken marble statues, the dark spruce trees, the pagodas flooded by standing water, the hull of an old fishing boat swept up, the rotted masts and canvas sails, she walked her certain way along the crescent beach, stepping at times through uncertain surf the color of the pearl moon half embedded in a cloud the color of the rain lilies, and in the first streaks of the tentative light breaking through clouds, and in the blazing noon which colored the sea like fire, and she would never spare herself another effort in the right direction, and she could not be induced by any example but her own. It had been her plain observation, made long ago, that useful work for the benefit of others and strenuous physical exercise and self-forgetfulness prolonged one's useful life on this old terra firma which was certainly no cloud, and she would never see necessity for any other existence but this which had its beginning and its end, nor could she have deceived herself by all these idle dreams of all these vagrant dreamers, nor could she have been happy had these dreams been realized, partially or fully realized, had they come true, truer than truth, had everything been according to the thoughts of the irresponsible dreamer, for she would still have been, though the whole world should suddenly change and get itself off on a new foot, her sensible self with her mind unclouded and her mind unconfused. She would have held to her usual ways, in spite of great change, perhaps because of all other things changing around her. It was surely best, according to her way of thinking, never to indulge one's self with somnolent or wakeful dreams of those things which the conditions of this mortal frame could not simply provide, for the deprivations were always and would always be the deprivations, no matter what they might seem or by what means they were concealed, and one should be clearly honest, even though plain. One should mind his own knitting, his own cooking, his own household duties even though he had no house. One should learn to build a fire upon the beach, perhaps a signal fire for some poor sailor clinging to a life raft and searching the darkening waters and not knowing where the land was until he saw this fire or the gleamings of the embers as of the ember stars like ashes in the wind. Life was made up, in short, of the necessary deprivations, even at best, the sorrows we did not create, those things God in His haste had forgotten, and we should create no others to take their place, and we should mind our own business, making just such little improvements as we possibly could but no more and being no more than we were upon this old earth which was quite plain, bare and simple and unadorned.

God's business had never been ours, perhaps had never been God's, and all men were alike, certainly, and there was not much room for the individual, for those who should lift up their heads from the foaming waters of the dream and imagine themselves as other than they were. Poor servants were not fine gentlemen, and simple housemaids should give themselves no aristocratic airs as they trailed their long lace petticoats in the dust. The dust should be swept away, along with the patterns

employed. We dealt with the injustices done to the Africans working in diamond mines blazing like fields of light. We pitied the lighthouse keepers who had no union and no organization, who must watch the changings of the seas and stars and be isolated by storms and hurricanes and frozen seas, and our hearts went out to the united brotherhoods of the sleeping car porters riding in lonely trains and of the truck-drivers driving their trucks all night long, often hardly keeping awake, perhaps not seeing the other traffic lights.

There was no space for the imaginary rainbows, the fish-scaled mermaids dreaming on the moss-covered rocks, combing their golden, tawny manes as their scales glittered with the colors of the waters and of the clouds, no space for the things which were not, for the things which were sufficed and were perhaps too many, and our bones should be as clean as the whistle, our eyes bright with only the burning sunlight. Honesty found no refuge nor even a dark harbor in which to hide away from the storms of life, and we should never lose our way nor be deceived by these deceptions which were less than the shadows, less than the winds, less than the waves. The shadow created the light, but the light created the shadow. There would be no light without the darkness. One was not better than the other. Perhaps no light but its own was needed by an honest mind, for the light which came from within was the only light by which to steer our way. It behooved us at all times to be simple and direct with our minds made up and our conscience clear and our shoulders at the wheel, helping those who were not the children of fortune. But once when we had lost our way, for the darkness had suddenly descended when we were far away from the house, and we had never seen the sunset, Miss MacIntosh found an old glass jar at the edge of the dark surf and made a lamp by filling it with fireflies, carrying the lamp up high like a lighthouse over the dark waters, the light of the fireflies streaking her chalk-colored cheeks and her light-colored eyes and the milk-colored shadows until suddenly the moon came out from behind a cloud, and the waters burned with the glitter of fireflies seeming to fall from the moon, the burning cloud.

This flat-footed Middle Westerner, Miss MacIntosh, my darling, so plain, so unadorned, and very far from feminine or fickle, a woman utterly unlike my sleeping mother, a woman completely without affectation or exaggeration, as she seemed then in my eyes, was far too simple, far too clear to be seduced by the soporific luxury which she could not even care to understand, the Oriental magnificence of dreaming mandarins and ivory and jade pagodas, the monstrous enormity of that old New England sea-coast house with its golden spires and broken cornices and galleries of iron lace, black flags, many roof levels, many distorted weathervanes, flooded paddocks and grassy tennis courts, my mother's unearthly citadel of dreams and visions and memories, all those ghostly tides, all those bare or ruined gardens covered by fog, all those Romish graven images, all those Greek busts, all those broken marble or porous statues sloping toward the edge of the wild sea, the Stygian river flowing through a bedroom shrouded against the living sunlight, the draperies of flowing gold, the golden crowns, the ruby crowns, the coins unearthed from graves, the whirling dervishes, the imaginary lute-players and rainbows and chauffeurs. It was not that she spoke against my mother, only that she spoke against unstable imagination and feverish delight, for a child should simply respect its parent, being in no position to judge of the adult sorrows, of those sorrows bringing our grey hairs. She was too salty, too forthright, too sensible to envy or be impressed by these unstable and floating or drifting things, real or imaginary, these she could not even begin to understand, she seeming not always to distinguish between what my mother possessed and what she thought she possessed, for it was all the same to her, poor Miss MacIntosh who owned nothing but the coat on her back and the umbrella over her head, just so much awful nonsense, whether one owned a vast estate with many winding roads and walks or supposed one owned it, whether one owned an automobile or merely dreamed one owned it, this life being so short, so earnest, so full of woe that one should not place his faith in earthly things, for all would fade like the gold-topped clouds trembling above the waters in the evening light, and nothing would endure, whether it was silver or gold, just as the waters closing over the head of a drowning man would keep no memory of him. She dismissed the insubstantial fabric of the dream. She seemed to feel that the pearls my mother owned were imaginary, too, not real, those green pearls which had been manufactured by the secretive ear oyster, those pink pearls formed by the winged stromb in warmer or tideless seas, and little would she have cared to own them even if they had been real and she could afford them or pearls of greater price, a pearl as big as her head, for they had belonged to the sick oysters, and nothing exaggerated appealed to her vigorous common sense, her lusty view of things, her certainty that everything had its place in the mortal creation, that nothing should wander outside. God had doubtless put us where He had intended, at least as far as was possible, and that we should not leave our place, He also intended, for He had never left His.

She did not wear a jewel, for that was something she could do without, quite simply. That would be, according to her way of thinking, pretentious and vain, allying her with those of whom she obviously disapproved. No jewel needed to lend its light to her, coloring her skin with opalescent hues. If sometimes she wore a grey feather tucked into the band of her old grey wind-battered hat, it was a seagull feather which she had found on the beach, something which had drifted through a drifting cloud. That was something which was already lost. That was something which did not cost money. That was something even a poor nursemaid could afford. She did not believe in wearing silks or satins or flowing draperies, long trains of cobwebbed lace, or cold sapphires shining like ice in the winter wind. She never heard the ghostly rustle of satin skirts on the marble stairs in the cold winter midnights. She did not believe in wearing coats of fur, for the fur had belonged to the animals, to the pine-martens, to the foxes, the rabbits, the polar bears under the northern stars, the ermine with their coats turning as white as snow. The jewels had belonged to the dark rocks, to the hidden lodes, and none should ever have been cut or polished or taken out of their places. The best diamonds were the diamonds in the rough, staying where they belonged. She even disapproved of the crystal prisms of the chandeliers lighting the dark clouds. Nothing outside of nature's wheel, though it should be a wheel casting foam and spray, appealed to my salty, sensible darling, so sensibly walking, fully clothed, knowing so well what her own limitations were, those she had been born with, those which had always been, those she had acquired, that she was no beautiful lady, that her feet were too long and long-toed, that her hands were too long, that her nose had been broken in a traffic accident and never correctly mended, she having gone to no doctor, that she was always alone, single and single-minded, accompanied by no guardian angel who would uphold her when she was failing, her way hard and certain and finite, for never once did she propose the infinite, her old black umbrella lifted above her head to protect her from the eyes in the clouds and the eyes of water birds as she took her constitutional in the grey, whirling rain or heavy fog or thin mists creeping along the ground or creeping surf or sudden squalls of raindrops burning as if with interior fires or clouded starlight or invading sunlight that was ambiguity enough for any human being, her eyes severely purposeful and fixed upon an immediate goal, the next step, her heart not stirred by any phantom.

What should she care for any naked marble statue with the grasses growing to its hips, she with her broken nose, her aging heart? Little she cared, though she could not have expressed herself, for the things of the mind which others expressed, all these illusions, hallucinations, false perceptions, exaggerations, marble statues opening their eyes, double-headed persons, imaginary pearls, pearl-divers blowing pearls out of their mouths, emperors, kings, queens, jesters with bells, dancing girls, these things dreamed by those already rich as Croesus for whom all things had turned to gold, even his bed and his bread, these things dreamed by those who had already too much, too many opal pavements and coats of golden fleece, those who owned enough stocks and bonds and real estate to sink a battleship. Little she cared, her old black umbrella buffeting against the dark wind, sometimes turning inside out, sometimes whirling, sometimes causing her to whirl, for all these wandering, drifting, homeless visions, those of the end of time, the black-winged angels of mortality falling into the burning sea, those of the beginning, for she was in the middle passage, as she would always say, not far distant from her extremities, and there was no time, no time to waste. When we were gone, we would be gone. For herself, she would have no tomb, and her grave would be in a plain place and unmarked. Little she cared for these end-of-the-world visions staining the atmosphere, these constant acts of revelation and betrayal, for though they had been mentioned in the Bible, certainly, they had appeared in the end and not in the beginning, so far as could be told, and they had not been intended for daily life. We must hasten, and we must not loiter nor imagine we could gather up all the broken sea shells on this old beach, even though we should gather sea shells until the end of time, for some would always be missing. It was better to begin a task we would have time to finish. We must run, galloping, an old nurse-maid and a dreaming child, her head heavy with dreams like the long roar of the surf which caused these tangles in her hair whitened by surf so that many might have asked—Is it the child who is old?

The sands of time, as Miss MacIntosh would say when we were walking on that lonely quarter-moon beach in the trembling evening light which gilded but a few far spars and stars, were running low, very low, indeed, for the individual life was both the beginning and end of life, and we should have no other. Man was but a breath, a puff of smoke, and quickly gone. Time was short, growing always shorter just like a candle burning in the wind. Our history upon this earth had been quite brief, beginning with the cradle, ending with the grave or no grave. The present moment, this last ray of light, was the shining one, also the dark, and we knew now all we would ever know, it was her opinion, of misery or happiness, all we would ever need to know. We must not waste our lives in the vain expectation of that which might never happen and had never happened and was impossible and would not be good for us if it did happen. She was sure that we get our just rewards and our unjust punishments upon this old earth itself, or if there was some after-life, then we should not anticipate it by running toward it, by running to-ward the unknown. We were put here for some purpose, and the way of our release was never yet in sight. To kiss the rod was better than not to know self-discipline, than to imagine we were free and our own archi-tects, building heaven as the sea builds its shells, as the birds build their nests. We were the nestless birds, even like the seagulls wading before us through lines of surf, even like the baby sandpipers who were the color of the sand which sheltered them and whose mother might have been the sand. Or so I thought then, not yet understanding the origin of life, not yet understanding time or eternity or the shadow, not even the shadow of Miss MacIntosh with her face lighted by fireflies.

Little she cared for all these fine-feathered birds of paradise, the dream of heaven as it should be realized on earth, the table set for the wanderer angel who, she was quite sure, would flee this place, or not be caught alive, or be caught only when he was dead in the windy garden. He would be caught with the tears streaking his face, with his feathers blowing around him like snow. There was no heaven which mortal frame with its old aches and pains should realize, or if it could be realized, then it should come soon enough, too soon for her if there should be only phantoms, and little would she care to associate with these in some won-derful mansion set above the drifting clouds like woolpack or the threads of sea nettles, something exceeding even these clouds or filaments of light, for she was human, plain and flat and angular, and would never lose her common sense, her earnest clarity, her way of dispensing with the awful nonsense, all these drifting visions which had no place. She would not care for six-winged seraphim with crowns of gold or for the angel cloaked in light or golden towers reflected upon dark waters or any luxury or any exaggeration whatever in the nature of things. If there was any heaven, it should be bare and plain and unfurnished, she was quite sure, a place of strong head winds and dark rains and dark tides without these pearly breakers, for God was not a harlequin with a shaven head and a masked face and parti-colored tights and a sword of lath, and God was not a harpist harping, and God was not a vain peacock strutting in a windy garden where no peacock was, but God was rather an old harness-maker or an old harpooner or a simple carpenter, she supposed, if she must speak of God and things not seen. Old earth was simply good enough for her, and nature was so splendid, especially when it was not too luxuriant, too overgrown, a morass of flowers and tangled weeds and tiny sea shells, for the bare rocks seemed truest to nature, and the dead tree in the tidal pool where the white crane roosted, sleeping until the tides came in, and the dark sands patched by snow, the sand and snow blowing into our eyes as we walked against the gale, and the hard way which closed behind us, which had provided no way of turning back, of walking twice in the same path, of living once again in memory.

Life, she was quite sure, was intended to be a challenge and not a bed of roses, and we were given our opponent in order that we might struggle with him and overpower the darkness or else go down in it. She believed, with all her simple and aggressive and loudly beating heart, in accepting the plain reality as it was, not in self-indulgence and these corrupting dreams of incorruptibility, of what was never possible to the poor, the starving, the cold, those who died but once, those who could not afford to die twice, and she believed not in the making of false promises which were never to be realized, the building up of false hopes, false pleasures. A rich man's heaven would surely be no place for her, she preferring to do one simple service for those who lived, to nurse a wounded seagull back to life as she once had done, carrying it against her bosom under her faded mackintosh until it had mended its wing and recovered its strength and could go upon its wavering journey through the clouds, she preferring to give First Aid to seagulls, to feed the hungry seagulls crusts of stale bread from her reticule, for she would scorn these golden thrones set above the mortal clouds, these crowns of silver and of gold which none had ever worn, these lute-players strumming in fields of asphodel above the stars, these weeping nymphs in a place no human being had ever been that anybody knew of. Her feet were too big a size, number eights, long and narrow, pointed outward. Her corset, this stout Admiral Dewey corset with its canvas strings and rusted wires and whale-bones and water-stained canvas flaps and sails, its girders as of a ship made to cut the Arctic ice, and surely she had seen many storms, many hurricanes, many dark seas, was drawn too tight, jabbing at her bare ribs, her breast bones so that she had difficulty breathing, and her cheeks were darkened to this purplish tinge by the great efforts of her navigating herself along the glassy shore covered with comb jellyfish like a mirror mirroring the glassy sky. Being so much exposed in spite of her head coverings, she suffered from head colds. Sometimes she seemed asthmatic, her voice turning coarse with the great effort of shouting above the icy winds. Her voice rang out like a buoy bell above the clanging waters. She shouted even in the peaceful days of calm when the sea scarcely moved or only turned in its sleep. There was no heaven, but there was earth, surely, and we were put here to be tested. This earth was but a testing ground for the squids, for the starfish, for the sea urchins, the chambered nautilus, the periwinkle, the hermit crabs, the horseshoe crabs, for herself, for Mr. Spitzer, for us all. Man was but a broken shell. Woman's heart was folly.

This earth was the testing ground, and there was nothing but the test, so far as could be realized. This earth was the testing ground even for God, often making His own mistakes which had perhaps been unavoidable as He had wished to leave man free, and also, it was the testing ground for man with all his fleshly weaknesses about him, all those temptations which he must ignore, for he must develop his strength and character. Time was not given to be wasted in vain pursuits, such as that of false knowledge, the argument as to how many angels might stand on a needle's point or whether a camel shall enter through the needle's eye or a rich man through the gates of heaven, and we should rather be concerned with the anatomy of the clouds, the directions of the winds, the positions of the stars. Every shining moment must be filled with action, ideally for the good of someone other than ourselves, for each life was given little time, the rushing of days, and opportunity knocked but once at the door of the sleeper, and we must not be tempted by useless dreams even when we were sleeping and could not summon our dreams, dreams which should be like the friction of the great waves upon the great rocks, and we must not be tempted by vainglorious riches, by torches burning in the dark wind, by slothful ease, these graven images, these empty husks like the old moss-grown boats going with the tides when the fishermen were no more. We should fight against the cloud, the shadow, the wave. We were to be proved, and the truth was better than the lie, even should the lie seem truer than the truth, every lie containing a seed of truth in it, no doubt, but ours was the freedom to make a choice between the truth and the lie and the truth and the truth, to do what was good and right, leaving no uncertainty. We must prepare ourselves to live in the service of others, the cold, the starving, the poor, the maimed, the crippled, for the opium paradise was never God's way of life. Surely, it was not Miss MacIntosh's way, never influencing her to dream or even to sleep more than would be necessary to keep her going.

Miss MacIntosh was always, therefore, very industrious, even in the hottest days, always bustling back and forth, enthusiastic, her red cheeks always blowing out as she guided me in those hard ways of poverty for which our environment had not really made provision, and I must lay up the damp hemlock branches and the driftwood gleaming with silvery weeds and tiny sea shells so that they would crackle in the winter fires. We burned the things which came from the sea. We were always preparing for another winter when there might be no sun, perhaps the six months' darkness or perhaps a longer winter than man had ever known. In spite of the circumstances which surrounded us, poverty was still our bare-faced lot, perhaps because her old ways of life could not be changed, she going according to her schedule which so few other than herself should be expected to understand or even its necessity, albeit it was very clear to her and needed not to be explained. If she changed her schedule, if she suddenly interrupted one task for another, that also was necessary and part of what she had intended so that she was never wrong. She was always right. Hers was not the undefined mentality, not even, when her eye-glasses were misted, steaming, the vague and absent-minded watery facial expression which would overlook one's immediate faults, ignoring these perhaps for the sake of future virtues, yet though she would not inquire into the secret valves of the poor human heart. It was not her business to ask, to inquire. She was surely no one who would have encouraged the intimacy of strangers, much less of friends, and she had no friends. She was doing her best here, certainly, compensating to others for their loss. She had given up other employments for this comparatively isolated position, this rich, privileged, secluded waterfront estate which few living persons had ever visited, one so little fitted to her, a hearty visitor surely upon this lonely shore as should be quite obvious and often squawking louder than the raucous-voiced sea birds and seeming almost to flap her wings, a gregarious and social-minded woman who, as she said, had walked the streets of great harbor cities and had been connected with various institutions, a lighthouse for the blind, asylums for the orphaned, the feeble-minded, the mad, the idiotic with their mouths foaming like the foaming tides, a home for old sailors on shore leave which would be long or short as God intended, though she was always, it was true, sufficiently cryptic when she mentioned what, precisely, she had done with her life and with the darkened years, how she had spent her time, for she did not believe in delving into the past, blowing up a cold spark among the dead ashes, arousing old ghosts of a personal nature, old memories, vacant faces which there might have been, the color of ashes upon the wind, their eyes glowing like embers. If ever she saw a phantom, it was not while she was conscious and in possession of her senses, and she was always conscious, her harness bells tinkling. She did not believe in letting her hair down, so to speak, in talking of old triumphs, old failures, this long struggle as it had been already enacted. She would rather crack nuts on a rusted flatiron, rather shell bean pods or stir the waters, yet though her cooking left much, she knew, to be desired, and she was better at feeding the seagulls than feeding man. After our picnics on the beach, the seagulls would sail down to eat, in the roseate light of the sunset causing their oily wings to gleam with patches of silver and green and gold, even like the sand, like the distant waters, the pieces of bread we left on our plates. Sometimes even before we had departed, perhaps not noticing us because of the heavy fog, the seagulls would float downward, their wings drifting like snow. We used paper plates which the sea might wash away. We would leave upon the sand the lace-edged table cloth which we had spread there and which the clouded breakers would sweep over by and by, carrying it away. We must have left many of my mother's beautiful table cloths which were intended for the angels and which were very old, edged by archaic lace, and my mother must have wondered where so many of her table cloths had disappeared. Perhaps she would have approved of the waves and of the winds and of the seagulls who were the inner guests, angelic guests. But Miss MacIntosh disapproved of lace, whether upon a collar or a petticoat or a table cloth or an altar cloth, even the patterns of the lace upon the breaking waves, the foam like spectral lace upon the waves and winds and sands. She disapproved of goblets of silver and goblets of gold and turret salt shakers and silverware. Ours was the simplest bone-handled tin cutlery which we would gather up and put into her picnic hamper along with her grey knitting. She would stamp out the last of the picnic fire with her well-shod foot, stamp out the last ember before the great waves came. We would walk toward the dark house with its many lighted windows, passing through the garden of the blind as I inquired as to that past which perhaps never was and should not be revealed, her ashen face lighted by the ember star as she turned her head away.

Merely, from her various brisk, casual remarks, often outside of any context, it could be gathered, over a period of years, that she had severed, long before this present employment, her connections with various institutions, that she had been, as it were, wallowing in a Slough of Despond, almost the gutter itself, and had been persuaded to take this present mission because of her profound conviction that one soul was as worth saving as another. Not all, as she would frequently remark, could be blind, yet though each had his burden and must accept it. What hers was, she never said, not through all those years before, at last, I knew her, before I saw her plain.

No one knew her past, in all that house where the past was always present, and her remarks were never revelation, a phosphorous light playing upon the darkened waters—and in future time, would seem the darkest, the most obscure. There was only her own account of what her preparations, equipment, and experience had been, what previous life she had led, if any, for Mr. Spitzer had hired her, as would be remembered through future years, without making any inquiry as to who she might be or might have been, he having been so impressed with her reality itself, it had not occurred to him to be so unchivalrous as to ask, and no one else had inquired into her character references from former employers, anything which did not meet visibly the eye, and none had ever looked beyond the surface of Miss MacIntosh, she seeming so sensible, so alert, so direct. Perhaps the surface itself was not seen or was seen by only one or two. Mr. Spitzer had noticed her because of her honest face, and she had drifted toward him because of his baffled face, his attitude of inquiry, of not being sure. She had kept to herself since coming here. She was ordinary, colorless even in spite of her high coloring, the ruddy cheeks polished by wind and sunlight, the definite ways, and not inviting that close scrutiny one might give to those who had more time, to those who loitered, those who would sit quietly. In fact, in relation to others around her, she was certainly the most sensible person imaginable, having never lost her major senses, her common sense which would never depart. She knew nothing at all, apparently, of the necessity of self-destruction, these cold, dark, negative things of life, these self-aggrandizing denials of reality, the flight away from the heart of life.

She always proceeded directly, straight to the point, never dilly-dallying, not shifting her course with every new blow of the wind, every squall of the lonely surf against the lighthouse rock, the tides coming in, the tides going out. She was impatient with all delays, all hesitations, all excuses, all ambivalences, even as of the wavering foam like mother-of-pearl. She was no turncoat, no one who changed her mind according to the imploring circumstances none could have foreseen, for her way had been set long ago, and she did her utmost to succeed within the watery fields she plowed, grey and plain though they might be. There was nothing at all unusual about Miss MacIntosh, in fact, but that she was so usual, down-to-earth, straightforward, her red hair gleaming and seeming ready to burst into fire even when she was not angry so that I was often confused as to whether she was angry or merely energetic, her strong character being certainly that which allowed no nuances of lingering interpretations, no finer shadings than just those of nature, those which had been provided, her greenish, greyish eyes glinting with unconfused determination behind her shining or her misted eye-glasses, even with uncontrollable anger if her will was crossed by so much as a word, a drifting feather burned by fire, a winged pod, a piece of driftwood, a wreath of foam, for all things, she seemed deeply, sternly convinced, should know their place cheerfully as she did, she always doing her utmost, sacrificing self-indulgence or self-pity or even her pity for others, not giving in to these powerless temptations which had no power to tempt her. She was neither a high brow nor a low brow but just, as she was pleased to admit, a plain middle brow, a Middle Westerner, trying to steer her middle course between these jangling rocks, and that was life. Was she not doing her best, steering true as only a simple-minded person could, keeping her head above the waters and ignoring these whirlpools of complications?

In fact, however, her red, gleaming hair, perfectly coiffured and smooth, lay low over her dreamless brow, though through the partings of the waves one could see, if one looked closely, a high, receding brow and deep furrows made by pain and no hairline to alleviate the lonely distance. One did not, of course, look closely, she being, because of her very flesh and blood and bones and immediacy, this comparatively colorless person, the one person who could be counted on never to fail, oppressive of strength, plainly visible like her angular frame, her nature so robust that she could not endure confinement in anything but her whale-boned corset tightly laced, that necessary harness, her stout out-of-door clothing which should protect her bosom from the long-reaching fingers of the sea mist, the feathers of the mist, the cold sea winds sweeping the crystal sands, her old salt-and-pepper tweed suit and grey shirt waist, for example, her heavy woolens, her grey knit stockings patched and darned, her British tan oxfords, her grey fedora. Any phantom, coming into her lusty presence, would certainly have fled, tearing its hair out by the handfuls, for there was something so terribly earnest about her, some-

thing which suggested nothing but the correct time, the front of her
faded shirt waist being armored always by her silver dollar watch and
battalions of safety pins, needles and pins, and a needle I had always
threaded for her because she could not see the needle's eye in the starlight-colored air or in the air too brightly colored, just as she could not
see the purple hairstreak moths among the evening flowers, and her old
black umbrella lifted whenever she went out of doors, whether it was
raining or shining, morning or afternoon or evening or night, and sometimes under the leaking roof of an old house with its ceiling of discolored
or fading angels, sporting shepherdesses, centaurs, naked gods of love,
wreaths of flowers. She had no eyes for these. Her oxfords scuffed by much
hard walking, her salt and pepper stained by many weathers since her
coming to this unusual employment, there was that about her which
discouraged loitering—even when she confronted incurious adults—her
movements being always so brisk, her cheeks taking on the rose color of
the fire-lighted air but seldom rose in a grey light, her strangely smiling
eyes seeming scarcely to notice the person she saw, for she treated him as
if he were the phantom, her way of life being so infinitely practical and
mundane that, though others might be foolish, there seemed simply no
responsive foolishness in her flinty character. If anyone touched her hand,
her hand was immediately withdrawn, the skin turning pumice grey or
rose where her hand was touched, and her cheek throbbed. It seemed
impossible for her to communicate with a fool, to establish a common
ground. She was fond of saying, over and over again—I am no fool. She
was not even a fool's fool. Indeed, she would make short shift of a fool,
quickly dismissing him—no doubt to the outer limbo. She would be
repelled by fools and dreamers and liars as by beautiful queens or ancient pharaohs wrapped in cloth of gold and silver lace—for what were
they to her, this woman who was so plain, so far from beautiful, so
obvious, no one to mystify a dreamer or elicit a second thought?

Her objectives were few. Her mind was clear as to the few essential
things, and the others were hardly worth thinking of, and she was dressed
in those durable clothes which would last her for this life, no doubt, and
she had no other life. She patched the holes when they needed patching.
Her best suit was her good pin-striped grey serge with the shining elbows,
but she wore it only for special occasions as when she went away and took
a train to the city. Her wardrobe, made up of the bare necessities, as she
would say, and no more, included no frilly dresses or trailing robes—only
her shirt waists and her simple skirts and a few old sweaters with turtle
necks and not even a trimming of braid or a fichu of lace or an unnecessary button, for if there were an unnecessary button, it would be only one
more button to lose, one more button to sew on, and the only ornament
she ever wore was a ribbon of green around her brilliant hair through
which the light shone, though perhaps her silver dollar watch hanging by
a black ribbon pinned upon her left breast was also an ornament. Her
wardrobe had been purchased, for the most part, out of her first salary
which Mr. Spitzer, with his usual far-sighted kindness, had advanced
to her when he had hired her, and she had chosen only the finest

quality, the stoutest material from the weaver's loom, as she would still insist when it was nearly worn out, much patched, much mended, for it still seemed sufficient for her needs, covering her, and she was in all ways the seemingly conventional nursemaid, one who, at a mere glance, might be accepted, perhaps never looked at twice, perhaps not even once. If, however, as the years had passed, she had become slightly less conventional, at least in those unimportant matters, the externals, wearing as often as not, both in-doors and out-of-doors, a whaler's hat, her muddy sea boots to which the seaweeds clung, her patched mackintosh faded by soughing wind and rain and surf, its hemline uneven, all its buttons lost except one, its pockets sagging because she had carried so many rocks, perhaps as ballast, as she would remark, and perhaps some day she would sink like that ship which sank of its own ballast in a quiet harbor, sinking without a sound, it was only because of the isolation of her situation, the fact that, as she might have said, so few people saw her.

We walked by the loud sea, taking our constitutionals to build our bones and characters, the surf fishermen not turning their heads as we passed, the sun-blackened clam-digger not looking up from the sand. Sitting upright in a funeral chair by the long-sighing waves at sunset when the departing light striped the waters with bars of gold, her black umbrella uplifted like a canvas tent and casting its shadow around her, her silver dollar watch shining, her rusted safety pins arrayed across her shirt front with perhaps a needle threaded with a milky thread, her wicker picnic basket on her broad-spread knees, her ankles crossed, she would busily knit, even when the darkness hovered over her, a grey hood for an orphan in a cold country as I either recited the lessons of the day, the known facts I had memorized as to the deaths of kings and facts as to geographical expeditions to distant shores and locations of major industrial centers, or read aloud from a book good for the growing soul, such as Pilgrim's Progress which she preferred to even the Word of God, for the Word of God was that which should be taken with a grain of salt and was that which could be subjected to so many contradictory interpretations and laid over with so many human exaggerations, the angels falling, for example, into a dark sea like this sea, whereas old Bunyan was fairly safe even though not altogether trustworthy as a guide through this great wilderness, this mortal life which was a path of thorns and very narrow and very uncertain. There were chasms on either side. There were roaring seas. I would begin at the beginning, reading straight to the end or skipping only a few passages, and sometimes I would begin at the end, reading straight to the beginning, working from redemption backward, perhaps skipping the same passages, and she would never seem to notice, perhaps because her ears were filled with nothing but the long, receding tides, the wash of the waves upon the shore, the winds and their antiphon reminding me of all who had died. Barn swallows darted out over the long, looping waters. Sometimes there was a strange white bird, an Arctic tern stopping upon the rocks or a long-winged white heron drifting through the clouds. The snow-white seagulls honked, descending through the late or early darkness as if they knew no time of man, and the sky was gradually or swiftly darkened as I read on, she not noticing these omissions, she almost seeming to snore, and she would droop her head, yet though she knitted on, missing only a few stitches in the dark. The sins we committed were worse than those of omission, it had been her plain opinion always, and she would argue with the world's greatest preacher if she knew him. As a matter of fact, she would have abjured all learning but what pertained to fact, and suddenly, obtruding upon old Bunyan, she would ask, nasally as if she had caught a cold—What is the best time to plant corn? Which part of the ship is abaft the main-mast? If you turn starboard, where are you going? She thought very little of all this higher education, anything that did not bear on use, for this world was a harsh place, a Slough of Despond, and we were put here to be tested, yet though all should fail the test. The deaths of all these old kings, as she would always say, her false teeth clicking like her ivory-boned knitting needles, were far less important than instructions in navigation, how to get from one point to another in the shortest possible way, how to make something, a pin-cushion, a pillow slip, a sleeve, a handkerchief, how to cook, especially those recipes which required no unusual condiment or garnish and were within the possibilities of a poor man's purse.

She would snap open and shut her purse which she wore attached by a rusted chain to her waist. There were never more than two pennies in that scuffed purse of hers, two pennies with which, she used to say, her eyes would be closed when she was dead, for her eyelids would be trained to settle. She always hoped, when she folded away her warped knitting, the grey fog swirling around her face, that I would see America first, for the normal life was the only one worth living, and it was better than all the principalities, all the powers of darkness, difficult though it might be to realize.

For herself, the conscientious, forthright, sensible nursemaid, Miss MacIntosh who had never been on speaking terms with any phantom, she had originated, quite simply, in What Cheer, Iowa, a small town like any other, as she frequently pointed out, and no different from its neighbors. If anything, it was more like its neighbors than its neighbors were. She was certainly out of her water here in a rich invalid's opium menage, blowing out her cheeks, making as much noise as she could, slapping her knees, and nothing angered her so forcefully as this, that she herself might be mistaken for illusion by some of my mother's unhappy friends or acquaintances who, at least in the earlier years before they had been discouraged, were frequent and parasitic visitors, coming to this old house as to a magnificent summer hotel, coming to tell my mother their most difficult problems, what phantoms had pursued them in their evening walks, what their great disappointments had been, what their hopes always were and would remain in spite of their disappointments, perhaps because of them, how their characters had changed because of great shocks or chronic woes, or that they could change no longer. Few ever saw Miss MacIntosh, who was usually in another part of the house, the private part, and would not countenance self-pity. Few ever greeted her. She was ignored by most, and the most they would ever know of her would be when they heard her laughter like a daft seagull screaming in the wind, when they heard her bouncing footsteps over head, or when the prisms of the many chandeliers shook with those reverberations as if a polo game were going on, and sometimes a prism broke. They cared not to inquire who the active servant was. All were imbued by themselves, self-pity, their own ghostly, creaking problems, though all might seem to her to be but the willful exaggerations of their problems which should have been suppressed or ignored, nipped in the bud by a wintry blast before they had got started. She could not have understood a merely mental sorrow, that arising from no physical source or caused by a cause so small, it could not be located at a glance. She better understood the broken bones, the actuality of a physical trial which had not been anybody's wish or desire, the trials of the courageous spirit, and she was impatient with all else, with all these visionaries, these thinkers of sad and empty thoughts.

Among all those who came to the house, only one had ever greeted Miss MacIntosh with any real enthusiasm or feeling, it seemed, of recognition, of wildest ecstasy, a look of eagerness lighting up his blood-shot, bulging eyes, his thick wrists trembling with uncontrollable delight as if he could hardly contain himself, as if at any moment he would spring upon her and take her by her shining hair and drag her away into a dark corner, there to perform his nefarious deed, to despoil her honor, but this would be no old maid's romance, it was her unbiased opinion, and she was far from favorably impressed or even vaguely flattered by his complimentary attitude and his guttural ravings which sounded to her like groans, and for the most obvious reason which should have appealed to anyone yet in his senses and with his common sense about him and with his head upon his shoulders—her admirer was a head-hunter. He was an Australian bushman wearing a loin-cloth, great hairs growing in patches out of his mottled skin, his wild curls hanging like tangled weeds around a very primitive, broken, pock-marked face which yet had, in spite of its strength, a peculiar delicacy like something ethereal and far away, something which should disgust her. His eyes lighted up whenever he saw her, but this was an unearthly fact, along with many others, which she could not quite stomach, as she would say, and could not understand even if she tried, doing her utmost. Many things about him, she disapproved of, having no shadow of doubt in her own mind, none of those marginal feelings my mother might have entertained when, not sure at all that he was real, she entertained this bold head-hunter, feeding him little crumbs of her wedding cake. Miss MacIntosh, with her usual certainty in the face of any mystery, was quite sure this head-hunter should not be trusted, for he was deceitful, someone who should have been put out of doors and made to fare for himself and who had preferred, to the living sunlight, these unhealthy shadows, these chimeras, these phantoms of phantoms. He was just semi-civilized and half baked and confused, a head-hunter who, instead of acquiring social consciousness and a feeling for his poor fellowmen, a knowledge of how the other half lived, had become a sculptor of heads, forming out of barnacles the heads of old Catholic saints or

Jewish patriarchs but indefinitely realized and vague as faces under water, leaving much to the imagination, for his dreams, so self-centered no matter how foreign they were, were that he might go over to Rome and be joined with the angels and with God's love, yet though he had never been in Rome, a heathen and monstrous city idealizing the dead, it was her plain opinion, a place which good Christians should flee from as from a plague, a place of cinders, one where she would not be seen, nor was he even a good Presbyterian or Free Methodist or Shouting Baptist or Jehovah's Witness, nor did he believe in total immersion, for he believed in sprinkling, and he gave himself these attitudes of lonely grandeur as if he might even some day become the Pope wearing turrets of gold, and he dreamed of a city of gold and marble with many splashing fountains, with many stone horses and stone curls lighted by the spray of fountains, with pavements of pale opal and walls of bones in beautiful designs like lace and roofs of gilded clouds.

He had certainly never been in old What Cheer where there were no graven images or ornaments or vestments embroidered with pearls or coats of feathers or cloth of gold, where God was worshiped in a building of plain walls such as befitted God or out of doors where there were no walls, where baptisms were total immersion in a cold or ice-bound stream, a great hole being chopped in the ice, and sometimes the baptized were drowned, and funerals were simple matters, the dead burying the dead until there were no more to bury. She was outraged, moreover, by his attitude of familiarity, by his bold courage in presuming that he must have seen her somewhere before, perhaps in another life and in a darker place, for he simply could not have, she having never been outside America or in New Mexico, the place from which he had most recently come, their paths having never crossed before, not if she was in her senses. She had originated in Iowa among the primitive Christians of great works and little faith, not of great faith and little works, and this head-hunter had originated in the Australian bush away down under where he should have stayed if he had been a proper head-hunter with his own mind about him. He was no proper head-hunter but another derelict, and as for staying in this house with him, this wanderer, she was convinced that one of them must go, for his proximity to her was that which was offensive, an assault to her common sense, her rigorous view of things, of what was possible, of what was impossible. She would rather have seen him skulking in the bush than skulking among the golden harps and the shrouded grand pianos and the black-draped marble statues in the music halls, skulking among the shadows and the stuffed lute birds, stopping to admire a broken Apollo, a dreaming Psyche, a fat-stomached cupid with grapes in its hair and its nose broken when it had fallen from a Roman roof, the wooden huntresses in ruined gardens overgrown with tangled weeds and flowers which were like his native bush. No head-hunter was worth his salt or his board and keep who engaged in such exaggerations of nature and who, though outrageously half naked and only half civilized, could balance an egg-shell teacup perfectly on his bare knees, acting as if he might have been born in a drawing room instead of in his native bush among bush-whackers and the Christian missionaries who had come to lose their heads and save his soul, and she had simply no patience at all with this head-hunter's unhealthy aspirations for a better life, his sitting all day at my mother's shadowed bedside, talking to a mad, sick lady who supposed her head was the only world, that nothing existed outside of her and her inflated imagination, not even this head-hunter with his wild mien and calculated, incalculable eloquence, his flow of broken rhetoric ranging from heaven to earth and bird babblings and unintelligible speech and imitations of a lyre bird, the love songs of a lyre bird who had fallen in love with an Australian spinster and had built a tower of earth to her window. Miss MacIntosh was utterly disgusted by my mother's teaching him fine table manners and by his eating from plates of silver and plates of gold and not mere paper plates such as Miss MacIntosh preferred for our lunches upon the sand dunes and by my mother's trying to teach him to read an old Ritz menu no longer understandable to her and by her giving him an Etruscan mirror and an ivory comb encrusted with jewels and the name of a tailor who would make him a fine gentleman from head to foot. For if he were fully dressed, then who would be warned of his former appetites—what dreaming lady, attracted to him, thinking that he was a lady-killer, might suddenly lose her head?

Nothing could be less attractive than a head-hunter to a simple-minded person like herself, Miss MacIntosh, snorting with her broken nose, ready to show this corpulent savage that, though he might lead some other lady down the garden path, he could never tamper with her private feelings and her sense of honest dignity, that she was not one to encourage these wild dreams of his or lead him astray. He was an affront, in fact, to her feelings of her own separate and lonely existence, her energetic life which rejected self-love or the love of any other person, her own life which kept its distance, even as she had kept her head upon her shoulders, losing her head to no man. Her head had never yet been turned by earthly flattery or even by the divine truth. She was surely no one to encourage his exaggerated ambitions, his desire to use her head as a model and to sculpture a great stone head which should be like hers, one of which the periphery should be lost in clouds, for he had said so, mumbling brokenly with thickened lips, his eyes livid, that he would hide it in a dark place, that it should be crowned with no flowers and put in a desert place and void where no traveller should ever come or there should come only a few, where none should see and live. He had promised.

His compliments had been just those which made her cheeks turn red, even in retrospect, and yet he was always seeming to hunt after Miss MacIntosh's head, always trying to stop her in her lively walks and tell her that he preferred her head to all the other heads he had ever seen, both living and dead, both human and inanimate, both flesh and marble, that for his purposes, it was practically unique, God's greatest masterpiece, a head such as he had always dreamed of. He was always putting his head in where his head was not wanted, parting the curtains, trying to surprise Miss MacIntosh, to take her unaware, always likely, when she least expected him, to confront her in a dark corner and try to pass the time of day with guttural and broken ravings which, though he was eloquent, seemed to suggest that he might still revert to the noble savage, for his enthusiasm knew no bounds, and his anxieties were very great when he asked her how she was or expressed that peculiar delight he found in looking at her head as if her head had been rare, very rare, indeed, something not quite of this world, as he would say, something of the last or of the next, he seeming unable to make up his mind. She was almost ready to believe that he had never been a head-hunter at all. She scoffed at his admiration, but he must have admired the high cheek-bones, the delicate contours of that coarse and often high-colored face, the flaring, broken nostrils ridged by a red line, the thin lips so colorless in a grey light that they were almost invisible, the furrowed brow, the flat, close-set ears.

He had not pleased her in the least. She would always vociferously express her doubt of him who had been her great admirer and whom she had seen through instantly, seeing that he was but a poor head-hunter who came each afternoon in a black-curtained cab for fear of startling the simple country people, the natives on the roads who might have seen the wild, half-naked man of Borneo if the storm curtains had not been drawn, a poor head-hunter, indeed, for if he had been an honest head-hunter with all his wits about him, he would not have hidden himself away. He would have hidden his neighbors away, it was her opinion. Nothing had outraged her sense of the fitness of things so much as this, that a head-hunter should be in the same house with her, that he should exalt himself above all other head-hunters, that he should walk among the stuffed reindeer and memories of Eskimos and memories of Egypt, that he should think himself a Sphinx, that he should sit relaxed by my mother's curtained bedside all afternoon and half the night when honest men were sleeping, talking of subjects which certainly would have passed over Miss MacIntosh's head, such as cherubim, many-faced angels with plumes of gold and fishes' fins, Charon on his great ferry boat crossing the dark river Styx with passengers who were the souls of the dead, the ghost of Cheops, St. Simeon the Stylite and what he had thought of this lower world, Daniel encompassed by sleeping lions, the Appian Way and houses of the dead, St. Augustine in the city of God, all those things which, strictly speaking, were nobody's business. What should a head-hunter know of Georgian architecture, of Spode chinaware, of Delft, of silver urns, of golden teapots, of things which should have passed his understanding? He talked too much of the dead and had no feelings at all, apparently, for the living, or only the most corrupt feelings, and thus this head-hunter's passion for a higher intellectual knowledge had seemed to her always, if she might say so, a bit too personal, he drawing all things into himself as if he ate them and yet could not digest them. He could not digest the golden steeples and streets of gold, the rippling towers. He had better never have molested her, that old head-hunter, or she would have taken care of him, quite simply, giving him a blow with her black umbrella, for he had never frightened her. Perchance meeting him in a hallway distant from where he should have been prowling, distant even from his usual haunts, distant from her usual haunts, she had not been afraid or startled by that terrifying visage, merely turning up her poor, broken nose with sharp disdain as he looked at her or lifting her eye-glasses so that she should not see him, so that she should blot him out, not losing self-control an instant, not even when he asked her if he might borrow one of her shirts or if she would thread a needle for him, not even when he said, growing more personal, that he would like to close his eyes and touch her head with his fingers dreaming, that hers was the most beautiful head he had seen in creation, that hers was a head outdistancing all others and one which should go far, that she had a greater imagination than anyone who lived.

She knew these men, how soon their flattery would die, even at one blow, and she was not afraid, ready to put him in his place even if he was an Australian bushman, his hair curled like a bush, someone who, for all she knew and as she would always say, might have been the graveyard of his own brother or sister or father or mother, someone who perhaps had killed little children and had cooked them and eaten them to gain their strength, someone who, as a matter of fact, could she have brought herself to inquire, might have told her where her brother was, for her own dear brother had disappeared among these gaping cannibals, quite some time ago. Her own dear brother had gone out as a primitive Christian bishop from Iowa to convert the heathen of the Easter Islands and had never returned, yet certainly had not intended to be so successful in his efforts that they should be converted utterly, that head-hunters should sit in faded drawing rooms painted with centaurs and should languish in an atmosphere of this civilized corruption, splitting silken hairs and cultivating refined appetites and engaging in these various refinements. This Australian bushman, this sculptor of anemic cherubim out of barnacles which had already sculptured themselves and needed not his help, should have stayed in the bush, working to save other souls, to increase the Christian mission as best he could, and if he had failed, that failure had been best. He should never have come to enjoy the luxury of a rich invalid's house which was like heaven in his eyes, the rugs muffling all sounds as if he walked on moss and wet leaf mold, as if he walked among the tombs. Dreaming among her satin pillows, my mother gave him the names and addresses of beautiful Roman ladies who would entertain him with lavish grandeur—though she forgot to say that they were the ladies mentioned by Plutarch, and the Rome they lived in was six feet under the Rome he should visit, for all their dining rooms and their divans were submerged. She asked him to look up her chauffeur. She asked the head-hunter to leave her calling card on the tombs of certain old Bostonians who were sleeping in the Protestant graveyard where Keats and Shelley slept and who after only one week in Rome had died of the marsh fever. She gave him the names of dead cardinals to whom he should bear her greetings, the names of popes no one else had ever heard of, popes not mentioned in any papal history though theirs had been the longest papacies in golden ages. She told him that the best hotel would be the Quirinale but that if he should not be admitted there, then he should try the Pantheon.

Miss MacIntosh had no patience with such pale pretenses of life, at least not while she lived, and she was living now, and she could never be influenced by that which was not and perhaps had never been. This cloying atmosphere of perfume like ashes of roses, wet and cold, the dark, spacious interiors filled with mummery and flummery and junk, could not but offend a natural out-door woman, Miss MacIntosh who saw no merit in wealth but only the untold virtues of poverty, of deprivation. She scolded the head-hunter long years after he had gone. For herself, she asked nothing, knowing that it would be impossible to improve her own affairs. There was to be a great change in the affairs of men, however, she was profoundly, cheerfully convinced, that things could not go on forever drifting as they had gone, that these illusions and self-deceptions and errant luxuries must all be stripped away and the past buried like a bad dream no one had ever dreamed and no one remembered. There would be no servants, neither real nor imaginary, none of these imaginary coach-painters and piano-tuners and glass-blowers such as my mother dreamed of every Saturday morning. There would be no lamp-bearers. All this trumpery and frumpery and junk, all these prized possessions should come to nothing, should be swept into the sea where they belonged, and the waves should wash them away even as the canker eats the rose, as gold and silver rust.

Walking along the beach in the early morning light, in that dim hour which seemed another twilight, for the moon had faded and the sun had not yet appeared, and sometimes the days were very grey and the sun as cold as the moon, and seldom was there a day without drizzle and fog and spindrift floating like the wraith of a star, slapping her knees, slapping her hands, almost tumbling as the wet-washed winds whirled against her broad skirts and long, thin legs, wading through the thin line of leaden-colored and foaming surf which cast its twilight on her face, her water-colored eyes peering above her misted and rimless eye-glasses, her cheeks spotted with hectic rose as the grey light was streaked with rose, she would stop to kick old driftwood back into the water, to poke at a dead lobster or broken hermit shell or lion's mane or mop of livid sea-weed which she would throw back into the sea, and sometimes she would fight to assert her will when the waves returned it, when the waves washed up the same sad thing again. Or if the same thing came not again, it seemed to her the same. Doubtless one sea shell was like another to her.

There must be, in fact, a revolution, a great change, she would always say so, blowing her poor, broken nose as her eyes watered, for nobody could afford to wait for evolution, no more than for a glacier moving in the night, and the naked sparrow could not wait, and the bare branch could not wait, and she most certainly could not, the sands of time already running low, she being only mortal, the plainest. Man must overthrow these powers of darkness, must go down fighting. What had this Darwinian evolution ever done for anybody? What had God done? How should God answer for God's omissions? God's was the strength of the unicorn, and God should bring us out of Egypt and to a clear place, but were we not still in Egypt, the waste-howling wilderness where we had pitched our tents which were so easily capsized? Revolution was the only answer, quick and sharp, for what was necessary was a great, an overwhelming change which should sweep away iniquities, the dreamers and the dreams, which should kill the dreamer and the dream. Honesty was surely, and it had always been, the best policy, never to hide one's head in the desert sands like the poor ostrich, never to hide one's iniquity in which one was shaped, for iniquity should have an end, even as earthly princes, and iniquity should not be found on our lips nor in our hearts nor in our eyes which had looked upon iniquity. The mystery of iniquity should no more work when the laborer should be paid for the sweat of his brow. The joys of the hypocrite were but for the moment, shining and brief, but the joys of the honest man were everlasting, lasting just so long as he should last, and our good works should not live after us. We must take these human affairs into our own hands, certainly, so she would say, beating the air with her hands as her breath ran short, as the gaspings of a physical pain struck her, and she would say no more, for words were very cheap, and she had no time.

She would explain never in leisure, of course, her remarks being always brusque, straight to the point, never winding in circles like the whirlpool, but yet it was obvious that what she meant was not the left wing of which so many fine things were said by my rich mother—not the right wing, that which poor Mr. Spitzer would sometimes seem to embrace, if only for the sake of a continuing argument—but something more immense, an honest point of view, the whole bird, as she would sometimes stoutly remark, stamping with her foot upon a dying ember, her old black umbrella still uplifted and bugling on the wind, for the wind was quite contentious—never to flee from the heart of life, always to live in the services of others, to know no soul but the soul of man, no heart but the other heart, no self-protection, all souls as equals, all men as brothers and alike.

If she spoke no further, it was because she was interrupted always by another blow of wind, another sea-swept spar which, clothed with feathery goose barnacles, had drifted into her watery path, and palings washed by waves, a bare tree branch with its empty nest of seaweed like human hair, the necessities of the present moment, the necessities of making haste. For we must build a sea wall to resist the encroachments of the slowly approaching sea, and we must carry ballast, our pockets full of rocks, and we must weight down the sand, burying old tramps' shoes which the tides had brought in, old refuse, oily rags. We must eat our breakfast, the eggs which we had gathered from the matted grass, and we must pack our lunch as we should take our lessons on the beach which seemed sometimes to me only the thinnest crescent between two worlds. Miss MacIntosh, under her black umbrella, sometimes with a handkerchief placed over her eyes, would seem to be waiting for the last tide. The waters whirled at her feet.

Why, then, had she fled, leaving no way she could be traced, no forwarding address but the cold September sea, dark and roaring with darkness or grey as an asphalt pavement spotted by golden lights, by great moons? It seemed that she had walked into the sea. The waves had carried her away. What proof was there? Her clothes strewn on that lonely beach, her Pilgrim's Progress water-logged with marks of sea shells on its pages, the great tides roaring like lions where she had walked alone, her broken black umbrella beating like a bird's wounded wing at the edge of the sea which had returned it, all her old properties left behind her, nothing taken, nothing missing, nothing claimed. The two pennies were in her purse under a rock, and she should never close her eyes. I could think only of these fugitive details. Such trivial things by which to remember her, yet now more precious than crowns of silver and crowns of gold! Her sea boots were filled with sand. Seldom could I bring myself to think of her unless I saw a shadow moving far away in the whistling wind or the faded colors of an old plaid raincoat laid out upon the sand where she had left it. She had buttoned the one button at the collar. There was a folded handkerchief in her pocket. Her eye-glasses, rose in the sunlight, were laid on the sand.

Who but I had caused this terrible thing, her disappearance or her death, who but I, the last person who had seen her, the last person who had spoken to her, the last person to whom she had spoken? Who but I could have predicted this sudden, unpromised end, perhaps not of our lives but of her as she was, as I had always known her—who but I, the shrieking, weeping child—who but I had made her go—who but I though I might blame the sun, the moon, the stars, the winds, the actions of the tides, the seaweed drifting at the bottom of the sea, the human faces, the carelessness of God, the malevolence of nature? Nature had always threatened us. Who but I had been responsible for that last decision which she made? Though my heart should nearly stop with this great grief of mortal shock, who but I had killed her?

Why had Mr. Spitzer, after only a few preliminaries, refused to trace her but that, as he had solemnly said, she was the heir to nothing, and for whom should he search? For whom through all the avenues of time, of space? He might better search for others. Certainly, he would start upon such an adventure if there should seem the slightest use or hope or chance, but he was by no means convinced that she was dead. He thought that perhaps she had disappeared for reasons of her own and would be very much disappointed if she ever found out that in the minds of others, she was dead. She would be very sorry if we thought that she, so good, so stable a character, had killed herself. In the dregs of the city he had found this pearl of light, and to the dregs of the city she had probably returned, fleeing this shadow. Her body was never found upon this shore, and without the dead body, there could be no proof of death in a legal sense, he knew and patiently explained, being a lawyer. So that the best we could probably do would be to maintain an attitude of secrecy as to this disappearance, here upon this shore where so many lost souls had appeared, flickering for but a moment where the fireflies gathered. Of course, he might instruct fishermen along this coast to search for her, search in the harbors and estuaries and tidal pools and rivers and under the long matted marsh grasses, and he might instruct sailors and lighthouse keepers to search for her through all the waters of this world—or he would send out a darkened boat to search where the dolphins rode— or even a lamp-lighter—but who would know her when he saw her, and who remembered her as she was?

He was so vague as to what she had looked like when she was here— how would he recognize her now that she was gone or if the waters had washed over her brow until she was no more? Perhaps, indeed, she might return. Perhaps she might never return, and we must wait and see. The wait-and-see policy had always been his. He had never jumped to quick conclusions. As for the two pennies in her purse, he would sequester them for her Treasury. Carefully saved or invested, they might some day bring a vast fortune, multiplying like the sand dollars on the beach. If we could not save her, we should save her clothes for that day when she might return, though never through the waves which had taken her. The waves themselves would not return. For we all must change. We must save her mortal clothing for her body when she came, as for the body of reality. As to the shock of her death, no man knew, unless it was Mr. Spitzer, the hour of his death. Death sent not always its harbingers. They were fortunate who died without a warning, sometimes without even a tap on the shoulder.

Mr. Spitzer's memories, not being reliable as to his own life, were somewhat baffled by his tendency to remember false memories, to remember only his forgetfulness or thoughts at second hand, at one remove from his own sad being and life. He lived by generalities, by perilous assumptions, it was his own acknowledgment. So he made many mistakes. In gathering up Miss MacIntosh's clothes from the beach, he had certainly picked up some things which had never been hers—an old black stocking, a shoe buckle, a petticoat edged with flounces of lace. He had no eyes for these chaotic details, these phantasmagoric events passing at the dim margin of his consciousness or even unnoticed by him. Frankly, he had never noticed precisely what Miss MacIntosh wore. Her beauty had never been physical. It had been something almost as intangible as the light, the darkness on the water. Yet as he would always say, it was always very surprising to him that he knew as much as he knew, at least in retrospect. Perhaps he should have asked questions when he was hiring her, but he had not done so, and it was too late to ask questions now. If he had not asked for qualifications then, he should not inquire now. What he had not done in the beginning, he should not do in the end. He had thought, quite simply, that she would make a good nursemaid, providing a much needed contrast to this environment of phantoms and of shades, of suicidal persons, some only dreaming that they were dead, some only dreaming that they lived, that she would stand out as a stout-hearted practical woman who could never be fooled by the vagaries of others, including his own vagaries which had certainly fooled him. She had surely been, at the first glance, a woman after his own heart, even if after the heart of no other man, as he would always say when she was gone, and he had always felt, though timid, though keeping his distance, a tender regard for her, a very genuine fondness increasing with the years and now like a dark whirlpool blowing around his heart.

Perhaps, altering his memories at the dictates of the moment even when he was unconscious that he did so, Mr. Spitzer had always known that there was something strange about her, something setting her apart from others, something not quite definable, and that was why he had been drawn toward her as if he were magnetized to a dark star, or else she had been drawn toward him because of something wavering inside of him and his inability to foresee the next step, his inability to make up his mind and be absolutely certain that the next step he took was right, that he would never live to regret it. Two people did not seek each other out in a crowd for no reason. Life was reasonable even in its finest moments. Even accidents had their rationale. Ah, yes, perhaps it was she who had recognized him—though he did not know her and would not know her if he saw her again.

Mr. Spitzer, as he would vaguely recall many times in the years after her death or her disappearance and always with increasing indefiniteness, after her so suddenly passing away and leaving no trace but the old clothes strewn upon a beach which had seen so many wrecks, so many silvery spars brought in by the tides and torn canvas sails and balls of warped string, had been seeking, in the course of his legal business, a lost heir, his mind far from the immediacy of the physical fact, and then he had remembered that he should be looking for a nursemaid, too, and he had hired her at the moment he had seen her, a woman whose honest face had made an instant appeal to him, so that he had not hesitated, so that he had asked no personal questions, for none were necessary in such an obvious case, and there had not been a moment's rapturous doubt in his mind which was usually of two opinions. He had always preferred a dark lady. She had pleased immediately, even when he had first seen her, his baffled and myopic eyes, yet though he had been somewhat vaguely surprised when, having hired her, he had seen her again, a different woman from the shawled figure he had encountered upon a shadowed sidewalk, for he had rather been under the impression that she was a brunette, that her forehead was overhung by cliffs of darkness, that her eyebrows were dark and beetling cliffs. Yet he might have been mistaken, his mind abstracted as it was and far away from any practical purpose, and so he had never thought, in the after-years, to question her or his own intuitions which had led him to make this choice. She had emerged as from a crowd of men upon a sidewalk, she with that definite air about her, that pointed and aggressive chin, her skin so moth pale, the color of the faded twilight, as he indefinitely remembered, for he had nearly not noticed her, having been wrapped in his own sad or empty thoughts, preferring abstractions and reasonings to the particularities of harsh, incalculable experience or to these lost perceptions blooming in his path, shadows of blackbirds, of clouds. He had almost passed her by, but perhaps she had brushed against him, for he could not recall every detail of the fleeting episode, and now he might have changed his point of view. She had seemed, if he was accurate of memory, obvious and set apart, standing a little outside the crowd at the doors of an employment agency which was turning away the unemployed, the men who dreamed of working in green fields, and under the sign of three golden balls of a pawn shop like golden apples blooming in a dark air, and she had been very shabby, a creature forlorn and yet sensible, cloaked in oyster grey, so he had chosen her instantly and without further thought and had believed that he had never had occasion to regret the spontaneous act so unlike himself and his usual caution, not even when he had seen her walking along the snow-patched beach with her red hair gleaming, with her face reddening in the sunlight. He had only been happy for her that she had improved her lot, that she was more robust. She had been very fine, she being all he had supposed she was and somehow qualified, as could be seen at the first glance and as he had sensed immediately, for a position he had had in mind, and she had not disappointed him, for she had been a good and dependable woman, he always would insist, even when she was no more, when possibly she was dead, that she had never changed, that she had never wavered as to her original intention.

CHAPTER 4

Long years after her disappearance or death, I had dreamed of no one but Miss MacIntosh, my darling, poor lost soul, her cheeks reddening in the terrible sunlight, her hair red as the red rooster's wing. Long years after she was gone, my hair cropped, my body slothful and immense, my flesh increasingly vapid and vacant, I had been somnolent, the creature of ease, my glazed eyes staring at the wall, the fish scales blown against a wall, the shadow of the sea, my mind still, employed by nothing but the dream, the dream of what was normal, and this in spite of the fact that my mother who had previously not noticed me as she doubtless had seldom noticed Miss MacIntosh, believed that I was losing my sanity, my last ray of common sense and knowledge before I had acquired my first, that I had lost my hold on life, that I must be drugged, that I must partake of the opium paradise in order to avoid that certain fate awaiting all who lived and breathed and walked. For those who died in the midst of life would never die.

My mother was not even serious in this discussion. She twirled her white umbrella in her swan boat, and she called to her polar bear to come out of the mirror, and she called for her hair-dresser to comb her long black hair.

A great, staggering blow had been dealt to me by life, that disappearance of my poor darling who had left no trace, no way by which she could ever be found, and I had staggered, shrieking like the winds, striking at shadows, lashing like the waves, tearing my hair as the phantom should, speaking to no one, seeming mad. Sometimes the sound of the sea was faded to a single cicada's cry. Sometimes the sea itself would seem to cease to breathe. Sometimes the sea was swollen, reaching higher and higher, and I felt as if I were at the bottom of the sea and looking upward through the dark waves of the storm clouds tossing, there where were but a few distant life rafts of stars which I could never reach, not even if I walked on stilts like the stilt birds. It had seemed to my mother that I might lose my mind if I had not already lost it, that I might be, if I walked, the greatest idiot who walked upon the face of the earth or water, a fool or a mad man or both, and so I must be stilled and put away, kept among the interior shadows and the crystal prisms which reflected only the dream of sunlight, the dream of refracted starlight. For what, she would ask, had ever been real, and who had ever known reality? And Miss MacIntosh, though she had not known her, had disappointed her by this very fact.

My mother had decided, perhaps too quickly and with little thought, that the crucial time was come when she must acknowledge her defeat, when I must make that compromise which she, a poor invalid sleeping in a charity ward or under the roofless heavens, had made years before me, when I must accept, even at so early a year, long before the cruel hand of experience had been laid upon my brow, my death in the midst of my life, that I must lie still, the companion corpse of her eternal illness, for there was no other way by which I could live, and the alternatives were always worse. It was better to think of walking than to walk, better to think of dancing than to dance, better to think of playing tennis than to strike the ball, better to evade life than to face it and all its enormities, the things which never would be understood. My hair would turn grey if I lived, my forehead be covered by crow's feet, but if I died this seeming death in the midst of my life, my beauty, she had promised, would be immortal like hers, and I would not live to regret my choice, for I would have no memory of time's passage, and the years should not bring me age. The years should bring me youth. Time died when my love died. I should have many rare jewels, the inexhaustible jewels of Golconda, moonstones and lapis lazuli, filagreed coral reefs, sapphire pavements, all the pearls of the sea and pearls no pearl-diver had ever found, hectagonal crystal spars of seven or eight feet in length, fire opals in clouds, cat's eyes, many servants to wait on me, some with jeweled crowns, many supernatural beings beyond the ken of rational knowledge. I should have my ermine cape and diadem, shoes of gold, gold wishing rings. I should be like a nymph in a mountain cave where are husbanded the everlasting snows, the fairy grotto where the lone traveller is lured.

This was my mother's greatest act of love, the only sign that she had a child, her acceptance of me when I was no more, her acknowledgment that I existed only when I had ceased to exist, her offering me oblivion as if I were born into death, as if like a meteor shooting far off its mark I had by-passed this world and all its wondrous experience, as if I had reached a barren star, her offering to me as something merely curative, secreted in a gilded coffee cup, in my food, in my drink, seeming also to be in the very air I breathed, in the noxious marsh dews, in the curling mists and fogs, in the salt pools where stood the white angelic birds with folded wings, in the wild or slumberous sea, the opium paradise which should bring the power of wakeful sleep, of sleeping wakefulness, that great play of illusion which must take the place of the world thereafter, all things changing their forms, their shapes, all things blurred as if seen under water. She had promised so many pleasures—fashionable sailing parties though the boats had gone down, leisurely rides on horseback through Poland, many balls, many evening guests, such a splendid coming-out party. I should be the greatest debutante of any season.

Her lace and white satins draped around her in her ivory bed, her skin seeming as cold as the white satin she wore, her feet shod in white satin slippers with paper soles such as are worn by the dead who have not far to travel, she was always radiant, and few should know the six months of darkness which had preceded one shining moment, and few should see her with her eyelids swollen and blackened, her face swollen like that of the drowned—and if I saw her thus, then I closed my eyes in order not to remember her, ignoring this sad time in favor of that time when her beauty should return, when she would seem to have no memory of a thousand roaring voices, when she would entertain once more her evening guests, the great round face with eyes which never closed, the small round face with eyes continually opening, closing, or perhaps a thousand canaries blown here by the storm and singing in the candle flames.

I could not compete with her dreams, and I would never have been, though I should never wake again, as beautiful an embalmed corpse as my mother was, never so lively, never so charming, for I was soon become the creature of my own sorrow, the fat, stupid, indolent girl, great balloon of meaningless flesh with negligee ribbons streaming as I lay upon the sand, my eyes glazed, staring at the winds, the tides, the wild, storming sea, the night which seemed endless, for the night had brought my love, and the night had taken my love, my mind employed by nothing but the dream of escape, by nothing that was strange, no enchantment of unworldly gliding image or animated furniture, nothing that could not be realized in immediacy and in flesh, only the dream of one who had been so good, so true, so kind in the ultimate sense, only the dream of one who had never dreamed and who had given her life to prove that dreams were false, Miss MacIntosh, my darling, her red hair gleaming in the sunlight spotting the fog where she took her lonely constitutional, an old dog barking at her heels as I could hear him barking long after she had gone, only the dream of that normal life which she had always spoken of in no uncertain terms and from which she had fled long before she came to this dark house, the things that might be found by those who lived, the other America, the interior, the small town, the routine of Monday following Sunday, Tuesday following Monday, the washings on the lines, the voices of little children, baking day, recipes, knitting for the mission at some far Arctic post.

Others might be surprised by what a rich girl dreamed, that she did not dream of riches. I did not dream I lived in marble halls, for I lived in marble halls. For years I dreamed of nothing but a shoemaker's awl, an old tramp's shoe which needed mending, a hammer, a nail—never of the sun-lit tapestries fading on walls, never of the hawking and hunting parties. I built a house of driftwood, though only the seagull came to the door. I lit a fire upon this beach that Miss MacIntosh might know where I was—that she, far out at sea, might see this light gleaming—long years after she had gone. Perhaps she might see this star. I had searched for her everywhere, and yet I had not given up the search even when others had said that she would never be found, neither in a great sea of humanity nor in the sea. Yet years after she was gone, I had found her ivory knitting needles in the sand.

I had walked along the surf, searching the waters for what the waters might never return. I had gone out in a sail-boat looking for her upon the face of the deep, looking for her through shadow and sunlight, had sailed in scudding winds, had talked to old fishermen drying their silvery nets on the beach, had talked to the red-faced lobster-trappers red as the lobsters they trapped, to codfish fishermen returning from the Great Banks with the full boats followed by the empty boats, to sailors of the deep, to all who were wayfarers of the sea. Staring through tears, my eyes blinded by tears, I had tried to write a book by the wavering light of the sea, but I could not compete with four snails crawling across the open pages, crawling into the sea, for their writing was more beautiful than mine. So I left the book by the tide.

I had escaped, and the slow years had passed, and I had grown thin, and my hair had grown long, sometimes hanging like a curtain before my eyes, but my heart had not grown older, and I had not gathered wisdom. But sometimes I thought that I had given up the search for Miss Mac-Intosh long ago. No longer dreaming, no longer I searched for her as she once had been, for she was dead, and my search was for life, this life as it would become. Here, where now a squall of rain drove against the bus-window, here where only a far lamp gleamed for a moment like a great moon and went out, here where the night shrouded the night of the soul which the daylight should never reveal, I knew what I had always known, that the unknown had always been, must always be her place. That was why I had come this circular way—by no direct route.

To have gone to Iowa direct, to have inquired at every door with a hopeful face—had anybody seen Miss MacIntosh, my darling, she whose face I could not quite describe after these years of oblivion—would have been too suicidal and foolhardy a journey, for that had been the place of her origin, of her essential deprivation which had accompanied her through life, and she had certainly depicted nothing which was ideal, even in the remotest sense. She had said that Iowa was very ordinary, that the life was hard and certain and finite, that all but a few atheists went to church and they were very kind people, that all the people were visible or almost all, that they had known each other very well from birth to death or as well as could be expected. She had said that the winters were cold, that the children's ears were frozen, and that was why she wore ear muffs. One must break through the frosty ground with his hoe, and the ice creaked like a glacier moving. The sun was frozen in a cloud. Sometimes the sun was small as a pumpkin seed. The children's toes were frozen. The horses were frozen to their plows in the frozen fields. The carts were frozen to the frozen roads. The beards of men were frozen. The snow piled up in great billows even in the spring, and the early birds were those who died, frozen to the crystal branches. The cherry buds were nipped by snow. The smoke was frozen in the chimneys. There were frozen flames. Once a farmer driving his wagon with a team of four horses went through a hole in the ice of a frozen lake, and in the spring when the ice was melting, when the great boomers were booming, he was brought to shore with his hands frozen to the reins and his four horses rising through the foam caused by the breaking ice, the mist and spray.

But this was not Iowa, that ultimate realization which I dared not face, the fact that I should inquire for no one. This was only the stopping ground, Indiana, the promised land of which I had read in catalogues of wild flowers and seed catalogues, as near as I could go without being confronted once again by the bitterness of the facts, by the cold, the lonely, the unfulfilled, the unforgiving, the unforgiven, the murderer, the murdered.

Though now this night landscape was clouded and blurred, the splotched cheek of the dreaming invalid, morning should bring the sunlight. I should be free of the dream, requiring no medium of the dream to stand between me and the clear reality of simple days, for life itself should be enough, and no further illumination should be required, none but the sunlight on the new buds and leaves, the robin redbreast singing.

No longer, by a momentary quiver of the dreaming eyelid, should the external world, all these colors and forms be banished, and no longer should I grope, feeling through the darkness, exploring with my fingertips those surfaces I dared not see. There would be the wind and the sunlight and no nightmare in the clarity of the sunlight, no dream lifting its forlorn head covered with hoar-frost, its head of snow in sea foaming like a field of undulating snow, of moving and white-capped waves.

There would be cherry and apple and peach and persimmon trees, their blossoms blowing like foam, meadows of wild flowers as closely packed as mosses, shaggy, sun-lit hills the color of a new-born pony's coat, the great, wild river overflowing, many tributaries, many streams, brackish pools of standing waters, the wilderness turned to waters standing, green fields or flooded, old rail fences broken down by the wild mares, the foals running against the clouded morning sky. Gradually, even imperceptibly, the wounds of an eternal mourning healed, I would be merged into that charmed life, the familiar community of souls, all souls equal and alike, that soft, velvety, shifting landscape of rivers and streams and low, beautiful hills and bluffs where the wild cherry blossoms hang as big as baby ears. There would be the laughter of little children, and there would be little lambs at play, the ewe and the ram and the old grandfather and the little shoemaker, and there would be nothing unkind but nature's bounty, nature's forgetfulness.

I, Vera Cartwheel, daughter of Catherine Helena Cartwheel, nee Snowden, and of a father unknown, perhaps of many fathers, would be a part of that other world, the commonplace, the essential goodness of life which asks no questions of the moon or sun or stars. For they are their own answer, shining through clouds. All people would greet me by my name, Vera, that which stands for truth and not merely the fickle promise or dead substitute for that life which was never to be realized, and none should dream or sense that background of illusion from which I had fled to reach this central heart of an essential life, even as it is experienced by others, those simple persons I now imagined. I would be freed of the past and of its obsessions, those driving ghosts white sheeted with ice, those voices calling my name upon the many winds, calling Vera to remember the lie as if it were the only truth. The dead past would be buried, and my eyes would be awakened, and I would be a Lazarus of these awakening joys, these country pleasures. There would be no dark hallucinations staining the air, no interior self-deception, no long sleep of empty years. There would be a continuity of blessed events, births and weddings and wedding anniversaries, natural death at the end of a long life, the silver, the golden, never the leaden bells.

There would be family picnics under the flowering hedges or in the orchards of peach and pear and apple blowing like surf. There would be the wild hedge rose and the burning brimstone butterfly and the pebble moth, a ribbon to the youngest baby, a medal to the oldest citizen. There would be contests of endurance. There would be foot-races between the fat and the thin.

Never the leaden bells. Yet how had I come to make this great change, this turning away from all I had experienced before, from the insubstantial fabric of old days, old nights, I still must ask myself as the bus plowed on through clouds of ethereal darkness or sunlight splashing so thin that it might be a dream? For all those persons who had ever pointed the way, all were dead, and some had been suicides, and I had come because of nothing I had known, because only of the unknown, because only of that which I had reached for, life, the unreachable. I had come because of a dead girl's love letters strewn on the floor of a room like a cell, because of those letters she had written but had not mailed, each accepting the proposal of a man she had never seen, Cuckoo, Bud, Jim, Bob, Henry, Bill, the farmers in deep countries who had never seen her, she being different according to each description she gave of her face and of her height, because of her yearnings for a beautiful domestic life and for only the simplest things imaginable, marriage, the union of body with soul, children, chickens, a little farm with a vine-covered gate. To casual acquaintances and strangers up and down a waterfront street of painted streetwalkers leering under the lamp-posts, the iron trees, and of darkly illuminated show windows displaying waxen brides in their wedding gowns with their long trains and veils, waxen ring-bearers, waxen flower girls, she had said that she was going to be married, that she had found him, the ideal mate who should be the bridegroom when she should be the bride, yet though she had no father who would give her away in holy matrimony, for she had lost her father at the age of three, and she was going a thousand miles to meet a stranger who was tall and dark and handsome and who wore a waxed mustache, an old-fashioned handlebar. Her straw suitcase was packed with her crushed veil, the pallid velvet flowers which she had torn from an old hat which had belonged to her mother who had been an Irish wash woman, her bedroom slippers which had never touched ground, her lace negligee with its ribbons and rosettes, even her portrait at the age of three in the arms of her father who had worn an old-fashioned handlebar and whose face was dented by the shadow, and it was only a question of time now, her wedding and the wedding feast and the wedding guests assembling, they who should come from many miles in all directions to eat her wedding cake, come like the wild swans flying over the city of night. She had left in a taxi cab under a shower of rice and old shoes for Grand Central Station, the train which would be pulling out in another hour or two for a place about which she was very vague, for she had named several states, but she had changed, at the last minute, her mind, directing the taxi driver to turn another way, perhaps because of the love which would always change its face, the love of which the only face was a cloud. She had returned almost to the same neighborhood from where she had started, one so like it that it would have been hard to detect the difference, there being the same rotted warehouses, the same tailoring shops and tallow-colored tailors, the same huge spools and scissors against the sky and signs of fishmongers' wares, anchors, ropes, sails, fishing nets, the same lamp-posts with lamps like the eyes of insects gleaming through the dusk, the same dives, the same billiard halls where the boys were making their lucky or their unlucky shots, tramps sleeping in doorways or on the sidewalks or in the gutters, even in enormous baby carriages, their empty whiskey bottles tucked under their bleeding chins, and then she had paid the driver and thanked him for his courtesy, walking on alone as the twilight fell over the quivering moth-colored city, as the city lights went on, as the tall buildings were suddenly honeycombed with golden lights reflected on the oily waters of the dark fog-bound bay, a few squares of window lights burning where burned the lights of grey freighters and coal barges and ships going out to sea. With her suitcase still clutched in one hand and the other hand holding her hat, she had jumped from Brooklyn Bridge at the main-mast, screaming like the ships' whistles as she went, and she had taken a long time falling. Clutching her suitcase all the way down, she had disappeared into the purple darkness of the waters.

Had I made, after all these long, circular windings, the wrong choice, the dread suspicion crossing me now that we had passed, long ago, the choice point, a dead star, a dark star, that there was no choice? So many turnings, so many windings, so many blank walls.

A fat, soft-faced lady on the train out of Grand Central Station had warned me, her voice screeching owlishly above the grindings of train wheels as we passed along the frozen Hudson where fishing seagulls skimmed above the breaking ice or perched upon the jagged ice floes and where only the tops of bare tree branches and winter grasses and towers of drowned watch houses emerged like islands above the thinly gleaming and ice-coated waters draped at their far edges by cold black mountains with heads of clouds and snow, that where I was going, it was a place out of this world, if she had heard me aright, that there was no social life, no communication, no human contact, that there was nothing but desolation and weeds, she knew, for she had just come from there, and she would never go back, never so long as she lived. Her chandelier ear-rings, her waterfall necklace jangling like nervous discord, her fat blonde head bobbing under its burden of filmy veils and pale blue ostrich plumes, she had said that where I was going, it was the jumping-off place, the end of the world, and she would not go back to such a place if someone gave her a million dollars, a yacht and sail-boats, all the land as far as the eyes could see or even farther, all the rivers, Renaissance chairs and feather beds and vestments of gold, for it was all loss, no gain. It would be better to think of the place, never to go there to a place out of this world. Why, she had asked, her eyes rounding and flat as dinner plates, would any young person want to go to such a desolate place? Why would anyone want to go there if he was in his right mind, if his senses were unimpaired, if there was any other chance in life whatever, any prospect? She was more experienced than I and knew her way, what she was talking of, and she must warn me that I was headed toward disappointment, that it was nothing, that my expectations would not be realized or would be rudely disappointed, that there was a chilling of life, a withdrawal, a numbing of senses, and one talked only to one's self in the long nights. If she were I, she would go to Boise or Reno, where she had gone to get her divorces from all her living husbands, where she had sometimes flown and sometimes gone by train, where she was going now, and she would not be confined to any man on earth. I had chosen this other way as she could see, her eyes vapid or sorrowfully smiling, and perhaps I had never been married to any man on earth, but marriage was better even if it did not last than to be unmarried forever, to be the old maid. Perhaps I was already married, and my husband was dead, but I should remember, even if I had lost him, even if I had lost him after only a single night of wedded bliss, after that one night passing like a dream, that there were just as many fishes in the sea as ever were caught, and love had never been unique, one man being like another, and love could always repeat itself, even like the flowers of spring, and there was a second husband for everybody.

In that place, I would find nothing but the bloom of disappointment, she knew, for she had been there and knew that the houses were empty with staring, cobwebbed windows like blind eyes, that there were bats in every broken belfry, bees making their honey between the papery walls, weeds growing up to the doors, that nobody was at home. I would find myself hemmed in, shut away, forgotten, that it would not be at all what I thought, that there was nothing to live for, as breathlessly she explained, that nature was the cruelest mother, that the much-vaunted beauties of nature had been exaggerated and over-esteemed by those who had never come close to nature, that nature was never kind to nature's children, that there was no nature at all, that there were only the weeds and the glowing ashes in all that land.

Where I was going, all the young people had fled from, and the old were half in their graves, and nobody remained but the old, and nobody could hear a word that was said. All the old people, those who remained, she must insistently warn, her ashen blonde head bobbing with vague emphasis, her eyes lighted by cold astonishment, her icicle ear-rings jangling, were deaf as door knobs, as wooden posts, and the human voice was not heard, and there were funeral wreaths hanging on all the doors, she knew, for she had been there, and no one had heard her screaming. The voice of the turtle-dove was not heard in all that land, for the golden bowl was broken and the wheel broken at the cistern. Nobody knew what time it was, for all the clocks were stopped. She must warn me, one so unexperienced, untouched by life, that there was nowhere such as I dreamed, that in the place where I was going, my cryings should not be heard, for there was no person left to hear. All the old persons were deaf, stone deaf, carrying old-fashioned ear trumpets which they did not turn on, the reason being that they did not wish to hear, and their ears were mere empty shells filled with no roarings of the outside world, the train whistle, the traffic horn, the grindings of wheels. Their ears were filled with only the roarings of the world inside, church bells, lost voices, the cries of infants in their graves, frozen bird song, echoes. They were deaf, for they had taken quinine to cure their malaria which was caused by the festerings in the river bottoms, the marsh butterflies, and their malaria had not been cured, and the cure had deafened them, killing their ears.

CHAPTER 5

No stars, no sign-posts now, a crazy bus-driver losing his way that he knew too well, his loud mouth singing to while away the hours, "Oh, the old grey mare, she ain't what she used to was," as the grey miles drifted by forever and forever. A pregnant girl—rather, a thin woman of faded complexion, and everything about her artificial, everything but the one thing that mattered—moaning thinly in her precarious and broken sleep, accusing everybody, all the Toms, Dicks, Harrys, all the glass-blowers, the night watchman, every man but her husband who slept at her side, and no other voice to answer hers. We were stopped by the shunting cars of the Pennsylvania Railroad, the watchman's lantern swinging like a great red eye in the mist, a washed-out wooden bridge, a fallen tree-trunk, and we must detour a thousand miles, it seemed, to advance one, and we must always go back through the chill and empty air, the sighing monotone of winds upon a flat expanse, watery and vague. There were rain-lit pools in our way, splashing against the bus-windows—upon a far horizon, sudden fountains—though now the rain seemed only to hover, pebbling the grey sky as with pebbles in a brook.

"How much longer?" I asked, impatiently.

"Three shakes of a dead dog's tail," the bus-driver answered, peering over his shoulder and obviously startled by my question. "It's the jumping-off place. It's where creation stops. Hold your horses." Some people said, of course, it was just the beginning, but whether the beginning or end, it was where the lamb had got no fleece, where the little birds had got no feathers—where the old doctor, practicing only in his crazy dreams, had now no patients other than in his sick imagination, of course, seeing the breath on the mirror where there was no breath, the feather move where there was no feather. We would soon be there, and we would have a long time in which to wonder why.

He winked, his eyes lighted with red lights, his drunken face purple as a swollen sunset, draped with his great black beard like a coarse-grained cloud, his teeth like a yellowed piano keyboard of which some of the keys were missing—and definitely, shouting at the top of his lungs or whispering in a voluminous voice loud enough to awaken the dead, he was not in tune with that which went on now undiminished in my heart, with the elegiac music of the spheres or with those heavenly harmonies no

78

mortal ears could hear, the angels accompanying those spheres down the accustomed road, the great dolphins uplifting the stone boats of the dead upon the turbulent waves, for he was only, somewhat erratic, this wild-eyed bus-driver, driving his stuttering and wheezing bus through the roaring spring floods under the pale, chalk-colored evening sky—or just galloping along, galloping along on a white horse in his imagination, coming like all the furies to a place which should awaken when he came.

"Giddy up, giddy up, little cherub dogs," he cried. "Giddy up, giddy up, little churchyard owls, little churchyard mice. Giddy up, little rabbits, little stars, for we are coming home," he said in a conciliatory voice, "and Papa is very drunk." He was not used to hearing these complaints, for it was very lonely out there, very lonely, the track circling around and around, and his horse could not hear a word he said, and the tree branches were weighted down with heavy snow, hooded and cloaked, and the stars freezing and cold, and the skies turning black as midnight, and his hair burning, streaming like the tail of a comet in the winter wind. His head was whirling.

If I had any complaints to make as to the distance, the elastic miles stretching out between one place and another, the whirling, shooting stars, the way these places moved around, playing leapfrog before us and behind us, make them to the company, not to him. He was not responsible. He had not created the world nor the distance between one place and another, and now if all those sign-posts were gone which had pointed the way, the familiar landmarks no longer guiding him, the Burma-Shave signs, the broken rail fences, the gate-posts, if all the roads were washed out, the road-beds rushing like livid rivers under these rusted wheels, he had not created them, and he was just doing the best he could, driving along with only his memory of the polar star, the sheep shed, the next turn, only thinking he was the bus-driver. Sometimes he felt as if he had missed his calling, as if he ought to have been an Arctic whaler lassoing a drove of pasturing whales, as if he ought not to have been the bus-driver and driving this old bus, trying to find his way past vanished orchards, passing the places which were no more but only in his imagination, of course, the cherry trees bending and breaking under their weight of snow, the snowbirds, the snow clouds.

He drained off the last drop from the bottle, the empty whiskey bottle which still went to his soft, coral-colored lips for which he must search, search through his great and coarse, silky beard hanging like a fringed mantle from his chin. An immense, fat hand, feeling around his bushy hair which seemed also filled with spines, was dimpled, soft and vague like a woman's or like a great white hovering bird with a fluted wing—an angel of this deep, I thought, but whether for good or evil, life or death, I did not know.

"Why don't you cut your hair?" I could not help asking, even though the sign above his thatched, amorphous head, there where many oceanic birds might rest, lifting one wing, where many homing doves might perch in a stone-colored evening light, seeming themselves to have emerged from the inanition of stone, urged that no passenger engage in conversation with the bus-driver whose eyes were always on the road and who had been chosen for his efficiency in getting from one place to another—perhaps, I thought, from this world to the next, for so unevenly he drove.

Ach, God and the angels, jumping Jesus, jumping toads, holy Lucifer and Lucifer matches, dead cherry trees blooming with sudden flowers, hell and high water, his mother's breasts—why should he cut his hair if he wanted to let his hair grow long, hanging over his eyes so that he might hide himself away from the face of God, away from woman, away from man, away from the cold starlight, away from the crazy old doctor who might tamper with his living heart and tell him to wake up, that he was dead, that he had died in his sleep two or three years ago and now only thought he was driving this bus with these four passengers, one as yet unborn? What question was that? Why should he ever cut his hair if that was not the idea in his mind and so long as he was a man in a free country, so long as he could call his soul his own, if this was his own old bus to drive whichever way he chose and still arrive where he was going, taking the road to his own perdition, the road to heaven that was the road to hell and back again, passing the same things again and again, the same rail fences broken down and horse fountains and hitching-posts, the filling station that was always closed, the same old barber poles in the country of the bald-headed men? Did I think his hair had grown longer during this ride, long enough to cover his naked skull, his burning eyes, and would I say that a naked skull should never be his fate even if he should live a thousand years?

His hair had grown three inches since he left Persia at sunset, just when the sun was setting over the empty box factory, over the bare razorback hills snouting like wild pigs against the dark sky, over the trees naked of flowers, the leafless bushes, the foundry that had no bricks and no fires and the bell-tower that had no bells and the flour mill where the flour was black as coal dust, when the sky had been filled with red-winged blackbirds so thick it might have been the middle of the night, and his hair would grow three inches more before the coming dawn which would be another form of darkness, purple as midnight in a town of the dead sleepwalkers, there where the spinster ladies, their prim umbrellas uplifted, walked with their empty market baskets, where the little boys walked with their naked dogs and their fish-tailed kites, the little girls pushed their doll carriages through the sun-splashed, shadowed streets, everybody sleeping but the bus-driver in his four-postered bed there at the old hotel in the room which was the bridal chamber where his old mother was, dreaming that she was young and beautiful with her breasts filled with milk and her baby in her arms and her young husband at her side, nobody hearing, through the thin partition between soul and soul, a word, only old Miss Pebbles, deaf as a stone in the midst of a rippling brook, turning her broken earphones off and on, off and on, turning, tossing in her sleep in a narrow bed, overhearing only the conversation she dreamed of hearing, and she would complain to the desk clerk of how she had been kept awake all night, hearing dead lovers quarreling, those who had pinched each other black and blue in their sleep, crows cawing, peacocks screaming in the windy gardens where there were neither peacocks nor gardens, horses neighing in the stables where there were no horses, an old watch dog, he who had been shot to put him out of his misery, barking at a shadow, a shooting star, moving clouds, the things which were not, the things which never had been, which never would be, the landlord's snoring, ears of corn rustling where there was no corn, where nothing grew that had ears, where nothing grew but the bus-driver's hair burning with eyes, with ears, with tongues, with whisperings. Nothing grew but the bus-driver's hair, his hair growing like his wild imagination, his black hair like golden tassels tossing in the wind, like flying manes, like fields whirling with drunken blackbirds mirrored in glassy pools, and his hair was full of burning eyes like the eyes of Argus if he had lived, full of eyes like the peacock's burning tail, like the many-eyed river, his hair drifting always around him, soft as a cloud, as a feather mattress and a soft pillow, as a bride in a bridal chamber, and his hair would not molt as would this mortal hair, and his hair would grow when nothing else grew. His hair was his angel, his dead mother who lived in him, his dream of life, his angel's downy feathers getting wet and clinging to his cheeks when he slept, and his hair was his burning beard, his sense of his being different from other men, for his hair was a personal dream and lively with his thoughts, his thoughts always of himself, his chin to his knees.

Perhaps his hair, if given a chance, would grow six inches more before the coming dawn, or if ever the feathers and burs were combed out of this old horse's mane with its knots and its snarls, was already longer than it seemed, long enough to wind around his feet and tickle his toes and keep him warm like an angel's folded pinions in the coldest nights and in his flooded grave, this womb of time, of time which was his dream. Hair was a very fine thing to have, it seemed to him, both in this world and in the next, so he had got his fleece.

It seemed to him that a fellow must express his mind somehow, even if only by his hair, by his hair covering his hollow skull, these burning eyes, and that was why he let his hair grow, never cutting it. He was just hanging on to his life, sometimes it seemed to him, by his hair, a single hair, a single hair that would never break, a hair hanging between him and a star. Or he could always, if things got too much for him, hang himself by the hair of his head—but at least, he would have his hair to hang himself by, and that was something to be grateful for, considering the way things were going to wrack and ruin, the way the Democrats were running this old country straight into its grave.

"Hell, yes," the bus-driver said, aggressively, arguing, trying to find his way through that great obstacle, his hair which, with his itchings and scratchings, almost drove him wild like the buzzings of gnats. "This hair is mine, I said to the barber who was turning bald, bald as the pumice stone he sharpens his razor on, and damned if you will ever cut my hair, even as a joke, for I like my bed soft, not hard like yours, and I like a feather pillow. I will be an angel in the next world. Go shave your own bald head, I said to him, and don't come at me with those old, rusted garden shears of yours, for my hair is all I've got that is my own, all that the government has never yet claimed, has not turned into public property, has not turned into a public park for the little birds, for the little white birds and the little black birds and the little red birds and the red-winged blackbirds and the little children that nobody wants, and nobody hears them crying in the bushes. Squirrels, I said to him, squirrels chattering in the tree-tops. What with all these free-lunch counters, it's getting so a man can't live any more or call his soul his own, and that's the way the Democrats are running this old country, straight into the ditch, and they will tax the shirt off my back, and then they will tax my hair. I will be naked. So don't come at me, I said, with that wild look in your eyes, for no hair of mine will ever line that old crow's nest of yours or keep you warm, and I'm no Democrat but just the same old bus-driver I always was, my mother's son driving along on three wheels, two wheels, one, no wheel. They say we are all equal in the sight of God, but God, said I, did not create us all alike, and you're the barber. I'm the bus-driver. You'll never shave me. God liked a little variety, something to keep God awake, and God must have been asleep when He created man out of the dust. God forgot to create some of us, and some of us created ourselves, and some of us were nipped in the bud by the coldest, darkest wind that ever blew across this old creation. There's my old mother, creating again. She's in the bridal chamber where there's that old rug with its picture of an old retriever, a dog with a bird in its mouth. It's a wild duck. There may be only one way to get into this world, I said to him, but there is more than one way to get out of this world, and I know all the roads or almost all, so don't think you will ever cut my hair, you with your head that is bald. You've got no business cutting the hair of other men." Spiders' webs. Perhaps the hair of the spider was all there was any more growing in this old country—the spiders' webs covering the barber's chair, the mirror, and the door. But the bus-driver was no fly to be caught in that spider's web, that illusion catching the stars, so he would keep his hair.

"When you cut my hair, I said to him, I will be dead and not the man I was, carried out by the pallbearers singing and drunk to sleep in the country churchyard, but you'll be going against a dead man's will if you touch one hair of my head, remember that, and I'll come back to haunt you. Poor old fellow—his head is hard as rock polished by axel grease. An owl mistook him for a street lamp only last week and landed on his head. Be seeing you next week, I said to him, when the lights go out."

The bus-driver got so mad, arguing politics or talking to himself, trying to keep himself awake, and anybody would think it was a mortal sin, his letting his immortal hair grow, but his hair was his only virtue, and it showed to the whole world that he was none of these Democrats who were ruining this country.

"This hair, I said, will cover me with a coat of hair, will cover me with a coat of hair like the wild asses that live in the desert places, and I will live in a desert place and wild or on a mountain top ere I will cut my hair, for my hair is all I've got that is my own, and I'm no Democrat, never will be, so help me God and all ye angelic choirs, but just the drunken bus-driver, rolling along here in my own feather bed. Hell, yes, I bet all the old pool players who have not a hair on their heads I would not cut my hair until Roosevelt got out of the White House and all those Brain Trusters were busted with their W.P.A. projects and their public parks and their marble bird baths and their rotten roads and their free skating rinks that nobody wants when the river is frozen over and their free kindergartens that nobody wants and the way they have furnished the houses of all these old madames with four-postered beds. And that is why I have quarreled so with old Doc—thinking of him, it just makes me mad even though he has a long white beard. His beard is longer than mine. His beard reaches almost to his toes.

"He should be careful, I said to him, old Doc, about bringing into the world more of these starving Democrats, these old rabbits crying in the winter grass, old babies crying in their water holes, old babies with long white beards, moths, woodpeckers. Said I, why bring more misery into the world that has seen enough misery already, and why don't you just let them rest in peace, and why don't you just close their wombs, tie the knots? Shut their mouths? Give them an anesthetic? Play soft music so as not to awaken them? Put away your medical case, Doc, and get out your violin."

He was addressing his remarks now to an old doctor who had evidently given up his practice, who only thought he was practicing medicine, for he had lost his mind. Rather, perhaps he had gained his mind. The bus-driver, of course, would speak to him in this way only when he was not there. "You've got no more business, you poor old fellow, than the barber who was once a blood-letter, too, even less, and your office is emptier than the barber shop, for there's not even a spider weaving its web any more, none but in your wild imagination, not an old dog barking at a crooked stick, and it's all a drunken dream of yours, a mad man's dream and not my dream, and there are none of these pregnant women you think there are, none of these women rolling on the floor, rolling in the flood, giving birth, beating their breasts, gnashing their teeth and wailing all night long like the babies in the brook, and you could take life easy now if you wanted to, retire and dream sweet dreams. Dream that you are young again. Dream that you are practicing, but don't practice here. Rest your old head on your stone pillow. Rest on your laurels, on your past achievements, and no one will hold them against you, for there is no one left to complain. Said I, is the blood of Abel crying from the ground that I should live to see these bloody flowers? Said I, have we elected a king or a congress? What's the senate doing? Said I, remember that you are a good Republican and that we shall never have free medicine. Am I not my mother's son? When was I born? Has my own mother ever seen me?"

As for the bus-driver, never talking one way, acting another, he was a life-long Republican, at least would be if he voted, if he could just see to sign his name, if he could just get to the polls in time for the next election if ever there were to be an election again. Everybody knew that he would not speak to a man if he knew the man he spoke to was a Democrat—for if there was anything he could not stand, it was a man's talking one way, acting another when he got into the secret ballot box. He would not trust himself in that secret box, so he made his politics public. He had taken an oath maybe two years ago, maybe three, swearing on a stack of Holy Bibles as tall as a church tower and by all the heathen saints and by all the fallen angels, swearing like an old crow in a graveyard, so help him God and as long as he was his mother's son and her only provider and bread-winner and as long as the Democrats were running us, he would not cut his hair, not if he was not crazy, if he was not out of his head, and he had kept his word, keeping also even those promises he had not made and those promises he had made when he was too young to know what the promises were, such as his promise never to leave his mother who thought that he was a baby crying in her arms— though he had never promised not to drink. She did not know he was the drunken bus-driver with the long beard. He had never promised to lay off the bottle, his White Horse, his Long John, his Johnnie Walker, his fire water, and he never would, for his only consolation was to drown himself in drink, even to drink from an empty bottle. Sometimes it seemed to him that he had been drinking from an empty bottle his whole life long.

"I have not cut my hair an inch since then, and it will be wrapped around my feet in my grave before that old fool gives up his sceptre and his crown of stars and his golden throne. It won't be long now."

God, though, the things that went through his mind in a dark night, in a dark night of the human soul, the things a man could think of, how time had ended, how time would never end and just went on and on. God, these pregnant women screaming, rolling in the waters of the birth flood, these naked men screaming, white tree branches clashing against each other in a perpetual storm, stormy petrels in the way of the old bus-driver—and where was he, and who was he, dreaming in the midst of his long hair? Jezebel! Was it his birth or his death he was living through once again? Only God knew, and God had never told him. God, though, the lice in his matted hair, the woodticks ticking like old town clocks that went on after they had stopped, the dead talking, the broken church bells ringing again, the gongs gonging, the woodpeckers pecking, pounding like hammers, boring these holes in his cheeks until he felt as if he could scream, scream his head off.

Sometimes he felt as if there was but a hairline's difference between himself and them, old Doc's imaginary patients, those pregnant women who were dead and whom old Doc seemed to think were living again, sometimes seeming to mistake the bus-driver, because of his long hair hanging in his eyes, for one who needed his help in parturition, in being torn apart, limb from limb. So that was why, when he was very drunk, he screamed, yet not tearing his hair, never so drunk as that, for his hair

reminded him who he was. His hair, of course, had come from the distaff
side, just like his lips, his eyes, and he was Penelope weaving this web,
not Ulysses who wandered over the wide seas, he just staying at home and
minding his own business, letting his hair grow, for his immortal hair was
the part of him that was immortal, that would never die, that would keep
on growing, he had been told, when a man was no more, when he was
dead and buried in a narrow box. He had been told of people buried
alive and crying in their graves, of people buried by mistake and how,
awakening, they had been so shocked to find that they were in their
graves and were not dead, yet though put away and mourned by their
relatives and friends and also those who had never loved them, they had
died again, tearing out their hair by handfuls, rolling, turning, twisting
in their graves, screaming like mad men or like women in their labor
pains when there was no one to hear, trying to push themselves toward
the light, toward the radiance of a star, toward the sky, but the earth was
heavy above their heads, and there were all those tombstones which they
must roll away, and the way was long. Sometimes only their hands
reached out from their graves, their hands holding great clumps of
human hair which they had torn out of their heads, and there would be
those bushes, those dead hands lifted in a flat, grey, rain-washed land.
Sometimes, their graves opening in the spring floods and rains, they were
washed up, years afterward, after the first funeral and the preacher's
sermon, and then it could be seen that they who had been buried alive
had torn out their hair, for their hair was in their hands, and their heads
were bald, and that was how you knew the ones who had died twice, once
by mistake, the old doctor said, and once because of reality.

If the bus-driver, though, should ever find, by any drunken mis-
adventure, that he was not dead, that he had awakened in his flooded
grave, he would be content, not knowing the difference between that
grave and this life, pulsing among his own feathers, feathering his own
nest, and he would have his mirror in his grave, and he would count his
hairs, and he would not pluck a single hair from his head, and he would
not creep out of that old water hole, not even if Gabriel should blow his
horn to resurrect us all, the living and the dead, for it would be of no
use, and probably things would be just as they had always been, not
much different, the Democrats still ruling the roost, the old doctor still
practicing in his empty office which was his bedroom at the old hotel, still
thinking he was bringing this imaginary birth where there was no one, so
what would be the use of resurrection and of eternity under the stars?
There would still be those rusted forceps of his on the wooden dresser in
front of the cracked mirror, the apothecaries' weights that he used for
paper weights, the weighing machine where no one was ever weighed, the
women's clothes, everything the same in the old doctor's office, the wreck
of his old automobile strewn around his bed, bare footprints in the dust,
long and light, some with webbed toes, footprints of things unhuman.

So far as the bus-driver could see at present, looking through his hair,
his burning hair, there was nothing ahead but political corruption, the
Democrats ruling the roost, the roosters not crowing at dawn and their

rusted cockles not swelling up with the old, auroral song of beginning
again, and the setting hens were not setting, were laying no more eggs in
the dreaming grass, the long grass that whirled in its own torment, and
the thin-branched trees were twisted, torn up by the roots, and the
starved cows only dreamed, thinking there was milk in their dreaming
udders, and the wild mares were not really pregnant, rolling on the
bedroom floor, rolling in the flood, and all the single women were crazy
and wild, just thinking they were pregnant when they were swollen up
with nothing but the waters and the winds, the winds and waters of
imagination, when they were like the carcasses of drowned horses rising
on the flood. No crop this spring would there ever be, none but the bus-
driver's hair, for there would be desolation—the old river overflowing its
banks and the dead fishes thrown up on the land, the seeds drowned, the
marsh flowers drowned under the standing water, the wild mares flooded
in the flooded pastures where there had been no male, no man, no
stallion, the wild mares dreaming that they gave birth alone to death,
their limbs interlocked like whirling tree branches scraping the clouds
and the distant sky and the sky where there were no stars, the old birds
flying under the streams and under the floods, everything upside down,
dreaming like the foetus in the mother's womb when there was no
mother, when the mother was dead. There was no father. That same
stream which a child could wade in was that same river which a man
could drown in, and there was no life but a dream going on and on when
you were dead, a dream swelling, breaking. Maybe there were just a few
dead cocoons stuck on the barren trees, a few infants hanging by their
hair, old hornets' nests, old woodpeckers pecking, knocking at doors,
town clocks striking, but who wanted to be born alive into this world of
death, of living death? This country was in a bad way, no matter what
the old doctor said.

This birth would bring this death, according to the old doctor's way
of thinking, and you died every minute that you lived, got a new skin
every seven years, and you were born every minute that you died, went
from baldness to hair, from hair to baldness, but he was just crazy, of
course, and living in the past, living in his imagination, and there was no
medical practice to speak of, and there were none of these pregnant
women clawing the empty air, cursing their husbands, rolling in their
beds, tearing at the old doctor's long white beard as if he had been old
Father Time himself, none of these pregnant men begging to be put out
of their misery. The stars did not turn in the sky when you were dead,
and you remembered only the last thing you saw.

It used to be different, of course, before the Democrats ruled over us,
the bus-driver said. It used to be that the undertaker, a very prosperous
fellow in these parts, had done an excellent sidetrade in the furniture
business for the honeymooning couples, a branch of the tree of life, as he
had said, of his original affair which was to paint the dead and make
them seem alive and younger than they were, but now things had gotten
so bad, even he was going to seed, and there were no calls for tables or
chairs, no calls but for the beds, the only beds there were to sleep in, deep

under the earth, soft pillows, sweetest dreams, little cherub dogs, little churchyard owls. The only other real business was that brought in by the bus-driver himself, it seemed to him, taking the wrong roads because the right road would have been too direct, too short a way, taking this infinite detour through nowhere, repeating these sunsets, still getting, of course, no credit in the book of human life, none by the recording angel, none, not even though he was bringing these four passengers, all four of them, all alive and one unborn, and he would be cursed for his infinite pains, cursed by everybody, and still considered no rival to old Doc with his broken stethoscope, his pill for heart's burn or sleeplessness or both.

Perhaps, who knew, though, the bus-driver sometimes thought, driving along here as the bus reeled from side to side, the doctor was right, just because he was crazy, and it was the bus-driver who was always wrong, in the wrong again? Perhaps he only thought he was the bus-driver with his rolling stomach, steering his old bus through the roaring floods while all the time he was at home in his four-postered bed in the bridal suite that was furnished with tables and chairs, the only place that was big enough for two or three, and he was just turning and tossing upon his feather mattress, tossing and turning and raising the roof, trying to keep his mind when everybody else was crazier than the stormy petrels, the wild swans, and that was why he had never married, why there was no old woman to complicate, to ruin his life, none but his mother, of course, and curtains between him and her. So why should that old doctor be always knocking at his door, telling him he should be married before it was too late, that the hour was about to strike, and what did he mean, and why should he not practice what he preached if marriage was so grand? Old Doc was smarter than he seemed, smarter by a long shot, and the bus-driver could not help laughing. The old doctor, too, had never married, he knowing too much of where that road should lead, that it was straight and had no turning back, that it went from one place to another, and so he had decided not to take it, just to encourage the others, and he was taking the bus-driver's road, taking all the roads that went nowhere, trying to push him off into a ditch, into the weeds, trying to build up his practice when his practice was no more and was unnecessary, when it was all this mad man's dream.

Were there even, when it got down to rock bottom, when the illusions were cleared away, the old doctor's illusions, his pregnancy practice going on and on as if it were real, real to him, as if there were these honeymooning couples, these shotgun weddings, silver wedding anniversaries, golden wedding anniversaries, for who was he but an old fool in his long white nightgown with his webbed toes, deaf as stone or a gatepost and with no license to practice medicine any more, even to make out a prescription, no instrument but a pair of rusted garden shears and a broken stethoscope with which to hear the beatings of the dead hearts, a mirror, no patients but the stormy petrels in a land where were no stormy petrels, the wild mares, the crazy women of his wild dreams, none crying, none crying but in his memory that had heard the birth cries too late, the birth cries like the cries of the dying that came to their hour of life only when they came to their hour of death or were already dead? The old doctor, poor old fellow, the bus-driver said, was drunk in his imagination, imagining he was drunk on ether and starlight, he being senile and long-bearded and in his second childhood, of course, and if he was not watched by the night desk clerk if there had been a night clerk in that old bridal hotel, he would walk in his sleep at night, crawl out of his four-postered bed and go knocking at all the doors and go out barefooted in his long white nightgown with his long white beard flapping like a bird's wing in the winter wind and his old, wheezing heart that still would beat and could be heard for miles and his broken stethoscope, and he would want to give you those pills to kill the pain you did not feel. Crazy old doctor, thinking he was right, that people needed his pills, those already petrified and hard as pebbles, those faded prescriptions he had written long ago for other people, people who had already taken his pills and were already dead and needed none of his free medical advice and would never pay him. For some were dead-beats. He should have been a horse-and-buggy doctor. They had not a cent left in their pocketbooks, not a cent with which to pay old Charon when they crossed the river in a leaking boat.

It was a dead country, everybody sleeping but the old bus-driver keeping himself awake in the longest nights or longest days, tossing in his wakeful sleep, turning and turning, his hands upon the steering wheel even when he slept, his eyes upon the road, feeling as if he were still on the road and driving this bus through hell and high water when he knew he was in his four-postered bed under a heavy blanket and crowing because the rooster would not crow, cackling because the setting hens would not set, and the grass grew over the roof-tops, and nothing was coming. Nothing was coming but in the old doctor's guilty imagination, of course, his just thinking he was forcing the babies' heads out of the dark water holes, his just thinking there were these married couples, these honeymooners, that someone was calling for his help. Nothing was coming, though, only dragonflies as big as stars, the moths, only the old bus-driver with his long hair hanging in his eyes.

Only the old bus-driver was rolling in his bed, bringing these four passengers, four angels at four bed-posts, Matthew, Mark, Luke, John. He said that there was no one else. "Bless the bed that I lie on. Conceived on boxwood, born on cedarwood, died on wormwood, died in my sleep, never would have known I was dead if someone hadn't told me, if that old doctor had not awakened me, shouting in my ear. So you leave me alone, I said to him, you damned Republican trying to fleece me, and I'll take care of my business, my end of it, and you take care of yours, and go and have your babies somewhere else but on my bed, these moths, these owls, and don't come after me with those old pruning hooks, those tuning forks, for damned if I'm going to sing in paradise or put up forever with this sort of thing. Take away your bellows. There's no living spark. There's no sunlight. It's my head on my pillow, not your head on your pillow, said I to him. I'm not pregnant, never will be, so help me God, wasn't made that way, and it's my old rooster crowing in the dark, crowing at midnight, cock of the walk, lord of the morning if he thinks that way, my old roosters fighting in the night, bloody spurs, flying feathers, coxcombs, red eyes, jesters with bells. There's no old hen cackling here, never was, never laid an egg on my pillow, never set, and damned if I'm going to have you crawling through my beard, my hair. You've got your own tail feathers. Go crawl through your own beard, old Doc, I said to him. Go play your double flutes somewhere else, not in my ear, and don't come creeping into my four-postered bed, trying to warm your old, cold feet in my feathers, your sharp shins, your lean shanks, and stop scratching me with those long toe-nails, for it's my life to lose the way I please, not your life to lose the way you please, I said to him, and I never called you, so help me God and as long as I'm my mother's son and not my mother's daughter, never asked for your help even once, none of your old pills to make me sleep, and I'll howl the loudest when I'm dead, just like the old watch dog that barks at every cloud. Get out of my bed, you old fool, I shouted till I thought I would die, or I'll be calling the police yet, even though I've got no telephone, but what's a little thing like that to you? What's a telephone? What's communication?"

What was a little thing like communication to old Doc, drunk on infinity, on eternity, and how beat any sense into his empty head that heard the angels crying, crying like loons upon the breasts of the waves? "You are deaf to my cries, I said to him, so just turn on your other side, you black Republican, and go to sleep. Sleep as you slept the day you were born, as you've been sleeping ever since. Sleep in your mother's arms. This is a free country, free so far as I'm concerned, and I'm going this road, and you go yours, and let me be. Just turn and go back, go back from where you came. You know me, the bus-driver. You knew me when I was a naked pup. You brought me into this world, and now would you take me out of it? You are the bringer of pain. You killed the ones you cured. Now they have all come back, and they are killing you. It's their revenge. It's the revenge that nature takes."

What were all these screamings and shoutings and cursings about, and did old Doc, crazy as a loon, always pursuing him with confused dreams of birth and death, always reflected in the rear view mirror above the bus-driver's shaggy head and driving the bus-driver crazy, think that he was one of those who needed his help in parturition, in giving birth to death? This was the sort of thing that made the bus-driver mad as hornets when the nest was disturbed, mad enough to go off his beam and off the road and into the next ditch, rolling with his feet above his head, screaming, tearing his hair out hair by hair, counting the stars, and so old Doc would have something for his troubles and a greater practice than any he had known before. This was the sort of thing that made the bus-driver see crooked and made him so mad inside, he felt like driving straight ahead, never stopping until the horizon stopped, until the stars fell from the starless sky, and he felt like by-passing the old hotel and the empty jail and the country churchyard and the old woman, leaving the doctor to dream with no help of his, to carry on by himself, to bring birth there in the world of the dead where nothing should make any noise but the woodchucks, and there should be no lights but the lightning bugs like little stars in the long grass, the shooting stars.

"It ain't going to rain no more, no more," the bus-driver sang in the midst of the driving rain, now pouring like a deluge. He whistled with shivering, reedy tunes. "The old grey goose is dead. Died in the morning," he sang, "died in the morning, died in the morning with a pillow under her head."

He mumbled to himself, his head drooping, "Oh, let us not marry her. Oh, let us bury her."

He felt like screaming, but he could hardly hear his own voice now, shouting above the storm. It seemed to him, driving along through these endless miles, that he had lived through all of this before, every last breath. "We're on the next to the last lap now, as sure as creation," the bus-driver said, "so cool down, dearies, and hold your horses, little cherubim, little churchyard owls, and take your time, and let's not hurry things. You are naked as the moon, as the dead moon, as the day you were born, and father cannot help you, and mother is dead. Make their bits tighter in their mouths, little dearies, and draw the reins, little churchyard owls, and stop them short, and let them dance, the winged mules, but don't break their necks. The next step is the end, said I to old Doc, or maybe it's the beginning, and maybe you are right, but which of us will live to know? It's only, I said to him, the cigar store Indian puffing his pipe, only the same old barber pole. It's only the water buffalo. You know me, Moses Hunnecker, the bus-driver, my long hair streaming like a curtain over my eyes, but I can see better when I am drunk than you can see when you are sober, you old fogdog, luminous spot upon a far horizon, and I can see through the windshield, and I can see what's coming from before, behind, having this rear mirror view.

"It's always the same, whichever medicine you take, always the same result, I said to him. It's always only my old, heaving, wind-broken heart, my spavined hocks, my broken sides, my flying hair, always my own nostrils foaming in the wind, and the angels were looking the other way the day I was born, the day I died. A doctor ought to bury his secrets, bury his mistakes. I never saw life come, but I have seen life go, and that's more than you can say. Who called you out on a winter night, a freezing night like this when the tree branches are heavy with last year's snow, humped and bending down, when there's no lamp at any window, when there's nothing to disturb the peace, not a cry, not a bird, not a hand reaching out of a grave? You are the bringer of pain, old Doc, so let us go."

Still, he thought maybe, as the night was so wet, he was getting a chill, imagining things, and maybe he should have let that excellent old doctor look at him, feel around his heart, look down his throat, look at his tongue, his bulging and blood-shot eyes, tell him what he saw and what it was—this new mortal complication that made him feel so bad, cold and burning, burning and freezing, burning and drowning all at once, living long, too long after he was dead, feeling a pain he had never felt before, and perhaps he should have worn, driving his old bus, his long white nightgown or shroud.

He sang no more, his fat shoulders sloping over the wheel, those old woodpeckers and red-winged blackbirds pecking at his wooden cheeks, boring these holes, sticking their heads in and out, in and out. Tree branches scraped against the bus-window at a sudden turn. A far light twinkled like a tired star far away, and the sky was suddenly reddened as if with a sudden but hallucinatory dawn, fading as of one moment in which had been lighted up the bare and livid branches of old trees, leafless bushes, a fuzz of thin saplings, whirlings of weeds, little bird houses on poles, a rooster's red comb and livid eye, the low and naked, distant hills, the attenuated distance.

CHAPTER 6

THE thin tree branches bending and scraping, there were some with ropes of last year's withered yellow leaves, hanging like human hair, some with waxen, tightly folded buds, and now the road was turning and turning upon itself, and we seemed to be going back the way we had already come. One branch flowered upon a withered tree, its flowers like purple smoke against the sky, like something spontaneous as in a dream of apparent disrelations which were secretly related, and now there were again, in the midst of vastness, these familiar signs, these broken gates and fallen pillars among iron-colored weeds, barns with gaping doors, old carriages set in the midst of empty fields, plumed thistles blowing, large as human heads, straggling orchards the color of wool steaming in the amorphous mist and seeming to be filled with phantom shapes which came and went.

Fleecy clouds scudded along the sky both dark and luminous, indeterminate as if this haze of fitful twilight were the hour before dawn, the roosters crowing in a nocturnal dream. A derelict windmill stood in the midst of a flooded and vaporous field, its broken silver arm turning furiously in the wind. A roan horse ran along the road, its tail straight out, racing perhaps only its shadow against the pale, rain-speckled sky. A bony mule, grey as the flooded mist, its eyeballs rounded and flat, stared from under a broken and twisted apple tree, the color of the mule, even as if sterility and creation were one, and the grey, spiny weeds whirled past, and there were the roarings of streams, some livid under the dark sky spotted with silver lights, flashings of green and gold as from a lonely watchtower.

This land was like a dying sea, hills swelling, valleys perceptibly moving. The roofs of the sky were filled with holes, space invading everywhere, no objects seeming tangible as yet, and all was this cosmic sadness which could not be defined in terms of humor, this mournful journey continuing as the tired, drunken bus-driver, his bushy hair curling to his shoulders, slept at the wheel, snoring, whispering in his demented sleep. Yet somehow he remembered the road, just as old carriage horses, their heads nodding in sleep, remember the road, turning where the road turns, turning through the gate.

Against the dark sky, there were thin-ribbed, distant trees bending like smoke in the wind, the smoke puffs of an evening train without lights. There was the shrill cry of a train, seeming near, yet coming from far like something heard in a dream as one awakens, unable to determine whether one is awake or asleep, whether the sound was heard before or after the dream was broken, these continuities persisting from one world to another, it seemed, so that there should be no other world but this which was many-valved, an intricacy like the roaring of the sea which knows no limitations but its own.

Perhaps I slept, but the pregnant girl had awakened, and I seemed to hear her crying in my dreams. Perhaps she dreamed, and it was I who was awake. Perhaps it was a border world between the waking and the sleeping, for many things were said which would not be said by those who knew what they were saying. Her face was dark, twisting with cold, furious rage, but she sat stiff and upright so that her coiffure should not be disarranged, and she jumped whenever the bus lurched upon a rutted, rain-flooded road, the bird on her hat bobbing on its thin, brittle branch, staring with a glassy, winking eye at the tree boughs bent by wind, the landscape passing like a dream no one had ever lived through, no one had ever completely understood.

Her situation grew constantly worse, minute by minute, she approaching that hour when she must be delivered of herself or of a stranger. She was this dead center of life, her face crossed by tiny, enraged shadows, shadows of birds, leaves, moths, tiny feet making it seem more animated than perhaps it was, than it would be if ever she were completely awake and staring upon a void, uninteresting world, her face expressionless, betraying no emotion other than the lack of emotion which was the greatest of all emotions—but in her sleep she was self-betrayed, crying in her sleep. She was pregnant and married and coming to her early grave, dead, knocked up, fixed, betrayed, everything happening to her, it seemed, in this one moment of wild astonishment, this wild sequence of meaningless and accidental events her delicate, fragile, breaking mind and body could never live through, her shrill voice screaming above the dirge-like wind, above the dying stars as cold as metallic flowers, above the empty places, her face hard, contorted with somnolent furies, and that was why, oh, by God, she could not endure this awful competition, all these old men dreaming of themselves and of their wombs, all these imaginary women beating their breasts in the bloody flood, all these screamings, shoutings, cryings, gnashings of teeth by those who would never give birth as she must give birth. What were sun and moon and stars to her, and what were street lamps, streets, houses? She wished to God she was already in her grave, her little hands reaching above the earth, wished anything but that she should give birth to her, that she should be married to this stranger and coming to her grave, all in one instant, for time had never touched her. Ah, how could she have been taken by so many men, she who had loved no man? How could she have been caught in this terrible trap—she who had always had something with which to defend herself, maybe only her hat pin? Maybe she had had only her little foot with the jangling heart. Maybe she had

had only her little fist. Maybe she had had only her flirtatious smile or a handful of dust to throw into their eyes.

And was it fair? Why should she be taken by these white churchyard owls with roaring wings, their eyes as big as city lamps—poor little thing, light as a moth or a sparrow, the prettiest dancing girl she ever knew, so light on her feet, her little, tinkling laughter like harebells tinkling in the winter wind when she had passed away?

Just as she shrilly complained, biting her lips with little sharp rodent teeth, her little face sputtering, darkening with this regret, she had forgotten too many things, forgotten herself only once, forgotten the heart of an adorable flirt who never was caught before by any man, and she had forgotten her dark bridegroom who was not this husband sleeping at her side, and now it was too late to forget, for now she must remember. It was too late for self-forgetfulness, it seemed, for this oblivion of faces and forms, and all she could do, crying in her sleep, was remember her, now when she was no longer that which she had been but only that which she would become, now when all her past discretions could not make her discreet, now when she must shed a ton of tears, all the tears she had ever saved, had never wept before, and rivers would flow from her eyes before she was through weeping. She was gone five months without shedding a drop of blood, and she had four months yet to go, and she lived now by the calendar, by time which never before had touched her or darkened her brow or turned her hair grey. She would give birth, but there would be no old doctor ever there to say to her that it was all a dream, this life, this other life, my dear of dears, and you were only imagining it, so now turn over on your other side and go to sleep, for you will awaken as you used to be, for you are dead, poor little dancing girl, yet though your little heart seems to be fluttering something like a moth or a star, and I can detect the faintest pulse, the faintest quivering of an eyelid, and I can hear you crying.

So go to sleep, sleep in peace, my little child, she cried, for you are the only child there ever was, ever will be, and there is no one but you, and in the morning when you awaken, you will feel better, and you will be as small as the butterfly over the brook. You will be two butterflies. You will dance again, leading the dance in your little glass shoes, and no one will know that you are dead. You will wear your snood of pearls, your tiny lace veil and tiny lace gloves. You will wear your ruby ear-drops.

She remembered, crying in her broken sleep, her little, light footsteps that had made flower patterns on a floor of dust, how beautiful she had been and how she had made a little map to locate her breasts, her navel, her still pools, her hands, her feet, her toes, her fingers—and now if this dark pregnancy were only an evil dream from which she would awaken, discovering herself as she had been before she was taken, she would be happy even though she was dead, and that was why, by God, she could not endure any form of competition whatever, be it even herself, this old rival gnawing at her dead heart and taking her eyes, her hair, her lips, why she was going to get rid of it and hide it in a water hole, tear out her hair by the handfuls if necessary so that no one would know her, she cried, tear out her bleeding eyes, feed it to the little birds that hopped and hopped about, hopping on one foot the way she hopped, feed it to the little birds pecking, pecking at a withered cherry, pecking at a dead tree trunk, a dead face, feed it to the woodpeckers and the red robins, feed it to the wingless things that crept along the ground, to the things that crawled, feed it to the rose-breasted wood ibis, to the little woodcocks, the little woodchucks, the wood lice, the beetles, feed it to the butterflies, the gnats.

She would feed it to the wild turkeys gabbling in dark forests, to the sandpipers wading in dark streams, feed it to the purple moose, the Arctic hawk, the crows on the fences. For why should she be responsible for what was not? She would do as she pleased, not as she must, she being caught like this, trapped in her own glittering trap, knocked up, washed out, poor little thing, ravaged by an old ghost with bleeding eyes, pregnant and married and coming to her watery grave, yet though she was dead, for she was the only one whose dream was real, unreal to her who was unreal to herself, and she had perished without a sigh or cry, dying long before she had ever lived.

How could an insincere moment become sincere? Should she give birth to a prime minister? Should a flea give birth to a star? Why should she not bleed?

She sat upright, the stuffed bird bobbing on her flower-laden hat, mechanical as consciousness, always in agreement with the dual-minded wearer of the hat, she who wore, dressed for her honeymoon in a long night or her funeral or both, so many little flowers, little faces, winking jewels, beetles and bees and tennis players, so many little hands like bird claws, so many little eyes, so many little ears, the skiers skiing among the apple blossoms white as snow, the horses' heads, the old-fashioned sulky racers, the painted skyscrapers toppling like toy building blocks and Brooklyn Bridge like a spidery web and ferris wheels and wagon wheels and cascades of nymph and seed pearls, so many bits of colored glass to cover her, she seeming herself this hothouse flower, this carefully guarded creature of artifice, someone who had preferred the shadow, someone who had scarcely ever seen the living sunlight and who had never walked bare-headed in the purple rain, exercising herself for a great conflict with the angel of death or the angel of life who might be its other face, her own. Things which were very deep or far away had never concerned her complicated mind before, and she had fled from her bare face. Her yellowish hands closed stiffly over her cracked patent leather vanity case, that which was decorated with other hands, tiny and tarnished, peeling gold with red finger-nails dripping like blood, she slept her narrow and rigid sleep which was, so many ornaments tinkling around her as if to set off a belated alarm, like a form of watchfulness, of consciousness continuing even now when she was unconscious, her thin eyelids continually fluttering, shedding tiny flakes of powder, and her painted lips continually opening, closing upon a new protest, that urgency permitting no self-forgetfulness, no giving up of self to a deep river of creative sleep and of oblivion, no identification, apparently, with another person, neither the living nor the dead. She was always thinking, it seemed, of herself, no matter what form she took. If she should forget her now, who else would remember her silken hair, her little hour-glass form, her little, light, glassy footsteps, her little, shrill cries like the breaking of glass?

She was shrewd, wakeful even in her sleep, it seemed, her mind never still, her little thoughts running and running about as if they could not stop. Her little thoughts ran and ran about like a mouse in an intricate cage of which there were no doors, of which there had never been doors, and there were no walls, only these mirrors of illusion as if there were many little mice—and how could she escape, finding her way out of this mortal life or into it, whichever way might be? She was turning on this turning wheel. She could not stop. She could not cease. She was dancing.

A star dropped upon a far horizon, making no sound as it fell, not even one splash as when a stone falls into a river, and the tin roof leaked, water streaking the bus-windows, and the pregnant girl screamed, feeling that she had lived through all these things before. Was this that honeymoon which she had never planned, had never even dreamed of, that she should be returning to the same old river town she long ago had escaped from, riding in this same old bus that had always leaked, and everything the same as it had been before or almost the same, the same old faces smiling at her in the whirling, moon-colored fogs, these dead tree branches scraping, whirling, these dead clocks striking again, these spiders crawling over the endless snow? She had taken this bus out when the bus-driver's hair was short, but now his hair was long, curling below his shoulders, and he had put on weight, so she knew how time had passed, even as in an empty dream which she had never lived through, how many years had fled on silent wings, leaving no trace, and that was why she cried, cried again and again, her little face wrinkled with sudden age when she thought how she had changed, when she thought of her withered breasts, her empty womb, everything happening to her in a single moment, it seemed, of horrified recognition, and yet she had no personal memory by which to remember her, no consciousness which was her own and not somebody else's. Why must she outlive herself, the tiny butterflies dancing in the winter wind? Why should she have to go like this, giving up her little ghost, her little breath, yet remembering her when she was no more?

She had done everything seemingly for herself—everything against herself, she knew, and she saw now that her mistake had been her recent marriage, hollow and sad, passing like an empty dream. She had been married just recently, it seemed, to him, this old husband who was oblivious to her, this poor football player wrapped in his own sad dreams and sleeping at her side with his long-lashed eyelids trembling upon his dreaming, beardless cheeks, the mark of a razor where he had tried to shave away the beard he had never had and would never have. He would never live long enough to grow his beard, never grow old enough to be her father who had killed her, she cried, crying in her sleep. No one else remembered what had happened to her, and no one else had ever known. He had killed her because she had killed her mother in being born. He had made her grow old. She remembered, though, herself, poor little thing, the night she had died, and no one had heard her crying that night and the many nights that came after that night. She remembered her little bony hands clutching pale flowers in the winter grass, clutching her father's grey beard, her glassy and unclosing eyes staring at the dark and lonely wind, the winter sky. Oh, what she had lived through.

She had been married only because she had never married before, because she was already dead and deflowered—and the second tragedy, her marriage, was greater than the first, her death, for tragedy grew, repeating itself. Tragedy grew like life, like death. Tragedy grew like this empty and hollow and ghostly marriage, this dark consciousness growing inside of her and having an unreal logic of its own, more than life should ever have, this exceeding death, this exceeding life. There were no wedding bells ringing for her, and there never had been. There were only these funeral bells ringing for her over a dark plain. It was something which should have happened to her worst enemy, to her best friend, something which should never have happened to her. She was breaking into two, herself and the other, this face unknown. She was this sad, unfamiliar reflection in her powdery looking glass, this other face which smiled. She was dead, the dark tree branches scraping like scalpels against her wounded heart, for she died in giving birth. She heard dead birds singing.

She was this poor bride, indeed, her marriage being unreal to her as time when she was no more—this pregnant girl shrilly crying as the old bus jolted on through rivers of foaming darkness and light, through sun-lit and star-lit streams covering these naked fields—as she thought of all the things she had forgotten, herself, her other face, her eyes, her body. What little clothes had she to come to child-bed with? What should she wear? Should she be naked when she gave birth to this other child? Should she not wear, even in child-bed, her little dancing shoes, for should she not dance? She had nothing to wear, nothing to clothe a dead child with—not even a little, silky, winged milkpod or cobweb or cocoon or black butterfly with which to cover her waxen cheeks, her hollow eyes, her hands clasping the tiny bouquet of the withered flowers which had already turned to dust. She had not even a blade of grass to cover her, not even a dead bird or the wing of a bird, not even a dead spider. Where was her little wedding cake bridegroom with his polished mustache? Who then should marry her?

If her wedding had been her funeral, where was her funeral, that which should be her wedding? If she was the bride, where was her little bride with the ravaged face, the torn wedding veil like a veil of starlight? Where were her two brides? One should be clothed, but one should be naked. Why should these cloud banks always move, clothing one, stripping the other? Where were her tiny lace gloves, fit for the smallest hands, and where was her looking glass, her little hand mirror, fit for the face of a dead bird, a withered flower, a snowflake melting in the dark air?

Where was her little red stag? Where was her little stalking horse? Where was her little knight with his black plume, his silver meshes under his golden snood, he whose little paper shield and bright paper sword had been lifted to defend her, poor little thing, against the monsters of the night, the faceless beings of the deep, these dark clouds changing their shapes in the wind?

Where were her little pallbearers, little black beetles who should carry her away, little red-winged blackbirds where the snow was falling, little snowbirds, white wood lice? Where were her little woodchucks? Where were her little flower girls, her little train-bearers, little boys with pink cheeks, with sleeping eyes, with long white hair, with long white beards? Where was her wedding gown with a long silver train like the tracery of the frost laid upon the winter grass—where was her birth veil, soft as a film of water laid upon her dead face, this other face which she had hidden away from man?

Who carried her little coffin now? Where was her little ring-bearer who should carry her wedding ring on a white satin pillow, this sign that she was married, that all the things which were happening now had happened long ago? Her wedding ring would be, if she was dead, this circle of creation, all of one piece having no beginning and no end, gold that would not melt in crucibles of fire. Stars would be married with her, roses and snow, water and fire, beginning and end. She would forget herself, the hour of the day, the day of the week, the time of the night. She would forget who her husband was.

But now she cried for all she had ever missed, for the years which had passed, leaving no sign. She was alone, out in the cold, and where was her little door key, and where was her little door? Where was the keyhole? Who had opened the door? She had no marriage bed in all this world, no little bridesmaids with their little flower baskets, no funeral candles lighting the sky. There had been no marriage of body and soul, and there was no way to prove that she was married. There had been no wedding feast, no wedding guests but only the red-winged blackbirds wheeling in the burning sky, plucking out her little, burning eyes, only the dead moon floating behind the floating cloud, only the falling star, only the splash of a white wading bird in a distant stream.

There had been no father to give the bride away, no loving relatives to see her go, none to mourn for her. If anyone had thrown upon her a handful of rice or confetti or white rose petals, she would have been the magical bride, blushing under her long lace veil which had been her mother's wedding veil. She would have thrown her bouquet, and it would have been caught by the next bride, the pale girl dancing herself to death.

All had passed as in a long dream, and where was her little bride, so light on her feet, light as a thistle, and who had danced at her wedding? Who had played the wedding music, the music thin and shrill and sad? Where were her little choir boys sleeping in a row? Where were her little flower girls? Who had mourned for her when she was no more? Who had played her little harp? Where were her red-cheeked oboe players? Who had carried her, poor little bride, her dead face, her streaming hair? There had been no other bride, no old bridegroom to carry her in his arms as a mother carries a child, to carry her across the threshold from one life to another life, that sleep of death from which she never would awaken. There had been no threshold. There had been no bridal bed. There had been no music but of the wind whistling through the hollow reeds, no tears but of the falling rain.

There had been no old husband but in her imagination, and she was married to this pale ghost, and she was still alone, crying in her wakeful sleep, and there was no one, no one but herself, it seemed, her poor little dancing girl with the shorn head, the bleeding mouth, the lips which cracked in the ethereal cold, the purple eyelids, the eyes turning purple in the darkness, and yet she remembered her as if she were another person.

She remembered, as if it were yesterday or the day before, the night she had died, and no one had known but the mournful fireflies lighting up her dead face, the little field mice squeaking where her heart had been, the rustlings of the winter grass when something moved, dancing on one foot, the plaintive reeds, the ears of the tall corn listening, the roots of dead trees, the empty wasps' nests and whirling water holes, and there was this dead rose in her tiny, folded hands.

She opened, in a dream, her tiny, bright insect eyes, staring for an empty moment without expression at the dark and silver clouds torn like old lace, shot with gleamings of gold, pale pools reflecting reflections and gauze-shrouded bushes and movements of spidery twigs—and in a dream, having never awakened, it seemed, she closed her tiny eyes, for she was dead.

Carried upon no palanquin of silver and gold was she, her little feet turned outward, now she cried, kicking with one foot, foot that wore the little gold heart dangling. For never would she be stretched out so that the great lover could take her. She would always dance, dance in the wind, dance among the whirling stars, and no one should stop her until the stars stopped in the sky, until the autumn leaves, whirling above her watery grave, should never fall again. She was this dead child dancing, naked in the storm.

Might there not be, now she cried, remembering her and her tiny breasts, her funeral since there had never been the wedding, the wedding march so slow and sad, the marriage of soul with soul, of body with body, and should she not dance, dance when she was dead, dance at her funeral, her last dance, dance at the old dance hall, dance at the river saloon where the old dogs slept, dance with all the boys, dance with the old men who remembered themselves, her hair streaming across her eyes so that they should not see who she was, this naked and grinning skull, so that they should not see this faceless skull reflected in the dimmed looking glass?

Why should she give birth, though she had worked in a pottery, to an urn, to a stone angel, to the face of a cracked sundial? Why should she be, she screamed, this common clay, this tortured dust?

Why should she not dance? Where were the little dancing shoes, winged with light wings, her little shoes which danced and danced without her? Where were her little shoes which danced and danced when she was dead, her little feet never touching the earth? Her little shoes, she cried, would always dance, dance in the wind, dance when she was no more, her little eyelids fluttering like moths, her little harebells tinkling in the wind. She remembered, crying in her sleep, the night she had died, clutching with her little hands, and no one but herself had ever mourned for her, poor little dancing girl who had cried. The slow stars had danced, wheeling by. The thin reeds had whispered, breaking in the wind.

Always before, guarding her virtue, she had escaped, in various ways, these ugly, brute men who were hounding her to her grave, she cried, and far beyond it, far beyond these purple hills ranged like old faces smiling in the fog. Always before, she had deceived them, making them think she was someone else, and maybe she still had, she cried, her little ways, a handful of dust to throw into their eyes, maybe only a thin shadow moving in a dream. She would make them think she lived when she was dead. She would make them think she was dead when she lived. She would paint her face. She would tighten her coat.

Thin tree branches clashed in this whirling dance, even as she cried, and purple thistles were blown along the wind, and there were red spots in the dark, glassy sky, and she heard the zoomings of the wild bees like comets in the empty skull, in the silver box.

Her beauty had always come out of this little box on her lap, and she had always put on her other face, had always deceived herself, smiling with this frozen smile. Where was her little lace handkerchief with which she would wipe her eyes? Where was her ivory comb to draw through her long gold hair? Where was her little skull? Where was her dew-tipped blade of grass, and where were her little feet she should have worn? Where would be the funeral for her dead bride, the dead sparrow, the spider, the bee, the withered flower, the evening moth, the sleeping dragonfly? Where was her little hand mirror, stained dark and burned and cracked?

Might there not still be, she cried, her funeral since there had never been her wedding, funeral for the little mouse and its grey whiskers? Might there not still be, she was busy making her little plans, the little mouse's funeral, the little mouse's pallbearers carrying her away under her little wedding veil of torn lace, her shroud which was like the cobweb torn in the wind, a wreath of the grey field flowers upon the little mouse's head, this tiny cross in the little mouse's hands, the little mice angels flying in the mouse-colored sky, the little mouse's funeral song of the little grey bird, the dead sparrow?

Yet too many confusions were breaking upon her all at once, it seemed, breaking like a dark wave upon another shore, sweeping over her with one wild cry, sweeping her away from herself. The stars rushed past her like rivers of burning light, and she was fording these cold, dark streams which made her tremble, yet though she was dead. The dead child should wade through many streams, cry with many voices. She was sleeping under the grass. She was sleeping under the stars. Sometimes she thought, crying in her sleep, screaming where there was no one who heard, she was just a poor skeleton in armor, the girl who never should have married any man on earth, not even the poorest, not even for chivalry, she having been already taken by the stars, the waters, and the winds, married to her father who was dead and who had lost his bride, and should she be awakened now, made to feel the feelings she had never felt, to believe in the life she had never loved, had only seemed to love?

Would she not suddenly grow old, wrinkled and bent? What virtues should she defend, now when the last great harm had happened to her or was about to happen? She did not know who her opponent was. It was a nameless something crying in the wind, a face she could not remember. What evils should she pursue, lifting her burning sword, fighting with these unknown shadows, foiled, foiled again, driven back, defeated by nothing but defeat? Should she be forced to take off her helmet and her golden mail, her silver meshes, her mailed gloves, to show her beard, her burning eyes, these dead genitals which were the withered flowers of woman? She was already fallen in the field.

She dreamed strange dreams, she who had never dreamed before, she who had so carefully closed her eyes. She dreamed that she was not herself. She dreamed that she was a sundial in a ruined garden, the shadows covering her face so that there were no hours, and now the darkness did surround her, and this was the everlasting night.

The things which were incomprehensible had never struck her until now when she was dead, her blood spotting the winter grass, and she was this pale bride, this naked skull who had passed beyond recognition.

She was amazed, thinking of all the men she could have married, of all those she could have chosen, just by lifting her little finger. She could have married any of those old pottery hands back there at the pottery, any face of clay, the men whose feet were clay, any old potter turning the wheel that threw the clay, and all those who had kept the furnace fires, for all had wanted her, and the night watchman had wanted her, and the day watchman had wanted her, and the greatest potter had wanted her, and she could have gone on both shifts, the day and the night, and she could have escaped, escaped this life which she could not now escape. She surely had been, back there at the pottery, the most popular girl she ever knew, the prettiest telephone operator and receptionist, talking on four wires at once, never getting the messages mixed, giving all the men the messages from their jealous wives, jealous old hags, and now she was trapped, trapped in her own plot, trapped throughout eternity, married to the wrong man, one she had never talked to. She had not even slept with him until it was too late. And then he had not touched her.

It was marvelous how popular she had been with all the men when they thought that she would never marry anyone, how all had pursued her, asking that she keep the evening for them when they knew it was already taken. She had surely led them all a merry chase, going from dancer to dancer, dance to dance, sometimes two dances at once. If she was not seen at one dance, it could always be said that she was seen at the other dance. She had never had a moment free. So she could not understand, not to save her life which was already lost, why she had married, even in an empty dream, of all the men she knew and might have chosen as her mate throughout eternity and time, as her husband for better or worse, one she had not known, why she had married this poor football player who was too young to understand the mysteries of life, for he was innocent as a new-born babe himself, his cheeks suffused with a darker red than hers and blushing like a bride's as he dreamed of himself, never of her nor of her pleasures, the things which he would never dream of, never that she was dead. He dreamed of his mother's face which he had seen when he had first opened his eyes. His mother was old, but probably he dreamed that she was beautiful and young again. She was younger than his bride. Why had his wife allowed herself to be deceived? He was dreaming of the old hunter, of the old, dead dog.

Maybe she had thought that, as this boy was big and husky, he would carry her as an old dog carries a dead bird in its mouth, back to the hunter's feet, but oh, she had been wrong, wrong again, and he was no faithful retriever, and he was easily deceived, and he was barking at every shadow blown along the wind. He was deceived by every shadow, by every stirring of pale and ghostly wings in the long, billowing grass of a dream, flickerings, flutterings, the dead moon riding along the sky, the winter sun, flashings of silver and gold. He was betrayed by every motion of her hands, her tiny hands, betrayed by her bright eyes, by her shrill screaming.

He was betrayed by her little foot kicking, kicking him in his sleep.

Where was this aging bus-driver taking her now that he should take so long upon the shortest road she knew, that he should turn and turn about among the wheeling stars, especially when the places were the same, when only she had changed, moving like a bush? She had changed her face, her little face before her eyes, growing so suddenly old as in a single night, wrinkled and bent, her hair turning grey between the uncertain darkness and the grey-streaked dawn, and all her life had been this empty dream, and this estrangement from herself, it seemed, was almost complete, even as she shrilly cried, her little soul flying out of her little body, roosting on another roof-top.

She was the dead child dancing naked in the storm among the whirling stars, the whirling leaves, the dead child dancing, dancing on one foot, and what cared she for these old, human faces, faces of the sleepers?

She had always evaded life, never once had dreamed of life which should follow life when she was dead, never once had looked beyond the superficial face she saw. Never had she known another person, not even herself. Never had she been a fisherman of these old human hearts. So why should she be born to die, die again?

Street lamps glimmered for a moment like moons in the fog-swept distance now as she cried, her blank eyes staring. Now she must pay, just like any other old whore or streetwalker plying her trade under the city lamps shining in rows like drunkard's lurching moons, for all her virtues, pay for the life she had not lived, pay out her last cent out of her own pocketbook, pay for her wedding, pay for her birth, pay for her funeral, and she would have to go down through this dark, thorny valley of this shadow of life with no one to carry her, no pallbearers singing and drunk as bridegrooms who had come to the wedding feast and had stayed for the funeral and now would spend all their lives married to each other because they had never married her who had no bridegroom in this life, poor little thing with her torn veil, her withered flowers in her tiny hands, her stuffed bird on her hat, her trailing petticoats making patterns in the dust, and she would also have to carry, all the way, her own suitcase, all the way to her grave, burying her youth that had been so light and free, so thoughtless, her little dead heart where the marsh reeds were trampled down by heavy feet, and the milk-colored moths trembled in the evening light, and there was no one. There would be the phosphorescent gleamings of reeds in the purple darkness, the fireflies gleaming like sudden stars, dead twigs moving again.

So she had cried, knowing how all things would be, having always known the future as if there were no future, even as if this future were her past or the present already fading, as if it were completed except for one wild cry which would be forever heard. Nothing was as she had planned, and nothing was right. She had no bridal trousseau, no negligee ribbons, no clothes to come to child-bed with, no dance programs, no suitors, no husband.

What good was this poor football player at her side, sleeping his deep sleep and heavily breathing, his breath roaring in her ears and roaring like the stars of heaven above the roaring river, his face turning red, he who no doubt imagined that he was running, he who was the all-star athlete of the past, captain of the dead crew, champion baseball player, pitcher and catcher upon the baseball diamond overgrown with silver weeds, captain of the dead football team who had carried him upon their shoulders and captain of the dead basketball team which had pitched its ball into a net of stars, he who would never make another touchdown, he who would never make another basket, he who would never make another home run, champion skeet shooter, shooting the clay targets thrown up to imitate the flight of those who flew upon the wing, champion pole-vaulter and high-jumper and long-distance runner, champion where there was no partner, champion in all the fields of the outdoor sports except her field where she was fallen?

What good, she cried, was he to her, he who would never again come to victory or to defeat, he who would never again wear the laurel wreath, he who would never again be carried upon the shoulders of the crowd, never again win the loving cup or the silver football player or the golden archer—or if he was victorious, who should know? Who should know his mournful failure? It was that failure which only the woman sleeping at his side should know—the girl never sleeping.

She would rather walk across the glassy, burning floor of hell than come to child birth in his mother's house as she was coming now, bearing the child that never would be hers. It never would be his. This much was surely clear to her, that the husband was not the father. Whoever the father was, it was not he in all this world. Of all the men she knew or did not know, she had married the one man for whom fatherhood would be impossible as the realization of the dream of heaven on earth. Never would he carry her child in his arms. She had just married him in a hollow ceremony in order to bury her, and that was the truth. She would rather tear out her hair, her eyes than sleep in that old widow's house, giving birth to her old, ugly rival who would live when she was no more, when she had parted from herself, when she would be forgotten.

She knew every minute where he was, every minute of the day and of the endless night, yet though he slept at her side and might so easily evade her as only the husband can evade the wife, and she knew every dream he dreamed, yet though he was this empty skull who would have no life except for her, this headless man who dreamed not of her no matter of whom he dreamed, and he did not deceive her, not for a shining moment, not for a split second passing before it was realized just like a comet one had not seen passing before one's eyes, not now when she was no longer herself but was another person, not now when she was married to him that she might give birth to a form of death taking her eyes, her hair as if she saw her reflection in a shadowed mirror. There were only these outward forms, these shadow shapes in all the world. He was never where she was. He was always running around with the old crowds of the old river towns and boats. He was always hearing the river boat's whistle tooting as it rounded the bend, hearing it only in his mistaken dreams as she could tell by the twitchings of his rose-colored cheeks. She knew when he heard the old dogs barking. She knew when he heard the shot of the gun.

He was always dancing around, dancing with all the girls at the old dance pavilion with its roof open now to the tented stars, dancing at the old river saloon where the dead drunkards were drinking, dancing with some who were already dead as little did he know. When the river froze, he skated on ice with a partner whose face he had never seen, for her face was covered with the snow. He was not faithful to her, poor little dancing girl. He was surely a philanderer at heart, or else he never would have married her.

He was married to a human football, it seemed to her. He was always out kicking an old football on the practice fields of his dreams, always kicking the wrong ball, and never once did he think of her, his mortal wife who soon must give birth to one who would be so soon immortal, poor little thing with her feathery hair streaming over her eyes, her tiny, closed eyes, her cheeks streaked with tears because she was born, never of her who had been kicked from pillar to post, kicked from goal line to goal line long before he had played this field, long before she had ever married him with her eyes closed. She had been kicked into the next field. She had been kicked from field to field. She had been kicked beyond the farthest goal post, beyond the farthest field of his imagination, kicked beyond the sun, the moon, the stars.

So she could not forgive him for deserting her in her hour of need, especially as she would not need him beyond her hour. She was watching the old town clock very closely now. Tick, tock, and she was running around and around the old town clock, driven wilder by its striking, wilder by its clock bells splitting her ears. For should she give birth to time who so soon would leave it for eternity, so soon would leave all human faces? He had already left her, she cried, to face the eternal darkness alone, and he was not fishing in her dark river, for he was fishing in a stream of light. Yet had he not faithfully promised, when she had married him—until Death did them part—to see her through this dark, thorny valley of this shadow of life, to stay with her as long as she lived and, if she died, to carry the dead child in his arms, even to say that it was his, the seed of his loins, that he was the old father though she was not the mother of the child? He would never live long enough to be the father, never long enough to be the mother with the withered breasts, the shrunken sides, these false memories of life. Never would he be the old man, and never would she be the old woman. Never would she lose her beautiful face. He would always be the child.

She had had to think of everything. He would not assist her when she took her downward step. He would not carry her suitcase or help her through a door. She walked ahead of him. He stumbled as if he were sleeping or still kicking a ball. Surely, he had no chivalrous instincts such as she had been accustomed to expect from a gentleman, for she had paid the passage, paid this old bus-driver to bring her back to this old river town of the night and the shadows and the old ferry boat sleeping under the bridge, to bring this sleeping bridegroom, this sleeping beauty who never dreamed of her, his mortal wife who soon would be immortal like the old ball-players, poor little dancing girl whom she remembered now, the bleeding wound which was her livid mouth, her shorn head with its grey, flying curls, the bleeding eyes in the sunlight. She had paid for him and her, for herself and her husband and this ghost. She had paid for the ghostly triangle which would destroy her marriage, for his love would be dead. She had paid for three crescent moons interlinking. She had paid for reality as if it were real to her, as if she might live. She had paid for many weddings and wedding anniversaries, the silver and the golden and the lead, for funerals and births, for cherry blossoms and peach trees and crab apple trees, for the faces of children as yet unborn and for the dead faces, for family reunions though there would be no family, for old ghosts crying, white-sheeted in the winter wind, for snow-laden orchards and the soft bloom of spring, for old hitching posts with human faces, for broken bridges and broken gates.

What was man that any girl, caught in this dilemma, breaking into two, should depend on him, always dreaming only of himself? He was a beast, she shrilly cried, biting with her tiny teeth, kicking with her foot, prodding his side with her sharp elbow, for he little knew of woman's suffering in giving birth, of what it would mean to bear a child that never would be his, never would be hers, to have his body torn apart and lose himself as she must lose herself, her little finger of which she had been so proud, her little hour-glass form which had not kept the hours, her hair, her eyes, her egg-shell complexion, her ruby ear-drops, even her teeth, her mental independence, her freedom, her little stalking horse, her red stag, her little black knight with his flying plume, his lifted shield, his paper sword, all those brave illusions she had ever lived by when she was free to make her choices, she accusing everybody, both women and men, all the men who had gotten her into this almost irredeemable position, man who was free, free to follow the fox with his spotted hounds, free as the wind to come and go, free to bird-dog the dead birds and sleep in the grass, sleep wherever he chose and everywhere but in her bed, for she had no bed to sleep in, not even the grass, and he was not taken by another shape as she was, and he was not shaped by the great potter, and he had not, she indistinctly moaned, these aching, pin-prickling breasts, small as withered flowers, these burning eyelids, this body wearing last winter's coat so tightly drawn and shrunken that she could scarcely breathe and might die, this tight corset with its rusted stays jabbing her sides, these tiny feet stuck into these glass-heeled shoes because she still must travel, travel so far through this dark, thorny valley of the shadow of life and far beyond it, far beyond these purple hills, through freezing winds and snow. She was so thin, so tiny, almost a child herself. Should she be swelling, giving birth to death, she sobbed, to the dead moon, to herself alone, to the dead child dancing in the storm? Surely, she could not be killed. Surely, she would always dance, leading the dance, going from partner to partner in a sad, whirling dance—or when there was no partner, dancing with herself, poor little dancing girl, or with her shadow. She would squire herself around and be her escort to another world. She would wear a tuxedo and a high silk hat. She had danced among the midges, so she would dance among the falling stars, the falling leaves.

Her taut voice shrill as it must have been when she was a telephone operator talking over the long distance or over the short distance, screaming as if she were talking to the other side of the world when she was talking only to the next sleepy town, she cried and cried in her broken sleep—her thoughts as restless, as animated as her dress which seemed the memory of the world, the spiders weaving their illusive webs, the spinning wheels spinning a gossamer fabric, the spindles with their drifting threads, the long-billed humming birds flying among the flying snow-flakes, the jockeys riding red birds and the horses flying like birds, clowns and dancing girls, starfish patterns and moon crescents and fishes' winking eyes and horses' heads, so many images that she was like a mosaic or bits of mosaic still sticking against an ancient wall, powder cracking her face as if it had been a mask of clay, another face, a face repeated in many dreams because of its incompletion, its evasiveness which was a prelude to birth or death. She was almost awake, restlessly moving in a shower of glassy sound like the breakings of icicles, the stuffed bird seeming ready to take wing, to leave its precarious perch, its brittle twig, the fox of her fur collar seeming ready to leap at the cry of the hounds, her spirit alerted, old bird dogs pointing their long noses, her transparent eyelids fluttering, shadows stirring in the long grass of a dream which, though personal, seemed almost impersonal at this stage, starting up so many other dreams, so many little cries, shrill and sharp, so many whirrings of muted wings, whisperings of dead voices, of no known form, and no wakefulness protecting her from those dark plans which had been growing, maturing in her thin and broken sleep. She solved, it seemed, no problem by her being awake, almost awake, and she was only worse off than she had been before, time having advanced through timeless dreams, for still there did continue, raging like the storm which displaced the stars or snuffed them out as if they had been candle flames, these old rivalries, jealousies which tore her apart, just as she complained, and she was not herself any more if ever she had been herself, and she was becoming, with every jolt of this old bus upon the rutted road, that other girl, the girl her sleeping husband loved or thought he loved, that old creature withered and thinner than the winter leaf in the blast, in the whirlwind, that old, dead thing who would always live and always be beautiful in his sleeping, prejudiced eyes. He would always love her more than his wife.

She would rather be dead than look like her, that withered rival her husband loved because he had never loved, and what in the hell had she done, she screamed, with her pot of lip rouge, the bright orange red, and how should she laugh at her funeral unless she should paint her face to make her seem happier than she was, wearing this mask to hide her natural sorrow over anybody's passing away, and how should she dance if there was no partner? And what would her marriage be if there was no rival to make him remember that he had, no matter how far his mind wandered, a wife?

He never thought of her but always of that other girl, the girl he had never dreamed of marrying and who, if the rumors could be trusted, was also dying, dying a fast death, having all these unfair advantages over his mortal wife who must take her time, for that other girl was thin as a moonbeam and was not heavy with a stranger's child, and she would never give birth unless to her own image like the ghost of the perfect love, and she would never be dead in his eyes. She would never have to endure the test of marriage, the daily friction. She would not have to rub wet wood until it broke into the flame of a star.

Sometimes his wife thought, her face darkening with furious grief as her eyes sparkled as if she were suddenly coming to life, that there was no other girl but only one she had imagined, that ever since she had found herself with the child of a stranger hanging to her heart, she had been imagining things, that she had surely imagined herself into this terrible triangle from which she could not extricate herself. The triangle remained when love was gone. Sometimes she thought she was her own old rival, already grown old, taking away his love because his love had never been given to anyone on earth and never would be, surely never would be given to her, poor little dancing girl who was buried long ago under the leaf mold and who would be forgotten by him without his wife to remind him, awakening his memory.

She shook the powdery dust out of her coat, the dust settling back again upon her shoulders, just in that single instant, for everything was self-contradictory, it seemed, as she was, and perhaps life must always have, so long as it is life, these double motions like the progressions of delicate planets, circles within circles, wheels within wheels, orbs within orbs, and death should not be simple.

Death should be involved, such complexity as life had been, such breathings, such whisperings, laughings and cryings, the imaginary lovers quarreling, pinching each other in the livid darkness, and beauty should last beyond beauty's unmarked grave, and stars should deceive us when they shine no more, when we only imagine that, because we see them, they are shining in the sky—though long ago, they did perish, rustling like the autumn leaves, whirling, falling in the ghostly dance. Perhaps, when life is gone, life continues in the mind, and all we should ever know of death would be what we imagined, this vivacity of roaring stars, whirlpools, whirlwinds, this illusion that we lived or died.

She powdered her sharp nose with a dust-colored powder puff, wiped away the red smear from her lips, bit her thin lips until the color returned, blew her breath against a dust-colored hand mirror, blowing away the dust of the pottery which settled back again like a wreath falling. She was always, it seemed, taking off, putting on her other face, pinching her clay cheeks, biting her colorless lips. She was never satisfied with these results, none of which should be ultimate—there was always the necessity of self-improvement, and she must paint her eyelids purple, and she must comb her blanched hair, and she must view again these tentative results. She frowned, for she was not pleased with her image in the dark glass. Heaven itself should not please her. With thin, brittle movements as of a tree in the wind, a tree too brittle to endure the storms of life, she moved restlessly, arranging herself, rouging her thin cheekbones with a red rag, pinching her cheeks, making a tiny curl upon her forehead, a curl like a feather at the back of her neck, seeming also to arrange the shadows. She plucked her already invisible eyebrows with an eyebrow tweezer, then marked with an eyebrow pencil where her eyebrows should have been, somewhat missing her aim. She was like a tired archer. Perhaps she would always miss her target. She pulled her short skirts down below her knees, now when it was too late. Her skirts crept up again, showing two hearts, but she did not seem to notice.

Now she was arranged, stiff and upright again, at least for another moment—though the dust was still clinging to the mildewed velvet flowers and ribbons of her hat and the bird molting a moth-like feather, the powers of disintegration being great, as great as those of life, and fog a greater clarity than light, than clarity. She drew her head down, the scrappy fur collar up around her thin and scrawny neck, and her sharp nose was sniffing the cold air current, and her little beady eyes were bright with shrewd, speculative gleamings as she complained, continuing, in a lucid interval, those dark complaints begun in sleep.

All the men were alike, old beasts with their coarse, whipping tongues, old beasts nuzzling at the coldest lily bulbs there ever were, and this old husband at her side was no different from the others. He had never touched his wife's cold heart, never would—never, just as he would not touch that other girl's cold heart or awaken the dead by his love. Marriage, what was it but only this awakening which had disillusioned her, wrecking her lost soul, and which had opened her eyes? When the men got you, they treated you differently from when they were only dreaming of you, she said, and your beautiful hair.

She seemed to be trying to explain though perhaps she was talking only to herself or to the dead ears in the clouds, to the silent stars, to whoever might listen. There should have been a heavenly harmony, but there was none. Marriage should have closed her eyes, it seemed to her, and she should have slept a deeper sleep than if she had been in her grave with the waters roaring over her. But everything was different now that she was legally married—everything fading so fast. She would have been happier if she had married the great potter. She would have been happier if she had married a glass-blower blowing ethereal shapes of color and light. After all, as she could only console herself by thinking, it had not been a marriage of true souls, and it had not been a marriage of bodies, for each had missed his love and the image of his love. They were married because love was impossible for them. If they had loved, they would never have married. Certainly, they would never have married each other. Someone else had ruined her, had taken away her youth and robbed her of her beauty, her little hour-glass form. So much had happened recently. It was only a marriage of convenience, she cried, now causing her this great inconvenience, now tearing her apart, limb from limb, so that she was no longer herself and was hopping on one foot, poor little dancing girl, poor little clown. She had married him to give a name to the child, a father to the child. Here on her honeymoon, dark without a moon, she was already planning her divorce, her separation from him. Marriage, what was it but always, even if it was convenient, this inconvenience, the violence of the night which the day remembered even when it was forgotten?

Marriage was not the realization of a young girl's dreams, even when she married a great athlete and when all the other girls envied her. Marriage was not, certainly, what she had thought it would be, and it was never tailor-made, never as she had planned, for she was married to this poor shadow of a man, this poor substitute for the love she had never loved, and he was married to her, this poor shadow of herself, so pale that she was scarcely visible. She had thought she was marrying one man, someone who would be good and kind and true to her, someone who would be faithful, and she was marrying another, even as if her marriage were an empty dream from which she had awakened, seeing with horror whom she had really married so long ago that she had forgotten the time, his old, cold, blear eyes staring at her through the murky light of dawn after dawn, seeing with horror his grey beard flapping in the winter wind, his face like a death's-head melting in the light, his ghostly hand with no flesh upon his long fingers, and yet this poor husband did not know her father who was his rival for her dead love.

He certainly had changed since the night when she, with her little eyes closed, her little fists clenched, had married him, and he saw her now through different eyes, always holding it against her that she was not the girl he had thought he had married, that she was not young and beautiful and pure as the new-fallen snow but old and broken and grey, an old woman before her time, old enough to be his mother, and her chin was grizzled like that of an old man, and she was bent to earth, and she was scratching the air, the glassy wind, the cobalt clouds. Not that he said these things, of course, but she knew what he thought even when he was sleeping.

So they were united by disunion, she and he, the poor shadows of themselves in earthly life, their marriage being such perfection as death itself could never break. For what was death? It was the falling of the snow. It was the opening of a flower. It was the singing of a bird.

Maybe the disappointment she was experiencing now, though, was just what everybody else had to go through, even in the best of families —maybe marriage was always like this, even when it was ideal, when it was one of those true marriages which are made in heaven. Maybe marriage never put an end to things, never laid the whirling ghost. It was the glove which never fit any hand. She laid her bridal veil over the face of nature cold and dead.

Maybe marriage came always only with these mortal complications, never saved the soul who was already lost, never solved one's problems as one thought it should—and you were always married in this fog—not knowing who you were or who the other person was—and in this fog, you died.

Marriage was always marriage to something you had not foreseen, something surprising, she said, these terrible shiftings of hearts, of faces, of forms in the night—and when you awakened, you were disillusioned, naturally, seeing the other face. You were as surprised as if you had been out all night drunk, marrying when you knew not what you did or where you were, marrying a stranger, a perfect stranger to you, someone you had never seen before, and when you awakened, if you had married a man, there was that old man whose face you had always known, ever since your childhood, or if you had married a girl, there was that old girl with her purple, blood-shot eyes, her bleeding mouth in the cold light of dawn, her body as cold as a corpse. Maybe you had married both.

It was not the girl you had thought you had married, not the man. It was the other couple always, the other love, the other death, and that was why she cried, her little eyelids fluttering like moths in the long grass.

"That old Adam never tempted me," she indistinctly said as if she were half asleep, "and I never tempted him." Why should she have tempted him? She had had everything a single girl could ask for, always paying her own way. "You know I did, asking nothing of anyone. I was the apple highest on the tree, hardest to reach. Boys would have given their eyes for me. Old men went crazy. I lived on crumbs." What now, though, had she got—what to show for her mental independence, for was she not dependent, and could she not hear the flutter of a moth in her ear? But why was a moth reproaching her? Was a moth reproaching her for what she had never done?

"Where's my trousseau? Where's my bridegroom? Where's my bride? Who pays the bills? Where's my child's bed? Little child's bed with the gossamer canopy over it and flowers in her little hands? Where's my funeral?"

She kicked at the football boy with her glass heel, kicking so hard that the bird shook on her hat and lost another feather, kicking to try to wake him up, make him see the light, she said, before it was too late, for the light was fading from her eyes. He should understand, in the brief time he had, life's tragedy which had already taken place, probably before he was ever born. "Wake up," she said, jabbing with her sharp elbow. "You poor boy, you will sleep your life away, and don't tell me it's these fumes. You're dreaming again, dreaming of her, the girl you know you love, the one you never would have married, for it's not your wife you dream of. She was taken by that old man. You're not the bridegroom. You only think you are. I'm not the bride."

Her face was triumphant, yet though her voice was an accusation, rasping and shrill as if it were she who had lost, for he did not awaken. He seemed to sink into deeper sleep. "She's dying, and will you not go with her? The girl you love is dying. Crippled, dearies, dancing on one foot—she's gone and laughing all the way. Now you think you would have married her, now when it's too late for giving in marriage," she prodded, "and you just know it is, and you would have to share her with the dead boys, the other team.

"You always did play on the safe side, taking none of these risks or leaving them all to me or someone else. I'm the one who bleeds when I should not be bleeding. My heart bleeds for her. How do you think I feel? Where's my lost girlhood? My youth? Where's my little red stag?

"You think you always loved her, that you always will even when you can't remember her face or recognize it when you see it again, even if you should forget her name. I grow old here, you think, but she does not grow old, and you do not grow old. Oh, Romeo, oh, Romeo! How wrong you are. The rain falls on her, and the snow falls, and the wind blows. She is not different from us. She has her phases, too. She waxed, but now she wanes. When I wax, she wanes."

He thought she had no age, that time would never lay its cruel hand upon that other girl's brow or turn her hair grey, that she was as beautiful now as when she had been young—but how wrong he was, for time had already touched her.

"She has lost her beauty that she never had, and it has turned to dust and ashes, and it was only what you thought you saw. She was never ravishing. I was. You were prejudiced, and love is blind. Love never sees our faults as you see mine. You even see my faults where they simply do not exist. She was not shaped by the great glass-blower, blown into a beautiful form. She has no little hour-glass form. She was not molded by the great potter. She is no urn. She is no sundial. She is no great stone bird. She is no angel in the churchyard. It was only a dream," she added after a moment of silence, talking to herself, "something you should have known better than to have believed, something you never should have touched. If you were in your right senses, we would be travelling the other way. We would not be travelling down this dark road."

Still, though, why argue with him, this sleeping boy so innocent of life? It was too late for putting sense into him now. What he had missed, he would forever miss. He could not be influenced by her, his living wife whose conscience suffered many twinges, many pangs because he did not suffer, not even vicariously. He did not suffer through a third person. He loved that other girl, thinking his love was immortal because it would not change even if she changed. Perhaps he would never see what time had done. Perhaps he would escape them both. Perhaps he would love her more now than he had loved her before she was bent to earth, suddenly old without his help and withered and twisted into another shape than hers—almost over night, some people said when they discussed her already as if she were something of the past. Perhaps they had already buried her. For there is a quality of impatience in love, the darkest love, dark without a moon. They said that the bull frogs were mourning for her. They said that the butterflies were whispering. They said that the dragonflies were spinning their threads above her face shadowed with the wings of dragonflies.

"Some people say it all happened in a single night, and some think it was two years or more before her condition began to show, before the skeleton was visible shining through her flesh. Perhaps it was three years, for they have almost forgotten the time. They say she is almost transparent now—so thin, she is almost like glass. You know when you look at her that time is running out. They say you can feel yourself growing old, and you shiver even in the sun-lit days, and it is like night's shadow over you. In the morning of life, you die. You do not die in the evening. They say you can see her little bones now like mother-of-pearl or something shining in the darkness of the night. She is like something that was dragged out of the dark river long ago and now is going with the river. You have to be drowned twice—once when you come into this world and once when you go out of it. You are drowned in the womb, and you are drowned in the waters of the grave. Her face is floating on the dark river. They say she is losing her big purple eyes, her hair, her teeth. She is almost blind though you would never know."

His wife did not know, for she was not there to see. She was far away, working in the pottery. She was in another town. She was flirting with the old glazier who had told her that she was a glass girl, that he should put the glaze of death over her eyes if she did not love him as he loved her. She was flirting with the oldest glass-blower. She rustled, shaking the glass jewels, the glass bells hanging from her wrists, the glass beads rippling from her neck, scraping her glass heel with a sound like icicles breaking in a cloud. "It was two years between the sunset and the dawn, a long night, and some say it has not passed. It might be nearer three years than two, for no one remembers the time now. The clock struck. The clock bells struck forever, for they were stuck in the church tower, and the bell-ringer is sleeping. The sexton is sleeping. The old hunter is sleeping with the old dogs sleeping at his feet. Ding, dong, bell.

"They say that nature mourns for her—ding, dong, bell—and the valley is filled with shadows, with shapes nobody knows. Ah, yes. So true it is, so false. They say she went to bed one night when she was young and beautiful and white as snowflakes falling from the clouds—and the next morning when she awakened, but nobody knows when the next morning was, she was old, old and broken, and you would not have known her withered face if you had seen it then. She was shriveled and had grown smaller. She was not as old as your mother. She was as old as your grandmother. Her skin was covered with dark spots like the skin of a frog, like a rain lily. She was spotted like a spotted cloud. Her face was spotted like the face of a clown, poor little dancing girl. Your kiss will not restore her beauty, for it will not awaken her love."

But what would this poor boy know of a former love unless his wife reminded him that though love could never die, the object of his love might die, might change, might alter her looks? And was that love which did not die, change, alter, grow old with time? Indeed, he was like all other men, indifferent to the facts of life or to the passage of time unless someone reminded him, for he thought time had never passed. He thought he was young. He was the king of heaven, but woman was the queen of hell. "You were sleeping with somebody else, you old fool, and I just know you were, and you were not faithful to her, the only girl you think you ever loved," she cried, "so why should I deceive myself into thinking you would ever be faithful to me or any woman on earth? Why should I grow old? You were sleeping at my side when you should have been sleeping at her side, so how shall I trust you when I know only too well where you are, that you never loved? I know you, you old fool, so don't try to crawl away or hide your face. You used the love you never loved as your excuse for never loving any woman on earth. See, it figured, didn't it?" she asked the empty air.

There was hardly even a transition period, she knew, between these two girls, the young, the old, for they were one. The great things were those which happened without any way of knowing them or knowing when or where or how or why or to whom they had happened, just as if they had happened to no one or were happening now. That was why it was so difficult to know where the walls were or how one person was divided from another. Where did the cell split? Where did the star begin or end? She had never thought of such things before—not once, not twice.

It was like a sultry summer day suddenly followed by a long winter night of a sub-zero coldness, the cold and furious blast of the eternal winter setting in, the land turning to a sea of seething ice, the teeth of winter gnashing in the gale, the snow bending down the naked trees, hooding the long-haired bushes, the snow piling up upon the crooked fences, the snow piling upon the buried roofs, the crystal snow blotting out all the roads and the glacial star which was breaking in the wind, and the telephone wires were broken by snow, the telephone poles lurching in the wind, great snow owls spreading their wings as the winds changed. The church steeple was broken, snapped off by the winter thunder. The snows of winter blotted out the face of the clock, weighting the pendulums. There had been no period of transition, of preparation for a gradual end. There was no autumn, no Indian summer. There was no sudden flowering of orchard boughs as if the ghost of spring were returning once more to earth. There were no whirling leaves of gold, gold leaves piling up where the old hunter walked with his barking dogs. The quail rustled not in the long winter grass. Never would there be another spring. The birds of summer were suddenly frozen upon the glassy bough, and the horses were frozen upon the icy roads, and the river was frozen like the roads, and the ice-skaters were frozen upon the frozen ponds. Death was her first lover. Death was her first husband and her last.

"So don't talk to me about next spring," she petulantly exclaimed, "or what we will do next spring. There will be no next spring, dearies. There never is. There is not even this. There was not even last spring." Never again would he see the cherry trees in flower. The buds were eaten by the great snow owls with their horns reaching into the clouds. The snow would be her bridal veil. "Oh, where's my little ice-skater? Where's my little football player that was hanging from my arm? I've lost one of the team.

"You will love her more when you carry her in your arms, when she is dead, when she is forgotten by everyone but you. That is your kind of love," she accused, "always the love that comes too late, the love you could not love. It is the love that does nobody any good. Neither the lover nor the loved. Her face will be as cold as the snow upon the hill. You will have to dig for her. You will have to dig under the old, swollen roots. Once you will mistake her for the wing of a white pheasant. You will mistake her for the horns of the great horned moon." In memory all things were possible, of course, and even the impossible things were possible as she suddenly seemed to realize, shaking herself from head to foot, shaking her glass jewels, all her little trinkets. "You will love her more when she is dead. The dead will remember you. The dead will remember you when you have forgotten her.

"Wake up, you old fool. When you're dead," she said, "you will be happy, but it's a long ride until then. You've got a long way to go," she cried, pushing and pulling, "you old, tired dog, and you'll pull your own weight. I can't carry you. Men are brutes. The oldest glass-blower told me never to trust them. He said that they would break and shatter in the least wind. What did the great potter warn me? He told me that all were clay, all men and some women. He said that he was quite sure that when some of them were turned upon the wheel, the great potter was looking the other way, was looking at a flight of red-winged blackbirds.

"You would be a naked pup if it were not for me," she moaned. "You would be a naked bird. It was I who rescued you. I tried so hard.

dear, to make a man of you. You would not have the clothes on your back if it had not been for my paying all the bills. I paid for the old fox."

She had paid all the bills that were ever paid, and she had paid the Justice of the Peace to tie the knot and anchor her, anchor her to him, and the bill-collectors were still pursuing her, trying to collect though it was not her money that they wanted, for they wanted something else, something they would never get. She would pay with a kiss, a wink, a smile. She had already paid. She had paid her last cent to the old bus-driver with the bushy hair. "Tell them that I'm dead, gone over the hill," she moaned, "and I'll pay them all over there. I'll pay them all next spring, next winter, any other year but this year. Tell them there is no man in the house. Tell them that the old bread-winner has gone, taking his old dogs over the hill, and they're barking on a frosty morning, and you can hear the glass breaking. Tell them Papa's gone a-hunting the rabbits, the little white rabbits sleeping under the snow with the little white flowers."

She knew, by that innocent smile on his broad-cheeked face, his mind was still on her, the rival with whom she could never compete. Indeed, if she could compete, she would not—for what was a man that she should want him or risk her life for him, either young or old, and what man could fill the vacancy in her heart which was vacated long ago? His eyes were closed, and there were shadows on his purple eyelids, and his mouth was open, the softest smile playing around his full red cherry lips, and he blushed like a bride, and he had hardly stirred. He had stirred no more than the grass blown over by the wind. He had not acted as if he had heard her. So she was going to awaken him.

"I told you to get her out of your mind if you were going to live with me and start a new life. Forget the past which never was. She's as good as dead, and you've got no grey hairs. She died in body, and then she died in spirit. Or perhaps it was the other way, for I forget now. She died in spirit, and then she died in body. She died in spirit and spirit. She died in body and body. Oh, who will bury her, I ask you?

"She died in the spring of last year or the year before, the way I figure time now, for it's all been a dream ever since, her living on. Before the first leaf falls, she will be dead. Some say she was dead when she was born. Some say her old father killed her. She'll never see another winter, and that's why she's so happy. Oh, my God! Should I wear my eyelids at half mast in mourning for her? She has gone to the great glazier. Oh, God! Do that which man cannot do. Let her be beautiful again."

Never would she see, with those big, staring eyes, the feathery snow falling again, and never would she go ice-skating on the frozen river, leading all the boys to where the ice was thinnest. Never would she take another boat.

"The lambs are nibbling away the flowers. The honey bees are buzzing around her even now. They will make their honey in her skull. She's sleeping in the grass, and you can hear the dead birds singing. The spiders are weaving their birth webs across her ashen face. What do you see in her that you don't see in me, your wife?" Did he believe in the double standard—was that it, that a girl should live with her past, that a man should be free to come and go? He was carrying the torch for her. He was carrying the banner.

"Do you ever give me a thought, remember what I looked like?" she asked. "Yet I'm the one you married. You married me with your eyes open, not closed. My eyes were closed."

What had been her marriage but a hollow ceremony, something forgotten, something which had left no sign? Marriage was never, she said, the way of a man with a maid, for the beautiful girl was always married to a poor scarecrow. It was never what you thought it would be. It was not what was written in the books of life nor what your blind-folded guardian angels said when they stood around your mother's bed, guarding you. It was what was written in the books of death, and they never told you until it was too late, and you had opened your eyes, and you saw who your old husband was, and you saw your old wife with the smile painted on her face.

"So wake up. It's your wife," she said, "and you are married to her, to me, and it's for your inconvenience. If you are miserable, you have no one else to blame. Stop kicking me. Kick her. She feels nothing now."

Had his wife thought twice or soon enough, everything might have been different from what it was. Perhaps she still might think of a way to get him out of her mind. "Quit bird-dogging me," she said, "you old fool, and go bird-dog her for a change. She'll never care. She'll fly away. Go hunt the dead birds with the dead dogs, dearies, and leave me rest with my hands folded. My helmet is drawn down over my eyes. My head is pillowed on a stone. I've had no wink of sleep since the night I married you. Do you keep me awake?

"It's always your future I am thinking of. It's always your future, my past, my poor little boy," she moaned. "Where's your old father sleeping now with his dogs? Were you as pure as the lilies when I married you? Were you as innocent as you seemed? Were you wearing a veil? Did you trip at the church door?" He had stumbled, and she had had to assist him many times.

Soon she would be in a place where looks were of no importance, where all faces were alike, but little did he know that this was true. That was why, kicking with her foot, she gave the football boy no rest—helpless though she was, and she would be happy, she repeated, if only she was already dead and looking back on this life, and then no one would hear a word of complaint from her, from Madge. Not even a little mouse's squeak would there be from her, not even a stirring of a winged pod in the winter grass—and Madge, crying into her thin-boned hands, would laugh, laugh like the maddest girl who ever lived. She would dance with the dead boys and with this poor widower bereaved, this poor scarecrow, her husband growing old. For a perfect marriage like this, one should be dead, and one should not live, or they should both die together, it seemed to her. Why should she not mourn for her, poor little Madge—she who had been so light and free—no one else crying, no one giving, she cried, a tinker's dam? Oh, who would solder this great hole in the burning cloud?

She cried into her webby, streaked handkerchief, and her face was streaked with mascara, with purple stripes, seeming like the cup of a white flower around which the bees should buzz all summer long. She wiped away her tiny mustache, a streak of paint. She painted the mournful shadows around her eyes. She stared into her little looking glass.

There was not even a distant ray, it seemed to her, of living hope—so why pretend? All her life—what had it been but this sense of something lost? All her life had been this poor parody of life, this sad pretense she could no longer countenance nor endure, for she was dead, and she had died at the hour of her birth. Should the dead give birth to the living? Should the child give birth to the mother? It was this feeble imitation of herself—and who was she, poor little Madge, and where was she wandering now? What in the hell had she done, she screamed, with her bright ruby red paint with which she had touched up her face when she was saddest, giving it a few high-lights, and would she never get off her body the dust of the pottery, the feeling of clay around her eyes and in her hair and under her finger-nails?

Had she forgotten her little flower basket of the glass flowers, her little flower girl who looked like her, her golden hair that was almost silver like ashes? Where was her other heart, that little heart which had never stirred and yet was perfect, and where was her other face, and who should mourn for her?

Why, she asked, was she carrying a great iron key to an iron door, door to a star when she knew she had no house, no door, no bed, no four-postered bed and no canopy, no roof over her, no old bridegroom? She was leaning on her crutch. She was old and crabbed with age and bent to earth. No man would ever look at her.

Death was birth, and birth was death, she said, so why go through all this suffering, and why take all this trouble when she already knew what the end would be? Why go through that which everybody else went through? She had no pillow for her head. Her head would be pillowed on a dark wave, a stone, a cloud. She must sleep in the great four-postered bed where her husband was born. She must sleep in his old mother's house with Remember Thy Creator in the Days of Thy Youth Ere the Evil Days Come on Thee hanging on the liver-spotted wall and all those old family portraits looking down on her, old grandmothers and old grandfathers who long ago had gone to their just rewards or their unjust rewards and his mother and father at their wedding with five spotted hunting dogs crouched at the bridegroom's feet and ready to jump when they saw the bird and the bridegroom straining at the leashes and looking as if he would jump out of the picture—as he soon had done, going with his old hunting dogs. And what right had they all to look down on her when she was no different now from what they were?

His old mother, that old widow woman who was left so happy with her little husband, never had liked Madge. Now should they both be left as widows in the same house, and must they breakfast every morning at the same table, thinking of their dead husband?

Of all the triangles she could think of, even the ghostly triangles, this was one she definitely did not want to live through. Her voice fell, rose, screamed, whispered. "Leave one of us out of it. Count me out. I told you," she whispered, her voice still loud enough to awaken the omniscient dead, those who, having all knowledge, have no need of further knowledge, neither of the past nor of the prescience of unknown events which hover ever at the threshold of life and are never seen, "that she was no good, that she was all skin and bones, no meat on her—but would you believe what you have not seen, what eyes have not seen, what ears have not heard? You thought she was better than I am and better looking. You think that beauty is as beauty does.

"She was no Venus Adonis, no handsome girl with a broken arm. She was no Helen of Troy, no face to launch a thousand ships. No one stormed the gates for her even though those Greeks inside the wooden horse had not seen Helen for years or perhaps had never seen her, for I am convinced that if they had seen her, they would have stayed inside the wooden horse, and they would still be there.

"I told you to stay away from where you do not belong, even if it's only an evil dream, and it was never life, and that which was never life should do no harm, I said to you, dear.

"Her head is naked as marble. Here's a field without grass. Here's a tree without leaves. Quit barking up the wrong tree. She scares away the little birds, I said to him.

"She is the one who is walking the streets at night, sleeping with all the dead boys, for the dead cannot resist, and they cannot defend themselves. That's your old grandmother she's gone to bed with now. That's your old grandfather. They have no faces, but they have long, cold feet with webbed toes.

"I am the one you married, I said to him, but I never married you, you old fool. You married me of your own free will, and I did not marry you of mine."

It was no shotgun wedding, no matter what people might ever say. Sometimes it seemed to her she had been too strong, being too weak—that her weakness was her strength. She had carried him in her arms, and he was as light as a transparent leaf. She had stumbled on her way to the altar, and there had been no altar. But if there had been no church wedding, might there not be a church funeral? Perhaps not, she sighingly considered—perhaps her funeral should take place out of doors under the sky which would seem to have shrunken to the size of a handkerchief, a sky so small and grey and lacy and webbed with the dying light, seen only by the dying eyes. But who was dying?

"Go chase after her," she shrilly advised, "or leave us both alone, and see if I care, and see if I will lift a hand to protect you from her. Your way is lonelier than mine. Men don't know the half of it. They don't know either the one half or the other half, the half there is or the half there is not. Whichever side it is, they do not know it. You will never marry her or creep into her lonely bed, not on this side of creation, dear, never on the other. For if you have not slept with her over here, you shall not sleep with her over there. Really, dear, you shall not. So why not take your chances now? Sleep with her." She knew what she was talking of, for she had already been over there and knew the way—only in her dreams, of course, and she had already crossed the bridge, and she had paid the old toll-keeper her one-way fare. She had not paid for the return trip. The simple reason was that she had planned no return trip, really.

"In heaven," she remembered, "the angels do not marry, for they are male and female in one body. The angels do not have children. God makes us forget who we were. Marriage is an earthly institution. I read it in a book. Marriage parts us. It divorces our souls from our bodies, and you are left alone, sometimes when you are young, sometimes in your old age. Better to be left, I say, when you are young. You learn to take care of yourself.

"You will never marry her," she whispered, "never until death do you part, and things are different over there, and you change your shapes so many times just by being dead. You are tall, and you are short. You are big, and you are little. You are fair, and you are dark. There are no couples at the dance, no twos, no threes. There's not even a lonely solo dancer pirouetting. There is no music of a violin. The other person was always only the one you dreamed of, yourself, and you never loved her who was outside yourself, and you only thought you did. You never loved him. The water flows. The way is farther. There's the whirlpool whirling. There's the waterfall falling. You will search for her through the crucibles of creation, and you will never find her. A comet shoots as a firefly glows. They both will pass. They will seem to have passed together. They were many miles apart.

"You will never find her though you search through all the world of the dead, my dear of dears, and look into every face, shadowed or sun-lit. You will not find her in the world of the living if ever you find that world. The world of the living was never discovered by anyone. Waters whirl. Waters divide. It's too early, dear, or it's too late. She's dancing, crippled and old, dancing on one foot.

"The other foot is gone, walking alone over the bare hills, and it's all a dream, they say. The clocks do not strike or strike only in your sleep from which you will never awaken. You will never awaken at dawn. The red rooster crows at sunset, and the moon rises at dawn. You should have thought of all these things before."

If he thought she was going to stand for it, his running around after a crippled girl, then he had another thought coming—he really did. For how could she compete with someone who did not care how she looked? That careless girl! "Wake up," she furiously insisted, jabbing with her elbow, pounding with her delicate, glassy fist. "Listen, dearies, the knot is tied, and it's too late, and I'm too old, too old for this sort of thing. I'm too young, and I'll never grow old. The womb was the grave. The gates are closed. The waters of creation have already flowed. The ice is broken."

So everything had gone wrong, she being now on a different road from what she had imagined, she being on this familiar road, turning and turning, passing these same gate posts twice, three times, these same old orchards flooded to the tree-tops.

That was why she was fixing her face again, trying to look her best even though the everlasting darkness should surround her, trying to deceive the angels who were not there, and there were no other eyes but hers. Her eyes were closed.

"I'm the one you married," she cried again, her voice breaking because of her certainty, "your wife, your mortal wife, the only wife you'll ever have. You'll never marry her when I'm gone, so wake up. I think she's playing on the other team, boy. She's playing with the other town. Say, don't you remember me whom you promised to love, honor, and obey? Come when I whistle!"

She had married him, yes, but what did that signify? Who could prove that she was married? She had no marriage license—having torn it up just to show him that, so far as she personally was concerned, her marriage to him was meaningless, and her marriage did not exist, and it never would. She had married him not for her own sake certainly, for she could have gotten along without him. She had married him only to make him a man in the eyes of this world. She had lifted her flaming sword. He had never been nearer to her than he was now, this roaring chasm dividing him from her, and they were playing on different sides. The stars shining down on him were not the stars shining down on her. He was kicking a comet with long gold streaming hair.

"I'll show him yet," she said, "he can't escape, and it's not so easy as all that, or I would have. I would have gone myself before. I would have paved the way. He can't run around and around all night and leave me alone like this, alone with my past."

She was not going to live in the future, for she had never lived, she was certain, in the past, and time could never claim that which had never been the subject of time.

"He'll not leave me this old widow. She'll try to take him away from me, just to show that she can. The needle points to the star. But does the star point to the needle?"

Her voice soft and blurred, she whispered to herself, for there was no one else who cared for her, she knew now. "Who can see that I'm married? What proof have I? What living proof? I left my wedding ring in the pottery the night we were married, the night I married him. I stuck it into the clay mouth. I slipped it into an urn—but after all, it was not gold. I was not married in the gold of the furnace fire. I was not married to her. I was not married to him. It was only a poor imitation, a dime-store ring of brass, one of those things that come for a dime a dozen—so who could blame me?" she asked. And why should she not have thrown it away, for had she not paid for it herself out of her own pocket? Maybe some other girl would find it now and slip it on her finger and be the bride. But who would be the bridegroom if a girl married herself? She, Madge, poor little girl with her head whirling, had slipped it off her finger the minute she was married to him. So her marriage seemed illegal now like something which might have happened to someone else, and she had no way to show that she was married, for she had destroyed the marriage license, had burned the papers. Her finger was so tiny and thin-boned—that was why—and even the fat-bellied Justice of Peace had remarked that the wedding ring was too large for her—for the brass ring was so large, large as one of those brass rings that are tossed out to the lucky riders at the merry-go-round so that afterwards you can go again without paying the old ticket-taker, riding around and around on a horse or a swan, and she preferred a swan because a swan left earth and a horse did not leave the earth—large enough for the bridegroom even though it would slip off the bride. It was as large as a ring of stars.

"It looks so real, no one will know you bought it yourself, poor little girl, I said, and you are the only bridegroom there is. Always the bridegroom, I said, never the bride—and the bridegroom is not faithful.

"You should have left her standing at the church door. I should have gotten a dozen wedding rings if I was going to leave them around like that.

"Twelve pallbearers walking up the hill would do me more good than one bridegroom, the way I feel now, my belly so big. Twelve men are better than one if none can do you any good or if they've already done all the good there is, poor little Madge. That other girl's no better than you are, though. You haven't got so long to live, outlive her."

Now what should be her plans, now when life was as good as over, Madge coming back to this, Madge with all her ruined pride, her skirts trailing in dust? "I haven't any drapes," she said. "I haven't any curtains at my windows. I haven't any windows. I haven't any doors. There is no roof. I haven't any furniture. I have no living relatives. Neither the living nor the dead.

"Oh, my God, where's my other face? Where's my other mouth? Where's the girl I was when I was free, before I ever married you? Where's your grave? Where's your womb?"

There were always, it seemed, two conflicting motives in her mind, and she was always confused by these considerations which should have worked for harmony, for the union of souls. She was divided, becoming someone else—and so she tried to hold on to her memory, hard as she could and though she was an evanescence like smoke fading in the wind. How could she have known, until now when it was too late, all her thoughts, all her loves, all her vague, unformed desires? Did she know them now? How could she have known her life, its beginning and end, what her life was still to be, what it might become? For there had always been another person like a veil through which one saw the burning star.

There had been, she knew it now and perhaps had always known it, always that other girl, the one he was head over heels in love with, the one who was dying—Madge's old rival, name he called in his sleep, name of a girl who was not aware of Madge. It was not the name of his poor wife.

Had she ever succeeded in putting one thought into his foolish head? Had she ever awakened in him, as in herself, the spark of his desire for what he should not attain?

"So that was what I was trying to tell you, you numb, dumb skull," she shrilly cried. "Stay away from her if you want to live. Forget, forget that old Jacqueline White. She's no girl for you. She never was." Ah, yes. She was little Jackie White who would scarcely remember Madge. Jackie would escape from her body, leaving no one to inherit her big purple eyes, but Madge could not escape, and that was why she was fiercely jealous, seeing these dark clouds. Was Madge expected to sit at home with his old mother, holding her hands, comforting her because Jackie was dead, and he was gone with her? His mother had always thought that Madge was the fast one. "Oh, good Lord!" she said. "Jackie was fast. May she be surrounded by the little jacks-in-the-pulpit, little Johnny-jump-ups. May the white moths attend her. May the softest breezes blow over her. May she sleep in the long grass with my little football player. See if I care. It's not my business now. May the field mice mourn for her, and may the little squirrels mourn. May the little stars go out with grief."

But who would believe that Madge was married if he passed his time with Jackie, she who would never again have to face the music of existence, never again hear the old dance band, she who was going to her grave as if she were going to a dance and laughing all the way, laughing fit to kill all the boys, to kill Madge with grief, to take away her little heart, her little heart so cold? Who would think he was married to Madge if he was sleeping with Jackie, she who had always ignored him and yet was the one he had always loved—perhaps for that very reason, for man was strange—long before he had ever so much as thought of Madge or dreamed of her, his wife, or of the security which marriage might give him? Madge was heavy with another's child though she was a child herself. Jackie was light as the purple thistle blown along the wind. And was this fair to Madge who should have been so light, so light on her feet?

"Avoid her. Stay away. Do not return—she intends no good to you, and she never could have," Madge insisted so furiously that it seemed as if she might be trying to put the opposite idea into his mind, the idea that he should pursue her, follow her. "It's not in her nature to think of you, dear. She thinks of everyone before she thinks of you. You're the last man on earth she ever thinks of. Why, you come when life is over. You know she is fast. She is playing on both teams, playing to win. But what would she win except the silver loving cup?"

The boy, an exaggerated skull, yawned sleepily, opening his eyes which were blurred with sleep, stretching himself, shaking like a dog coming up from a stream. He leaned with his cheek against the cold bus-window—away from his wife. "Who stayed away?" he moaned, talking in his sleep. "Didn't I do the right thing? Didn't all the other fellows think so? I took the responsibility, and I carried it all the way. I carried it in my arms, and it was as light as any feather drifting in the wind. I dribbled. It drizzled. I hardly knew it."

"All the boys congratulated you, not me," Madge intoned. "They said you ought to be crowned as the great football hero. You had lost the great football game. They said you ought to wear the bridal wreath. Or was it the laurel wreath? Ha, ha! I have forgotten. They said you ought to be crowned, drowned." Madge could not help laughing as the bird bobbed on her hat. Perhaps they had known that he would not support her. He was strong, yes, but what was physical strength? It had deceived her so many times. "Why, for all the good he will do me now," she cried with her little face knotting and darkening as she searched for her handkerchief, "I might just as well have married the shadow of a man. I should have had the glass-blower blow me a glass girl. Put the glass tube to your lips, I should have said, and blow me a girl. Blow her of silicates. Blow her of sand. Blow her of wind. Blow me a goblet, an hour-glass, a window pane, a mirror, a thermometer, a pair of eye-glasses, binoculars with which to look at the glassy stars, I should have said to him. I should have had the potter make me a clay man. Make me a clay pigeon." Now she hid her face with her handkerchief. It almost seemed as if she were playing hide-and-seek.

But he continued as if he had not heard her, as if he had already learned to ignore her. Didn't he do the right thing, the right thing by everybody, all the Toms, Dicks, Harrys, all the boys who had played around with her and thought she was so lovely and so lily white and a spotless lily, poor little Madge whom he had taken as his wife, all her admirers being not worthy of her little finger, her little ring finger, and had he not taken the burden on his own shoulders because he was a man, because he was not a boy—saying the child was his, even when he had never so much as dreamed of becoming the father of a little child this year or next year? For he had so far to go. He had two or three years. The only little child he had ever dreamed of had been himself who had lost his father before he was born. He had dreamed that he was his mother's little boy, never that he was the child's old father, never that old hunter.

How often, she asked with her handkerchief covering her eyes, must she repeat herself? He was a poor numbskull, a poor numbskull, indeed —for she was not talking of the past but of the future, of their married life together, their sharing everything, even their innermost thoughts if they had any thoughts. "Stay away from that old Jackie White, for she has sores in her eyes, and her lips bleed, cracking in the cold—and that was why I said to you what I said. You will lead a long and happy life if you live with me. She will make you chase after her, even when she is dead, I warned you. She will come between us," Madge promised. "You will die in your sleep." Yes, if he went skating next winter with Jackie, he would be skating on the icy river with a ghost, the snow falling on her eyes, on her muff, on the violets on her muff. But whose ghost, she asked?

She removed her handkerchief, wiping her face once again—her eyes sharply gleaming as if she saw the frost, her face cracking under its coating of white face powder streaked with grey. Perhaps she seemed, even to herself, that person she warned against since it was so hard for her to tell the difference between one person and another now that she was not single. It was getting harder every minute. Why should they have an old ghost coming between them, crawling into their bridal bed—for why should she endure this marriage of three, or should they ever be four?

"You know you wish you were married to her instead of me, and you would rather mourn at her funeral than mine—any day in the year," she accused, "no matter which year it is. You think there is no time. There is no time for man, but there is time for woman. Time, dear, is passing. You would rather be married to her because she will be no more, and the years will go on without her, and she will be forever young. It's easier to be married to the dead—not half so hard as life is. I know. I might lose my life," she promised, "and then would you love me as you think you loved her, or would you even know the difference between us, or would there always be the three of us, yourself and her and her? Would you consider us as one or two when we were gone? Or wouldn't we melt into one like gold in the fire?

"She haunts you even now when she is still alive, so what will it be like when she is dead? She'll be worse, more active then—I can see it all coming. You know it will, and we never can be happy on this earth," she warned, her voice soft and lowering and almost indistinct. "It's this eternal triangle that does so much good or harm. There's always this stranger in my house. Why do you call out her name in your sleep, little boy? Jacqueline, Jacqueline, you cried last night, and that made me remember—she has forgotten you." Yes, how long did he think a memory could endure? Even if it was a simple memory, it would change, alter its shape. And she was not simple. "Why do you forget and call me by the name of that old high school cheer leader? Was that an insult?" she shrilly asked. "Was I supposed to take offense at what I cannot see, feel, hear? Do you think I have no heart?"

"It was a compliment," he said. "It was the highest praise I ever gave if I called out her name. If I was sleeping with her, I would call your name. Oh, Madge. You know it was you I loved. I never think of any woman." His eyes were only half opened, his mouth yawning and wide so that one could see his large pearly teeth and his red tongue and his red throat. "It looks as if I am just an old married man, boys and girls, and I have been married a long time. So quit buzzing. I only think of you, and you're the one that puts these weird ideas into my mind." Why, what was she trying to make him do? Was she trying to make him leave her, leave before the bride was cold? He had not thought of Jacqueline for almost two years now, maybe almost three years, not since that last dance when she had danced with all the other boys, never would have remembered her if Madge had let him even for one minute forget an old love, an old girl friend whom he had loved so long ago that he had almost forgotten her. He had hardly ever thought of her. He had been quite helpless in his love, never had spoken it. For he was too shy. But Madge was always digging up the past, always kicking old hornets' nests, and she had reminded him of Jacqueline as vividly as if the years had never passed. She knew now, of course, his love, it seemed to him. But how did she know? All the other fellows had loved her, and he was no different from them. Things were always very simple. He did not believe in anything that was complex. For the great things were those which went on in silence and mystery. Silence begot the mystery of the dream, and he would always be true to her. She was a part of him. Without the dream of the past, a man could have no dream of the future.

"The last time I saw her," he said, "she was Morality in the high school pageant, the most beautiful girl in the senior class, but it was more of a beauty of the spirit than of the body, and you were not even in that class, Madge. You had graduated so long ago. Or did you just leave?" he slowly asked as if he saw the dawn of wisdom. "Didn't you get a diploma? She got high honors. She was away ahead of me. She was Morality, and I was Honesty. She wore a long white dress and a golden crown. I was draped in the American flag. They were playing taps for the World War soldiers, and then she kissed me, and then I awakened and strewed paper roses on the crowd. She was Juliet, and I was Romeo. She wore a long white gown as when she was Morality, but my kiss did not awaken her, so I committed suicide. Then we went to the popcorn festival. It was snowing popcorn. She was the drum majorette. We were graduated together, and you had gone so many years ahead of us. You were so much older. I hardly remembered you until I saw you at the pottery. So how could you be jealous?

"I did not know what you looked like," he patiently explained, "or I would never have looked at her. She was so beautiful then, a beauty queen, and now you say she is dying, and she is old, going so far ahead of us, just as she always did, leading the boys to victory. Oh, Madge. How could it have happened? It all sounds like something that might have happened in the last five minutes while I was sleeping."

It did not sound reasonable, he sleepily muttered—not reasonable that Jacqueline was dying, too.

"She could skate like a comet," he remembered. "She was not afraid to skate where the ice was thinnest. She was the best dancer. She was the best girl basketball player in the entire county. She made the most baskets. She rooted for the team, making us win when we were losing. She was first in everything, taking the first prize every time. She was first in love, and now you say she is first in death, too. First in the hearts of her countrymen. She never took a second prize. She never got married. Perhaps it's reasonable, though."

"She was never compromised," Madge accused. "Skate like a comet! Yes, she'll skate right into that old ice hole. How you imagine these things," she said as eagerly as if it were not she who had perhaps suggested them. "She's changed. She walks with a crutch. She leans on your arm, and you would never know if somebody did not tell you it was the old girl you used to love. Your old flame that burned so cold. Her hair is grey. How you dream, not knowing that time passes—two years for her, five months for me. She has been going now for more than two years. You know she is never far out of your mind.

"So I am telling you now while you are still here for me to tell you. You'll be going over the hill with that old Jackie and the pallbearers carrying her all the way to her grave, and they'll be going over the hill next week following her. It's your funeral."

"Well, why not?" he grudgingly asked. "They were the dancers who danced with her, just as you said. I heard you before. Why do you always repeat what you said—when I heard you distinctly the first time? I'm not deaf. She is never in my mind."

That was his way of saying, of course, that she was never out of his mind, he guessed. He did not think consciously of her. He thought of her when he was not thinking. It was like the sunlight and the wind and the rain, like all those things he never thought of, things he did not have to remember, for they were always going on somewhere and even without his help.

"You don't have to think," he said, "of everything you think of in this life. She probably never gives me a thought. She was the forgetting kind. She lived for the present moment only and always will live for the present moment. The sky never asks me when it wants to rain, wants to snow. I cannot make the wind stop blowing."

Just when Madge resurrected Jacqueline, then did he suddenly remember her, the beautiful girl she had always been, would always be in his forgetful heart. She would be beautiful in his eyes when she was buried under the leaves, under the snow, under the falling of the rain. She would never change. She had been the girl cheer leader at the old football games when the crowds roared, roared with her, and that was why he had kicked the football. He had kicked the ball clear over the stars.

"She excelled in all the sports and was the best girl athlete I ever knew," he said, "next to Tom Cricket—remember him?—and yet her bones were fragile. She was a girl who knew how to toss the ball and make you run a mile under it. She wasn't strong like you. Oh, it breaks my heart. What for would I want to stay away from her now if she's dying the way you say she is and if the sunlight is fading from her eyes, if she can't even make another basket or jump another fence or go anywhere but to her grave? Shouldn't we all be kind to her? Shouldn't her last hour be the happiest she ever knew?" She had not been proud. She had been aloof. She had loved life just the way he did, it had always seemed to him—that she had always had a good time, running around with all the other fellows from midnight till dawn and dawn till midnight. No one ever knew when she had slept. She had never shown her preference for him—unless it was by ignoring him, he thought now, and that was especially true after they had died together in the class play, after he had kissed her and cried over her tomb and nearly forgotten his lines. After he had died, someone had had to throw cold water on him to bring him back to life. He had passed out. She was just affable and gay and spirited, treating all the boys the same, all as equals to each other. She never had thought of them or of herself in all her life. No one had ever known whom she had loved, for she had never spoken, and so they had all loved her. Perhaps she had loved no one, for perhaps she had not yet awakened to life when they knew her, and they had not awakened.

"Wouldn't it be a good idea, if she is dying, to have a class reunion?" he asked. "Shouldn't we invite everyone who was graduated from the class? We could not invite Tom Cricket, of course. He's dead, and besides, he did not graduate. He died two or three years ago, it seems to me. But maybe he has graduated now. Maybe he has got his diploma over there and taken first honors as the first in his class. Though mathematics was always so hard for him, especially algebraic equations, and he failed in Latin. Still, what difference does that make?

"We could not invite Timothy Grackle. He's dead. We could not invite Bob Tucker, of course. He's in Louisville."

"Where?" Madge sadly asked, showing probably more surprise, more horror than at any other time as if there were something she really could not comprehend.

"Louisville," the boy sadly replied, shaking his head. "It's too long a journey for anyone to make. We could not invite little Jack Fleet. He's gone to the Upper Michigan Peninsula. Old Bill Roberts has gone to Australia, I heard now. I heard it some time ago. We could not invite poor Archibald."

"You keep on like this," Madge said with her voice high and shrill, "and pretty soon you will have named the whole class."

"We could not ask poor Archibald's brother, poor Theobald," the boy continued as if he had not heard her. "He is back there in the pottery town. He told me last week he never would go home. I saw him only last week, and I never would have known him if he had not spoken first. He used to be brick red, but now he is white as snow. He's working in the flour mill. He's making flour—used to make bricks. He's a flour miller now, and he's covered with flour from his head to his feet." There was flour on his eyelids and flour on his eyelashes, flour on his cheeks, his mouth, his chin, and flour streaking his clothes with long white streaks and flour on his shoelaces. "He looked like his ghost, flour falling all around him and in the dark air. I surely was surprised when he said he was Theobald."

"You and your immortality!" Madge seemed to feel as if all things were fading in the air. She shivered in her coat, her glass beads jangling. "It is not the flour mill. It is the dust of the pottery. If you did not know Theobald, how will you know her? If you cannot remember the living, how will you know the dead when you see them again, I ask you? Oh, the brevity of life. The oldest glass-blower told me that life would be short, a rose fading in the summer air. He told me that you will never pluck last summer's rose. I never knew until now how short life was. So what is your immortal love if you have already forgotten her? Will you remember me when I am gone?"

"She was not like you, Madge. She would not notice if I was not there. She never looked forward to the future the way you do, and she never lived in the past. She was light-hearted. She could jump the highest fence, landing always on her feet. No one ever helped her."

"Jump the highest fence! There you are again." Was he dreaming again, Madge asked, if he thought that two years had not gone by, thumping with wounded wings, that the girl he loved was not two years older and hobbling toward her early grave or being carried there by all the old boys, the dreaming football team of which he was the only one who had been away for all this time? She would take the baseball boys, too, and the old river crowds.

"Don't you let me see you pushing her around that dance floor, Homer Capehorn. You will die if ever you dance with her. I will die if you leave me—sure as God made little owls."

"Then don't be jealous. We are all going to the same place in the end. Some might go before others, but we will all wind up in the same old river town."

Why must he avoid an old sweetheart if she was really dying as Madge said—if Jacqueline was really breathing her last in the spring of this cold, dead year and soon would be no more, not even the memory if there would be no one who remembered her? It was true—women dreamed too much, imagining things which were not there, and sometimes they brought them to life. Sometimes they made them happen, just by imagining. He would never have thought of leaving Madge, not now on their happy honeymoon or even long years afterwards. It was Madge who thought of leaving him. She was jealous, it seemed to him, of an old love never touched, one which had never been realized and had broken no heart except her own, a love which had no mortal issue. She was jealous of many persons she had not known and even of his old mother who had lost her husband, and such jealousy was as unreasonable as life after death. For the dead should not be jealous. The living should not be jealous of the dead. The dead did not love.

If Madge had not wanted him to remember Jacqueline, that flame which had burned so bright and brief, why had she mentioned the past, blowing the dead sparks to life and making the dead ashes glow? It was just a little firefly girl. Why did Madge continually remind him of a girl he had always loved from the distance and had never touched, never got close to because of the great crowds—a girl who had always been too much a part of him?

"It was not even one of those great romances you read about in books. It was just an old puppy love affair," Homer said, smiling and sad. "She was the most popular girl in the senior class, and she was always surrounded by the boys, the other fellows, even when she was beautiful. I remember her poodle-dog hair-cut. Madge, you were older than we were. You were already broken by life. You were already gone.

"I came last. I was the last man with her, even as with my wife, Madge, so what is there to envy now? She was the president when I was the vice-president of the senior class. She was the girl cheer leader when I was the captain of the football team, when I was making all the touch-downs and carried on the shoulders of the crowd and when I passed out because somebody kicked me—but I never did get over the line with her, no more than with you after I married you for better or worse and in the eyes of God, or else I just seemed to always kick the ball too far, away out of the field. The umpire said it was a game which should not be counted. No one ever read Jacqueline's mind or knew what she thought.

"You see," he continued patiently, his voice fumbling and slow, "it was this way. She was all of us, and she was none of us. We elected her to be immortal. She was Abraham Lincoln's sweetheart and Lincoln's mother afterwards and Jenny Lind and was going to have the most brilliant future of anyone who graduated and was going to be a great singer, for it was written in the unhuman stars a long time ago. Her star would never go out. She was going to sing in a great choir. Little Sir Echo! How do you do? How do you do?" Yet she had never been ambitious at all, and things had just seemed to come to her without her asking. She had won a prize when she had not entered a contest.

"I remember her better now," he said, "as time goes on, her poodle-dog hair-cut, those short curls that were always lifting in the wind. She wore a T-shirt, and she was always up in front, cheering the team when we panted. I never got off home base with her. I never made a homer. It was the same with basketball. I missed the basket. It was the same with skating on the frozen river. I missed the hole. She led you on. Her skin was dark. Her hair was chestnut brown streaked with darker streaks, and now you say it is streaked with grey, but I do not believe what I cannot see.

"She wore a yellow evening gown. She carried the yellow tuberoses at the commencement and gave the class speech. She chose the class motto—To thine own self be true, and it will follow as the day the night, thou canst not then be false to any man.

"Maybe she still will be a great star. You never know. It takes time to work out destiny in—things don't happen just over night, you know," he said as if he were enunciating a very important truth which only he had discovered though perhaps he had just discovered it. "She was a fast ball."

"Maybe she still won't be a great star. Time has already passed," Madge said. "Time has done a lot of things to Jackie in this time you have been gone. If you loved her so much, why did you leave her? Do you think she thinks of you? You are a slow ball. She was a fast ball. Do you think she remembers what you look like or who you were or were not?"

"Probably," he said. "Probably and probably not." If Jacqueline had forgotten him, he still would think of her. He had not asked to be remembered. Had he ever said that he had loved her in a fleshly or earthly way—any more than, of course, all the old boys had always loved her? The athletes had loved her because she cheered for them when they were rolling in the mud, when they were running in the rain and snow. She was the mascot of the team. She brought them all good luck and many wreaths of gold or silver or bronze, many silver loving cups, many banners, many trophies of football and hunting and field and stream and river. She had led all the boys to victory, yet never had been herself the victor over anyone, never had asked for triumph. She had been so small, the tiniest thin-boned girl. No wonder if he was always crying out her name. Jacqueline, Jacqueline, he said with his tongue thickening—and it was her spirit he remembered, anyhow, not her body, not something of the flesh as Madge thought. It was something that could not be defined. It was like his youth, his life, his love.

Though the flesh might wither and die, even as the grass, the flowers of the fields, the spirit could not die, it seemed to him. "You know very well that the soul always does triumph over the body, the preacher said when he married us. You know you can't prove anything in this life or the next. Death comes to every wedding feast. The bride is that poor skeleton who wears a wedding veil to hide her naked skull. Her eyes burn like flames. You do not know who she is."

"The bridegroom is the skeleton," Madge said. "It's just the other way around."

There had always been, it seemed to him, something about Jackie that had been more beautiful than life, something more beautiful than this existence as if she had already transcended it like the wandering star, something illusive and far away, so there would never be any change. There would never be any sudden transformation. She would be beautiful even when she was old and grey and withered, for he would see her as she had been in his eyes, not as she was. No lover saw a lady as she was. Besides, what was more beautiful than an aging face through which one saw the face that one had loved? In fact, he always would believe in the best and not the worst. He was not like Madge.

The boy, sighing, was half asleep again, his pale eyelids trembling, his red face smiling lingeringly with the thought of an unbaffled time when there had not been these complications and these amazing rivals, when he had never thought, perhaps, of Jacqueline or Madge. He had thought only of his mother and of his father who had gone with the dogs. Why awaken him when there were so many miles yet to go, so many curves to turn upon a turning road, and the old dogs were baying?

"She was always going to do something unusual," he said. "Maybe she still will. Nothing would surprise me."

"Maybe she still won't. The unusual things have all been done to her, and she's not the same girl she was, the girl you used to know. Perhaps you never knew her. You would not recognize her now if I did not tell you. Death is catching up with her. Death stole away her beauty which she never had. She'll have to pay for all her past sins she never sinned—just when she is already broke, too. Yes, that's what hurts," Madge said. "Even though you spend all your life without loving anyone, you die for love. No one escapes. Everyone pays the piper."

Time had done a lot of things to old Jacqueline in these two years or more he had been away, evading the responsibility for human love. Time had broken her. Old Jacqueline, for one thing, was two years older—age had come so fast, galloping upon her like a wild horse, for she had been so fast—living too fast, dying early because of her fast life. Now she was eighteen years old and would have no bridal bed but the moon—and though she should have been in the first flush of her youth, just now opening her eyes, she was like an old woman with grey, mangy hair or hair which ought to be grey, and she was closing her eyes. Death had been coming for a long time, Madge had no doubt.

Her eyes turning red or purple in the darkness, that ridiculous poodle-dog hair-cut and the chestnut brown curls flecked with gold and the wing-like movements of her arms, Madge remembered, just as he had reminded her, for she had almost forgotten, of herself, what the girl had looked like.

Now Madge asked—what could the boys have seen in her, even when she was young and they were young? She had had, from Madge's point of view, no feminine charm—no allure. She had never worn perfume, not even ashe-of roses. She had not even painted her lips. She had been angular and thin-boned and had never seemed attractive to Madge, who believed that a girl should paint herself—show her best face to the world.

Now, though, Jacqueline was old, dragging one foot after the other, going to her grave, just as Madge had said, and how could that old thing be even more attractive to the boys and the old married men than she had been before she had lost her beauty and her charm, and how could she still seem to draw them by a thread, a silken cable? She had lost her job at the saw mill. She had lost her job at the restaurant. She was not even working at the restaurant any more because of those germs she had been spreading out to the customers, trying to take the whole town with her when she went, it seemed, thinking she would never be lonely over there, for she had never been lonely over here. Fellows would drink a glass of water to show that they were good sports and that they still loved her and that she had always brought them good luck. She had always been surrounded by the old football crowds talking of the old touch-downs, the old baseball crowds talking of the old home runs, the old hunters talking of the old dogs, the old athletes—and they were still surrounding her—and that, it seemed to Madge, was Jacqueline, all over again, always so inconsiderate of other people's feelings. But now old Time had caught up with her, with Jacqueline who had thought she was outside its reach but who was no different from all the others, for she was old and grey. Time was no respecter, Madge said, of persons. Time cut down them all, the young and the old.

The county health agent, even though he was Jacqueline's father's cousin by marriage, had finally forced her to quit working because it was not the malaria poisoning the air—because it was something else, something galloping, the galloping consumption she was spreading around. He said that her lungs were spotted with black spots like a clouded sky before the rain.

Those big eyes of hers were turning different colors. The whole town was coughing when she coughed. All the men were coughing with her, and it was like a chorus of the bull frogs in the misty marsh land. Even the old health officer coughed. He coughed the most. The preacher coughed in the pulpit. The horses coughed on the roads. The old violinist coughed in the saloon, shaking with palsy from head to foot whenever he played the violin, and he was always playing only one tune. His music was the shakes. The whole orchestra coughed, and the leaves shook on the trees, and the stars shook in the clouds.

Some people still said it was just the usual malaria, the marsh butterflies spreading around the old sickness that made them cough and deafened them—but Madge knew, and she could never be convinced otherwise, it was always that old Jackie who flitted about, running the streets, trying to break up the peaceful homes and take all the men with her when she went. She was coughing, spitting up blood, Jackie was. Some of the men had gotten as crazy as hoot owls in the graveyard, hooting at every shadow.

That reminded Madge of something else which tormented her, keeping her awake.

"Her own father won't have her now," Madge said, "so she need not think she is so smart and so much better than I am just because she was the banker's daughter and lived in a brick house with a steeple and a butler's pantry and a four-postered bed with a canopy and tassels and that dining room table always set with the plates turned down for the members of the family that were already dead.

"You could tell the living from the dead, they say, by looking at the plates. The plates of the dead were turned down. Who cared if there were monogrammed napkins and silver toothpicks, especially as no one had been invited to dinner for years, and the flowers in the vases were withered?

"They say her father has already turned down Jackie's plate in front of Jackie's chair.

"They say she is going the way the other sisters went—one following the other to the grave. One left that blind, deaf baby that nobody wanted, that even the old man would not have, and some people said it was his, but she kissed it before she died, and pretty soon, it followed her to the grave.

"It was dumb, and it could not talk, but it knew the way it had never gone before. But who cared, and who shed a tear? It all happened without anybody's ever saying a word. That little baby ran through the grass chasing a butterfly.

"That last sister," Madge said after awhile, "kissed Jackie on the lips, and so she caught it, tuberculosis that was probably the easiest way out. It is easiest to go because of something you cannot help. She'll go now where her sisters went and never think of you, never kiss you. I don't think any of them really wanted to live.

"Their love was too great. It was something awful, the way that family loved each other and the way that old man loved all his daughters and loves his only son. They say his only son will be his only daughter now.

"They say as long as the old man has that son of his to ride around with, hunting the dead foxes, it makes no difference how many daughters are lying cold and dead.

"They used to ride to the hunt together, all dressed like British lords in scarlet coats, and now every year, it's just one fox-hunter less, and they never catch the fox. They don't catch anything. There's no fox to catch. Just tuberculosis or something like that. It comes from riding in the chilly wind.

"They say it changes your color before you can say Jack Robinson. First, you are pale, and then you are flushed, blushing like a bride, and then you are pale again, white as chalk—or maybe you die when your cheeks are the brightest, when your cheeks are the reddest, dear. You are six months gone before you know it. Five months gone. That's Jack."

"Jack who? Who was that other fellow?" the sleeping husband asked, turning his head toward her.

"Jack Robinson. Jack Frost who paints the window pane white. Frost flowers on the glass. Little Jack Fleet. Little Jack White. Jack-in-the-pulpit. Jack jump over the candlestick. Nobody. Quit accusing me of what I never did. I mean man in general and no man in particular, you numbskull, poor Homer Capehorn. Don't you ever listen, ever speak? When will you see the light, get the water off your brain, stop dreaming? She's a fast one, faster than you are.

"She's sleeping with all the team, the fullback, the halfback, the quarterback, all except you, of course. You were always so slow to catch on, to understand. You always fumbled, stumbled. You always missed your man. She's sleeping with the baseball team that won the loving cup, don't you remember—the rival team? You played with the losing team. The only fellow that won't have her is the oldest pinochle player in town. He wants to live, and he does not care how the other players change, who comes, who goes. He's only interested in his pinochle game, the one that has been going on for twenty-five years now, and he has never won. He has always lost, but he says he is going to win if it takes him another twenty-five years. He will win when he is the last player. But there is always a new player cutting into the old game. He says he does not know where these new players come from.

"Don't you keep in touch with the old town, with all these things that are going on? Doesn't anybody tell you what is happening? How do I know?" she seemed to ask herself. "Things that people tell me, and the rest I can imagine. My intuition tells me what I do not already know. I hear the birds sing. Oh, a little birdie told me. She is sleeping in the grass."

The boys all slept with Jacqueline behind the billboard because they were all such good sports, and they knew she was dying, approaching her last hour—that she would never tell, would never get them into any trouble with their jealous wives or mothers—that she would never ask anything of them again—but just this farewell kiss. It seemed so little to ask, and she was this dying girl, and they wished to remember her, be remembered by her. They knew that she would never be the full moon or even the half moon or quarter moon. She was the crescent moon, and she was waning. She was as thin as a thread in the sky. She was the crescent moon waning as thin as one pale sickle in the cloud, and so they gave their love before the light of the dawn should efface her from memory, the little heart-shaped face which once had throbbed with life.

Or so Madge imagined, pitying her as she pitied them. They would be the pallbearers now to take the girl up the long hill when the full moon was riding in the clouds, for they were such good sports, such fine gentlemen and true. They thought that they would mourn for her. Never once did they dream how soon they would be with her, sleeping at her feet with their old hunting dogs. And yet, of course, perhaps they dreamed that they were already sleeping with her, that time had passed, Madge sometimes thought—she did not know. Viewed in retrospect, the longest life would seem short. It would seem as short for Madge as for that other girl.

"She's sleeping with all the men, all except you," Madge said, almost as if she reproached him. "Love's the ghostly reaper now. He asks not what flower he reaps or where or when or why. She's sleeping with the whole town. She's sleeping with the out-field catcher who's catching the ball on another star, the left-handed pitcher, the whole diamond, the basketball players, the girls and the boys, the pinochle players who won the game, lost the game, the harpist who plays on the harp with the broken string, sounds like the wild turkey gabbling in a dark forest, the river-boat crowds who never again will hear the boat whistle, all the Toms, Dicks, Harrys, taking them all over the hill and far away, just like I told you last night and the night before.

"Wake up, you poor fool, before it's too late. She'll soon be gone. Oh, my sides are splitting."

"Harry who? Which Harry? I thought you said Jack."

"Jack White. Nobody, you poor fish. Jacqueline. All the boys in general, nobody in particular. Oh, why are you trying to confuse me? Not you with your slow ways, for you're married to me, it seems," Madge said, pursing her lips, both smiling and sad as she snapped open, shut her purse. "She'll be after you, but you're already married to me and taken, and there isn't even time for a divorce. There's no time in which to get ourselves unhitched, the old teamster told me. She'll try to break us up, dear, break our perfect marriage, break it into pieces. Perhaps I don't mean that she'll have to try. A moth's wing could break it. A snowflake could break it. She'll break us by being—or by not being. She'll do it just the same. If she is not, I cannot compete with her. I already know, for I already lost out to a ghost, dear, long ago, more beautiful than she will ever be."

"Whose ghost," Homer asked, "are you talking of now?"

"My mother's. My father's. Never mind," Madge said. For she wanted to talk about Jacqueline's family history and not her own. All the White girls, even those who had stayed at home and were respectable and snug and smug and would not look at any man on earth, were mad and sad, and all had gone from bad to worse, just like Jacqueline who was running the streets all night and must die some day. "Didn't that last sister get married when she knew she was dying, just to leave that baby the name of some other father, and didn't the little baby who never spoke and could not hear and could not cry die, too, and follow her through the long winter grass, looking for its mother? They found its little footprint in the frost on the grass, just when the cherry trees were beginning to bloom. The cherry blossoms were falling. There was no summer. Autumn came soon. Then there was the longest winter and snow upon the grass. Those White girls never seem to know when to stop." In fact, they never seemed to fall in love until they knew they were dying. Then all of a sudden, they would become very anxious, and their eyes would brighten, and they would begin to blush just when they should be fading, and they would marry a bridegroom no one had ever seen. Death was always the bridegroom, Madge admitted. Death with his grinning skull. Agony was the only love. They had followed each other to their graves. But why should they look down on Madge as if she were a strumpet? "I was taken a long time ago," she said. "I was married in my winding sheet. I was married to my old father. We are all the same."

"That was different, Madge Edwards, and you know it was," Homer said, opening his eyes, seeming to be awake though forgetfully addressing her by her maiden name—for perhaps he was still half asleep. "Jackie was always popular—and pitched the first ball. Maybe it fell on some other star. Maybe it always falls on this star. Did it fall on this star or some other star? Was it a spark or a star? What did you say? I did not hear you. Speak louder. It must be the static in the atmosphere—there are so many voices now. It's just like a baseball game. She could have married half the town if the other half had not been so jealous. You were just jealous of her and wish that you were where she is," he teased, his eyes brightening with sudden radiance as if a light were passing, "but you can't be. You can't be she, Madge. She can't be you. It's mathematically impossible. Two bodies can't occupy exactly the same position in space—or if they did, they must be one, one star and not two stars. One must be a spirit not anywhere in space. It must be outside of space. Is it a bird? If one triangle is laid over another triangle and they are not the same, it must be two triangles. See what I mean? You are you, and she is she. I am I, or am I? Am I? Are you? Is she?

"One box is one box. If there are two boxes, one must be inside the other or outside the other, the way I look at things. Jackie is in her body, her box. She is not you. She is not a spirit until she is dead." And then, of course, who would see her, touch her, love her? Were not all the boys after her, forgetting that they had been divided, and were they not united by their love for her now when she was dying, Madge had said?

"You mean," he asked, seeming to grope for his words, "she's better-looking now, even more popular than she was? The fellows still such good sports and she cheering them on, cheering both sides? Who's opposed to whom? Is there darkness, or is there light? Maybe she will never die. Life has a way of going on in the darkness under the surface, even when you don't think it will, when the sky is clouded. There is always someone else to catch the ball." He just could not look at life in this dark, cynical way, he said, closing his eyes—he just could not, and he would rather sleep, and he had never wished to do anyone any harm. "I always will look on the sunny side. The sunny side of the street. The sun is shining over there. I never wanted to hurt you, Madge. Forgive me if I kicked you. There was a lot of mud. It was a muddy field." He closed his eyes though his eyelids still fluttered on his cheeks.

"Poor little Madge Edwards that was," she sighed.

"Not you, Madge. Jackie. I was no more to her than the others—just lost in a crowd, just like you say. We never got past the gates." He could not come closer to Jacqueline, even when she was alive—so how come closer to her if ever she should be dead, lost in the wide reaches of star-lit space? He was alive now. He would not be alive then.

She was the best pole-vaulter he ever knew, jumping over the stars, the best dancer he had ever dreamed of, so light on her dancing toes. But she had always been elusive, and he had reached for the wrong girl. He had reached, time and again, and had missed. He had failed in all the sports, so what kind of champion was that? Who wanted to be a dead hero?

She had never been so wild about the boys in those days of their youth, he sighingly remembered, turning his head from side to side—but they had been wild after her, quarreling among themselves, some not speaking for years. They had fought it out, rolling in the grass, locked arm in arm. They had wrestled with each other because of a love they had already lost, and they had never won the prize, for there had been no umpire, no one to blow the whistle and break their long embrace which was so near to love. They were locked like lovers in Death's everlasting embrace. If anyone had been the victor, they probably would not have loved him. They probably would have envied him.

"Now they are all speaking again," Madge said. "They are all triumphing over each other. Their victory is that they fail."

"It's because they all have something in common, so what's wrong with that?" Homer asked as he turned his head toward Madge and opened his eyes, reaching out his hand until it almost touched her hand on which the glass jewels glittered—but she withdrew her hand. "Sometimes, I have been told, only sorrow will unite you. Death will unite you, even when marriage can't—or at least, that's my way of looking at things." Did not all Madge said prove that Jacqueline still had what it took, that she was still attractive, a big star pulling at a little star or many little stars? Some were as small as fireflies reflected on the winter grass. She could lead a drove of fireflies home and never lose one. "She was always to have had a place in the brightest constellations, you know. You don't know what beauty is until it's dead. For if it was beautiful before, then it's even more beautiful when you have to remember it through a cloud. You don't know time until time has passed. She must be better looking now if she is dead, and you only remember her, her dying face. I always will say that there's nothing like an old face that once was beautiful, especially if only you remember it."

"Don't tell me. Dying," Madge insisted, "dying, dying on her feet and won't give in, now when there's only one foot, when the knee is gone.

"They say it's just an optical illusion. They say it's something awful and would break your heart to see her going so fast, losing her hair in the starlight, her eyes, her teeth, and one knee gone, and she's dancing with one foot in a cloud. How often must I tell you, Homer Capehorn—will it never penetrate that thick skull of yours? She's a mere skeleton, a plucked bird, and she was plucked by the storm. There is not even a feather drifting through the sky. The time is short for her. There is no time."

Not that some pity would not have stirred in Madge's heart if Jacqueline had been married when she was alive, if she had settled down with one man who would have kept her away from the others. It was not her death she held against Jacqueline, for death could be forgiven us all, cutting down alike the evil and the good, and death could be understood, at least in retrospect. When it was passed, it was over. It was her life, that which could not be forgiven by Madge who still must deliver her child.

"You should see her now, those big purple eyes in the darkness. She's chasing after all the boys, the whole county and the next, dancing with them, going from partner to partner, and she's even dancing with the girls. She'll never dance with me. They think they are going to carry her over the hill. They think those are only her flowers she is wearing in her funeral wreath, and it's only her funeral, but there will be flowers for all. There will be wreaths on all the doors. Who will mourn for her when she is dead? I won't."

"You will. You will mourn for her. You already are. She never kissed any of the boys when I knew her, not even me, Madge," Homer said, "and yet it was I who loved her most. She was not like you, Madge, at all, no one to talk. She never said no, but she never said yes, and that was the way it always was, always will be, and she went before you knew she had passed. You knew there was no hope, but you just kept on hoping until you died. Of course, you never died. You got married." So he had married her, and he had never lived to have any regrets. He was probably just as happy as any other married man. His hunting days were over. He was warming his cold dogs. Poor little Jacqueline! She had always been like the angel looking for a human host, never finding one, the angel losing its feathers. Poor little bird forever in the storm, fluttering with broken wings.

Then why, Madge asked, did he think so much of Jacqueline, and why had he not married her instead of Madge if that was his secret desire, so ill concealed? No secret could be forever concealed. It would always come to the surface of life even though working through aeons. Even the dead would return. The grave gave up its dead as the river gave up its dead. The waters of the sea should not contain the dead. This was all she knew of life. Perhaps it was all that anyone knew.

So the spirit of Madge's old father had returned from the river. He had been a drunken fisherman who had mistaken Madge for her mother when Madge was twenty-three years old—the age her mother died in giving birth. After twenty-three years of reproaching Madge that she was not her mother, that she had taken her mother's life by being born, that she was born with blood upon her forehead, that hers was an evil star and a cold heart, that she had rejected him, he had come into Madge's bedroom one cold winter night when Madge was sleeping in the starlight

with her glassy eyes wide open, afraid to breathe, afraid to move, trying
to still her wildly beating heart—for no doubt as she realized now
when she looked back, she had always imitated her dead mother and had
tried to take her mother's place, had tried to compensate to him for her
and early death and nights without stars—and had always been fearful of
him who was her father, more fearful of him than any stranger, for she
had always known in her heart of hearts that he had always loved her,
and she had feared his kiss more than his blow—but what had he said
which had so frightened her that she had awakened and had screamed,
had cried out as if she saw her father's bearded ghost or the ghost of
someone else with snow upon his beard and water-colored eyes, someone
who was not her father? Oh, my poor wife, you have returned! You have
returned in your winding shroud. You have returned with your cold
heart. You have returned from the grave so cold and clammy and dark.
The grave's worm has not eaten you. Death has not decayed you, oh, my
dear. You are beautiful and young. You have not grown old. You were
never born. Oh, my poor spirit! You have found your body. You have
knocked at every door. You have returned with your flesh upon your
bones, with your eyes, with your lips, with your hair, with your screaming, crying. Oh, my poor wife! The grave gives up its dead, and you were
never killed. She has not killed you. So he had leaned above Madge's bed
where she had lain with her hair spread out upon the pillow in the
moonlight, but she had killed him—she had kicked him out like an old
dog whining for a bone. Everyone in the town knew this, how she had
made him go that night of the howling winds, the great snow storm, the
freezing cold which cracked the stars. He left his footprints weaving in a
drunkard's crooked walk upon the snow which covered the frozen meadows to the river's edge, his footprints zigzagging in the snow upon the
glacial frozen river between the snowy hills, his footprints like the drunkard's walk which was the pattern upon the faded quilt over her bed, that
which had been her mother's marriage bed. He had gone down to the
frozen river, and he had not returned, and she had known that she would
never see him again, never in this life. The river was frozen, shrouded
with snow, and he had gone down to fish through an ice hole.

Madge had known that he would not return, that never again would
he fish for her cold heart, dead heart, sleeping heart, but no one else
had believed her, for he had disappeared for long months many times
before. People had thought that he had crept into an old sheep-herder's
empty hut. Madge had known that he must have fallen through a hole in
the ice, a hole in the frozen star. She had wanted to search for him, but
no one would search. She had waited for a few weeks, but he had not
returned. She had broken up the bed for fire wood and had sold the
furniture and had thrown the plates out into the mud, and everyone had
thought she was very heartless, for thus had she masked her grief—by her
cold and furious anger. She had left town and had gone to work at the
pottery. After she was gone, the ice had melted, and the river had
flooded, and her father had returned with the spring floods—but she had
never come to see him buried. She had never returned until now.

"I was the prettiest telephone operator flirting over the wires. I kept the wires singing just like the birds in the spring, and all kinds of strange men called me, asking me for dates. There were some I had never seen. Then how did it happen, I keep asking myself, and who was that old man? I saw this old man coming in one day, and I kicked at him with my foot, my glassy heel. I said—Get out of here. I'm busy. Can't you see I'm busy? Hello, hello, hello! I said. Is this long distance? What's that buzzing in my ear? Here's your party—the long distance operator said at the other end of the line. Hello, I said. Then I heard somebody say in a thin, cracked voice—Hello, hello, hello. Is that you, Madge? Yes, I said— It is I, Madge. I'm right here. Who is it? Is that you? Is that you, father? Get out from under my feet, you old dog. Who are you? What are you doing here? Where did you say you were? Then I heard a long buzzing like a busy busy signal, and it sounded as if a cloud-burst or a rain storm in Illinois or a snow storm in Kansas had come between us, or maybe it was static coming from another star or the buzzing of honey bees in the long winter grass, and the operator said—Your party is disconnected." Poor Madge. She was disconnected then, just when she had made the connections. She had been disconnected ever since. She was cut off. Her wires had gone cold and dead.

She was confused not so much by her own confusion, of course, as by that of beastly man, this human beast molesting her. So her husband could leave her, for she was giving him his freedom now, his choice to make a choice if that was what he wanted, and he could go either way, leaving her alone with her grief. Had he married her just so that he could throw Jacqueline up to Madge and make these comparisons, so he could always have Jacqueline in his mind, in his heart—while poor little Madge wandered out of doors and shivered in the celestial cold? She believed so. His intentions never had been honorable. What man was ever faithful to the image of a woman's love? Really, no man could be trusted.

"Why think so much of her? Her days are numbered. She can't last five months at the outside." Madge laughed into her cupped hands, her face darkening, for perhaps she was already outside. Madge heard her laughter.

"Four or five months can be an awfully long time," the boy argued, "a long baseball game in the freezing cold." He was thinking of a long baseball game and of the stars flying over head and of the pitched ball moon and of the homer shaking the floors of heaven, for he was making a home run, he guessed, or something like that. He was running among the stars, for he was dreaming. "A great many things can be accomplished in just four or five months. As to time, it's where you spend the time that counts, that makes it long or short. They say a babe lives centuries in its mother's womb before it is born. Stars shine there, too, and light the dark waters. I wonder what time it is."

"Sometimes they are accomplished in a single night, just in an instant," Madge said. "It's like the flashing of a star, bright star. You are gone before you know that you are gone. The time goes fast for me, slow for you. I'll die when she is born."

"You'll live, Madge. Really, you will. They always say in the pulpits," the boy said, "that death is a kind of birth, and you should rejoice in it. They say you are born again, body and soul and spirit, and you have a different face, and your old sins are forgotten, washed away. For instance, if in your last life you were a blonde, in your next life you may be dark, quite dark." That was just the way he looked at life or death, always on the brightest side, always with hope.

"They say that youth is eternal," he continued, "though time is fleeting, and you do not grow old over there. No one changes but for the good. You die as a little child in the sight of God, you know, no matter how old you are. He plucks you up and carries you in His arms, you and the wounded bird. God never dropped anybody. God never dropped anybody from God's mouth. Or if so, He will retrieve you. God will find you again. There is no autumn. There are no winters. There are no seasons of the year. It is always spring." So why should Madge worry over what would never be again except in her own mind? If the fellows were such good sports, living over their youth again, then what was wrong with that—if Jacqueline was a little child in their eyes? What was the harm in just one last dance?

Madge's jealousy was just a woman's jealousy of something she could never know—the love of a man for a woman—so he believed it would be best to put these thoughts away and sleep. "It's only the lead in my system makes me want to sleep. It's not Jacqueline I think of any more, not even Madge," he sleepily moaned, yawning, closing his eyelids which were as heavy as lead, stretching his weary limbs. "Every time you think of her, every time you press the lid, it's she who jumps out like a jack-in-the-box. It's you who think too much of her, too much of Jacqueline."

Madge was the guilty one and could not get Jacqueline out of her mind though Jacqueline, he was quite sure, would never think of Madge if it were the other way, if it were she who was dying, breathing her last. Jacqueline would not even think of herself. She would think of everyone before she came to her own heart. Madge was the one who wanted to go with Jacqueline, leaving him. He was not himself these days, was not so physically fit as he had been in other years. He guessed his old mother would not know him, the unnatural color of his cheeks, how he had changed. He had put on several pounds.

"She won't want me to go to work right away," he whispered. "After all, she had no husband. Her husband left her. I was her only son. She'll say I should stay home and rest. I have worked too hard. She'll say— Death is an old hunter. Wait until you hear his winding horn. She'll say—Wait for a frosty morning. Then you will hear the old hunter whistling at his dogs. The old hunter will be coming again, calling his dogs. Death is your old father. I used to listen when I was a little boy— on frosty mornings, lying in my little bed upon a lace pillow that was like the cobwebs, I could hear the old hunter whistling and his old dogs barking as he passed. I got so I could tell one dog from another dog. Sometimes I could hear far away the shot of a gun. It was a bullet whistling, that with which my father killed himself when my mother got pregnant. I could hear my father passing in the winter wind. My father was the North wind. My father was dead."

He was lost hunting just as Madge's father was lost fishing in the dark river. It was strange how many people disappeared even in a small county, how many were lost. Perhaps that was why it was called the county of the lost.

"That's why I don't want to go there," Madge said. "Can't you see?" She was not herself these days either, anyone could see, for she had changed just as he had changed. Though their marriage was unreal, yet marriage had changed them both, it seemed to her, in many ways, some which would never be seen.

"It's just that we two are married to each other until the end whenever that may be," Madge said, "and I don't want those old ghosts coming between us and crying in the wind, voices I hear even when I am asleep. Sometimes I think they are talking about me. Sometimes it seems as if the lights were still going on and off. It seems as if I am back at the switchboard, still plugging in and plugging out, but that's not possible." That was all she had been trying to explain. Madge might die, too—and then what—if there were neither Madge nor Jacqueline, neither one heart nor the other heart, if both should go together? What if they both should die, Madge asked, and then there should be no one? There should be no cherry trees, no cherry trees in flower, no rabbits under the snow, no winking stars in the clouds, no crooked fences in the sky. She leaned closer to him, trying to put her head against his arm, but he withdrew his arm and turned away, slightly kicking as he turned his head toward the misted bus-window, for he was already sleeping as if he had not awakened, his cheeks a darker red and faintly touched with green and blue and gold as if he burned with inner fires. Perhaps he burned with some inner jewel greater than she would ever know. "She's free, not married to you." She would not have to come to child-bed as Madge must come, bearing the child that was never hers, never his, never would be theirs, the child of the dead father.

"So different from us," Madge said, "the most popular girl I ever knew. Never pregnant, never married."

Madge's heavily powdered face was streaked again with purple tears. Madge was crying, looking for her lace handkerchief, her wedding ring which she had thrown away, she had forgotten where now. She was rubbing paste rouge on her lips, for she had forgotten her lipstick as she lamented once again, and her fingers were smeared with red. She had forgotten too many things. She had forgotten—almost forgotten her other face which she must wear, seeming alive when she was dead. She was painting her lips with a cupid's bow as the old bus jolted, travelling through showers of sparks, its windows dashed upon by spray and foam and wandering lights, its wheels scraping against pebbles and rocks as if the only road were a river bed forever winding—and oh, my God, she screamed, looking at herself in her darkened mirror. What had she done? She had painted two mouths—she had painted two hearts.

"She is never alone," Madge said.

CHAPTER 7

❧

THE bus-wheels turned through great pools of oily and many-colored rain which had drowned the gulched dirt road, water running under the rusted wheels, water spraying the bus-windows with livid fountains as the motor sputtered, growing cold. The mist hung low like a curtain across the sky suddenly gleaming again in its middle reaches with tentative green and gold and pale translucence as if the sky were made of moths' wings which had fluttered against a glass. The lower sky was dark, and the upper sky was dark. The middle sky was streaked with transitory lights which soon must fade, for darkness came not all at once but only gradually, by slow degrees, even like the recognition of death, the mind continuing to dream of life when life was gone. Earth itself might be like a moth's wing lost in the enormity of space. On either side of the flooded road, there were these low and clouded and purple spotted, mirroring, pale fields of indistinction, tips of grain like rusted spears lifted above the glassy flood, clumps of indistinct, huddled trees. The bus, wheezing like an old horse, lumbered down hill, passing a stairway of stone covered by a sporadic waterfall. Upon a ragged bluff, the bell-tower of a grey, rain-washed wooden church which leaned against the drifting, illuminated cloud, the mackerel sky. Like some vast, ominous bird of passage, an indefinite, many-gabled house with broken chimneys, ruined balconies, an exterior stairway climbing to nowhere, mottled eyes like great rose windows lost in the blowing clouds, silent wings which were fluted and scalloped and scudding past among blurred, enormous shadows, shadows so massive that they might be these wings. The house might be only its shadow. Spiny bushes with claw-like hands, splotches of weeds and winter growth and great thistles like lost medusas, rail fences broken down, perhaps by stampeding cattle with stars upon their noses, perhaps by storm driving the stars to pasture. Transition seemed the only permanence.

In the midst of the shallow, finely pebbled waters rimmed by obscure, dwarfish hills, the waters still rippling around it as if it had just stopped, there stood the ruined chassis of an old Ford among poles, its top dented as if there had been an accident, its sides curtained by windows of torn isinglass through which shone a light so very dim that it might be the light of a firefly or of consciousness.

"Damned if it's not old Doc out on a night like this," the bus-driver said, having awakened only to continue the thoughts broken by his apparent sleep, "as I live and breathe. Angels of creation, and the motor's flooded, flooded to the gills, and he's drowned, and I'm still going on, passing him, him and the drowned moon, the dead world.

"Am I seeing with my eyes? Am I hearing with my ears? Is my heart still beating or not beating? Is this my body corporeal? Am I in my body or out of my body? Which would you say it was? Where am I, said I to him? Who will tow you in now if I don't? Hitch on to me. I'm the carriage. Tie yourself behind me like a boat. Bring on your passengers. Don't put out my tail light."

Oh, no, he must be only dreaming this, for it was not possible that old Doc's car could still be stalled out there in the whirlpool and the old fellow's face still staring upward through the murky flood, just the way it had been last week when this old bus had slowly passed him upon the crumbling shoulder of the hill, not possible that he was still tinkering, trying to start a spark of life in that old car which was only its skeleton with so many missing parts that it was almost entirely missing. Old Doc had always driven without lights or no light but an old carriage lantern that was so smoky no one could see its flame. He had always driven with a white flag to show that he was not the undertaker. "I said to old Doc— It's not a woman. It's not even a horse and buggy. It's not even a horse. It's not even the winged mule, the old grey mule flapping its wings on a lonely plain and laughing. Ha, ha, ha. She'll never breathe the breath of life again. Where's your ignition? Where's your spark? Where's your star? You've lost your guiding star. You've lost your fifth wheel. Where's your rudder? Where's your sail? Where's your anchor chain?

"There are no dead eyes staring through the flood water, I said to him, no dead eyes that will awaken again, old Doc. It's the sparrows perched on an old mule's back. It's the dead rabbits or an old squirrel or a dead fox. It's not what you think it is at all. It's changed its mind. It's the porcupines in the woods, I said to him. It's the angels chattering in the tree-tops. It's the porcupines."

Yet might it not be that it was just as usual the old bus-driver who was still wrong, and might not old Doc's imagination count for something? Maybe the old bus-driver had really seen, had really heard these things that kept him awake in the long nights—this old, dead baby crying out there in that dark water hole of old Doc's dreams. Maybe the baby's head was coming, and old Doc was always right in a world where you could not prove that he was always wrong, in a world where no one had ever been born, and no one had ever died.

"There's a new fool born every minute, and an old fool never dies," the talkative bus-driver said, scratching his head, turning his head from side to side, reasoning his way through densities of ethereal thought as if they were profound. "He ought to know these things better than I do or where he is now, what's his practice. Maybe he's practicing music. This will teach him a lesson, my leaving him now to find his way back.

"He never should have answered a call on a night like this, especially when he's got no telephone, when no one is ringing him, and he never should have come out riding in that old wreck, especially when he's got no automobile, and it's always his crazy imagination now. Nobody's being born. We've passed beyond his help."

God, though, how did old Doc get out this far, riding in an old wreck of an old automobile without a windshield or side-curtains or wheels, not even three wheels which the bus-driver could see now, and with no guiding star? God, Lucifer and all the angels of creation, the brightest that ever fell with burning hair—you could not stop old Doc when he got started. He always spoke so politely when he answered the telephone there at the old hotel. He always knocked on your door down the corridor, asking if the baby was coming and saying he would need hot water and clean towels. Sometimes he would say to take a headache powder. Sometimes he would play his violin. It was always the same tune. He said it was Mozart, but it did not sound like Mozart to the old bus-driver who many a night had awakened to this weird music. It sounded more like the music of the shakes, like old dogs howling, tree branches clashing in the winter winds. Many a night he had been awakened when he was resting from his journeys, perhaps only dreaming he was driving this old bus and wondering why he could not be paid for a longer journey than any he had taken, why he could not be paid for over-time like the fellows working for the government, like the road-menders who mended no roads. God, though, how did old Doc make it on these icy roads, he without a windshield wiper or any other instrument to wipe away the falling stars, he with nothing but his old medical kit which was a violin case?

"You've got to hand it to him. He's never refused a call yet and would come if it was Napoleon Bonaparte being born or George Washington's mother, just like I always said. If the baby's head is coming or even if it is not coming, he will come even if you have not called for his help and did not know he was coming, and he will pull like wild horses, or else you will die when you are only half born, he thinks, and he will die, and there will be no one. There will be no loving couples. There will be no crying women. He will come in the dead of night, away below sub-zero when this world is like a frozen star, in the coldest of the winter weather when the horses are frozen in the snow clouds just like you say, and it's always cold and freezing when he comes, it always seems, and you can see your breath, and he's got no winter overcoat, and the bird has got no feathers. Most people think he thinks he's driving a car. They even know which make it is. It's a Model T and gone to wrack and ruin. Sometimes I think he thinks he's one of those old horse-and-buggy doctors driving his horse, lean white horse that is nearly all bones, and the fringe is frozen on the surrey top that is over old Doc now, and there's no top but the frozen clouds, and the icicles are frozen in the clouds, or they might be the glassy stars. That's why he's got that old carriage lantern and plays his violin even when the string is broken.

"It's an old habit of his, going out like this in the middle of the night. He'll come like this even if he's naked, if his toes are webbed. He'll always close your mouth and give you something to ease your pain you do not feel.

"Used to be," the bus-driver said, steering around a bend as the bus seemed nearly to go off the road, "he would not answer your calls if he was asleep, but that was when he was young. That was before he grew old and lost his mind and lost his practice. More brilliant now than he used to be, has more patients, as many as the stars, as many as the autumn leaves. Some are already dead and born again. They say he's the smartest doctor you ever did see. Always was cautious."

Always increasing his sphere of practice, that's what old Doc was, and in spite of all the odds against him, hell and high water and old angel Gabriel blowing his tin horn to tell him to get out of the way.

"No steering wheel, no tires, no windshield, no motor, no head lights, no running board. He's off his beam," the bus-driver said. "I truly know he is. No crank, no driving license, no road, no gasoline, no horse, no horseless carriage. He has no top. He's lost as the stormy petrel, and did I ever see one?" A fool, Lear in the storm, old Doc was, fifty mad men! Who called him out on a night like this? Who wanted cauterizing, the gap stopped? "Who called him? It must have been that wounded bank-robber." Still, on second thought, it must have been that crazy barber. On third thought, it might have been almost anybody. The women were always hysterical, thinking they had been raped, even by their old husbands.

"He'll come all the way, farther than you are, and you'll not know he came. He hasn't got a telephone, I said to him, so why does he answer it? Let it keep on ringing. Why do they keep on calling? Why does old Doc answer when nobody calls? Life could be simple, Doc. It's all over now. Sleep." No voice but the old doctor's screaming like bloody murder! No practice but that in his memory. That was the problem.

"Crazier than fifty mad men playing at badminton in an insane asylum, and what's that? What said the night watchman to the owl? What said the owl?

"Damned if I'll stop to tow him in," the bus-driver said, his eyes bulging with light as he looked back. "For I am the bus-driver. He's the doctor." He could get in as best he could. How did he get out if he could not get in? He was a menace, old Doc was, always out driving at all hours of the night with no head lights, no steering wheel, no wheels, always burning the roads, skidding on ice.

"Old arteries hardening," the bus-driver said. "Palpitations. Blackbirds. Too much drink. That's what it is. No color. Who cures the doctor?

"Jumping Jesus, though, his car there on the road, off the road! Old Doc under the water and crying in his water hole. He can't cure us." Anybody would know he would have to be wrecked on a stormy night like this.

"Solomon, Bathsheba! What can I do? If he's drowned, he's drowned. Old car turned to rust, no wheels, this mortal chassis that has no parts. I got to look out for myself. I warned him. I told him to stop hogging these icy roads. Death, I said to old Doctor, will catch up with you, too, but no reason could penetrate. Those generations of his, that's all he thinks of, the poor humanity that was dead before it was ever born. Reuben, Gad, Manasseh, Jahaziel, Eliezer, Luke, Dan, Saul, blind as a bat," the bus-driver recited names in a broken jeremiad for a watery mile, "the children of Ham, deaf as a post, all these people begetting, begetting, begetting shades. I never saw them. Old Jesse Ferguson, John Simon, William Williams, Hannegan, Flint, Stein, old Tim Dorey and Red Mayhew and Skinflint and Buck, all gone over the hill.

"It's a stone without hands. It's a headstone, a corner stone, a stone of stumbling, a rock of offense, a living stone, a tried stone. He searcheth out stones in the darkness The stork knoweth her times. The footman, the forerunner, the mediator, the daysman, the interpreter, the inter-cessor, the advocate, the keeper of the seals, the strayed sheep, the unjust steward, the wedding gown, the candlestick. Jack, Jack, be quick. Who ever saw one? Say, who's talking now? Who does old Doc think he is, telling me I'll go first? I don't want him worrying over me. He's sick. It's my health. It's my laburnum." Did he care if old Doc was wrecked or not, for why had he been out driving in the first place with no steering wheel, no windshield, no clutch, no motor, no reason but the reason in his head? Who were his passengers? "I never saw them." Never did the bus-driver see them though he had been driving this road for more years than he cared to remember and knew every tree, every bush, every changing cloud.

"Holy angels! Shall the zebra lose its stripes? Shades, he's drunker than I am, that old greybeard. He's rolling in the flood, trying to start her up. Water on his brain, bats in his belfry, and I don't care what you say. He's bringing them in, all those old idiots staring through the wind-shield, some as small as moths, some with big, watery heads, no hands, no eyes, no ears, some with only their eyes, some with only their ears. It gets you. There are ears without eyes. There are eyes without ears. So now what has he got for his trouble? Nothing that you can see, nothing that you can hear. All these old cretins rolling in the flood, smashed like birds' eggs against a broken windshield, all these old birds' nests in the chim-ney pots leaning against the clouds, all these old bell-towers with the broken bells. Yea, and these hills we climb, this star which was never born.

"No tires, no spare tire, no instruments, no instrument board," the bus-driver said, "no lights, no rear view mirror, no side mirrors, no tongs, no bellows, no fire, nobody ever pregnant, no star ever born. He's got no match, and where there is no spark to start with, he can never start one. The branches are wet.

"He's pinned under the steering wheel, and it's rusted in the flood. He's tinkering with her old heart, dead heart, tin heart. He's wrecked from the shoulders up. Let him rot where he is. Quit following my tail lights. If it was just a matter of my personal choice now, I might have rescued him, might have towed him in even though I could not carry so much additional weight. Hitch your old tin lizzy on to me, I might have said, even though it is light as a feather and has no parts.

"He wants me to be one of his patients and take the medicine he gives to everyone, no matter what his sickness is. For it's the morning sickness, he said to me, or the evening sickness, and I can see a shooting star. I can see a breath of life, a light upon the other shore. He said he used to be a member of the amateur star-gazers' association, but he's not star-gazing now. It's real. When did he ever cure anybody, he with fingers that can't light a match to see whose face it is, if you are one of us or if you are someone who was never there, someone no one ever saw before?

"Isn't there trouble enough in the world already with the Democrats running the country and telling the woodpeckers the little woodpeckers can't peck the old cherry trees any more, and the bluejays can't scream in the windy mornings, and the peaches can't ripen on the boughs, and the moon can't wax, and yet the tax assessor is assessing us all, even those who never were, never will be born? The old Doctor's been retired long ago. He could enjoy his old age. Practiced himself out of his profession long ago. The way I see it, he's not even practicing in our sphere now, so why won't he leave me alone, go practice on some other star? His office is his bedroom. He resigned from the star-gazers because he said he discovered a new star which they said was an old star. Already discovered. It was just about then that his peculiarities began, and he began to act in an odd way, some people think. But I think they started a long time ago, probably long before anyone ever knew. And those who know can't tell. A doctor buries his secrets."

Ever in the Tavern hallway or on a public street corner or in the poolroom where the old pool players were pushing a few slow balls and arguing about the past and the plays of the players who were no longer there, why did old Doc try to stop him with that long bony finger of his, try to tell him what was wrong with his health when he felt so well, try to hand him an old prescription blank made out long ago for somebody who had already left this world, try to tell him to take pills, ointments, oils, elixirs, mercury to awaken his vital spirits, albumen, aqua regia which the bus-driver, being distrustful, had ascertained was that which would dissolve gold or platinum and burned like a star, zinc, lead, iron, all kinds of tonics, even hair tonics for a bus-driver whose hair was already so long that some day it would wind around his feet? Who had asked for medicine to help him out of this world? It was always the same medicine—something to put us to sleep, something never to awaken us until we were dead. That kind of doctor could never lose a patient.

"He says I'm suffering from a floating kidney and a swollen bladder, lung trouble, hemorrhage of the brain, palsy, quivers, liver spots, that I'll be taken by hardening of the arteries, hardening of my joints, hardening of my bones, calcifying, petrifying, turning into stone, turning into water, heart failure, spots before my eyes, woodpeckers pecking my wooden cheeks, bluejays screaming in the tree boughs, that old coxcomb screaming at me, he with his little burning beady eyes, he with his burning tail feathers. Who does he think he is, the angel Gabriel blowing his horn? So put away your medical kit, Doc, said I to him. I'm not diseased. I'm no spirit. Put away your fiddle. Go play your music to someone else. He says it's groin, gangrene, gall, fossils, whirlwinds, storms—that damned old whippersnapper warning me as I warned him. How did he get out this far?"

No head lights, none following the old bus-driver, none which he could see through his misted mirror, for what he saw was a warped star, no steering wheel turning like a wheel of blackbirds turning like a wheel of stars turning with the turning sun or moon, no wheels, no tires, no flat tires, no skid chain, no motor, no license plates for his old chariot now. No windshield, no motor. But that was just it—he did not need a car. He did not have to have his tires retreaded now or his motor fixed or his carburetor changed or his gasoline checked.

"I'm hungry. My stomach is roaring," the boy said. "We can stop at Iosh's All Night Spot when we get to town. There will still be a light burning for some old trucker on the road going the other way. Josh's Night Spot will still be open because it always is. I want a hamburger."

"You know I'll never set foot inside that drinking joint where those poolroom sharks and card players and wild women foregather waiting for the dawn," the girl said, "those old river rats all staring at me as if I killed my father. You, Homer Capehorn, what do you take me for? You know that's where your girl hangs out."

"I do not know. I never saw her there."

"Don't pretend innocence now that you are a married man. You know all these things and many more. Besides, I already told you last night and the night before. Old Josh is gone over the hill, so his place will still be closed in mourning. There's black crape across the windows, and there are black streamers hanging from the electric fans over head. There has to be a decent interval before the drinkers start drinking again. The drinkers are drinking somewhere else, you know, in memory of him. If he were alive, he would set them up. I think perhaps he did."

Was she still talking to a deaf man, a man with ears of stone? Did she waste her breath and her finest efforts? Didn't she tell him herself last night that old Josh had kicked his traces, kicked the bucket, crossed the bar, gone with the river's flowing?

"Caught on fire last Friday, joked with his pallbearers last Saturday, was laid out last Sunday, was buried last Monday by that drunken sexton at noon with all the old drunks standing around in the graveyard and not a tear shed. It was raining cats and dogs, knives and forks and spoons. Or if they cried, they were crying for themselves. They were thinking of the times they used to drink together from an old German helmet that was their loving cup. They were standing with their hats off and thinking of their next drink. As he was in the World War, they played military music. They should have played taps, but they made a mistake and played reveille. Men don't sorrow. When they buried that old football player, they all yelled—Rah, rah, rah. This time they were thinking of the horses running over the river at the next horse race, what old Josh had bet. He gave his ticket to someone else and said—Good luck, old fellow. May yours be the winning horse. If you win, you can spend the money on my brother's widow. Then he seemed to laugh. He died with what seemed like a frozen smile on his face. There were lights in his eyes for a long time, and then the lights went out. Things don't stop. Sometimes I think they are still happening. Things start up again."

Maybe, though, to be sure, Madge was mistaken, for maybe it had all happened not last week but the week before, Monday before last, Tuesday before last, Wednesday before last, but anyhow, the truth was the truth at any time, and she was sure of the day of the week if not of the week, not of the month, so why should Homer Capehorn deny it, deny the truth that everybody knew? Couldn't he face the truth for one sad moment such as this? Had she not told him only a few nights ago and many times how it was, and had he not been sickly sad, and didn't he say it made his stomach turn, that he had lost the best friend a man ever had and that he had lost the job which might have been his, for old Josh would surely have given him a job washing the glasses behind the bar, filling them up? Cleaning the tables? Strewing new sawdust on the floor where the old dogs had vomited? For that was the place where the hunters brought their dogs.

She was the kind who sorrowed over everyone's death, but she was glad old Josh could not give him that job now, that he must go over the river to the mines and be the paymaster, or he might dig coal in the pits though he did say he always liked the brighter side.

"There's just one temptation going to be less," she said. "He burned to death. His wife killed him. What did he expect, marrying his brother's wife and looking like his brother she had already killed? She's the one that did it all, killing two brothers with one stone. I know old Gertrude from away back. She's younger than he was. She's older than I am."

"Don't talk so loud. Someone might overhear you, and you might cause a suspicion to float around," Homer said, "attaching to all of us. We all have to turn in our checks some time. We all have to pay our passage through this life. Old Josh was not killed, and neither was his brother. Old Josh never showed his age. He was not even sick except that he was always pale from never being in the sunlight. He kept himself in the darkness like the old wine. He surely was proud of his old blackberry wine. He died, and the way I figure it, everybody has to." Blissfully, Homer smoothed back his tousled hair with both his hands, still yawning though his eyes had brightened. His forehead was sweating great drops. "I have always believed in the after-life, and I always will. The lights do not go out. They are just dimmed. It's better over there. It's just the same as here but better by far.

"The way I figure it, old Josh is still handing out the drinks, only more of them. The drinks are on the house. There are free drinks. Do you know what I dreamed? I dreamed I was rounding Cape Horn."

"No matter what you dream of, it's always yourself." Madge would, too, talk if she wanted to, even though she might as well be talking to a stone wall as to him. The whole world already knew, and there was no such thing as a secret, no lock which could not be opened at last by the locksmith. "Old Josh was killed by his dead brother's wife," she said, "because she had already done this thing and had to repeat herself, and you cannot deny it, Homer Capehorn, trusting the whole world and never looking beyond. He knew what was coming. He was murdered in cold blood. He was burned to death and was a long time burning. Didn't he always say—That woman will be the death of me? Didn't she wear black when she married him—still in mourning for his brother? There were only a few days between the marriage and the funeral. She was Mrs. Hathaway, and she became Mrs. Hathaway, and now she is Mrs. Hathaway who was twice widowed. Was she not already thinking that Josh would soon go where his brother was? Josh knew. Didn't he say that he was suspicious—and that was why he was marrying her—to make sure, to find out? One thing sure. If they did not love each other, they always loved his brother. At least, that was what they thought. But I heard she always loved Josh, and that was why she got rid of poor old Rudolph.

"They always kept Rudolph's picture in the house with the black crape tied underneath. I think it was his old bow-tie they hung there. His picture was in their bedroom. It was Rudolph who owned the bar, you know, and poor Josh worked for him, and he did not pay him. He never got paid until Rudolph died. If you had been hired, you would not have been paid. You would have worked for nothing."

"Then don't call it murder, Madge. It was a fatal accident if it happened like that. She could not help herself. You always look on the dark side and take the opposite point of view, no matter what it is. It is just as I say it is. Nobody ever killed anybody. You ought to try to be more broad-minded."

"I just face the truth when I see it coming," she protested, her eyes glittering and hard, "and it's inevitable. It's always there no matter what you do. You trust everybody. I don't look in the other direction the way you do, Homer Capehorn."

He knew as well as she did, Madge said impatiently, that the door of the coat closet where old Josh was locked in was locked from the outside. Old Josh could not have crawled through the top window. He was in there with a lighted match looking for an old overcoat, and there were all those empty coats hanging on their coat hangers, his brother's coats with moth balls in their pockets. He wanted to change his clothes and go out. He wanted to put on his brother's clothes.

"What for?" Homer asked. Undoubtedly, he was not paying close attention. He might have asked the same question as to almost anything else.

"What for? How can you ask such a foolish question? There is no reason in life. Everything was burned but the key in the keyhole, the undertaker said, and some old woolen coats that were never touched by the fire, and that the door was locked from the outside, and he ought to know, for he's always the first that comes at the last, and he fixes your face when you are dead so that you wouldn't recognize it. The door was shut like a tomb. It was locked from the outside. Old Josh must have howled, but nobody heard him. He had to kick his way out."

The key would have melted, too, if the heat was so great. The key never did melt. The key never did turn to open the door. No hand was placed upon the key to turn it. Old Josh had had to kick the door open, just as if he had been drinking his own drink and did not know what he was doing, and when he ran out, he was on fire in the middle of the dark street, even his hair burning like a torch, his coat burning, his eyeballs burning, his skin burning like ribbons, burning straws blowing around him and igniting the dead leaves, the wind blowing so hard that trees broke into fire and leaves burned for days, somebody saying it looked like the phoenix, somebody saying it looked like the end of the world, the skies opening, pouring down hail and brimstone, the headless horsemen riding with their torches like stars passing through the clouds, but he lived long enough to joke with his pallbearers, those old fellows always hanging around in that old saloon of his long after closing hours, old pool sharks and horse betters and card players, fishermen and drunkards and old coal miners with their faces blackened with coal dust and their eyes red-rimmed and their smoky lanterns still attached to their hats although the mines were closed and the drunken sexton who used to dance a merry jig when anybody died and the old tax assessor to whom he said he would pull through, and it would be a free drink on the house and a hot time in the old town next Saturday night or some other night, or if he did not make the grade, then they must stand at the bar and have a glass in memory of him, and he would be seeing them all soon over there. If he did not set them up over here, he would set them up over there. He would see them all next week. But he did not know Gertrude. She never set them up in memory of him.

"Did Gertrude so much as shed a tear at his funeral? Did he so much as ask to see her or say a word to her? When he saw her, his face froze. The lights went out of his eyes. She could have heard him screaming. How did the door get locked? Was it nobody's hand? He seemed to die when she came in. All she ever said was—I'll still be Mrs. Hathaway. There is no other brother now. I have married both brothers, but when I was in mourning for the first, I lost the second. But I'll still be Mrs. Hathaway. The way she talks now, you would think she was married to Rudolph. She never speaks of Josh. She had killed him."

"In the middle of the night like that, she would have been sleeping, off her guard," Homer said. "His voice would have been muffled under so many coats, so many mufflers that no one could have heard him. Those old pioneers built the walls thick. There are bricks with layers of straw. I saw an old evangel church torn down. It surely broke my heart. It could all have seemed like some terrible dream to her. There was no foreknowledge." The way he figured it, things just happened of themselves, and nobody was to blame.

"She was wide awake, old, greasy Gertrude that married two men, brother," the girl said, "wide awake, sitting there with an empty whiskey bottle in her hand, and you can't tell me any different. That big, bloated face that never scared away the house flies or the spiders. The place was hung with cobwebs. Those water rats running across the floor, bigger than life. Nine o'clock in the church steeple, and she could hear those bells. She never moved.

"She killed him, or she thought she did. The door was locked from the outside with that old pioneering key. She must have locked it. She must have got up and walked across the floor." Then why, if she had killed those two brothers in different ways, had she never been arrested and thrown into jail? Who was there to arrest her for killing her second husband, and who cared if she had killed her first? Who cared, for it was just another temptation less, and this was the toughest town on the river, and things like that happened every day along with the things that never happened?

"Nobody cares. Nobody could prove a thing. That is why. That is why," she said, answering her own questions. "They would all rather pretend that it had never happened. They would all rather close their eyes and just go on as they were, whoring and roaring, or they would rather suspect. The better element wanted to close down on old Josh anyhow. They wanted to lock the door."

"If you were not there, how did you know so much about it?" Doubtless his question was natural, but it was rather startling even to her.

"Use your head, Homer Capehorn. Have you no imagination? I didn't have to be there. If I had been there, I might not have known so well. There are some things you know better through never having been there. You do not live to tell of them."

"She was sleeping, and she never walked in her sleep," he argued. "You can't prove she did it. You ought not to say anything you cannot prove. If it is not true, it must be false. It stands to reason, doesn't it? It cannot be both true and false."

A fine world it would be if there had to be proof! Nobody would ever speak a word, the whole world knew, Madge scoffed at him. "She was sleeping the other time when the other brother was taken. Things like that just don't repeat themselves. Old Josh knew what had happened to him. that other brother with whom he had not spoken since the marriage, she having married his brother instead of him. So when his brother died, he married her. She married both brothers, and she killed them both. Rudolph's ghost was in the house. She could have turned the key in the lock as easy as anything, and who could prove that she didn't?" Was it somebody else's hand? What other time? Was it the heat from the fire, the great warping which might have warped the stars? The key could not have turned by itself, so there must have been a hand, even a ghostly hand. "Keys never turn by themselves. Somebody always turns them.

"Somebody is always guilty. Would he just stand in there and burn to death? Wasn't she in the house all the time? They say she has ordered two funeral wreaths."

"She could have been asleep. Keys do turn by themselves."

"Could have awakened. It was no dream. She gets it natural, I guess, killing them, for her own mother tried to kill her. Her mother killed her husband."

"What for? It was so long ago. You could not even have been born then, and you're older than the rest of us by a long shot, so how do you know? You know you're thirty."

"I am not," Madge protested. "She's thirty-five if she's a day. You know what she saw when she was little, sitting in the high chair, and what that younger sister saw, crawling on the floor, her mother killing the other one because it didn't have its right mind. It was an idiot. At least, its mother thought so. Maybe it was the smart one."

"Which one?" Homer asked. "You get me confused. I never knew there were three. Were there two or three? Which one didn't have its right mind now? Gertrude?

"Besides," he argued although without conviction, "nobody could ever prove it, for nobody ever saw it. Old Mrs. Tidings was never put into jail. She's just peculiar, always was. There never was a Mr. Tidings that anybody knew. Nobody ever saw him. They say she just invented him. Which one didn't have its right mind? You don't mean that same old Mrs. Tidings that has the parrot in the window, she killed one of her children? Which one, though? Which one was it?"

"Oh, yes, there was a Mr. Tidings. They say she killed him," Madge said. "She kept his old coats and his old hats in the house. It was that skull the children played with, used to set on the mantel piece, for she would not bury it. She let the children play with it on the floor. Some old rabbit-hunter's skull, I think it was, and that was all that was ever found of him. She didn't kill Gertrude. She aimed for the wrong one. See what I mean? She made this big mistake. She killed the one she thought was weak-minded. The baby that was put up too close to the fireplace and was killed before it could talk.

"The baby that was supposed to be the green idiot and was burned with the rotted log, and I don't know why I have to tell you all these things. The whole county knew at the time. It was something that was just passed over like this. The mother killed it. You never understand these things that go on under the surface. Men are so dumb, but women are so smart. Gertrude was looking on, never moved, never said a word."

"Which didn't have its right mind?"

"Not the baby that was killed, not the baby that was never named. Gertrude thinks she is so smart, marrying those two drunken brothers that had always loved each other until she ruined things. It's her sister that I feel sorry for. Musidora. She's the one that's kind of strange. I don't know where she got that name." He knew Musidora as well as she did. That idiot woman, Gertrude's sister that grew up with the water on her brain and was always begging for rags from house to house. "She begs at Gertrude's and her mother's, and they won't speak to each other, and she does not seem to know them, and they do not act as if they ever saw her before. Musidora. I don't know whether she's crazy or sane. Maybe she's sane. She never speaks." Why not? Maybe she had nothing to say—

that was why. "She works off and on at the Tavern. She lives down there in that old house boat with the holes in the roof." The starlight shining through, the water at the window when the river flooded.

"Crazy thing," Madge said. "Maybe she's sane. She never speaks. She helps at the Tavern for scraps of the landlord's bread. Maybe his wife's dirty petticoat that was used for a mop. Then she goes home."

"I remember her."

"Everybody does. She's flabby and grey-colored, kind of shapeless. The butcher sells her the rotten meat not good enough for the landlord's dog. She's got so many to feed, so many mouths, so many children. It's awful the way these common people reproduce themselves. They just go on and on."

"What for? They could stop."

"That's what I don't know. She grew up kind of peculiar, never explained," Madge said. "You know how she walks around the streets with that curly old grey hair hanging in her eyes and that look of not seeing anybody's face and kind of slobbers if anyone speaks to her or asks her how she is. I never did. You know I don't associate with everybody, can't afford to. In a place like that, people talk. That's what you don't understand, you being so faithful. You got to hold yourself high. Hold your head up. Don't lower yourself the way that old Musidora does, associating with everybody." Who would speak to Musidora? Wet, dirty thing, old, groveling Musidora, crawling on all fours at the Tavern, cleaning the slop out. No shoes, those big, bare feet with the blackened soles, her breasts sagging, those marble-colored eyes, that mottled skin, those grey, ragged curls, water running down her legs. "Gertrude need not think she's so smart with a sister like that. Old Musidora."

Old Musidora, pushing a battered baby carriage down the street from house to house to pick rags, and nobody knew why. Sometimes her face would be smiling. Always a baby inside, always another outside, something planted there by that old man, her husband, something that would grow. He plants no corn.

"What does she do with the rags when she gets them?" Madge asked. "Torn nightclothes, corsets with broken stays, old hats, men's hats, baby's clothes that are a century old. Throws them into the river," Madge said, "for she knows not the value. Dirt streaking her face and her hair never combed. You don't know whether she remembers anything or not. Sometimes there seems that look of recollection in her eyes, but she was looking beyond you. Someone gave her a nice dress once for her new-born baby. She threw it into the river, too. I heard she could laugh out loud even if she couldn't talk. I heard she could cry and kind of babble and reach for things."

"Her baby?"

"No, the rags were the ones she threw into the river. She didn't throw her baby, none of her children. That wouldn't have been right. The law would have caught up with her and put her into jail. Don't you ever listen? Why did I marry you? She shakes her head from side to side. It seems too big, and there is water on her brain. Her lips keep moving, but she never speaks." Poor Musidora! All those mouths to have to feed!

"All those children and always another coming, but nobody's sure she feels anything. She never speaks to them, and they don't seem to speak to her. She's just a child, too. The old man's the one that shouts at them and is the father of them all. He buys them bottles of pop. He seems to know they're his."

Which old man? Why, the one she was married to, naturally, the one who was their father.

"He's sixty-five years old and on the W.P.A., could have been Musidora's father, but he's Musidora's old husband. How does he do it?" That old man, Musidora's husband, was always taken by a terrible tide of coughing, and his looks were so haggard, his skin shriveled, his face like a naked skull, but the embers were always burning in his sunken, watery eyes, and some said he could not be trusted with children, not even with Musidora. He certainly would not let Musidora alone at night, as was well known, and there was always another baby coming, and people forgot how many there were. There in that old house boat with the starlight shining through the chinks in the rotted roof, what had Musidora's children seen that made them look so scared and thin-boned? Murder, they had seen murder, too, their father murdering their mother. "She's always got scratches and teeth bites on her arm like mosquito bites, but she never says a word. She can't complain. She just smiles."

The way it happened was this. The old man bought her from her mother for sixteen dollars and a new roof he promised. "The way I heard it, though," Madge said, "he paid twelve dollars down, and he still owes four, and he never put on a new roof for Mrs. Tidings, and she was going to sue, and it made her mad, for he had Musidora. Anyhow, she did not want Musidora. She always did know she had killed the wrong one. That's how it must seem."

"Which one had she killed?"

"Not Musidora, you stupid thing. She had not killed Musidora! That's the one that lived." The girl was almost too disgusted to speak. How could she make things clearer than she had made them? Really, it looked as if she were wasting her breath, talking to this stone wall, to these deaf ears! He knew as well as she did that it was not Musidora the mother killed and did away with in the roaring fireplace that time, and it was not Gertrude.

"Musidora's the one that is going on, I told you. She sits up there at the top of the graveyard hill. She takes that old W.P.A. worker's lunch to him. He's her only husband she has ever had, her only father. Nobody knows how he could have children. He's an old goat. Her mother sold her when she was a child. Then she always climbs the graveyard hill with all those half-clothed children stringing after her, their faces so white and peaked. You would think it was the first time they had ever been in the sunlight. Their eyes blink. They're as pale as moths. They are as solemn as little owls. They all have the same color of yellow hair. It's more like down than hair."

"Why does she go to the graveyard? That's a depressing place. I'll never go there unless I have to."

"To eat, she goes there to eat, that's why. She can't eat in the restaurant. She's too dirty. She hasn't got the money. She eats in the graveyard instead, for she's so simple that she does not know she should be sad. She's afraid of a lighted match.

"You can find her sitting up there any day at noon among the fallen birds' nests and slabs and all those rusted tin cans full of withered flowers, Homer. She sits up there among the tombstones and those old French angels with all those children running around her, half naked, little bird bones sticking out, their stomachs round. The grave-digger never disturbs her. He does not even speak. She eats raw hamburgers out of a paper sack, feeding the children, feeding the naked sparrows. The children play with the skulls, I suppose. If you tell her to go away, she cannot hear. She can't reply. She can hear, but she cannot speak a word. I doubt if anyone ever heard her speak." She always babbled like the brook babbling at the foot of the hill. Sometimes she wore a rusted old tin laurel wreath she had found in the grass and fanned herself with an old feather fan which had belonged to someone else and looked as if it had come out of a tomb. Maybe it was the wing of a bird. Sometimes she slept as her children ran around her. Many a time when she gave birth, she carried the baby in her arms immediately afterward. She did not know how many children there were. No one else knew. Her children played ring-around-a-rosy and hide-and-seek in the graveyard, hopscotch among the tombs, hopping on one foot. Her children raced with the shadows. Why could not the county put her away where she could do no more harm?

"Why should they? She's happy. She's doing all right."

"Anyhow, they're going to take that oldest child from her when she is twelve years old and give her to Musidora's mother so that she will not be ruined by that old man, her father. What is sorrow? Is it happiness? The county will pay her board and keep. She will need to be clothed. They will tie a ribbon into her hair. They will tie a sash around her waist. They probably will give her shoes. Ah, perhaps she will have lace mitts and a little lace veil trailing in the grass. They probably will give her a doll and a book. They say she's too smart to go on living with Musidora. The child already knows too much. She has seen too much. You've surely heard that saying—Little pitchers have big ears. The old potter told me—and he said—If you want to awaken the dead, just whisper. You don't have to shout. I can hear you." Some of the people thought, in fact, she should be taken away from Musidora now, Madge said, and given to Musidora's mother who had no husband and needed money, but what excuse was there, for Musidora was married, and no laws had ever been broken?

"Gertrude could take her, but Gertrude drinks and sees those water rats crawling over the floor. She's no housekeeper, you know, and never was. She's more like an old man cursing over her bottle. And now she has no husband. I guess she's Mr. Hathaway now. Old Mrs. Tidings, though, would do anything for money. She lives in a nice house with lace curtains and that parrot at the window. Oh, the things that parrot could tell if that parrot could talk. There's never a fire in the fireplace. She threw the skull out the door. Gertrude wears old Rudolph's coat."

"Musidora loves those children," Homer said, "or else she would not have them. She could have gotten rid of them if what you say is true. She could have thrown them into the river. Nobody ought to interfere with a mother's love. It's bigger than all of us."

"It certainly is. Did I ever say it was not? Nobody will," Madge agreed. "Nobody knows whether Musidora remembers what happened, for she's a child. She may not even know she is a mother. Unconsciousness is not always followed by consciousness. Nobody knows what she knows. She never talks. That little Wonet, though, is already old, too old for her age by far, and will surely be ruined if they let her stay on with Musidora after she's twelve, which is the age of wisdom, for the child will begin to notice things when she is old, don't you see, and she will remember what she never saw? Twelve is the age when Christ went out to preach to the wise men and was followed by the Apostles. I was told that there were twelve. What were their names? The dawn light creeps through the cracks in the roof. Then there is the dawn though it is not the dawn of innocence. Then there is the daylight, but everything looks dark. She will remember the things of the night, and she will tell. She will tell the other children. Or maybe she will run off with some old man. Or maybe she will just stay at home with that old man."

She surely would be better off, Madge argued, with Musidora's mother than with Musidora who knew no modesty and threw old clothes into the river so that the river might carry them away. "You cannot say that old Mrs. Tidings is not respectable and clean. She's a pillar of the church though I don't know which church. People forget. It's just too bad both her daughters turned out so badly, disappointing her.

"Gertrude sleeps, and she's already murdered two. Musidora does not know what time it is or whether school keeps or not. She's always picking flowers. Anyhow," after a long pause, the bus climbing up hill, wheezing and chugging and seeming ready to lose a wheel, "she will see another winter's snow, another dawn, and she'll be always with us. She'll be safe. No one will frighten her."

"Who, Musidora?"

"No, Jacqueline."

"What's Jacqueline got to do with it? I'm still hungry," Homer said, "hungry enough for two."

CHAPTER 8

✣

WE HAD passed through cloud-bursts accompanied by peals of thunder and flashings of stars, through the rain falling like a deluge, and the
night was dark without illumination as the bus plowed on through
whirlpool and whirlwind. We had come into that region of almost indistinct hills and valleys toward which we had travelled, here to where the
cape of the glacier had reached, inching like a crystal sea, leaving, when
it had passed, this rich soil which was to be populated by wild swans and
wild geese, wild herons and cranes and kingfishers and chimney swallows,
horny-tongued woodpeckers and marsh butterflies.

Yet there was only this greyness as if we had by-passed, long ago, the
spring of the year, and now the bus plowed on through darkness and
whirling waters toward no known season or toward one season which
should be all seasons. The windshield wiper was broken, and the road
was a river running under the wheels, the earth itself seeming to shake
like a funeral bell in vast, sonorous, conflicting dirges of wind and water
even after the storm had passed. Perhaps it was the beginning of creation.
Perhaps we had said farewell to earth.

The old bus-driver, knowing his way, had needed no affirmation
from the exterior reality, the storm being like only the established
routine of his marauding life, something he had experienced only too
many times before. Now he stopped the bus at the side of the road, just at
that moment when, if we had continued, we would surely have come to
the end of our endless journey, or so I had believed. On one side, fenced
in with a broken fence, was a graveyard hill, just where the road divided,
a branch passing through the open, rusted gates, climbing to the crest
lighted by a white carbon lamp like a moon in the pale arc of which were
fluttering moths and old, slanted tombstones with names of Stonecipher,
Longtree, Thistlewaite, Chesterfield, Dalton, Grebe, Thomas, Whitehill,
and there were other names in the darkness and names effaced by erosion,
the other branch of the road turning surely downward toward that obscure village I had dreamed of, the beautiful life toward which I had
travelled, that land of promise through eternity, there where the trees
would blossom and where no flower would fade, there where the children
would dance, where the young would not grow old, where the old would
never die, for time should cease. On the other side, now where the bus

head lights were turned like searchlights over the waters, there stood an old tin house in the midst of a dirty, slimy, flooded yard oozing with mud and refuse, its flat roof weighted down by innumerable tin flower pots and chimneys made of stovepipes, a low ridge of blurred hills flanked against its back and almost not to be distinguished from the greyness of the watery sky where burned one dim light beyond a cloud. In the beam of the bus head light cutting through curdled mist and darkness, the rain-filled hollow was lighted up only in that way in which one might see a realm of visionary hypothesis or uncertain speculation. A white chamber pot in the midst of the yellow flood, clumps of old rags, broom handles, twisted bedsprings, tin tubs, a soggy mattress laid upon the drumming waters, barrels, empty chicken crates, a broken rocking chair, wreckage. And yet someone had survived. The bus-driver signaled with his head lights. A light at the window was dimmed, raised, dimmed —though for a moment I thought it was only the reflection of the bus-driver's light.

"I got to change horses," the bus-driver said. "That old horse is tired. We can't go further unless we stop. It's the last stage." His fat hips rolling, he stepped with light-footed grace among flagstones lifted above the flooded yard, then disappeared into the dark doorway as the lights went out at the window.

Madge said, "She always puts out the lights when she knows they are coming, so they won't see her. Why does she think the darkness will help her? They can touch her. A man knows who she is even in the dark. He has seen her in the daylight, hasn't he, so why should she think she can fool him in the night or hide away from him? The way I look at life, he knows the woman he is sleeping with. Do you think it is possible that a woman can be ugly in the daylight but beautiful or someone else in the darkness? You know that a man cannot be deceived unless he wants to be deceived. That's why I always leave the light on. That's why I sleep with my pale gold hair spread out upon the pillow. I want him to know who it is so that afterwards he cannot say he did not know. He can see that I do not have to hide my beauty away. It's only a beautiful girl who can be deceived. It's always that same old one-eyed Beatrice there in the dark-ness, and now he's going in to see her. Old dirty thing. He knows she is the ugliest old hag for miles."

"She's clean. She brings my mother's laundry," Homer said, "and washes the clothes so clean. I've known her all my life, and no one ever worked so hard. In winter, she pulls the clean clothes in a wicker basket on a little red sled over the snow, up the hill and down the hill. Her face turns blue. They say she's royal, that there's blue blood in her. That's because her name is Fitzgerald. Everything that begins with Fitz is royal in this country. Fitzwater, Fitzsimmon, Fitzhugh, Fitzpatrick, Fitzgerald. I don't care what it is, just so it is Fitz. That was because of some woman that was never married to some old king but had a child by him. It's the bar sinister. It's the bastard line. Or otherwise she could have been a queen. That's why the dogs bark at her."

"Royal! She's nothing but a common prostitute, washes nobody's clothes, not even her own, and you know it better than I do. The whole baseball team used to go there, the pitcher, the catcher, all the old boys. You were on the team. She took them in the darkness. That's where they learned to toboggan, too."

"I never did know. All I know is what I saw. She was pulling that little red sled in the coldest winter, and the snowflakes fell into her eyes." Yes, that was how she had lost an eye. "A little boy shot at her with his bow and arrow, but I don't believe he lived around here. She never said who he was. She acted as if it were a hailstone that fell out of a cloud."

"She's the oldest prostitute in all this country. That's why she turns out the light. She never did want anybody to see her. Now she is losing the other eye."

"See no evil," Homer said. "Hear no evil. Speak no evil. The bus-driver's just gone in there to get a drink."

"You couldn't have hung around Josh's Place the way you did and not have known what I'm telling you. That's not why the old bus-driver stops out here by the graveyard where the loving couples sleep."

"I thought he was a faithful son. Maybe he's stopping for his mother's clean clothes and some shirts or to bring a message."

Did it look that way? What was ever washed? "You know she is nearly blind, so what can she see? Her clothes are streaked with dirt."

"Poor old Beatrice Fitzgerald," Homer said. "Away back, they say she had a son, that fellow that joined the Navy and went to sea. He must be twice my age, for I never saw him. He sends her postal cards from all over the world. He has seen all the world's great ports. But he never forgot her. It was his little red sled she dragged through the snow."

"What son did she ever have?" Madge asked. "What are you talking about? Are you out of your head? She would not have been so dumb as to get caught like this."

"Old Doc used to go in there, and she had a son by old Doc, but old Doc never claimed him, young Doc. Of course, it could have been any-body's son. Old Doc never knew that he was a father. I don't think he knows yet. That son of his grew up awfully smart and handsome and joined the Navy so he would not be around any more and would not wear rags and could wear a uniform and could see the whole world. Borneo, Singapore, Japan, the China Sea, the Rock of Gibraltar."

"How do you know so much about it?"

"Everybody knows. I only know what I heard. It's named after the Moslem general who landed there and invaded Spain away back. It's the impregnable fortress. You can storm against its gates. It's the life insur-ance ad."

Heard? What business had he hearing? "You always act so dumb. Besides, if he loves her, why does he not send her beautiful clothes?"

"It just shows," Homer said, "you haven't heard everything there is."

Three, five, ten minutes passing—who could tell, and where was I that I should hear these voices, see these faces? I heard the drone of voices now but not the words, not the meaning, for my head was heavy with the grief unexpressed. Part of my mind was submerged in my mind, thinking—was it really true that one relived, in three minutes, all one's life as the drowning are said to do, that old scenes pass before one's eyes, childhood and youth? Can a drowning person remember everything, even those things which none had seen? Whose life? I was sinking for the first, the second, the third time, though yet it was not myself who sank or my life which I remembered. It was another, another's ultimate face, cold and unchanging, those features I did not recognize, that face pillowed upon the oozy tides of time. That face staring through the dark waves. Great waters roaring to the sky, that head covered over. Where was Miss MacIntosh, my darling, now aloud I cried? Who had killed an old woman or an old man? Who had killed a child?

"The door just locked by itself," the boy said, stubbornly. "That happens sometimes. The key just turned in the lock. There was nobody's hand."

His face a darker purple, wooden and expressionless and coarse-grained, his eyes bulging and expressionless and without light, his hair dripping with wet and curling around his face, the bus-driver had returned after a long period of waiting, this small eternity within eternity, and now we were heading toward the village which, as I understood, was sheltered on one side by these sheltering grey hills, a semi-circle, and on the other side, edged to the wild, turbulent river and the open plain beyond.

"You heard about old Josh getting killed?" the bus-driver asked. "Old Josh Hathaway is dead. His wife killed him, and he never should have married her if he had not wanted to die." That was the way of these secretive women. They shut you in, or they locked you out. If his wife didn't kill him, then who did?

"You can't prove it's murder, but God and the avenging angels," the bus-driver said, "you can't prove it's not, so you are right, whichever way you look at it or if you do not look at all.

"As God is my only witness, so help me God, and may I never witness God, it's murder, no matter who done it, for old Josh is dead, gone to join old Rudolph. If the key turned by itself, that key in the lock, it's murder just the same, for old Josh is killed, dead last Wednesday, or if God done it, the way some people say, it's murder. Old Josh is sleeping with old Rudolph now. It's what he always wanted. Perhaps they have forgotten her. I don't care who done it. Who killed the old horse? Who killed the sparrows? Who killed old Jim? Who killed old Tom? Who killed old Dan? It's murder. I wouldn't hesitate to say so to God himself, for look, I'm an honest man, got nothing to conceal." Would he trust God if there was a god? It was a fine thing, trusting God, for who had caused all this trouble? "The politicians. There's no one I'll trust," the bus-driver said, "not even old Doc who is practicing medical science no more and thinks that he can cure you. No, sir. No, sir."

He would just go out in his own way, the bus-driver would, and take the shortest road.

"It's all in his brain, you understand," the bus-driver said, talking to himself, "and I never take him seriously. Old Doc means no harm, but he's under the water, flooded to the gills, and can't see us. Medical science, woodpeckers! Mocking birds, by Jove! Rejuvenation, what? When you got to go, you got to go. He can't be disturbed or suddenly alarmed. Repairing, tinkering with my old heart, pulling me through the storm, that's what he says, says he! Bats in his belfry, says I. Did I ask him? Say, when was it he practiced last or used his stethoscope? Did I embarrass him by asking questions? Did I ask him who his patients were or where? Where's Moses Hunnecker, the old bus-driver, now?

"Some say he went out of medical science in the influenza epidemic that struck us shortly after the Armistice. Those German germs washed up in Boston Harbor. Ach, Gott! Do I care? What's that to me? Some say he eased out of his practice about ten years ago. That's more like it. Nobody knows when it was.

"Was I not made," the bus-driver asked, "as man in all his glory to rule over the peacocks and the pelicans and the polar bears and the whole benighted universe? Am I not in my right mind? Is this not my body? If it's not mine, whose is it? My foot, my eye! My hand, it looks like my hand. What's that? Who shall stop me in the Tavern hallway and warn me I'm losing my health? Tell me my heart's beating low? Will I come around? Will I weather the storm? How's my stomach?

"Damn his hide. He thinks these things. He's just out of his mind, that's all, not practicing, just relapsing, poor old fellow, just thinks he's a doctor. You understand, he has no car, no windshield, no chassis, no wheel. There's no wounded bank robber anywhere. There's no bullet hole in old Doc's windshield.

"Hell and the furies! There's no hell, and there's no heaven, and there's no doctor. There's no beautiful movie star dying unknown at the Tavern, so what does he want to cure her for? There's no cure for what ails her. Who called him with those old pruning hooks, those old garden shears? Who wants it lifted out? Who's pregnant, and who's conceived?

"Am I pregnant, are you? You understand, it's not that he wouldn't be all right if he were all right, and it's not that everything he thinks he's doing isn't right, but the fact of the matter is, he's not doing what he thinks he's doing, so it's not all right by a long shot, and I don't want him to meddle with me. Splicing, tying, untying, stopping my artery! Prescription, pills, antiseptics so I won't fester, anesthetics so I will not feel! Gauze, ether, butterflies! I left him in his bed.

"Yes, away behind the times, old Doc is, skidding on ice, blowing out his tires, couldn't cure a butterfly, hasn't kept up with the changes in medical science, might as well be dead, I told him last week, hasn't a pulse. It's all in his own brain," the bus-driver said, "and he thinks it's mine, so we argue like that. Delirium tremens, mocking birds, snakes, women! Antidotes, prophylactic, cough medicine, but damned if I wouldn't prefer my patent medicine to his, my tonic, my pick-me-up! Did I ask him to look down my throat or tell me what it is?

"Plaster, he says, plaster, plaster! What's that, vulnerability? What's that, a key and lock hospital? What's that, a bird mason? What's that,

snatch me from the jaws of living death? Kill or cure? Who killed anybody? What's that, me hanging by a thread? What's that, me trusting to a
broken reed?

"You understand, he means well. It kind of makes your heart give to
see a doctor going like that. It makes you begin to suspicion yourself. You
get to thinking that there's nobody else. Nobody. You take that poor
little Jacqueline now. Death never entered her head. Kind of infatuated
with life, she is, prettier now than she ever was, going to see us all next
Christmas, going to dance the light fantastic. It'll be light. Kind of makes
your old heart give.

"The best doctor couldn't help her. Old Doc certainly couldn't. Who
asked for help? Barmy, old Doc is, screw loose, unhinged, off his head, off
his beam, beside himself, galloping mad. Stark, staring, raving mad, running amok, hogging the road, taking up all the space there is, and would
not know the difference between a bug and a star. Mad as a March hare,
gone in the upper story, wouldn't know a microscope from a telescope,
that's what he tells me, that old knight errant curing them all, taking
poor folks by surprise in the middle of the night, for some don't want to
be cured, rather hear death knocking than the doctor. He says it's a boy
or a girl, male or female. If old Doc comes, they say, to wake us up, tell
him we are dead, that we just passed on.

"A clean bill of health! Who wants one? What good would it do? Fit
as a fiddle one day, in high feather one day, gone the next, and nobody
mourns for you. You went so fast. Nobody knows you went. Galloping
consumption, that churchyard cough, old Doc, old Father Time, horse
feathers, hooting owls! Who cares? You got to go, say I, I say, when your
time comes.

"You got to go when the tide goes. You're on your last legs, you're at
a low ebb, somebody turns the key in the lock. When you're washed up,
they don't know you. Look at him. The way I see it, we are all mortal,
and there's no difference. The way I see it, there's no immortal case.

"Lightning bugs in the woods! Not even the lightning bugs. Rabbits
crying in their holes. Not even the rabbits. Shallows, rocks, crossing the
bar, who cares! You go some way. Sore, ulcer, abscess, fester, boil, a
scratch! Greatest kings have died. A turtle falling on your head.

"Well, I'll be damned. I got here the same way he did. Who cured
anybody, any mother's son or daughter? But the thread never broke.

"Understand, old Doc would be all right if the world was. That old
life stream, passage of time, things like that, hearts, arteries, he just
thinks they're going on when they're all washed up, when nobody asked
him, nobody phoned. His memory's so tenacious, just three sheets to the
wind and skidding. It's just a brain storm he's always passing through,
damn him, nothing else, and he's got no car, no passengers. Stormy
petrels! He's got no horses. A frail vehicle, this life is. Who's he to stop
me in the corridor and ask me how I am? God damn. Yet you can't help
giving him your hand when he gives his hand to you. You can't help
asking him how he is. Still under the weather, Doc? Roof still leaking?
How's tires? How many yesterday, did you say, how many last night,

those crazy women in labor pains? How many bastards? Was old Lethe roaring, making you forget? How was old Charon that rowed the boat?

"Damned, though, if I'll take his cheek! Damned if he'll peck at me, trying to remind me of the things I don't want to be reminded of! My age, my change of life! Mutations, migrations of birds! If I don't care, why should he care about this old body, this mortal corruption? Let it go. Alpha and Omega, beginning and end! Trunk, bole, hulk, skeleton. Slice, scale, morsel, scrap, one eye, two eyes, three. Flesh, blood, stuff, substratum! Where did I ever see my substratum? Turnstones. Tangible, real, corporeal, evident. What's evident? Figurehead, who's a figurehead? Where are any woodpeckers?

"Am I not well? Is there anything eating on me? Echo, what's that? Man of straw, where? Groin, my elbow, bone of my bone! Whose? Render unto Caesar the things that are Caesar's! Render unto Doc the things that are Doc's! Cicada, who's got one? Gullet, where's my gullet? Cardiac, where now?

"Canst thou draw out leviathan with a hook? Canst thou put a hook into his nose? Bore his jaw through with a thorn and open his eyelids like the eyelids of morning? Open his tongue with a cord which thou lettest down? Wilt thou take him for a servant forever? Will he speak soft words when you speak to him? Wilt thou play with him as with a bird, or wilt thou bind him for thy maidens? Make a banquet of him? Canst thou fill his head with fish spears? Do no more. Who can discover the face of his garment? Who can come to him with his double bridle and bring him in? Who can open the doors of his face? His teeth are terrible round about, and his scales are his pride, shut up together as with a closed seal, one so near the other, no air can come between them. They cannot be sundered. Out of his mouth go burning lamps. His breath kindleth coals. Sparks of fire leap out. Smoke and belching. He roareth like a great locomotive.

"What happened to Julius Caesar? Stabbed by his best friend! Hercules, what happened to Hercules? Wormwood, dust, ashes. Hewers of wood and drawers of water! Where did they come in? Was I not made to be the king of the earth? My long hair wrapped around my feet. No partridges in these mountains. Nary a one. Was I not made to rule these damned bluejays?

"Mock me. There's no one needs a bone set. There's no one broken any bones," the bus-driver said. "Ossification, what's that? Dividing membrane, who's got it? There's no bleeding. It's all up there in the upper story of that old Tavern, just where we're coming to, old Doc practicing away, just like I said. Flies, horse flies! Babies crying. Mothers' sons. Not a baby born this year. Who threw that poor little baby into the winter grass last winter? 'Twasn't I, 'twasn't you, 'twasn't there. Damned if I ever saw what I saw. Damned if I ever heard what I heard. Damned if it's not still crying in my ear.

"Damned if I don't mow him down! Old Father Time, old Doc. Who does he think he is? Roosevelt in the White House? But what makes it so bad, though," the bus-driver mused, "old Doc's a Republican, too.

Don't believe in free silver. Damned if that wasn't his hat on the road away back. We're just bumping in according to schedule."

A row of upright houses like coffins standing against the sky, the houses tall and narrow, bleakly grey in the wet, dripping moonlight, great spaces yawning between, tattered awnings, broken hedges, a pale, dented moon like a skull seen through thin, contorted, leafless trees, their steaming branches that danced above a porous sidewalk. A spectral village was gliding by, seeming a conspiracy of illusion and not of brick or stone or wood, but this was it, and we had come, here where no sound might disturb the peace, the dead ear, no sound but the past, the dead, loud voices. Upon a thin steeple, a fish weathervane in a drifting cloud. Little bird houses outlined against the cold, wan, silver-streaked sky. In a bare front yard, a flock of wooden geese. A bicycle leaning against a telephone pole. Hanging on a clothesline in the wet wind, sheets, drawers, shirts, stockings. A light going on in an upper window. A light going out. The far whistle of a train. Signboards lurching, the winter weeds, a tall, humped man disappearing into the shadows.

To come to a village at night may be never to know it with that clarity which one realizes if he comes to that same village in the beautiful sunlight of day. Had I not come to a land of eternal night, that of these voices, forever the aberrations, the irregularities, old, amorphous shapes like those which creep through mist and fog, Cyclops, men whose heads do grow beneath their shoulders, dead souls, unsoluble mystery, that fleeting image, that dream within the dream?

CHAPTER 9

WHAT terrible deed was this which I had done and which I never should forget, not until all the seas are emptied, until the waves fall away from the sea, not even then? What dreadful crime had been committed that all my life I should be pursued by this vain remorse, this dark possibility that I, even as a little child, had killed Miss MacIntosh, that I had done so only perhaps by opening my eyes, that had my eyelids remained sealed, she might have lived and might to this day be seen again with her black umbrella lifted, there where waded in the milky fog the sandpipers timing themselves to the tide, the seagulls moon-breasted, the nestless shore birds long-limbed, taller when they craned their necks and spread their wings? Who killed her, she who nursed beneath her shawl, against the coldness of her breast, the seagull with its wounded leg, taking her constitutional with this companion though many days? Who killed my darling? And the seagull died when its wound was healed.

Was it murder or the key turning of itself in the lock? Whose hand at the door knob? Was it God's hand, and if it was God's hand, was it still murder? Was it nobody's hand or desire? Was it the light, the night, the failure of creation which brought about this failure, this vision of the beginning which was also the end? Did she kill herself in some unimaginable way escaping definition?

Whom had she wished to kill, what image of another in her lonely heart? Was there no other, not even the created world and its necessary disappointments? Had she merely disappeared? Did she kill me?

"Forget, forget, forget," she said, "you ever saw me. Desire be to thy husband what thou hast never been to him. Live well in a useful circle, and do not seek that which you shall not find. All of us are mortal, and some of us are more mortal than others."

The self-deception of our lives, Miss MacIntosh's and mine, how we were self-deceived from my seventh to my fourteenth birthday, playing at good housekeeping, I remember. Everything had to be as it had been in What Cheer, Iowa, where Miss MacIntosh was born and had spent her unprivileged childhood as she constantly reminded me. Cheerful, I supposed she had been in What Cheer, and always skipping a rope, and always playing hide-and-seek with her brothers and sisters or racing them in the wind, she being the youngest of a large Christian family—for I simply persisted in my refusal to acknowledge the possibility that her childhood had not been a happy one. That was before I knew Miss MacIntosh so intimately as I was to know her after my fourteenth birthday, in that one last crucial month before her disappearance or her possible death by drowning alone, in sight of shore, the shoreline disappearing when the waves arose. Those die twice who drown in sight of shore, had she not always said, but that there was little danger of her drowning, for she could not swim an inch, hence would never go by sea? She was the land-locked sailor.

She was always trimming, in her own mind, of course, her sails, or letting them out, and her speech was so often nautical, filled with imprecations to the waves, the winds. She was always going at a good clip. She was always scudding along, and never had she been becalmed before, not until she had taken this present employment.

In seven years, I had lived with a stranger, someone I thought I knew. In one month, I had lived with a dearly cherished friend, someone I would never know. Perhaps in seven years I had hardly noticed her, taking her too much for granted, colorful though she was, for she was less a part of my life than the water birds among the water reeds, the shadows of the purple rocks, the tidal pools. She had been only someone who had interfered with my precious thoughts, those which she had not strictly approved, those she had not countenanced, those focusing on no object or human character, those mere molecules, fragments, specks, dabs, dots, shadows, tiny perceptions like sparks floating free in air. To me she had been nobody but what she had then seemed, a very forceful and single-minded character, sure of her own life, there being nothing notably uncommon about her but her strength, her insistence that we should gird ourselves for some great struggle in the open air, and I could have dispensed with her company and have felt no emotion whatever except a breathless sigh of sharp relief.

She was just the cross I had to bear. She was merely Miss MacIntosh, always in my way, always interfering with my contraband thoughts, those sparks made by mighty hooves, those curls of foam and light. I would shut my eyes to keep from seeing her. I would look toward the wild ocean when she spoke, for that seemed a vision more secure, safer for my wandering dreams. Through my indifference, I was insolent and proud, even when I seemed most humble. Her elongated windpipe so amplified its cry that it could be heard, I used to think, two miles away. There was never the luxury of a private room.

"Vera Cartwheel, child," she would storm, her red hair gleaming fiercely, her cheeks as red as her hair, "what are you doing now? Why are you dreaming this poor life away? You have but one. Opportunity, it has been said, knocks only once at the door. You have missed your opportunity. Sit not there dreaming of Triton among the minnows, for there is no Triton, and it was all a dream. Time marches on. There is no time. This dollar watch deceives me.

"Vera Cartwheel, do you hear me when I call you? What is the

Twelfth Commandment? Run, fetch my needle and thread, for we must hem a handkerchief before the sun sets, and we must have the clothes to cover us, and we must not be seen naked as in that day when we came from our mothers' wombs, poor, flailing infants who had not hope. Hope dies hard in the human breast.

"When, Vera Cartwheel, did the first Viking land upon this bleak New England shore?" she would intrude upon my delicate thoughts which were so personal. "Let us waste not our spirits speaking of Christopher Columbus, for he was but the second or third or fourth explorer to arrive here in this new world. He was but a mere pretender, and that's the baldest fact of history. Many an old sailor had already been washed up here and did not live to talk about it. Many an old drunkard at many a Spanish port could tell of it, this undiscovered continent where the tides had brought him. There was already a great colony of seagulls. Where are my scissors, and what's become of my darning egg?

"Do you sit there dreaming again, even in spite of all I can do to save you for some useful life? Locate my scissors, and locate the Grand Canyon, and don't point to the map of Africa, for that's not where it is. There is some arrangement in these matters geographical, I have no doubt, even though our history be mad and overgrown. Tell me where's Seattle, Washington, and where's Spokane, in what latitude, that where I broke my nose due to a bus accident which could have been avoided? I was standing in front of the bus with my umbrella blowing in the storm, but the driver could have seen me. I was a foot passenger. I was always a foot passenger. Where's the Mississippi River now, my dear, and can you locate its source? Go wash your face in the basin. Stop biting your fingernails. Stop acting so nervous.

"Vera Cartwheel," she would storm, walking back and forth, always restless, "you must keep your mind on your work and the thing that is at hand, for we were put here to be tested and not found wanting, even though we want. Our desires are nothing. Now look about you. Tell me exactly where in the sky we may find Charles's Wain, the Hair of Berenice, Orion's Belt, Cassiopeia's Chair. When to plant corn, when to plant oats? How much are two plus two? Always four. Six plus six? Twelve. Twelve hours in a day, twelve hours in a night. That is all we have."

Although we lived in that strange household which was filled with inscrutable marble statues and rustling draperies and rooms which had not been opened for years, my room was not private, for Miss MacIntosh intruded. My life was simple, utterly simple and austere, since Miss MacIntosh was training me for domesticity and marriage when I should be my own servant, waiting on myself and picking up my own clothes as I did now, or I should be the servant of another, waiting on him.

A woman's place was certainly in the home and not in the streets, Miss MacIntosh held, and a woman should guard her own hearth, and she would not have me walking in the streets. I should be some day, for all I knew, a poor little shoemaker's humble wife, so I must learn the essentials of good housekeeping now and how to make ends meet, and I must begin saving candles for the darkness. We must always prepare for a rainy day. How did I know what fate awaited me? Had I yet seen my husband's face?

No matter what one's situation in life, as a matter of fact, there were dark days ahead, and there were clear duties and responsibilities at every level. A rich girl should be taught to sew like a poor one, to make her basting stitches straight and even, and Miss MacIntosh would have no laggard in her care. Large, straight basting stitches were more easily pulled out than small or crooked ones. What! Could I not even put in a sleeve? She used to tap my fingers with her heavy thimble, quite sharply, when the stitches I made climbed up hill and down dale as if I were sewing no garment or only the garment of a dream. Should not my clothes fall off in the streets at this rate, and then what man would have me, if ever he saw me as I was? Men like, she would say, a mysterious woman, one who shall not lose her mystery.

Marriage, she said it not once but many times, was the only normal state for a woman, and perhaps it was the normal state for man. At least, it was customary. All the creatures of the earth, all the creatures of the air and of the water were married, or if not, then they would reproduce themselves by breaking into two parts like the worm, and thus the world went around and around. Bees carried pollen on their feet from highly colored flower to flower. Flowers were colorless if they were impregnated only by the wind, but with a woman, there must be a man, not merely the wind. Between persons of opposite sex, there should be a preacher to seal the bond, and in the Catholic countries, priests were very useful though pretentious. A preacher was, however, even in the Protestant countries, no necessity, as she would often say, blowing her broken nose, that she herself could dispense with him, this third party, for he might be an impediment if the spirit were true, and she had always worshiped out of doors. After several years, a loving couple need not ratify its bond by marriage, she believed, not at least if the spirit was honest. On the other hand, ever since Man's Fall which came from Eve's eating an apple of the tree of knowledge, and the apple was no sweet macintosh such as grows on the pinkish boughs in Iowa and throughout the temperate zone, and she was quite sure that it must have been small and green and sour and bitter to taste, there had been marriage, a human institution and very fine. The sparrows of the air were married. The birds, the bees were married, too.

God had approved of marriage. God, Who had divided the light from the darkness and created great whales which spent too much of time asleep, had said that the whales should be fruitful and multiply and fill the waters in the seas. Often, they spouted on the near horizon. The salmon were married in their great rivers without the benefit of the preacher, the wedding veil, the wedding ring, and even though a wedding ring, according to the newspaper which Miss MacIntosh read, had been found in the mouth of a dead salmon, and who knew what would come next? Their wedding was followed by their funeral in the vasty deep where their young were spawned, for the old did not return, and that was life, and marriage was the custom amongst most of the created creatures. Obviously, those who married were fortunate—and though, alas, Miss MacIntosh was unmarried and a poor fish, as she would say, that fact was not so much her fault as her misfortune. She had long ago given up hope. No man was ever tempted by her. No man had ever looked at her twice, to be sure. She had always been a homeless rover.

Meanwhile, as I was being trained for early marriage, for settling down with some suitable husband in an uncomplex life, that which should have no space for the dilatory, the tardy, the slow, I would have to do the smallest pieces of Miss MacIntosh's personal laundry—innumerable large white handkerchiefs embroidered with the initial of her first name only, the G which stood for Georgia, her shirts, her collars, everything in fact but her bloomers, which were red jersey and very voluminous. Her winter bloomers were red jersey. Her summer bloomers were plain white cambric, not frilled, though even in summer she might prefer her woolens, for she was always very cold on a hot day. And in the coldest weather, she would complain of the heat. Miss MacIntosh detested frills and feathers as she detested the luxury of my mother's house, too many involutions of the sea shell. She had been brought up in that severe way which seemed best to her and which now she tried to reproduce. When she was a child, her underclothes had been made of bleached flour bags. Her ears had been frozen. Her head had been naked. She had never had a velvet dress or a lace collar. Though her father had been a poor shoe-maker as well as a coffin-maker, she had worn broken, hob-nailed shoes or none, and she expected to have no coffin.

I would even have to scrape the mud and sand off Miss MacIntosh's sturdy, sensible, very expensive British tan oxfords which she wore in spite of her being, as she would often say, so entirely anti-British, opposed to all things British and corrupt, the British Empire, the king, the queen, the House of Lords, the House of Commons, the country houses, the London Tower where the ravens were chained, the exploitations of the natives and of the workers in the dark Satanic mills. She was always talking about the poor workers in cotton towns. She was always thinking of useful things for me to do, and I never dared openly resent any task for fear that there would be a worse one, one I had not foreseen.

Miss MacIntosh was the one authority over my life, but who watched over Miss MacIntosh, her life? Our existence was cut off from that of others, as we were the living branch. No one inquired into the details of our lives together, ours in that isolation as remote as if we had been shipwrecked inhabitants of some undiscovered archipelago or coral reef or desert island, an island of flint. Miss MacIntosh was the missionary, and I was the dreaming savage, the disciplines of life being enacted for my sake, and I must show no slight resentment but be cheerful as are those in What Cheer, Iowa, an average small town where there were no flamingoes, no palm trees, no pearl divers.

Miss MacIntosh herself recognized, of course, that she had not completely succeeded in forming or reforming my character, that I had always left open some door by which to escape from her authority. There was always, as she recognized, the quality of seething rebellion in my obvious obedience. She was not entirely sure, though I seemed subdued, that she had cured me of my early habit of lying—she would look at me, quizzically, when I made the simplest remark, for back of it there might lurk a mystery, and mystery was what she most despised, all things being clear to her because she rejected those which were not. I must not revert into that earlier chaos I had known before she came, and she must correct, with some sharp statement of fact, some dreaming statement of mine, for there were no fifty white horses struck by lightning in the garden, no sail-boats moored in the lily ponds, no imaginary persons ambushed in the fog that was the color of pussywillows, and I was simply lying, and there were no wooden eagles. The dream was always the lie.

There was, therefore, a secret tension, a secret drama in our lives. Nothing was ever quite settled between us. We did not bring the drama out into the light, surely—we kept it hidden. In fact, our lives were necessarily crowded with the austerity of good housekeeping, and this though we had, as Miss MacIntosh herself would admit, neither a rookery nor a cookery. Things were very bad, very unhealthy and corrupting, not at all as they had been in old What Cheer where the children's feet were frozen, where one broke the ice on the brook in order to get a bucket of water for the family wash, the few clothes that were to be washed. Winter and summer, Miss MacIntosh insisted that the windows be kept open at night, for our health's sake. Winter was so cold, we both wore ear muffs in our section of the house, and Miss MacIntosh would not take off her gloves. We would walk back and forth in the shrieking wind, trying to keep up our circulation, and I was afraid I might freeze to death and be found preserved unchanged through centuries. The old ship would be entombed in an ice block with its captain still on board. The rest of the house was overheated, Miss MacIntosh said, and smelled like its old, rain-washed, discolored velvet draperies and cold marbles, like a funeral parlor, in fact. All that we needed was the fresh air, the wind to blow away the dust. We needed no butter on our bread.

I was always looking for Miss MacIntosh's embroidery hoops, which would roll under the bed as if they were trying to get away from her. Her fingers were knotted and yellow-stained, though not from nicotine, I thought, and her fingernails were always dirty and cracked. She kept herself well polished, she said, washed her own face and polished it with an old rag. Sometimes she would dust her face with an old feather duster. She would rather be caught dead than in a beauty parlor, having some stranger pawing over her, for she cared little for all this feminine fiddle-faddle, all this forlorn pretense which deceived no one, and was content to be as nature had made her, apparently, and would add no thing where God had not, she being as she was. Even at that period, however, it often seemed strange to me that a woman of so much energy should have wasted her life embroidering tea towels and pillow cases with the initial of her first name, the G which stood for Georgia, and why did she never add M, the initial of her last name? I would feel sometimes quite apologetic, thinking that I was wasting Miss MacIntosh's life and that I must make amends. She seemed to have no friends of her age.

We had, however, our many endless tasks, our exercises which should teach us motion. We had our lessons, mostly in geography, as Miss Mac-Intosh had found so many mistakes in the history of this world, and she did not even trust sacred literature, for it was profane, the dreams of corrupted Pharaohs, of headless horses, of those who spoke in dreams and those who flew away as dreams, of those who suffered in dreams and those who stayed in dreams. We extracted only the moral lessons, the examples. I must also memorize, for discipline's sake, as these required no illumination or interpretation other than their names, all the genealogies of the Moody Bible, the sons of Levi, Judah, Er, Onan, Issachar, the sons of Tola, Phuvah, Zebulun, the names of those who had sacrificed the heave shoulder and the breast wave, those who had worn breastplates and built cities in the wilderness and built arks.

Our only companion, other than ourselves, was a great giant turtle who shared our living quarters and recognized us by the timbre of our voices, the voice which was gruff and loud, that which was thin and low. The turtle lived in the bare, dreary schoolroom which had been my mother's. The same cracked blackboards lined the walls. There were maps of sunken continents. There were the same pictures of the same pyramids, the camel-drovers driving their camels across a desert of stone, Hannibal crossing the Alps with his elephants. The same proverbs were framed in frames of peeling gold.

This turtle was quite ancient, one who might have carried, as in some legendary preadamite time, the whole world on his back. Generally, he carried only a clay flower pot in which I had planted a red geranium which smelled like tobacco. Wearing this, he would move with scraping steps across the bare schoolroom floor, taking his meditative constitutional which quite provoked Miss MacIntosh, scraping, she said, against her nerves. Besides, the tobacco smell of geranium was very unpleasant to her. His name, which Miss MacIntosh did not approve of but which she could do nothing to change, was Solomon, my mother had insisted when she gave him to me on my twelfth birthday, and that he had been given to her by one of her dead guests. Solomon, Miss MacIntosh objected, had had too many wives and too much of mortal glory, too many tables of gold, lamps, snuffers, pomegranates, too many ostrich eggs, more worldly goods than any one person ought to enjoy if he was in his right mind and had his senses. She could see no wisdom in a turtle, very slow, very slothful, indeed, that class of being which has a toothless horny beak and carapace into which it may draw its head, its tail, its legs, as if it carried its own bed covers always or was its own castle. What wisdom in an old turtle sleeping its life away and unaware of happenings on Wall Street or Threadneedle Street? A turtle should be no example for me.

My twelfth birthday, Miss MacIntosh said, was the dividing line between my irresponsibility and my responsibility, for I had reached the age of wisdom both in the eyes of God and in the eyes of man. She had always promised that after I was twelve, I was to make my own decisions, for she should not be responsible and held to account in the book of life. When that birthday came, however, she was quite as much the authority as ever, and even a little more impatient when I dreamed. She would rap my fingers with her thimble, just as she had done before, and she acknowledged no change in our lives.

At about that period, I began to rearrange Miss MacIntosh's life and mine. Our lives, after all, were not to be, as she thought, domestic. Though I would be busily sewing or ripping out stitches, I was also living a totally different existence from any medium she, in her wildest apprehensions of disaster, could have imagined. That was why I smiled inwardly and often. I was, back of my dreaming eyes—could she not suspect it?—a bareback rider wearing pink tights and jumping through her exaggerated ivory embroidery hoops which were her luxury.

She, Miss MacIntosh, was the ring-master, wearing a high silk hat, a white shirt with a soft collar, a checkered vest, her silver dollar watch which, in fact, she always wore, her red jersey bloomers, her flopping sea boots in which she sometimes walked in the mud-flats by the sea. Her red, marcelled hair was the same as it always was, no hair out of place, but now she had a red, curling mustache like a waterfall, and she had bushy eyebrows.

Miss MacIntosh, of course, did not suspect the details of this other life, that which could be realized only as an undertow of nameless suspicion. Her cheerfulness continued like her salty common sense. Miss MacIntosh, however, though she was the soul of order—at least, she said she was orderly and circumspect in her personal behavior, and I believed then all she said—was sometimes absent-minded, too, perhaps concerned with her own troubles. When I was in my twelfth year, I asked her, one morning as she sat behind her newspaper reading the news of the Stock Exchange, reciting aloud the prices of eggs, leghorns, longhorns, and shorthorns, "Miss MacIntosh, where are your ovaries?"

Ovaries, I knew, were little brown pods filled with seeds, those of future life which should be better than the present, and I supposed those seeds blossomed of themselves after a heavy rain or could be started up by someone's look of love. As yet for me, all love was in a look. There was a picture of a flower's swollen ovary in one of my school books which had to do with growth. Miss MacIntosh herself had told me of the mysteries of marriage, that I had been given two ovaries which were like little pockets filled with seeds, and she had warned me also of the necessity of taking care, that there might be, in such a seafaring neighborhood as ours, old hooligans and sick drunkards lurking in the spectral sea fog at night to waylay a young girl and steal her youth which was unprotected, that these bad men were those to be feared and not the sixteen bleeding Greek metropolitans taking their constitutional nowhere and not the fifty wild horses struck by lightning, for there were none. She also had imitated the mating cries of birds. My mother had exaggerated.

"In the bottom drawer, dear, you will find them," Miss MacIntosh answered, absently, "next to the spare corset, I have no doubt. And be sure to put them back exactly where you found them," more absently, "or we will memorize all the genealogies from Abraham to Abraham, and we will not go driving in our pony cart this afternoon. Indeed, it looks like rain blowing in from the North Atlantic."

I looked and looked, but I never found Miss MacIntosh's ovaries, for there were only wads of old grey stockings, a card of pearl buttons, a spool of darning thread, a darning egg, nor did I mention the subject again, for I soon forgot it or put it away in the back of my mind as something of no conceivable importance to anyone. Some time later, however, perhaps many months, I asked her one day, as we were walking in the bright, burning sunlight of noon by the swollen and purple sea, the sea scarcely moving, a question which seemed to me of the same order, perhaps slightly more bold, more personal, for I marveled at my foolhardy courage in forming the words, and I was afraid she would think me very stupid, indeed, and that she might make me swing dumb-bells an hour by her silver dollar watch as often was her custom, she believing that the development of the body is more important than that of the mind which can always take care of itself. Where, I could not help asking, were her eyebrows—that which astonished me being merely that I had never noticed their absence before. She had no eyebrows, bushy or thin.

Whether she heard me distinctly, I was still uncertain, for all she answered was, "You are undoubtedly too young, Vera Cartwheel, to re-member the great Chicago fire in which so many people perished. Living people do not remember it, the screaming, the crying. What was the cause of that great conflagration? What was the date? How many were unburied? How many were not identified?" As I hesitated, she continued quickly, even impatiently, "Very well then. We see you are ignorant. Name other great catastrophes this world has seen, the floods, the fires, the earthquakes, plague or famine or drouth. Where was that moving glacier? Where were those showers of grasshoppers? Where were those seven years of lean? Who shall divide the wheat from the tares? Who hid his lantern under a bushel? Say to yourself when you see one less fortu-nate than you are, some poor beggar in the streets—There, but for God's grace, go I. Has God protected him? What is the population of Kansas? Where is Missouri? Where is the Bosphorus, a narrow strait, and where is that sea of light?"

I was so busy trying to answer these various questions, I did not realize, until long years afterward, that she had never answered mine, that she had evaded the issue.

Our lives were thus extremely dull except for the drama of our constant opposition. There was no incident until I came to my four-teenth birthday—that which, had all things been normal on this earth as it is constituted, might have passed without a mark or trace—that which was to be, in childish memory, the whirlwind, the flood, the fire, for that day was the beginning of the end. There was perhaps no way that day could have been truly avoided. That day was like every other day except to myself as I celebrated the beginning of my fourteenth year. Perhaps that day should have passed in utter emptiness, for it was an experience in the absence of being, the absence of life.

I received, on that occasion, my first formal party dress, a filmy white creation perhaps too mature for me, for Mr. Spitzer had chosen it in an abstracted moment when thinking of someone else who was also young and lovely in his own heart, perhaps of my mother, he admitted as he shyly kissed my forehead and pressed into my hand an old Roman coin but recently turned up by excavators. His face had definitely lighted up, and he had smiled. Fair as a bride I should be, he promised, and he wished the whole world could share his happiness to see me on my fourteenth birthday, my mother's image, and he personally was very sorry that, due to circumstances beyond his control, he should not be present for the celebration of this important event when I trembled on the threshold of life, that only my excellent guardian and boon companion, the good Miss MacIntosh should share my feast and see me blow out the candles one by one and cut the angel food cake and pass the wine among the merry guests, for though his heart urged otherwise, that he must stay, yet his affairs and those of a dead man were of such complicated nature that he must go to Buzzards Bay to trace a lost heir, one who had died a decade previously and who claimed to be egregiously alive, and these matters would prevent Mr. Spitzer's presence. It would be impossible for him, even if he made all the right connections and saw all the right people, to get back before the following evening, perhaps the evening after.

Miss MacIntosh declared that Mr. Spitzer had rather let his imagination run away with him when he chose an extravagant party dress which had no sleeves and an uneven hemline and such a low neck that my bosom should be exposed. He had shown poor judgment, and she was glad that he should not be present. Long sleeves would have been better, a high neck, something which should not arouse slumberous temptations. The tempters were more guilty than those who were tempted, and only God could not be tempted.

The only other person who had been invited was not coming. He was the thirteen year old son of a Portuguese fisherman, a poor little boy who, the day before, had swollen out with mumps and then had caught the measles. A blind violinist and a deaf dancer who danced only to the vibrations of strings had been invited by Mr. Spitzer to perform for me, but they had missed their train, one hearing its whistle but not seeing it, one seeing it but not hearing its whistle, and there was no one coming. My mother, busy as usual, expected her dead guests, the tapestry princes and the gilded wooden fawns.

Miss MacIntosh thought it would be just as well, as there was no one coming from near or far, that we should follow our usual procedure. We should have a game of shuffleboard or dominoes, and so to bed, for tomorrow was another day, and the poor were starving. Early to bed and early to rise makes a man healthy, wealthy and wise, and we should be up by cockcrow to face new challenges in the natural order. I insisted, just the same, on wearing my beautiful party dress, for this had been Mr. Spitzer's special wish, as I reminded her, and it was my birthday which only came once a year. Miss MacIntosh, though she had to give in, was dumbfounded by Mr. Spitzer's extravagance and my rebellion, by all this fuss and all these feathers and all these fine preparations, especially when there should be no one. Were we not born alike and equal into this vale of tears where all should be tested and found wanting? It would be better to celebrate, not the day we were born into this world but the day we were born out of it.

What guest did I expect this evening, Miss MacIntosh inquired, sourly and glumly, her face ashen-colored as I persisted in having my light-hearted way, and should I not better wear my long-sleeved white nightgown and blow out the birthday candles with one breath and go to bed early? Tomorrow was washing day. Tomorrow was ironing day. Why did I smile, for who was there to entertain? Was there even a dark angel at the gate? What horseman reining his horse at the door? What sense was there in dressing for a great occasion when there was no one? So she insisted.

With whom was I dancing, and was I not ashamed of my immoderate, expensive dress, its tiny net ruffles embroidered with tiny seed pearls as she could plainly see, the innumerable stitches which had cost some poor seamstress her eyes? Did not my heart bleed for the orphans in cold countries? Was I not ashamed of my revealed shoulders?

My mother lay in an unearthly coma all that evening, entertaining, in crystal-lighted darkness, the many P's in her extensive circle of acquaintances, those never yet listed contemporaneously in any social register of blue bloods even though it include also their dogs such as the snowy Great Pyrenees, the Irish setter, the Alpine retriever, the French poodle which is the dog of kings and always wore, in her presence, a crown. She was being at home to her distinguished circle which never diminished and which included Pythagoras who had a golden thigh and had discovered heaven's harmony, the symphonious music of the silver-toned spheres, her circle which included also Proteus who changed from fish to bird before her eyes. The P's were crowding upon her—Pandora's bottomless box, pyramids, peninsulas, pebbles, prologues, pterodactyls. The P's were crowding upon her—planets, Pythian games, polygons, Prussians, petunias, pseudopsias which are the delusions of sight, pseudosmias which are the delusions of smell, and there was no other guest expected through all that empty house.

I danced alone. I danced with my shadow. My hair unbraided, whirling, my cheek shadowed, I could imagine any partner I pleased, for no one else would ever see him, and he was entirely mine.

Miss MacIntosh sat in the shadow where the lamplight ended. She was perspiring heavily, her skin seeming to glisten as if she had just come out of water.

"With whom are you dancing now?" Miss MacIntosh asked, heavily, her eyes red-rimmed.

"I am dancing with Death," I said to Miss MacIntosh, just as I whirled past her.

"I thought I had cured you of lying, for Death is not yet," Miss MacIntosh said, bitingly, severely. "Things are getting worse, for the canker eats the rose, and the green leaves fall before the fruit is formed. There is vomit at all tables. The greatest sailor of the waters is swallowed by the waters. Take off your clothes now and go direct to bed. Enough is enough." She was not at all amused by my childish fancy, she continued, firm and stern, and chastisement was probably that which was in order —but when I lay still with the sheet up to my chin, she stood at the foot of the great, canopied bed and asked, almost absent-mindedly, with her muscular arm around the bedpost and her eyes slightly smiling, "What did your companion look like? Can you describe him?" The bedpost was carved with a woman's head such as might be the figurehead of a ship.

I thought that my companion looked like Miss MacIntosh, whose face glistened in the watery distance. I began to laugh.

"There is really nothing very funny about Death," Miss MacIntosh said, pronouncing the word with a capital letter. "Death is quite commonplace and occurs in many forms and is something that befalls all men even as the ephemera who last but for a day which seems eternity to them. Death levels the mountains, ironing them out like valleys. The grass fadeth, as do the small flowers. No one should laugh at Death," she continued, her severity unabated. "Died Abner as a fool died, laughing, One died in his full strength. Another died in bitterness of soul. How died the wise man?"

"As the fool died," I said.

"When thou diest, I shall die with you, the flowers of the fields. Tomorrow I shall tell you what you must do to make up for this disdain of life. I shall have to punish you for your insolence in the face of naked truth. Experience, as I have heard, is a much harder teacher." Miss Mac-Intosh, however, did not look as if she meant a word she said. She was looking in all directions, and she had perhaps already forgotten me. Her facial expression was vague, undefined, her eyes watering, and she loosened her collar.

"If only I had somebody to kiss me good-night," I said, "I would be happy in this present existence. If I knew Love, I would not dream of Death."

"What makes you think they are not one? I have never believed in kissing," Miss MacIntosh said, her voice high and thin. "Perhaps a kiss on the forehead would be all right, but even that I doubt, for it has its hazard, so I am told. Kissing is unnecessary." Did a husband kiss his wife good-night? She supposed so, answering my question, that if they had not been married very long, they might kiss each other good-night when the light was put out, though not before. "But no wife ever knows her husband," she added, almost at the door, "until after she is married to him, and then it is too late. No husband knows his wife. There are many gay deceivers. They deceive each other and their own sad hearts. That is the fact."

This fact, that man and woman should not know each other, was probably the first which had ever fascinated me. I lay thinking of it in the darkness. It was a thought which begot a thought. Who would be my husband, and was I never to know him? Where were my wasted fourteen years? Was it too late for me to find a man, even one I should never know, and what would be his complexion, dark or fair? If I were not always dressed so plain, surely I might be, as I had been this evening, the center of attraction, as popular as my mother had ever been, and many ambiguous lovers might whirl around me, asking for my hand in marriage. On the other hand, should I need many? Perhaps one lover who would be true would be better than many who would be false. If my heart were pledged to him, it could never belong to another, and if he died some early death, I should be the inconsolable widow. I should marry no second man, for I should still be married to the first who was the ideal. I should search for him through heaven and hell, through all the roads, streets, and alleys of earth. I half arose from my bed, my heart pounding with this knowledge, that true love comes only once in a life time, that every other love is but the echo, hollow and thin and reedy, that I should prefer, when love was over, the silence.

Should I not be always faithful to my husband, then I asked, but where was he, for we had never met that I knew of? Whoever he was, he must be somewhere far away, someone I had never seen and might never see. There was one thing I was very sure of, my hair streaming across my cheeks, my eyes brightening with the expectation of this man. He must not be ordinary, and ours must not be an average life. We would be as if we were unmarried. Ours must be some life of great, dark romance, some fearful, billowing voyage upon uncharted seas, the crossbeams crackling like frozen twigs above our heads, sea birds screaming in the many winds, and no shore imaginable. To marry some poor shoemaker in Iowa was not my ambition then, certainly. I had seen enough of that mediocre existence to know that it was not the one for me, and I would rather die than be stuck away behind a kitchen stove in a desolate country. I wanted something far more fearful, something that would take me away from it all, the washing, the ironing, the recipes. I wanted adventure on the high, rolling waters where the stars hang as thick and near as blackberries on the bush. My marriage would not be the impoverished isolation which had been promised. I would not want to do the ironing.

My marriage would be accompanied by the great, beautiful world as then I dreamed, the foreign countries, the European capitals, the Asiatic temples and cities hanging in the air, mountains and valleys of vision, deserts, remote interiors, the wide, stormy seas, all shores, harbors, inlets, coves, shallows, breakers, whirlpools, all anchorages, moorings, eyries, the beak, the headland, the ledge, the spur, the hummock, all promontories all coral reefs, all islands, the Islands of the Blessed, the Islands of the Dead, all local habitations and all names. Were not true marriages made in heaven, and could they ever be dissolved by mortal law or circumstance, I asked, hearing outside the rustling, drumming of leaves in the cold, salt rain, the rising waves that crashed against jagged, sea-worn rocks and naked roots?

CHAPTER 10

AFTER awhile, as I could not visualize my own marriage, neither my lover nor his rough, frost-bearded cheek, I began to think of some other wedding which might take place in the near future, some other bride blushing like a red, red rose behind her veil, some other bridegroom, the wedding cake, the music, the reception, the wedding guests. Should it be my mother and Mr. Joachim Spitzer who would marry each other at last and live happily ever after as in an old fairy tale which ends with inscrutable happiness? But it could not be my mother and Mr. Spitzer, for she had rejected him so many times and long ago, she having preferred his dead, charming brother who had not preferred her. And Mr. Spitzer himself had often said, diffusedly smiling and apologetic as he surveyed his own existence, that he would be married to no one now but his brother worm who was under the ground, that he feared there was no such thing as death. For the worm would eat him, making a banquet of Mr. Spitzer, and he would then be the worm, and that was life.

Was it so late, however, that he might not yet marry someone else, some good, simple woman who would keep his grey, impoverished house for him and brush his elegant, old-fashioned clothes, those which were of the style he had worn when his brother was alive? To judge by Mr. Spitzer's clothes, no one would dream of the dirt of his environment. There were in his bedroom twin iron bedsteads, his own and his brother's, and he was sometimes disturbed by the baffled feeling that he was two bodies sleeping in two separate beds, that there were two heads on two striped pillows. Of course, however, he knew his feeling was absolutely ridiculous, and so he whistled in the dark. Sometimes he migrated from bed to bed.

I must have been dreaming when the wedding march started up, pots and pans jangling in my ears, and I awakened to the sound of cacophonous kitchen music. Suddenly, however, I could not believe my ears, for it was a funeral march which was played at a perfect wedding, the sad, slow, paced tones fading away into the nether plain of great, grey silence. All the carriages were hooded like beetles. Mr. Spitzer was the bridegroom, of course, and who should be the bride but Miss MacIntosh carrying her black umbrella?

I heard the preacher's voice, clear as crystal ringing out, but there was something wrong, and it must be the continuation of my dream, as then I reasoned. All was going according to schedule, yet with that slight deviation which marks the most ordinary event in an unreal world, the preacher not seeming to know who was woman and who was man and who was beast and who was bird.

"Dearly beloved," the preacher said, "according to the words of the old text, we are gathered here in the sight of God and of this company to join man and woman together as is customary"—but which was woman and which was man, for he did not seem to recognize the subtle differences of persons? "They shall be joined together as the birds of the air are joined, as male and female who do cohabit without fear, as the rabbits of the fields, as the moles under ground, as the bee and the rose, as the fishes of the deep, both great and small, as the great whales, as seals and otters and butterflies, and if any man know reason why they should not be joined in holy matrimony which is the key to the temporal and to the eternal life, he should speak now or forever hold his peace, for the end of the world draweth nigh with lightnings and thunderings and voices when all shall change their nature as in the twinkling of an eye, when there shall be many gnashings of teeth, many wailings, many beatings of breasts, and as a matter of fact, to make a long story short, a mighty hurricane is blowing in from the Canary Islands or Hebrides this night of nights, though calculated to pass us at many leagues' distance, far out at sea where nothing is.

"Dearly beloved," the preacher said, his voice cracking like a tired storm bell, "this life is very short and full of mortal sorrow. Porpoises shall eat the drowned sailor. The waters of this world shall close over his head. He shall sink to the oozy depth, the ocean floor. Do either of ye know of an impediment to this marriage, a reason why it should not take place in the sight of God and of St. Michael and of all the holy angels, both those present and those past, Lucifer who was the brightest and is fallen farthest, Beelzebub, Chaos, Gorgons, Hydras, Chimeras, Chance, for I require ye and I charge ye, even as ye will answer at the dreadful Day of Judgment when golden thrones appear in the sky emblazoned with jewels, when great stars burn like lamps and when the sea shall turn to glass and when the secrets of all hearts shall be revealed, ye do now confess it and make clear why ye may not be married in the sight of God and in the sight of man. Unadvisedly or lightly, marriage should not be entered in, but reverently, advisedly, discreetly, soberly, and the drunkard shall not marry, and none shall take a wife of whoredoms, and the dogs shall not bark.

"Do you, Mr. Spitzer, take this man to be your lawful wedded husband, to have and to hold from this day forward?" the preacher said, addressing his hollow question to Mr. Spitzer who, with his usual indetermination, was nodding his head negatively as he replied affirmatively—"I do, I do, I do, indeed. Indeed, I do."

"To love, honor, and obey, forsaking all others and all property, all earthly goods, titles, claims, demands, estates, effects, all corporeal and incorporeal hereditaments, spheres of influence, feelings of neglect, golden crowns and thrones, heirlooms, appurtenances, to cherish in sickness and in health, to protect with your life?"

"Most certainly," said Mr. Spitzer, as he shook his head in dubious negation. "Certainly, certainly, certainly till Death do me part."

"Man that is born of woman," the preacher said, "hath but a short time to live, and he is full of misery, and his stomach is swollen with wind and many waters. His stomach is full"—for the preacher had changed, even without the flicker of an eyelid, from the wedding rites to the rites for the burial of the dead. No one seemed amazed, and he continued but with a slight deviation.

"He cometh up, and he is cut down," the preacher said, "even like a flower. He fleeth as it were a shadow, and he never continueth long in one stay. He has gone from Newport to Mystic, from Wellfleet to Buzzards Bay, from Boston to Boston. He has gone to Gloucester. May God forgive us, for we know not who or where we are, and we are our mothers' sons.

"Spare us, Lord most holy, God most mighty, holy and merciful Savior!

"Spare us from ourselves. Spare us from the light. Spare us from the shadow. Spare us from the earth. Spare us from the air. Spare us from the waters, the tempest, the whirlwind, the archangel trumpeting the last trump. Spare us from the woman.

"Spare us.

"Why stand we in jeopardy every hour?"

Then turning solemnly to the bride, the preacher said, his eyes lighting with wild recognition, "Do you take this woman to be your lawful wedded wife till Death do you part?

"Nothing thou hast brought into this world, Miss MacIntosh, and it is certain thou canst carry nothing out. No pot, no pan, no pot-holder, no pin-cushion. Gold and silver rust. Mortality is the common state, as is also our self-deception and yours. Some die by dying, some by departure, some in bed. What is man but a poor, two-legged animal?

"He is but as the stubble of the field, and yet he has no beard. His beauty consumeth away, like as if it were a moth fretting a woolen garment. In the morning it is green and groweth up, but in the evening it is cut down, withered, all but the weeds. All hearts shall melt to water. The strong must perish like the weak. The weak are the strong. So be it. Be it so. So be it ever and anon. Selah, selah, selah. The red rose is not red. The white rose is not white.

"Where, my dearest heart, is Issachar? Where is Nepthalin? Where is Reuben who begot a horde? Where is Manasses? Where is Kansas? Where is Iowa?

"Oh, death, where is thy sting? Oh, grave, where is thy victory? Oh, bridegroom, where is the blushing bride?

"Oh, man, where is the woman?

"Oh, woman, where are thy breasts? Where is thy womb of morning and delight? Where are thine ovaries? Who hast taken away thine eyes? Who hast taken away thine ears? Can these bones live? Where is the prophet of the past?

"Forasmuch as it hath pleased Almighty God, in His great providence and wisdom," the preacher said, his voice sonorously roaring, "to take out of this world the soul of our deceased brother, the lately departed, we therefore commit his body to the ground, earth to earth, ashes to ashes, dust to dust, brother to brother, deep calling to deep.

"As it was in the beginning, is now, and ever shall be, world without end. Where is Philemon? Where is Zipporah, a little bird? Where is the lost fleet? Where is the sunken ship of stone? Where are those wandering stars to whom is reserved the blackness of darkness forever?

"Clouds that are without water, carried about by fickle winds of chance. Trees whose fruit withereth, without fruit, branches bare and plaintive, twice dead as are all who die, plucked up by the roots.

"Amen, amen, amen. Strike up the music! On with the dance."

Miss MacIntosh did not reply. I never laughed so hard in all my life, for there had been this great mistake, the preacher eloquently asking Mr. Spitzer if he would take this man to be his lawful wedded husband, asking Miss MacIntosh if she would take this woman! Both parties were reluctant. I nearly died laughing at what transpired in murky distance. Though I could clearly hear, I could not clearly see, for the shapes were blurred by everlasting snow and ice as if the surface of the earth were some enormous, frosted wedding cake under the dark, blowing heavens from which the snowflakes fell with slow whirling like great, wandering feathers. There was no candle lighted.

Then suddenly, in perfect silence, the manifold skies were illuminated, pointed star by pointed star, and I saw that it was not the preacher who had been mistaken, that it was not even I, that this error was the error of the dream which had begotten nothing and no marriage. Mr. Spitzer was the bride, wearing a white veil. Miss MacIntosh was the bridegroom, wearing a waxed mustache like Mr. Spitzer's and a high silk hat and her silver dollar watch. There was no preacher anywhere in sight.

There were no wedding guests but myself, whom I could see quite clearly though I was not myself at all, and the only others present were the turtle Solomon and the red geranium and an old, empty shoe.

It was all so terribly confusing that I shook myself awake, though perhaps this dream, if dream it was, was only a sane prelude to the confused reality of one long night.

I lay in bed, wide awake, thinking sad thoughts. What had happened all this evening to make any person glad? There had not been even a birthday party, much less a wedding. We had not even cut the birthday cake, and I was hungry, my stomach aching.

It had been a hallucination, that was all, and nothing had happened to disturb the wild universe. The stars had not really fallen from the sky, and Mr. Spitzer had not married Miss MacIntosh, and I had not been the bridesmaid. It had been my fault and nobody else's, for I had been the only person present at these lost events, and there had been neither the wedding nor the funeral.

What had I done to Miss MacIntosh, and how must I blush when I saw her next, for suppose she guessed my forbidden thoughts, and they were written on my face as plain as day! What had I done to her but make a fool of her, the old maid, make her the handsome bridegroom who wedded herself to Mr. Spitzer!

Was that her fault or mine? The awful nonsense, how she would have thoroughly scorned it, blowing her poor, broken nose, for did she not know herself better than I knew her or ever would know her? The heavens should surely fall on my nonsensical head, not on hers, and I was the one who should be ashamed, she having no illusions, she being so clear as to her necessary limitations. None would have her, as she might say, and none would ever hold her.

She was not going to marry anybody in this mortal life, she had often said so when I suggested marriage, that the best man on earth would be the worst, in her opinion. She was certainly, from a matrimonial point of view, the least interesting person in the whole world, the most colorless. She was someone no man in his senses would think of looking at twice, much less of pursuing. A man would flee from her, for what did she have to offer? Her face was certainly not her fortune. Hers was no face to stop the traffic. She had stopped it only once, and that was in Spokane. Hers was an ordinary face.

She was probably just like any other woman, I thought, a little sensitive about her age, for she must surely have passed the zenith. She was more than fifty if she was a day. The rest of the journey would be only going down, and she did not believe in kissing or expressing one's affections openly. She would never think of celebrating her own birthday, not even by lighting one candle, she had said so this very evening, that the subject of her age was painful to her, that nobody should be proud of being old or young or middle-aged, for it did not matter how many years we wore upon our brows, and the oldest fool was the greatest fool.

Maybe, as I now considered, she felt simply that she was too old to marry and start a new life, that the time was too short ahead, that marriage would not be worthwhile from a strictly practical point of view. Yet her red hair was not streaked with grey, and she was domestically inclined, clipping the recipes out of old newspapers. If she were married, she could chop her own wood, build her own fire, wash her own shirts, be absolutely self-reliant. Maybe, therefore, my bad dream might still lead to something good, and she would find a man appreciative of her efforts and of her sterling character. Maybe she would still be married and live as happily after as she had lived before. She had no prospects, of course. Though she did not exaggerate, perhaps she was too pessimistic, and she might still find a suitable husband to whom she could be the helpmeet in case of some great disaster. There were many lonely men in the world. Mr. Spitzer had said so, that their numbers were legion, that every man needed a woman in his life.

Was there not a man for every woman, a woman for every man? A man might appear yet in Miss MacIntosh's life and sweep her away. Though he would be far from remarkable, might his not be, if not love at first sight, then love at second sight which she had said was probably the greater love, insofar as she understood these alien things? Familiarity breeds contempt. One who could know us and yet love us was undoubtedly the truest love this world has ever seen.

She was surely neither ugly nor beautiful, it seemed to me then, that she was just commonplace. She would still make, however, an excellent if erratic housekeeper for some old, blind, deaf shoemaker who needed a woman and whose tastes were simple like hers. She knew when to plant, and she knew when to harvest, and she understood the principles of navigation.

Poor old soul, I thought, the moonlight crossing my pillow, and it was the first embryonic emotion of pity I had ever felt for her, the first lingering sense I had ever had that she might be pitifully human, too, and capable of great error, for her capacities were always great for good.

What would it be like to be old and unloved? It was hard enough to be young and unloved as I was, to waste one's sweetness in the desert air, but at least, the future was mine, as then I thought, and she had no future. The sands of time were always running low, had she not said? I wished that I could go and see her, even though it was so late, past ten o'clock when all hands should be sleeping. Maybe she was wide awake as I was. She had complained once or twice recently of sleeplessness, of being under the weather, that she felt as if there were a sharp pain running from her shoulder to her hand, claws upon her forehead like the claws of a lobster, perhaps a touch of rheumatism which came from living so near the sea in this salt air. She said that she must begin to spare her right arm.

I wished that I could go and see her that I might be reassured that all was well, for I had wronged her, and I wanted to know she had not changed. While it would be impossible to apologize without betraying the wedding, yet she would certainly see in me tomorrow the greatest change for good. I should have matured. I should myself suggest the unpleasant tasks, that I should swing dumbbells, knock down bowling pins, recite the genealogies of all those old kings, prophets, locate her handkerchief.

Morning seemed so far away, perhaps I had reasoned then, and I was hungry, and we could still cut my birthday cake, making a feast worthy of a king. Like any two women, we could sit with our hair down, exchanging confidences, but I had not the courage to burst in upon her privacy. At night, her bedroom door, as I knew, was always locked from the inside, always double bolted. She had warned that she must not be disturbed unless there was some good reason. It was necessary to respect another's private life and need for unbroken rest.

I must not wander through the house at night for fear of all those wall-eyed phantoms, necromancers, shades, whirling dervishes who had no place, the unworldly creation to which my mother was the slave. I must not wander by the sea at night for fear of the old rapists lurking in the grey or purple sea fog, those against which Miss MacIntosh had lately warned, though I did not know who or what they were, and everything was very vague, very clouded—and what lay beyond the clouds, I dreamed, must be good, true, beautiful, perhaps like nothing I had ever seen.

CHAPTER 11

STARING at moonlight scissoring the darkness, I wondered—how should I endure this isolation, for I could not be like my mother, and no mere illusion would suffice me? I would always be able to tell just where the dream ended, where the reality began, even as Miss MacIntosh had taught me through her denial of those things which did not exist. Her mind lighted like an ocean liner at dinner time, my mother lay in a wakeful coma, entertaining the P's, the Q's, the R's, though by now, according to the schedule of her opiate voyage through nowhere, she must have passed beyond Pericles, Admiral Peary, Penelope's web, the Pleiades, the formal penguins.

She must have reached, in fact, the far more difficult Q's, for these were a naval battle, an island, and a continent. One was Queen Charlotte Islands with whom she exchanged always a word or two, asking perhaps only of the climate or of some pale courtier missing from her train, someone who had accompanied her in another summer, perhaps only a dead, snowy gyrfalcon who had been blown upon that desolate beach, a goldeneye no longer nesting on that rock like a honeycomb of goldeneyes, a goldeneye whistling in its flight, a wild swan absent, one wild swan more, according to my mother's mirage-like calculations which admitted no theory of loss in the universe where all things were lost. Another visitor was the proud, cold, utterly snobbish Queen Maud Mountains, colder than Boston society, an Antarctic continent on the south edge of the Ross Sea, a coastline of frozen, phantasmal peaks where the human voice was seldom heard if ever.

When Queen Maud Mountains came into my mother's velvet-shrouded bedroom, coming like the mountain to Mahomet, my mother felt as if her eardrums would burst, as if her heart would stop, and the bellropes were frozen, so she could not call a servant. Queen Maud Mountains, dressed in glacial white from tip to toe, towering and immense, was a most imperious house guest, indeed, exchanging no words with my mother, and her face concealed always by her white parasol which happened to be my mother's. Queen Maud Mountains was frigid. My mother saw, with eyes congealed by envious astonishment, that the skirt of Queen Maud Mountains was five hundred miles long and made of pure Brussels lace.

Perhaps my mother had already passed on, however, to the R's who were so much more charming in her eyes, they who were connected by the most subtle web of silken relationships though they had never met previously, of course, some having been separated by time, some by space, some being dead, others living as strangers to themselves. She would be extremely talkative when the R's came, greeting each separately as an old friend, and her eyes were almost blinded by the brilliance and paradox of the company assembled under one great roof. She shook hands until her hands almost dropped from her body. There were some she had never seen before, but she nodded her head to them as to the others. She would be afraid only that there would not be enough pyramid-shaped ices to go around, for more always came than had been invited, so popular was she as this great hostess who was in exile. There was, of course, Mr. Res Tacamah who was the drug bottle and any number of forms shifting and merging into each other. There was also a bemused Egyptian pharaoh who was, as could be seen, Rameses I, II, III, each wrapping being a different and older king as he realized when unwrapping himself in my mother's enchanted presence, that the beautiful, parabolic confusion of his dream life had been caused by the fact that he had been partitioned into many selves without his knowing it, without his consent, that as Rameses III he had dreamed the dreams of Rameses I who was already dead.

There were runes, roulades, rubrics, royal masts, rose windows, Roman numerals, many riddles, many red-caps in the Grand Central Station. There was Roland who was killed at Roncevalles. There was Rimski-Korsakov who never came except in Mr. Spitzer's absence, as my mother would afterward tactlessly remind Mr. Spitzer, that he had missed a great composer of music which was not altogether silent, that he had also missed the great English portrait painter, Sir Joshua Reynolds, and the constellation known as the Great Ram. What delightful company Mr. Spitzer had missed. He had missed Raphael's tomb, the songs of Ronsard, Mr. Res Tacamah. Tracing a lost heir to no property, he had missed Rhadamanthus, he who, for his justice on earth, was made, after his death, one of the judges of the lower world and had already judged Mr. Spitzer, as my mother would remind him, and had found Mr. Spitzer guilty of many forgotten crimes. Performing his dusty legal errands which no one really cared for, Mr. Spitzer had always missed her crowded musical evenings, the reflections without faces, the sister ravens, the brother doves, the realm of night which knows no boundaries. He had missed Sir Walter Raleigh in his marvelous white satin suit embroidered with seed pearls and pearl buttons and lustrous gems varying in color, that fine gentleman who, in my mother's courtly bedroom, when he removed his white plumed hat, removed also his head and who asked that he be addressed by his intimate name, Ocean or Water, for he had crossed many waters. He was also, as his head explained, the head of a society of night devoted exclusively to atheistic propositions, such as that man had existed before Adam, and God is nothing but an idea in the mind, and God is dog spelled backward.

CHAPTER 12

How arid this life of the imagination had seemed to me, the child. As I had missed my birthday party, should I not also miss my wedding? The night was lonely, seeking its mate.

It was now long past ten o'clock, according to the illumined face of the Big Ben alarm clock at my elbow, the clock which, though not carved with the ornate figures carved by dreaming horologers, was yet to be relied on, telling us with accuracy the exact hour for our rising up and for our lying down, and it was set with its alarm, for it was Old Reliable, according to Miss MacIntosh who kept it wound each day and would have no Tritons dreaming around the clock, no ladies weeping over dead birds, no sporting cupids or rosebuds garlanding its face. It did not repeat the hours, a day being gone when a day was gone, and the nights were no more extensive than the days which were quick and short. An hour was only that hour. There were just such similar clocks in the bedrooms of servants who must awaken at a certain hour, for though time was an illusion, it was not the illusion of servants. All the other clocks in the house were like enchanted cages, each clock having been stopped at a different hour over that period of time when my mother, retiring from the world, had gone to bed, by slow degrees and not suddenly, as if she had hesitated a great deal, as if her decision had not been an easy one to make. Sometimes, in a remote part of the house, especially at night, a stopped clock would suddenly start up, wheezing or musical, seeming to make this one last effort, just as I heard it now, three dim bells sounding in the midnight air, and now, from another corner, there were four bells, and I waited, but the darkness did not lift.

That night, yearning only for reassurance, for human contact, and unable to wait until the morning should make all things clear again, fearful that the morning should not bring the light but that it should bring instead the darkness, I went to Miss MacIntosh's bedroom—though the details must always seem, in retrospect, blurred, and for this reason, that they were not, even then, fully realized. Certainly, the visit was not planned and was like a sporadic moment. The details must be told only through a veil of oblivion which is itself a medium of memory, for there is no forgetfulness even of the smallest thing. If it is hidden, it is revealed through its absence, the sense of the void.

I got up out of bed in the luminous darkness and sat in a rocking chair by the great bay window, fanning myself with a palm leaf fan, Miss MacIntosh's, which had the words Drink Coca-Cola written on the back, I remember clearly. The next thing I remember, I had crept out of the silent, shrouded house, though where my courage came from, summoned by subdued powers, I could not have told, for it had come so suddenly, and I should have been ready to do battle with phantoms and monsters and things unearthly and things earthly, and nothing could have frightened me, I thought, not even some small, timid rabbit with purple eyes staring through the wild marsh grass, not even an old rapist had there been one lurking in the swollen, golden fog this night of illumination and of innocence when I felt my whole being filled with the inestimable beauty and goodness of life, when I felt that life should answer the quest of the heart. I was free, and my heart rejoicing. I had declared my difference from the dreamers and the dreams. I passed the quiescent faces of marble statues, the immobile, the becalmed who seemed ready to awaken from their sleep, the unmoving who seemed ready to move as small wings stirred sleepily in the moonlight almost as bright and refulgent as day.

The beauty, the unity of nature, the sublime harmony of this great enterprise, I felt, that the stars in the heavens were real, not merely flickering lights, that there had been no cosmic joke, no conjurer's trick played upon us to make us believe that which could not be believed, that all does not fade at a touch, that all does not dissolve at a breath, that we are not as shadows. The eyeball was made to see with, this nearly spherical mass having been set in the bony concavity of this nearly spherical skull for this purpose of vision, that we might see, and all the world repeated the pattern of the rounded eye. The organ of sight was repeated as the spot on a peacock's tail, the eyes gleaming among the tail feathers, the hole through the needle, the center of a flower. Also, the ears were made to hear with, they being the chief passage-way of the human spirit, the tongue to taste with, the nose to smell with, the skin to touch and feel with, and the skin was a drum of all our senses blurred and commingling, for the brain was but the infoldings of the skin, and we were the masterpieces of nature.

Also, the hair was made as filaments to cover the animals and man, the hair being an outgrowth of the skin like the feathers of a bird, the feathers ruffling in the wind, the hair being also like another sense, the hair raising to warn us of our mortal danger even when all other senses fail. The most beautiful ladies of history had been noted for their hair. Men, in olden times, had let their hair grow long, and Absalom was caught among the apple boughs and hanged by his hair, for he had rebelled against his father. The organ of sight, the orbit of vision was protected by eyelids, that part of the movable skin with which an animal covers or uncovers the eyeballs which, if there were no eyelids, even the eyelids of transparency, could not shut out the vision and could not give a merely tentative regard, could only look fixedly as in wonder or fear, and also by the eyelashes, the fringe of hair that edges the eyelids and shuts out fine particles of dust and sand and salt and protects the eyes from the burning sunlight and from watering or weeping as when one walks in the eye of the wind, going almost opposite from the way the wind blows, going nearest the wind. Without eyelids, one would stare at the face of one's love, even as one stares at death until another closes his eyes, for dead men are usually found with their eyes open. While we are alive, we are privileged to close our own eyes and sleep.

Also, the eyebrows are made to protect the eyes, but Leonardo had forgotten to give eyebrows to his Mona Lisa, or perhaps the omission was intended, I thought, to add beauty to the mystery of her face.

I was free, having no sense then of the imploring past, no sense of the power of the barren, the power of helpless and impotent things, nor the presentiment that what does not exist exists if we believe in it. The pregnant moonlight streaked the pebbled mist with fine golden hairs, braids and curls. There were faces pulsing in the vacancy of mist, and the wind was filled with flat or rounded eyes. There were sleek and shining backs, ethereal gleamings of scales and fins.

I stood in the garden of the blind which had been created for one whose eyes were as missing, for one who had suffered the absence of a sense, the absence of a world of vision and of light. My happiness seemed boundless. That this was the garden of the blind could surely in no way have influenced my own clarity of vision in that amorphous, wet, clammy night of clouds and whirling fogs—even though, I have wondered ever since, what is the influence of place? Are there places which seem to breed their special sorrow, that sorrow which colors the atmosphere often with the most illusive colors like the memory of a nature already dead, that sorrow making the stones cry out, the leaves fall, making the trees bend in contorted shapes as if under some imponderable weight of a more than human grief? Was it from me or from the world around me that sorrow came, just when I was happiest?

There were, in that invisible garden, vague, ghostly flowers and vines from which the flowers had been washed away. The ground was matted with wet, steaming flowers. There were grey spots as bare as blindness set in the midst of wandering vegetation. There were knotted growths like the malignance of abundance. There were here no marble statues, nothing which should meet the eyes alone, nothing which should be the obstacle, the stumbling stone to the blind. The bushes were thin-branched and full of eyes which gleamed with an unholy iridescence, and the pale colors of the night seemed not to take cognizance of the absent sense. One might see with one's fingers. Unthinking, my happiness self-evident, I stood in that sad, empty garden which my mother's methodical father, long years ago, had planted not for vision nor for point of view nor for even a hidden perspective but for the commingling of odorous blooms and the Braille texture of flowers, whorls, petals, clusters, stamens which should move under the moving, visionary finger-tips of his blind wife as, according to legend, she had used to walk with certain steps a circular path in the morning or evening light which had been but, enclosed in her far from imaginative brain, a practical household memory and nothing else, she being, when she was alive, the most immediate of persons, it was always said, given to no far flight of fancy, no understanding whatever of things chimerical, arguing with her voluble black coachman about the colors and formations of the clouds, whether it looked like rain or the clouds would pass away, and choosing from her wardrobe the dress or scarf most inconspicuous, a dim, muted shade, the rose, the grey, the neutral blue which should fade into a quiet landscape.

She had never cared much for works of art—only when she was blind, stone blind, had touched the stone faces, tracing the features which seemed to move, the lips, the flaring nostrils, the ears, the eyes, the stone birds roosting among the stone curls, the horned foreheads.

I had closed my eyes. There were only these flowers most heavily freighted with sensual odors, the forms without color and void as when darkness moved on the face of the deep, sweet william, cosmos, rose geranium, phlox, nasturtium, nicotiana, flowers of the old Jerusalem, flowers of the new Jerusalem, the suffusion of beings like an idea in the mind, one which hovers only at the threshold of realization. Under my dreaming finger-tips, there moved the lips of flowers, their tongues, horns, valves, their tiny ears like shells, their tiny feet and hands, their spines and ribs and hairs. I opened my eyes, that I might not feel estranged. My forehead throbbed. Little could I have realized, for my heart had been filled with preternatural joy, that my first vision of the wonders and glories of this planet, glimmer and shine of flowers and leaves and birds' breasts like multiple moons shining in ineffable light, the first vision would also be the last.

Could I have foreseen, should I have turned back? Should I have gone on?

I should be surely struck between the eyes by the cold horror underlying all mortal things and the beauty of that horror more beautiful than life. I should surely see, underlying the restricted routine of days and nights, another meaning than any I had seen, that nothing had been as it had seemed—that though there had been hallucinatory visitors in my mother's gold and ivory bedroom, such phantasmal beings as Mr. Chandelier or Mr. Chanticleer or the merry-go-round horses, their poles lost in the vaulted ceiling of heaven, or old pontiffs walking in the mist, they were as nothing. I had unwittingly entertained that which was far more horrible because it was real, the flesh, the blood.

What a different perspective then there should be on all that was past, how it should be altered, how it should be transmogrified when I saw, even in the candor of imperfect truth, the beautiful and horrifying disrelations of the spiritual, that there was no perfection, that there had always lain, just beyond the threshold of my secure vision, this other vision I had not been conscious of and had perhaps not even dimly glimpsed, significances which had escaped me, even though there had been, as Miss MacIntosh had always said, a place for everything, and if I was deceitful or wasted my time with day-dreaming, then I must box a sandbag dummy or run a mile along the beach of running sand in order to restore my circulation and my waning common sense. Always, over my head even then, though it had seemed more like a promise than a threat, she had held the rueful possibility that she might some day leave me. As she was not getting any younger, she might decide to retire, she had threatened, for there were even then those calm and airless days when her breath came short, when her lips turned blue and her skin lost its natural color, turning to saffron, turning as grey as stone and so full of minute cavities that it was very light. She might retire, and that was why she was so frugal and sparing, saving even the soap coupons to exchange for crockery. I should not need her when I was old enough to know my own mind and to live in a useful circle or be perhaps only a poor little shoemaker's wooden wife if that should be the way of the lost world.

She had sacrificed her life to a cause which was perhaps doubtful, lost from the first beginning. She had given up all vanity, all luxury, and personal preference, I remembered. Had I not been, when she first saw me, a much wilder person than I had become, as she would sometimes say, tapping my forehead with her great silver thimble on which was carved the inscription Juliet, 1899?

At the age of seven, I had been a nervous wreck, baying like a dog at the moon—pretending, in fact, that I was a dog and often digging for a bone in the garden. With firm hand and true, however, Miss MacIntosh had restored me to my senses when I had already seemingly lost them, when even Mr. Spitzer had been on the verge of giving up hope. She had taken over, solving most problems by ignoring them, never losing her clear way, her moral principles which distinguished sharply between right and wrong, her excellent, narrow mind. She had taught me a profound respect for who was real, such as herself or Mr. Spitzer, and who was not real should never stand in our way. If fog obliterated us, we needed no other obliteration, as she frequently remarked. Even if she was dead, she would not waste her time dreaming. No, siree, sir. She held my attention by yelling louder than the dead, louder than the waves.

How should I have heard, at the age of seven, a rooster crowing when there was no rooster, have seen its golden spurs and cockles, its red comb—or have imagined that a wireless was attached to my head so that I might hear the voices of the dead? How should I have been deceived to believe that I held musical discourses with an old-fashioned gentleman who wore a snuff-colored velvet coat and white breeches and white peruke like the crown of a bird and carried under his arm an ivory-lidded music box filled with the buzzings of wild honey bees? How should I have imagined, at that early age, that I was the reincarnation of Chopin because of the tinklings of piano keys so constant in my head, the patterns of old polkas and mazurkas in faded ballrooms where my mother, when she could walk, though this exceeded her memory, had danced with pigeon-toed, ambiguous Mr. Spitzer, perhaps with two Mr. Spitzers, one who had died, one who had lived? How should I, at that early age, have concluded that dreams are superior to the limitations of realities, that dreams are limitless, the thinnest walls existing between persons, that the sleeping life, that which I saw around me, was to be preferred infinitely to the cause and effect sequences of the waking life which had its reason and its purpose? For the disconnected, reflective, lily-margined pools I had visited each night in my sleep and the snowy train of twelve white swans like brothers or suitors bewitched who fed at the gilded margins shadowed by reeds, though these seemed disparate, these had provided greater beauty and enchantment and unity of life than the organic stream of narrow and visible experience could possibly have done and were perhaps, in fact, themselves also organized and continuous and streaming, so that they might go on separately toward an identical goal, even like dark rivers, I had concluded, that though the dreamer waked not again from sleep, though his breath should be stilled and should stir no feather in the air, yet death might be proved, as his dream existed and continued and merged with the dreams of others, to be nothing but an old humbug, an imposture, an imposition bearing no grain of truth. The truth was only in the erroneous dream, the bridge between life and death.

This was not to be, however, as I was taught, the case, according to an old nursemaid taking over with tight reins. When nothing had happened, I was supposed to admit, quite simply, that nothing had happened, that not a leaf had fallen, that not a blow had struck, that not a wave had broken, that not a shadow had stirred, for neither I nor any other mortal was God, and omniscience had not been given to us, fortunately, so that we could not see everything—or we should all most certainly lose our minds and go stark, raving mad, screaming, tearing our hair.

There was simply, one must deduce still from all her energetic, caustic certainties, and I believed then that Miss MacIntosh, even though she might go against the grain, was right, no shadowy borderland where that exists which does not exist, where headless horsemen ride about in purple fog or old emperors play water polo or men have heads like dice, or if there was, then it was God's murky business and not ours to tamper with or change, for God had suffered due to this erroneous creation and had quite frankly been filled with the greatest remorse ever since the day of the beginning which was not too far different from the day of the end. Things had not turned out exactly as He had expected. Things had not developed. Things had gone somewhat awry, but that was not our affair, for God did not ask us to set up in His trade, and God did not ask us to understand His traffic, and we should do well enough to attend to our own knitting and frugal wants and take our constitutionals in the sweep of sunlight barred by fog. We were very plain. We were intended for no high and mighty office, no vast estate, no imaginary diadem, no fine feathers, nothing which should set us apart from others. The wisest man was a fool in God's eyes, and there was a fool bound in the heart of every child. The oldest man was but an infant, puny and crying, reaching for the stars which should not be very different from this old, lost earth with its vexations. We could not command the waters to stand still, the stars to subside, nor was it our task to move the heavens and the earth and the earth's foundation. They would doubtless move of themselves soon enough. They were already moving.

Indeed, we were put here rather to endure ourselves than to test

God, Who required no judgment of ours and not that we meddle in His remote business and not that we unlock His deep mysteries and not that we dream our lives away. We were not like those fishes who must seek only the darkest waters, those flowers which open only at night, for the honest man was he who walked upright and showed his face to others and had nothing to conceal. He cheerfully spoke to his neighbors.

Love, what was love? How should Miss MacIntosh know what love was? She could only guess, her face blurred by watery vagueness, Love was not an inquiry beyond what meets the natural eye. Love was undoubtedly greatest love which could see another's face in daylight and hear another's voice. There was no better test than harsh experience.

As for herself, her face was not, it was simply not her fortune, being just one face in a million, for who was she but a plain, old-fashioned, unvarnished spinster, her shirt waist bristling with needles and pins as if to forbid inquiry and to suggest that hers was not a good shoulder to weep on? Stuff and nonsense that perhaps there was a time which had not passed, that perhaps it was we who passed through time! She would not give a pin for such innocuous suggestions wavering like crests of foam. They made less difference to her than a leaf falling, for it was her self-evident position that, when something is gone, then there is no return, nor did she seek discoveries which might disturb the earnest thought. Her fortitude was this, to keep her feet solidly planted on earth which was not solid, never to let her head drift among the drifting clouds, to do her work of retribution for some old guilt not conceived by her, to make the best of matters and indulge in no self-pity. She could not soar upward on wings of words to heaven, she had always said so, for words were meaningless to her, and she was very stout-minded, carrying a stout umbrella, and she was a middle brow, and she was a Middle Westerner, and she was middle aged. She had only one face, one form, one heart, this old body which would not last a life time.

She had not two faces, one to turn toward the world, one to turn toward heaven. There was not even the remote possibility of something else. There was nothing of the errant dreamer in her character, and none should catch her dreaming. Little could she have understood, it seemed then, these necessary dualities of darkness and light which others seemed to live by, the self-contradictions, my mother's often-entertained suspicion, for example, that Mr. Spitzer was far and away from being the altogether substantial, fleshly character he seemed, that sometimes, as in a protracted, wakeful dream, he imagined himself to be his dead brother and, with a remarkable knowledge of horse flesh, considering his own ignorance, put his bet on the dark horse which would come in first and which he considered to be spiritual, a phantom like himself, or he would seem to be on familiar terms with dead jockeys humped upon their saddles, those of the tramontane regions, those lying beyond the snow-peaked Alps where his dead brother had never been.

CHAPTER 13

FAREWELL to the last certitude, even that tender night of my fourteenth birthday when I trembled on the margin of sentient life—farewell to Miss MacIntosh, for though I should surely see her again, yet she should have so greatly changed in my eyes that she might have been, to all intents and purposes, a perfect stranger I had lived with for seven years without so much as realizing the ominous fact. I should see that I had taken for granted the strangest being on earth, that I had even reluctantly washed and ironed her shirts and collars and handkerchiefs as I would have done most cheerfully had I known the facts. I had thought of her as probably the only ordinary person I knew, as far from mysterious, no one to compete with the moon and the waves, and all the while—who had she been, who was she?

My ignorance had been perhaps my salvation. I had been like the weary traveller who rode over Lake Constance in a night of crystalline sub-zero weather blotting out, for forty-six miles, all vistas and landscapes and signposts, all bushes and houses and trees, snow pebbles driving against his cheeks, burning against his eyelids and his eyeballs congealed, snow shrouding both the horseman and the horse, so he could not see their reflection, his breath freezing like a burning sword, and who did not realize that he had left terra firma long ago, his horse's hooves striking sparks like stars, that at any moment that which he took to be frozen pasture land for the sheep and pasture land for the brood mares and the foals and slumberous meadows of wild flowers would be the grinding and roaring and breaking of ice, the icy waters of imperial darkness suddenly closing over the rider and the horse as if the earth had swallowed them up, and who, when he reached the other shore and looked back and saw where he had been, that no one had ever lived and crossed frozen Lake Constance which was never completely frozen, that he had done the impossible, that he had crossed that waste expanse which was said to be impossible to cross, the Alpine peaks mirrored as on a trembling sea of glass, had dropped dead with the shock of the after-knowledge. Everything, as I looked back, would be different from what it had been, the simplest gesture having a different meaning, the smallest word being weighted with a different message. Never again should I see Miss MacIntosh whom I had known so well in daily life, whom I had hardly

195

stopped to think of or speculate on as to some other life I had not known, whom I had even rebelled against—never again, except in memory's dim or golden light, should I see that simple-minded, fussy old nursemaid, secure in her authority, her always being right—her black umbrella up-lifted against a darkened sky, her dripping whaler's hat drawn down below her ears as, with her face pale and twisted with unuttered pain, her lips blue and drawn to the thinnest line, she had used to plow through old, forgotten cloud-bursts taking her constitutional though it might be a bitter pill for her—or had briskly walked back and forth across the sun-splotched nursery floor, slapping her knees as she would ask her bawling question—Where is North Dakota, and what is a monsoon, and what is a mirage, Vera Cartwheel, or is there such a thing as a mirage in nature?

After this night of change, that which should take place in myself if not in another, I should not be sure of anything, not even of that old creature who had seemed, in spite of some few oddities which were her own, so very average and unassuming, the one person who had not veered suddenly before my eyes, whose ways had appeared fixed like the North star and unchanging, and who had been neither the unstable voyage nor the voyager—in all that great, glimmering, many-roomed house where my mother feigned death because it was an enchantment greater than fleeting existence, the one person who was not chimerical and fading, who was by no means the phantom filled with color, with sonority, with delusive vision of what was not, the one person who was not the dreamer and the mistaken, egregious dream displacing life. But farewell to Miss MacIntosh as I had always known her, nor should the surrounding ob-jects, moons, suns, stars, waters, give assurance that she had not given. And farewell to the unity of awakening life, the superficial consciousness which omits so many hidden things, and farewell to the old moralities, the proverbial wisdom, the rote questions and answers like the rote tide, the routine of our humble days, the narrow schedule, all that fabric of self-deception we two persons had lived by, and farewell to the past and its illusion, and farewell to the reason, the purpose, the goal, the future, and farewell to What Cheer, the cherry blossoms billowing like surf, the peach orchards, the globed fruit, the dusty lanes, for all had been as if they were a lie.

Farewell to the dream of the past, for it should be laid bare like a corpse before my eyes, and I should see that there is nothing which does not bear the capacity to surprise and shock us with the absence of all those qualities and properties we had supposed—perhaps, too, with the presences of others.

I wandered through dense, neglected undergrowth of dew-drenched, steaming gardens which, laid out non-symmetrically, had not been planted for the ravaged eyes of the blind—immortal gardens where, ac-cording to my mother's scheduled, disruptive visions, those which saved her from the absolute darkness, one might meet so easily, just as one turned down a winding path of broken shells, with Dr. Galen, who was a

Greek physician and medical writer of perhaps the second century, very, very brilliant, with Dr. Harvey, who had discovered the circulation of blood in that greatest of all sublunar mysteries, the human body, though his own blood no longer circulated, with Oliver Goldsmith or Ben Jonson or any number of distinguished persons—for life was only this, a perpetual garden party omitting the tragic spirit, even the dead hostess. Her guests would surely understand why she herself could not make her appearance, that she was indisposed, suffering both chills and fever, her eyes bright with love.

Delicate vapors of colors drifted like scarves and veils and plumes before my eyes, like rustlings of old, cracked, water-stained silks, yellow and green and rose, like cuffs of foaming lace, like powdered wigs and ribbons and hearts, like wheeling skirts, anti-masks and masks, snoods embroidered with pearls, like bony fingers carrying bouquets of faded, mildewed flowers, and there were congregations of pagodas and um-brellas, and there were flutes and choral voices. Had it been a real garden party, of course, such a one as I had never attended, there would have been something to eat, and I was hungry enough to eat the flowers, the moths. Upon the darkness checkered with golden light, a chessboard of which the squares moved and changed positions in the mathematical wind, the life-sized chessmen seemed, as they emerged from corruscated mist, their rounded eyeballs lighted by the reflection of the absent sea, to be moving, too, as if played by invisible players who could perceive an order in multiple confusions of movements and sounds, a secret plan. A somnambulist seagull drifted anarchically on motionless wings through an opening in the curtain of enormous shadow and light, the dark or gold-veined, shimmering fog. Stars speckled the dark blue sky, smooth as a bird's egg, and there were marble statues trembling on the brink of supernumerary consciousness, and there were stone helmets gleaming in the finny light of the sea, and the Venus was bearded by patriarchal fog, and many familiar things were increasingly unfamiliar as if, until I had seen them in the illuminated darkness, I had never seen them. The mist flowers drooped their purple, langorous heads, seeming a part of the mist. There were flowers opening, long-lipped, bright-eyed, hairy and sticky, and there were spotted flowers which, when I reached out to pluck them, flew away like luna moths, leaving the grey branch bare and moldering. Upon the cheeks of cherubim which had been formed of barnacles as by the action of a meditative sea, there were shadows cast by white, dwarfish roses in a continual stir of musical sound, even of ghostly sound, that which should not be heard, for I had come to the garden of the deaf. In this garden, as my mother would always say, the ear is dead. A frog screamed. A fish hawk dived. I stood still, hearing all around me the stirrings of leaves and flowers, the splashings of waters, even the voices of crickets against the roarings of the sea. There were water-spouting gar-goyles, those which my mother described as family faces, and there were pigeon-breasted marble statues and their reflections cast upon reflections.

Her hair spread like gossamer upon a green silken pillow, her eyes as bright as pebbles in a brook, my mother would moodily insist, talking to

Mr. Spitzer, his face grey and many-folded in the turgid evening light, his great head bobbing and nodding, that this was the garden of the deaf, that the ear was dead, a fact which he knew certainly as well as she did, so why deny it, and why pretend that he could hear? The ear was dead, she would repeat to Mr. Spitzer, and that was why, for so many years more than either he or she could realize, she had not dared go out of doors, for she could not endure the silence unbroken by the sound, and she feared the silence, feared it most when a frog screamed. She marveled, over and over again, that this was Mr. Spitzer, her old friend, that he walked abroad, that his fat cheeks twitched, that his forehead throbbed with thought, that he lifted his hand. She marveled that Mr. Spitzer argued law cases in dusty courtrooms, that he said yea and nay, that he made important decisions, for who could hear him in all this world, and who had heard his voice for meaningless years, and what difference had his legal practice made? Was it a star? It was not even so much as a straw blowing in the wind. Why did he come to see her? The ear was dead, she would lovingly sum up his case, and urged also that he needed not trouble himself to attempt now even a brief reply to her regrets, for there was no sound, not even the creaking of starlight.

When he asked whose ear was dead, she would always answer that it was his ear, and how should he deny it? She naturally did not mean his dead brother's ear, and why should he try to confuse her, his old friend? When he walked through the garden of the deaf, taking the short cut to the sea road which was sometimes lost in booming surf, did it not give him pause, the dead ear, so she would ask, her voice running like water when the ice was broken? Did he not stop to think of the dead ear, to drop perhaps a flower upon that silent grave? Did he not tremble slightly, surrounded by such silences as few living men had known, for was not his heart silent, too, like the dead ear?

Mr. Spitzer, however, would sometimes insist on speaking, even though he should not, he believed, be heard. He would argue that, after all, if she referred to his dead brother's ear, he must point out that his brother had not been buried anywhere on this vast, amorphous estate and came not among her dead guests.

As for Mr. Spitzer, it was true that, of course, in his right ear, there was always a subdued roaring, a noise which came from the head only, a noise which, his dead brother's dead physician had assured him, did not come from this world, though he had learned to live with it and many traffic signals blowing even in a silent, empty street. Mr. Spitzer was try-ing to learn not to turn his head every time he heard a traffic horn.

But my mother would not be persuaded that Mr. Spitzer was right. For in this garden of the deaf, she would vividly insist, talking louder and louder, arguing with pompous, beclouded, many-valved Mr. Spitzer who did his best not to betray his real confusions, his possible agree-ment with her at some level other than reality, arguing with Mr. Spitzer even perhaps long after, sighing, he had departed, the sense of the vision remained, the bud and branch and falling leaf, but the ear was dead, and the sound was fled from the universe, and he could not hear another's voice, not even his own voice speaking. All the world which entered through the ear, reason and imagination and human argument, it was also closed and soundless, and there was not a sound to be heard either by herself or Mr. Spitzer, and that was why his music was the silence. One should see the bird and the shadow of the bird, but one should not hear the song. One should see his lover's face but never hear his voice speaking farewell.

CHAPTER 14

※

I CAME, in my wanderings, to the grave of the black coachman, he who had used to drive, upon a circular avenue, the carriage and the four white horses, taking for their constitutional my mother's father, his blind mother, his unmarried sister, his blind wife, and who had survived them all, just by a shade, as my mother would point out to Mr. Spitzer, he who sat at the foot of her bed, his face almost extinguished at times by the darkness.

Always my mother, at certain points of her illness, would come to the subject of the black coachman whose grave, she believed, was hypothetical and changing, for she had not visited it for years, perhaps never had visited it. She had arranged, however, that the black coachman should visit her. She had requested that the black coachman be buried in this or an approximate grave by the sea, beyond the last line of stunted, blackened spruce and hemlock, there where the waters swept up and covered the land with brackish ponds, with gleaming eyes and starfish and moon shells, there where, if her instructions had been followed, one might still hear, in the reverberations of foaming, clouded waters, the cloppings of horses' hooves, the grindings of forever turning carriage wheels, the barkings of spotted coach dogs running beside the wheels.

She would ask Mr. Spitzer whether he knew where the black coachman was now—whether, according to her specific instructions, he had been sunken into his grave with the carriage sinking, the four white horses plunging downward, their heads turned toward the moon-colored waters? If she knew this, she would know whether she was right in often hearing, on a sunken avenue, the clop-clopping of hooves, whether there might be at least this certainty in the midst of times transshifting and perceptions distorted and seas whirling and dreams repeating themselves as if they had another life.

Mr. Spitzer was usually so careful to try to please her, his dark lady with her endless torments, but as to the black coachman's present whereabouts, he maintained his silence, perhaps because he believed the answer would be ridiculous. Mr. Spitzer, his face almost blotted out so that he might be thinking his own thoughts, whatever these might be, would sit in the darkness which was filled with the broken gleamings of watery silver and gold and glass, reflections of candle flames like fishes' eyes in the dark mirrors, and he would make no answer, perhaps because he had been over the disputed ground so often before. He perhaps did not understand why, after so many years, she should wonder where a dead coachman was, especially as she was so inconstant, why she should now be concerned, at this late date, as to the black coachman's position in interstellar space, as to whether he had passed through the last postern gate or was drawing up under a dark porte-cochere. His own impersonal theory was that the dead were never angry, that they had attained, as he would have liked to have expressed it, perfect silence.

My mother believed, though, that there were two worlds, just as there had been two Mr. Spitzers, both continuing though one could not now be seen. There was always the invisible world which she saw around her, was there not? Her drugged vision provided more of reality than reality provided. There were still, of course, some beings missing, and they were visible. Where was the other Mr. Spitzer? This was, she believed, peering into the shadows, the one she had never loved, Mr. Spitzer, the lesser one, the lawyer with the broken law practice, the recessive mentality, the forgetfulness, the evasiveness, the taciturn regrets, perhaps only the imaginary clients or the dead such as herself, trying to locate her black coachman. Why should she not ask a question which it was not practical to ask—she being, as she knew, a poor, hallucinated invalid obsessed by voices which could not be heard by Mr. Spitzer because of his dead ear, she being obsessed by the buzzings of the wild honey bees of Libya? Where was the black coachman, so gallant? He had always offered her his hand.

Where the black coachman was would make no difference, however, in the conduct of this world, for this world would be the same chaos, the same madness rolling like waves around our heads, perhaps it was Mr. Spitzer's opinion—nor would there be any marked difference in my mother's life, the same pale duchesses coming to tea, the same mosaics cracking in the cold, and Boston continuing indifferent as before to these phantasms in her bedroom.

My mother, however, felt quite otherwise, that the black coachman must be located even now, that everything must be regulated, really, and not left to thoughtless chance, as surely Mr. Spitzer must agree if he were absolutely honest. Nothing should be missing from the chaos, not one leaf that ever fell, nothing, unless it was Mr. Spitzer—and in some way or other, it was the black coachman upon whom all things depended. It had been the black coachman who had already circled through endless chaos, driving the four white horses on and on until the end was the beginning. If she could find him, she could perhaps find herself, the bewildered passenger. If she could not find the black coachman, how could she find her Seeing Eye dogs, her gondolas flitting like swallows through the dusk?

The black coachman was a landmark to her, and she would remind sleeping Mr. Spitzer that the black coachman had been like the dead, flowering tree she had always passed, a white sea bird roosting on its blackened top. How very careless of Mr. Spitzer, her lawyer if not her lover, to have misplaced the black coachman and the white horses, the family carriage! Her father, ruling all things with an iron hand here, had thought a great deal of the black coachman's future welfare if not his present welfare. That was why she had asked, long, long ago, that the black coachman be buried with the carriage and the white horses, that he should even be wearing his livery, his high silk hat, his plume, his silver buttons in his grave, so that he might crack the coachman's whip, driving the horses under the earth, the thin tree branches driving with him.

Besides, the arrangement had been the coachman's idea, not hers. He had wanted the carriage and the horses, just so that he might continue his old employment, and she remembered, quite distinctly, that she had made sure of this provision in her last will and testament. Had Mr. Spitzer forgotten her dying wish?

Had Mr. Spitzer, locating all other lost heirs, cheated the black coachman out of his employment and inheritance and gone against her dying will? Mr. Spitzer, my mother said, needed not look so indefinite, so far away, his face blotted out by blackness, his eyes white and staring at nothing but the void. She knew him well enough to know that if he had followed out verbatim her instructions, if he had sunken into the grave the black coachman with the family carriage sinking, the four white horses plunging downward into the abyss, their faces turned toward the foaming, swelling sea, it should have made sufficient impression on his vacant mind that even he, with his absent-mindedness, should not have forgotten it, this grand funeral, not even after so many years, so many soundless tides.

She would accuse Mr. Spitzer of having buried the black coachman in some other grave and having sold the carriage and the horses after she was dead. The black coachman had complained to her only recently that this was so, that he was buried in another's grave, that someone else was driving his horses around the long, shaded avenue. No one could be so forgetful as Mr. Spitzer unless, underneath his indifference, he was really quite brilliant, a shrewd dealer taking advantage, she believed, of her weakness. Was she not weak? Was she not poor? To whom had she childishly, innocently entrusted her practical and financial affairs, her investments, her great, empty house, her vast, undefined estate, her carriage, her horses, the black coachman, her jewels—to whom but Mr. Spitzer, who could not be trusted and was not so different from his brother as he sometimes liked to feel? Think how Mr. Spitzer would feel if he had been buried in another's grave, himself the food of worms, separated from all he loved, hearing the marsh bull frogs croaking over his head, the songs of butterflies! How would he feel if he had been deceived by the living? How would he feel if he had been his dead brother, loved by her, yet never loving her?

Mr. Spitzer would sit there in the blowing shadows, his face as grey as wet ashes, a slightly yellowed white rose or tiny tuberoses always in his buttonhole, his hands folded above his dusty high silk hat which might have concealed another vapid, smiling face, even his brother's. Of course, his brother had hardly ever smiled. About other and important things, he might try to make some lucid explanation, even concerning his brother —but not about this black coachman, a matter which, though ponderous, he had always protested, escaped his passive memory, already over-whelmed by shock. The black coachman had died, as he believed, several years after his brother's death and at a time when he himself was still laboring under great shock, trying to adjust to a world which should not include his suicidal brother.

What, my mother would ask, had been that black coachman's name? The name, like so many other things, had slipped her mind, a sieve which could not hold the water—but what was a name? Poor black coachman, whoever he was, wherever he was, she would recall, his shout-ing at the horses, King and Queen, Prince and Spade, old and lazy things which should have been retired long ago. The black coachman had had no wages for years, even before his death. Money had meant nothing to him. As to the hour of his death, his expiration, she believed it must have been before Mr. Spitzer's loss of his brother—about that, she must be vague, too, often changing her mind as her mood changed, depending on what hour it was or where she was in space, and there had been no cause.

She was quite certain that she had wanted a grand funeral for the black coachman with the white, rolling eyes. She had definitely asked that, instead of a winding sheet, he should have, in his grave with him by the pounding sea, the carriage and the four white horses, and perhaps a passenger or two—so that she might still go driving, her dead self propped among the velvet pillows, and she would wear her large lace garden hat to shade her eyes, this instead of the coach's roof, her eyes staring at winged fishes and creatures of the waters and undersea flowers. She had always intended, of course, something more generous than a well-furnished grave—she had not been selfish and self-centered like Mr. Spitzer.

Mr. Spitzer, being her executor and lawyer, knowing that she had no survivors, knew as well as she did that she had remembered the black coachman in her will, of course, in many wills—and when he was still living, too—when there had been no way of knowing which would go first, herself or him—that in codicil after codicil, she had provided for him in all respects, leaving him first one thing and then another, her father's house and her private jewels and the three clavichords, the twelve grand pianos, the family portraits, the empty picture frames, her father's coin collection, the golden dishes, the fountain pen which, hav-ing a crystal point, wrote under water, leaving him something different with every new will she made, always changing her mind and adding or subtracting—and when it had seemed that she had outlived him, she who was dead, this jeweled corpse, had she not done away with her earlier scruples and left him everything? Or when he was dead? She had left him the falling leaves, the golden sands, the sweeping waters, the tassels of gold, the carriage and the carriage horses, everything that was hers, every-thing that was not hers, and she had not been unduly influenced or coerced, and she had been possessed of all her mental faculties, feeling no great pressure. Mr. Spitzer surely remembered that, with one grand sweep of the fountain pen which wrote under water where eyeless fishes gleamed, she had left the black coachman everything, even her old, empty gowns, her nightgowns, her hats. What better could she have done for the black coachman? Where was the black coachman now, and where was the carriage turning, and where were the four white horses, so old and fat, and where was she, thin and shivering, and where was the other Mr. Spitzer who, she had no doubt, had prospered even in his grave? If she could just locate the black coachman, she could locate everything. The black coachman had known her since childhood, and he had known her brother and sister who had not known themselves, and he had known both Mr. Spitzers, identical as twin buds before the one was fallen away, and he had known which one was fallen. He had known the directions of the winds, the colors of the sky.

Her eyes starred with tiny lights, she would become very angry, trying her best to break Mr. Spitzer's stubborn silence, to make him speak to her, even if only to comment on yesterday's weather. Why, to her simplest questions, could Mr. Spitzer not answer yea or nay? She knew very well, she distinctly remembered, as a matter of visual memory and not of what he had explained, that it was his left ear which was dead and buried in the garden of the dead. Why should he appear to lie to her? Why must he always look in the other direction, cupping his hand over his right, good ear, shutting out, she had almost no doubt, her plaintive, beseeching voice, listening only to the roaring sounds which do not come from this world, the sepulchral traffic horns and foghorns, the withered leaves whirling in the winds of the past? Was he a vision or real? Where was his heart buried?

She would ask, her eyes quizzical and smiling as with a new illumination, what were all these snowflakes falling against her cheeks, and where did all these flamingoes come from? She was a face floating on waves, her dark hair streaming, and she had forgotten both Mr. Spitzers, and she had forgotten the black coachman. At least, she had forgotten him for the time being.

Perhaps Mr. Spitzer, his dignity only slightly ruffled, was sustained by an infinite compassion. Perhaps it was only his endless tedium which drew him toward her as if he were magnetized and made him sit out an otherwise empty evening. How else should he have passed an evening except in her enchanted presence? Though he was often bewildered by the flood tide of her visions, by her shifting points of view, it seemed that her confusion brought a kind of splendid alter ego to him, that without her, he was almost nothing—for surely he had led, since his brother's sudden and unexpected death, the most retired, the most unassuming life imaginable. Of himself alone, who was he? His life had hardly been, by and large, a shining success, at least not according to the ordinary standards. He had been a failure although, of course, in some ways a distinguished one, surpassing any success he knew of, and operating on a cosmic scale. This much, he was fairly sure of. Sometimes he felt as if he were hibernating a long winter through like some old grizzly bear who, enclosed in a dark cave, will never again eat the buds of spring.

As to my mother's irrational ravings, perhaps there was no rational answer anyone could make unless, facing the truth, she should be relieved of the oppressive illusions of life, of her erroneous perceptions of things where no things were, of many people going and coming in an empty room, a great hubbub, a constant uproar deafening to his ears— and who was he to rob her, to disturb the dreamer and the precarious dream? She would never recover from her prolonged illness unless, when she was cured, she should die. From the brink of ultimate truth, she would always draw back, therefore, he hoped, not taking the steps he took, preferring her many mistaken visions, always so superficial—and he would silently encourage her ravings, even though, as he must often have assured himself, he was literal-minded, stodgy, not easily taken in by scintillations of the dying dream.

His facial expression, however, was always one of both denial and flight. He could not say no unless he should say yes, though yet the perfect truth was that which he must always search for. He would seem filled with a stupendous self-doubt when, returning from some dark voyage though she had not stirred an inch, she would tormentingly remind him that his brother lived, tormentingly ask him whether he was quite sure who Mr. Spitzer was, whether he had not always been deceived by some great jokester who had played upon him, by sleight of hand, this trick of life when he himself was dead? Were the thoughts he thought his own or his brother's, perverted and distracted by this monstrous presence, faceless in the deep? Could he be sure that some superior intelligence had not dreamed this enormous, moribund joke, his living body, his flaccid face with the sunken, glistening chin, the dusty hat in his hand, the black suit he had worn ever since his brother's funeral, the twelve moons shining over Jupiter, the stars, the clouds, the clouded waters? Were not these his brother's cuff links he was wearing, double horses' heads carved of mother-of-pearl, he having appropriated these to wear to his brother's funeral, and was not the ivory-headed cane his brother's, too? Had he ever paid his brother's gambling debts? Was the funeral even paid for?

Did his right hand know what his left hand did, my mother would further ask, talking through a haze of wakeful sleep in which all objects shimmered and changed shape, and the gold-framed mirrors drifted toward the clouded ceiling—was he a good man or a knave, perhaps even, in some obscure way she could not define, a thief, a purloiner of the things and ideas that did not belong to him? Though it was his avowed profession to upturn rightful heirs, sometimes already in their graves and covered over by their own tendency toward forgetfulness, had he not taken the properties of others, a dead ear, a slumberous face? He was a stranger to himself, certainly, in her opinion. Perhaps he might meet himself some night, quite suddenly, on a dark street such as he often frequented when looking for some lost heir, and then what should he do? What should Mr. Spitzer do if there were really two of them, not one?

Would he drop dead or just go on as if nothing had happened? She would ponder the answers to these and many other questions—the answers which she herself provided.

She knew that Mr. Spitzer must be often surprised, even in his daily life, by the fact that, though he was a lawyer, he was in flight from the law. There were ways in which he was disturbed. Why should he be afraid of the law, the mortal law if she was not? Had she not seen the law of gravity defied and golden apples falling upward? How should she be surprised if a candle's flame should burn under water? Would his brother be surprised by any of these things?

She knew that Mr. Spitzer must be often surprised by many minor discrepancies, cracks, flaws, such as he himself had more than once reasonably remarked upon, his forehead breaking out into cold sweat as he confessed that, for example, when he searched through the pockets of his great coat, he was always turning up something which he had not anticipated, his brother's black-rimmed handkerchief, other things which had been his brother's and not his, a tip on the horses which were no longer running, a ticket for a boxing match between two dead boxers, the name and address of a fallen woman. He would have been less surprised by the cold hand of death, by wandering stars, stars out of their places, stars falling like cold summer rain, heavy as surf, even as he himself would sometimes confess, doubt crossing his face, his domed, throbbing forehead, for he felt strange things sticking to him like weird barnacles to a spar, and he felt himself overgrown by curious growths, even as to his own ultimate consciousness, and it was he who should have died, he who had preferred the lonely ways, his brother who should have lived. But always, disturbing Mr. Spitzer's peaceful life, there was his brother's life, these incongruous incidents repeating themselves with nightmarish certainty, just as my mother had guessed, Mr. Spitzer must admit. There were always disturbances which, after all, had impressed him, it seemed, with their vast significance, that which he would have liked to have escaped—how he had found, in his coat pocket, for example, his dead brother's cigarette still warm at the stub or burning like an eye, though fortunately, he had been able to smell the burning wool and had extinguished it before it had done any harm to his old coat. A playing card dropping out of the sleeve of his dead brother's butterfly-sleeved purple dressing gown, just when, after a sleepless night, he wished to be relaxed, to contemplate, in fact, eternity, the tired music of the dying spheres. His brother's high, cynical laughter disturbing his most peaceful sleep, arousing him so that he could not close his heavy-lidded eyes, yet though the hours were serenely flowing toward their source. His dead brother had taken every chance, even the last, had taken a chance when the odds were even or all against him, unlike Mr. Spitzer who had never hoped to win anything for himself but, as Mr. Spitzer carefully explained, if it were possible, if it were not too late, his brother's love, and if that were not possible, my mother's changeable love at the last minute, of course, he knew only too well, waiting here all her life for her to change her mind, waiting for that moment when she should prefer him whom she had never loved.

And though, because of his turbid sleeplessness, he might wish to drink, after a night so disturbed, a second morning coffee, and though his old manservant, the excellent clam-digger, would swear that he had brewed enough for two before going out to dig clams and listen to their dying voices, yet there would be no second cup, and who had surreptitiously drunk it? His manservant, though clam-mouthed, a man who knew Mr. Spitzer's personal habits as well as he knew those of the clam, and he also knew the Medusae of the beach, all the creatures swept up or almost all, all the broken shells, and he had also known Mr. Spitzer's dead brother, would swear or indicate that Mr. Spitzer himself, in an absent-minded, sleepy moment, his head roaring with old tides which opened old valves, must most certainly have drunk the second cup, too, perhaps while, with indifferent, sleep-clouded eyes, he was reading, at the overladen kitchen table covered with an oilcloth and broken pottery, the water-stained newspapers of a week ago or a year ago or a decade ago, trying to catch up with current events, trying to follow, to the best of his unconcentrated ability and in spite of the multiple confusions around him, the Manchurian or some other conflict which made him always wish he were well out of this sad, mistaken world. He found himself always on the losing side with the fallen as to these lost battles.

Undoubtedly, there was some reasonable explanation which could be made, according to Mr. Spitzer, though as yet he had not found out to his own satisfaction what it was, who drank the second cup. There was almost no avoiding it. When he returned from the dirty stove to the table, which had always been in plain sight, which had never moved, he would sometimes find that his knife and fork, which he had carefully crossed above his plate in the sign of the cross, his plate unwashed since yesterday, had changed in their positions. Sometimes his plate had been upturned, or someone had spilled a glass of water. His manservant, the grey clam-digger, would swear that Mr. Spitzer himself was responsible for these confusions, that he had moved these things around, perhaps by a slight gesture of which he was unconscious or somebody else moving his arm, but Mr. Spitzer knew better than that, for there was never anyone else in the kitchen at the time. He had watched himself in a broken kitchen mirror which reflected also the crooked table, the stove, even the stovepipe, the two chairs, and he had retraced, with mathematical accuracy as if he were a general reliving a lost battle, every step. He had checked and double-checked. Yet sometimes a goblet was upturned, just when he turned his back, and so he often felt his heart shaking within him.

He had thought of these things perhaps too much, and their solution was perhaps more simple than he understood. Perhaps, Mr. Spitzer believed, his face bewildered by these times when he would consent to argue aloud, they had not been caused by him or any mistake in his perception of reality, that they were caused by the general confusion of his own house, the poor clam-digger's poor housekeeping when it came to human beings. They were due, in fact, to his manservant's inefficiency in all matters not related to the economy of the clams which were so highly organized, the way things, for many years, had been left at loose ends in that house where he lived, the roof rotted, the shutters banging, the windows broken and stuffed with old newspapers and covered with cobwebs and fish scales to belie, when Mr. Spitzer walked out upon his punctual evening visit, ivory-headed cane in hand, high silk hat at a jaunty angle, black cape sweeping around him like the waters of darkness, his altogether elegant appearance which he, in his own shy way, was tremulously proud of, it being practically all he had, he having suffered irreparable losses on a grand scale, those the world knew not of, would perhaps never know of.

His troubles at home were not, however, all his troubles. He was also being approached constantly, when he walked in distant city streets, some of which he had never walked in before, his mind filled with nothing but the score of his unwritten music, by strange men who, as my mother knew, mistook him for his dead brother and who, moreover, had apparently never been apprised of his brother's unexpected death or of his own protracted existence, that it continued, broken though it was, and self-effacing. The idea had occurred to him, of course, that perhaps some in his brother's circle or many circles had not known of his existence, for undoubtedly, his brother had not been one who would have mentioned him indiscriminately to casual strangers. It was Mr. Spitzer who now mentioned his brother and sometimes, in fact, as my mother knew, would not correct, in other minds than his, the illusion that he was, indeed, his brother. Thus his brother lived. At other times, of course, he would find that he must simply deny his brother's continued life, that he must simply and tersely disclaim all knowledge of what the other fellow had been up to, or otherwise, he would be involving himself in all kinds of present difficulties, some quite beyond his means, even old lawsuits, suits for heart's balm, for wounded vanity.

It was apparent that, much as he had known of his brother, there were still ways in which his brother's life could shock him by force of new circumstances—for the other had been, in spite of his outward carelessness, the deeper, more brilliant fellow and capable, though indifferent to music, of far greater variations on one theme than he. Large areas of his brother's life were still unknown to Mr. Spitzer. For the most part, therefore, when approached by strange men or women on unfamiliar streets, those claiming to recognize him as an old roué of the gambling circles or as some old lover of their youth, Mr. Spitzer tried to protect his brother, to act in that way which he considered to be, even now, to his brother's best interests, to surround him, in a manner of speaking, with the capacious cloak of his own protection.

There were many considerations. There was, of course, the pitiful consideration that his brother seemed to live in other eyes, enjoying a vicarious immortality, and there were points at which it was thus perhaps best to allow the delicate situation to take its own course, times when all explanations would seem an awkward fumbling and stumbling, as he knew so well, times when it was best, in fact, to allow the fleshly illusions to persist, even at the expense of, if necessary, his own life. He would merely be silent on ambiguous occasions, hoping against hope that there would be no further ramifications or echoes, for his own life was now a comparatively simple thing, devoid of all romance, and he had thus avoided, he hoped, those difficult involvements his brother had most avidly sought for, his brother having associated with shady characters. All these connections had not touched on Mr. Spitzer. They had touched on his brother. My mother must surely recognize, as well as he did, he would suggest, how deceptive the outward appearances often necessarily were, that though there had been, she herself had said, this great physical similarity between himself and his brother, and their cosmic union in the womb of time, there had also been many sharp differences as to their daily lives.

There had been differences as to their inclinations, the influences to which they had succumbed, even sometimes when they had not recognized these differences. His brother had been impatient, unable to wait an hour, and Mr. Spitzer had waited, loving my mother through all these empty years, no thought of revenge ever entering into his heart as it would have entered into his brother's heart. His brother had been quick-tempered, quick to take offense, and Mr. Spitzer was slow, stumbling, fumbling, barking his shins in the dark, sliding on icy pavements, bumping into lamp-posts. He was not half so colorful a fellow as his brother had been. He was almost colorless, and his brother was dead, as he so frequently told himself, that the mistake which had been made was not his mistake, that he was by no means responsible now for his brother's affairs, that he would never have wished to encourage, if left to his own choice, the idea that his brother lived. Why should Mr. Spitzer be obsessed now by memories outside his own somewhat limited experience, things which had never happened to him but had happened to his brother who would not have confided in anyone his dark secrets, his double life? Why should Mr. Spitzer be stopped, in his aimless peregrinations through city streets, by faces leering or smiling at him, by people who thought they recognized him when, so far as could be ascertained, they had never seen him before? In fact, he had suffered greatly through the persistence of his gambling brother's very involved problems and the failure of many people to recognize that he was not his brother, who by now should have attained to peace. Mr. Spitzer was pursued by people who believed that he owed them money—and by others who suddenly wanted to pay a debt to him, much to his surprise.

My mother would be emptied, however, of understanding as to Mr. Spitzer's present problems, her eyes lighted up by some other vision, perhaps of a vast, sunken city with trembling pavements of moonstone and black umbrellas and sunken, globed lamps like enormous pearls, perhaps the tidal return of a swiftly receding past, wave upon wave, her own swollen, bloated face upon the dark, whirling waters. What had she ever seen outside herself? There was no Mr. Spitzer.

Mr. Spitzer, however, perhaps not sensing that her mood had changed, and hoping to avoid, by his seeming candor, further probings of his private life and wound, would make, to her unlistening ears, his sombre confession of a being not his own, of a dark counterpart running through all his nights and days, his dead brother's life, the plural melody which was not Mr. Spitzer's composition or choice, the melody not single or alone, the melody moving or attended by one or more related but independent arrangements of sounds distracting to his ears, the ocean gale, the child-like twitterings of barn swallows in darkening heavens, the alien music of chaos which disturbed his peaceful mind and which was not his present responsibility though surely, if he waited long enough, as he would ponderously explain, there should be some further clarification, some ultimate harmony—for it was he who had preferred the last footstep, the last doorway, the withered rose, the music of the perfect silence beyond the chance of the brittle and falling stars and the shifting clouds and the invisible winds. His brother had preferred the last chance. Mr. Spitzer would ask, his forehead gleaming with what he hoped was his pardonable pride that he had been, though literal-minded, so expansive —had my mother heard him, and could she see him now? Could she see his face? He had never cared for loud colors, never for many guests, never for competition. He had rather enjoyed the muted colors or only his illusive memory of them, the slats which were toned to a beautiful color by the salt air, the opalescence of the shifting clouds, the invisible, sighing winds.

My mother would amaze him by replying, with sudden liveliness, that she had heard every word of his faded, muffled speech, that he had made his point which was an important one like a crisis in one's affairs or a point beyond the ultimate point, that he had spoken to her out of the whirlwind and in the midst of the black, billowing waters where the black swallows whirled in that black, billowing sky, that it was all quite clear to her, this which came after life, a beautiful tumult of undying confusions in her mind. He had not attained to heavenly harmony. If there should be a heaven beyond all chaos, then in that heaven the leaves should fall, too, and there should be the same cracks and strains, the same confusions as to Mr. Spitzer, the lost stars blowing like the incoming of the morning surf. There should be the same irresolutions, the same flaws in the heart of God as there had been in the heart of man. The only solution was a further problem which could not be solved. There should be the same divisions and multiplications, the same additions and subtractions, the lawless image of the dream, the same Mr. Spitzer with his covert hesitations. She imagined, surely, these phantasmal things she saw, these goings and comings in her bedroom, the battle of the roses, the funeral gondola with the corrugated angel at its helm and also the angel looking backward toward the shore as the oars swept out to a still, glassy sea, carrying the body of the dead to its last resting place—she imagined, surely, Mr. Spitzer, his head nodding in unwilling acquiescence, or God imagined him, for he was a dream like all the others, and so was God, that invisible quality through which the visible must move until it should be seen no more. Had she not mourned for him all her life, often when he smiled? Was Mr. Spitzer blind that he could not see the golden cock perched at the foot of her bed, that it was really Pythagoras shedding his golden feathers?

My mother was always tormenting Mr. Spitzer by seeing what was not there, by sometimes not seeing him, though it was his own position that he, with his obesity, took up a great deal of space.

Sufficient, in her eyes, to the fleeting or protracted instant, was the appearance of the reality, and it was not her way to challenge, as to some quality beyond the visible, her evening guests, Mr. Chandelier with his seven bent flames lighting, to its four corners, a dark, empty heaven, Isabella of Spain, any other hallucination or presentiment. She entertained imaginary street Arabs, camel-drovers, rug merchants. All were real in her enchanted eyes, and she asked for no further verification, ordinarily, than just that she saw them. Her house of the dead was visited by many birds and beasts, each of the present moment, some fading before her eyes. Though under the tracery of the present vision, there might be old and precious communications faded or illegible, a palimpsest of many hieroglyphic writings which had been effaced, she would ordinarily not ask for the appearance beyond the appearance, mainly because she was aware of it and knew that the dog was Socrates. Ribald jokes were cracked in the still air around her. She was dazzled by so many guests. Only Mr. Spitzer aroused, as she did not like to admit, her feelings of hostile doubt, perhaps because he was flesh and blood and real, making her feel that there was that about him which exceeded her comprehension and might be vastly different from anything either she or God had dreamed, yet though she was omniscient, for she had a third eye in her forehead, the eye of her omniscience, a heron's blue, milky eye which sometimes, she saw it, floated out of her forehead, disappearing among the evening clouds. Mr. Spitzer was always in danger, it seemed, of passing beyond her scope of knowledge, of threatening her omniscience which knew just what there was to know. He was the lost perception.

She would endlessly question Mr. Spitzer as if, among all the appearances and visions which no one else saw and which needed no explanation, he was the most doubtful, just through his being visible to others. She was no more impressed by his faltering speech in which he tried to explain himself than by his grudging silence, for who was he, and where had he come from, and was that the dew of the grave upon his cheeks? She would see him calculatingly through a haze of distance. Where had all these moths come from, their shadows as big as the wings of birds? When did he last see the black coachman?

If Mr. Spitzer was, as he claimed to be, merely this frame corporeal, then how could it be that he had gathered flesh in his grave, that he was not a skeleton with an hour-glass in his hands?

Something about him evaded her definition of what was possible or true to life. Was he only a great hermit crab without a soul? Or did the crab have also its soul in eternity? How could it be that he wore the coachman's hat and coachman's silver buttons and coachman's black, flowing cape, for he was not the coachman? Where were his law cases—in what realm, that of the moths, and why should he not answer her questions as to the present whereabouts of the black coachman, the white horses, and her dead self?

Sometimes she would dream that she was taking this long journey which she had never taken, and there were many carriages, many coachmen. Was it her funeral cortege? Which coach was she riding in, as she would always ask? She would stare into the darkness of the imaginary dawn when the sky was streaked with only the thinnest lines of light like foam upon a dark sea, lines as thin as silver hairs, foam trickling from the corners of her lips, and now it might be known by those who knew her best that she was going somewhere.

She would cry out to the absent servants that they should bring her body, bring her soul, bring her fourteen white rabbit jackets, bring her hats with the white plumes, bring her falconer's gloves and hooded birds, bring her twelve tiaras and her heavenly constellations, her chandeliers which were like the tears of kings, her imaginary diadems, bring her thirteen planets, bring her pearl necklace of pearls big as goose eggs and her burnished gems and her peacocks and her twelve Catholic popes, for she was dead, and she was going somewhere, going to a place where Mrs. Astor could not go, and Mrs. Vanderbilt would not be seen. My mother had always been, she would say, the great hostess, the first to go to any distant place. Didn't she hear the rivers flowing under the ground? Didn't she hear the coachman's whip cracking like the thin branches of trees in the winter wind? Wasn't that the coachman's voice shouting to the horses, King and Queen and Prince and Spade?

As she would say to Mr. Spitzer, she was very much confused by clarities, and her mind was left in an almost total darkness, and she could not see the coachman's face. What image did she clasp, what icon lost? How many carriages were there, and were there many mourners, many who noticed that she was gone? There were a great many carriages circling the long avenue, and she did not know which one was hers, the last or the first, and the carriage was hooded with snow like the horses, and she could only see, as she would say, the back of the coachman's head. There were no carriage lamps to light the way, not even the eyes of owls. There were no street lights, not even dimmed, though yet there was the moon in the clouded sky, and she could sometimes see, through a whirling fog, old tenements with bare ribs outlined against the sky, with great domes like skulls, dead, flowering trees, hour-glasses in the dark heavens, and she was shivering in her white silk nightgown. Where was the black coachman taking her?

Why, she would ask again, could she only see the back of the coachman's head, nodding as if in heavy sleep, his high silk hat like a chimney pot? Why did the black coachman never turn his face toward her?

Sometimes there was only this one carriage, always going down a dark and endless street, so she was not always sure which city she was in, whether it was the city of the living or of the dead, and could Mr. Spitzer tell her? Sometimes she thought she was in Moscow, for they were passing under the shadow of a crenelated wall, its tower of bells, so it must be, as she would suddenly exclaim, the Kremlin, and she nodded her head to greet Czar Kolokol, the King of the Bells, the iron bells which, because of an engineering miscalculation, had never tolled. The tired horses stumbled in their walk. She saw their frozen breath. She saw, through great flurries of snow, through blinding snowdrifts, through snow as black as soot falling from the sky, old beggars wrapped in rags or burlap horse blankets, and they stared at her from lonely doorways and at every street corner. Was it before or after the Revolution, could Mr. Spitzer tell her? If it was before, it was after, and if it was after, it was before, my mother always said, so she had never broken off her diplomatic relations with Moscow.

Her body was the carriage, and her soul, now it seemed, was the passenger, and her horses were her will, and the coachman was her conscience, but who was this passenger in her carriage, she would shrilly ask, and who had taken her place? Who had stolen her fine carriage? When had the carriage ever stopped that she remembered? When had it ever waited for anybody? Had the coachman frozen to death while waiting for his mistress to emerge from a dark house? When did the last passenger get out? When did this one get in? Who was this spirit not hers and staring through her cold eyes? Who was the coachman, and who was this passenger, and where were they riding now? Why so many totem poles like telephones poles, so many wooden birds, so many wooden faces?

Was it any old beggar, this passenger picked up at any street corner, any old passenger riding in her carriage and wearing these old rags? Would any old horses do?

She would cry out to the coachman when Mr. Spitzer perhaps was gone, when perhaps she was alone, the sunlight streaming across her face as her eyes stared into the darkness. How often must she be betrayed?

Were these not her fine horses but any old crazy tatterdemalions half asleep or dreaming or dead, their skin hanging in rags as they turned down a darker street of a darker city? Was it any old carriage and not her own? Was it any old coachman, and had the coachman changed, or was it the same coachman with whom she had started out, so long ago, on this long journey? Was the coachman dead in the coachman's box? Were the horses dead, frozen to death in their sleep? Was it any old coachman drunken or half asleep or dead like her dead consciousness fantastically dreaming as the carriage wheels turned and turned on a circular avenue? Where was the black coachman, and where were her white horses, and who wore the coachman's purple plume?

What was the case of Spitzer versus Spitzer? Why had he never told her of that most distinguished legal adventure which the world knew not of, the lamentable case of the late Spitzer versus Spitzer, that in which he must appear as both the defender and the accuser, the defense and the accusation? This case, he might have safely told her of, for she had always guessed it, that it was this which took most of his time and destroyed his silent music, even the unwritten score, and made him seem a man who did not know himself and who was disturbed by the beautiful minor discrepancies, those she loved, those his dead brother had also loved, the things which did not add up, the green leaves blowing in another's path, the lost perceptions which were never his, the alien intuitions, the many voices. Had there been no accusation or only a weak, phantasmal one— and if so, then why this vast bulwark of defense, this constant sparring with a shadow? Which was he, the shadow or the man, she often wondered, peering toward the broken shadows—and was there to be no decision, no outcome but a constant irresolution and suspension and doubt? Which was alpha, and which was omega? Which side had he appeared on? Who was versing whom and where, she would vaguely, indistinctly murmur—were the blown clouds versing the transient stars, and was the wind versing the water, and was the rose versing the cuttlefish? Where was the black coachman with the bulging eyes, and where were the four white horses, their sides foaming, and where on blackened boughs were the cocoons of some eternal waiting? She would fall back suddenly, seeming to sleep, but she would be wide awake, aware of every rustling, every shadow, and Mr. Spitzer's silent breathing.

He would move, and she would note the slow, surreptitious movement as well as the golden cock drifting toward the ceiling. Why, if Mr. Spitzer was himself, should his calling card have fluttered down from the ceiling among all the others, those of the dead guests? Was there not some explanation he could give?

He had lived through winters which he had not known, as was apparent to her, as was perhaps apparent even to him. Naturally, even in spite of himself, his fugitive law practice must continue, but she could not help wondering why he was always so inscrutably indefinite about almost any subject pertaining to human law, why he disclaimed knowledge of the laws governing disunion and the severance of heart from heart, for example, why whenever she asked him how she could get a papal divorce from her dead husband, he would sit with his fingers drumming against his dusty hat rim and his mind wrapped in a vast slumberous inertia, cold and unresponsive as if he had not heard her questions or had heard them across a roaring, many-pinnacled distance. She knew, of course, that there were many clouds blowing before his eyes, that he had never been an expressive person, that the silent music had been his only form of expression, that he had denied disharmonies and differences, that he had thus differed from his gay, gregarious brother who, when alive, had never meditated an instant beyond the instant of his meditation and had been secretly, shrewdly aware of every flicker of the eyelid, every intonation of the voice, all the discrepancies, all the chances, the one chance in a million, and who, as a gambler in the horse circles and other circles, had figured everything in relation to optical illusion and a fundamental human weakness which was the desire to be deceived. Mr. Spitzer really maddened her.

She would naturally not expect the law-abiding Mr. Spitzer to be as sharply observant as his charming, lawless brother had been, his brother having noted every card in the other player's hand, the clouds darkening and their portent, the high roaring wind, the color of the sky, and his brother having known, as Mr. Spitzer apparently did not, the chameleon colors of human nature which takes no colors beyond the colors of this world. She saw no reason why, however, when it came to the divorce laws and the maritime laws and the financial bubbles, Mr. Spitzer should not have spoken in order to enlighten her as to the fable of the modern world. It seemed to her that the greater secrecy was never that which is unexpressive, that it must continually speak, announcing itself under many forms, and she wondered that Mr. Spitzer did not speak more often, that he maintained a dubious silence or spoke with reedy whispers. It simply was not true that, when he sonorously tried to explain the law to her, she would not listen or preferred some other vision, lawless and unkind. She always listened to all those wonderful things about the law, the Admiralty Law, the Lords Justices, the Vice-Chancellors, the Masters of the Rolls, the King's Council, the big wigs, the little wigs, the scriveners and copyists and minor clerks, the pettifoggers, the stuffed gowns, the silk gowns, the black gowns, the suits, the lawsuits—and she had entertained them all, and she had entertained Rhadamanthus, the judge of the underworld, and she had entertained Mr. Spitzer who was so obscure and frightened of his betters.

Why was he so secretive about the things which were none of his personal concern and could in no way have involved him and were surely matters of public knowledge? It would seem to her as if he had something personal he wished to conceal, something very unimportant—and in the act of concealing that, he must conceal all others, even yesterday's vanished weather, even the black coachman. Why could she get no satisfaction out of Mr. Spitzer? Why was he ever evasive, looking the other way when she asked him of her many faded investments, her consoles and floating debts and intangible properties, her water marigolds, the numbers of her orient pearls under water, the carriage and the white coachman and the four black horses, what had become of the color line? Where were the Alps? Were they above the water or under the water? Peering through the soft folds of luminous darkness, her eyes shining as with a sourceless light, she would suddenly ask—what had become of the stone fleet manned by stone figures, the stone figureheads, the stone sails unfurled in the winds far, far from any shore? Did Mr. Spitzer, a stone figurehead, sink with the stone fleet? What could Mr. Spitzer tell her of the satyrs? What could he tell her of the antinomies, both true, each contradicting the other so that each, if true, must be false? What could he tell her of the octave, the eighth day of the week?

Mr. Spitzer might here complain of inundation, of not being able to keep up, for woman's mockery was a delusion and a snare against which man must guard himself, even by his seeming ignorance. My mother was so illogical. She travelled out of the record, driving a coach and six through a legal statute as if it had been a shimmering cobweb. She reasoned in an erroneous circle, proving that white was black or that black was white, just as the mood took her, beginning with false premises and ending with debatable conclusions, as he had always seen. He would sigh, shake his head, disparage his importance to anybody, even to himself. He was no better than the next fellow. He was no worse. Only the usual things had happened to him, this life being as it was. He trusted that this life was not as it was not.

My mother still attributed to him, however, some unusual fate which must have overwhelmed him in times past, something of which he did not dare to tell her. Obviously, though Mr. Spitzer, often blurred by her distorted visions which displaced him, tried to keep up, perhaps only for her sake, the bravado of the vain appearance and his faithfulness which she suspected of being the chief aspect of his faithlessness, he was hopelessly backward, in her opinion, and weighted down by a burdensome past which was not altogether his own, exceeding him as heaven exceeds a star, by failures of memory as to those problems most closely pertaining to his person, by the memories which were not confirmed by haunted sense, by the like not befalling the like. Even before his brother's sudden and untimely death, he had been slipping, disinterested in the things which had interested him. Though he had always said that it was after the death of his brother that he had stopped writing an oral music, a music which could be heard by living ears, she knew that it was before. She knew that he had already given up his music, the compositions which had been played to empty halls.

Why should he deny this now, she often wondered, for it was a mere question of time—why should he deny the date at which he had chosen to write only the silent music, that which should reach to dead ears and stir dead hearts and awaken the dead to consciousness? His unspoken words were all too many. The void was not filled by Mr. Spitzer. Was he the simulacrum which she had witlessly entertained, believing he was the reality, the flesh and blood which also faded into starlight? Her mind would waver among many possibilities. At times, her fever heightened, she would feel that there had been some vast mistake which she had not previously realized, that the Mr. Spitzer who loved her was dead, that the wrong Mr. Spitzer was buried in his grave, that the Mr. Spitzer who had hated her was he who sat by her bedside, his face tenderly smiling. The undying love of the one Mr. Spitzer seemed too near the undying hatred of the other Mr. Spitzer, she would complain—and which was which? The eye of her omniscience could not report. Only by his stultified slowness could she recognize Mr. Spitzer, the plodding and unprofitable brother with whom she had been fated to pass the best years of her life. The other Mr. Spitzer's had been a short life but a merry one, even like hers—so why should she have been left with this, this mere appearance? She doubted, though Mr. Spitzer had often explained that he was merely growing older, his undying love of which he spoke too much, for she had seen it dying.

She often accused Mr. Spitzer of this indifference, of not contributing in any way to her sense of present life. Mr. Spitzer seemed to know, of current events, nothing or less than she did, to be hopelessly out of touch, yet though he walked about in the world and rode on trains and dined in public restaurants, though he did his manifold business errands which had no specific purpose. His brother had seemed to live only in the moment, whereas Mr. Spitzer, she would say, was living in the past. Mr. Spitzer seemed to know nothing of the moment, and this in spite of his well-known punctuality, his jeweled watch which told the positions of the slow planets moving through autumnal space, moving and whirling. He might know where the planets were, but where was he, she would ask, peering through the darkness which gleamed with many sporadic lights —where was the real Mr. Spitzer? Something of Mr. Spitzer had died when his beloved brother had been buried, the clods of earth falling on that other face, the white roses falling into that open grave, though how should she know unless he had told her?

That funeral, too, she had not attended, nor any other, not even, as she would conclude, her own, for she had been so very busy, filling her social engagements, her crowded calendar, and she had gone for a long weekend in Newport. Mr. Spitzer had attended Mr. Spitzer's funeral, and that was why he was so hopelessly benumbed, why he knew so little of all these current events, these current months, these currents in streams, these air currents, this passing or flowing onward.

Mr. Spitzer had forgotten so many things he had used to remember, yet sometimes remembered for her sake the things he had forgotten, such as Mr. Spitzer's funeral which had been an all-star event. Mr. Spitzer, in loving memory of his brother, had jockeyed his brother to his grave, and there had been, as he remembered, this grand funeral, the great banks of white roses sent by his brother's friends, the roses white as snow, the roses woven in the shapes of horses' heads jockeyed by old jockeys to his brother's open grave, and Mr. Spitzer had been the chief mourner, perhaps was the only one who now remembered it, his brother's unusual death, for now even, as he supposed, the jockeys were all dead. The coffin had been covered with a mantle of green turf, a horseshoe of white roses, even in memory of his brother's racing life. There were saddles of roses. For his brother had been a great figure on the turf. There had been many old, faded racing flags and banners flapping in the winter winds. My mother's racing colors, Mr. Spitzer had thoughtfully included. The coffin had been lowered into the ground, but only Mr. Spitzer, standing with high silk hat in hand, had mourned at Mr. Spitzer's funeral, the wind ruffling his wet curls, the tears streaming down his cavernous cheeks. The sky, having been livid, had darkened suddenly, and the cold rain had begun to fall, heavy as surf, and some of the party had lifted their umbrellas, and some had turned away, and some had gone to another horse race or another funeral, as Mr. Spitzer had almost no doubt. The tears of the dark rain had mixed with Mr. Spitzer's copious tears. It was like an optical illusion, the apparition of himself, for many people had not known until then of his dark existence, and many had been surprised to see that the corpse was the only mourner at Mr. Spitzer's funeral.

Yet he had lived. True, according to his own descriptions of his activities, he was always pondering over old obituary columns, last year's shipping news, old horse races which might be of interest to my racing mother, the weather reports of yesterday, always trying so desperately to keep up, to be found not inaccurate, but she was not impressed, for his knowledge even of times past was filled with vacancies and mortal hallucinations, to say nothing of the present tense. He was trying to remember, for her sake, things which had never interested him. True, he had even looked up, as she would gently observe, the Phoenician fleet, the Battle of the Roses, the Thirty Years' War, and Dr. Galen, and he was perhaps on speaking terms with Copernicus, the author of that great celestial revolution which had exiled the dear God to the void and had robbed us of the evidence of our senses—but nonetheless, his memory of history would mark him as a total failure in life, even as to his personal life, she still believed.

What difference, these impersonal things to her? What should he have to do, she would suddenly ask, with the weather—what concern of it was his, even if it was only yesterday's faded weather he tentatively spoke of, much as if he wished to apologize for his continued existence? If he spoke of the weather as of the moment, she was not impressed by his keeping up, for he might complain of the heat when, as he could easily see, she was frozen, the snowflakes whirling around her twelve white parasols. Such was his inconsideration, his lack of true perception, she would say, fanning the air furiously with her lace handkerchief to ward off a drove of orange-colored butterflies. How few people understood her.

Mr. Spitzer might at least have told her about the world of the commonplace, the ordinary things which, she imagined, must be so wonderful, exceeding imagination at the last moment. She was tired of these cerebral regions, tired of Mr. Spitzer and his pontifical dreams of self. Could he not explain to her at least the fickle human law if not, as she had always hoped, the celestial mechanics? She was disappointed. When she asked him a question as to anything specific, he was ever evasive, shaking his head from side to side, protesting that these affairs were not in woman's realm, that she should rather be concerned by starfishes and rainbow fishes gleaming through the darkened carriage windows, by subaquatic flowers, by a thousand magpies chattering in a dark forest, by anything that crossed her beautiful mind, by five jockeys with skull faces, that the world had long ago outdistanced him, or that he had outdistanced the sorrowful world, in either event the result being the same. What kind of answer was this?

The world, Mr. Spitzer believed, was woman's world from the beginning. It was not man's. Man was necessarily the alien here, the lost soul, he would explain to my mother. His brother had fallen from a tall building and thus had left the world, there was almost no doubt in Mr. Spitzer's mind. Mr. Spitzer, however, long before his brother's death, had dreamed that he himself had fallen. He had dreamed that he had climbed a tensile rope to heaven, that there were silver-toned trumpets blowing, the faded voices of violins as he passed upward, that because of something crossing his path of vision, perhaps the whirlings of dead sparrows which pivoted around some lower sphere, he had lost footing, much to his embarrassment at the time, and had fallen downward, his head roaring with old dreams—but obviously, this had never happened, for he was sitting at her bedside, in plain view, he would point out, so why should she make so much of his absence? He would explain to her that, about many things, she was right, and he was wrong. He took care of her interests to the best of his present legal ability, was trying to locate, he said, her ruddy turnstone birds perched upon her turnstiles, her surf birds and many shores, her coach dogs, the Dalmatians running behind the coach wheels.

His face suffused by wintry thought, the law, he would carefully concede, was the practice of liars, just as she supposed—that he, as a lawyer, had been a greater liar by far than his poor dead brother, with all his debts, had ever been. The only implacable law was the divine law, the heavenly harmony, that which kept the planets in their course, that which controlled, with mathematical accuracy, the falling stars, the music of the spheres, the silent music, that which was not based on the roulette wheel stopping or games of chance, such as the marked cards, the loaded dice. He must capaciously confess, of course, as to much of life his ignorance and his limitations, for he had outlived, by many years, his brother who, by now, must know it all, who must know the silent music, who must know the language of the mute, and who must have long since become, though he had been disaffected by the laws of harmony, a greater musician than he himself could ever be, he being only that brother who, alone on noisy earth, groped toward the sublime understanding, his ear still distracted by wild geese honking in an empty lane, by variant traffic signals, he being only that brother in the chaos, as he knew, and disturbed unwontedly by all these minor but palpable discrepancies my mother always spoke of, these things which did not add up, the principle of nothing but confusion plus confusion.

Mr. Spitzer was not, he would insist, disorganized and disoriented as my mother thought. He was only aware of the dark counterpoint running through his life, the darkness which can be explained, as he would say, by nothing but the further darkness.

How often had Mr. Spitzer tried to explain himself, sometimes through his silence which seemed to him more expressive than speech, a mere gesture denoting more than words could say, sometimes by long, fumbling explanations of the fact that, to be sure, one understands the mystery only by proposing the greater mystery, the unknown only by seeking the greater unknown.

My mother's mind, however, would then be perhaps contracted to a needle's eye. She would hear many voices weeping in unison, and the mourner was invisible like the corpse, and she did not know whose funeral it was now. She would call out that Mr. Chandelier should light the windless sky beyond the sky, that she was going somewhere, that she wanted her opera cloak and her opera glasses. When she reached some other star, she would know what this had been. Where were her slippers, the velvet toes covered with dust? Where was the black coachman? Where were the stars, big as poinsettias?

Impressively, taking advantage of this or a similar opportunity to expand upon these hidden themes which had chosen him, Mr. Spitzer would still try to explain that, as a matter of fact, he had passed beyond a stage of selfishness, that he came to her only to protect her and to assure himself that he had been forgotten. He had found, however, that she had remembered him as he once had been, the sad youth whom she had rejected because he was the slow one, the plodder who had been filled, as she had not suspected, with seething excitement and torments unexpressible. All things would finally confirm with her belief. It was true that, with the passage of meaningless time, all she had once believed of him had come about, even like an inaccurate prophecy somehow realized. The quick heart of the young man had been stilled. He was not the same man he had been. Inwardly as well as outwardly, he was greatly changed. He was often breathless, especially when he tried to climb a flight of stairs or catch a train. She should no longer think of him or who he was, he having reached to utter self-forgetfulness and selflessness, so far as was possible in this life, all souls seeming alike to him, their mothers' sons, he knowing now and without a trace of remorse that she had never loved him, though once or twice, and even quite lately, he had almost been persuaded otherwise. Then his heart had pounded. He had surely been persuaded that her love for his brother was also her love for him, the dead musician.

He was surprised, even sometimes chagrined by the number of persons who remembered him, that they were those he had forgotten, even along with himself whom he often felt as if he had outlived, he being incapable at this late date of attaching significance to the incidental variations of the human countenance, as he would say, the human voice, the human gesture, the human scene, he failing utterly to recognize, when he passed them in the streets, old friends whom he had known in his buried youth, persons he had naturally assumed to be dead but who were living and who, in some instances, had attained to positions of great eminence, corporation lawyers, railroad magnates, high financiers, Supreme Court justices who clapped him on the shoulder and, greatly to his embarrassment as perhaps to theirs, they having mistakenly assumed him to be no longer a citizen of this planet, had asked him to visit them in their houses and break bread at their tables as he would never wish to do inasmuch as he would not know what to talk about with such distinguished gentlemen and would have to confess, before the second cup of coffee, his own stupendous failure in life, the fact that his appearances were deceiving, that he was not so well off as he seemed, that life had failed him. He was afraid he might make some awful mistake with these successful friends, some of whom he perhaps had never seen before.

He might, indeed, betray himself, show his hand, disillusion them as to what seemed his prosperity, for there had always been in him, as in his brother, a suicidal streak, as he had often realized.

The only way he could come to terms with himself was to forget himself, and that was what he was always doing. It was undoubtedly why, as to his own habits, he was conservative, preferring his wakeful nights, his slumberous days, and never going out of his way except for some purpose, even those aimless wanderings having to do with business interests, the locating of lost heirs. There were always, of course, new adventures in his path, though he himself was in no way adventuresome and measured every step, often retracing his steps or nearly retracing them. The highest, the lowest people clapping him on the shoulders—international lawyers, great manufacturers, doctors of law, broken-down lawyers who had steadily lost out in the lottery of life, physicians, broken-down hags and nags who were as pitiful as the horses they had bet on, old dancing girls who would dance no more, bookies with tips on dead horses, hunchbacked dwarves with snaggle teeth and lidless eyes. There were always old cripples who had been the kings of speed, or thought they had, and that was the same thing at certain levels of debate, old tarts, old hearts, old sweethearts, old lovers, those who had failed to win their loves, those who had gonged against Cupid's cracked bell, blind violinists and deaf pianists and footless dancers, many who could not have known either himself or his brother, for their numbers grew in time.

Though my mother might make fun of him if she knew what he had done, he had been surreptitiously reading some of those paper-backed dream books sold by fortunetellers in poor neighborhoods where, of course, there were so many kings, so many kings dethroned. These dream books were so much trash and nonsense. Their calculations as to the stars were based upon a mathematics which began with error. They placed the planets forty degrees off their course to begin with, and thus nothing was ever quite right, and there were many errors from beginning to end. So he was not surprised by many illusions, even as he read over the predictions of future events already of the past, days which, though they were said to be lucky, had been unlucky for him, times when the gods had not smiled. The day of his brother's death was a lucky day for Mr. Spitzer, he had read, a great day for embarking upon a new adventure, a great day for conquering new worlds, an excellent day for beginning a new relationship or ending an old love—and yet had it not been a most unlucky day for Mr. Spitzer, for had not his brother died, and had not Mr. Spitzer lived? Had he not lost his beloved twin brother, so like him in the flesh? These dream books told him, moreover, nothing of his day life, the meaning when the thing was not the dream, when it was not predicted, when it was utterly gratuitous, when he could touch it with his fingers, and that was why he always wished my mother would enlighten him, even though he feared she should not be able to do so. She had told him that she had detectives following him through all the reaches of star-lit space and to places where the stars did not shine, and it was true that he was often surprised by her knowledge of his new activities, some of which had escaped his memory. If she had really traced him with exactitude, as he very much doubted, then he would like to see the reports as to all those things he might have missed. Perhaps she could also trace his missing brother. Mr. Spitzer could see then what had happened or if there was nothing. He was certainly much amazed by the excitement of his life.

The playing card dropping from his sleeve each morning had nearly always been an ace—a run of aces—the ace of hearts, the ace of spades, the ace of clubs, the ace of diamonds. This fact had given him pause in each instance, making his forehead sweat, making his heart tremble. The ace, though he was unfamiliar with cards, he had ascertained to be, as it was one, the lowest, and, as it was an ace, the highest. Yet why these aces since he was not the gambler and it was his brother who had died?

My mother could not imagine why the four cards if not an entire deck. Why the four cards, she would ask—where was the suite, the flush of cards, the hand which should be made of many cards? Who were the other players? Old parables of childhood floated before her eyes. She remembered that the Devil plays with man for man's soul, that man is an absent-minded loser, that angels weep to see man losing the game of life. Playing cards would seem to flutter from the clouded ceiling. She would hear the dice rattle, the bird cages shaking in the winter wind, the bones rattling. Now all would become quite clear to her and her eyes many-faceted by the refinements of her visions.

As to why there were four cards, all aces, which had dropped from Mr. Spitzer's brother's sleeve on various occasions, it was because there had been four brothers, four Mr. Spitzers, and she could count them. There had been, in some remote beginning of time and space, one Mr. Spitzer, conceivably, of one heart, and that was many. Then there had been two. There had been two identical Mr. Spitzers, each mirroring the other's distorted image, so there had been four, including two who were not. Each Mr. Spitzer had been reflected in the other's dark heart and hand, each like his living host, and that made four. Each Mr. Spitzer had wished to get rid of the other heart, by some quick movement or slow, some master stroke which should take the opponent unaware and send him shivering into a cold, empty universe. The Mr. Spitzer who had killed himself, having been the quicker to play his hand when he foresaw the other's hand moving, had not meant to take his own life but only to kill the Mr. Spitzer who was the pale reflection in his own heart, to get rid of, to cancel out that other, the silent heart. He had taken the greater chance, and he had lost, but the loser was the victor. The spade had turned over the dead heart, over Mr. Spitzer's heart which had been so quick, and then there was one Mr. Spitzer, the loser, vacant and slow and smiling. There was one Mr. Spitzer, so that made two, for the Mr. Spitzer who had killed himself in order to kill the other Mr. Spitzer was still the shadow in Mr. Spitzer's heart and living to this day. There were enough Mr. Spitzers to make a club, perhaps the deuce, the deuce of clubs portending death, the head, the arms, a sign more volatile than life. The club, which was trifoliate, might be transformed into the sign of the cross. The cross might be transformed into the rose. The rose might be transformed into the snail. The snail might be transformed into the head. There were many transformations, many butterflies. Nobody ever knew himself or who he was, whether Joachim or Peron now. Nobody knew the watery landscape or where the road ended, for it ended where there was no end. The landscape shifted even as she watched. As to why the cards were both highest and lowest, that was clear to my mother, also, if not to Mr. Spitzer, his face dully shining in the evening fog. The odds, she must point out, were still equally great. The players continued. His brother was the highest person she knew, and Mr. Spitzer was the lowest person she knew, and there were no degrees between the highest and the lowest, for both Mr. Spitzers had fallen. He had fallen first.

He was just the lowest person she knew. She accused Mr. Spitzer of greater indiscriminations than were possibly his—either that, or he was deliberately lying in order to becloud the issue, in order to add to the confusions of her present life, already confused beyond endurance. Why, if he was always being approached by all these distinguished persons, these great men who controlled the world, had he never brought any of them to dinner so that she might ask them how the world was, how the practical world fared without her? The house was always ready for these innumerable guests.

The table was always laid for twelve or thirteen or fourteen guests or more, as Mr. Spitzer knew, and that there was a place set for the dead, and that there was a living servant to stand behind every chair, or at least, an imaginary servant to wait upon these living guests. Why, during the years of her isolated invalidism which had yearned so for life and which had reached out for every straw in the wind and every nuance of meaning and every speck of starlight and every faded rose, had he brought into this many-chambered house, now and then, only the lowest person he could find, no one from the higher walks of life, only someone he had picked up in the streets, a perfect failure, someone who made her sicker than she was, a thief or a clown or a broken person like himself? She remembered, in lucid moments, those who had been real, and all had been failures in life, only making her feel that she had been right to retire from Boston society. A priest who was cursing God and who still wore his priest's robe and who said that he had died a thousand deaths while listening to a thousand confessions of a thousand dead whores, an old public dog-catcher barking like a thousand dogs, a horse doctor talking as if he were an argumentative centaur, a Bostonian camel-drover who had never been outside East Boston and had never seen, until he came into my mother's bedroom, a white camel in a snow storm. A duke who was no duke, a duchess who was no duchess, a thief who had stolen nothing but sequins and was a fish sliding through dark waters. If these people were real, then where was the reality?

It was Mr. Spitzer who walked about in the world, but it was my mother who knew, through her absence from the world, the world, as she insisted, and who could tell him quite scrupulously his errors in perceptions of these things which were the facts of the case. Of course, the errors might be real. She knew how often he mistook himself for another, that he had waded through imaginary storm-bursts wearing, as he had supposed, another's high silk hat which he had picked up by mistake in a public restaurant but which was really his own, as she could clearly see, the same dust furring the brim, that often, at shrouded parimutuel windows, scarcely aware of what he did, he placed a bet on a dead horse for his dead brother. His brother would have made no such error. She preferred, to Mr. Spitzer's many errors and indecisions guiding him through precise and punctual days, the many errors of Mr. Res Tacamah, those which were nobody's responsibility and had happened of themselves before her eyes and were without effect, the dolphins plunging, the eyeballs of foam, the funeral wreaths upon the waters of the formless past and of the unformed future.

It was she who must point out to Mr. Spitzer, time and again, the differences between what he said and what he did, she who must be, through knowing the greater dream, the authority on the reality, and this in spite of the fact that she was not responsible, a poor invalid dependent upon visions and rumors and winds of chance. It was Mr. Spitzer's responsibility to know the facts, the differences between the illusions which were all of her mind and the bare truth, and yet how often he had failed her, he who walked about in the world and changed trains and saw people, and how often he had not distinguished between the real and the unreal. Each day he would waken up, he himself had frequently remarked, with a sense of reeling, a feeling that his heart had failed him or was about to fail him. Surely, however, he either understated or overstated, according to my mother's view of matters, for there was no single truth such as he insisted on.

If she had not passed into some delirium of her own, her finger-nails scratching against the sky, she was sure that it was Mr. Spitzer whose conscience was not easy and who had lied to her about the most unimportant matters as if they were important, even yesterday's weather which she had already forgotten or had never known, the colorations of the mental, the inaudible sounds of incongruent harpers harping congruously, the conspiracy of the melting snow, the intangible bird, the rose turning into the crab, the secret points of a dissolving compass, the idea which is always antagonistic to the existence, the things he had perhaps never spoken of. He had lied to her about the most unimportant, fleeting things, even as if there were the things he thought of. He might be at least sufficiently responsible, with all his punctuality, to read a railroad time-table, she would say, not to say that he had changed trains where there were no trains to be changed and where there was no railroad station. There was not even a sleepy station master at a point which he described.

Mr. Spitzer, my mother insisted, could not have changed trains at this station or that on his way between two destinations, that it would have been easier for him to have travelled from the world of the living to the world of the dead than to have changed trains at such and such a point, she must make clear to him, perhaps several evenings after an evening in which he had hesitantly recalled a journey in the distant past and not in the present as she mistakenly supposed. He perhaps had spoken of a journey taken many years ago, but she had not paid sufficient attention, particularly as she had just heard a distant train whistle. It would be easier, she said, to have travelled from the world of the dead to the world of the living than to have changed trains at Hartford, so why had he lied to her, lied outrageously about so small, so trivial a thing? Did he imagine she did not know what modern travel conditions were?

Why had he spoken of waiting for an hour and a half at this station or that which was no more, not even an old landmark or chimney pot, of the cold, biting winter dawn or evening light where was no light, of his walking back and forth on a windy platform, counting his paces, waiting for a train which he thought would never come, of his almost freezing to death though wrapped in his great coat? He could not have waited for a train at this point, wherever it was. If he had waited, he would still be waiting, and he would wait a thousand years. If he had ever left Grand Central Station, running to catch his train when it had long ago departed, then he must ride straight through, for these modern trains never stopped, my mother said, and some arrived at the next station before they had left the last, so great was their speed, great as the speed of the starlight, and there were no stations. Why then did he say he had changed trains at Hartford, that he had got off one train and on to another, having waited two hours at dawn, that he had drunk a second cup of coffee to keep himself from freezing in the cold winter air? Why did he say the sleepy station master had recognized him? The trains through Hartford never stopped until they got to New Haven. The trains sometimes by-passed New Haven, too. For she knew more about the conveniences of modern travel than Mr. Spitzer did, and she owned half this railway stock, and she had travelled in these trains quite recently. He could not have ridden as far as Hartford, talking to some fine upholstered gentleman as old-fashioned as himself, perhaps the president of a Hartford life insurance company who had recognized him as his oldest living policyholder, then have waited for the electric train which long ago had been retired to a graveyard for old, broken trains and dead conductors. He could not have ridden in the old electric train with children who were crying at their mothers' ample breasts and many cackling hens, could not have heard, at many way-stations, the newspaper boys hawking their news that Queen Victoria was dead. He could not have passed, in this journey, the shipyards which were building the ships which had already sunken. He could not have seen the masts of sunken ships.

Obviously, there must be some great mistake, my mother said, for the countryside was vanished, and so was the many-colored sea, and so was the old electric train with its stained-glass windows and green plush seats and friendly ticket collector who had come for the last time, and so was Mr. Spitzer, hat in hand.

How often, moreover, he had said that he was going on a distant journey when he had not stirred a step, when he had merely sat at home, writing his silent music, a dirge for a dead clam, an evening sonata to a dead ear, a fugue without instruments or voices, his chords, his tetrachords which should not be heard on this earth! She doubted that they should be heard upon the earth hereafter.

She would continue to speak, even after Mr. Spitzer, having consulted his watch for the last time, had punctually departed, as she would not seem to recognize. She would talk on, increasingly quarrelsome and argumentative, complaining to Mr. Spitzer of his gross inefficiency and slowness, the stupor of his life. She would see him where he had been, his vacant chair, and she would not recognize that he was absent. Though he was a lawyer tracing lost heirs of lost estates, perhaps those which never were, had he not shown, in every way, his untrustworthiness to locate person or place? Who, where was he? Had he not sometimes upheld the illusions of false claimants—encouraging, even by his silence, their ravings, the ravings of those who believed they should inherit, in the next life if not in this, the many golden mitres and the purple robes and the lost crowns, the thrones? Had he not sometimes discouraged the true? Where was the black coachman? Where was the carriage—rounding what sunken avenue shaded by cypress trees? Was Mr. Spitzer sure that he had not surreptitiously chosen, instead of a carriage, a sarcophagus for the black coachman, that he had not arranged his transportation to a distant place where, of course, though there should be many excavations at many levels, the black coachman should not be found? Where were her surf birds, her turnstiles, her rain lilies, her marble statues? If Mr. Spitzer had buried the black coachman by the sea, yet how could he still be sure that the place of the grave itself had not changed, moving and stirring, for everything else moved and stirred, limpid as water? Where did the grave open?

Mr. Spitzer's left hand would make, before her eyes, long after Mr. Spitzer was gone, a quick movement. She would complain of the light shining in her eyes. She would almost feel that he was ready to give a rational response to her irrational questions, that maybe he could tell her now where the black coachman was and where her father was. Where was the grave, she would ask, of the other Mr. Spitzer, the slow one, the sick musician she had always loved? She would talk until the stars, pale as jellyfish in an evening tide, faded from the dawn-lit sky, at which point she would sink into sleep until there should be again the night. The night was the only light.

CHAPTER 15

THUS in that night of my fourteenth birthday, night which should be greater revelation than the sunlight which conceals so much—I stood by the tumultuous sea, listening to the long, melancholy roarings of black waters under the near sky where, in the partings of the curtain of streaked fog, the bloodless moon was like a white, thin skull drifting without purpose over the many roofs, the dark towers, the abandoned golf course, the grassy tennis courts, the hidden archery range, over the foaming headlands, the saddle of rock, the spur. The waves broke like primal memories of things unknown breaking on my consciousness. I was filled with an almost unbearable excitement as I realized the immensity of life, that which, through its necessary imperfections, might weave a higher perfection than the faultless and restricted days such as I had known. What if everything should be false and nothing true, nothing true of these humped, naked dunes wreathed with seaweed, patched with bayberry and beach rose and meadows of billowing Queen Anne's lace and clumps of wild grass, nothing true of the low, stunted, blackened spruce and hemlock, the leaping tides, the tongues of surf, the sudden sparks of diminished stars? Then all false things should be true, I thought, as true as Miss MacIntosh who was so very truthful, her red hair gleaming in the sunlight, in the stale nimbus of familiarity, her eyes severe with a resigned but cheerful purpose, her ways methodical even though the winds should blow her athwart. If all false things were true, however, then all true things should be false like my false mother who postulated merely as her theory the outer world, the blowing cherry trees beyond the surf line, the lanes where she had never walked. Where was the truth which should not fail?

I laughed aloud, running to meet the black, whirling waters sheeted with foam, shells like white roses blooming at my clouded feet, my body gleaming with finny phosphorescence and shining like a mirror, my hair wet and shining. My hair was wet, streaked with salt as with greyness. I trembled with cold in the hot August night. I should surely catch my death of cold and have a mustard poultice placed across my chest to burn it out, as Miss MacIntosh would say, as I knew so well—this remedy being her favorite cure-all for broken bones, whooping cough, measles, spots before the eyes, ringings in the ears, anything that might be wrong with me. In any event, as I had already erred once before this evening, dancing with nobody, I would have to box that old sandbag dummy as if it were the dark angel of death with whom a prophet met upon a barren hill, or I must knock down bowling pins, or I must pitch horseshoes, or I must tear out the hems in last year's skirts. I did not care, however, in this roaring of black tide, what the routine of the morning might bring, what hackneyed proverbs and moral aphorisms to stare me in the face until I learned them by heart, until I knew everything that old Benjamin Franklin had ever said about early to bed and early to rise or a bird in the hand being better than two in the bush, until I knew everything that old John Bunyan had said on the evils of swearing and lying and gambling and laying a snare for an innocent maid. Never again should I be afraid of the outer darkness, and there was no rapist skulking anywhere among the thin, leafless bushes, his eyes blear like the eyes of time, and there was nothing to be wary of but nothing.

All those old people in the house could not be expected to understand the heart of youth which reaches out for experience, even the forbidden, and would rather die than live in a vacuum. I laughed aloud again, thinking how surprised all those old people would be if they could see me now, thinking how I had escaped them and their adult fantasies which were empty as air, that they were the older generation, that they were as crazy as loons in a whirlwind of centuries ago. Only Miss MacIntosh was sane, of course, but she had never really understood the deeper things of life, the undertow which carries away the strongest swimmer, the waywardness of the waters and the winds. For if she had and had still been sane, then she would have been insane, I thought, but she had only skimmed these surfaces, so she had kept her sanity. Why had she no friends of her own age? What did she ever cook, though she talked so much of cooking? Could she even swim a stroke? Did she not always avoid the greatest waves when they came in? She could not swim a stroke, for example, no more than could I, and in that tide going out, she would have been dragged down at the first blow by her rainproof, her oilskin hat, her sea boots water-logged, and so many needles and pins and safety pins. She could never have breasted the roaring tide, so what was her practical knowledge? What did she know of life as it might be lived? Men and melons, she herself had often said, are hardest to know, and still water runs deep.

Miss MacIntosh knew less than I did, hers being, as I now thought, a deadness, a dullness, a coldness of heart. In spite of all the plain wisdom of that old Ecclesiastes and of Exodus and of the Farmer's Almanac, what did she know of life as it might be lived—what did she know, in spite of all the dates of history and famous discoveries and scores of ancient boxing matches and the correct breast-stroke which one should practice out of the water? Why did she keep herself bundled up in hot weather as if it were cold, and why did she sometimes carry her umbrella uplifted in the house when it was not raining, when there was no rain leaking through the roof? In winter, she left the windows wide open, so that the snow feathers drifted into the bleak schoolroom, and we must wear our ear muffs, and our breath was frozen like plumes, and the ice crystals formed on our hair, on our cheeks. Was this some more of her famous common sense, this certainty that she would freeze? Her great, windy bedroom was empty and bare of furnishings except for a broken-down brass bed with peeling curlicues, a harp as the headpiece, a harp as the footboard but no angels to play these harps, as she would thankfully remark, a table, a broken chair or two, the hearthstone streaked by the ashes of the past, for now no fires were ever burning there, she preferring the cold in which she slept, or she would add a crazy quilt to her bed, another blanket cold as snow. Also, though she never looked at herself in any mirror if she could help it, there was, pushed against a darkened wall, my grandmother's mahogany dressing table with its three stained mirrors reaching to the ceiling and dusty powder dishes and tarnished silver brushes and combs which had been hers when, in her blindness, she had used to stand before her crystal image thrice reflected, matching the colors. Sometimes, to see better, she would walk into the light, and never once did she believe the shades of death were creeping on her.

Why, when I asked Miss MacIntosh some personal question which should be of no consequence to anybody as she herself had so often remarked, would she never answer except to ask me the date of the sinking of the Titanic which was struck by an iceberg in the fog, the date of some lost battle? He is bare whom virtue hath not clothed, she would always say, peering above her eye-glasses at the slate-colored or sunny waters, the grey or golden sky, the clouds, and that this world is very naked, indeed, and one swallow does not make a summer, and a thin meadow is soon mowed, and winter is summer's heir, and the night is no man's friend, and the night is filled with darkness. It was easier to clothe the body than the soul, according to her flat opinion, often stated with that lack of equivocation with which she also said that a straight line cannot be made straighter and is the shortest distance between two points. Man, she said, should beware of wandering, and the narrow channel is the greatest ocean if we drown.

Death, like our mother and our father, she had always said, her ivory-boned knitting needles clicking, is an old harpoonist who will capture the swimmer in narrow streams. The old go toward death, but death comes to the old, and that was very certain, and the apple falls not far from the apple tree. Our cradle stands in the grave. Death has many faces and one and none, she had observed long ago, that we know not who or what we are, not even when the hour is late, that nobody knows the face of death, that none should ever see it and live. Death loves a young maid and an old man. Death loves a shining mark. The dead have few friends, and few remember the dead, and that was just as well, there being more dead people absent from this earth than living people present, there being so many doors to let out life, so many doors which should require no key and no lock and should open of themselves. But there were few doors to let life in, she had observed.

Death, she had said only this morning at breakfast in the grey light of my fourteenth birthday, is always the bridegroom—but wedlock is padlock, she had hastily added with an absent air, rustling the newspaper behind which she spoke—and all women should marry, certainly, but no man. Perhaps no man should marry woman. Man was but a bubble breaking on a dark shore. Man was but a shadow and a breath. Man was but a poor, forked animal. Here she had continued, her newspaper rustling busily, that the wheat market had slipped a point or two quite recently, and there was a drouth in the West, but black hens were still doing well, laying white eggs, she would suppose, and eggs and oaths were soonest broken. What we needed was order. Disorder was the order we were not accustomed to. Peering above her newspaper, her brow slightly lifted, she had read aloud the scores from the sporting page, the news of the bowling alleys and tennis matches and billiard halls, things of motion which concerned her more than things which never moved, and then had paused to ask laconically, her eye-glasses misted in a beam of sunlight, her eyes red-rimmed, her face grimacing, whether I had heard the old sheep dog barking in the night, that which had kept her awake, her head tossing on her hard pillow, or had I slept the sleep of innocence as she hoped? The old sheep dog barking in the night had not barked for nothing, as does a young dog who barks for the pleasure of barking, and there might be, she must warn me once again, someone who would take a young girl by the hair and drag her into the shadows where her cries should not be heard. I must keep close to the house. She did hope I would be careful, now that I was coming into my age, and remember what she had always said, that ignorance is no protection, that the fairest flower is plucked the earliest. She had given me my domestic training for a humble marriage, for one wedding which begets another wedding, and that was why she had often been of a sour disposition, she had no doubt, and why I had been forced to iron her shirts and skirts and learn the genealogies of all those old kings and simple cookery and proper navigation as between one shore and another. She had not wished to see me unprepared when the hour came, unprepared for a rainy day and harsh weather and long, cold winters which should have no fire to light them.

All day, it had been raining, off and on, and she had stopped, more than once, to explain the practical life which, in her opinion, should need no further explanation and no apology. Music does not fill the empty stomach, and music tells no truths, and life is very earnest, the great moments happening in silence, and the grasshoppers are always surprised by winter as if there had been no winter before, and that was why I must be far-sighted like the industrious ants who furnish their houses and the bees who store away their honey and the birds who build their nests in a high place. Some day, looking back on her, she had always said so, I would see that she had been as right as mortal could be, that she had been self-sacrificing and self-effacing for my sake, that she had only thought of what was best for a wayward child, and she had been a good shepherd and had tried to lead me in safe paths, yet though there were these jagged rocks and many pitfalls in the old sinner's path. Indeed, she sometimes feared that all her work had done no good, and she had plowed a barren shore, and I was like the wild swan which can never be taught to lay an egg that is tame, and I was like the crooked crab which can never be taught to walk a way that is not crooked. She feared that I was still wrapped in foolish dreams and paying no attention to her.

All day, she had been preaching, often grumpily, though many words bespeak an unsound heart, and children should be seen but not heard, and the apples of speech were silver, but the apples of silence were golden. Better a castle of bones than of stones, she had said severely at dinner, at a table almost bare, and woman's heart is folly and deception, and man is born to trouble as the sparks fly upward, and man is a little soul carrying around a heavy corpse, and man is a substance clad in shadows. Men are fallen. As for me, I would certainly marry, she hoped, when the first opportunity came, but marriage had always been a lottery, and this life was a way of thorns, and there were many who made false promises and many who were jilted at the altar or on the night before the marriage night, for true marriages were few and far between due to the sins of our first parents and the high cost of living. Husbands must be taken with their faults, for men were never perfect. They were never tailor-made, or else they were made by poor tailors and were like coats of which the sleeves fell out before the night was over. Good tailoring, certainly, was much to be desired. Good housekeeping, also, was much to be desired, even though one should keep house in an igloo and have no modern conveniences and have no feather bed and no broom and no stove and no husband, no companion but perhaps only a lonely soul or two, perhaps a walrus or a seal. Before marriage, she had said later, her mouth yawning, her hair as red as a candle flame, one should keep one's eyes open, but after marriage, one should keep them half shut for fear of what he should see, it had always been her unbiased judgment, though she could not speak from the narrow experience which others experienced, for she was single and single-minded, no man looking at her a second time or perhaps even a first, her life being almost over and the battle perhaps already lost. The old, she had said, were the wise. As for herself, the sheet anchor was gone. But there was this to be grateful for, she hoped. She was not one of those to be borne down by her own anchor.

Death, she had said, is the bridegroom—so no wonder if, my teeth chattering with cold, I had laughed in the pitch-black darkness which was filled with the roaring of winds and waters. The moon was like a white skull drifting. I had laughed, thinking of my secret dream of the false wedding, that which should beget no other wedding, that where Mr. Spitzer was married to the bridegroom, that where, as now it seemed to me, the only wedding guests had been the northern light beams, the stars, and droves of seals on a solitary shore in a crystal void where no hunter ever comes.

Far out at sea, there were sudden lights like a many-tiered ship burning or a storm which passes at the world's rim, the waters turning to oily green and gold, and the dark sky was lighted up with other colors as if no reflection, not even of the waters mirrored in the skies, could be accurate, nor that of God in man's mind, nor that of man in God's mind, nor that of man in man's mind. Water hills and valleys broke upon the sands with myriads of sparks like fireflies, shapes of waves like poplar trees or weeping willows streaming foam, corpuscular lights of the same colors as were the far waters burning in the wind. The crescent beach, when the waters withdrew, glimmered and shimmered, sheeted with pale, translucent jellyfish like ice, with conch shells and bones and burning eyes. The sea was like a crucible of glass, and the moon was a ball of fire, and the clouds were swollen with lights, and there was such illumination as I had never seen before, colors so intense lighting the dark sky that they seemed outside the mortal spectrum. For one moment, it seemed that the moving waters stood still, and I could hear a sound as of harpers harping on those seas of glass which man shall behold at the end of time when the heavens are parted, when the sky rolls back like a scroll. The sea turned to rolling blackness again, rolling toward the sky, but the clouds remained for a long time pregnant with momentary colors passing from brilliance as of unearthly jewels into darkness without face and void upon the deep. Leafless bushes, uprooted from their shallow moorings upon rocks and sands, rattled and clattered in the wind, for this earth was but the testing ground, as I remembered, and all should fail the test, and all should be found lacking. A dead seagull, wings folded, lay cold upon the narrow shelf of rock above the flood. The black waters rose to the black sky, drowning the accidental moon, and it seemed as if the sea would sweep over the land and drown the sleepers and the marble statues and the granite birds, the empty paddocks and pagodas and coach houses, the golden towers and porches of the old, sea-blackened house, its weathervanes turning crazily, its shutters banging in the wind, no light at any window.

Sometimes, it was true, the sea had swept up through dripping and ruined gardens and over the fountains, leaving a bare garden strewn with mysterious wreckage, the prow of an old ship, an empty coffin, and many playing cards. Once, the marble Saul had been swept out to sea in the departure of a musical tide, but a strange marble head had been swept in and was found resting in that place. Saul had never returned.

Now far away, the old, blind sheep dog was barking at the waves, the winds, a shingle.

CHAPTER 16

WHAT is a child that its heart shall be so superficial, so unthinking? What is a child?

The fierce, exultant pride that was mine that bountiful night of my fourteenth birthday, riding my black pony, Falada, his dish eyes shining like two moons as his hooves pounded through silvery, foaming darkness from which he could scarcely be distinguished, even by the rider! His sides were coated with foam. He was very old and had a sagging back, a scrappy mane, a knotted tail, a short breath. Light as a spirit, he moved with me, his eyes protruding and strained by the excitement. I heard, like a door opening on rusted hinges, the raspings of his heart as we turned and turned in all directions following the movements of an imaginary polo ball which he could see before I saw it, for it was the reflection of the moon. He was controlled only by the actions of my knees. I laughed aloud, chasing the ball. We rode through vocal darkness beaten upon by the far sobbing of white-lipped waves.

We rode down dark alleys which, even in daylight, the sunlight had never penetrated. We passed the burned and stunted spruce trees, the orchards of crab apple trees, the untended kitchen gardens, the turreted stable with its old wheels and carriage bodies and pieces of broken furniture, the paddocks where were broken torsos and marble heads lying in the grass, the grassy tennis courts with their faded marquees and dragging nets like fishnets and ghostly players like swans running back and forth in the moonlight, the many fountains which made a splashing music under the loud music of the sea, the old gargoyles with livid eyes and many chins. We rode around and around on a path that made a circle like an eye through the garden of the blind.

Oh, how startled Mr. Spitzer would be if he could see me now, I could not help thinking, if he could see me, Vera Cartwheel, who had escaped all those old people and arid phantoms, my hair between my teeth like a comedian's mustache, my polo hat cocked back at a jaunty angle, my riding crop, a bare branch lifted in my hand as Falada and I charged through the moon-lit night, swifter than wind, almost as if the little black pony were winged. It was a steeplechase, and we would jump over all the church steeples and ride with the seagulls in the wind. I was a bareback rider, wearing a plume, a pair of pink tights, doing all kinds of wonderful tricks. Falada could dance on his hind feet. He was a great waltzer and loved the music of Mozart. He wore no saddle, and yet the rider did not part from the horse even when we soared, soared over the stars and the clouds and a tiny city and train lights far away. I brought Falada to a slower pace as we dragged through the long grass wet as velvet tongues licking against my legs, the wiry bushes scratching as if their spikes were rusted nails, the wild flowers steaming and billowing around the pony's feet, the wet, streaming leaves. I lay on Falada's back with my arms around his bony, pulsing neck with its long, straining tendons and my face against his diseased, withered mane with its dust mop feathers. His heart was pounding and his sides sweated, but his nose was as cold as frost. I whispered, into his drooping ear, my deepest secrets—how I had no mother and was an orphan, how I had never known my father, how Miss MacIntosh was an old witch who kept me enchained in a dark tower, how I had escaped her domination. Pink was my favorite color, and strawberry was my favorite ice, and I was going to have seven stairstep children with long blonde hair. But I had not yet met my husband, the man who would ask me for my hand.

Falada and I took the low hedges. We cantered past the melancholy potato fields, desolate as the landscape of another planet, marsh reeds at the moon-lit edge through which there were the dulled gleamings of indefinite, brackish pools like eyes.

How kind, how considerate of Mr. Spitzer to have given to me, for another birthday, Falada! He was my rose, my heart, my love. So light was he that he moved as if he were magic. He was almost only an idea of a horse, Mr. Spitzer had said, and in his youth this prince of equines had served as a model for merry-go-round horses because of his grace in keeping all fours off the earth at once when he was in a canter or jumping a hedge, such as now we jumped. When we jumped, it seemed as if his life increased. He was very old and tired and wind-broken, easily winded, just as Mr. Spitzer had carefully explained, yet still had a spark of life in him like the sparks now in his dish eyes, the starlight gleaming in splotches on his sides, the stars like sudden shoals of fireflies breaking around his feet, breaking like milky pods and winged spores as big as marbles and seeds of burning light, and had been sent to Mr. Spitzer by someone who had admired Mr. Spitzer's brother and who had not known, naturally, that Mr. Spitzer's brother was dead, no longer a member of the horse circles, or so Mr. Spitzer must presume, and he had given Falada to me that he might enjoy a peaceful retirement. Mr. Spitzer had thought that Falada might live for many years, that he might always accompany me, live with me—and surely, I had taken excellent care of this little horse. I had combed his hair with a jeweled silver comb and brushed him with a jeweled silver brush which, tarnished by age and the dews of the grave, had belonged to a beautiful dead lady now sleeping in her marble tomb, and he had looked into a little hand mirror where he had seen perhaps his clouded face and eyes with long eyelashes and perhaps the gleamings of a moth with dew upon its wings, and I had tied blue ribbons upon his tail, and I had told him all my secrets, secrets which even I had never known until I spoke them, for I often did not know what I thought until I heard myself speaking the words. I was frightened when sometimes, though whispering, I heard my voice shouting among the stars.

It occurred to me now that Falada was old and tired and that he was the kind of horse who might sleep on a gold divan, rock in a rocking chair, look at himself in the life-sized cheval glass trembling toward the clouded ceiling—that he might be, I thought, as much at home in a house as in the star-lit night, the out-of-doors. For the night was cold and damp and dank and dark. Mr. Spitzer, believing that it was necessary to know a horse's pedigree, had made the most careful inquiries as to this little black flyer with the star upon his nose. Falada, with his light grace, was descended, Mr. Spitzer believed, from the horse which had inspired not only the jewel-studded horses of the merry-go-round, not only the carousel—he had inspired also the cabriole, the furniture of good Queen Anne's day, whole forests of Chippendale, tables and chairs and divans with curved legs and ornamental feet such as might be seen today in the best Boston houses. Mr. Spitzer believed that this was why, among old-fashioned gentlemen wearing snowy perukes like caps of snow and modest, bewigged ladies wearing hoop skirts and blushing behind their feather fans, the legs of a chair were referred to as the limbs. The name of this horse, Falada, had accompanied this horse when it was sent to Mr. Spitzer, and this was a fact for which he was very grateful, for it seemed to him that the name of a horse was important as the name of a man, and he never had held with those who believe that a rose by any other name would smell as sweet. What was in a name? All things were in their names, Mr. Spitzer believed. He, of course, had paid for the bill of freight, for though the horse was small, it had come from a long way. He had forgotten the name of the sender.

Falada, Mr. Spitzer had later ascertained, was the name of the horse in an old Arabic fairy tale which had its parallels in many countries, in many ages, Falada being that horse whose head was cut off and nailed above the city gates and whose head, after its death, had spoken to the people. This horse's head had spoken oracles and parables to the people passing through the gates. He had spoken secrets and perhaps was speaking now.

We turned toward the sleeping, shrouded house. Falada was very difficult to manage, going his own way, going so fast that he seldom needed a spur and never needed a whip, for he turned with my desire. We turned into the shadow of the great sprawling house, the angular shadows of gables, towers, steeples, weathercocks outlined on the grass, the clouds with their stars, gleamings of stained glass windows. We came to the marble-pillared doorway which was like the portico to a tomb containing some vast population of which all the members would never be known. We passed the sleeping marble lions which had once guarded the palace of a Venetian doge who long ago had joined the world of water. As in a dream we passed through the interior courts where were the mosaic emperors like the faces of old playing cards. We passed the kings with the triple crowns. We passed the black funeral gondola in the interior fountain, the long-nosed stone dolphins which were visible in the thin flow of water, the fishes winged like birds, the sea horses, the small Triton, the great mother-of-pearl mollusk which might have contained the form of Venus. And now we were passing under the thin spray of ethereal foam, foam like an arch so that I thought I should be carrying an umbrella. I should be the umbrella medusa rising to the surface. Was this a water castle, this with its gleamings of moon silver and gold and great stone boats at the bottom of the sea and garlanded candle flames blurred like underwater flowers and so many half-visible colors and forms, curtains drifting like water over me? We passed through curtains of crystal beads palely drifting as if from the phosphorescent clouds, each crystal gleaming with interior fire as if water were the coffin of fire. We passed the phoenix outlined in jewels above the great stone fireplace reaching to a roof of ruby glass, the phoenix rising from those cold ashes of the dream. We passed the empty tomb of some old musician who had gone to join the world of music, the tomb which was a gold grand piano upheld by cherubim pallbearers with folded wings wading through a musical fountain. But where there was only this world of water, there was no sound, for water muffled the sound of water. Water knew no echo. I was surprised to see a mammoth swan among the shadows—then suddenly remembered that it was lead and weighed three hundred pounds. It was as heavy as leaden water, as leaden bells. We passed the effigy of a sleeping marble boy lying on his tomb with a marble book opened in his hand and marble rose petals upon its pages and his marble dog sleeping at his feet. No one knew whether there had ever been an occupant of this tomb.

We climbed the marble stairway carpeted with purple velvet which muffled every sound and which, reaching up and up, was wide enough for a span of seven vast white horses climbing through clouds as if they had just come from the shells of mollusks. I would have sworn I felt a snowflake whirling against my cheek. I would have sworn I was hit by a hailstone. There was no sound but of many-colored crystal prisms moving as we moved, moving in a stream of wind. We passed the dim tapestries of angelic beings in golden cuirasses on fields of washed-out blue, angels blowing golden horns, angels riding long white dogs, roses in the cheeks of men, angels who restored sight to the blind and hearing to the deaf. We passed the stuffed elks, the velvet ravens on the velvet boughs, the stuffed lute birds, the dead children's sleighs with their rusted sleigh bells moving in the wind, the family portraits framed by golden frames. We might almost have passed into the dreaming landscape of some faded wall-hanging where the shepherd plays his flute to the sleeping shepherdess. We made of ourselves no sound. We might have been a pair of moths.

Perhaps I should have called on my mother who was entertaining her imaginary guests, I had no doubt—or who might be submerged so deep in her dreams that no one knew what she thought. Perhaps at the deepest level there were no dreams. Perhaps she was rising to the surface and seeing visions, beings so strange that no one else might ever see them—and so I dared not visit her, dared not confront her with horse and rider dancing in her bedroom for fear that, if she knew that we were real, she would become hysterical and pull the bellropes, and there would be a ding and a dong and a bell through all the rooms of the great, many-chambered house. She might even disturb the sea shells sleeping on the beach, the shell which was the great turbaned Turk, the phaeton, the winding stairway—or little fish sleepers among the reeds under the waves. All things might suddenly come to life. She might think we were phantoms, of course, and then we would be safe. If we were phantoms, she would not be afraid—fearing us no more than if she saw a centaur rising from the sea or a flock of city pigeons coming out of Mr. Spitzer's high silk hat. But if we were real, she might die of shock. I could not take the risk. So we climbed another stair or star, whirling star. We passed without a moment's hesitation to that far wing of the house where we should find one who was real, one who was plain—Miss MacIntosh who, though she might condemn us, would know that we were real. Indeed, I scarcely guided Falada, his light footsteps clattering on stone and ivory and wood. He seemed to know the way, and I could not help laughing. He seemed to be my head, my intelligence. I was the headless rider.

Falada pushed with his leaf nose against the plain wooden door of Miss MacIntosh's bedroom. I leaned forward, ready to turn the white china knob which was painted with a spider's web, but the door, which was usually locked and barred from the inside, was creakingly opening of itself, and in we charged, horse and rider charging like a whirlwind, the bare branch lifted in my hand. I rode Falada in. His hooves clattering against the uncarpeted floor, his head lifting, he snorted as if he saw some unexpected obstacle or hazard, a drifting oak leaf which distracted his vision, a blown newspaper, a veil blowing in the wind. He whinnied, and his whinnying was like my laughter, like the crying of a bird. It was all darkness, however, except for the scalloped bedspread, cold as snow, and two moonbeams cutting like a pair of large, rusted garden shears across the space where Miss MacIntosh stood by the tall, white-curtained windows.

I shall never forget the way she looked, that first impression made upon a youthful mind—never, though I live a million years and have as many husbands as Solomon had wives. She had greatly changed since last I had seen her, and she was unbelievably not herself, and yet—how was it that I recognized her instantly as if she were something I had always dimly known, and the shock of this knowledge was but the affirmation of some older shock which had been forgotten and laid over by the autumn leaves, the snow falling, the first buds of spring?

CHAPTER 17

Miss MacIntosh stood by the blowing curtains, the tall windows, a figure dimly seen, her corset stays sticking out like the quills of an angry porcupine, or were those the rays of the moonlight? Where her head should be, there was another moon, cold and dented and shining, seeming to float upon the waves of corrugated darkness. I could not see her head but only that dim dome like some enormous ivory ball such as perhaps a god should play with, but only her body which was more angular than curved, the body of a weird wrestler ready to meet with the opponent at a single move, the muscles protruding, the skin taut and gleaming in the moonlight as if she stood beyond a wall of water, her metallic corset supporters gleaming like the eyes of a fish seen through a dark, translucent wave. It seemed as if her eyes were misplaced, as if her head were down where her knees should be. Falada, his ears cocked, did not move. There was no sound but of heavy breathing, the white curtains blowing, unfurling like white wings, the wind blowing through empty corridors and lanes. There was no other sound but, against the moon-streaked window glass, the faint tappings of a spectral branch. She might have been, wrapped in this vast expanse of whiteness, a figure of a tomb, something old and timeless, and yet she moved, her arm lifted as I watched, the instant seeming the hour, that zero hour, the hour of midnight when strangest things do often happen and leave us mad. My hair crawled against my cheeks. Great drops of dew stood out upon my forehead, cold as a frog, and I could not find my voice, and I could not hear my heart beating. It seemed as if my eyes were frozen in my head, as if I were entombed in fields of everlasting ice, and mountains rose above me, their peaks lost in clouds. I heard, far off, the shriekings of some distorted seagull, the moaning of waves against a shore which was never this shore. She moved, her arm lifted, a branch of foam. She stepped out from behind the curtain which, blowing like a shroud or torn sail, had concealed her head, and I saw her head, that great dome, that sphere devoid of being, saw that there was something missing from the mortal woman, that all was not right, for she was bald. She was bald as the egg or as the rock where nothing grows. She had no hair on her head, no hair at all, not one hair to cast its shadow, and her face was as absolutely impersonal and expressionless as a face may be and still be human, and she was this monster moving toward me in the darkness. Who was she? Her beautiful hair was gone as of one terrible blow, some sudden shock or amazement or illness, I had no doubt, for she had changed so greatly since last I had seen her, since she had said good-night when she stood at the foot of my bed talking of love and of life and of reproduction, and now she was this ghostly stranger moving toward me, her eyes standing out like striped marbles as she moved through beams of broken moonlight, her head cold and sweating, a great mirror where one should see one's self if one looked closely and did not lose one's mind and fade into unconsciousness, but I was ready to faint away and be dead rather than endure this terrifying vision of a woman who was bald and shorn and naked in the moonlight and in the shadow, too, the checkered shadows blowing. From whence came my courage? I could not endure for one moment longer this spell, and I must break it, at all odds, even though it meant that I should meet my death in this unexpected way, at this very height of life. I waited, breathless, Falada himself not moving.

Who was this woman in the darkness, her face uplifted, her hands crossed against the flatness of her breasts? She was bald, coldly, stonily bald, with goose pimples on top of her head which seemed out of all proportion to her body, and she was this monstrous stranger, but yet I knew her by her broken nose and something that was definite in her manner, something suggesting the intimacies forgotten. She was not herself, certainly, seeming suddenly, irrevocably changed. She was someone else and moving toward me with an attitude of strange, fearful beseechment in the darkness crossed by moonlight as if, of course, she was familiar to me, and she had known me for years, and we were certainly old friends who had played at many a quiet game of dominoes under the storm lamp when the waves leaped high, many a game of battledore and shuttlecock. There floated through my mind, even at that long-drawn instant, a parable or a proverb repeating itself as in a dream—perhaps that the mountains shall never meet with the mountains, perhaps that you shall praise the bridge that carried you, perhaps that man is not born to happiness and is a bubble.

I should have been less surprised to see old pharaohs voyaging to heaven upon clouds of incense or buffeted by hailstones in their long voyage from this world to the next, an identical world, one with the same lakes and swans and mountains! I resisted what I saw, the knowledge that this was my friend. Scarcely without thinking of the past, therefore, and its changed significance, a different face which now was put on everything, a different light, I refused to accept the simple explanation which I myself proposed, refused to believe that she had not changed, that only I had changed, that she was still herself entirely and without flaw, the same plainly sensible woman she had always been, for she was also this phantasmagoric being who loomed before my eyes, this visible stranger, jagged and broken, bald and bare as the naked rock lashed by waves, the most pitiful example I had ever seen of human nature. There was not a marsh reed, not a tuft of the wild broom grass. She was bald as the rose stripped of all its petals, as bare as the winter winds blowing over the

Arctic Circle. Where was her red, shining hair, tawny as an August sun-set, and where were her sun-lit or shadowed eye-glasses, her eye-glasses like dark pools or pools of light, and where was her black umbrella, and where was her Pilgrim's Progress? Was this that same plainly visible woman I had always known, counting her stitches, slipping her stitches from one ivory-boned knitting needle to another, going back to pick up, unless she was distracted by a blow of wind or ripple of surf or fluttering shadow, the lost stitch before her hands moved rapidly forward again? Better it had been King Magnus, the fleshless being! Now I saw what, at that instant of sweeping revelation, it seemed that I had always dimly seen, in some far, hidden corner of my mind—that she had never been herself at all but someone else, this appalling apparition clothed with flesh and blood which should fade, and yet I knew her, for who knows not the grinning skull? I knew her by her polished, glossy, sudden bald-ness which, though it surprised me, making my hair stand on end and the chill wind creep down my spinal column, making me shake like ivory-keyed music from head to foot, yet should have surprised me equally if it had not been true, if in another instant I had seen that all had been an error of my own perceptions or that I was this lost soul. She was other than herself, and she had deceived me, I felt now, with that long knowl-edge which could have come only from a vast experience—that all during the years of my acquaintance with her, she had been pulling the wool over my eyes, and she was the bald pretender, she whom I encountered now in her own bedroom, she who now approached me, her arm lifted, drifting like some pale plume upon the darkness. Where was her strength? She seemed so frail, almost an indistinction, something which, after all, could not possibly be there, and yet I heard her heavy breath-ing, the sharp intake of breath, a rasping sound. She was even perhaps that old, lurking rapist she had so often warned me of, some Irish hooli-gan or drunken sailor who had reeled through miles of mists and fogs, and I laughed aloud, feeling no pity for her but only a kind of wild triumph that I had been right, all along, in visualizing her with a red, curled mustache, that I had been right in assigning to her the role of the bridegroom, that she was certainly never the bride blushing behind a veil of gossamer, her cheeks rosy with the wonder of being given away. She was only this old man who had only one breast and no hair and no future prospect. Her baldness gave her away, coldly and utterly. She was as cold as a codfish swept up upon a barren shore. I laughed, though I should have cried, the shrill winds screaming, too, and the sea birds screaming at some far horizon, and waves rising and sobbing with the intuition of some devastating thing which might take place, for nature often foresees that which man cannot foresee, man being as if blind.

"Miss MacIntosh, you are a man!" I screamed cruelly, though had I stopped to think, I might have been silent and might have stayed my hand, for I was not so serious-minded as I seemed. It was a horse ballet, a Spanish carousel with many mirrors, many horses, many riders. It was the realization of a dream, and like all realizations, it had brought with it both that which was expected and the unforeseen, the unforeseeable nothing which changes everything and stops us in the midst of our laughter or makes us laugh with joy when we are filled with tears. My ecstasy knew, however, still no bounds, and I was ready to plunge into whatever abyss lay ahead and ask no questions of this night until long years afterward, perhaps when I was old and grey and had no other occupation but to search through memory, asking the why, the wherefore, composing, recomposing, finding perhaps no answer. I laughed, Falada leaping like my own excitement, Falada pawing the empty air or only white, whirling branches through which shone the brassy-edged clouds and that cold, dented disc, the moon, dimly radiant but distant, invulnerable to our assault, the moon which draws the waves in its wake and has no life of its own. I was going to jump through Miss MacIntosh's steel embroidery hoops now, in actuality, though they should encircle the sky, for she was the ring-master—if only she had worn her high silk hat, such as mourners wear at funerals, if only it had been a dream like the others, a dream from which I should awaken. What shall we do when, fleeing from illusion, we are confronted by illusion? When falling from illusion, we fall into illusion? Have we not deceived ourselves? Where was the real world? Where was Miss MacIntosh, an old nursemaid and true and severe, the last person to deceive herself or others?

What next? Borne along by some will which seemed not my will, determined to vanquish this phantom, this bald pretender who had no business in Miss MacIntosh's bedroom, did I strike at Miss MacIntosh first with my riding crop, that bare, unflowering branch lifted in my bony hand, or did she strike at me, dragging me down from my proud height of vision which should be the vision of nothing, or almost nothing? There was then, though it has faded now in significance and seems less important than one rose which canker shall not eat or one door which shall not open to our knocking, our physical encounter in the darkness and the light, my head whirling with new agony, and I was borne along by mighty wings, and yet my feet had struck the bedroom floor, and yet I struggled against this unknown, bald opponent who surprised me with his strength, his amazing biceps and muscular expansion and chest expansion, his perfect control, the left jab which annoys, hurts, and stings, the straight right. My head gonged like a bell, and still our unequal battle continued, even though my blows were as feeble as those of the moth striking against light. I went down to my knees, still striking against an object that could not possibly be there, one which was certainly all my imagination, for no blow of mine could have caused the blood upon that other face, the skull broken, the eyes blackened like burned-out holes. There was surely, I told myself, some deviation from the laws of nature, and that deviation should be the law. There was such brightness shining in my eyes that I could not see an inch before my nose, and my head roared in brightness which might have been the utter darkness, and my body seemed divided as if now there were two of us, one who fought, one who lay still and watched it all. The stars fell like dried seed pods upon a dark and barren plain, a desert of salt and stone.

Myriads of dark horsemen thundered against a sky in which there was but one dark cloud extending from pole to pole. There was one beam of searching light, and then there was none as I felt my head roaring again like the whirlwind itself, and blow after blow was still delivered—the rabbit punch which cracks against the base of the skull, the upward punch which thrusts upward to the heart, the Sunday punch, that which is given under the ideal condition for the victor. We wrestled, caught in an everlasting clinch, my long hair streaming across my forehead, and I could not see my enemy, and I had forgotten who he was. There was nothing but the blackness like a wave, the premonition of death, and yet I wondered, even as my consciousness faded, going out like a light—who was this mad being who had come to life in Miss MacIntosh's bedroom —was it some fallen angel, some livid creature of the deep, or was it the angel of light, such light as blinded my eyes and made me cry out even now for my mother? Where was my mother that she did not rescue me from this old, bald-headed man closing my mouth with his hoary hand, lifting me up from the floor, laying me out upon his bed, the bed of death or something which might be worse? Where was Mr. Spitzer? He was gone from Boston to Boston.

Who then was this massive, ruthless combatant dealing such skillful and decisive blows, even when I lay still, staring at ambiguities which were far distant from my present situation—for surely, it could not be Miss MacIntosh who held me with her arms piniored against my back, my limbs rigid as if my spirit had departed like a breath? Surely, it must be someone who did not exist, someone preternatural who should take advantage of a poor, ignorant girl, only fourteen years old, just when the whole future had opened before her, I remember—surely, it could not be Miss MacIntosh, the guardian spirit who thus assaulted me and lifted me high and laid me low? We travelled so fast. Where were we going? We travelled so slow, I could hear the bangings of the window shutters, the creakings of the oldest weathercocks. It must be, I reasoned, even as my consciousness faded into my consciousness, someone else who had assaulted me, dealing such a thunder shower of blows now scarcely felt, stripping the tulips from the tulip trees, the roses from the midnight bush, perhaps some ancient Sumerian or Greek wrestler or Roman gladiator who should astonish the world, perhaps a Christian knight in armor charging against the Turks and the heathens, someone who wore a breastplate and upheld a shining spear, someone who wore a jumbo corset whale-boned and girded like a tired battleship coming victoriously into port with all its chimneys blackened and its streamers streaming like corset strings and all hands dead on the upper deck, perhaps even that holy angel with whom Jacob struggled at Peniel. Perhaps it was a reindeer. Perhaps, I reasoned, my consciousness slipping like a train through an airless mountain tunnel, it was no one, after all, but the sandbag dummy come to life, he who bled, he who dealt the rabbit punch, the sickly final blow, the left hook over my right shoulder, he who was the southpaw, the north, the east, the west, he who was the arms of the compass, the animation, the shadow boxer moving with such rapidity that his blows were impossible to block. He met with me on each horizon.

There was no use, my screaming and crying, my wailings and gnashings of teeth, my battle with pillows and curtains, for none should hear me, and a great hand was pressed against my mouth, a hand as implausible as death which one may sense and yet not judge. There was no one near me but this bald opponent whose surface was so smooth that it evaded touch and was an icy peak. It touched me, but I could not touch it, and my numbness was like the anesthesia provided by nature before she strikes her final blow which shall be followed by another. I was conquered, feeling my hair pulled out by handfuls, though there was no pain in this but only my sense of distant, speculative wonder that I should be snatched bald, that I should be bald, too, in the light of the cruel dawn, a creature robbed of her feminine beauty, her ravishing powers of illusion, and I should have to hide my head as if it were some terrible mistake, God's error—even though, the next morning, of course, my long braids were exactly braided down my back, and there were no scratches upon my cheeks but those which might have been made by leafless branches.

CHAPTER 18

WHAT next? That night's passage, unlike any night before or afterward, that when I was confronted by the phantom of change, phantom which had seemed fixed, the flesh and blood and nothing else, nothing escaping definition. Then what was done that crucial night, and what escapes now the verbal memory, memory which, though it may seem all-inclusive and final, is always moving toward something else, the something which cannot be put into our paltry language and which is so very simple and clear that no one can utter it except by infinite winding and winding among those subtle complications providing more complications, mysteries begetting only further mysteries, questions which can have no answer but the void where we are not? Memory is surrounded by the unknown, the void, and there is so much that we have not heard, much that we have not seen. Memory sometimes provides the one flower more than ever blossomed. Memory sometimes omits the only flower there really was.

I am not sure now that Miss MacIntosh, who had been at dinner that red-headed, plain nursemaid and at midnight was bald and naked, having no hair to cover her, not even one poor feather of pretense, I am not sure now that Miss MacIntosh did say all I remember her as saying in that night's passage when nothing seemed certain, not even that the night should ever end. Perhaps, in retrospection, every lost event must be changed by the illumination larger than that of any instant, larger than life. We can never see an old face as new, not even though we look upon it with new eyes. There is no new experience which shall not have emerged from the old. There is no surprise but of our own slow-wittedness, our own failures in understanding that the thing was always present.

I was taken, that night, by quick surprise, though yet like some angelic demon this thing seemed also to have emerged from the depths of my own consciousness, an image which had already haunted, perhaps unperceived, perhaps dimly seen, the chambers of the mind, an image which had already followed like a cold shadow through all the ins and outs of thought, this phantom of change which was the flesh and blood, the fixed, the true. That night, the curtain of illusion had been stripped away, it seemed, even as if the illusion were the only reality, and our self-deception was the only rose. That night, I was confronted suddenly by the forlorn something which had been hidden like that in everyone's heart which no one dares to face, the knowledge that each must wear a mask which screens him from himself and pushes him farther and farther away into the reaches of the imperial darkness, the knowledge that the external world we take for granted is but insubstantial as a mad man's dream, all we know or shall ever know, and we are always bald when we are robbed of our illusions, and we know not who we are or where, for we were only these and always fading.

I heard the curtains blowing, the shutters banging, the weathercocks creaking to their own rusted music, a strange and mournful concert of which the score was never written and was lost in that night's passage. I heard quick, definite footsteps moving, and surely it was a familiar sound as when, in dark or sun-lit days, Miss MacIntosh would walk back and forth during our lessons, and I heard her hands slapping against her sides as when she had used to keep up her circulation, as she would say, and ward off death. All the while, however, there was also this other Miss MacIntosh, this fearful man who had lifted me on to his bed and whose bald, furrowed head loomed above me like a skull, the eyes missing from the eyeholes. There was this great shell like a mollusk or coffin with loose hinges and filled with the roarings of the sea, opening, closing in the darkness. Would that my lover had been a man! It was neither man nor woman but some angelic demon, the flesh and blood with features missing, with senses missing, and yet with something more than sense had provided. It was almost nothing, and it was more than the whole world besides, though then I could not realize this thing as I would come to realize it in the after-years. The lover who had emerged was surely no man but only such a man as is hidden in the woman, just as there must also be, in every man, a woman secret and recessive, the forever fading image of the other self, the lost soul, one who combs her long gold hair upon the rock, one whose body is scaled with silver scales gleaming through fog and tide, one too beautiful ever to have reached the shores of mortal life, one who trembles on the margin of heaven or hell, she who may be seen only in the tremblings of broken intuitions, she who fades away and yet is always present in the darkness and in the light. This now looming above me, this was surely the secret man. The secret man was he who held me pinioned in his mighty arms, his limbs too strong to fight against, he whose voice I heard, gruff yet familiar, crying out as if above the storm of life, crying out even when there was no other sound but of the cross-beams creaking, the winds blowing through empty chambers so that the house seemed swollen with music, the waves white-lipped and sobbing for all ghostly things.

Who was that old rapist if not Miss MacIntosh, she who had warned me against him, that he might be loping through purple fog where there should be no ear to hear my crying? Who else could it be but Miss MacIntosh, an old nursemaid who had been very plain, her eyes protruding and purple as a rabbit's—whose but her enormous head, looming above me in the foggy darkness, that head which was chalk-colored as the dead moon which draws, in collaboration with all the planets, the spring tide in its wake, the waters piling high in quiet bays—whose but her amorphous forehead, forever sloping upward like a snow-topped peak— whose, that lifted shoulder cold as snow and sharp as ice at some high altitude—whose, that hand pressed heavily upon my mouth—whose, that knee driving against my ribs—whose, that heart which pounded, vast and resounding as the hammer of heaven upon the anvil of earth? Whose, those pointed ears in the starlight? Whose, that voice crying out with broken cryings, heavy as the drag of the undertow, then high and thin like a lost sea bird screaming above clouds in a world of water, the timbre changing so that there seemed two voices?

Sometimes near, sometimes far, that voice crying, moaning like a fog-horn, "Oh, how ephemeral are we! Oh, how transient were we, my child! The earth has known us not. Our mothers and our fathers never knew us. Watchman, what of the night? Who goes there?" That bald, scarred head floating above me, pillowed on waves of darkness, those blank eyes star-ing at the void sky, the stars eclipsed, those eyes filled then with light which came from no reflection, no searching beam, that forehead without brows or hairline, that peak cloud-topped, that viewless summit! Some-times I nearly swooned away, and at others, my consciousness was ex-tended to the breaking point, even as I heard, in the midst of this great strangeness which was the departure from the feathered security of the past, familiar statements repeating themselves as if all were normal, as if everything were in its fixed, accustomed place, as if even this bald head, smooth and hard as a billiard ball, should be an apparent, familiar thing, eliciting no comment from those who knew it best and had always lived with it. That head which was now so cold, for the first time touching mine! The old foghorn voice, the voice that had often changed to thin and high, the nasal twanging, the clearing of the throat! Those false teeth clicking, clicking like old bones or dice in the wind, should I not recognize even in a dream? How could I live through a night which would never pass? Who now should save me? Had I not lost my mind, even at the first blow of fateless fate? Who now destroyed my body? Was this love, or was this death?

"Dead men tell no tales." I heard that hoarse, pained voice scraping, "and I am dead, wrapped in this house of clay, these mortal vestments! Thus did sparrows fall. God pity us. God pity the small fishes and the great whales beached on this beach.

"God pity my right arm! God pity my left! The left breast is already gone. God pity the stars, the moon, the empty places, the uncreated, the created! Oh, where's my old heart? Oh, where's my hair?" I tried to break loose again, but those arms held me fast, and this voice moaned with awful resonance in my ear, "First things come first. Ladies before gentle-men. Oh, plunge me in the purple flood, that I may lose myself in thine! Oh, bear the sinner up! Oh, wash our sins away and leave us white as snow! Oh, where's What Cheer, Iowa, and where are my eye-glasses, for the fog is blowing in my eyes?" Where, I wondered, were the cherry blossoms and crab apple blossoms blowing like surf, the sumac trailing the grey fences, and where were the green fields, and where were the happy children? Where was Miss MacIntosh, her red hair gleaming in the sunset?

I cried, but my voice was not heard, and there was no other person but Miss MacIntosh, her head as cold and bald as the moon sweating in the murky darkness, the grey, swollen fog heavy as the sea.

Surely, I thought, Miss MacIntosh it was. Surely, I thought, Miss MacIntosh it was whom I should have always feared, and I was harrowed now by fears greater than if I had never known her before, greater than if I did not recognize, even at the edge of oblivion, certain of her features and her characteristics which had seemed so much a part of her person-ality in the light of day, that hers was that breath which rasped like a rusted hinge, that hers was that knob where the breast was missing, that hers was that strong right arm against which my feeble blow should be as powerless as if it struck now the invulnerable air. That head curving upward forever, no brow, no brow that was high, no brow that was low, none that was middle, no ledge, no limitations, a surface greater than eyes should encompass. I screamed and tried to die, fighting with shad-ows, with surfaces which were not.

"Unfold yourself," she cried, her voice as stern as it had often been before. "Do not resist. Struggle no more, for it is useless, and it would not be common sense, my dear. Be silent as the corpse. Each must lose the last battle. Each much lose, in fact, the first, as I have often told you, so let us not give away to surprise, for it was always so, and it was never any different. This earth is but the poor testing ground for the king rail with the bleeding throat, for the paper nautilus torn by wind, the horseshoe crab broken by surf, the dead clam, and all oxen are our brothers. Oh, ephemeral are we," she cried, her voice rising, thin and high as the dream of ethereal surf which reaches no shore, "and we shall pass as the small birds, the leaves, the grass, the snow, and we shall leave no trace which can be followed. Only the worm is clothed, and the worm is our little brother, and our own mothers shall not know us. Our nakedness is God's nakedness."

My head roaring, I heard her say, her voice as male as something I might have dreamed in a young girl's dream of love, "One kiss is all I ever asked, and that was never given. Where is Issachar, my dear, my dear of dears? Where is Reuben? Where is Nabal? Where is Mr. Spitzer? Where, oh, where's Miss MacIntosh, that old fool we used to see here? No fool like an old fool! My skull is laughing. Out, out, brief candle! Man was but a shadow and a breath. Where are my knitting needles? Where's my heart? Locate the left breast."

Those false teeth clacking like a pair of weird castanets, everything whirling around me, old playing cards, suns and moons and stars!

"God help us all," she cried, pushing against my shoulder, greaves of brass upon her legs, a target of brass between her shoulders, her spear like a weaver's beam of solid oak, her helmet shining. "One leak sinks a ship, and one sin sinks a sinner, and we are sinking far from any shore." God help us! All hands were lost—that grave voice moaning—all heads like meteors in the wind. Our sails were burning. The islands sank like the great continents. We should be found as missing when the roll was called up yonder, when the countless stars were counted, and God Himself should not know us, and our own parents should not know us. "Child, we are sinned against more than we are sinning. I can go no farther. God pity the withering of the right arm, the left! Oh, who am I, what shepherd? I am the lamb, the fleeced lamb. God pity the heart which beats no more! God pity Miss MacIntosh and Mr. Spitzer and all who died!

"Clubs are trumps," that low voice cried, hollow and empty, the nostrils flaring, the eyes lighted with an unholy light. "Luck is for the few, but death is for the many. Long ago, I died and was not buried. Never married, never buried. An old man's love is a young maid's sorrow, and so I always told you. The bald head is soonest shaved. I never denied it. No grass grows on a busy street." Her bald head touching against mine, her cheeks sweating, her forehead cold as cracked and frozen marble. "Child, have you lost your senses? What do you imagine? Nothing that you think is happening is happening! Nothing that you think is true is true. Nothing that you see is real!" She shook my shoulders. Her bare knee bone scraped against my knee. "It is all a dream, a poor man's dream," her voice common and flat, "and it was always this, but you were living in a fool's paradise, and now you know there is no answer.

"Heaven's nets are woven very wide," her voice drifting and high as if she were far away, "but none shall escape them. You shall not escape them. We each must die and know that this life was all a dream, and there was nothing. Oh, where was my hair? Oh, where was my love?" Oh, where had she taken her constitutional, and where was her black umbrella, and where were her sea boots, and where was her faded plaid which she had worn buttoned at the chin, and where was her fishnet bag with her Pilgrim's Progress and a loaf of bread for the seagulls, and where was that old Miss MacIntosh whom I had always known, an old, red-headed nursemaid spouting proverbs? "What bitter pill is this!" she cried. "Would I deflower the rose, I who am the last rose of the last summer on earth? God loves you! God loves the wind, the empty places. There is no God." There was no God, but the true lover remembers everything, and the true love is that which does not alter when it alteration finds. The true love wears an old shirt and is familiar. "Do you remember me," she asked, "Miss MacIntosh, poor soul, God's poorest creature who worked here for her living and whose shirts and skirts you ironed? Did you not know me? Will you know me when you see me again? If you have seen me every day and do not know me now, how will you know me in the future? Ah, there will be no future. There was no past."

There was no use, my groaning, my flailing, my trying to struggle against an antagonist who took so many forms and yet had none and was this surface without depth and was as bald as the skull uncovered, the naked rock, the crumbling tower. Perhaps, however, the lack of deception is always another deception. I am not sure now that Miss MacIntosh did say all I remember her as saying, though I heard her voice bellowing above me, and we seemed to be riding in the icy wind, and we passed through many a starry ring in unknown skies, and we plunged from abyss to abyss, yet did not lose our balance. I am not sure that, when Miss MacIntosh put a feather pillow over my head and sat with her long legs like those dulled garden shears cutting into my sides, she really did tell me to jump a fence, trot, get down on my knees, eat meadow grass and wild flowers, dream no more, for we ourselves were the dream, the rider and the horse. These would have been, under the circumstances, facetious remarks, as if I myself had become Falada, as if she were now the rider, her face pale and drifting, a skull that rode upon a cloud.

No, indeed, it was only Miss MacIntosh I saw again, Miss MacIntosh who gave me something to remember all my life, the heavy, claw-shaped mark of her hand upon my forehead.

"There, that will teach you to remember me," she said, wiping my foaming mouth with a wet cloth. "There, that will teach you—oh, I hope—charity."

Ever since, in a moment of extreme revelation when I have seen that people are not exactly what they have seemed to be, I have tried to be charitable, not only for their sakes but as a retribution for my cruelty to my darling who had seemed so very plain. For I had been cruel to her, and I had discovered her essential baldness.

After our physical encounter and struggle and her triumph, perhaps we both were crying like two children in the streaked darkness that was cold and sad and unhuman. Perhaps there were only my own cries I heard. Had I truly lost my mind? Was I only some poor sleepwalker who had stumbled upon this dreadful thing, the secret of another, the lonely secret? How should I face her in the morning light again, or should all things be as they had been, oblivion covering over this bald head?

She scolded gently. She tried to talk reason to me, even there where I lay in the crook of her old arm, staring with wild unreason at the head which still was bald, the bald head where nothing grew and which seemed to have no character of its own. Her voice was plaintively intimate and reassuring, but I knew even then that this dear intimacy could never last, and I was as disappointed already as when one looks back upon a faded dream evading final description or definition, yet seductive through its very evasiveness, and seeming more of the future than of the past. The dream is never complete. The dream is always partial, even when it is whole. There are certain features missing, others only vaguely sensed—and something new arises through their absence. And in this case, the dream was a goal toward which all headed, but I had already outdistanced it, and I was looking back upon that which would be another's future—or so I felt, staring at the essential baldness of one creature.

Under our interlocked bodies, the aged bedsprings creaked like the distraught music of the errant weathervanes, and there were white sheets blowing in the wind, the shutters banging against the sides of the house all night long with the slappings of waves against rocks and broken oars and cries of seagulls. There were rustlings of tiny wings in the sagging eaves, the many ruined chimneys which leaned awry under the floating clouds. There were dark, shrill wings in the interstices between the moldy walls, knockings, hammerings as of all kinds of lost sensations. I knew even then, as she held me in her arms, that our proximity was doomed, that we must part, that she must always leave me.

She drew me close to her, kissing me wetly on my eyelids and my eyes until I knew that my sorrow was not my sorrow, that these were all her salt tears which streaked my cheeks and made me sad, that it was her weakness. She was almost timid now, rubbing her smooth cheeks against my cheeks until my cheeks burned, her voice whispering into the shell of my ear. Her voice was gentle but brisk, her hands as cold as lilies on a grave which is filled with water to the brim. She was so very near, her bald, furrowed head spotted with dark splotches as of blowing rain, her rigid limbs wrapped around mine, her strong arm under my shoulder, and yet I knew her weakness, that her strength was itself a delusion, that she had lost some greater battle than ours. The first sunlight bisected the shadow, one rounded eyeball lighting, and I saw her ear like a conch trumpet, her bald head foaming in the whirlpool, one breast of milky whiteness lighted even as she tried to explain that what I saw, I did not see, that it would be banished with the honest dawn which should dispell these vagrant, foolish dreams. She was only herself, she said. She was not one who could hold with the hounds while she ran with the hares, and little would she care to live in a house divided, to stand with one foot in the sea and one foot on the shore, for common sense forbade it, and she was no deceiver, not even of the deceiving, but very plain and clear, and always had been, and doubtless always would be. She could not deceive even the blind. For the blind had fingers.

Her fingers reached through the livid darkness. She was so very near, brushing her cheeks against mine, trying to hammer in, she said, a little reason, trying to restore me to my senses. The bloom of my youth was not lost. There was no deep cause for regret. We should live through this night, even as we had lived through so many other nights. She was still my guardian, the monitor of all my normal days, and she would never cease to be sincere, even though subjected at times to my misunderstandings. Fiddler crabs should play their music at her wedding if ever she were married. How should she impart to me a grain of common sense, that salt of earth, or her failing strength which grappled against such great and overwhelming odds like some poor swimmer who sinks in sight of shore? Her breath blew against my mouth. I felt the flutterings of her eyelids. Her voice complaining, wandering and sad, her hollow cheeks touching against mine, all flesh, she said, is as the burned grass, and heaven wills our pleasure even as it signs our doom, and the brief candle goes out, and every heart is married to death who is the bridegroom and the bride.

All of us, she said, her voice sighing like a tired wind in that long night of love where already the first light wavered, lighting with momentary gleamings her bald head, are guilty of something which the seas shall not wash away, but we must get along with just our makeshift garments, and many a fool is caught in a golden net. God pity poor sailors with their faces upturned on the leaden waters at dawn. God pity the poor streetwalker whose heart is virginal, and pity the virgin whose heart is the heart of a prostitute, and pity the lazar, the dope fiend, the tramp, the thief, and pity us all, for we are all alike in our being mortal and lost, and the greatest king is no better than the king of rags and patches, and the greatest king must go to bed at last with a spade, and we know not ourselves. God Himself, she said, does not know God, and the night is long which has no ending, and a watched pot will never boil. Better be stung by a nettle than pricked by a rose. He who covers us with his wings will bite us with his bill. A woman, a wig-maker, and a wild horse are the three things never to be trusted. Better go to hell with rags than to heaven with embroidery. Child, I was still a vain and foolish child, very, very ignorant of life and its seamy side, the shoals of human nature where all are wrecked, and I believed the best until I believed the worst, but this was a grievous fault of mine which should be corrected, for neither one was truth. The best are often the worst, she said, and the lowest are the highest, and we are all our fallen brothers, and we are looking for ourselves, but no fisherman can seine the entire ocean or drain it of its gold, and we are lost with the bright light. Where, she asked, had I put her heart which was not her heart?

Where now were her eyelids, her eyes, her ears, her other breast, and whose red wig was that upon the carven chair post, and who was walking back and forth with heavy steps—who, for she was so near, her arm above my shoulder, pillowing my head? Who, for she had never been in Iowa or Kansas, and she knew not any place, and she was lost? All she had ever asked for was a kiss, and that was but a good-night kiss, the kiss of farewell, of one who does not come again and will not be seen even in the dark, blowing days of rain and fog and lifting seas, of one who would so soon be gone, this bald head fading like the moon in the first light of dawn which restores our senses, this bald head covered over by the waters of oblivion and our forgetfulness, and she would be forgotten, and no search would find her unless it be a search through all eternity where she was not. Thus had it always been, and the end was like the beginning when she was bald, and the bald head still was bald. Was she not flesh and blood and bones, poor thing though she might be, ill-favored and far from handsome, a poor creature who had lived by patches and had tried only to earn a roof above her head and make ends meet and be like other people, the fair, the dark? Why had I opened the door that was not locked, or why had I never opened it before?

She hovered above me, her face in the blowing fog that was veined with light, her face neither dark nor fair. Her bare, rough-furrowed head barred by starlight in the blowing fog, her browless eyes uplifted, her face not a face I would have recognized had I encountered her in any city street or crowd, she kissed my wet hair, my eyelids, my eyes, my unanswering lips, my ears, the palms of my hands, the soles of my feet as she tried to explain, her voice coarse-grained and sometimes shouting, that nothing was happening, for I would live, that it was all a dream from which I should awaken bright and early, for early to rise was still the rule, and there was nothing to fear but sloth and the crooked way of the crab, the stingings of the sea medusa, the tentacles of the seaweed, and I should attain to reason and greater stature, and I should mend my manners. Why battle, she asked, with a shadow that cannot strike back and has no being of its own? Why bark if one keeps a dog?

I heard, far away, the old, blind sheep dog barking, perhaps at a spar, perhaps at the last falling star, a pebble, the waves, the skull of a seagull, or some danger greater than any I could have imagined. I saw the face of the clock, the vague outlines of a table, a chair, the dented light of a mirror.

The first light was playing upon her bald, spotted head—the first light of the first dawn which seemed a falsehood. What, she asked, kissing my forehead, was the chief industry of northern Michigan? Where, she asked, kissing my hair, were the world's great iron fields? Where was Egg Harbor? Where was Aldebaran? Where was the lost star? Where was Tobias Smollett? She swore that nothing had happened to disturb the course of the universe, that it was all a dream through which I had lived, and in another dream, we die. Where was her corset? Where was that salmon-colored monstrosity which she must wear for her support? Her voice roaring with tumult in my ear, she cried, even with her cheeks against my cheeks—where was Skagerrak, an arm of the North Sea which should be south of Norway, and where was the Battle of Shiloh, and what was the population of the Society Islands and of the Easter Islands, and who spoke only with a whistling language, and where was Shakespeare? Where was the Palace of the Doges? Where were her sea boots filled with holes, her whaler's dripping hat, her silver-dollar watch that told the time which was no time? Where was her handkerchief? Where was Ratisbon? Where was Paul Revere? Where were the Pyrenees? Where were those veins of coal, those pockets of diamonds, and what had we done with our natural resources, our great timbers and rocks?

There was this jargon of old saws, old proverbs plucked from the World Almanac or farmers' journals, those I heard repeated now, yet with some brooding premonition of sorrow which I might never have realized before, some sense that all was not right, that all was not normal, and this in spite of her protestations that things were the same as they had always been and would be, that nothing had changed between us, that she was still that authority which deserts the dying king. She was trying to explain, with her voice croaking like a bull frog in some distant marsh, those things which seemed to have no bearing on what seemed to me to be our remarkable situation. Was she trying to diffuse my attention, to turn my eyes away from her, the bald head dented and fading like the moon in the pale, washed sky of some first dawn?

He who plays false with one, she said, will play false with two, and the night is the absence of the day, and there is neither night nor day, and the joker is that card which has no face but is the highest card when it is used in euchre. The gambler is not to be trusted even with himself, for life is the game he loses, and the other player has all the cards. God pity the highest card, and God pity God. One dupe would be as impossible, she said, as one twin, one heart, and most men are conceived in the night and die with the ebbing of the tide, and most men die at dawn when the pulse is low, the spirit departing from the body. The night is a cloak for sinners, but the day reveals what the night has been, and virtue has no need for repentance, the remorse which is the awakening of memory. Where had she put her clothes? Where were her red jersey bloomers? Where were her eye-glasses, her false teeth, the various paraphernalia which she might need in this illusion of time?

The Roman Circus, she said, her voice gruff and astonished, was undoubtedly an un-Christian institution for the sports of kings and fools, and the early Christians were martyrs torn by lions, so we must pay these taxes, and she should surely not be able to keep these lions sleeping much longer, or were they angels in the furnace fire? She pitied the lions who ate the Christians in deserts of stone.

How, though, I wondered, could she go on talking like this, she who had seemed the salt of common sense, the one sane person I had ever known? Was she dying in my arms, I being too ignorant to recognize this first death I ever saw?

God pity us all, she said, for winter is summer's heir, but it is a bull market in Wall Street, and maybe our stocks are slipping, and we do best to look the other way and mend our clothes. The tallow is burning low. We have no oil. Put not all your gannet eggs in one basket, but scatter them among the rocks. The Arctic Sea is that which does not melt, but the rose at the North Pole is the rose immortal. God pity, she said, the dreamer whose dream comes true and who is confronted with the uncreated thing of his creation, even that which will pass and leave no mark. There's not the mark of a sleigh's runners over this eternal snow. What time was it in Iowa? When did the next train leave? God pity God, she said, for God had doubtless dreamed or had been most absentminded, not tending to God's knitting, and she could never face her Maker if she had done such a dreadful thing, if she had been the cause of it, this old, ugly, meaningless baldness which was nothing but a bad dream intruding on her peace of mind, her peaceful ways. Had she not always done her best to correct the situation? What if the whole world should turn to salt? There would still be her work to do, and that was man's.

In the morning, everything would be all right, shipshape, she said, all things restored to their usual place, the tide bringing back what the tides brought back, and my senses should have returned to me, and I would be myself again, no better and no worse, no more and no less. The morning should find us the same as we always had been, two simple wayfarers in a thorny way, two grey pilgrims climbing the naked rock as we overwhelmed the temptations and improved our characters and minded our manners. Everything would be bright and clear. It would be the brightest day she would ever know, only a slight drizzle darkening the air. Everything would go according to our fixed schedule which was to overwhelm the powerless temptations and lay them low and be so cheerful that adversity should flee before our faces, that sloth and ease should know us not, that ours would be no soft bed, no silken pillow. A good husband makes a good wife, she said, and a good wife makes a good husband. She would build up my character, for my life lay before me, just as she approached the end of hers, and I must sleep in whatever bed I made. One makes one's bed, then lies on it, even this bed of rock. The wife is the key, and the husband is the door which will not close, and there is no such thing as a new love in an old house, and there is no use barking at the wind, the waves, the shadows. The old ways are best because they have been tried.

I would surely forget, when I had come to my senses, this baldness, for she was not a man, and men are but mortal, poor shadows and vain, and their days like unto the shadow. This baldness would disappear, and her every hair, bright and shining in the sunlight, would be in place again. She had so prided herself on her beautiful marcel, her shining hair. Nothing had happened to turn the hair grey or age the heart which was no heart, and her own heart was giving out. She was turning her head to leeward. In the morning, she said, her voice brisk and too cheerful, her cheeks still touching mine as the hovering light seemed ready to depart, collaborating with us, everything would be all right, and I would know no more than I had known before, no more of life, for there was nothing to cry over that there had not always been. We would be fit as a fiddle. There would be none of this business of robbing Peter to pay Paul.

Things would be fine and dandy, the old routines persisting like another dream, and we must prepare to go into the winter solstice, the cold and vapid sunlight and shorter days, the freezing rain when the sun should apparently stand still in its southward motion at the farthest or highest point in the sky. Fishermen should recognize her, an old, red-headed nursemaid sunning on the rock, her black umbrella lifted, for nothing would be visibly changed. A husband loves a silent wife, and our innocence does not long outlive our modesty, and I should help her in those little tasks which were our plain domestic bliss, the washing of her shirts, her ivory collars, the ironing with an iron polished by bee's wax, and I should keep house with such simple means as if our house were an igloo of durably constructed ice spars and packed-down snow at the roof of the world where should be the whistling winds, where walrus kings should be our dinner guests, and I should study recipes for dishes which would not be expensive, and I should pursue the genealogies of those garlanded shepherds and triple-crowned kings who were no more, and no one should know that this night had ever been, for clearly, it had never happened but in a naked dream which should be forgotten. We should surely find ourselves in our usual traces, and I should scrape the mud off her walking shoes and help her mend torn sails and her winter wardrobe if by chance a moth had gotten in among her clothes in this old, sea-dampened house, and we should take again our constitutionals, our sprightly foot-gallop even in the shadow of death, she promised, and locate perhaps the Anatolian coast, the Bay of Biscay, the Shetland Islands, and Archangel, and Archimedes.

Stuff, fiddle, and balderdash—she suddenly exclaimed, the light beam dancing against her chalk-colored head in the dove-colored dawn—what was she saying? What were these angelic rivers to her, these fountains of unholy light, these immortal roses, these golden shores? What were they to her, a sensible woman? Little would she care for anything out of the ordinary which should attract attention. Little would she care for luxury or the least pretense, fuss and feathers. Her ways were so plain, yet insecure. We would have a busy day tomorrow. We would find there was more work to do than could be done. We would run a mile, and we would knock down tenpins, and we would say our lessons which were practical. We would hem a grey skirt, patch a worn shirt with leather patches, accept the disciplines of life, for this mournful baldness would fade with the candid morning light according to its schedule. When the evening came, this baldness would not be seen.

O, tempora! O, mores!—she moaned in the first lifting of sunlight washed by moonlight. What day would be tomorrow? Would it be Sunday or Monday? Some might call it Tuesday if that should be their pleasure. If it was Sunday, we should not rest, for we never had and would not until the poor orphans of this world were clothed and fed, for he is unworthy to live who lives only for himself and not somewhat in others.

Still, that promise of the normal life returning, what did it seem to me then as I thought of the day which lay like a grey plain ahead of us, that nothing would be changed or more expansive than yesterday had been? Still, in spite of all she promised, the old time returning with the dawn, her phantasmal baldness had not yet disappeared, and her bald, spotted head brushing against my cheek was less like a moth's wings than like a man's cheek, smooth and hairless. Was I to live with this, even if only in memory? Was I the only one who would ever know of it, this bald pretender whom I would remember every time I looked at her, a weather-beaten, red-headed nursemaid, her face twitching in the light and seeming to give off sparks? Bending my arms under my back, she held me fast, whispering, and there was, just as there had always been, a thorn under her tongue. She said that I should forget this foolish baldness long before she did. She said that if ever I told what I had seen, she would kill me, for it was nothing another should see. She had never seen it herself except in a mirror.

Still, perhaps because I stared with widening eyes, she argued on, even weakly. Oh, how many years she had wasted in forming my character, and now it was, she saw, defective as natural man. I was still what I had always been, the little liar, the little sneak who had entered her bedroom without knocking though well knowing that a man's bedroom was a man's castle, the little day-dreamer like my unconscious mother who had fled from suffering and could perhaps be forgiven because she had evaded responsibility almost entirely. What kind of wife would I make when I grew up? What woman could be trusted? What on earth was to be done with me if I should continue to behave like this? She had done her utmost. She had tried everything, severity and absolute kindness, but nothing yet had worked. She had tried to woo me away from my mother, believing I was more nearly her child than my mother's, but had she succeeded in restoring common sense? Common sense was the rarest jewel, more precious than rubies and diamonds and great crystals, for they were as glass by comparison with common sense lighting the darkest corners of the sky. She had all but failed. I needed a father to guide me, to keep me from losing my balance, to keep me in safe paths. She did not seem to realize that my father had fallen while walking a frozen cable stretched between two snow-capped mountain peaks. So that gradually as she talked, I felt guilty, just to be looking at her, and was ready to close my eyes even in the swimming of golden light. I had stumbled on to a great secret, and now that secret was my sin, and my heart was the heart of the night, the darkness.

She rocked me back and forth in her arms, whispering thickly as I drifted toward the thin haze of sleep, "You are hysterical, my dear. I have lost my hair in your service. When I came here, I had all my own hair, a thick mane of it, pale gold hanging down my back. Alas, I was several years younger then than I am now, for tempus fugit. Will you believe me when I say that I am not so old as you think? I am no older than the day I was born. Age is the most difficult thing to achieve. Alas, when shall I grow old?"

CHAPTER 19

THAT was the false dawn, surely. I slept, my mind buzzing with thoughts which were often self-contradictory. When I awakened, thinking that the night's passage had been a dream already faded and was surpassed now by something else, the visible world, that the night had been a dream for which no one was responsible, the tremulous dawn light swept, with the murmuring of distant waters, Miss MacIntosh's bedroom, that vast chamber so barely furnished, one which should have no dust-catchers. There was not even a mole-colored rug on the wooden floor. There were no hanging tapestries, no floating angels in this bedroom, no unearthly creatures as I knew or only those which could not be avoided, for Miss MacIntosh would not have them in her sane company, and she had always wanted to put everything out of doors that was indoors, and I recalled that there was no ornament but the bust of Martin Luther on a pedestal. There was also a large sea shell, but this served a useful purpose—it was used as a door stopper. There were also the crumbling heads of cherubim like cinders around a blackened fireplace, but they had always been there and could not be removed unless the walls were torn down. However, Miss MacIntosh, when she first moved here, had hung a thin webbing of cheese-cloth drapery over these cherubim who had already lost their wings, she having always said that they never would remind her of herself or anyone, for the walls of her room should be plain. Everything was broken like the acanthus leaves in the molding. There was a cherub's ear which had fallen on to the floor. Or was it an alabaster rose which had fallen during the night?

My mind was lucid as day, but I had hardly dared open my eyes, even in spite of my profound conviction that the dream was not the reality, that there should be no continuation of the night's revelation, and this although retrospectively, feeling the twinkle of burnished light upon my closed eyelids, I had already begun to consider certain little things about Miss MacIntosh and her characteristics and features which had never seemed overwhelmingly important before. After all, she was no invalid and was not always lying prone like my sleeping mother who called herself the horizontal person and never walked except in her imagination. Whereas Miss MacIntosh was perpendicular. Where were her eyebrows, had I not long ago asked, and had she not replied eva-

257

sively? Even before I opened my eyes now in this moon-washed morning, I wanted to ask her, tactfully and with studied detachment as if one were considering a land one had not visited and would never visit—why was her face always so sensitive, trembling in the wind, the bright or watery light? Why did she try to be so rigid, bucking against the broncho wind? Why did the colors of her skin change so fast? Why was she pale one minute, red the next, blushing for no reason? Why had she always worn, in the mornings, an old baseball cap or any other old cap she could find, the cap of a sleeping car porter, and why did she always wear a whistle around her neck? Why had she always worn, in the evenings, a ribbon around her hair, a ribbon of Irish green when we had used to sit under the storm lamp playing at dominoes or jigsaw puzzles which always turned out to be the faces of presidents or the maps of foreign countries or playing tiddlywinks or stitching pot-holders, mending old skirts, patching old patches? Why would she never walk in the wind without a hat tied by a veil under her chin, sometimes acres of purple veiling over her whaler's oilskin hat so that, with all this head gear, her head seemed twice its size? Why, in rain or shine and often even when she was in-doors, had she carried her old black umbrella like a shield uplifted where there was no gale?

I opened my eyes. There, in the morning light of grey and green and rose and gold and opalescence, there in the full flush of dawn, there on the hard pillow next to mine, like something long polished by the sea and the action of the tides, was Miss MacIntosh's bald head as cold as marble seldom touched by sunlight, and her veined limbs were wrapped around mine under the tufted coverlid which was quite threadbare, al-most transparent. Was I awake or still asleep, even though I saw with such crucial clarity the cleanly sweeping dawn, tremblings, washings of pristine light in the room of this nocturnal confusion? This was surely Miss MacIntosh, my strange bedfellow, that lost, reflective moon continu-ing in daylight which should drown it by twelve o'clock.

Her red wig, almost purple as the light shone through its ragged edges, was perched like a rare tropical bird on the hat rack on the marble night stand next to her plain bed, within easy reach of her gnarled hand should she stir and awaken suddenly, even at the slightest footfall, for she was no deep sleeper wrapped in the sloth of sensuality, and she had always said so, and death should never catch her napping. Her whale-boned, salmon-colored corset, stained by water and wavering light, was draped over the back of my grandmother's rocking chair, the woven bamboo which rocked in the gentle wind, the metallic supporters still staring at me like a pair of lost eyes which I had seen before, perhaps only in a dream. Her silver-dollar watch was pinned to a window curtain dirtied by the rain. There were several black patches on the curtain. Her false teeth were in a jeweled water glass. Her best hat, which I had always thought of as a man's hat—a grey fedora with a simple black band and one burned, greenish feather she had recently found on the beach, a plumage beyond recognition—had been kicked on to the bare floor, along with her undershirt of horizontally striped blue and grey, the convict's garb, as she had described it, faded grey stockings of ribbed wool with patches at the toes, and her faded, patched and darned shirt waist, that still bristling with rusted needles and pins, that which ordinarily would have been hanging on a hanger in the almost empty dressing closet with her twelve other worn shirt waists of identical pattern and vintage and her salt-and-pepper tweed and her good serge and other woolen skirts stained by water and mud and her long white woolen, fleece-lined underwear. There were a pair of white fur ear muffs on an unpainted and rickety end table with her warped knitting of a grey, ravelled hood which caught the August sunlight in one full blast and of which some of the stitches had unravelled. Her whaler's hat was not in view, but her dim mackintosh was spread across the foot of the bed, much like a tarpaulin, the tarnished harp strings of the footboard seeming to quiver with music as the murmur of wind and water filled this lonely bedroom. Her feet were not covered. There was even a kind of abandon in the way she slept through this still dawn. There was an old-fashioned porcelain chamber pot with doves and wreaths and rosebuds, something which had belonged, I believed, to a late king of France, and there was an empty picture frame, and there was a world's almanac, its torn pages turning in the wind, and there was a broken ship's compass she was intending, I remembered, to repair, and there was a Moody's hotel Bible. I noted that she had chained it to a table. There was a Pullman towel. There was an Atlantic City paperweight.

There were ends of white candles, stubs of sealing wax, bits of soap in a cheap soapstone dish, things that had been carefully saved for a rainy day, a dish of unmatched buttons, a reed sewing basket brimming to the lid, balls of grey yarn, and there were those knitting needles ivory-boned like that bald head glistening on the pillow next to mine, and there was a quiver of wind upon the high cheek bones, the lashless eyelids, the thin, ascetic mouth, not one soft fuzz of hair upon the upper lip, not one long hair growing out of her chin. The pillow had no pillow-case but only the bare, striped ticking. The pillow was wet and stained.

Upon the marble slab, within easy reach of her work-knotted hand, were some almost translucent playing cards with curled edges and Dutch windmills on their silken backs and one card upturned, a low card, the deuce of clubs, that card which signifies the test of tears, that card which is the omen of death, and this though she had ever criticized gambling as the crafty Devil's handiwork and chief insult to the integrity of God, for there be those who stack the cards, she had said, and yet will play to lose the game, they perhaps forgetting how the cards were stacked, in what order, their own forgetfulness tricking them into making mistakes they always wished to make, and the Devil's cards are marked, and she was a Christian woman with an honest mind, and she was no weathercock turning with every wind. She was no turncoat. She knew not, she had ever said, of these dualities in one heart, these double motions, and beauty is as beauty does, and beauty is more than skin deep, and there is much that does not reach the surface, and it's an ill wind that blows nobody good.

Her eye-glasses were hanging on a chair post. The dark mirrors trembled in the moving light. There were an old-fashioned swan pitcher and wash basin in the oyster-colored, spotted, moving light, a half-eaten apple, the peeling of an orange, a piece of sponge, and the walls were cracked in many places, and the ceiling was claw-hammered and discolored by stains of water, cornices and molding broken. The hunting scenes were dimmed or covered over by patches of plastering. The door, I saw with dulled amazement, was barred from the inside, a clump of blackened seaweed hanging on a nail on the door, much like some other wig, barnacles clinging to it, and her red jersey bloomers were hanging against the light of the northern window, and her sea boots were toward the southern hemisphere. There were mud-tracks everywhere, grains of sand, gleamings of salt. The heavy-ribbed black umbrella, opened, was on the floor where it had rolled as if, during the night, she might have upheld it for her protection.

Miss MacIntosh herself, sleeping, was singularly unaware of my scrutiny. I observed what I must surely have always known, the fact that one breast had been amputated. What was left was no bigger than a baby's fist.

CHAPTER 20

Dawn, the slamming of a far door, rustlings of salt-encrusted leaves, cries of moon-struck sea birds, washings of waves. Oh, diamond dawn and pure, many-prismed, oh, radiance of heavenly light which shall bind up the wounds in our sides and wash away our sins that they may be no more, that they shall not be seen again on earth, that we shall not die like Saul or Solomon or Sennacherib in the midst of our corruption, our decay! Oh, celestial aureole of thinnest, finest gold fine-drawn as hairs when we shall put on our shining armor like a bony carapace and go forth to slay the senses five, those who dwell in hidden caves beneath the overhanging, moss-grown rocks in places dark as the ace of spades along an ebony sea-side! Yet was it the light which had already killed the heart of Miss MacIntosh, my darling, even before her death, that which I must already have had some premonition of, as I have said? For the light revealed these wounds which would not heal with time, these deprivations which were surely hers and everlasting, and some were older than the pale or burnished light sweeping across her fearful forehead which seemed now the climax, the culmination of simplicity's mysteries no one can solve, though pitiful are they, tugging at our heart-strings.

It was surely the light which had already killed her, my plain darling, stripping her bare as roses of their petals, the light returning now with haunted rays of Aurora Borealis in her bedroom so sparsely furnished, this field of snow, the polar spectrum tremulous as if this were the first experience of light upon waters and the things which were never to be created, the things uncreated but hovering at some dim threshold, as if this were the experimental light of the first day of crazed creation lifting upon a face forever problematical or upon a face already dead, and that face was hers I saw, strange but familiar as if I had always known it. My eyes widened with recognition and old surprise of long surmise as I saw that the renunciation of life had preceded the struggle, that all was lost before the necessitous conflict had begun, that victory was failure as when some dead king is borne aloft upon the shoulders of mourners celebrating his triumphs over the Devil and the flesh. My hair crawling as I saw, with bemused acknowledgment, who was hairless in the hair-like light of the surf's immemorial reflection, who had not one hair at the bald and naked, cloudless summit, and yet had been but yesterday, if yesterday was possible in the knowledge of this new experience, the one authority I had truly known, a very bleak, a very singular-minded and a very forceful character of old-fashioned vintage and proclivities, a hale and hearty, a red-headed nursemaid carrying a valiant black umbrella in the dark or gilded light of the tormented, answering sea which sweeps upon all shores with forever tentative, changeless and changing music of which the score was not written, is only probable, of which the ultimate themes cannot be resolved. I should have been less surprised to have found her with a red beard than with no hair at all.

It was the breaking up of rock to see her thus exposed in thought-less daylight, her face so sublimely peaceful even in its broken, anguished beauties such as I had hardly noticed or appreciated before, her thin-lidded eyes closed in thin sleep from which she might suddenly awaken, moving her hands which now were crossed above that narrow and in-tolerable vacancy where there should be the other breast of woman or of man. The bald top crowned by light's refulgence, there was that which, even in this light of day, was absent from the woman. There was no crowning glory of woman's hair to crown her, no subtle, single hair of dark or golden light to suggest a possibility of future growth or what had been the unknown and troubled past, wrinkled as waters of the sea, no tuft of hair like a bird's soft down upon her lips or cheeks or limbs or the bald top shaved smooth as the shell of some old, stony egg, this surface which, laid bare to every chance, seemed to resist impressions of light and color and sense. The limitless invaded the limited. It was the faltering of all that was real, sensible, and true to see her thus exposed, a barren, impoverished landscape without flower or bush or hedge, yet still inscrutable, this one invulnerable truth I had taken for granted in a material world where everything else had shifted like the irresponsible waves of the white-capped sea or like my mother's dreams which were so mad.

Should Miss MacIntosh be held responsible for this poor thing who was Miss MacIntosh? Whose work, I vaguely wondered, was this? Whose accomplishment, this sad masterpiece? Oh, who had robbed her of her glorious hair and when? Ugly is a field without grass, a plant without leaves, a head without hair, according to Ovid. Hair adds beauty to a good face and terror to an ugly one, according to the Greek. Was it hair by hair she lost, perhaps through many hesitant years, or all at one blow in some troubled, unknowable past escaping my sphere of life's experi-ence? Was it her broken heart which had caused this? Was she in mourn-ing for someone dead, for a dead lover of her youth? Oh, who had robbed her of her feminine nature, the woman's delicate contours and hidden being, the wheels within wheels, the seeds of stars, the vague evasions and whimsicalities more profound than Calvinistic rigors and denials and aggressions, her hair which should have been her crown, even that shadow of a single hair which might have been and was not? Had some old crow plucked each hair away? Was she deserted at the altar by her bridegroom or her bride? Was she her only lover?

There, though I saw her clear and plain, I was determined, my childish heart furious with resolutions, to go on as if I had never seen her, just as she had saltily advised, determined that common sense should be the mind regnant, that all of this lack of balance should seem but a mere meaningless spark in view of our run-of-the-mill ways, our moderate tastes, and our good housekeeping. All of this, the forlorn head upon the striped pillow, should seem the foolish dream without mortal consequence and not the reality, I was bleakly determined, that by no reflex flicker of my eyelid as when a grain of sand might lodge underneath should I lay bare my secret, ill-won knowledge of her dearly cherished, secret baldness and hairlessness, this which was like sackcloth and ashes, this which should never again seem really elated or flushed with triumph, this which gave to sorrow no words, this plaintive forehead without brow which was high or low or middle or could be defined, should we even use a mariner's compass or guide ourselves by fading or faded stars. I was resolved to close my guilty eyes again that they might open only on the commonplace where nothing should be deranged, and discipline should be a protection against the wildness of the universe, for I could not now blame myself entirely for what I had seen. Heavenly morning had revealed her, but high noon should conceal her, and darkness should not find her again, not even should I open my eyes.

I would awaken upon a day of old, beloved routines repeating themselves, some average way of life the world had not displaced, the existence which is the phenomenal beyond which we do not inquire, for it is good enough for us, this flesh and blood which fades. Her false teeth should be in her bony head and not in the ruby-colored glass, and she should wear her salmon-colored corset tightly laced and with stout stays and double reinforcements, her breast pad, her brick-colored wig of bright, metallic curls and waves, her white collar with its moldy black velvet ribbon tied at her throat, her shirt front glittering in the pale sea light with threaded needles and rusted safety pins which made her prickly as a pin-cushion or a hedgehog or a star fallen on a lonely beach or some strange underwater growth gleaming like a star, her silver-dollar watch hanging by its black cord, her mud-streaked skirt with the parti-colored patch upon her knee, and she should not in any way be undermined or challenged or made clear, and my vision of what lies beyond should be locked securely in my own capacious heart, dislodged by no unthinking accident, revealed to her not by my slightly lifted eyebrows or some wandering gesture as when of old I pushed back my curls or dreamed of things too wonderful and rare for her comprehension. It would be simple to pretend that we were simple. With what alacrity now, I would iron her man-tailored shirts and run her household errands. With what eagerness, I would skip the rope and knock down bowling pins and serve at tennis in the evening light and recite the genealogies and names of those who fled into a desert.

I would be more attentive, more conscientious. I would learn the measures of ancient Hebrews, the digit or fingerbreadth, the tophach or handbreadth, the cubit, the fathom, the reed, the foot. I would learn the weights and coins, the value of the Attic drachma, the gerah, the beka, the maneh, the talent. I would learn the Jewish calendar, Nisan which is

March, Jyar which is April, Sivan which is May, Thammuz which is June, Ab, July, Elul, August, the hottest month of the year, and I would learn the cold months, too. I would learn the names of the antediluvian patriarchs. I would learn the itinerary of the children of Israel from Egypt to Canaan, the stations such as Rameses, Succoth, Etham, Pi-Hahiroth, Marah, Elim. Where was the mouth of Wady Feiran? Where was the site unknown? Where was the desert of El-Tih? Should some die, she had always asked, on their way from Egypt to Canaan, the blessed land?

She would surely never be able to suspect what empty vision lay beyond my eyes, for she was not endowed, as I remembered, with intuitive imagination which sees beyond the commonplace or which wishes to illuminate the darkness. These whirling fogs, these low clouds had been kind to her. She had been content with things just as they were so far as personal desires were concerned, had objectified herself, and her hard lot was her hard lot, and she was always getting down to bedrock, always facing the obstacle. Hers, she had always said so, was a face which should break all mirrors, though until now, of course, I had supposed that it was her humility or her modesty which had dictated the appalling statement. Now I saw that, after all, there had been a grain of truth in it. She would be the first, however, to forget what she wished to forget, what should be put away and out of mind, the gloomy forebodings of impending misfortunes already of the past, I was certain or almost certain, there where I lay with my eyes staring widely at her pale deprivation as I tried to figure out what should be my attitude, as I tried to organize my own transient point of view in such a way that the old moralities should not be disoriented or lost, sent shivering like ghosts at dawn. This bald, imploring head was surely that which a woman of her unusual common sense would not be able to understand or even to suspect, I trusted, that it was something outside the beaten way, something too strange and visionary for her tastes, something she would deny and say did not exist. Her well-known common sense would provide, even in this mortal extreme, her salvation, so she would awaken with her usual robust healthiness, having forgotten, even as if it were a dreamless sleep, this night's lawless doings, just as she herself had promised. A ghostly past had never haunted her vigorous mind, each moment being enough for her, perhaps too much, and she was cryptic as to any forlorn romance of the past, always disclaiming knowledge of any tragic love affair or any heart she might have broken. It would be easy to deceive her, even as I had often done before when I could not focus my mind upon one simple object, or if again I let my foolish, fickle thoughts wander far and wide, I should pretend that it was someone else I dreamed of, perhaps someone who had never existed in our sense, that it was surely not she who was the enchantment of my days and cause of all my vain pursuits, that I found her, in fact, if anything, an obstacle to the ultimate happiness of my life, that she stood between me and my love, that she was not my secret lover or husband or cause of the smile playing like a lost sunbeam upon my lips. I remembered that she had never wished to travel or see the world, for she had seen enough of it. We were settled here—in this old house which, my mother sometimes thought, was a busy Etruscan seaport. A place where the dead came and went.

Though she stirred restlessly, her lips slightly opened, her eyelids fluttering, yet she stared with sightless eyes, and she had not yet awakened, her grave baldness like a mirror catching the light played upon by wind. One could sleep around the punctual clock, surely without fear of some further revelation, evade through sleep's escape from life this contraband commentary on realities which have no business to be real, awaken animated with the same assurance as before or almost the same, with scarcely a shade of difference as between yesterday and bright tomorrow, take up again the dim and beautiful tasks and duties assigned as if they had their meaning in the generations of man and beast and bird, that rigorous training for the ideal marriage which may never occur or which occurred so long ago, we have forgotten it.

But now this routine would have a different meaning for me, would be already of the elegiac past, and I should hold to every moment as if I lived with a dying man, and I should protect her from the knowledge of herself.

Not that she would ever really die, of course! Yet she would be lost, covered over by all the extraneous details of life, and only I would remember her, even when I had forgotten her, for only I had seen her clear and plain, this bald head so pitifully asleep. Bemusedly, with tortured slowness, my mind wandered already through far waters and narrow straits and passages, searching for that which was lost. How should I believe anyone again? How should I believe myself? What was old age? Better were two heads than one, I irrationally concluded, and that grey hair does not signify a necessary wisdom, that many lives are lost before their beginning, that this seeming new-born baldness as of a babe cast into purgatory was never to be held against the creature as denoting failure to acquire mortal experience. This was the tree stripped bare of leaves before the tree was. This was the dead tree of life. Perhaps she was older than those whose hair had turned grey. Perhaps, in fact, it was through a greater experience than ours that she had acquired her bald top, her mournful baldness, that now striking my awakening vision with subjective pity for all mortal things, for all who are exposed to blows of unthinking chance, for all who know not their own nature. There was, livid before my eyes, the missing breast like a door knob, the reality of that which is missing. There was, through all this theme of dark negation and flight away from life, her affirmation, strong and positive, that which God Himself should tremble to see should ever the problematical deity be confronted with the problematical creation.

Was God bald, too, I wondered, or bearded so that birds might hide themselves behind His dreaming hair, behind the cloud? What was God, defined in so many terms—as a fuller's soap, as a refining fire, as the light of the morning when the sun arises, even as a dawn without clouds, as rivers of water in a dry place, as a hiding place from the wind, as a stone of grace? Was God as a friend that sticketh closer than a brother, a brother born for adversity, a root out of a dry ground, a nail fastened to a sure place, as the tender grass by clear shining after the rain, as a casket, as an ark, as a crown of glory, as a diadem of beauty, as a belt of stars, as a friend that loveth at all times, as the shadow of a great rock in a weary land? Was there the plant not planted by God? Were there the strayed sheep? Was there the relapsing demoniac? Truly it had been said, I had come close to something which none should see and live to relate, the image of life failing before his eyes.

CHAPTER 21

EASY it would be to concentrate tomorrow, however, upon the red and baleful hair like shining armor, the scaled vizor of my rugged individualist, this triumphant, plain companion who knew not of refined hesitation, the quick barking of some command which she should give without shallow illusion or vain pretense when we should take again our evening constitutionals as the first cobalt star pricked the sun-streaked heavens and as, with habit unchanged, the old, blind sheep dog running ahead of us on three legs through milkily churning surf and light, guarding the pasture which was no more against the thief who would not come, should bark at every stick and stone and cavernous shell and mariner's rope, the worm-eaten rock, every clump of livid seaweed, the carapace of the dead animal, the living eyes.

For there would be no great alteration but only a deepened feeling as to life. For that love is love which is love forevermore and unchanging, which does not alter with the changing circumstance and does not ebb, does not wane, and I should accept as ultimate the palpable disguise of the average man, the inarticulate mediocrity which covers over such dead and vanished glory as this I saw on the pillow next to mine, this great baldness as of the moon sunken beyond a watery horizon of iron waves, though yet I should also remember this bald head baring my heart of all deceit, making me know what lay just beyond the surface, that the strongest heart was also the very heart of phantoms and of chaos. But I should not betray astonishment, and I should not betray this knowledge of this experience I had stumbled on to in a dark night, not seeking it. Daylight should cover us. She would put on her old clothes, be as she had been. She would be, forever in my memory, even in daily life, as something washed over by the sea, this great head which was the secret pearl.

This was surely my good intention, that I should deceive her into accepting herself as but a usual being in the light, a creature not unlike another and not merely her poor likeness, one who conformed to her own methodical standards and calendar of dreamless days, one who was incapable of grand or feeble impersonations or plain hypocrisies, one who had not built her house upon shifting sands, one who was no mere simulacrum to be shattered at the blow of a feather or of a single hair, even a hair of light. For she had always had her wits about her, loved only the physical things, cared not for spiritual pretence. Yet I should have remembered that evil has many forms, and the good has only one and has no other face. I should have drawn back, considering some prospect other than the future which would be like the past, that now repeating itself. I should perhaps have thought—was there no other way than to go on much as we had gone before, for should our lives be only this living lie? I should have remembered, even then so early, that the road to Hell, as she had often grimly said, is very broad and very wide and is paved with bones and good intentions, and life is this valley of dry bones. So we should not be easily deceived by these mirages. The Devil does not always wear horns, she had said so only yesterday and would say so tomorrow, and he may be quite charming, a very handsome fellow, and that is why we must guard against him and improve our country manners, be not easily deceived by fine feathers which make fine birds. For all she knew, the Devil wore a red coat and a pair of green breeches, she had said, laughing with her most ribald laughter, slapping her knees, and he was a fine dancer. The Devil could quote his Scriptures, too, chapter and verse for his purpose which might be good, and he might even know more of good than the good could ever know, for once he sat at the right hand of the throne of God and was a favorite son of Heaven, and some there are who still confuse the brothers, he who fell, he who is not fallen and is not apparent, he who died for us. The Devil, she had said when opening her black umbrella in the sunlight, is God's ape, wearing God's suit at court, God's crown which is a crown of stars, and better the Devil you know than the Devil you will never know. He might appear as the angel transfixed by light or as the angel of darkness. The greatest sorrows were those not described. The King James version of the Bible was not to be trusted because made for the vanity of earthly kings and for the unification of the British Empire. A man who is a pig is still a man.

Though what awakened now with me was pity, yet had my pity been of some deeper nature and had I understood the sorrows greater than baldness which was itself phenomenal, it would have been I who would have fled, I who should have disappeared rather than embarrass her, when she awakened, by my continued presence. This bald head remained, even oblivious to my staring, to my laughter which should have been my tears, oceans of tears. It was only the beginning of pity. It was not the end.

The pity, pity, pity of that head where nothing grew, the Alpine frozen slopes, abysses, chasms, vales, no single flower to crown the top, nothing at the summit but some further summit, no identity but the individual stripped bare of individuality and vain pretence. I had found the dream of the night repeating in the morning, doubled and made visible, the night's nightmare plain as day, my darling who slept now without her wig and who in all her life had entertained no dream that she remembered and who would have been incapable of dreaming this unfinished thing, that which had no business in creation. This unfinished thing, tentative and unbelievable, my darling in the impartial morning light which covers us with utter mystery as does the darkness and the whirlwind, this which had persisted in the grey, uncertain dawn, this everlasting baldness so like my love. Her forehead furrowed and brown-freckled like a wintry field beneath that dome of smooth whiteness glacial and far away, that jester's wig which caught, in the wrong place, the light, for she was bald. The mystery of that head where nothing grew, the head itself concealing all that was not revealed in the sweeping sea light which seemed to come from no source but the sea.

The truth was that it was best not to look too far ahead, to take each day as it came, to be short-sighted and practical, to mend our ways. Her vague snoring, still I heard. I saw her pale, vapid mouth open and toothless, her face serene but anguished in sweeping sea light that lighted the dark corners of a bedroom, the stalk of a breast which had been cut away so early, the scar, the tissues like a baby's fist, the pity, pity, pity of nothing, of something, for nothing is always something, her wounded side like polished marble clammy with dew, a pinkish gleaming in the rose and mauve and golden light which was not of the sea but of the light, those absent features which are present through implication and association and habit, no eyebrows, no eyelashes, no single hair or feather, the hairless body shining in the whispering sound of surf that stirred and rustled and withdrew with a long, wan sigh or cry, her gnarled hands with veins knotted by old labors like the veins upon her forehead, her gnarled feet grown over seemingly by barnacles though yet the seaweed had not covered her, this denudement of the substance and of the shadow, this reality which was less substantial than the wildest, saddest dream that man had ever dreamed, her woman's clothes not folded but strewn in pieces over the carpetless floor, bundles and rags and a dirty corset, the window curtains wet, the spectral rose staring through the window glass, the flat wooden eyes of sporadic dolphins staring from the rain-stained ceiling with its cracked places and gaslight chandelier, one crystal prism left, her wig like another and sinister presence, a brassiere with a wad of cloth which had been concealed, that there had been this member lost above the heart which still was beating, her Irish green hair ribbon looped over the bust of Martin Luther wreathed with foaming curls of light's reflection of light.

It was my good intention that she should always believe herself to have been the first to have awakened, that she should be completely deceived by my apparent ignorance of her, that she should have gone before me, for I would not be the one to open a final door. I must have fallen asleep again, dreaming of blackberry bushes, of summer rain, of all the beautiful things I knew, the natural things, the surge of the summer sea, showers of pollen darkening the air, for the next I remember, Miss MacIntosh was up and fully dressed and standing at the foot of the bed with her muscular arm around the bedpost, her red, waved hair shining. There was only a look of mild reproach in her cheerfully smiling eyes beyond her light-dented eye-glasses. She had not changed at all since the evening before. I looked at her without the slightest astonishment, completely forgetful that she had ever been different than now she seemed, for this, her standing at the foot of the bed in the early morning, was a familiar scene which had long ago been imprinted on my consciousness, my waking life. It was true that, however, I was in her brass bed and not in my wooden one, and this was something which had never happened before. I was sure that my being in her bedroom would not seem to her worthy of her explanation, so I did not question her as to how this transformation had happened to take place, how it was that I was not in my own bed but in hers. Her bedroom was neat, even though shabby.

Miss MacIntosh herself was in a remarkably good humor, very robust, radiating her kindness which was barely tempered by her severity. Never did her skin glisten so much, exactly, indeed, like the skin of the deep-sea fish in a silver light, though doubtless due to the fact that her face was freshly washed and that she did not use face powder to dull its shine and clog her pores. She was wearing her green hair ribbon to hold her hair in place. Also, as if she foresaw a brisk morning, she was wearing, over her pin-striped shirt waist, a faded turtleneck woolen sweater with holes at the elbows and, over her shoulders, a faded woolen scarf pinned with a large black safety pin. She was wearing, as usual, her silver-dollar watch, its face blotted out by a pool of the cold sunlight.

"You have been very sick and unusually stubborn, but you have recovered," she said. "For awhile, I wondered in my old heart what was to become of you. What a way to have behaved at your first birthday party, even though no guest came, and it was a very simple business. Dancing is never to be encouraged by this old lady, not even—," she paused, smiling, looking about her, "when there is no one, no partner, I'm sure. I'm sure you did not intend to tear your party dress, but the highway to Hell is paved with more good intentions than shining cobblestones, as I have always said, and anyhow, it was immoderate and most unnecessary. However, let bygones be bygones. We shall turn over a new leaf. You must learn to be more careful and more far-sighted and not to act upon a foolish whim or impulse and to foresee the consequences before the deed. Life will surely punish you if I do not. History is made up of those who did not think."

She lifted to the light my party dress, and as it was a filmy, floating creation, cloud-like, I could not see a hole in it or even a seed pearl which was not in its place, all the little ribbons being where they had been, each rosette of yellowed lace as intact as when Mr. Spitzer had taken it out of its long white box. Oh, I should have worn white roses in my hair!

"What on earth," she asked, "was Mr. Spitzer thinking of? It cannot be mended," she said, looking unusually pleasant. "We should only have to tear it further. We shall have to throw it away. There'll be no new one. Into the ash bin it goes."

CHAPTER 22

AT BREAKFAST, where we sat at a table by the bay window overlooking a faint line of foam, the sea which often seemed an astral light as of some other planet, I was seethingly irritated by Miss MacIntosh's very usual cheerfulness, her aggressive eagerness to pursue this new day's affairs, her failure to inquire as to how I might feel. How I had passed the night, could she at least not have asked? For some reason, that which I could not name, I was unusually tired, and my spirits were drooping with a nameless disappointment. There were scratches on my arms and legs as if I had walked in my sleep through patches of spiked brambles and an infinity of grey marsh land, perhaps only a neighboring bog. The base of my skull seemed knotted as with a huge, supernal growth, that which I could not define. Waftings of plumes in the air, angelic, void eyes, and yet I could not see them! My breasts ached. My knees were black and blue. My lips were dry, cracked and scaling, and my eyelids burning feverishly at this beginning of a morning so little different from any other in our two lives.

Miss MacIntosh, having eaten her breakfast, a meal both hearty and spare, as she described it, just that fuel she would have needed to keep alive had she been a Pennsylvania coal-miner or engaged in some other strenuous labor below the ground or above the ground, was monotonously reading aloud, both for her moral illumination and for mine, as was her immortal custom, her morning newspaper which she upheld to shield her eyes and beyond which, when she turned a page to remark upon a Brazilian rebellion or a needle-workers' strike or a new garment union or the obsolescence of schooners and mail coaches, the fluctuations of Wall Street, a bearish market, the instability of islands, the insecurity of British funded government securities when the world should be organized, the recent visit of a British prime minister whom she personally would never have welcomed to these rude shores of freedom, the tonnage of water falling each day over Niagara Falls where was a honeymooners' paradise, the high cost of living, a great drouth in the sheep-raising lands of Western Alberta, a fall in sea island cotton, the news of sports, the water polo scores, a project for draining gold out of the sea, the lost regatta, a shipment of cocoanuts, the deposition of another Balkan king, I could only see, my eyes staring with utmost fascination, the brick red top of her head, the redness as of the rooster's comb or of some rare jungle bird. The print was blurred. The headlines were jagged. The newspaper was water-stained.

Upon her plate, there were broken egg shells. Her knife and fork were crossed accidentally in the sign of the cross, just like Mr. Spitzer's. She had already eaten, as was her custom, a Bermuda onion in order to thicken her blood, so unaccustomed to this invidious sea damp which crept into old manor houses within the sound of the invading sea, the dampness of the air tarnishing the silver and making the gold peel in curls off the picture frames, the near proximity of the loathsome surf which, with her flattest Middle Western manner about her, she complained of when, staring through misty or fly-specked eye-glasses, she half lowered her newspaper, encouraging me to eat my breakfast in order to gather strength, for all hands must be on board. We must plow the ocean, as was her way of describing our routine. Perhaps we would devote this day to cleaning out our bedrooms.

"Heave ho, my hearties!" she cried out like an old salt, one who had weathered many a North Atlantic gale, and yet she had never been to sea, she being land-locked though she sometimes wore a long-waisted black bathing suit with a voluminous skirt and long striped stockings and a black bathing helmet and bathing shoes so that her toes would not be nipped by crabs and barnacles as she stood with her black umbrella lifted as the thin waves of a tidal pool licked at her feet—and would have been dragged down by the weight of her clothes if ever she had tried to swim. Yet she was always talking as if we were far out at sea—this morning was no different from any other. "All hands to the ropes!" she cried, her voice hoarse as if she cried above a heavy wind. "Pull away! Spread the sheets to the wind! It looks like a storm brewing at the far horizon. Calk my sides! Man the rigging, Vera, and scrub the floor. Throw out the ballast. The sky is turning very black.

"Eggs up another cent. Ah, well," she said a little later, "we shall see what we shall see. There's a great deal of washing to do, all my handkerchiefs, all my camesoles, my fine linen. There's a great deal of ironing, and the sea is full of wrinkles, though it has neither age nor grey hairs, I'm told. Don't gape. Some people say that the sea is full of memory though I'm rather of the opinion that it has no memory. What does the sea remember when it swallows the ship?"

Really, she could talk quite foolishly, too, especially when I half listened to her as now this morning, my mind seething with discontent. Her language was colorful, but the day would be colorless, as I knew, and my spirit protested against our activities which were inadequate because reality was missing. Man the rigging, indeed! With what? Where was even the beginning of a man? Was this to be just another work day, the old tasks and duties still staring me in the face, the genealogies of the Biblical shepherds to be memorized, the proverbs, the jeremiads, the harbor lights, the locations of distant harbors and ports of call to be repeated by rote as if we could sail upon those voyages which others had sailed although the waves had long ago closed over their heads? What good were these old voyages? I would not have them once again.

She was clacking those ivory castanets, her false teeth, making her usual throaty noises, snorting with her broken nose behind the wet newspaper which still, oblivious to my offended presence, she pursued, reading aloud that the price of corn had fallen, that General Electric had gained a point, that Commonwealth Edison was doing very well. Hong Kong funds were frozen, and the British were rank imperialists, and there was a great famine in China. A younger brother had been assassinated in Java. A new star had been discovered in the Northern Hemisphere.

Why, however, were we being so tardy, I kept wondering, and at what hour had she arisen that she had eaten before me? Had she ever done this in the past without my noticing? Already, our schedule seemed somewhat off course, perhaps by a point or two which ordinarily I would not have noticed.

Of course, as I knew, Miss MacIntosh, though she seemed so regular, had been noted always for brusque changes of her mood, for sudden shiftings from her usual line. She would walk through the still house at dawn, scaring the Irish housemaids or any guest who, like the Australian bushman, might then think of taking his obscure constitutional. As likely as not, she would open her umbrella under the roof of the house, and she always carried her knitting bag or something which would make her useful. Often along the shore through the purple fog which was veined with light, she had been seen by early fishermen rocking in their boats or by Mr. Spitzer's close-mouthed old houseman with his clam buckets and his seine, an old tennis net which he dragged through tidal pools upon the salt flats as if he were searching for lost tennis balls—at least, according to Mr. Spitzer who always said that, whatever he was doing, he was not working for him. She had been seen standing upon the salt flats in the low tide, a figure clad in grey like the fog through which there shone the dented moon or sun, her grey skirts blowing around her long grey-stockinged legs. She had been seen moving like a pale phantom in the dense, curdled fogs, her black umbrella upheld in that personal darkness in which she would always walk. Then, however, she had not eaten before me, as she believed in taking her physical exercise on an empty stomach when her faculties were at their clearest and sharpest.

Now the breakfast table was decorated as if for some special occasion, the nature of which I could hardly imagine, for it was nobody's birthday or wedding anniversary, and we believed not in the luxury of any ritual, heathen or Christian, we being as plain persons and poor who must earn our daily bread. We loved no graven image. The breakfast table, three long slabs of coarse, unpolished oak, was covered with a counterpane of time-yellowed Irish homespun linen and medallions of rare, medieval Italian lace work which was filled with holes like another subtle pattern. The sunlight was watery, and the earth had not quite awakened. There were flickerings as of the shadows of invisible birds who must be milk-white. We were usually so modest in our arrangements, using only the broken crockeries which Miss MacIntosh had bought dirt cheap at an old fire sale, but now we were using the Haviland china and a silver service, one of the hundred and forty or more silver services under our roof. There were forty silver soup tureens, four hundred finger bowls, five hundred salt shakers not one of which would work. There were enough dishes of royal design to have run a grand hotel, but we had never used them, for they had been much too fine for us, so I was surprised to see the table laid with vermilion and silver and gold. There was a hammered silver bowl of white roses glistening with coarse water-drops, cabbage roses such as grew, if not in What Cheer, Iowa, then in some other heavenly place. We were certainly being festive for some unknown reason, we who did not celebrate even Sunday as the seventh day of the mundane and temporal week, the day of rest, for Sunday, Miss Mac-Intosh had always said, was the first day on which God had doubtless started the creation, dividing the light from the original darkness, and we threaded our needle on Sunday. On Saturday, which was also our work day—when we nailed old boards or unnailed old boards or swept the shore with our brooms or searched for the vacated houses of whelks—God had stopped, and that had been His second great mistake. The first was to have begun what He could not finish. The second was not to have finished what He had begun. Therefore, we worked on both Sunday and Saturday as well as all the other days, observing no period of rest, though it was not our privilege to question the wisdom of God Who had left so many unfinished things upon this beach and Who should have created the world in seven days and rested on the eighth. We gave no thanksgiving. We sewed and patched on Sunday, often in a blowing fog, and all our days were crowded with duties which gave no time for the luxury of thought. We pitched horseshoes or ran back and forth through surf like the sandpipers which were so punctual in their running that they might have been keeping time with a great clock under the sand, under the surf. Sometimes lying with my ear to the sand, I heard its ticking, gonging.

There were twin many-branched golden and crystal candelabras, intricately carved with doves and leaves, which had once been used as altar pieces upon an altar to the dead, perhaps in some ancient Eastern church visited by Mr. Spitzer in his youthful travels when he had encircled the terrestrial globe, returning to say that he had found it unsatisfactory because he had found no monsters guarding the waves at the edge of the world and no girdle of clouds and stars which should encircle it and nothing at all which should contain it, no shell of starlight, no mantle of darkness. This world was not wrapped in a cocoon.

Miss MacIntosh apparently did not notice our present luxury, the fine tablecloth, the swan-breasted coffee urn of silver chased with palest gold, centaurs and cherubim small as a baby's finger-nails. She saw only the old place at What Cheer, the old oilcloth, the broken crockery, the smoky lamps. She could not get used to anything else. There should have been an old-fashioned wash basin, a roller towel, a shaving glass. She had no eye for artificial beauty or anything which man had made, caring not one straw, and she had always said so, for the works of any flattering silversmith or goldsmith who had been employed by the idle rich to hide their poverty, their failure to understand the living world and its rough edges. She would have preferred plain bread and butter to pheasants' tongues served by imaginary servants. None of these imaginary kings and visitors were for her. She would have preferred a plain face. She would have preferred, to all the throngs of heaven storming with their horses at the gates, a tinsmith, a practical roofer to keep the rain out of the impractical house, so overblown, so exaggerated, a monstrous growth of dark rooms cluttered with helmed cherubim riding in boats and stuffed reindeer and royal sleighs with rusted sleigh bells and triple-crowned griffins with gold eggs between their gilded paws and stringless harps in empty music rooms. On the other hand, that this rich man's castle should slip gradually into ruins, there being no man, was perhaps the best of penalties which could be devised by careless nature, the winds blowing and hammering upon the unstable roofs, the rains falling like blows, the drifts of snow piling high on ruined chimneys and towers. Sometimes the soot fell like black snow through the chimney places. Black snow fell upon the pillow of my bed. The sundials walked through the rain-flooded gardens in the perpetually whirling fogs under the dented sun, and great bells rang all night long without purpose like the great waves breaking against rocks.

How often, during her seven unwilling years here, Miss MacIntosh, though ordinarily reserved as to any direct criticism of a poor, sick lady who had seen so little of the sunlight, had laughed loud and long to think that people passing on a distant sea road were of an opinion entertained at times by my deluded mother, that they shared her illusions to some extent, that they believed the crazy-roofed, leaning house with its many galleries and widow walks lost in seas of clouds and hurricane lamps burning like the day's stars was but a vacant-eyed façade or was but an old, empty hotel not fit for human habitation, chambers roaring within chambers, chambers filled with broken sea shells and bits of glass, clumps of seaweed, reefs of coral, spars, barnacles, pebbles, the shells of clams, horseshoe crabs, goldeneyes and seagulls and barn swallows, the tracks of sea birds blown here by the storm, all kinds of oceanic debris. Sometimes the sand glittered brilliant as mica or the dust of stars. Miss MacIntosh herself was almost of that opinion when the sand blew into her face. In fact, had she not warned me, time and again, against some unexpected visitor, some old prowler or tramp who, tired of sleeping out of doors or in doorways or under a shelter of rock, would come to register at the empty hotel, loudly demanding room service, breakfast in bed? My mother always insisted that the hotel entertained many dead men, people from a lower world or from a higher, but Miss MacIntosh did not refer to these, for the dead would always find, she believed, a safe harbor from the storms of life. She referred to the living, the coarse-grained, the tired.

We were carrying on as usual, Miss MacIntosh testily reading her newspaper aloud, stopping only to scold or to ask me some question of a new day's old lessons which I should have memorized by heart if not by head, just as if my marriage in some distant future might be accompanied by the need of, it seemed to me, this discursive, useless information. No one had ever died, certainly not for years. There was, in the air around me, that sound of her heavy, quick breathing, the rasping as of a pair of rusted hinges or rusted weathercocks which now in the morning winds were frozen in one direction and would not turn again until the night fell, releasing all sad dissonances. Her breathing was always inordinately loud, difficult like that, I supposed, of a drowning man who sees the approach of a wall of water, and I wondered that she did not spare either herself or me, that she did not take life easier, loosen her corset strings, talk of our more intimate problems. What did I care that a bee and a horseshoe crab should never lose their way? I was increasingly impatient, perhaps more with myself than with her. Why must we always, every morning at the breakfast table, even all day long, review the whole history of this problematical creation, especially as there were so many things uncreated as yet and never to be created, and why could she not notice, in me this lucid morning, a quality of lingering sorrow? Why could she not appreciate a sorrow which would never recognize the difference between one day and the next? Surely, there was a timeless moment which she should have understood. Why must she ask, instead, with her usual insistence, what God had created on Wednesday, the fourth day of the week if one counted from Sunday forward—whether God had created the signs in the heavens, the stars, the moon, the sun, the lesser light to rule the night, the greater light to rule the day? Why must she ask the same old questions every morning, ask when God had created the great whales, leviathan, the sea anemones, the waters of the deep, the beach grass? My spirit rebelled. Why must she always ask what God had created on Thursday, the fifth day of the week according to the old calendar which she still rigorously held to, even in spite of the general opinion, even in spite of the Emperor Constantine's having changed the calendar when, shedding his tears of repentance which fell around his feet as pearls paving the pavement, he went over to the pagan Church of Rome and got us all off on the wrong day of the week, resting on Sunday which was the day God had not rested?

Men did not live so long as in the past time, she muttered behind her water-stained newspaper, and that her eye-glasses needed polishing, for this which she felt could hardly be the failure of her vision.

"Great whales," I said, "and creatures of the deep, fish of the sea, winged fowls of the air were created on Thursday last. I think it must have been around four o'clock in the afternoon. Miss MacIntosh, can you not give me your undivided attention?"

"Did God, indeed?" she asked, laconically, not looking up from her wet newspaper, her mind already wandering to considerations of the economic order or chaos, soil erosion, the waste of our natural resources, the treatment of the underprivileged. "At this rate, we shall soon be unable to eat a square meal. How does the other half live? Who clothes the poor prostitute, the tramp, the orphan? Organized charity omits some, I am afraid. There is no money for coal. There is no money for flour."

That vexed, hoarse, loud, cracked voice of hers, grating against my ears, setting my nerves a-jangle like broken harp strings, making me realize that there was no difference between today and yesterday, today and tomorrow, Saturday and Sunday, that all days were the same! We would work the whole week through again and never pause. Things were just as usual here—only, if possible, more so. She might well have been my lord and master. I might well have had no mind of my own.

World affairs were in a sorry state, going from bad to worse. She paused to stridently complain, over her newspaper columns which divided her attention, for world affairs were in a sorry state and many governments changing their heads and the Democrats very backward, almost as bad as the Republicans or the Tories, against my laggard carelessness in the last few weeks as to all matters pertaining to good housekeeping which, as she understood it, was every woman's privilege and duty or almost every woman's. A man, when he came home from his work in a hard world, wanted to find peace. He wanted to find that there was food on the table, that the bed had been made. She complained of my laziness, my indifference to my most transparent duties, the fact that I let things go, the fact that there were dust furrows gathering upon the schoolroom floor and under her simple brass bed, curls of dust, that her long-toed foot tracks were outlined in the dust each morning, and the porcelain door knobs needed polishing, and the windows needed washing, and there were spiders' webs in the corners. Not only the cherubim should be covered. There were spiders' webs draping those void, startled, foolish angelic faces which congested the atmosphere and made it difficult for her to breathe. The angels should be covered with white sheets or canvas sail cloth. The interior gargoyles needed going over with a feather duster. The mattresses, she noted briefly, needed turning. Solomon's tub should be changed. Everything indoors should be swept out of doors, including, she had no doubt, Solomon who lived in his own house, and perhaps we should wash the beach and comb the ocean. The workers were outrageously exploited. The mill workers were striking, and she would like to picket for them if only there was time. The needle-workers were starving.

"I wonder," she said gruffly, clearing her throat, "whether I could possibly induce you, with your lily-white hands, to sew a button on my Sunday shirt? What of your housewifely duties, my dear, your share of the bargain?

"As to the socks, there seem to be no two socks which will mate," she continued, morose and grumbling. "The heels are full of holes. One golf sock is checkered, and one is of some other color, and what a sorry appearance I should make on the golf course if I were ever to think of such luxury. Of course, maybe it makes not so much difference here on this old beach," she added, almost dreamily, "but what of the city?" Things had come to a sorry pass when she could not find the clothes to cover her—when, in the mornings, she hardly knew which way to turn, trying to put herself together so that she should make an at least respectable appearance. "What if I had to go out for business purposes?" she asked. "What if I had to earn my living by the sweat of my brow? What kind of wife will you ever make to a good man, one who must earn his living in the busy places and be seen by his fellow men?

"Here's Norwegian shipping. Here's a great storm. Look in the bottom drawer and tell me what you see there."

It was there she kept, as I well knew, her grey yarn, bunches of old rags used for dusting and polishing, her spare canvas corset that was also water-stained, her darning eggs, a baseball autographed by a dead St. Louis Cardinal who had been a friend of Peron's and was Mr. Spitzer's favorite to make a home run in this new season playing against the incorruptible Brooklyn Dodgers or some such outfit, this souvenir which Mr. Spitzer had thoughtfully passed on to her. Mr. Spitzer, though he knew nothing of sports except by indirection, had been, as he had explained, the brother of a man who was a great lover of sports, even though always a bystander. Miss MacIntosh had been, she always loudly stated, the best baseball player in little old What Cheer, playing baseball every Sunday. She had made the quickest home run ever made. Her brothers had said it was as fast as if she had never left base. Georgia had run faster than any of them.

Already, as I lingered crumbling bread crumbs into my plate, wishing I might have a slab of marble birthday cake or of wedding cake, Miss MacIntosh had turned back to her current events, forgetting me for some new injunction which I had always heard before, the fact that I must mend my manners. Her voice, rising and falling, pursued the day's news, that which seemed always the same news. This was surely the second major storm blowing off the coast of Norway or Portugal, off the Canary Islands or the Islands of the Blessed or the Islands of the Dead.

"Eat your oatmeal. Straighten up your shoulders. Well, if you will not, then do not. Take time by the forelock!" she suddenly cried, her loud voice booming as the crystal prisms of the chandelier danced above our heads with pale, reflected lights, the rose and green and gold of some chromatic aberration. "We will have no errors, no dawdling so long as I shall rule the roost here. I drive with a tight rein. God's errors are God's own. What created God on Monday, a very busy day? Do you remember God's creation on Monday, the firmament in the midst of the waters to divide the waters from the waters, the waters above from the waters beneath? Don't bite your fingernails. It's a heavy sea running," her voice now droned. "We are running against the tides which overwhelm us. Where appears the dry land? Tuesday or Wednesday? Last or next? What's the starboard? What's the larboard? What's the fore, and what's the aft?"

The longer the orbit, the longer the planetary year, and the longer it would take to circle time, some people said, but she was one who doubted this. Time was circled in a single week. Siberian wheat, she was pleased to observe, was grown successfully in some of our Western states where the climate was similar to that of Siberia, where the winters were as long as those on some other star. Cold struck everywhere. Cold was no respecter of climates. Cold winters struck the Dakotas. Grouse ate the buds off the white cherry trees in the long winters that were blanketed with snow. This old New England coast had seen some rough weather, too. The American divorces were increasing, and soon there would be more divorces than marriages, she said, and it was a wise child who knew his own father, but she knew hers, make no mistake about it. Here was a man who had found a hen's egg laid in his high silk hat. What might she find laid in her hat some dripping, chilly morning? Here was a woman arrested for stealing her husband's false upper teeth and pawning them, then stealing his lower in order to get his upper out of hock, then stealing his upper in order to get his lower, then pawning his lower to get his upper. So the judge had granted him a divorce, and now he would have to pawn his teeth, Miss MacIntosh supposed, to pay the alimony, and there were many other items which showed how badly the world was going. God created man on Friday, the sixth day of the week according to the best of authorities, but it seemed a shame. Today was Friday.

"Your goose flies too high. Man is man's wolf," she said, blowing her broken nose, grinding her false teeth. "Homo hominy lupus, according to the Latin proverb, and I know no Greek, less Latin, less Hebrew. The sheep cannot guard the sheep against the thief. An old dog barks at nothing.

"Ah, it's a confusion of tongues, the very Tower of Babel. That's plain to be seen. We must catch the old Devil by the tail. I am told it was made of the burning stars. He sat next to God, and he thought that he was smarter than God." Her voice drifted on, high and scraping and sad, for now she would have come to the obituary columns, the columns which advertised real estate for sale, old Newport houses with boarded windows, hunting lodges with family portraits, the things she would not have for love or money. "The first thrashing had its origin, I have no doubt, in heaven, and one fell. He was fallen from morning until seven o'clock, from evening until morning dragging the stars with him. Sometimes you can see a star falling now. Old bull fiddles going at a low price. Piano-tuner wants job.

"Which state of the Union is named for its green mountains? Which for its snowy peaks? Here's a horse," she said, "that is half-brother to an old plow horse and has won the famous steeplechase at Aintree where is the dreaded water-jump, that where many horses fall with their riders. It should interest Mr. Spitzer. Here's a horse of a different color."

Differences of opinion, she would suppose, made for horse racing, a very luxurious sport. Many jockeys broke their heads, but those who broke their heads in sport should not complain, it was her flat opinion. Here were the names of some very interesting horses, Royal Flamingo, son of Speedy Moon, who manhandled Pericles' Pride yesterday at sunset, Thine and Mine who beat by a nose Trinitarian in the Bahamas Monday last when God created the light. Here were horses running in a heavy fog. A heavy wind blew the horses to starboard. A horse had won in that way when it would win in no other way. Here was a race-track at Pimlico still dead from the heavy rainfall, a fact which doubtless should interest Mr. Spitzer if he had noticed it. Here was an old trainer making his death-bed statement, complaining that all his best horses were dead. Mud changed the course of a race. Mud changed the complexion of a horse. Here was a muddy horse which none should recognize, for even the jockey's colors were coated by grey, and the race had been run long ago.

Here was an abandoned race-track. "Cobwebs stretched over the empty grandstands, empty bleachers, old flags drooping, no scoreboard, a lost and grassy track," Miss MacIntosh intoned, "the kind of thing which should interest the late departed Mr. Spitzer." What was the world coming to? Here was a cock fight, and here was an ostrich cart race, and here were dog races. Fashionable people were going to church on Sunday morning to hear a preacher who wore the dress of a clown. He wore a tall peaked hat with a white rose. It was getting so nobody knew who anybody was. If anybody asked her, Miss MacIntosh would say that all preachers were clowns, but nobody had asked her. "Dog races, indeed! What next? Dog races in Heaven as on earth. Bowling is better, for bowling develops the right arm. Oh, my poor arm." She approved, though, always would approve of healthy sports, running, jumping, restoring one's circulation, playing leapfrog in a windy garden by the sea where the great breakers rolled.

I thought of Mr. Spitzer, and wondered where he was. I thought of Mr. Spitzer, the departed one, not the gentle, retired, meditative musician to whom we were accustomed but the other, the brother I had never seen. His life had been both gregarious and mysterious. He had often been seen at the race-tracks, putting his bets on the daily doubles, the longshots, those with such great odds against them and yet those which always came in first, the dark horses, the doped horses, even the dead fillies. In fact, he had sometimes been seen double, standing in two places at once, both on a street corner and at the horse park, some people had said, not having known that Mr. Spitzer had lived. It must have been Peron at the gates or window, Mr. Spitzer at the street corner trying to decide whether or not he should cross the street. If he had been his brother, he would have tossed a coin.

Miss MacIntosh's voice intruded sharply, for she would still permit no errant day-dreaming, even now when it seemed to me that the whole world was a mad man's dream. We must be very attentive, very sharp. "What is the greatest corn-producing state? What is the correct Chicago time? In what latitude is Seattle?

"Common stock watered. Securities floating. Fleet sunken and all hands lost. How recognize the coming storm? What is a hurricane sky? What is the color of opal? If a ship sinks and no one sees it sinking and there are no survivors to tell that it has gone, how tell that it has gone? What is a monsoon? What is a mongoose? What is a man?" How revive a drowned man? What were the rules for life saving which I should have memorized? What was a life buoy? The price list, she read aloud—tallow for candles, harness leather, tarpaulin, mariner's rope, sledge hammers, shirts going in job lots, slightly damaged by fire and flood, damaged church bells. "The evening primrose will soon be out. The neap tide is the least in the lunar month." Perhaps she should order a dozen out of her life's savings, for all had fine percale fronts, the best which Bond Street could offer to a poor woman, and the damage was hardly visible. She needed a dozen.

A dozen neap tides, I thought at first she meant, but no, she must mean a dozen shirts of excellent tailoring, and what would she do with so many in this restricted life, and why did I feel as if I were half asleep? I was only half awake. On the other hand, she said, shirts were a luxury she could not afford. The old, worn clothes she had would probably outlast her old, worn body if the holes were patched. Fine clothes were for those who travelled, for the rich who flitted from spa to spa. She was not thinking of taking any long journeys for her health's sake, failing though it might be, and very fast. Her work was still here. Old-fashioned celluloid collars were going two for a nickel in a flooded Boston basement. Well she remembered those old-fashioned celluloid collars and paper collars, too, the kind her old father had worn in old What Cheer.

Here was a recipe for gooseberry tart made of sea gooseberries, and I must learn to cook and sew for any possible husband, to serve my lord and master and be a modest wife to the poor little carpenter or shoemaker who might yet make his appearance. I should remember that those who fall in love are always blind and do not see the flaws.

"All in all, my dear child," she said, turning another page but seeming to read it upside down, "there is no news today that was not yesterday. Man does not change his nature. The morning is like the night, but the stars are hidden. The light is hidden in the light."

"Did you throw away my party dress for a punishment?" I asked, wearily, tired of all this mental wandering which now I recognized even in her. She was almost as evasive as other older persons I had known, some who had existed only in my haunted dreams of early childhood. There was something she was trying to evade. Why otherwise should she have asked so many questions?

What difference to me, either the lonely archangelic grandeur of God moving over the face of the dark waters Sunday, beginning the fable of creation, or now these current events of Friday which seemed themselves phantasmal like the dream of another world, the facts so fleeting and unrealized? What difference to me that a cargo of English setters and pointers had reached Boston Harbor Tuesday last just before nightfall and were in quarantine, that a Turkish emissary had arrived by the same boat, and what difference to me that there were two stars in the Great Bear, the lines which joined them pointing nearly toward the North star, of which the absolute location was only human guesswork, we being but the occupants of these poor tenements of clay? What difference to me that a shipment of human hair had gone down into the waters? Should I mourn because a man I had never known had been killed by a sea shell while walking on a lonely beach? How could these remote facts, these distant matters change or influence or magnify my life, so out of relation-ship with the external world which I had never seen?

Miss MacIntosh, her voice coarse-grained and severe and certain, doubted that the heavens should be alterable in our brief life time, they having been perhaps God's climactic masterpiece, that roofless cloud-work more comprehensive than the work of any mortal tinsmith, but this poor earth was in a very sorry state, and no one had yet found the cure for cancer.

"I shall dance again, even with my own shadow, Miss MacIntosh. You cannot stop me," I said. Youth was a joyous state of mind, an acceptance of life, and what did any older person know of my desire for a perfect happiness? Were all human beings equally evasive, surrounded by clouds of chance and doubt, by opaque ignorance no morning light could penetrate, and were there such dark things in the heart? How was she different from any other, the highest or the lowest?

She chose to ignore my daring question as to the present where-abouts of a torn party dress, to ask, with a sudden onrush, those questions which might serve as a blind to a restless spirit, for perhaps she saw that I had already dismissed her and all those sterling values of common sense which she had preached. Already, in my mind's shuttered eye, I had forgotten where I really was and was dancing to the muted, tinkling sound made by the crystal prisms of Mr. Chandelier who shook like a frozen tree in the icy wind, the sound as of showers of orient pearls or hailstones falling from the upper firmament of water to the lower. Had she asked no further questions of me, I might never again have ques-tioned her. I had forgotten Miss MacIntosh.

Her false teeth rattling, her eyes watery and vague but sun-lit with fugitive radiance, the red, marcelled top of her burnished head gleaming like the sunrise or like the sunset in chalky mid-winter of some sub-zero climate where the day is almost indistinguishable from the night's streaked, livid darkness, she asked, and it seemed to me that her cheerful voice was haunted by another's sad, imploring voice which I could almost recognize, for surely I had heard it before, perhaps in the distant past, perhaps in the treachery of wakeful sleep, "Where are those towers of gold which God created before creation officially began? Where is that sea of jasper and of light? Name clouds, early cloud formations, positions of lost constellations.

"Describe that heaven which is filled with mares'-tails, the cirrus merging into cirrostratus and altostratus, the cirrus merging into cir-rocumulus which is known familiarly as the mackerel sky, the practical importance of these to farmers and navigators and men. Gales may check tree growth. Salt may stunt and twist. Salt is wedded to this damp air. Old lace curtains offer, however, tolerable protection for bushy crops like currants and gooseberries.

"Where is James Bay? Where is the Sea of Azov? Where is the Coral Sea? Where is the North Pole, and where is the South, and how would you know the difference between them if you were set down at either, by what stars, birds, signs? What is the North equatorial current—and what, the countercurrent which runs the other way, my dear? Where is the Sargasso Sea, a sea of grass that's colored red and gleams with tiny shells like flowers? Sometimes, too, you'll see the lobster, the stinging ray. Sometimes you'll see the dead quail in the sea grass. Where are the world's great oyster beds, and what was the greatest pearl ever grown? Where are the Gilbert Islands, the Falkland Islands, the Shetland Islands, Coronation Island, Henrietta Island, Bay Marguerite, Port Royal, the Suez Canal? You may need to know."

The waters, the islands of the world, the hurricane belts, the horse latitudes, those of high pressure and calms, of light, baffling winds—would she name them all, I wondered as her voice continued, almost dreamily like something heard in an opium-colored sleep?

"Where is Fingal's Cave? Where is Victoria Station? Where is Charing Cross? Where is Trajan's Column? Where is Cleopatra's Needle?

"Where is Mt. Pisgah, my dear? Where is Mt. Everest, known among the Tibetans as Chomolungma? Where is Mt. Ararat, said to be that mountain where Noah's Ark was foundered with the couples of all animals, and shall they ever meet? Were there butterflies in the ark? Were there sleepers on the waters? Where is Pike's Peak? Where's old Jessup Land, far to the North? Sometimes in the glacier there's a tidal crack, my dear. Where's Herbert Island? The walrus ground is just off Herbert Island. Where's Cape Albert Edward? Where is Queen Maud Mountains, an Antarctic range, how high, how long, and what grows there if nothing grows there but ice and snow, the old snow, the young snow? Snow may age. The young snow gathers between the hardened packs." The mountains, the hills, the valleys, the rivers of the world, the glaciers with their vertical faces and crevices, the bays, the inlets, the narrow streams, the waterfalls, the annual precipitation of rainfall, the frequency of frost, the formations of ice caps, the nature of thunder, lightning, hailstones, the definition of a gelding. "Where grows the winter cherry, in what land? Where is the sole nesting ground of the Kirtland's warbler, first sighted by an English sea captain off the Bahamas, a species almost extinct, seldom seen in this world? Upper Michigan Peninsula." Her voice was once again thin and scraping and sad as she described the nesting place preferred by the Kirtland's furtive warbler, the low scrub, the sand where it could not be easily seen.

Should we pass to mortal history—should we briefly consider it, she asked, just as we were passing away—should we consider the mistakes of men, their lack of mature judgment, the fact that, as she had always said, grey hairs had brought no necessary wisdom?

She turned again toward her newspaper, the day's news which never seemed to exhaust her interest—and I wondered, where was Mr. Spitzer this morning, and should we see him again in the evening or perhaps tomorrow evening's light, the same familiar gentleman, his hair tinted a chestnut brown but slightly streaked with grey to make him seem much younger than he was, to make him seem more like his dead brother who had departed this mortal life with his first grey hairs? So Mr. Spitzer had never gotten any greyer.

"Where is Mr. Spitzer, Miss MacIntosh?" I asked. To be more friendly, I added, "Do you think we will see him again this evening?"

"Out on business," she replied.

She was not thinking, I knew, of the other Mr. Spitzer, he whom I referred to, the dead brother, that drifting, gifted man who had gambled his brief life away, his own and his brother's money, the whole or almost the whole of their patrimonial inheritance of which they had been equal co-heirs with share and share alike, their twin estates, the mutual effects, the assets, the liabilities, the remainders, their leases, fees, mortgages, bonds, chattels, goods, paraphernalia shared communally, things corporeal and things incorporeal, all of which or almost all had been lost at one fell blow. Peron had never cared for these twin arrangements, even during his life, and had lived in an apparent disorder, always introducing incalculable elements or discordant notes or a third party. The disorderly environment in which Mr. Spitzer lived was like Peron's now, Mr. Spitzer having had to give up those twin arrangements so dear to his orderly heart. He had had to give up the town house with its twin gardens, twin Apollos, twin parlors, twin mirrors with identical frames of acanthus leaves, twin fireplaces, twin hour-glasses and twin musical clocks, sets of twin fire-dogs, twin candlesticks, twin stairways, twin bedrooms, all those symmetrical arrangements of which Mr. Spitzer had been so fearfully proud. What remained was almost nothing, just a few odd city lots grown over with weeds, a few old lobster dories with broken bottoms, rotted wharves and empty buildings and sunken ships, broken seines, old birthday parcels of which the strings had never been untied, old heirlooms without mortal value, old glass brooches, pieces of water-stained silk wrapped around old figureheads. But she was not thinking, of course, as my mother might have, that the living brother was put into his grave, that only the dead brother was left, a poor musician unburied in the sunlight, for such a mistake would surely not have been sensible, and she was a sensible woman, reading the morning newspaper.

"Ah, this poor fiction of life," she said. "What dead king lies on the balcony at Elsinore? In what tower are the ravens the guardians of the dead? What Greek city prided itself that it had no wall? Who gave a sop to Cerebus? Who was King Canute? How long did he live?

"Where is New South Wales? Where is my brother Richard? Some said I looked like him. His hair was red. Where are the Easter Islands, the Barents Sea, the Sandwich group, Shackleton Shelf, Enderby Land, Keeling Islands? When one lives on a coast, one always wonders what the other coast is. Where are the world's great fighters?"

She paused, struggling lividly for breath, one hand beating against her empty breast, her face as red now as the full blast of the sunlight on her red hair, her face as red as a lobster.

"Where is the angel of death?"

"Miss MacIntosh, you are evading my questions," I cried, taking advantage of this pause, "and I will not answer yours until you answer mine."

"In olden days," she continued, her brow a controlled calm, "it was believed that the world was flat, for men did not travel so far from home, and home was the mystery. Where are the Antilles, by the way? Where are those insubstantial rocks, the Antipodes Islands which arise in the midst of the waters and then are covered over as with a shroud? Where is the Giants' Causeway? Where is the Golden Gate? Where is Brooklyn Bridge? Where is the Grand Central Station?

"Whose dog did not bark in the night?

"In bowling," she quickly said, determined to outdistance, to evade me, "when there are only two ninepins left, one at each outermost edge, what move will take them both at a single blow? What is a baseball diamond? Who were the great kings of baseball? Name them. Who were the great boxers? Name them.

"Had you been in the crowds at Parker's Arena on Parker's Island the first Monday of September in the year of the century's turn, 1900, what great fighters might you have expected to see in the flickerings of the gaslight under the gaslight stars, their shadows moving slowly as if under water, the one knocked out at the eighth gong, the other crowned with roses and bay leaves and carried away? Those were the fighters who do not live now. What, do you remember, is the Sunday punch which I have taught you, even with this feeble arm? What are the left hook, the right hook, the pause, the feint, the purse, the rabbit punch? Who is the umpire whom all men despise?" Who fought with John L. Sullivan, the victor until his last fight? Who was Hercules? Who wrote, she asked, the laws governing glove sports in the British Isles and in America, too? Could I recite the rules from the handbook of the Marquess of Queensberry? Death did not observe these rules, however, she quickly added. What sport was named after the Earl of Derby? What was meant in sports by a gridiron, a pitcher, a diamond, a basket, a home-plate, the pigskin, the foul, the bucket, the false strike, the home run, the needle, the net, the dope sheet, the score?

Something she felt as to the trend of my thoughts made her cry out in sharp protest, as so often when she suspected that I was woolgathering, that my mind was far away or concerned with such dreams as, when the fogs rolled in upon our beach, all those old emperors with church-steeple faces, with great silver bells hanging between their knees, all those beautiful and harmless terrors. "Phantom, indeed! Stuff and nonsense and fiddlesticks!" she cried, her brow contorted, her face paling visibly as she spoke, her eye-glasses misty, beaded with light. "Who ever saw one if he was in his senses? Who ever saw the ghost of his father? We are always the thing we see."

Her face, it seemed to me then, was hardly personal and almost featureless, drained of all color, a face which might be anybody's or nobody's, for I had not yet come to recognize whose face it really was, that it was only hers. Her face seemed suddenly to have no individuality of expression but was like the shifting character of the blown sand which lies in exposed locations near the tumult of the foam-crested waters, like the white dunes moving in the loud, discordant winds, those shapes wild and pointed and fantastical as forms sometimes seen in blizzard drifts of crystal, whirling snow, hills, pinnacles, valleys, the bareness unrelieved by any shadow of growth. Her face was like the bare sand when it is void of ground coverings, when it is not held down by trees with withered tops, by wire grass, clumps of wild, tangled beach plum bushes, beach cherry, holly, bayberry, barberry, the wild beach roses which seemed to flourish in the evasive fogs.

She was scoffing against the very idea of a phantom, that which was but a delusive appearance, an illusion, a figment of the disordered mind, a spectre only of ourselves, that which was something in the appearances but not in the realities. "It takes more than clothes to make the man," she said. "Phantom, indeed, the sorriest balderdash, my dear! I would not give a grain of salt for it. I would not trade an old candle-end, an old night-cap. Who ever saw the ghost of his father, the ghost of his brother? Why should a third party come between us, disturbing the even tenor of our days?" Who knew better than she did that there was no phantom or ghostly presence anywhere, that it was only a spar or an empty fish barrel or a shad-bush moving with the leeward tide, the tide running in the same direction in which the wind blows? She had been out already this morning in her dripping hat and sea boots and faded mackintosh, though she did not believe anyone had seen her. She had seen nothing extraordinary, just the usual haul of comb jellyfish and moon jellyfish coming in upon the glassy tide, the usual starfish and a few old sponges, a few lions' manes and dogwinkles.

I was half inclined to agree with her that this was just another of our usual normal mornings, to feel that she was completely right, that I was completely wrong. Nothing had happened which was out of the course of usual events, at least nothing which was my personal responsibility and because of which I must feel the stain of this great woe. I should not try to remember that of which I had no memory. There might have been, during the night, one of those wild storms for which our coast was justly famous, and this was another wreck. My stomach churned with nausea like a rolling sea. It was a hulk, a spar, a star that I had seen, but it was not a man. It was only, I thought, cast up by the night's storm through which I had slept, such old wreckage as often littered our wild coastline where had been found so many drowned things and men, old coins, the helms of sunken ships, the stays, the shrouds, antediluvian pianos, some with their legs missing, piano legs, playing cards, Moody's Bibles, many black umbrellas. Sometimes there came a sea shell from a distant sea. It was only, I thought, and I well remembered this, cast up by the storm which disembowels the waters, that which the old clam-digger had mistaken at first for a man, that which had seemed a man, well dressed, lying with his face in the sand and his heels in the water, and it had been a well-dressed store window dummy, one of many that had gradually floated in. Mr. Spitzer, with his usual thoughtfulness, had introduced him to my mother, and my mother had thought he was very lifelike, much more like Mr. Spitzer than Mr. Spitzer who was also wrecked and whose house was furnished with the wreckage of old storms and old estates. Miss MacIntosh herself had used to say that, if it were necessary to do so, if Wall Street collapsed, if my mother lost her fortune, we still might furnish our little house with wreckage such as we had seen in the early mornings when combing a storm-littered beach—tables and chairs from the oceanic deep, their sides encrusted with barnacles, chests of bureau drawers, shaving mugs, broken dishes, such things as one might also find in an old Jew's pawn shop under the sign of the three golden balls where the end of the creation is also the beginning. The sand dunes were piled like cracked and rumpled satin under a sea of glassy clouds, the sun like a watery eye staring through a cloud. Good housekeeping, if one was an industrious and humble wife, could surely begin, Miss Mac-Intosh had always said, with these old odds and ends, even though dripping with seaweed, with seaweed like the nests of birds. A little paint here and there would help a great deal.

Many sunken anchors lay off our coast, this magnetic harbor—many old pieces of iron-mongers' ware, many ships' bells which affected the compasses of surface fishing vessels.

Riding the rocking horse waves at a far horizon, the ships would suddenly stand on end, and the compasses all went crazy. The magnetic needle, instead of pointing upward to the polar star, suddenly pointed downward as if there were, in nearer proximity than heaven should afford, a sunken polar star. There were intricate shoals and bars and hidden rocks. If ever the sea withdrew, we should surely behold a strange landscape, for the sea just off this tumultuous coast was a treacherous place, a graveyard of ships, so many ships going down in sight of shore that they were more than all the numbers of all the dead sea birds. Buried in the oozy deep, yet not deeply buried, for sometimes there would be, just above the water's troubled level, a mast or spar or lonely hull which, rising for a moment, disappeared again, there were many old whaling vessels, frigates, trawlers, merchantmen, perhaps only their prows with prodigious figureheads. Sometimes, in a loud, storming night which seemed to move the earth's foundations and which disturbed my mother's dreams, my mother could hear, penetrating her deepest sleep, the bells of sunken ships ringing through clouds and waters as if they were all sailing in, some having sailed from another hemisphere in another century, and that was how the house would be overwhelmed suddenly by other guests, so many Greeks and Romans and Turks, so many mandarins with long cues burning like fire, why shoals of silver fishes drifted out of the candle flames and fluttered like swallows past darkened mirrors in eternity.

Once as if to justify my mother's dreams that she entertained the dead, an empty ship was driven ashore in the whirlings of snow at low water, her frozen canvas torn to shreds, her spars rotted, seagulls perched on the masts, and the captain's table still set for two or three or four. There were many broken ships' lamps floating in for days, for years. Once there was a weaver's loom cast up, warp and woof still clinging to its cords. Once there was a stringless harp. Once there was a cardinal's hat. Once there were twelve rosaries with black crosses strewn along the beach from here to the farthest point, the saddle of rock, the lighthouse burning like a star.

Often the migratory orioles, mistaking the lighthouse for the light, the reality for the illusion, would dash themselves to death against glass. Sometimes there were strange sea birds dead upon the spur of the rock, those which, until they were dead, no one had seen before in this latitude.

Miss MacIntosh, blown often from starboard to larboard as she waded through shallow pools, was surely as strange a sailor on land as a horseman might seem riding distant waters. She never went out beyond her depths, neither as to her thoughts nor as to her constitutional, it seemed, her stout black umbrella being always handy. Whenever I ran out to where the waves came up, she would always call me back, and she would call back the old, blind sheep dog that barked as it ran toward the sea, the quiet waves piling up like sheep or the loud waves storming, running wild as if an old bellwether had lost his way through mist and fog. She never let me wander far from her. She would blow the silver whistle which she wore around her neck, its sound being so much like that of an old screech owl that sometimes she had not blown her whistle when I heard it and came running, and she would say that it must have been an owl screeching in daylight. She would say that I should pay attention and not be misled by the wandering foam or octagons of light in mist and clouds.

"Best to keep fit," Miss MacIntosh was glumly saying, much as if I could not see through her sad pretence of life, "and to mind our knitting, dear, to knit hoods for orphans in those cold countries, for we must, and winter is coming on again, baring its angry teeth, and we shall have no baby of our own, none to lay its head on this cold and empty breast. How handsome it might be with its curls, its three-inch hair, its closed eyes and long eyelashes. We shall save ourselves this trouble. We are not married, my dear. No man has asked for my hand. No hand is tugging at my sleeve. Ah, dear me! I fear it's just an old crab."

Much work was there to do. Why speak, she sternly asked, of that which never was, of the flowers which perished in the seed, the children who were not born, the children who were not wanted? Why, however, should a dirge for one's self issue forth from one's living lips? Never was her heart so cheerful, so sound, her head so clear, and she was not like Mr. Spitzer or some of those who looked for trouble, her troubles being always with her and those which she had long ago accepted. They were the ones she had not acquired. They were the ones she could not get rid of by any pretence whatever, by seeing a phantom painted in the air. For many years now, she had never looked into a looking glass. She could not remember the last time she had seen herself.

She was denuded of all pretence, a barren land where nothing grew but that which was barren like level tracts of land, like those which were commonly covered over with light, sandy soil and poorly forested, such as the pine barrens, and she was this poor face which should make an honest woman tremble in her boots. As for herself, even be there another and beautiful, what phantom would look at her twice, for who was she that she should attract a poor, shivering ghost to come from one world into another? What would he find here that he had not already found? She would frighten even the living if once they looked at her. As to the others, the dead, she would frighten them.

Emperor Hadrian, indeed! Who stole the mosaics off his tomb? Who stole the sea shells off this beach? Poor fools, all! Mr. Chandelier, Mr. Res Tacamah, these vainglorious illusions festering around her like the unnatural growth of time, of space, like cells corroding with slowness and with fatality, these selfish evasions which should have no meaning in a busy, active, healthy, out-door life! She would rather sow the whirlwind and reap it. Her mind would never fail her, and there was much new business which should leave no space for sorrow over a lost mind. We must keep busy. The old ship must be patched, the old sides calked, the old deck scrubbed, and we would hoist the old sails. We would move up into the forecastle where the sailors lived. Best not to look for unnecessary troubles and further complexities as of these generations of man, for there were difficulties enough surrounding us immediately on all sides, and we must steer our narrow passage among overhanging rocks, and we must not lose possession of our senses and our powers of moral judgment, of making quick decisions. We must surely do for ourselves, and surely nothing was sadder than the wisdom which did not help the wise, and she had always said so. Fortunately, she had had, she said, a good night's rest, a sound and unbroken sleep, and had arisen early as in What Cheer.

It was I who looked peaked, dawdling at the breakfast table, my shoulders hunched, my hair stringing in my eyes. What was I dreaming of now, Vera, she asked, her voice slow and sad though her eyes continued to read the baseball scores? No hits, no runs, no errors, she read aloud, and wished that she could have seen the game. She would not care for the loves and the hates of the dead if she were in my place, if our places could be exchanged as easily as our plates, if she were a young girl with all of life before her, with nothing to sorrow over, nothing to regret. I should eat my breakfast, straighten up my shoulders, push my hair away from my eyes, for there was a long day ahead of us, and the nights would soon be growing shorter, and the winter would be long and dark.

"Baldness is no cure for sorrow, my dear," she muttered sleepily, her voice like the continuation of a dream I had almost forgotten. "Spinach is the best bone-builder. We all require a little salt in our blood—but not much. Death has a salty taste—the same as tears. We came from the sea."

Was she all others? I wondered.

She would scare any phantom, and that was a fact, she said, broadly laughing, showing her false uppers, her false lowers as her face reddened in the coarse-grained sunlight, the color flooding back. She was a plain, red-headed woman, very honest, very quick to show her temper if her will was opposed. A homely woman, she said, could afford to be honest, very plain-spoken, forthright. What cared she for the false opinion of others, the adverse winds whirling around her like the whirlwinds? Opinions, all being false, should be perhaps highly polished as jewels, set in a beautiful setting, but the truth was very dull and plain, always had been. She was armed with her black umbrella, her needles and pins, her feather duster, her old dollar watch which was given to her by her dead love, and she was protected by her lack of all pretence or vain imaginings. She could not be seduced out of her senses by a mere shade drifting in her path, and she would certainly tell him so, that she was not taken in by that which could not be seen by other eyes, that she was nobody's fool, the mirror to no one. Indeed, she was only as she seemed, no other soul but hers, and sometimes it seemed as if her soul were not her own. Sometimes she doubted that there was a soul.

Sometimes it seemed to Miss MacIntosh, she gruffly said, that the inner man was all that counted—not the outer man, this poor visage and mockery of himself, so every image should fade, and the dead should not return. The inner man might be an altogether different being from the poor outer man. Only the poorest fool would judge by the appearances, by the outer visage and these poor clothes a man must wear, these mortal garments so ill-fitting and not his choice at all. Sometimes she thought the inner man was battered, too, impaired by much hard usage. Her soul itself must have, she laughed, this broken crown, these weak and watering eyes which could scarcely endure the sunlight or its reflection on the water, this poor, broken nose, these false teeth, these knotted veins, the large hands, the large, long feet.

Unlike my mother, she was no one to entertain, it seemed to me, these multiple, invisible beings whom my mother supposed she entertained every evening of the week and who, of course, were visible to my mother—prisms expanding, ruddy turnstones perched upon great rocks, square Cossack faces with the feathers of ravens on their hats, minarets and spires and domes. These would seem to come from nowhere, but there were also, always in my mother's bedroom, the images suggesting others. My mother saw everything but mistook everything she saw for something else, my mother suffering not from physical but from mental blindness. My mother's mother's blindness had been only physical, her mind flooded with light and the correct memories of colors and shapes and dimensions, even of the most difficult perspectives, and she could see the wind, and it was believed that long after she could not see the coachman's skin like the black cloud she could see his eyes burning brilliant as stars. Nothing was fixed in my mother's eyes, not even the image of the dead. My mother, who could see everything, would suppose a dish of apples to be, however, the portrait of a lady, perhaps one of her marvelous duchesses, a basket of white grapes to be a ballroom chair, a golden harp to be a fan, a fan to be a door, a rose to be a swan, a swan to be a washing basin and a pitcher, and that was why it would have been so very dangerous for her to have walked among so many obstacles changing their shapes before her eyes which were lighted like spindrift in the shining darkness and saw no darkness. When she reached for a book, it was a pear. When she reached for a glove, it was a basket of peaches. When she held out her hand to Mr. Spitzer, he was an umbrella stand or a store-window dummy or any other image which might occur to her. A bouquet of lilies was an elephant, and a door knob was an apple, and a high silk hat was a ship's chimney, and a glass of water was a window, and a window was a glass of water, and sometimes the floor was the ceiling. Sometimes there were stampeding icebergs, and there were cracking mirrors.

Yes, surely, I was still half inclined to believe—the errors and the faults and the flaws were all mine or my mother's or Mr. Spitzer's, and none were shared by unimaginative, bold Miss MacIntosh, she who was always protesting, perhaps only to herself, that she preferred the essential facts, bare and unvarnished, that illusion was not her meat and drink and bone-builder. What were illusions of any kind to her who lived not by illusions or memories or dreams and who never would, whose face elicited no interest or recognition or memory? Bosh, twaddle, nonsense, Jeremiah! What cared she for Issachar, Aaron, Absalom, Togarmah? What cared she for any translation of the Word of God and flatteries to earthly kings, for those who walked in the light or in the shadow, for those whose garments smelled of myrrh and aloes and cassia, for the beautiful clothing which came out of the ivory palaces of the dead?

Nonsense, she would tell these strangers if ever she saw them, for she was just what she seemed, a very plain-faced and earnest and flat-footed Christian woman who knew what the score was and was far from having lost her mind or her corruptible senses or her vision seeing through every lie and pale pretence of life even in this heavy fog blurring boundary lines and who was far from self-pity. Self-pity was not her mortal weakness, and she had developed, in the bowling alleys, a strong right arm, an arm which should have vanquished even the angel of death. If ever, when taking her constitutional, when navigating with her black umbrella beside the rainy sea, an aft wind blowing her along at a lively clip so that she would not have time for idle conversation with any phantom or shade of her imagination, if ever when coming through the treacherous fogs rolling like great combers at dawn when the sky is streaked by the setting moon and the rising sun and the last stars or at twilight when the sky is streaked by the setting sun and the rising moon and the first stars, she was accosted by someone who was not there, she would certainly give him a solid piece of her mind, be it even the Emperor Constantine whose tears were no rivals, as she would flatly say, to the sea-pearls embedded in the fat of mussels never yet converted to join the Church of Rome or even the Baptists or even the Free Methodists. She would ask him why he had changed the calendar, disturbing our schedule, making the preacher preach on Sunday, the day we worked the hardest. She would give him a whack with her black umbrella which shielded her from the curious eyes of women and of men.

CHAPTER 23

"VAIN man, the Emperor Constantine, festering with sickly illusions! Brambles, weeds, a marsh land, a Slough of Despond this life is, in fact. Vain, these aspiring mortals, giving themselves immortal airs, imagining what is not! When the door of the heart slams shut, it will not be opened by man again. The heart, my dear, was locked from the inside, and that is that." She paused to drink noisily a glass of water. A house fly buzzed around her head, the hair hanging low like a roof above her brow.

Wasps droned against the window panes which trembled in the amber, watery sunlight. The light increased. A drove of yellow butterflies was navigating now the distance, the astral light of the sea which seemed to melt into both the sky and the earth. The pallor of the day was different from the brightness of our interior.

"Vain man," she said, "great Caesar crossing the Rubicon, a small river, indeed, as I would say were it my doubtful pleasure to meet with him, a Roman! Who knows that he crossed the Rubicon or that there was a Caesar? What man alive ever saw him? Has time accumulated or taught us any wisdom? History lies, and geography is uncertain, unstable as water or a sick lady's dreams, and we know not who or what we are in these modern times or which star we inhabit. Still, that's no excuse. Ignorance of the law is no excuse," she said without conviction, her head turning from side to side, "and I should certainly never consult Mr. Spitzer as to the law if I needed a lawyer. I would not ask him for the time of day." Her head was drowsily nodding as if she were ready to fall asleep in this broad daylight which swept like brilliant starlight around us, but she was surely never one to be caught napping, either in the day or in the night. Her facial expression, however, could not have been less personal as she continued, "We make mountains of molehills, my dear, and ignore the truth, the simplest truths of life. We stumble in the broad daylight which God has lighted, even as He has lighted the darkness. Ah, these falsehoods which, though false, may be the face of another truth, so it would appear! How should I know what is true unless I know what is false? Poor mortals all and blind as bats in a cave, and shall I be different from these? Deliver not my soul to a turtle or a crab, an old moss-back with moss growing between its crevices. Am I my brother's keeper? One can be an epicure, I have no doubt," she added indefinitely, her face showing now a lugubrious uncertainty as she peered above her misty eye-glasses, "and yet eat nothing but chestnuts. One can eat nothing but grass like the donkey and be a saint. One can enjoy too much one's poverty, in fact, and make a great business of it. Dwarves may dream that they are giants, but never forget this—giants may dream that they are dwarves. The crab and the crane observe the same time, I have no doubt, as this old silver-dollar watch."

What was so rare a thing as common sense, that which she fiercely believed in, the middle brow, the middle way, the average life? Her common sense would never fail her, not until all the seas ran dry, she hoped, for common sense was just her greatest love, even though it should be despised by other men.

"Vain man, Benjamin Franklin!" she suddenly exclaimed. "It is he who has helped to put us in this bad way. It was he, paving the way for electric lights. It was he, trying to harness the lightning of the heavens as he was not asked to do, so now we must have all these electric lights disturbing our privacy, keeping us up all night, my dear, making the nights like the days, and a man has not the privacy of his own bedroom." In fact, if it had not been for electric lights, she would have been much happier, for she disliked the glare and the dazzle and the shine. Certainly, old President Garfield had seen well enough without them. "Even Skid Row," she said a little later, looking up from her newspaper through slanted eyes, "was once but dimly lighted, but now there seems to be nowhere a man can hide his ugly face. There's no dark corner. All these electric lights, electric lights everywhere! I do think it is a pity there should be no more darkness. About the only advantage is midnight base-ball, but even that seems a bit unnatural. Midnight golf, indeed! Midnight, my eye! Electric lights dashing against us everywhere, and who pays the light bills? The poor always." There were all those bright lights lighting the dark harbors, all those bright lights lighting the sky, and it seemed a pity that there should be such extravagance. God's starlight had not lighted everywhere. God's starlight has left us the privacy in which a poor man may die. There had always been, before this tampering with old, damaged creation and the original, uncreated darkness, a dark cor-ner, maybe a street without lights, maybe a lightless, snow-covered alley, maybe a man's own bedroom where a man could hide away, could at least hide his face from all but God. What good had electric lights done except in hospitals?

"Electric lights, electric lights, indeed!" she muttered. "Electric trains, electric irons! Benjamin Franklin, my foot." The sunlight dashing lividly against her face, she was talking above her newspaper even as she seemed to be reading something else or merely glancing at headlines. As if it were not bad enough that the Emperor Constantine had confused our days and our sense of time, then Benjamin Franklin had to come along, confusing our nights, making them bright as day, keeping us up half the night, and yet it was he who had written that early to bed makes us wise. We should arise early. The morning hours had always been the most useful, the brightest, had always brought gold in their mouths. Days were for work, and nights were for sleep. God Himself would never have made the nights as bright as the day, for God had realized that a man needs his sleep and his unbroken privacy and had made the nights dark, the shadows lengthening as the day advanced toward the darkness, and as for there being ghosts in the darkness, that idea was ridiculous. There was no ghost in the darkness who could not be seen in the daylight with only one's naked eyes. She was sure there was nothing invisible. Pfaugh, electric lights!

"Bayberry candles were good enough for our fathers to see by," she was grumbling, her face now concealed by her newspaper above which I could still see the red, ruffled top of her head, the part-line. "Only kings could afford many candles in those windy castles. The wind put them out. The kings, the candles, and the castles." What good had electric lights done to improve the happiness of marriage? Was Helen of Troy ever disturbed by electric lights dashing against her face? If she had been awakened suddenly, she would never have been Helen of Troy, the face that caused a thousand ships to sail, many which might still be sailing. Ulysses, if ever he had seen Penelope under electric lights, would never have come home, would have wandered the wide seas forever, and she would always have woven her web. "Electric lights, my dear, have ruined many a hopeful marriage. Many a blushing bride has been shown up for what she was, sometimes during the marriage night, sometimes the night before. As for the groom, I will not say—but look at the divorce rate.

"I have sometimes spoken to you," she grumbled, "of marriage, the sacred union, yours which is yet to take place when one day you will meet a man. In the olden days when the darkness fell, and it most certainly did, my dear, sometimes at noon when chickens roosted, though this was an aberration caused by an eclipse, sometimes quite early, an ugly woman was safe in her husband's arms, he knowing not those short-comings which he could not see when she was fully clothed. He might even think that she was very handsome. Then why electric lights suddenly going on? If he could not touch what was wrong, he could not see it, and beauty is as beauty does, my dear."

Couples, she had always said, undressed in the darkness, each being modest. Many a wife never saw her husband except when he was clothed. Many a husband never saw his wife.

"Then why all these modern illuminations which bring nought of understanding," she asked, turning a wet page, "all these dreadful fluorescent lamps and two-way lighting systems here I see as available in Boston, all these fireflies and glow-worms and stars, as I would say to Benjamin Franklin if ever I met with him in the darkness. What business had he flying a kite and stretching a string from earth to heaven? Was it his business or God's to meddle and tamper with creation the way God left it last Saturday in the eternal darkness?

"Electric lights, electric lights, indeed, electric trains! Stuff and nonsense and my old hat. What good have artificial lights ever done to preserve marriages which are still made in childish ignorance, I have no doubt, and in the darkness and which still require the continuation both of the darkness and of our ignorance? The wisest men are never married. Is woman more beautiful under these electric lights than she was in the darkness, whirling her hair? God had protected woman, at least when it came to that." God, though He had forgotten many things, had given to woman her mysterious ways, grumbled Miss MacIntosh, her beautiful hair, her eyes, her eyes to see with.

"Those who are fooled want to be fooled," she muttered, "and others want to be disillusioned. Electric light bulbs, what a shame!" A fine thing, she would say to Thomas Edison if ever it were her doubtful pleasure to meet with him, and that did not seem likely. "I would give him a piece of my mind. Electric lights, a fine thing, keeping us up all night like Roman soldiers, causing so many divorces and so many old maids and so many bachelors. Our fathers and our mothers got along without electric lights, and life went on for the most part, and that is surely something more than we can say. We be creatures of the darkness." Where now, with all these electric lights dashing against our faces, should we hide ourselves? Before electric lights disturbing our peace of mind and our unbroken slumbers, bright lights suddenly flashing in our faces, a man might never dream what manner of woman he was married to, and a woman might never dream what manner of man. "Why, a man had married a man, and a woman had married a woman, and no one had been the wiser. A pair of snuffers, in the old times, was all that was needed to put the light out, perhaps only a breath. Men were saving of the light. They saved for a rainy day. The North star was good enough to steer by, and I still prefer it. We are so very poor." Electric lights, electric lights, indeed, what nonsense! All these head lights turning upon us, all these foot-lights as of an evil conscience, all these flood lights flooding the fuliginous vapors, all these tail lights, these traffic lights, these lights like stars where God had left the darkness, these searchlights upon the leaden-colored waters of our natural oblivion!

"Where," she asked, "is Baffin Bay? There's one streak of starlight upon the dark waters." How, she asked, would I go about keeping house? Would it be a lighthouse on a distant rock, its light lighting the empty waves?

"It's always well," she said a little later, blowing her nose, "to have two igloos. It's always well to have the permanent igloo closed against wind and drifting snow, my dear, heavy as crystal stardust, always well to have a good supply of frozen seals and sea otters and kitchen matches, and remember that a new broom sweeps clean. It's well to have an additional igloo in case something should happen to the other one, but never build it on an old ice floe which might move away in a long night's darkness. It's very difficult to locate things up there at the world's roof. One should wait until the ice has ceased to move—listen for the crackle of distant ice," she said, "like the screaming of wild geese." She coughed into her napkin, and then she seemed to scream. "The ice might seem quite firm where we are, yet might be in motion, dear, miles behind us or miles ahead of us. These appearances are often quite deceptive. Old ice floes have a way of splitting into two. We might lose ourselves. We might lose our sleds and our dogs."

The sunlight dashed against her face. Miss MacIntosh, always so forthright and sensible and charged with energy as I still half-way supposed, though perhaps with a vague doubt arising in my mind, how could she be expected to care for the things which were no longer of this sad world or, as some might say, perhaps had never been, yesterday's tides, the shadow of yesterday's moth, the shadow of a leg or sleeve, yesterday's snowflake, even that underlying coldness and nothingness which always permits something, the present fleeting phenomena, a hand, a glass of water, fourteen tall white candles?

She could not care, I thought, for the things departed, the departed members, and could never remember having dreamed even her own dreams, let alone mine, for her consciousness, she had always said, ceased entirely when she slept, and her conscience kept guard, a lonely vigil. Certainly, she could never remember a dream if it was only mine or Mr. Spitzer's but not hers, if it was, in fact, somebody else's, if she was in no way implicated, and she would say so, quite frankly, if now I asked her, if now I attempted to bring to light the lost, the hidden soul of another. She would say that she snored, not that she loved.

She was not frivolous. She would never wear, as another lady might, in honor of a special occasion, a filmy dress, not even a white rose pinned to her old coat collar, no ornament or jewel, no jewel which would sparkle through the fog. Even if it was her wedding here where the dead souls wandered like flames, she would always be dressed the same—or if it was her funeral, I thought. She was dressed for just that life which she lived here on this rough shore, for no other life, certainly. She always would be as she was, so very serious-minded, wearing that practical clothing she had always worn, the old grey baseball sweater with its ravelling sleeve, the stout shoes which surely covered no angelic feet, and having all her rigging with her wherever she went, her old black umbrella which was like the sail, the mast, the gaff, the boom, the tolling bell, her whaleboned ice-breaker corset which was surely not necessary for the support of her lean frame, the salt-and-pepper tweed with patches over patches and perhaps an old tarpaulin draped over her shoulders in the rainy light falling like a precipitous star breaking from a cloud. Life was a very serious and immediate business, certainly no love affair which one carries on in one's dreams with a dead man. Yesterday was of the past, and today there was no occasion to grieve. No one had gotten married, and this was no one's honeymoon or morning of love or morning of disillusionment when the cobwebs should fall away from our eyes. No one had died. No one had been born. She had little patience with that which could not be seen by those who have eyes in their heads to see with, and this though her arena of struggle was always, in spite of her moderate nature and her middle brow which she prided herself on as if her only pride lay in what was commonplace, greater than that at hand, as now I recognized, and somehow involving cosmic or remote issues which must have transcended her ordinary experience and surely transcended mine as the waves transcend the sea-horse and the anemone and the clam.

These remote issues of which she spoke too often, considering her famous common sense, her narrow path which looked neither to the left nor to the right! These lost, vainglorious splendors, the first day of creation, the last, the first starfish upon the first beach of the first evening, the first cuttlefish, the first lobster, the first fiddler crab, the first moon drawing the first tide! Why had she spoken so much of the things which were far away?

It occurred to me, in the sunlight at the breakfast table, that first morning of what seemed, in some inscrutable way, our new creation which bore already its sense of loss and death—that these cosmic or remote issues such as phantasmagoric glaciers, submerged continents, the latitude and longitude in which may be located the Austral Islands, ice-locked Baffin Bay or the Magnetic Pole, these were dreams, impersonal and vast, and these did cover, as is said in gambling circles, her hand, for they did conceal her own limitations, the fact that there was something missing from the essential human, something she did not want me to see, and that was why, in the midst of our ordinary daylight, she evoked the starlight, the foaming waters of the world, God, Benjamin Franklin, Emperor Constantine, President Garfield, a monsoon, a mongoose, why she was always reading aloud, at the breakfast table, the news of yesterday. Of herself, of herself alone, what had she ever said that was personal and sad and revelatory? She was always, in spite of her attitude of direct approach or perhaps because of it, evading something, something too subtle to evade.

"Ah," she said, "we must get ready for winter's blast. It's the cold hand of death for those who are not ready. We must mend our old woolen drawers. Winter will soon be here again," she sighed, "very cold for those who are not clothed. A nip of brandy would be very useful to warm us."

The sand, I thought, would be covered wth crystalline snow hard as glass, snow blowing off the humped dunes which changed their shapes, dancing like mad dervishes in the wind by the sea. We would take our walks by the winter sea, I and Miss MacIntosh, she wearing her old plaid coat, her ear muffs, her grey muffler, and the winter sun would be small, shrunken and hard, and the nights would come early, and there would be heavier fogs.

Why, though, should we be talking of winter now in the August sunlight, heavy with the perfume of rain-washed flowers, and was there to be no season of transition, no gradual change, no autumn, no Indian summer like the Indian summer of the human soul, no time when the temporal leaves should fall, no time for the migrations of passenger birds, no time for farewell before the world grew colorless and dark? There would be fewer colors, a narrower spectrum when winter encircled us, when we were icebound, snowbound, and the out-door world would seem colorless, void and dark, and there would be only ourselves in the darkened house. Yet winter wore its coat of many colors, too, I thought, dimmed though they were, and there would be, lasting the winter through, these dimmed colors there had always been, the bronze of beach grass, the whiteness of snow upon the heads of the blackened spruce and hemlock, the pale iridescence of the seagull's eye, the purple and mauve and grey and gold of the winged seed heads. There would be the luminous colors of the winter sea like a great opal seen through a curtain of fog.

"Why should light," she asked, "be given to a man who is in misery and whose way is darkness and whom God hath hedged in and though the blind may see? A blind man saw me, certainly, and without electric lights. Electric lights, fiddlesticks! The stars have lighted the heavens from pole to pole," she cried.

CHAPTER 24

MISS MACINTOSH was certainly practical, unlike the others. She was certainly never a person who engaged in much foolish gossip as did the servants in the servants' quarters, some busily drinking themselves to death or imagining an order more than life provided, that they were the life-sized chessmen moving across parterres of black and white, that they had no choice of their own, some spending imaginary money, some loving imaginary loves. The servants, too, reflected my mother's chaotic but celestial dreams of a great crowd under this roof, old Beau Brummells coming to life in a crystal ballroom, old belles walking through an empty corridor in watery cascades of rustling, gyrating taffetas. The servants, entering into my mother's spirit, could hear, in the long nights, the carriage wheels in the driveway, the carriages drawing up under the dark porte-cocheres, the neighings of the dead horses.

The servants, reflecting my mother's dreams, were quite comme il faut as to their unusual environment, taking it all for granted, discussing the latest doings of this fine gentleman or that, one who had discovered a new planet, one who believed he dwelled on Uranus, one who had had many loves and had abandoned them all. They knew the habits of the imaginary guests, even as they knew or thought they knew the latitude of my mother's dreams. They knew when she was in the light or in the shadow. Some had seen the black coachman muffled under great clothes which dripped as if he had been driving through a heavy rainfall. Some had seen the white horses with their nostrils foaming like waves. Some had seen the black horses. Some had seen the white coachman.

In fact, just to hear the servants talk, anyone might have thought they were all real, my mother's opium dreams, especially when they were unreal. There was one who believed he did nothing but polish the shoes left out each evening at their bedroom doors by the imaginary guests, and he complained against these muddy boots, these horsemen. There was an old valet who, though there was, in all the house, no man to whom he should serve as valet, seemed to think that he was waiting on Wellington. He was called Wellington by the other servants, and even my mother called him Wellington, perhaps because they had discussed Wellington so much. Nothing amazed my mother, not even the four walls tottering or the furniture disappearing if there moved the vast, dead planets through her bedroom. She would always ask the old valet how Wellington was—and what were Wellington's appetites? There was still another who thought, perhaps because of his intricate discussions with my mother, he lived in a forest of cuckoo clocks. One imagined he was Hannibal driving the elephants over the Alps.

After all, however, how else should they keep their jobs? The servants, always so talkative, would sit disputing among themselves as to what place, what time it was. One would say that it was Roman in the morning but Greek in the afternoon or that the Duke of Wellington was surely expected. Admiral Peary was to be put into the blue room which was already occupied by Plato's boat, et cetera. Sir Christopher Wren and Jenny Lind were to be put into the rose. Spinoza and Shakespeare and Mrs. Sydington were already in the green. The house was always crowded to the roof, and the halls were lighted with a thousand imaginary chandeliers, and the bedrooms were filled with famous guests sleeping tier above tier according to rank and station but with little regard for century, and there was a mad lady retouching her make-up each night in the second powder room. If she was not there, then where was she? Who left, each night, dusty face powder streaking the dark mirrors of Venetian glass, dead rose petals upon a rain-washed marble stair? Or was she a unicorn wearing a necklace?

If there was no one, how could the drunken second butler have stumbled over a mad lady's train just as he went to pass out the free drinks and cigars to the imaginary gentlemen? One gardener, in all other ways normal, believed he was the spouse to Potiphar, the Egyptian captain. There was an Irish housemaid who would never open her mouth to speak if there was more than one person present, for in that case she would be confused by the numbers of persons. She spoke only to herself, and she was several fine ladies and a swarm of fly-catching warblers against which she must complain, a swarm of flies.

The servants moved about in the dimmed evening light, arranging flowers in crystal vases, flowers as big as human heads, the bronze-colored chrysanthemums which are the flowers for the dead, lighting fires in jeweled fireplaces to greet those guests who would never come. They polished the brass fire-dogs, arranged Renaissance chairs very intimately for conversation.

The most simple and apparently sensible persons, did they not seem to undergo, after an hour or a year or many years in this employment, a sea change, a transformation, to be other than themselves, to reach for door knobs which were not door knobs, to open doors which were not doors, to stagger to and fro chasing illusions like butterflies? Some would become snuff takers, and some would scratch their heads. Some had great Medusa heads. Some were lions with wings. There were sunken cities, cities sunken under the waters of the universal dream, chimeras clothed with flesh. There were trumpeters and desk clerks and bellhops, many rushings to and fro. How could my mother have endured, though, this vastness surrounding her if it had no face, no name, if there was no one, if there were only the bare walls—as she herself might always ask?

The refractions of that drugged, dazzling atmosphere produced snow crystals with their faces half inclined toward my mother, and there were not only the ordinary halos surrounding the sun and moon but also many mock suns and moons, many angles, triangles, hexagons, diamonds and hearts and spades and clubs, many mocking birds, many voices, and all was a wild ferment, a tossing to and fro.

The horizontal lady must close her eyes always, it seemed, upon the visionary dream from which she never would awaken unless, of course, she should die. She should die in the midst of her dreams and not be awakened, never know when she died, as tactful Mr. Spitzer always said, his fingers to his lips, for if she was awakened, she would awaken only to die.

My mother's dreams were taken, by those around her, to be real, at least to have their sequences in the realities. My mother herself might be, of course, the only genuine unbeliever, as everyone recognized, for she was very clever. My mother placed her faith only in the unreal. My mother, through endless shining and enraptured hours, would sit upright in her silken bed jacket, her drooping garden hat which shaded her eyes in the imaginary sunlight. My mother would furiously shake her head, demanding that the horses should be driven faster. Or they should be brought to a slow trot, a pace so slow that they would seem not to move. Or sometimes, for hours, she could not move because of the cormorant, the great sea bird laying its egg on her head, and everyone must walk very softly, and everyone must whisper. My mother would whisper, too, her fingers to her lips.

My mother would never tire of discussing her final obsequies which had already taken place or her colossal arrangements for some other great affair when there should be many colors and sounds and voices, the dead returning to life, most of the dead returning. There were some she might not invite. She did not believe she would invite, finally, Mr. Spitzer, though she might always change her mind. Some would come by boat, some by train. Some would come by ski train. Some would bring their dogs, all very fashionable, their Great Pyrenees, their Newfoundlands, their English Boxers, their Pomeranians.

My mother would discuss endlessly with her absent social secretaries these invitations and arrangements as to what wines and ices should be served on the terraces or what procedures to follow in the cloud-domed banquet halls if she were to entertain two equal ambassadors of rival powers, the emissary from Heaven which was Hell and the emissary from Hell which was Heaven, how not to offend, whether it would be possible to deceive these fine gentlemen as to who or where she was. Morning would slip into afternoon and afternoon into evening as she, still wearing her garden hat, sat poring over the lists of the guests she had not yet invited, some antiquated copy of the Boston or Philadelphia telephone directory, perhaps even of Amsterdam or London or Prague, circa 1905, and sometimes she thought she was an entire telephone exchange with many dead operators calling many dead numbers, for the people so rarely answered, or else it was the wrong party, only the night porter, as she would complain to Mr. Spitzer, he snoring in her brilliant presence like a tired bumble bee or like a busy signal or a disturbance when the wires were crossed. She was distracted, chattering wildly. She had called Athens, and she had gotten Rome, the Roman airport. She had called the Bishop of Hippo, but he had always just stepped out, was always expected to return in an hour. She had left her messages for the Emperor Hadrian, but Hadrian had stepped out into his garden and had not returned. King Canute had gone on a long voyage. She had asked that the parties be traced. How did it happen she never found the Lowells or the Saltonstalls at home, though she had left her invitations, her regrets with the second butler who expected them to return at any moment? He said that he was the Great Emir, so she invited him. She invited the Persian delegation, the Chinese mandarin tennis players, the medieval skiers. Why had Cousin Hannah never called, and why was her number disconnected long ago? Why had Cousin Wilbur never called, never since his sailing boat had disappeared with him in it? What of Uncle Ronald who was dead? What of Uncle Bernard who had died in Moscow while bringing a message to the czar? All she ever got, when she called Boston, was a cackle of old hen voices, a Boston saloon. The Duchess of Spode had gone to a watering place. What kind of long-distance telephone service was this, anyhow, she would ask Mr. Spitzer, she never guessing, apparently, that her telephone was connected only with the servants' quarters, even the servants not always replying—and who paid these extravagant bills? Perhaps to communicate with Cousin Hannah, she should send her gold-turbaned blackamoor. Who had made these transatlantic calls, these calls ship to shore, star to star, these calls from the living to the dead?

Sometimes, disappointed by her own adventures, she thought that Mr. Spitzer was a roundhouse of the trains which run no more, the broken trains, the trains of ruined sequences, the trains of vanished thoughts and dreams, for he was really very stupid in her dreaming eyes. How should he live through his forgotten past again? Sometimes, true, the nowhere trains were running nowhere, but no trackwalker had walked ahead of Mr. Spitzer to inspect the ties and crossings and bridges and clear away last year's feathery snow, the fallen tree boughs, the other wrecks, and the rails were crossed in the eternal darkness or the tracks lighted only by false signal lights, the red where there should be the green, the green where there should be the red, false moons, suns, stars, signal towers, directions, railway stations where, according to his own confession, there were no stations, and no trains should stop. Sometimes, in her opinion, Mr. Spitzer was a ghost ship with broken mainmasts and torn sails, the captain's table set for two, none aboard. He was never satisfactory as a companion to her eternal illness. Many images displaced him, and there were many evening guests, footsteps in the empty corridors, tinkling laughter, the music of pianos and flutes and conch shells, and she was entertaining her chimney sweeps, her coach painters, her iron trumpeters.

Then who, I wondered, should offer any contrast to these wild illusions and selfish or selfless deceptions, their concatenation here in the morning sunlight where two people sat at the breakfast table, the one so obvious, where there were only myself and that familiar companion to my illness which was only mortal, Miss MacIntosh who was coarse-grained and ruddy, her red hair gleaming like another light? To whom should I have turned that sun-lit morning, asking those personal questions which burned like low fires in my mind, questions as to the secret purpose of life, questions as to love and marriage and reproduction and death?

Should I turn to Mr. Spitzer, he who was so unsure of himself, remembering never his own memories as well as those of strangers, he whose powers of evasion were greater than even he could realize? He would be coming again in the evening light, filled with his usual euphemistic certainties that an ultimate Heaven should unite us all as one brother—but as to this earth, he was very uncertain, often silent. My imagination wandered like a dark and formless cloud, seeking that certitude it might never have.

CHAPTER 25

※

THERE was always, of course, as I knew, Mr. Spitzer, he who was useless as regret, he who had missed so much of life and for the most part was content to have missed it, he whom my mother, in evenings when she could hardly endure the continuation of his fleshly presence or of eternity, would accuse of having died, of having been buried, of having been married to the worm or to his brother. Mr. Spitzer's living flesh did not deceive her for an instant, for it was quite clear to her that he was not his living brother. He was this dead brother and this pale version of himself, of all that had perhaps been real.

The white tuberose or the white carnation in his buttonhole, the door knob or whatever it was he wore upon his mournful velvet coat lapel, did not deceive her for an instant to believe that this was Mr. Spitzer who lived, nor was she convinced by his attitude of inane apology, his vapid face, his air of only half listening as he plucked one ear, only half seeing as he closed one eye and thus blotted out half his field of vision and of hearing, perhaps to please her. She was not easily pleased. His omniscience, though he was dead, was only half of hers, for she was both living and dead, and she could see everything and much more besides, and she was an excellent judge of reality, that which was so unreal, an infinitesimal particle. The Mr. Spitzer who came to see her was not the Mr. Spitzer she saw, for she must entertain the other one, whichever one that was, the ghostly person. She would accuse him of shifting his position, of being in many places at once. Many images displaced him, yet though he did not move. She was the magician, drugged by magic.

No matter what she supposed, however, he was not inclined to deny completely the interesting possibility, he being rather willing to concede that there was doubtless some right in her point of view which shifted constantly, that the table might easily be a coffin of stars and two wing chairs set above a sea of clouds, that there were bumble bees droning in her bedroom, that the rose in his buttonhole was in all probability a lady's ear, that perhaps he was himself a tower of water or a basket of peaches or winter grapes, or perhaps he was a fat duchess drinking a goblet of wine, glass and all, for in this mortal chaos where we now were caught, this constant fluctuation of distorted mirror images and principle of nothing but error repeating error like a mad, sad dream, no man knew where or who he was, and no man knew what he might become, and even in the twinkling of an eye. Perhaps he had no life but that which was as insubstantial as she imagined, and all she thought was true, yet though he was always the same fat, polite gentleman, his features somewhat blurred by clouds and winds.

He existed only where separateness from Heaven could not be denied, it often seemed to him, the bewildered evening caller who did not believe in Heaven except as a state of mind. She knew him, he believed, only too well, taking him for granted, accepting his doomed punctuality as if it were an aspect of her opium-clouded dream, her erroneous fecundity which should be rivalled by no one, neither the living nor the ghostly flesh, not even by Mr. Spitzer who had ventured into the footless places with his memorial problems and who had travelled through darkness unutterable and miasmic fogs and the disenchanted airs of night, he who blamed the dust for that which the dust had not forgotten, himself remembering himself, he who, even in the midst of his silent elegy, destroyed the silence as if, in the reedy marsh lands, a dead bird should sing, or a dead hand should move, dividing the tangled bracken grass which covered his oblivion, or the blush of blood should return to a dead man's chalk-colored cheeks, or he should smile. Perhaps he yawned. In the still chambers which had never bisected life from death, its twin, the deathless dead returned like tides which cannot cease, a cloud of change shifting into a shower of phosphorescent and many-colored rain, of whirling leaves and mocking birds and winged flowers, pale moths which flew along the light, the sunbeam in the darkness. So he enjoyed this sense of unity he found here, found even through separation, through division from life, he being the ambiguous twin. There were new stars gleaming in the cold mirrors of Lethean streams and whirlpools and floods, of glacial walls, and that tempestuous music of the silence broke upon his living ear and made the walls dissolve and made those die who lived, die because they had heard the singings of the dead, the dead who lived and moved. How could he object?

Mr. Spitzer, himself a soul divided and at loss, was in no position to judge another's dreams or visions, and yet he did his best, and he was always very thoughtful, consulting his jeweled watch—though time had only seemed to pass! Time, he must agree with my mother, was like her opium illusions. So many mistakes had been made in this mortal life, and some were his, and some were hers, and some were nobody's, the erroneous perceptions such as she imagined he had often witnessed, a falling leaf, his brother's eyes burning in the fog, his brother's hands reaching toward his. But who was his brother?

His own ways were harmonious, every step being as if it had been mathematically planned by a higher power and even though there should be circles within circles, orbs within orbs, many spheres of influence, clouds of eyeless witnesses, dead sparrows falling—but what of his brother's ways? They were incalculable.

He, Mr. Spitzer, was this soul divided, for he was this twin, and one was dead, and one lived, this confusion reigning like order in his great heart. It was true, too true, that he had suffered egregiously for the fact that if he was the right man, then he was the right man in the wrong world, and if he was the wrong man, then he was the wrong man in the wrong world, he would sometimes plaintively admit to his dark lady with almost a look of wild, secret humor playing over his ordinarily quiescent face, one eye winking in that slumberous moment which seemed to overcome his usual discreet air of admitting nothing and denying nothing, of neither agreeing nor disagreeing without vast and perhaps forever unspoken reservations, for he could make no permanent commitments or engagements in this scene of meaningless fluctuations and of mortal chaos, his manner of procedure being tacitly to weigh all waning possibilities and come to no direct conclusion to be held against him afterward in the score of some new argument when he had forgotten the old or what it was, their argument as to whether there was or was not an imaginary elephant as smokily grey as evening light beams or as faded lilies, whether Mr. Spitzer's head was his head upon his shoulders. As he was not really drugged, not really enchanted, how could he argue in this realm? What could he say which should be final and conclusive, leaving no realm of doubt? He knew that he was likely to renounce his accuracy, to lose each argument. Time was like sand running through his loosely spread fingers, and the present had little meaning, he living in either the remote future or the past when they should join and be as one, as brother and brother. He had no capacity, he believed, for vivid thought, he tending always toward the abstraction of the taciturn last word. He had little memory of the immediate moment or image, even when it was presumably real, when my mother had not imagined it, when the impressions playing through his mind were only his, for they were as fickle as wind or water or woman, and he was but a man, a sad man in the wrong world, and his mind was watery and vague, not even his own face being real to him.

He remembered, as if he had outlived himself, that he had loved my mother, even with his dying breath—so should she not have treated him with greater courtesy, in deference to his remarkable faithfulness, the fact that he returned in the evening to her bedside, much as if he came among the dead? With her, he had found, he believed, a refuge from the unreal world, a safe harbor beyond the storms of life, doubtless such a harbor as Peron never could have enjoyed, even in his old age and had he lived to mourn. As for himself, if he had been fortunate, if it had been his happy lot to be among the blessed, if ever she had accepted his passive hand in marriage and his undying love, if she had asked for proof of his devotion, his life might not have been so different from this life of patience and of waiting.

At least, he had glimpsed what his sad life might have been, and that sense of his sorrow upheld him when everything else might fail. My mother was an enchanting woman as she had always been, for it was she who, by placing him on the defensive at points which could not really be defended, she who, by addressing him at times as if he were already dead, reminded him of those vast areas of life he had surely missed, all the irrational, feminine things a man's mind could not be expected to grasp and encompass. Doubtless he must have felt superior in her presence. Perhaps he was safer in her phantasmagoric bedroom than in his own where there were two iron beds and all these memories of his brother, where there were so many nocturnal disorders keeping him awake, a cough in the night when he had not coughed and was alone. All night, guarding against the thief, he was kept awake by listening to the winds and the waves and the high, disruptive tides which reminded him how feeble we all really are, how we all may be swept off our feet by the ghosts of old loves, by children unborn.

Besides the twin iron beds, there were those twin golden cradles which had been his and his brother's, and Mr. Spitzer would have sooner parted from his life than have parted from those cradles, they reminding him of infancy and death.

Perhaps, though my mother was delicate, always in her beautiful swan boat which was her bed, her soft silken hair half hiding her face which was always half in the shadow, she was stronger still than he. For he had found in her the bulwark of his own greater delicacy, the fact that he could come to no clear-cut decisions, that he was seething with uncertainties, his heart like a great whirlpool even at that moment when he seemed most accurate. He was indebted to her, he knew, for some sense of his own precarious being, his existence which she denied. Had it not been for these long, crowded evenings in my mother's company and her magnetic personality which drew him toward her as toward a sunken star, drew him even in spite of himself and his own will, had it not been for her accusing him of falsehood, even of subtle theft, of stealing the lanterns of the gods and the black coachman's property and many other floating estates, her water marigolds, many other dark flowers sunken under the waters of her dreams, had it not been for her constant, fickle reminder that he was insensate and unexcitable and inexplicably colorless, of unsound perceptions and faulty memories and faulty reasonings as to time and place, that many of the avenues of his senses were closed and grown over by tangled grass and that others were marked detour, road under construction, road under repair, he might have enjoyed even less knowledge of himself and his continued existence than he now enjoyed. He might have forgotten both brothers, the living and the living, the living and the dead, the dead and the dead.

He had lost, as a matter of fact, almost all feeling for himself or what might have been, at one time, his undeviating point of view, that of a man who had been rigidly circumspect and limited as to his tolerance for many mistaken things in this mistaken world, that of a man who, at this late date, so many years after his brother's sudden death, would scarcely ever have travelled by any vehicle whatever or associated with his contemporary fellow men for fear of losing, in a heterogeneous mob, those heavenly harmonies which he sometimes believed did control him even now when he, this old lawyer and ex-musician, went forth upon his obscure errands in search of lost deeds and lost heirs and bastard sons

and unnatural mothers and lost heirlooms and lost musicians, those
whose music, like his own, was the cryptic silence.

Food had lost its taste for him, even its texture, as he would often
hesitantly complain, and bread tasted like ashes in his mouth, and coffee
was tasteless or acrid as if it had always been brewed the day before some
other yesterday. It would have been a ridiculous gesture if he had attempted to drink that second cup of coffee which was never there when
he counted meticulously and conscientiously his steps from the kitchen
table to the iron stove, seeing that there was only himself in the empty
room, seeing in the cracked and distorting mirror which the waves had
warped and twisted out of shape by undue contraction and curving, only
his own concave or convex face startled in the midst of the absolute
loneliness, the face which was stained and vapid and had grown older,
older than his brother's.

Sometimes, in fact, Mr. Spitzer saw, though he searched and searched
through dim depths, no face, not even his own. Sometimes it seemed as if
he had outlived both brothers, his being this heavy sense of woe, this
stain of immortal guilt, and yet again it seemed that they had never been
born, and so he was always astonished by life's incompleteness, even when
it was complete, when one was dead and buried. His brother was surely
dead and was absolved, in reality, of any guilt or responsibility for what
Mr. Spitzer saw or felt—even though it seemed, at times, that Peron had
persisted, that Joachim had died under mysterious circumstances. Mr.
Spitzer was naturally puzzled, for he had been born first, the first of two,
he had always been led to believe. Should he not have died first, or
should not both have died together—or if his brother had died, why must
he always think his dead brother's thoughts, even at the expense of his
own conservative life? Why should he envy the dead gambler? Perhaps it
was true that as no man knew the time of his birth, no man knew when
he died. Mr. Spitzer had always felt, when both were alive if ever both
had been alive, his greater responsibility, the ominous burden of caring
for them both, and even now when one was truly dead, he continued his
old habits of thinking perhaps too much of the dead brother, of Peron's
tastes, his attitudes, likes, dislikes, furies and regrets, his loves and his
hates, his interests which had been so much wider than his own, of
course. Peron, a man of many superficial loves, had had no loyalties, no
fixed way of life which anyone could count on. Except, of course, he
would always gamble—take another chance.

Peron had been quick, quick to live, quick to die—but Mr. Spitzer
was stupid and slow, lumbering toward his own open grave and, as my
mother might sometimes dreamily accuse him, taking his time about
it.

He was not, he must admit, the sudden, untimely suicide as his
brother had been but rather the hesitant suicide who takes his luxurious
time and considers, weighs and measures all the lost possibilities and
disappointments until life ends upon its own account without anyone's
permission or objection or desire. His own desire had always been to die,
and he had died with every minute since his brother's death, perhaps

before, he having only vague memories of his present life, memories which baffled him at every point, demanding consideration. Unlike his dead brother, however, he had lived on, merely for the pleasure of being this perpetual and unconsummated suicide, this living death, this man who was always dying, dying with every hesitant thought and step.

His brother, though fickle and faithless, had had the faith, the finality which had allowed him to kill himself, and he must have believed in an after-life, that his situation would somehow be greatly improved if he should die—whereas, unlike his decisive brother, he who had been faithful had had no faith, and he had lived, perhaps because he had believed in no after-life of the individual, not even should he be himself, in nothing beyond this present life and all its remarkable dangers, all its hazards which everywhere confronted him. He had lived on, it seemed to him, only to prolong the agony of his present life or only in memory of his dead brother, his brother living through him, this fat gentleman with the trembling eyelids, the soft, sad, indefinite hands vague as the flutterings of white wings in a heavy fog.

Having died, even in this sad life time, so many fugitive deaths, having so often rehearsed his ultimate passage, he had hoped that the final and ultimate death he died would be imperceptible, that no one would notice when quietly he slipped away from this mortal chaos, as he would sometimes hesitantly remark, a look of wild regret crossing his usually peaceful face—for he himself might know when he was gone! He was caught between hope and fear. He might have to grieve for himself some day, he often told my mother, and so she nearly grieved for him now, even when he was present, coming each evening as her faithful guest. He came when the moon arose. If he did not come, she still believed that he was there.

Sometimes he felt, shaking with a new, implausible anguish, that the only music worth hearing was the music he had never heard, perhaps his own which he had never written, and the only friend was the friend he had never met, and the only loves were the loves he had never loved, those loves which, like my mother's visions, should exceed the human circumstance. He thought of the cities he had never visited, even the cities of the dead, all kinds of things which were not now his concern to think of and which lay quite beyond his mortal scope.

There were all kinds of sharp or dull pains going and coming in his capacious body which should have been undisturbed by unnecessary motions of disorientation or of orientation, and his was, he must sometimes admit to my mother when she accused him of an unbecoming and deceptive stupor, that dead ear which was filled with the undiminished memories of chaos, buzzings of the winter bees, iron bells ringing, foghorns, shatterings of glass, raucous noises as of crows discussing him, discords and tensions most dismaying to a man who loved, as he did, the eternal silence or the music of unknown Heaven, whichever it might be called and depending on one's fortuitous point of view. Did he not love my mother because she believed she had departed this life, because only he remembered her and the unstained beauty of her face? All was illusion, as she had so often said. Only in this life, should we remember the next, the next being only a dream as perhaps this life had also been. The dead, he hopefully believed, remembered nothing, not even themselves, for all personal features were lost, not even remembered by the rose in one's coat lapel, the cane in one's hand. Only through him, as he could not too often insist, his brother lived. There were moments when he could almost agree, as my mother at other moments insisted, that the door knob was an apple, that she entertained, through glowing evenings crossed by shadows, only Mr. Chandelier, that all the people who were more than three miles tall should be put out of the house, as she would say, for fear they should bump their heads into Mr. Chandelier with his candle lights like dim stars in some dim, glassy heaven.

Mr. Spitzer had his own sad, concentric problems or his dead brother's continuing but sporadic problems, those which were not confined to these marvelous evenings, those which were not his in reality but which he had assumed on the day he was called away from his silent music to the morgue to claim his dead brother's body which had been shattered almost beyond recognition, beyond belief. Only he had recognized his brother. All similarities had been lost—except that Mr. Spitzer was this twin. Mr. Spitzer daily encountered, through his brother's vicarious and many-faceted existence, many adventures in this lost, mistaken world, some caused by his failure to hear, some caused by his failure to see a transparent obstacle looming in his path, mountains which he had taken for illusions. There were also those illusions which he had taken for mountains. He was so easily deceived by physical manifestations of all kinds. He could not think and listen at the same moment, even when he was in association with living men and women and not in my mother's bemused presence where, of course, many persons would have been baffled by these curious transformations always going on, these substitutions taking place in her enchanted dreams.

Even when he was absent from her, when walking abroad, he would sometimes see things better in uncertain retrospect than when they were right in front of his face, big as life or bigger. He was always being overwhelmed, he feared, by the sudden shifting of a vanished scene, by another interpretation of a vanished moment. When a house had been torn down, he entered that house, finding the rooms intact. Yet there was always the slight veering of a fixed object toward the right or toward the left, whichever way the wind might blow. There was always, though he was painfully accurate, a slight inaccuracy, an unaccountable movement of any concrete or actual form. This was true when sometimes he had never seen the place before. That was why he would lean in the opposite direction from the wind, why he would disparage, with his large immediacy of flesh, the immediacy of any repelling circumstance.

What was this life, this life which was no life but a temporary incarnation, a mistaken embodiment? What death was this which was no death? How still those doubts which rustled like silken skirts in the wind where Mr. Spitzer walked, thinking of the dead who lived, of the living who were dead? And who would agree with him?

Sometimes he thought his brother's lamentable death had been an irrational accident, something never planned by his brother, something never thought of before the moment of its occurrence, something never thought of after the moment, something eliciting only these vain afterthoughts, these questions, Mr. Spitzer's! Perhaps Peron, the bright madcap, had never intended to kill himself at all, having been the jester with bells, intending to live—and if anyone should ask him now, would never know that he was dead until the question was asked, and he would reply, smiling in his grave! For Peron's problematical death had occurred in a fleeting moment, even like something outside of time, something we do not know of. It was Joachim who had thought so much, as Mr. Spitzer said, of death, of beautiful death and who, even before his brother's last departure, had often passed his lonely evenings here, talking of life and love, the life which was not lived, the love which was not loved.

It was surely at least possible, Mr. Spitzer believed—considering all lost possibilities, all avenues of thought—that Peron had not really intended to die, that Peron, the master of those ambiguous situations by which, of course, he had always lived, had simply been overwhelmed by them, that in one moment, perhaps because of a bright light shining in his eyes, he had been deceived as Mr. Spitzer so often was, increasingly since his brother's death. Mr. Spitzer should long ago have died, realizing a fine intention in his mind, and should have taken part of his brother with him into the outer darkness where was no individual life or memory. Yet Mr. Spitzer had lived to meditate on Peron's death which could have been so easily, he believed, this unpremeditated death and not this concealed suicide, this intention made to seem this irrational accident, this lack of judgment as to distance or place. Peron had rushed impetuously ahead, and he had fallen through a glass window on the fourteenth floor of an office building which, unfortunately for him, had looked out only upon the pavements of the evening clouds, the first gleamings of the first stars.

Yet perhaps, as Mr. Spitzer had once mistaken a door for a window, Peron might have mistaken a window for a door. If the floor level had continued on the other side, then Peron would certainly have lived, carrying on with his usual pleasures. If the floor level where Mr. Spitzer had walked had not continued on the other side, if there had been the void, then he, Joachim, would have killed himself or would have been killed, falling from the cobalt clouds to the shimmering sidewalk, falling like snow, as he would always reasonably conclude when he thought of his narrow escape. His face crossed by the anguish of sudden grief or doubt, he would consider that there would be no Joachim now, no Joachim coming with my mother's troops of winged evening guests to this great bedroom where she had implausibly slept through the years since Peron's death or perhaps since before the unforeseen event. Late, too late, as Mr. Spitzer dizzily remembered, shaking from head to foot, his head whirling like a top, late, too late his brother, screaming loudly as he fell, had recognized the moving clouds, the first tinsel stars, the void, the pavement of the city, and his nullification so final, so complete that he had perhaps hardly been able to judge of it. To judge was Joachim's duty now.

Mr. Spitzer was certainly inclined, at many points, to believe that there had been this unpremeditated accident, for he had made many such intangible or tangible mistakes, none, he believed, fatal, the result being always only his partial nullification, the loss of those features he could afford to lose. Indeed, he had gained weight as his sorrow had increased. A fat man, well protected by his dreaming flesh, this corporeal body he could not depart from, he was one who, walking always as if on thinnest ice, tread softly where angels feared to rush ahead, for he never knew, wrapped in his many ethereal abstractions, what the next step would bring, whether he would step on nothing, whether it would be a stairway or a dissolving stairway or a chasm filled with the songs of dead birds, whether he would stare at that wild, precipitous abyss which would stare at him.

He was ridiculously proud meanwhile of little accidents, little mistakes made by a man so punctual, so unperceptive as himself acting always according to his routines. Who would not be both proud and chagrined, dismayed? Had he not walked through a glass wall, as he would sometimes hesitantly boast, even as of many other little accidents befalling him, some of which he had never noticed or had not noticed until they were called to his passive attention by my mother or any casual stranger touching him on the arm?

Upon this remarkable occasion, he had been alone, visiting another lawyer's office where he had gone to present the claims of a poor fellow, a lost heir whose own mother, a famous actress of the gay nineties, now dead, had denied that he was her son. Mr. Spitzer had written a number of most painstaking letters, setting forth the poor fellow's pretentious claims. No estate was involved. That other lawyer had been all too prosperous, of course, and Mr. Spitzer had resented, naturally, the sumptuous furnishings of his suite of offices, the atmosphere of wealth. Also, Mr. Spitzer had been disappointed in his efforts and had been turned away without an interview for which .he had made the most careful arrangements as to time and place. The other lawyer had simply failed to see him, ignoring Mr. Spitzer as completely as if he did not exist. All of this had been so very irritating, of course. Mr. Spitzer had been filled with seething rage against that other lawyer.

As for Mr. Spitzer himself, he must have thought, when he walked through a great glass wall, that there was nothing, a transparency as thin as air or thinner, for he had noticed no obstacle in his path, no barrier, no wall between himself and the infinity of space. Perhaps he had thought that there was one great room, and he had not expected this division into two rooms, each so like the other.

Or perhaps, in the unconscious part of his mind, he had thought that the wall was a window, that the floor level would not continue, that he would walk on opalescent clouds which shifted in the wind. As to the exact details of this remarkable episode, he was always sufficiently vague, just as he could never recall or did not wish to recall the exact moment at which it had occurred, for it had transpired during a moment of his absent-mindedness, making no impression on him. It had made an impression only on the glass. He must have left, certainly, a hole in the glass behind him, it could not be denied, not even by Mr. Spitzer, and yet he had heard no sound, no sound of the fragile glass shattering, breaking and falling, and he had felt nothing, no sensation, no scratch, no mortal injury, perhaps because his ears were dead, perhaps because his mind had been abstracted, wrapped in his silent music like a shroud, an immortal elegy for himself or his dead, unmusical brother, and he had doubtless been thinking, as usual, of the lost chords, the silent keys, the broken strings, the disappointed hopes, the music which should never be written and which should never be heard upon this earth. Or perhaps he had been thinking of his butterflies, of velvet pockets. Whispering reedily, not knowing the wall was there, not knowing whether it was a window or a wall, he had tread softly, and the floor level had continued, the floor boards creaking under his steps, and the continuities of his sad, broken thoughts had not been disturbed, yet through no fault of his. It was the fault of the architecture. Perhaps he had felt the building shiver in the wind. He had walked from one room to another, not recognizing the partition thin as a membrane, a cobweb, the empty air.

Yet he had nearly killed himself, even through his absent-mindedness, his perpetual grief which often made him stumble in his walks. For as he must repeat, if the wall had been a great bay window and if the streets had been the sun-lit clouds, he would have fallen and would have been this suicide, either through accident or through concealed choice made to seem this accident. Or perhaps this accident would have been made to seem this premeditated suicide. Had he been successful, he would not have lived. He would have been this failure.

He had gone on about his many errands. He would never have noticed at all, doubtless, this accident of which he had absolutely no memory at the time—had it not been, of course, for the fact that his gentleman's valet, the old clam-digger, that evening in the evening light as the first evening stars appeared, pricking the dark sky, had noticed glass particles hanging behind his ears like, Mr. Spitzer supposed, the prisms of a chandelier. The old clam-digger had plucked out the glass sticking to Mr. Spitzer's ears.

And several days later, as if to confirm this lamentable accident about which, though trying to recall, to reconstruct the details, he might still have entertained, of course, a lingering doubt, Mr. Spitzer had received a bill for a glass wall which, serenely, he had ignored, it seeming to him that he was rather the one who should be paid, he having survived, he had concluded, an irreparable damage to his person. Indeed, though it was an intangible injury, this shattering of his already shattered self-confidence, yet it had seemed as real to him as if it had been tangible. He would have been willing, of course, to have dismissed the entire episode, to have asked for no compensation, had it not been for the fact that the bills had continued to come, and there had also been numerous insulting or threatening letters written from the other lawyer to himself. Finally, seething with fury, he had lost his patience, even as his brother might have done under similar circumstances. There had been still, it seemed, a spark of life in Mr. Spitzer. He had decided to end the whole controversy by collecting for his discomfort, by presenting himself as the aggrieved party.

But when he had tried to collect, he had been told, by an obtuse desk clerk, that Mr. Spitzer was dead, having departed this mortal life several years ago. And all his arguments had fallen upon the empty air.

CHAPTER 26

So scrupulous and conservative a mind as Mr. Spitzer's could not quickly unwind the factual truth of any immediate situation as of the present delicate and fleeting moment, as of unilateral time, most particularly as, in his profession which had been thrust upon him more by dour necessity than by early choice, as he would say—he having been always somewhat reluctant to enter the law and having done so only because of his father's wishes—his department was that of the dead. His special areas were those of the hidden past, the wills and deeds departments, the dusty archives and pigeon-holes, and secret drawers—and of necessity, he was always entering old houses, those of the dead, always searching through old secretaries in dim, ghost-haunted rooms where he had felt that at any minute the living might appear. He naturally dealt or had dealt with many eccentric persons, with both living and dead, with strange recluses, those who were rich and imagined they were poor, those who were poor and imagined they were rich and dwelled in many castles of illusion, those who had made a sport of writing many wills to baffle even the most conscientious attorney, especially now in his later years. There had been so many baffling situations, he had come to doubt, yet with great hesitation, that there should be any heirs whatever or any property whatever handed down in golden perpetuity through the generations of the dead who thus controlled the living. There had been so many lost heirs, so many lost heiresses, secret sons, secret daughters, wandering derelicts who could not be located or were shipwrecked on another coast. There had been heirs who had been heiresses, heiresses who had been heirs. He doubted we should even have inherited our features, our hair, our eyes, our ears, our hands, our feet. For these properties, too, had been very confused in metamorphic storms and were very, very makeshift, very uncertain, the properties, just as my mother had always imagined, of a dream, a dream which faded while we looked.

His professional problems were easier when they were simple, certainly, and not so involved as his personal problems. Such had been, in his youth, the case of an elderly Boston lady who, having imagined all her life that she was the reincarnation of Cleopatra, though there was no Marc Antony and no mysterious lover in her past, though she had lived next door to a rival spinster who had been a rival beauty in her youth and who was also the reincarnation of the dead Egyptian queen wearing purple plumes and whose lawyer Mr. Spitzer had also been, and having had, in order to taunt her neighbor who had a Sphinx in her garden, a Sphinx built in her adjoining garden grown over with spotted tiger lilies, a rival Sphinx, a greater pyramid than her neighbor could afford, had died without mortal heirs or issue, leaving her house and garden to her innumerable Siamese cats, with the provision that the ancient caretaker should live in her house and enjoy an annual income as long as the cats lived. Also, Mr. Spitzer was to supervise this arrangement, the old lady having left quite a generous sum in government bonds bearing a low interest, Egyptian securities, and New England shipping. Many another lawyer might have been unscrupulous, but Mr. Spitzer had been very cautious, very conservative in administering this estate which had by no means diminished. Such marvelous cats, too, each having nine lives, he would sighingly remark when he thought of these cats and the magic of their lives, how not one had apparently ever suffered death. Nothing could have startled him so much as a dead cat in the garden. He had often seen these cats sunning upon the great stone pyramid, these sleek, silken animals prowling through the windy garden where no birds sang. Of course, he had not visited the place now for a number of years, but he remembered that there had certainly been a little cat's door that led into the great, sun-streaked house where the cats had prowled about, whirring and purring and eating from golden dishes fit for the dead pharaohs. The cats had always been insolent, even when the old lady was alive—and after the old lady's death, they had seemed to know they owned the place—or so Mr. Spitzer had thought when, returning from the funeral parlor where he had identified the corpse and left a bouquet of flowers, he had hesitantly called to leave his engraved calling card, to pay, in fact, his respects to the new owners. There had been cats sitting upon satin pillows in the drawing room, cats walking about like flower-faced sibyls, cats purring at Mr. Spitzer's feet, cats on pedestals, cats swinging in hammocks. There had been a great white cat standing at the top of the marble stairway—less fearful than the raven might have been, certainly, yet giving Mr. Spitzer quite a start. There had been cats' eyes gleaming like gooseberries in the shadows, enigmatic faces of delicacy and disdain. A cat had walked up and down on the piano keys, playing a little tune from the works of one of the more obscure eighteenth-century musical composers.

The old caretaker had long since passed away, having been, even when Mr. Spitzer first knew him, like an old mummified pharaoh wrapped in his body which was his boat, and there was a new caretaker, but Mr. Spitzer had said nothing, for the cats were flourishing. There were as many cats as cattails by a marsh stream, butterflies gleaming among the shadows.

Of course, Mr. Spitzer, when he remembered such visits, was probably only teasing my mother who had accused him of never amusing her, and it was true that he himself was never amused by life, he being this old family lawyer with the sombre, weedy look, the attitude of a perpetual grief which could not seem to settle upon any one point of view. He recognized, of course, though my mother must often point it out to him, no practical value in his own situation of eternal paradox, the fact that, for example, though he disparaged the fickle operations of the law, he was a lawyer with a rigid, conscientious mind, the guardian of my mother's property. Was he not over-scrupulous, guarding my mother's life when she was already dead, and was it not he who hired the servants and paid these astronomical bills, often out of waning resources or an imaginary wealth? He had also his brother's debts to pay long after he surely seemed to have paid them. His brother would never have assumed responsibility as Mr. Spitzer had assumed it, he was quite certain—would never have paid Joachim's debts as he paid Peron's now with every new day of his life, it seemed to him. For himself, he had incurred no real indebtedness now of any kind for years. Yet his brother, distrusting the law, had had no use for any lawyer unless he was a crooked lawyer, one who could be fixed, one who would fix the witness and the judge. How often, not succeeding, his brother had tried to fix him, and Mr. Spitzer remembered that now his dead brother was this floater forever upon the waves of death, that his instability had increased.

Peron had had so much to live for, yet though he was shallow, and Mr. Spitzer had had only his elegiac music, that which still remained to console him, the music he had written only for himself or for no mortal ear. Mr. Spitzer, cupping his fat hands, drumming his fingers together with plaintive sadness, remembered that hour, that hour of terrible shock he continually relived, that in which he had been called suddenly away from his elegiac music to the morgue of a great city, there to identify, among homeless men and fallen women and faceless creatures and bloated corpses of the dead, his identical brother. Ever since then, his life had not been entirely his own, but perhaps, to be exact, to be truthful, it never had been, as he would always say, slightly yawning when he thought of the lost years, the words which were never to be spoken.

His swollen head nodding from side to side with those usual indecisions which he could not really resolve, he could only apologize for the fact that he had continued in his usual paths, that he represented the erroneous and arbitrary system of the law which should one day be, he hoped, of the completed past, for there would be no need of any judge or lawyer, just as there would be no need of any musician or sailor or lighthouse keeper. The future should be, he tremulously believed, the silent music which requires neither instruments nor voices, the heavenly harmonies forever fixed above the floods of time, dark time, those unmoving golden spheres set above and beyond these present fluctuations, the tides of discord moving not again to disturb our peaceful and our dreamless sleep. Perfect life should be perfect death. One should not die while one should live. One should not live while one should die.

He could believe in probably no hell more than this present individual life already afforded to the living. He was not sure that heaven should be so much a place as a state of mind when we should have completely forgotten who we were, when we should have put off this mortal clay and should have been united in heavenly mansions as equal brothers, one and the same. Peace should lie at the end of this mortal course. There should be no rivalry between person and person, none between the divisions of self. There should be no immortal derangement as of this present world with all its stains and cracks and flaws and irremediable ills. There should be a complete oblivion and not what my mother apparently wished for, a complete memory—she continually narcotizing, however, by the opium doses, by the needle points, her memory even of the most commonplace things, she allaying her sensibilities and sinking into a deeper and deeper, visionary sleep so that she should not see him, this old family lawyer with his brother's face, so that he should be displaced by many images, by sleeping car porters with golden roosters on their heads and headless horsemen and all those other invisible beings only she could imagine. It was never certain that even she could imagine them. No one knew her thoughts.

All souls should be equal when all were dead, as Mr. Spitzer would say, and all horses should come in first, if he might be permitted to employ in my oblivious mother's presence his dead brother's language for which he must elaborately apologize, his brother having been a most competitive soul and never satisfied, one who had lived in no sphere whatever but that incomplete sphere of competition, failure or victory or both, and his brother having often tried, by various means, to displace the visible realities, to confuse the spectator for the sake of some immediate but perhaps altogether hallucinatory goal. The immediate moment only had been his brother's, he having lived through the fact that life was always fleeting, that human memory was short, that impressions were not lasting and were inaccurate—and he had lost his life, or he had gained his life through death. Mr. Spitzer did not really know. For Mr. Spitzer, always and increasingly, remembered him, living his brother's life and dying his brother's death, it seemed to him, and so he looked back upon himself as one who was dead.

Mr. Spitzer, though he must admit that he had been outwardly identical to his brother—many people having been mistaken because of these great similarities, many people still confusing these brothers in their minds—yet had always had a different internal character and constellation of values, an almost cosmic serenity which had enveloped him even in moments of his greatest and most personal, most bitter disappointments as when his brother died, and if it had been his brother who had lived and he who had died as was so nearly possible, what memory of him would his brother have cherished at the cost of his own impatient, instinctive life? Would his brother have felt, for Mr. Spitzer's anguished sake, this great vein throbbing in his forehead, this quivering of his pulse, these flutterings of his eyelids, these trembling throat cords, and would he have spoken with this voice which now my mother heard? Would he have adopted this attitude of punctuality? Would he have endured my mother's pleasure in ignoring him?

If he had lived, would his impatient brother have spent so many empty evenings and hours here in this dead, turreted house by the cold, dark sea which moved and breathed and sobbed, almost as if it were trying to compete with him, to drown his grief—or have attempted to finish, as Mr. Spitzer would always ask, Mr. Spitzer's unfinished music, even to add a hesitant note—or ever have brought to a sick lady a bouquet of winter violets plucked from a secret place, even in the midst of the whirling snows, the furious blast?

His brother, certainly, it was all too clear to this living man, would not have been so faithful to my mother for the sake of his dead brother's continuing love and in memory of Mr. Spitzer whom she had always ignored, he whom Mr. Spitzer now remembered with almost a tear for himself, the poor, unappreciated musician who had turned so silently away when she had refused for the last fickle and unconstant time the dimpled hand which he had proffered to her, the passive hand, his offer of the ideal and incorruptible marriage, that immortal happiness which had been too great, as he realized now, for realization in this mortal life, within these narrow limitations. For of the flesh, it never could have been. Perhaps as this way had been, it had been best, both from his point of view and my mother's, Mr. Spitzer must concede, grudgingly, after so many years. Yet he could not help thinking that his brother would not have honored Mr. Spitzer's immortal love if, as so easily might have been the case, Mr. Spitzer had been the dead and the buried and turning to dust and ashes, as now perhaps his brother was, though precariously living through this approximate memory of him.

Mr. Spitzer was sure, his face lovingly smiling as if to conceal his grief, that his brother's love of life would have been too great, too impetuous for this prolonged moment of farewell or for the serenity which had been quite meaningless to him, a man who had preferred, to all conceivable dreams and visions transpiring in isolation, the great crowds of Derby Day, colors and raucous noises, phantasmagorias enough for him as of each present, fleeting moment. His brother would not have sat up all night with any corpse, for his brother had been afraid of death. His brother would never have watched, as Mr. Spitzer did, the passage of a dying soul from this world to the next, that which should be, Mr. Spitzer still believed, no world but the coldness and the darkness, that which should be void of consciousness, that where should be not a tree or a bush or a star, not a reed bird singing among the reeds. His brother would not have indulged, not even for one sad or happy moment, my mother's opium illusions. He would have swept my mother into the living sunlight, even for one magnificent moment of defeat, even though the living sunlight might be, of course, her death, the death of beauty. What had his brother cared for the immortal beauty of one remembered face? Peron had cared only, it had seemed, for old hags. My mother, Mr. Spitzer realized, held it against him that he did not rescue her, carry her away as Peron might have done—for she was restive, and she yearned for her escape from this illness, even though the years might crumble around her, though she might be suddenly old, though she might die if ever she escaped into the living sunlight.

As to poor Joachim, how could he play, however, Peron's role, Mr.

Spitzer knowing only, as he would always say, the darkness and the night, the cold and empty places as of a deathless dream? He might have liked to have obliged her, but it was always too late, and he could not kill his love, he being unlike his brother who had been without scruples, without reserves as to any other's life, even perhaps as to his own. His brother, now dead, could not have spent so many years and so many hours and so many quarter hours and so many timeless minutes with a woman he said he hated unless he could justify his hatred by marrying her, by sweeping her out of the darkness of this old house, as Mr. Spitzer, his face sweating with the awful thought, would sometimes suggest to my mother when, in a mood completely rejecting once more his apparent faithfulness as a mere façade which she could always see through, she accused him of subtle faithlessness, that he was absent when he was present, that he was wandering through the intricate streets of a dark city in perhaps the underworld, the world which lies under this and is always close to the surface of life.

Mr. Spitzer would seem to deny, of course, that he knew, except for his discursive legal profession and his sporadic continuation in other people's minds, the least thing about a lower world, that of the thief who had stolen bright jewels, that of the painted street woman leering under a lamp. Mr. Spitzer's interests, of necessity, were special and refined, somewhat remote—though it was also true, as he would sometimes eagerly state as if he were overwhelmed by an absolutely new idea, that in order to reach the upper world, one must first travel through the lower world, visiting all streets, lanes, alleys, and the journey might be endless like some of those journeys taken by my mother.

CHAPTER 27

※

Oh, why were these ancient people always so involved, turning for-ever and forever upon the same spiral problems, themselves, I wondered, and why could my beautiful mother never see the sunlight, the living sunlight of actuality, and why instead of acknowledging her situation and facing it must she imagine that she was someone else, perhaps Cathe-rine the Great sleeping in a bed with pillars of twisted amethyst, or that she was listening to an intricate dialogue between a swan-necked Chinese mandarin and a French clown whose head was a church steeple, neither of whom understood the other's language, yet though a perfect under-standing existed between them? Why must she interrupt, addressing a remark to someone who was not there?

Mr. Spitzer, unlike my mother whose pleasures never dimmed, was aware of most of his difficulties, perhaps of even more than my mother or Mr. Spitzer realized, as he would sometimes innocently acknowledge, his head nodding as my mother slept—for he was never immunized by any drug, and all the unreal things that happened to him were real and monstrous threats, disturbing the course of his pacific existence. Every experience, even that which he had not been aware of, had left its trace. There was always some right in what my mother said, even when she was wrong, her mind distilled by the juices of languorous poppy flowers which gave to her these perennial essences of thought running from year to year or recurring over a long period, even as a perennial joke caused by her consummate lack of faith. Indeed, it was this lack of faith which made all things possible to her.

Left to his own abstruse devices, certainly, Mr. Spitzer would never have stirred outside his own doorway, and no report could then have been made of his activities, and my mother would have been mystified, not enjoying her present sense of omniscience. Undoubtedly, he would have been quite secretive, as taciturn as he had always wished to be, and seldom would have expressed himself. He found it extremely burdensome to place himself, as a matter of fact, in the world of competitive women and men, he preferring his own isolation and sense of distance and curi-ous neutrality. Who was the dying spirit in a hollow house? Who was the wind? He would not so much disagree with the phantasmagoric facts which my mother always insisted she had resurrected concerning his present life, his mysterious goings and comings, as with the perverse interpretation which she placed upon them, her insistence, for example, that minor details were of major importance, that major events were of no importance, for it was she who was isolated, she who lay still among old, frothing laces and stained satin waves and wilted rosebuds in faded candle light which half revealed, shadows which half concealed her beautiful, lively, impassive face, she who might imagine what she would and find nothing more than she imagined or many things exceeding imagination or only that which pleased her in the empty hours, those devoid even of Mr. Spitzer's company, he who moved like a dead man walking in the difficult, indifferent world of rival interests and cruel delays and who knew too well, though he continued this mortal struggle, the uselessness of struggling now at this late date for human recognition, the paucity of lost events and lost loves which controlled his every present thought or step.

He went out only for business purposes, and nothing of world-shaking importance had ever happened to him, and the details were always trivial, and many of his practical transactions had no bearing at all upon present realities, and that was why he preferred the Pythagorean harmonies, the muffled planetary voices, the music of the silent spheres in a world which should come after this, and even my mother's company, and even the company of Mr. Chandelier. An evening away from my mother was always a very real deprivation to him.

Though she surrounded him with many incalculable hazards, his hazards were much greater in the world he visited when he did not visit her, she continually reminding him, by her eternal derision, who he was or who he was not, and he was prone to forget. His life, which should be continuous, was intermittent. He knew his deficiencies in respect to his self-concern and to his own personal memory, the aggregate of lost impressions, his fugitive thoughts, even that he was likely to walk through a wall of shimmering glass or forget the purpose of his immediate journey, practical or impractical, that he was likely to take the wrong train, get off at the wrong city, the wrong station, the wrong star—though he was painfully accurate, of course, and covered with exact reminders to himself. In case he should ever be found, even as the altered visage of himself, he should be recognized, he hoped, by his flowing cape of darkness and by his various paraphernalia, his high silk hat and black necktie and rosebud with maidenhair, the numerous calling cards he always carried on his person, an out-dated passport for a journey he had not taken, had not thought of taking, and also, of course, for he would sooner have gone unclothed than have stepped forth without it, a scroll or sheet of the silent music or perhaps several abandoned beginnings, mere preludes, perhaps several tentative endings, mere epilogues to the great body of his uncreated work, unfinished epithalamiums and dirges and vast recessionals to be sung during the recession of the clergy and choir from the chancel to the robing rooms, notes for the voiceless choirs, for the tongueless nightingales, for the deaf listeners. Thus should he ever show up in a city morgue among the drowned women and the fallen men, the poor brothers, all men should know that he had not been his brother, that his brother had not been Mr. Spitzer, that this life had been this illusion even before his death. There would be no more, tormenting to a man of his precise certainties, these uncertainties which were not his own, these cloud-like apparitions in his devious path, these dimmed street lamps shining through fog, these spectral shapes and whirling leaves, for he would be dead, not remembering himself, forgetting Peron, too, as if he had never existed, and perhaps even my mother would have forgotten Mr. Spitzer, her evening caller, time healing, he believed, all wounds, even the wounds of time, even his when he had disappeared, when his eyes no more gleamed in starlight.

In the meantime, to any engagement other than his evenings with my mother who so often ignored him in favor of God knew whom, he would come, it always seemed, too early, or else there would be inexplicable delays, shiftings of scenes, alterations of places, sudden snow storms or unexplained summers, light where there had been darkness, darkness where there had been light, laughter where there had been silence, and this though he frequently consulted his jeweled watch, timing his steps which were difficult to time. Indeed, if my mother did not interrupt him to make some irrelevant remark, such as that there were storks' nests on the roof-tops and long-limbed storks drifting through clouds, he would sometimes add that it was, as a matter of fact, his dead brother's wrist watch which he wore, the crystal unbroken as his dead brother, thus destroying, in some people's minds, the hypothesis of an impulsive, thoughtless suicide, had most thoughtfully removed this time-piece before jumping like a wild horse. Why should his brother have owned such a fine time-piece? Any old silver-dollar stop watch should have done for him, a man of blatant tastes, a man who had worn loud checks, a man impatient with the idea of eternity for which he had no time, a man who had preferred careless associates, low company, lapsed souls, void characters, dice-rattlers, and active nights and days, a man who had laughed at Mr. Spitzer's silence. But he had left, among his unwanted possessions, this accurate, fine time-piece, this which marked, now on Mr. Spitzer's trembling wrist, the course of the inaccurate planets, the recurring years, the unknown flow of time, the backward flow, seasons, days, hours, half-minutes, quarter-minutes, seconds as of a hair's breadth, every conceivable departmentalization, and yet Mr. Spitzer must lose his way, fighting against a great undertow of timelessness, searching through time for that which was already lost in space as undoubtedly almost any fool could tell him. Almost any fool, including himself, could tell him that there was no time, that it was all this artifice, even like my poor mother's opium dreams of life and love and death or her dream of some great coffin of stars which might contain the body of her love. Yet this elegant watch was a convenient time-piece for a poor lawyer, a poor musician dealing with the flow of time, the groupings of beats or pulses into equal measures, accelerated or delayed, so old Joachim always thoughtfully wore it, mindful of the fact that his own identical watch was that which was broken, that it had stopped long ago, its wheels rusted, its delicate mechanism being clogged with dust, its crystal shattered into a thousand pieces—probably several days after his brother's death—or perhaps several days before—Mr. Spitzer had forgotten, for he had been, it was true, in a state of shock negating memory in any personal sense. Perhaps while walking along the sidewalk under a light snow-fall, he had fainted and had fallen at about the time of his brother's death, perhaps through sympathy, for they had always suffered, except for this final accident, the same accidents, one not falling unless the other fell. Mr. Spitzer had found his broken watch again only recently, stuck behind some bottles and scrolls in the crystal dust on his dressing table, pale as the gleaming of a marine eye, and had begun to wear it under his cuff on his left wrist as a reminder to him that his brother's life had been brief, that all that life which Mr. Spitzer attributed to him now was only his imagination as when he heard a long sighing in the darkness or a sudden squall of laughter in the days of endless calm when not one wind would blow through the sails of a ship stuck at the far horizon, when not one cloud would move.

His brother's watch was surely that which ticked on and on, even like Mr. Spitzer's own heart beating, pulsing in the darkness. For surely, it was not he who had shattered time by jumping headlong into time with screaming stars, and he could have made no such great mistake. His brother's watch had been an excellent time-piece for clocking the horses, the long jumps over waterfalls—Mr. Spitzer sometimes timing now the great breakers coming in with their foaming manes and tails, the great mollusk horses with their flanks gleaming through tides and foams as he thought of the long horse race of life, these foaming horses and foaming manes and tails and the cloud-streaked sands when they withdrew, the salt cracked and barren like a great cranium exposed or covered with moon jellycombs reflecting the horses streaming through moon-lit clouds. This was his elegiac music in memory of his brother. It was an excellent watch for timing Mr. Spitzer's eternal music and the music of the dying wind. He must allow, of course, for the inaccuracy of the wearer, the fact that a watch has a tendency to be influenced by the beating of the pulse, whether slow or fast, and this old watch was sometimes slowed though still probably more accurate than the sundials in the windy gardens, particularly when they were shadowed by the wings of birds.

He, Joachim, the survivor of his own sad heart, had died a thousand deaths, from none of which he had suffered any mortal injury but to his spiritual peace, as he would say, and that only in retrospect when someone else had tactlessly reminded him of it, his perfect, corpulent dignity and external elegance of appearance being in no way ruffled by an irrational event. He should have been apologetic, but he was proud that he had walked through a wall of invisible glass, doing great harm, no doubt, to the wall but none, in the last analysis, to him, and he was proud that the old desk clerk had insisted that he was dead, as Mr. Spitzer would recall, chuckling softly, thinking of the joke he had played. The preservation of his dignity was now, however, all that remained for him in life, or so it often seemed to him.

There was probably nothing he feared so much as the loss of his dignity, that he might seem ridiculous in other people's eyes. He wished to make, of course, a good impression, and yet there were innumerable, unimportant instances when he came near to losing his external dignity or bravado, and everybody knows, as he himself must cautiously admit, that there is nothing funnier than a fat man slipping on a banana peel. He, of course, was always busy losing weight, even as he gained it, and he feared his elephantine avoirdupois, his size, the vast area of his response to life. He feared the icy pavements, the polished floors reflecting his image, the crystalline glare of the sky when half the sky is in darkness, and these loud noises ringing in his dead or deafened ear which often confused him, disturbing his own sense of order and justice. There was always this discord of the tone or the tones held over, confusing the simplicity of his arrangement. There was always the holding over of one or more tones of a chord into the following chord, a blurring of effects which produced, with every new moment, a terrible discord, the suspension of the concord which he had expected. He was always being caught ponderously in a revolving door. He was always being caught between two headlong traffic streams, perhaps those of some other year, always crossing the street or avenue just when the red light turned to green. Even as my mother had supposed, the signal lights were all wrong, undependable, and he had reached the wrong city. A mere stranger once had tapped him on the elbow as he was crossing a crowded thoroughfare and had asked him if he wanted to die, and when Mr. Spitzer had doubtfully replied in the negative, at the same time shaking his head in the affirmative, then had escorted him through a maze of traffic, the cars and trains which had seemed to come from all directions, blowing their traffic horns and whistles as perhaps of some other year or day.

CHAPTER 28

꡴

His faithfulness drew him each evening here as to a brilliant star, yet though he had outlived himself, he having, he believed, except for these enchanted evenings in a nightmarish world of my mother's narcotic dreams, little sense as to the immediacy of his own corporeal reality, the vastness of this trembling flesh enclosing his feeble spirit like a flame. He might well have been, he must admit, among my mother's irresponsible hallucinations, only another of the luminous and metamorphic dead she entertained, a bearded Russian bishop or an iridescent lighthouse keeper, perhaps the Antarctic Queen Maud Mountains with her snow-capped mountain peaks and white umbrellas and lace capes and great snow owls with horn-rimmed spectacles and human faces, perhaps Queen Charlotte Islands in a storm or a moon-faced duchess with rustling silken skirts and many brown-eyed lap-dogs barking, many music boxes tinkling old-fashioned waltzes, many astral voices, bird cries, insect whirrings, perhaps the headless horseman fording a brook, the flowers turning into serpents.

For all his life, in a personal sense, it seemed to him, except for his delusive evenings here, had been a dark and empty plain, and only here where he was still denied and turned away, he was still renewed, perhaps by my mother's obtuse faith that he would always return, he with his hesitant smile, smiling at him because he smiled, his unchanging ways. It was only problematical, however, his life which he had precariously lived, and it was also problematical, that spindle of creative flame which is said to sleep in the eternal darkness, weaving our bodies, weaving our separate souls, weaving the clothing of our dreams, weaving the nakedness. He was this living ghost whose terrible flesh belied, he believed, his late death or his brother's early death, and so his problems of being were greater than he knew, even as were his more comprehensive problems of non-being. How should he know the actual man he was? How should his brother know?

His brother would never return, never in this individual life, Mr. Spitzer knew, for the dead did not return except in our thoughts. His brother, his face veiled, would not be born again, even should there be the darkest clouds and whirlwinds, vortexes, stars out of their places, deserts suddenly flowering. Even in this drugged atmosphere, there were the things not possible, or they were possible through the deceived memory of the unknown.

He remembered his dead brother with an increasing vivacity when he had forgotten himself and most of his subdued enthusiasms, the meditative pursuits he once had passionately loved, just as his loud-mouthed brother, having no foresight, no patience to wait for the caterpillar to become the butterfly or for the rose to become the star, had loved the cruelty of actual life which was enough for him, or so it had seemed. It had seemed that he had given no thought to a future life, that the present hour or moment had sufficed—whereas, Mr. Spitzer had thought only of the impossible future.

Mr. Spitzer, search through memory's dim corridors and lanes though he would, had no vivid recollection that he, of himself, had ever deliberately sought, until after his twin brother's untimely death, the heterogeneous crowds, the motley crew, and he was still, he believed, this serene gentleman who, if left to his own choices, preferred his isolation and the darkness, though he came to see my mother and sit by her bedside as if he were drawn by the bright lights, here where were these wandering shadows.

For he still remembered her, he would explain, much as she had been in his youth, and here where there were these spiritual derangements, he found his only sense of his unbroken continuity in life, perhaps because no chair had changed its place for years, and there were these ethereal gleamings of gold and silver and watered silk and fluted ivory as of the great shell of Venus, these intricately woven bellropes, these bells which gave off a booming sound like that of the loud sea bittern, these candle flames reflected in dark Venetian mirrors, these semi-faces staring from the ceiling and from the floor.

He had even given up, two or three years after his brother's irrational death which had divided and sub-divided his own rational soul almost to the point of lunacy, that favorite pursuit which, during his brother's incalculable life, had often consoled him in the midst of his absolute or his tentative loneliness, his collecting, like emblems of each shining moment, beautiful butterflies of every coloration and kind, of every description and impression, of every realm, the Hesperides like spirit messengers, tenants of air, tenants of earth, winged flowers, gossamer wings reflecting many prismatic lights, brimstone-colored butterflies burning like torpid flames in the wind, bejeweled butterflies as precious to him as the most precious jewels or mosaic emperors or bits of colored glass my mother at least imagined were hers, more precious than the cuckoo singing as it flies, the warblers and the babblers she thought she heard, the griffins flying over the roof-tops, the imaginary house guests, the imaginary sea bishops with mitre-shaped heads and vestments of silver scales, the long-limbed and heron-footed citizens walking in the cool of the evening shade, the pagodas moving on the waves, the swan weathercocks lifting their wings in the winds and the empty paddocks and the drowned gardens and the mermaids feeding their infants at their breasts, the milk-white unicorn enclosed by a picket fence, all these beauties which he could no more see than if he were a mole under the ground and which my mother saw, even when her eyes were closed, and yet he had cared as much for his ephemeral butterflies as she had cared for things invisible made visible to her or as his dead twin brother had cared for the wastrel wheels of chance, the games of loaded dice, the croupiers, the billiard hall artists, the macabre clowns, the drugged horses, the swift horses, the harlequins, the painted ladies fluttering through the darkness of the night which had held no mysteries for him.

Of course, Mr. Spitzer's impersonal passion had been expensive, a great toll upon his system. He had had to carry on, for one thing, a large correspondence with other meditative butterfly hunters, this correspondence requiring a considerable out-lay for stamps and envelopes, even distracting him from his silent music, and he had had to do much research of a delicate nature such as thoughtless Peron would most certainly have scorned. Peron would most certainly have seen no value, no unearthly significance as to butterflies or any other spirits. As for himself, Mr. Spitzer had not added to his butterfly collection now for many years, needless to say, and many other things had come to an end on the day of Peron's devastating funeral, including, of course, his own capacious heart, the living heart, his way of life or most of it, the important part, yet though he had contrived to continue here, colorless as he had always been and of few personal interests, though still occasionally remembering, when his memory of his brother grew dim, the phenomenal world of the butterfly in all its illusive manifestations, seas of twinkling yellow flowers and clouds of yellow butterflies like flowers floating in the pale morning air. And why should he not remember, for his own sake, these almost incorporeal butterflies? What harm could he possibly do to anyone by his present butterfly memories and thoughts? Sometimes the butterfly perching upon the flower had seemed as identical to the flower as twin to twin, and the flower had seemed to fly away, and the winged petals had remained, much to his bewilderment.

Peron's interests, unlike his own, had been many and mundane, Peron having cared, or so it had seemed before his death by accident or suicide, for no theory of a life beyond this life, no after-life, nor could he have wasted his precious moments watching the amazed birth of a butterfly, the first tremblings of the feeble, dew-lit wings as they unfolded, or watching the last tremblings, the death, the expiration. The manifestations of birth and death were the same in this realm. Indeed, if one watched at only a certain moment, if one were suddenly called away in the midst of these proceedings, one should never know whether it was death or birth, beginning or end, as Mr. Spitzer would sometimes say, plucking at his almost invisible, feathery mustache or consulting his bejeweled wrist watch to see if there was time for his sporadic butterfly memories which, though for years quiescent in his mind, he still enjoyed. It was an early experience such as this ambiguity which had caused him to first embark upon his studies of impalpable butterflies.

CHAPTER 29

As to the subject of the butterfly, there were many mysteries, of course, and ambiguous beings not easily defined, creatures who seemed to be at the boundary line between butterfly and moth, evasive creatures who, though they were of the dawn, were so nearly alike in their almost intangible features as to make it difficult for even a great expert like Mr. Spitzer to draw, with absolute certainty, a map or boundary line, to say which was butterfly and which was moth, just as it might at times be difficult to distinguish between brother and brother or between the ecstasy of happiness and that of sorrow. Seldom did happiness and sorrow occur in pure and disrelated states, happiness being so often tinctured by sorrow because of the fear that happiness should be only temporal, having its end, sorrow being tinctured by that happiness which came from the knowledge that sorrow might endure.

It had certainly been, however, Mr. Spitzer's observation long ago, a butterfly performed its peregrinations by day when almost as many colors were revealed as were concealed, and moths usually flew by night which muted and subdued or exaggerated, changing familiar shapes to unfamiliar shapes, when the streaked plumes of the dandelions were like the Milky Way enclosing sparks of insect stars, when the white helmet flowers opened their translucent petals gleaming with the sourceless reflections of ethereal fire, when the trumpets of Jericho were blowing in the windy gardens by the sea, when the pale, luminous, trembling flowers were lighthouses to the wayfaring moths, those drawn always toward the dream of light, toward flame which should extinguish them—but there were variations as to this apparent law as to passage by day or night. There were also, he remembered, many moths which flew by day, especially in regions of great nocturnal moth-eating birds, such as owls and hawks and bats. So moths would sometimes avoid the night of stars. Yet there were great gold-eyed owls flying among clouds of luna moths with moons of passage upon their wings, so one could not be sure that moths feared owls around whom they broke like seas of moths breaking around the prows of boats rising upon the moon-lit tides, breaking upon the figureheads which had slept beneath the waves. Doubtless there were night-flying butterflies. If so, he had never yet encountered them though butterflies flew over his chessboard and butterflies landed on the brim of his high silk chimney hat and on his sleeve and on his flowing cape. Usually, he saw butterflies clinging to the honey-scented orchard boughs in the honey-colored sunlight and suddenly flying out across his path like winged flowers. He had walked through tumultuous orchards. He had yet to encounter a butterfly which performed its passage through the air by night, a butterfly which was abroad to see the cold stars shining through the bare, lacy tree branches and through the shifting, silver-lighted clouds, the moon shining on the breast of the sleeping wave. Yet all things were doubtless possible, and as clouds of migratory butterflies had sometimes been observed far out at sea, far from any shore, it might be assumed that they had performed their journey through the night. It might be assumed that they had been buffeted along by winds, through many days and nights. For the waves gave no resting place, and the sky gave none. The earth gave none, moving continually in its place, moving like the sea. There were those who believed that these butterflies were blown by hurricanes far off their course, perhaps that they were blown from star to star, travelling over lunar seas and planetary meadows and fields of distant light. There were those who thought that these butterflies sailed because of their own dreams, being these wandering psyches. According to the Greek, the butterfly was psyche, the word which signified the human soul or mind or mental life, the human spirit. Butterflies were wanderers seeking reunion with immortal love, Mr. Spitzer believed, so they might wander far off their course, flying each as his own mariner in his winged ship under the flying stars or flying in droves. He had seen many times the caterpillaring sea. He had seen wings of butterflies like sails of ships gleaming through distant clouds. As droves of nautical butterflies were reported far out at sea with a certain amount of regularity by the watchmen in lonely crow's-nests under the stars flying like birds, perhaps these oceanic migrations were intentional, not merely the result of accident or chance or whirling monsoons or blows of glassy waves or winds blowing them or great hurricanes making of day a night of the shining stars, the stars burning like great hurricane lamps in the dark clouds over the crystal sands burning like stars in the light streaked by long lights like lilies or the necks of the wild swans.

He had seen the caterpillar wrapping itself in its silken cocoon, changing into a chrysalis which was like a mummy sleeping in its casing or a shroud around the dead. He had seen the preparations of the cater-pillar for a future life, the leaf-roller caterpillar cementing together the edges of two pale leaves shrouded by glistening cobwebs, leaving but one aperture for its entrance, then crawling through the door into its little tent or boat where it should sleep until it should awaken, achieving immortality within the logic of mortality, as Mr. Spitzer said. The most hidden moments had been revealed to him, often when he was in agony of spirit, or when he was most melancholy and withdrawn, when the irises of his eyes had shrunken to pin-points, when his grey skin was mottled with rain spots like the rain lilies or seemed to be turning brown, when he spoke with hoarse notes as if there were a frog in his throat, when he seemed numb, dumb, dead, or sleeping.

Indeed, as Mr. Spitzer would sometimes say, his fat flesh rippling as he spoke, his voice this voice of unctious softness which was soporific in its effect, he was still obscurely, tremblingly proud of his brilliant butterflies, still the old butterfly collector at heart, he had no doubt, and remembering, as if he had seen them only yesterday instead of many years ago, his enviable butterfly collection, boxes of butterflies which were surely somewhere in the chaos of his house, classified and labelled and embalmed even like, he would suppose, his embalmed memories. Or perhaps they recalled to him now his fleeting, flashing, mercurial memories of that life which was no more, the fugitive thoughts old Joachim had tried to stay, the scintillations of the undying dream when it was already dead, the images of the vanished moments moving through his clouded and opaque brain, the lost perceptions which were never lost and which returned just when he had forgotten all other temporal thoughts.

He surely had had in his possession, he remembered, many beautiful butterflies, many mementoes of golden coppers dazzling as sunlight and white admirals white as Arctic snows under the midnight sun, one spots, two spots, four spots, six spots, eight spots, butterflies with dice markings like the dice cup flower, speckled woods and pearl crescents and mountain ringlets and marsh ringlets and foam ringlets, butterflies the color of the thrush's egg, saffrons with the rose blush upon the shimmering, glimmering wings, wings marked by intricate leaf veinings or veinings as of the transparent human hand, wings marked by horizontal bars and spots like, it sometimes seemed to him, opalescent moons, moons of his silent music written on his shirt cuffs or black-bordered white handkerchief which he had worn in his breast pocket over his heart ever since his brother's death.

He remembered the images of the children who, unlike these human children, were identical to their dead parents, images of the future life which repeated the ineffable past in every feature and whirled for a day or months.

The old caterpillar sleeping like the infant Moses in his cradle among the bulrushes by a dark stream—would he not beget this future life? Often in his butterfly walks Mr. Spitzer had used to find, in long-lashed grasses along the meadow streams and marsh ponds, pearly eyes and eyed browns, communities of butterflies which had started at his steps or the sound of his dark cape flowing around him even as butterflies had used to start up in great droves before the sleeping coachman driving his sleeping horses in the long avenue. Butterflies had started up like lights, lighting the way. Mr. Spitzer remembered that once he had found, in a dark and frozen winter when the ice shrouded the thin-leafed bushes and trees gleaming in iridescent light like frozen brides veiled by ice billows and snow and impregnated only by seeds of the moon or memory of refracted light, when even the sea seemed frozen and scarcely breathing in its sleep, the waves scarcely moving on this shore, the beautiful mourning cloak butterfly hibernating in a hollow tree trunk where, like some old grizzly bear dreaming of butterflies, butterflies in his tomb, it was sleeping a long winter through, sleeping with folded wings, and he had not disturbed the sleeper. Doubtless he must have seen other hibernating butterflies, others which slept the long winters through and which came to life again perhaps in the spring—though none had lingered in his mind with the beauty and pathos of that one mourning cloak, seen through a veil of snow and ice. When in the spring he had seen a mourning cloak fluttering over the daisy-starred fields, he had felt as if it were an old friend, and he had almost greeted it, had almost lifted his hat. He remembered many meadow browns, and though he had watched for growth, he had observed that a butterfly grew no larger after it was born, and neither did it seem to age, and its colors faded not, so it was somewhat difficult to judge of age in this realm. He had observed, of course, that butterflies were vulnerable to many forms of death, that death came in many guises, in many forms, and yet though they were most mortal, they had always seemed to him the most perfect symbol of immortality, each being the image, the perfect image of himself, a being woven in his sleep, such a being of perfection as doubtless a poor human could never be, never in this life and never in the next which was, he believed, improbable, not to be depended on. For we saw ourselves die while yet we lived.

He remembered, sometimes even in his sleep, the Essex skippers and the Lulworth skippers, the chalk hill blues flying above blue hills of sleeping butterflies and the orange tips with lights like port lights upon their wings and the large browns, the sleeping beauty marked by eyelashes and eyes, the bath whites and the pale veined marble butterflies who were lovers of marble statues in the wind-swept gardens by the sea and continually fluttering over their cheeks and bosoms and thighs and blindly staring eyes, pale clouded yellows who had navigated the darkest seas or perhaps only these flooded gardens, the purple hairstreaks and the black hairstreaks and the white mountain butterflies and the Arctic satyrs, wings of flame roosting in flocks in the dark woods, their wings like flames, monarchs who flew to the South with the migratory birds in the autumn and far North with the birds in the spring, butterflies who migrated with the stars, butterflies with passages of ice floes reflected on their wings, emperors and great turreted bishops with wings like cloth of gold. Their lives were extremely hazardous, and they were buffeted by many storms streaking the skies with green and rose and gold and silver lights like the waves of the burning sea. He had seen, in his various wanderings, regal viceroys and vicereines and small gate-keepers, keepers of the gates of Heaven, hawks and turquoises and walls, banded purples and red-spotted purples, colors as of the pied linnet's wing, colors as of the piebald horse, colors as of the agate or as of the sea when it is like a great, slumberous eye staring in the sun-lit wind, designs as lovely as those of stained glass cathedral windows, brilliance as of burnished jewels gleaming in hallways of leaden-colored armor and kingly tombs, brilliance as of the jewels of Aaron's breastplate, colors like Japheth's enlarged opals, butterflies of every imaginable color and hue and gradation, the colors rivalling those of Joseph's coat of many colors, colors as of the birds of paradise.

Yet butterflies were colorless—the colors being the effects not of pigmentation but of the illusion of light shattered on the gleaming mirror scales as if they were so many geometric prisms, so many prisms dancing in Mr. Spitzer's mirroring mind.

What had always seemed, in the butterfly kingdom, rather odd to him, for it was the reverse of the human order—though perhaps it was no more peculiar than that the male birds wore brighter plumage than the female—some of the male butterflies were perfumed, having feathery scent patches or discs upon their wings, so they left a trail of perfume even in distant clouds, each being its own little scent bottle and perfume atomizer, emitting sweet scent—but the female was scentless. Probably this perfume, Mr. Spitzer said, was to attract the scentless female, so that she might find her mate, sweet-smelling as honeysuckle, hyacinth or cosmos or heliotrope, tuberose, mountain laurel, lupine, jack-in-the-pulpit, his own eau de cologne which was a mixture of many somnolent flowers. Sometimes, in fact, closing his puffy-lidded eyes, Mr. Spitzer sensed around him, now after so many years, especially in the cold winter evenings of trembling starlight, the perfumes of butterflies, these tremblingly winged flowers, the aromatic emanations by which they should be recognized. He smelled odors like balm, musk, myrrh, attar, frankincense, yet different from any of these. He would feel that there were butterflies in the empty rooms. But when he opened his eyes, it was only the night of the cold starlight, so what he sensed now was probably the perfume of his thoughts. He swore that he could smell his thoughts.

Though he was not always sure, of course, whether his present ghostly thoughts were his own or his dead brother's thoughts moving now through him, whirling and shaking, perhaps it would not be necessary, in the last crucial analysis, for him to know this transitory difference of effects, and there would be no ultimate difference when the heavenly harmonies were established on a surer foundation, not moving like waves, when conflicts were resolved at every level of thought, when he was divested of desire, when Mr. Spitzer had put off this mortal flesh and sombre cloak. How should he know when this had happened? Who knew, and who would ever know that which must remain unknown, his life beyond the grave, beyond the sphere of our human experience with all its limitations and unsoluble mysteries and doubts, those doubts which might themselves comprise a kind of faith?

He was not, he believed, and had never been wildly imaginative, and he was only as logical as he knew how to be, unlike his illogical brother who had been spiritually unimaginative and whose reasonings and motives must remain forever unknown to Mr. Spitzer, himself unknowable. So were Peron's finer impulses unknown to Joachim, who had seen but little of the occasional moments of quixotic generosity which others had attributed to his brother. For Joachim had been useless to his brother except for those occasions when he had been called upon to help him out of an entanglement, a fugitive relationship which might have embarrassed him in some of his other designs.

Joachim, Mr. Spitzer lovingly remembered, his face showing his astonishment, had even had to act as his brother's reluctant go-between, a pander to his desires which had never seemed to touch upon his genuine feelings, and he had had, upon one or two terrible occasions which he never would forget, to play Peron's role, to seem to be his brother when his brother had wished to rid himself of a difficulty or to break off a seemingly meaningless relationship, though doubtless the third party, the duped person must have been surprised to sense in him that stupor which was not his brother's usual characteristic. But Peron, even if Joachim had needed his help, would always have turned a deaf ear, Mr. Spitzer still believed, for there would have been no reciprocation, no return for something done or given. Peron would have shown not a spark of gratitude, not even after so many years. He had been one of those persons for whom it had been all but impossible to acknowledge generosity or indebtedness. He had airily dismissed Joachim from his mind when a purpose had been served. For in spite of all they had had in common, yet they had been divided by many things, not merely by death when it came—Peron had been, Mr. Spitzer still believed, the greater mystery, and death had enhanced his mystery. Though Joachim could not pretend to know all the secret valves of his own being, though he had never yet gotten a total glimpse of himself, he had known even less of Peron, but Mr. Spitzer was always trying to learn more of the remarkable fellow.

He had been a being of so many volatile impressions and mad designs and fickle moods, so many sudden turns and twists, so many inexpressible ideas, who had ever known him as, beyond all the externals of chance and circumstance, he really was, perhaps closer to his twin brother's heart than most persons had realized? Had even his twin brother known him, or had this worldly brother, less responsible than Mr. Spitzer was as to the necessity of understanding his own or another's life, ever inquired into the heart of this old Joachim, ever tried to unwind the silken threads of his thoughts, the tangled skeins? Peron, he seemed to remember, had gaily fluttered through this brief dance of life, wearing so many changeable colors, so many fragile coats, indulging in so many innovations and variations, so many patches and pieces and transformations, being like that mortal moment which was the one immortality, dying as we watched, and perhaps, though he had sought for greater freedom in another life, to shuffle off these mortal coils, he enjoyed no after-life now except through Mr. Spitzer's literal-minded and mournful memory of him, the approximate repetition of this broken life through fragmentary gleamings until it should be no more, until Mr. Spitzer himself should be dead and beyond recall. Mr. Spitzer knew the poor butterfly dying each evening on the lip of the evening rose.

His sympathies were great. Perhaps it was Peron he remembered, even like that poor creature who would never see a second dawn, and perhaps it was Joachim who had grown old. Indeed, to him, the old attorney whose many-folded, glistening face trembled in the mother-of-pearl evening light, his recurrent butterfly memories, like his dead brother's thoughts which moved and stirred in his cold, dead, imperceptive mind, were surely as beautiful as figments of the absolute, beautiful as the fictitious and multiform persons who, the splendors of my mother's toxic dreams, were like the quality of her essential evasiveness, her inability or unwillingness to look directly at the anonymous face of life, and who were evasively wafted to my mother upon waves of eternal darkness, the purple pharaohs in their swan boats, the Irish poets wrapped in bands of fog, the enrobed captains and emperors and Greek bishops who, having crossed the darkest seas this life would ever know, left their calling cards upon the jasper mantel piece, left their white umbrellas in the umbrella stands, their hats upon the hat-trees, she believed and still insisted, just as she believed herself, both living and dead, this animated and bejeweled corpse, to be the creature of mystical metamorphosis, of many transfigurations and conversions, even like the expanding crystals of Mr. Chandelier, the golden cobwebs singing and flying away, the golden humming birds flying out of the candle flames, the glaciers moving through her darkened bedroom, the snowshoe rabbits, the frozen clouds. Or perhaps a dark stranger reined his horse at the door. Or she heard the tinkle of distant piano keys, delicate trebles of sound followed by the loud breakers booming against corroded rocks, changing the shoreline and all familiar things.

Though he was not one who was now perceptive, though fleeting details escaped the orbits of his present interests, and he must agree with my mother that his stupor had long, long ago nullified him, yet it was certainly most curious that, though other knowledge failed to answer to his summons, this phenomenal butterfly knowledge had grown and increased, even during the years when he had given no conscious thought to it, when he had had no time for the renewal of his earlier interests, no time for butterflies or butterfly pursuits. He knew, better than he knew the life of his dead brother and those previously unsuspected characteristics and facets and faces and aspects which his brother had enjoyed and which still evaded complete understanding, the life of the luminous butterfly in its many inviolable expressions, colors, and variable markings, the image which was like a miraculous revivification, an epitome of all that had gone before, a moment's summation of all vanished moments. Indeed, he was constantly struck with a dulled sense of wonder, considering that, in a long interim which was like the absence of time, like many moons which had passed without his knowledge, these butterfly memories, rather than expiring, had shown such durability, that these transitory and mutable things should seem immutable and lasting and protracted and prolonged. For they should have been only the essential transiency of life, the changeableness of mortality, a nine days' wonder at the most, fragile as mere bubbles fading away into the air, vanishing and melting into empyreal nothingness, fleeting and fugitive and short-lived and perishable as human life, precarious and impermanent, brief, quick, brisk, temporary, things of but the moment, things which should not last till Doomsday, twinklings, flashings, breathings, things extempore and sudden and abrupt. They should have been like his poor brother's life.

He knew the wings marked with eyes, eyes which had been caused, according to a rumor still extant in the whispering butterfly circles, by someone who, perhaps when he was dying, long ago and in another life which was this evanescence and this melting into light, had looked upon a butterfly with a peculiar intensity of rapturous and undying vision, leaving the impressions of his eyes, these eyes which had multiplied, eyes like the eyes of Argus, the hundred-eyed watchman who was set to watch over Io when she was changed into a white heifer and wandered through flowering meadows and wandered far and wide before she was restored to her original form. They were as many as candle flames reflected in dark mirrors, as many as the eyes of the dead.

From whence came, as he would sometimes ponder aloud, the first butterflies, and were they journeyers between two stars, even like my mother's evening guests, those who could hear the grass grow, those who needed less sleep than a bird on the wing, and could my sleeping mother tell him, a man who distinguished not between the reality and the dream? Did the first butterflies crawl out of holes in the ground, or did they come with the bright cloud, the unearthly radiance? Mr. Spitzer could not really say, for he did not really know, yet though he had studied, at his leisure, many illuminated butterfly manuscripts, many wings, their hieroglyphs engraved upon their gleaming wings as by their names, the nameless dead should still be known and recognized even when they had suffered the last transfiguration. Yet the origin was wrapped in darkness and in mystery scarcely lighted by this momentary iridescence, the rainbow colors moving through a darkened bedroom.

From his point of view, and he had wandered far and wide through many blinding clouds, butterflies were as mysterious, though they were the created effects and not the fountainhead, as some old castle-building Creator, dreaming this creation of His phantoms, making out of His reveries this chimerical life of butterflies and stars and barnacles and men. Mr. Spitzer, though he had sought through the wide heavens and earth, had not found the face of God and had not found the location of immutable paradise, yet though he had visited such phantasmal places as the Happy Isles, the Fortunate Isles, the Isles of the Blessed, Aldebaran, Venus, the Garden of the Hesperides, the third heaven, the seventh heaven, Valhalla, Nirvana, the happy hunting grounds.

God was not God in Himself, Mr. Spitzer believed, but in these pitiful images of God, these images which were but phantoms fading on the air, clouds driven by the whirlwind. It was God's business to create, fashion, make, form, mold, preserve and keep, perpetuate, bless, absolve, curse, forgive. Yet what was God, a being of so many forms, so many names that He should seem as none? God, it had been said, was the True Vine, the Bread of Life, the Gate, the Door, the Wine, the Mediator, the Only-Begotten, the Anointed, the Word, the Restorer, the Resurrection, the Great Spirit, the Light of the World. God was the Man of Sorrows, the Old Man, the King of Glory, the King of Kings, the Prince of Peace, the Good Shepherd. God was the Narrow Way, the Rose, the Thorn. God was many things to many people. He was the Risen, Immanuel, the Word made Flesh, the Advocate, the Intercessor, the Dove. He was the King of Light opposed, Mr. Spitzer believed, by the necessary King of Darkness, for if there were no darkness, then there should be no conception of light.

Here in my mother's bedroom, Mr. Spitzer must have encountered, at some time, though he had perhaps been unaware of the exact moment, many other gods, the god of the sun, the goddess of the moon, the judge of the dead, the busy clerk of the underworld, the goddess with the head of a cat, the goddess of wisdom, the jackal god who was the conductor of the dead. For undiminishingly, there were many familiar spirits going and coming, many guides taking many paths, good geniuses, evil geniuses, demons, screeching harpies, wailing banshees, salamanders, shades, shadows, straw valets, faceless doubles, all imaginary. My mother would spend hours, years talking to someone who was not there.

Who knew where the first butterfly had come from, Mr. Spitzer asked, whether from a velvet cocoon on a dead tree bough or only from the unexplored, vast darkness, the limitless night of creation? Did it come before the beginning of time, before the separation of the waters from the land, before the division of light from darkness? Was the first butterfly of the dawn or evening? Did it come through the strings of the golden lyre of the stars gleaming through a heaven of clouds? Did it come through the bow of the golden archer pointing his arrow? Did it ride before the prow of the old ship Argo lying near the small cloud of Magellan, keeling with its lights toward starboard? Did it fly over the cascade of stars falling from the mouth of the heavenly centaur? Did it fly above the Milky Way, the thin stream of stars streaming from the breast of Juno? Did it come with the wild swan? Did it come before the constellations or afterward? Did it come before the first penguin's-foot starfish or brain coral or cloak anenome or heart cockle or hermit shell or razor shell or ducal boat shell cast up upon a lonely beach, before the first gannet's egg laid upon a shelf of rock, before the first sandpipers running back and forth in the silken surf, before the nestless sea birds drifting over the roof-tops? The finest butterfly authors were, upon this subject, as abysmally ignorant as himself, this man who would have liked, with his entire being, to resist the suggestion that there should be anything beyond the powers of rational explanation, anything outside the logical sequences of reason and time, and yet who was continually confronted by a butterfly mystery like that of his soul. Perhaps the first butterflies, according to a rumor he must have heard long ago in the extensive butterfly circles, and doubtless it was apocryphal, had originated not at all upon this planet.

They had wandered through the dark sky before the whirlings of the first stars, the bloomings of the first meteoric wild flowers, the first feathered grasses and winged seed pods, before the sea had boomed and buzzed with light, before the first sea shells marked with the patterns of luminous eyes, the first ears of convoluted mystery. They had fallen from the void heavens to the earth when the earth was still barren and void like a demented woman in her imaginary labor pains, only dreaming that she lived, when the mountains and hills and valleys were as fluently moving as great, unearthly waves in a cosmic storm, or their creation was sporadic like something in an erroneous dream, like the note of falsehood which gives significance to truth, that lie which illuminates the surrounding darkness, and all of nature had been this dream for which there was and had been and would be no substance but this dream. There would be no awakening. Or perhaps everything was the devious imitation of everything.

The fat, whispering man seemed to be talking in his sleep, though his eyes were open, milkily staring as shadow or light crossed his face, and he was alert. Indeed, there was much uncertainty, and there were many possible explanations of that which could not be explained.

Perhaps the first butterflies had lived in a period of greater longevity than ours, perhaps at that enchanted time, Mr. Spitzer thought, when one bird should sing for a thousand years. Perhaps there had never been more than a mesmeric day or moment, and time's extension was another aspect of the dream, the dream of an hour.

Though these modern butterflies were small, mere pygmies, rarely bigger than Mr. Spitzer's soft, relaxed hands when he spread his fingers wide apart, thumb to thumb, making a butterfly pattern, yet the original butterflies, if he was not mistaken in his evasive memory, had had wings as large as the wings of seraphic beings or lazily drifting, moon-breasted and human-faced sea birds such as those who glided over the salt lagoons and misty marsh lands or stopped at my mother's many-roofed house on their way from pole to shining pole, from polar ice cap to the dim Antarctic cape. But these present butterflies were their diminuendos, even as in music there is a diminuendo passage or effect which melts into the aftermath of the charged silence, seeming to be the music going on and on until it fades, seeming to be the illusion of music.

Perhaps only the delicate things, perhaps only the small things endured when the great things were gone, even as our thoughts which outlive the thinker and his thoughts. Butterflies could be entombed in icebergs. Butterflies could be entombed in icicles, yet awaken in the spring, flying out of the flame-colored butterfly bushes and elder bushes, even like those suddenly animated blossoms which Mr. Spitzer had observed whirling around him in his walks. They had survived the deaths of stars, the cyclic whirlwinds, the ages of fire, the ages of ice. They had passed from islands to continents, from continents to islands. They had come down through the long corridors of time. Or perhaps they were only this vague cloud of perfume like Mr. Spitzer's thoughts which wandered on the trembling air.

Who was Mr. Spitzer now to impale a butterfly, as he would sometimes ask, to pin it down? Should he make himself ridiculous in his own eyes, trying that adventure he should avoid? And what would be more ridiculous, he asked, than a fat man with a butterfly net pursuing butterfly examples, chasing multi-colored butterflies through the checkered sunlight and shadows of his dead dreams, and why should he pursue ephemera now when he had outlived himself or his brother and the first impressions of his haunted youth, the faded colors of his thoughts, the orbits of his actual interests? Should he stumble, mumble, talk to himself or a shadow?

Such questions were always stirring dim whirlpools in his mind, causing other questions to infinity. Peron, the coarse-grained fellow, as Mr. Spitzer seemed to remember, had laughed at this quiet sport, even as he had disparaged preternatural butterflies, the diaphanous wings of light, the small pearl borders and the broad pearl borders.

And now old Joachim, Mr. Spitzer seemed also to remember, thinking of himself as if he were someone else and with that curious detachment which was sometimes his, was grown too old, too obese and short of breath to afford this luxury of butterfly hunting except in his nocturnal dreams, and they were his dreams which asserted themselves in spite of him, in spite of his present reserves. When to all appearances he did not move, yet he would catch himself out butterfly hunting. Indeed, why should there be an ascertainable reality, an outside world, he sometimes asked? Of what necessity was it to a man who seemed to include, within himself, so many streets, wandering stars, curl clouds, traffic lights, gilded butterflies? He should scarcely notice the world's absence. And as for his days, being this old estates lawyer who was always closing empty houses and winding up last affairs, the affairs of the dead, he pursued lost heirs of lost crowns because of his profession and because it was, after all, less arduous to do so, less physically exerting than to live by day again the life he lived by night, to pursue subtle butterflies through reedy marsh lands where the reed birds sang to the sleeping babe in his little boat among the reeds reflected in the dark stream.

Only his silent music and his memories of his recurring butterflies consoled him now for his brother's early death and for his continuing life, broken though it was by many interruptions, many disappointments and needless complications and by his great original disappointment, his failure to win the object of his love—as he would always say, softly smiling, his features almost radiant, his eyes enlarging in the evening light which was the color of a moth's gold mottled wing when a breath of wind stirred the candle flames, and he would slightly tap his ivory-headed cane to give vague emphasis to wandering remarks which needed to be in no way emphatic.

For my mother probably had not awakened, her bright eyes staring at shadows of foam and wind, staring beyond him. Perhaps she heard, beyond the wild oceanic gales, a canary twittering. Perhaps she saw, drifting before her eyes, a ball of golden, ruffled light. Why should he come each evening only among the dead? Why should he not come among the living, too? Or why must he come in an intermediate stage between life and death like that stage of life which follows death?

It was his own personal theory that a butterfly could hear, the seat of its hearing being—as a butterfly was not endowed with ears—the antennae, the clubbed, sensitive hairs, the delicate horns moving in the wind. Undoubtedly, a moth could also hear, though its feelers were feathery. These little creatures, both butterflies and moths, could hear a great many sounds never heard by human ears, perhaps even the thunder in the heart of the rose, Mr. Spitzer said. Though he doubted that a butterfly could hear the fog bells, the loud tickings of clocks, the slamming of a door, the whistle of a train, or any other sound disrelated to its evanescent life, yet he was sure that it could hear the voice of another butterfly, the soundless tread of its fellow creature winging in the air, the fallings of leaves, the whispering grass, a curtain blowing in the light, the opening of a flower, the creaking of a lid on a tomb, or perhaps his own whispering voice. He had made many tests, noting the reactions of butterflies to various sounds, to various keys of music and gradations of echoes, even to sounds which he himself could not always hear, his being, he must admit, the heart which had died within itself, the heart beating no more.

The air was filled with subdued rustlings, stirrings, tinklings of starlight, even in a dark night of the human soul, even when there should have been no consciousness, no memory. When the sea had turned from myriad iridescence of green and blue and gold and lilac to velvet darkness, then it seemed to him as if all the world were the spectre of this sad world—and it was the spectre butterfly suddenly gleaming in his mind, the spectre fireflies, Roman helmet snail, sea-polished rock fringed by the wild beach grass, livid medusa, starfish, eye shell, ear shell, wing shell, windpipe barnacle, foot, hand, mask, face, rose, crown wreath, starred wreath, wave wreath, golden mouthed wreath, and the blackened dwarf spruce trees were the ghosts of themselves, and so were the beached sailboats with the wind-tattered sails, and it was the spectre dead moon which drew the waves, and the waves were the ghosts of the white-lipped waves, yet though they should be different from those which had broken before them, and the humped sand barrens moved and shifted like the foaming waves.

The headlands were the ghosts of the ghostly headlands, broken and jagged against the opal diffusion of the sky, and the only conformation was a mad man's dream, and he was this poor ghost of himself, even as he would have been if he had had no brother. If he had been born alone, doubtless he would have felt this same great sense of overwhelming loneliness. His problems in all probability would have been the same and identical to these—problems which were, though they were his tendency toward madness and also its source, his only orientation and the renewal of his life, his weary spirit.

His was, he sometimes tentatively believed, the bipart soul—though whether already divided from himself or about to be divided, he could not say with certainty. And how should his brother be self-contained? And who was his dead brother now, he asked? His double-chinned face quivered with a weird, slumbering emotion, so like Mr. Spitzer in this life—his problems would always seem, to anyone else, an unnecessary exaggeration, as he himself would doubtless be the first to acknowledge —and yet they were this life's necessity to him.

His butterfly memories, those fanning from dead coals into glowing embers, were surely as important to him as my mother's convict chauffeur or black coachman, great toad coachman with coach lantern eyes and fireflies gleaming in his stomach, thirteen moons in a cloudless sky, her hunting dogs, her golden Labradors and great stone birds and dragons in the clouds, conch blowers, surf riders, her evening guests were to her who entertained them with such a lavish hand and at times entertained the droves of butterflies which moved and stirred through his sad, empty life, making him feel that he was not really dead, that he lived through others even as his dead brother lived through him, Mr. Spitzer remembering his butterflies, the wings marked with orbs in the nebulous light of the dying mind. His butterflies were as important to him as my mother's harpist, the lady strung through harp strings.

Or my mother, so easily deceived, might imagine that the migratory beds were coming with the migratory sleepers, beds of silver and ivory and gold drifting over the mountains and valleys and through clouds of amorphous images to come to her where she slept, beds of unearthly dreams, hypnotic dreams, mesmerized beds, murderous beds, poisonous beds, beds of Italian princes, Elizabethan poets, rakes, trollops, clowns, great beauties, the bed of the sleeping beauty who would sleep until she was awakened by the kiss of a fairy prince, musical beds, the bed of a fawn, the bed of an Indian rajah with four automatums at the four corners, four rosy nymphs dancing and playing sweetest music of bells and cymbals and flutes, the beds which were shaped like coffins which were boats, the stone bed, the effigy of the great stone knight sleeping on the great stone bed, his stone helmet and shield, the bed of Charlemagne, the amethyst bed of Catherine the Great, the bed of Cleopatra with the gold god of love perched upon the gold footboard, pointing its gold arrow straight to her heart, the bed of Martin Luther, the camp bed in which the great Napoleon died, the beds of Arabs whose beds were tents and shrouds in which they wrapped themselves and quietly stole away. Or perhaps my mother heard the furniture talking, an old-fashioned duchesse sofa talking to a circle of empty tapestry chairs.

Yet Mr. Spitzer was the only mysterious stranger here, coming so faithfully each evening—and surely, he was not sinister, he who talked of butterflies for hours or, if he was too greatly discouraged by too much competition, lapsed, like ripples which had spent themselves, into a pool of silence. He surely was surprised by the way, each evening, his butterfly knowledge grew, even during a few hours, seeming to evoke a world.

He knew butterflies of every region and of both hemispheres, butterflies of the antipodes, the frozen poles which once were clothed with grass and flowers, butterflies in Elysium, the place where the good dwelled after death, said to be located in the Western Ocean or in the lower world, butterflies and moths of other stars. He knew Urania Sloanus, Ornithoptera Paradisea, Saturnia Pyri, eyeless whites, green hair-streaks, butterflies of Boston Common where, a somewhat antiquated figure, he often took his walks smelling the butterflies, butterflies of the Himalyas, the Alps, the Andes, butterflies of Mt. Olympus, Homeric butterflies which were like persons who had passed through many unknown forms of being, many forgotten periods of enchantment, periods of metamorphic sleep, persons who did not awaken as the same persons they were when they went to bed, for they had changed their forms in sleep, butterflies which seemed to tremble all night long like candle flames in the ceaseless wind of memory, keeping him awake, Io Vanessa or the old peacock's eye winging through a sun-lit garden of flame, the butterfly Aphrodite, named after that goddess of beauty and love who claimed the golden apple of discord and who was later identified with Venus, goddess of bloom, the twelve-spotted butterfly Apollo, namesake of that god who was the twin of the virgin huntress Artemis, known sometimes as Diana, goddess of the wood and of wild nature, helper of women in child birth, associated with the moon as her twin brother Apollo was associated with the sun, butterflies fashioned by Morpheus, god of dreams who was known as the fashioner because of the volatile shapes he called up before the sleeper, shapes of sibyl and icarus and water nymph and phaeton and centaur and star, Leto Venus, beautiful as the goddess rising from the grey mother wave, Attacus Atlas, memorial of that divinity who was in charge of the pillars which upheld the heavens, the Titan forced to support the heavens on his head and hands, that king who knew the depth of every sea and who was metamorphosed into a lofty mountain, wanderer paraselene, Heckuba of the bewitched glades, Euphemia, Ebule, Sakuna, Sugrina, Thyria, Papilio Memnon, Papilio Antimachus, Papilio Homerus, butterflies like ourselves spinning out of ourselves who were these caterpillar spinners and these voyagers.

Had not Mr. Spitzer often seen, though his eyesight was myopic and likely to play him many tricks, the packed prisms like jewels in a box, plane above plane, the butterfly or moth emerging from that prison form, the sleeping chrysalis, unfolding by slow degrees like the unknown, unfolding its fragile wings, then suddenly glowing with colors more beautiful than the most glorious humming bird? Had old Joachim not seen this death, this birth? And as for himself, should he be, at the end of life, as he had been at the beginning, changing so much that he should scarcely be recognized? Or when should he come to the last infernal circle of this Divine Comedy of life and death?

When dark seas roared around him, when he was confused and felt as if this old body, this old hulk would split into two, splitting from the mast, or ride into port with its torn sails drifting like shrouds, casting great purple shadows, no captain, not even a ghostly captain lashed to the mast and wound in a winding sheet of snow, his eyes burning with the memory of iridescence, no individual consciousness, no ship's lamp or lighthouse to light his way, no pilot star to guide him, no memories of life, no gear and tackle, intricate rigging of the dream, no flying jib, no yards, booms, stay-sails, skysails, top-gallant sails, royal sails, studding sails, mizzen sails to swell in the gentle wind, gliding without apparent exertion, moving in a stately manner like a sea bird drifting through the air, like undulating wings, when opposite whirlwinds, like furies raging within, seemed to drive him in opposite directions, toward both the darkness and the light, when he was all but overwhelmed by chaos and the Stygian night, spinning in watery abysses, Mr. Spitzer held to the one life line, his phantasmal butterflies, these thoughts and memories surprising him even now as if they had come from another life, another and forgotten source. Were they his butterflies glowing in his cavernous mind? Did they belong to nobody? Should possession be significant in this realm?

Who could call his soul his own, defining the misty boundaries between his soul and another's limitless soul, his dreams and another's universal dreams? Were these two souls which moved through him, old Joachim, the dreamless one? Were these three souls or the amalgamations of many souls, the images formed by cloud fusions, flowers of the storm, by coalescences of incongruent beliefs and parallels of inconsecutive ideas and wild disharmonies? Should one soul be at the same time among both the living and the dead or a voyager between two worlds? How should he know which soul was living, which was dead? Who could truthfully say that he was in possession of his own body, that a new tenant had not taken over an old, empty house? Mr. Spitzer could not say, except for this assurance given by his memories his thoughtless brother would never have shared, not even had he lived.

To be sure, Mr. Spitzer had wished for the seal of hermetic privacy, and yet there was always the opening of a door. There were new reflections mingling with the old, new intuitions mingling with his traditional despairs. He was surprised by this atmosphere of mutability. He was surprised by his mental brilliance which others had denied, which he himself had often doubted, these shimmerings like fire in the midst of darkest waters, like flames reflected upon a far horizon or like that fire which burns within and would be seen if man were transparent, shimmerings like this sudden rainbow medium of his thoughts, even like the midnight rainbow.

Did he not remember, with a sense of expectation influenced only slightly by remorse, Clearwing Aurora with the first dew light of dawn upon its pristine wings, dew drops trembling like future pearls in the winds of memory? Did he not remember Croesus, the golden bambino in a golden cradle spinning from a golden web?

He remembered, as if he had seen them only yesterday, their luminous colors repeating themselves in patterns of lambent flame, butterflies miraculous as if they had come out of the whirlwind, out of the great cloud, out of the fire enfolding itself, out of the terrible crystals like the dark sky over head, out of the colors of green and rose and gold, out of the tremblings of his thoughts.

Could he not compete? Were not these butterflies as beautiful as anything my mother dreamed, perhaps exceeding her wildest dream of enchantment? They were as beautiful to him as the wandering surf, as silver fish scales gleaming near the surface of the dark wave, as ambient sea shells, as the plume of Raphael gleaming through gold and pewter, whirling fogs, as the horned moon, as the iridescence reflected in the feline eyeballs of great horned owls, as the sleeping sea ringed by light and scarcely moving in her sleep, as fireflies, as flying sparks, as evening stars, as the Venus-comb upon the beach, as the nebulous mass of golden light like hairs surrounding the nucleus of a comet and with it constituting the comet's seraphic head. How out of the heart of darkness could evolve this creation, sudden as thought? It was the triumph of night over death.

Did it come from himself or another? What difference did the ultimate source make, for should not the results be judged by their own merits? Should not one idea be surrounded by many associations—one rose evoke a garden, one sea shell evoke a sea?

His eyes gleaming in the webbed candle flames, Mr. Spitzer affirmed that, just as my mother knew the phantom carriages and whirling dervishes and wandering stars in opium comas, as she knew, in her dream life, dazzling balls in crystal ballrooms and many dancing partners, old Beau Brummells who had risen from their graves, such monstrous apparitions as men with heads or women without heads, so he knew, in subtle ways, butterflies which had been known by all the dead, by all of broken lives, butterflies of resurrection, butterflies of other selves which should be only when we were dead, when we had spun ourselves out, out of this mortal life, butterflies which he had known ever since that day he had been called away from his silent music to the morgue to claim his brother's body. For this extension of life had been given to him, though for purposes he did not know, for futurities which seemed already of the past, his brother having died at the high noon of life, just when he should have lived. His brother was buried, wrapped in folds of velvet darkness, and was no more to be seen upon the earth of men, no more to be seen in the crowds at the turf, no more to be seen where the turf meets the surf, where the horses run through foam, no more to be seen at the gambling tables under the shuffling stars, though Mr. Spitzer looked so much like him that few had realized this death, for the coffin had been sealed, and no one had looked upon his dead brother's shattered face, the all but obliterated features of one who had resembled Joachim, and his brother had not lived until the evening of life, this nadir of existence which was like the last departing wave of the sea.

His brother had not lived to grieve, to acquire the terrors of the widowed heart—to wait, like Mr. Spitzer, through this long winter of hibernation, this which seemed so much like death, to wait for that spring which, like promises deferred, might never come. He had not lived to remember him, old Joachim who had grown old and fat with the tremulous memories of his vanished loves, his vanquished hopes, his airs of deathless thoughts.

Though Mr. Spitzer had been a composer of funeral music—that music which, his brother had always said, had been too fine, too beautiful for human ears—there had been, in deference to what Peron's explicit preferences would have been could he have expressed himself, no classic music at his funeral, though for reasons very different from Joachim's silence. Indeed, there had been a heterogeneous crowd of the merriest mourners who ever were, as Mr. Spitzer said, persons with whom he should have had, except for his brother's death, nothing in common, merry andrews and fat aldermen and nimble Jacks and broken-down vaudeville stars, waterfront characters and cue-ball champions and dice

shooters, crowds of clowns and hooded dominoes and blind street singers
and old fly-by-nights and mad mountebanks and ruined gamblers and
old men with sea-shell memories, dumb giants and clever dwarves, such
persons as his brother had associated with for various purposes unknown
to Joachim—he sometimes thought now, only to embarrass the haughty
aristocrat. There had been a great deal of incomprehensible horse talk,
roulette wheel talk, bird cage talk, dice talk, talk of cold turkeys and
wild goose chases and pretty chicks, blind alleys and pigs in the poke and
wooden heads and spirit jockeys and glass bead madames, talk at the time
incomprehensible to Mr. Spitzer, though gradually his intelligence was
being illuminated, he hoped, upon such mysterious subjects, his sympathies for his brother having so continually increased that sometimes he
felt as if he were in a very noisy graveyard, listening to the conversations
of the dead. But at the time, everyone had thought that Mr. Spitzer's self-
containment and self-control, the serenity of his grief had been almost
supernatural, something strange and marvelous to behold, strange as the
phoenix, the perfumed bird of Arabia arising from its ashes, as indeed,
it had been, for he had been utterly devastated, shattered by a grief which
should have been recognizable, visible to the eyes of the blind if not to
the eyes of those who saw, a grief which he believed had surpassed in its
magnitude the occasion, great as the occasion had been for him. Few or
none had sensed his grief.

Only to one man Mr. Spitzer must have directly betrayed his grief—
afterwards on a windy street corner, his black cape whipping against his
heels, his face streaked with tears, he must have shown his grief to an old
lamp-lighter whose face was also streaked with tears and who had said,
speaking to Mr. Spitzer of Mr. Spitzer's late departed brother—He will
never light another lamp.

So that Mr. Spitzer had been somewhat surprised by the brevity of
human memory, surprised to see the lamps going on one by one down a
dark street where the old lamp-lighter moved like Jacob with his ladder
of dreams reaching to the clouds—as he had been surprised to see the
firmament of stars above his head.

He liked to recall his brother's funeral, perhaps more often than was
good for him, this being a subject to which he would always return. The
details had been blurred or cast into a double focus. Sometimes, even
now, he saw two of everything, two faces of every stranger, two chairs in a
room where there was only one, two moons in the sky, but he knew he
was mistaken. His defective senses had played this trick. He knew that
even one face was problematical, though it should be his own. He had
hardly been aware of his troubles at the time, of course, but it was clear
to him now that, after his brother's death, he must have gone into a state
of coma, a profound insensibility like the blurring of light, as if a cloud
of darkness were passing over him, for all images had been blotted out for
a long while, or else they had been but dimly seen, dimly understood,
and his had been this heavy, sluggish habit of mind, this lack of vividness
in his responses, even as if his natural faculties were permanently benumbed, and he had not been aware of many immediate impressions,

and there had been a certain denseness, an opaque quality as to all or almost all his thoughts, a certain impenetrability as to the ideas and emotions he might once have understood with that diplomatic grace, that tactful air which had been his, he having been noted always for an atmosphere of evasiveness which had made all kinds of things possible. He had sunk into a state of sleep which was, he now believed, the similitude of death, its twin brother.

He had suffered this great wound of death, and yet he had suffered more, this wound of life. He was pursued by this demon accuracy, that which, as he would always yawningly say, kept him awake, spinning these most wakeful dreams, even as his dead soul voyaged over a dark blue sea. How could one life endure this double life, that he should stay in one place, weaving these nocturnal dreams of death and birth, yet wander far and wide—or, as he sometimes suspected, oscillate between limitations, two fixed points? Why should butterflies, which should have been meaningless to him in the void inane, still be meaningful to him, along with so many buried hopes, so many exhausted feelings which he still must feel, even in retrospect?

He remembered, with remarkable accuracy, considering his loss of memory, the powdery pollen gold freighting the bright wings of transcendental butterflies, the veined leaf green, the milky midnight blue, all known butterflies and some which were unknown, even to him, the old Diomedes with planets and half moons and worlds upon its dark blue wings, butterflies with quarter moons or eighths, the ethereal tortoise-shell, both small and great, reflecting the icebergs which had once reflected them in Arctic wastelands under the frozen stars, the white-veined blacks, the black-veined marble whites reflecting the branches of frozen and leafless trees, butterflies as big as the wailing lapwing, butterflies of the Tropic of Cancer and of the Tropic of Capricorn, butterfly wings streaked with the lights of Aurora Borealis and Aurora Australis streaming across the darkness of the sky, the emerald, the amethyst, the coxcomb red, voyager butterflies, voyagers who were subjective voyages between two stars or poles, the red admiral of the light-wing fleet, harbors and gulfs and bays indented upon the outermost coasts of his burnished and double-edged wings as if by action of the waves or by sudden creation which was another matter, sudden as thought though noted long ago by the old butterfly geographers drawing their maps of this world, the white admiral going with the wind on his starboard side, the uniform of the checkered skipper patterned in squares of light and shadow like a chessboard moving against the sky, the uniform of the grizzled skipper sprinkled and streaked with grey, the silver-spotted skippers washed by waves, the dingy skippers who were the color of an oily sea, greylings, Adonis blues, wood whites, butterflies with Latin messages written on their wings, Io on one wing and Io on the other wing as if they knew they had two souls, the cabbage-haunting butterflies and those who shadowed marble heads of ancient gods, the painted lady fluttering through this brief dance of life, she with her breast fur like a golden fleece and her golden snood and her transparent, shimmering gauzes and pearl-embroidered silken veils, her brilliant mirrors in the pale sunlight mir-

roring the invisible wind, also the old swallow-tail with its tail tapering
and forked like that of the barn swallow or a swallow-tailed evening coat,
also the veinings of the underside of its wings, the wings reversed. There
were, as he must have frequently remarked before during his butterfly
passage, zebra swallow-tails and tiger swallow-tails and black swallow-
tails crowding through his mind in empty hours which perhaps could
have been no better employed at his age, his stage of life.

For though in his youth when his brother was still alive, he had
indulged in what he had believed to be the harmless hobby of knitting
fine socks for himself and his careless brother, he felt that to knit now
would be to make himself quite ridiculous, even as he must have seemed
in Peron's eyes—and, in fact, he could not endure—he hoped he might
be forgiven the pun, which he realized was the cheapest form of low-brow
humor which certainly would have appalled him in another life—the
ribbing, the ribbing he would get. So he wore, it was his frequent complaint, the old socks mended and patched over and over again, even to
that extent that he had lately begun to wonder, to ask himself the philosopher's question, especially as new holes still appeared like the holes in
the sky or in reality—as there had been so many holes, so many darns and
patches, were these new socks or old he wore? The ghostly conformation
of his old sock persisted, showing the ghostly shape of his leg, his foot—
and yet it seemed to him that, technically, he might be considered to be
wearing, made of so many darns and patches covering so many holes, new
socks—or that he would be when the last original thread had disappeared. Such new socks would be, of course, quite fragile, easily unravelling.

If he were to be perfectly accurate, it seemed to him that he would
be the sorriest old bindlestiff wearing a coat of so many tatters, so many
rags and patches covering so many holes that his coat was not his own, for
his was a coat of holes, and he would carry all his worldly goods over his
shoulder in his black handkerchief tied to his stick or cane, and all the
dogs of creation would bark at him, nipping at his heels.

And what of the regal butterflies, as he must repeat—should he ever
forget them, though they be pecked away by birds and storms? He knew
all nomenclatures and symbolic wings, heraldries and signs and orders,
butterflies of Byzantium, inlayings in patterns as of small pieces of colored
glass or stone, washings of mosaic gold, purple emperors the wind had
blown ten thousand miles from shore, infallible conformations which
seemed to change before his eyes, old monarchs with their orange-brown
wings black-veined and black-bordered as if in mourning for themselves,
queens and kings and pawns, old cardinals cloaked in scarlet robes,
mitred bishops saying high mass among the evening flowers, mass for the
dead self or selves. He swore that their chant would be almost Gregorian
if it were amplified—though perhaps it was something even older—
perhaps it was Arabic. And yet he was this dark atheist, this believer in
nothing, in no one—for who, as he might ask, could speak with greater
authority than he of the life beyond the grave? And who knew less of this
present life?

CHAPTER 30

THERE were thus these unreal persons whom my mother and Mr. Spitzer endlessly discussed, for hours as if they were real, as if the dead should live, walk about, clap their hands, sing and shout and whistle. The real persons were apparently the only persons who were unreal to my mother and perhaps also to Mr. Joachim Spitzer, who seemed to indulge, often through his silence, her every mood, even her ignoring him and his problematical being and identity. She would rather address her solicitous remarks to Eustace, seeming to hear his replies which no one else heard, for only she knew when he came, he being invisible. Of course, no one else had seen the phenomenal Eustace, so his appearance could be judged only by her rapid-fire remarks—and it would seem that he was many persons, varying according to her whims. Sometimes he was a mocking bird. Sometimes he was an old woman, and sometimes he was an old man bearded like the cypress—that beautiful tree which, though it casts its shadow, gives no fruit. He was limitless. In fact, he might be simultaneously many persons, for he was not confined to any one form by the laws of nature, which had been suspended in his case. Sometimes he was confused in my mother's mind with Wellington riding at the head of his troops. Sometimes he was a Venetian gentleman's murderous valet. Or he was the murdered gentleman who walked about in the midnight air. He was a blind astronomer.

My mother would cry out, quite suddenly, for no reason at all, often interrupting Mr. Spitzer's bewildered silence—Eustace, Eustace! Oh, is it you, Eustace dear, and the golden-antlered stags, the large planets, the small planets? Come in, Eustace, and do close the door, for there's a great draft. Blow out the candle, Eustace. The wind is blowing the door shut.

If Mr. Spitzer continued to be so uncertain a companion as he was —so unreliable and tentative and solitary, this great abstraction always yawning in her face like the idea of the uncreated creation, the stars before the beginning of time or after the last thin star had fallen through a cloud of starlight—she would invite an ancient uncle or aunt or cousin or cousin's cousin to spend a long, lonely winter with her, and they would play a game of whist or loo or poker, my mother said, if only there were four partners, an Elizabethan gentleman in his white ruff or a satrap clothed in Saturnian gold or a wild, bearded Cossack making up a fourth. Often, indeed, she thought of inviting Cousin Hannah, a soul of vast duplicity who had gone to join her fathers long ago and thus would make the ideal partner for a lively game of cards. My mother would have a full house, a royal flush, all the kings, all the queens except one. Perhaps if Cousin Hannah deigned to accept my mother's invitation, it would be necessary to locate only one more partner to make up four. For if my mother could not be two partners, herself and another, then Cousin Hannah could be two partners—being both herself and a gentleman who had apparently never worn the white plume of cowardice. She had rescued many fair ladies, many dark ladies, and perhaps she might rescue my mother from the opium dreams of her dead loves and the sounds of the long tides blowing like Gabriel's skirts upon this shore of darkness or light. Indeed, Cousin Hannah's entire history, it seemed now, had been a history of skirts.

Cousin Hannah Freemount-Snowden, the jolly old soul—or if she had not been jolly then, surely she would be so now, released from her long endeavors in this mortal life, which she had probably felt to be the only life and yet had managed to scorn as something intolerably beneath her dignity just as she had scorned personal immortality or its vague counterpart, her image handed down in memory through the generations of posterity—had never cared for the Spitzer boys, not even when they were promising and dreamy-eyed young men with all of life seemingly before them, and had stanchly predicted that they would come to no good end, that they were destined for an early grave and utter oblivion —for they were really identical, not nearly so different as they had supposed. She had often spoken of the musical gambler with his piano-playing and horn-blowing friends, the horse-playing musician, the gambling lawyer who would take his last chance, the philanthropic dice-rattler who had allowed all other men to win, and the suicidal butterfly-chaser chasing himself with his butterfly net. Both brothers were profligates.

But then, her views of life had been based on a knowledge no one else had enjoyed—so that always, no matter what had happened, it would seem as if she had already known, perhaps because she was in touch with so many couriers like thunder clouds before the storm. She had known of the murder of the Russian czar and royal family several days before the event. She had known of the murder of the archduke at Sarajevo several hours before the news had reached the rest of the world. She had known of the assassinations of archdukes in many countries, often before they had occurred, just as she had known of the deaths of great kings and captains, great turbaned Turks, great sultans of the past such as Saladin who was the opposer of the Crusaders in cities of minarets and of inverted minarets, Solymon the Magnificent who was the greatest of all the Ottoman sultans and kept ten thousand beautiful veiled ladies in his harem, Sardanapalus, king of Assyria who was sometimes identified with Ashurbanipal, Seleucus I, first king of Syria, Seleucus II, III, IV, V, many other Syrian kings and Babylonian kings, many Bengal lancers to dazzle my poor mother in her dark tower. Cousin Hannah had known the politics of all those nations where the ladies wear trousers and the gentlemen wear skirts, and she had gone by camel into places where no woman had ever gone before. She had been apprised of the secrets of bedrooms throughout this world, whispers behind silken curtains, dreams which were spoken out loud by men in their sleep, confidences poured into listening ears and into great stone ears, coughings of shieks in striped Bedouin tents in howling deserts, whisperings of great rajahs in palaces of ambient jewels, cryings of men in palaces of ice, neighings of horses throughout the nocturnal world. She had heard what the camel drover said to his wife in the night's darkness. She had heard what the water carrier whispered to his dead love. She had heard the farewell of the New England sea captain to his wife before he sailed for the last time, for the last time before he was engulfed, going down into those watery abysses where the stars whirled, that creation from which no man returned.

She had never stayed for long in one place and had had no time for long visits or for the exploration of any single character—certainly no time for long, luxurious conversations over the telephone which had nearly always rung in an empty house so that, when she was alive, my mother had sent her messages by a blackamoor in a fringe-topped surrey arising out of her opium dreams. Now when the house which had stood between two ivy-clad water towers had been torn down long ago to make space for an asphalt highway, for the new horseless carriage, when the Boston address was no more, not even a mirage, my mother called by telephone ringing and ringing through empty rooms which she imagined were still furnished with trophies of Cousin Hannah's conquests such as the heads of great stags with their eyeballs staring at shadows. Cousin Hannah had always rushed from country to country—so no wonder if she did not answer now. She had been so seldom in this region before her death. When she had come to my mother's house, she had not been announced. No trumpeter had preceded her. Not a wild swan had honked. Death seemed scarcely a greater absence than life had been. It was difficult to know on what date of the calendar her death should be marked—and how should my mother know? Cousin Hannah was never known to leave a forwarding address.

She had compensated for her superficial views by a marvelous certainty that was set above the peaks of time, by a ruthless sangfroid cutting through all obstacles as a sword of ice cuts through clouds and moving mountains as if they were moths. She had been a great archer in Persia, a great dueler in France, an expert with sword and gun in Rumania, a marksman who could shoot with unwavering aim through the ace of hearts at a distance of twelve paces, a great stag-hunter in Bulgaria, a great Swiss mountain-climber, a great New England boatsman, a great yachtsman who could reef and haul and ride into the eye of the storm, a great lassoer of mustangs and many graziers, the strayed, the wild, a great Chinese horsewoman who could ride herd longer than anyone, a tall Tibetan jockey who had ridden through whirlwinds and sand storms and mountains of stone. She had made many balloon ascensions and had once ridden over my mother's garden from which she could hear a music coming like a faded cloud-burst. She could hear the faded strings of violins in the clouds. She could hear faint silver alpenhorns blowing on lonely mountains. She could hear waterfalls like the rustles of skirts. Because of the loss of a skirt, it was known now, her entire life had been perhaps an act of sorrow and redemption. She could hear the whispers of a beautiful lady sleeping in a windy garden where slept the white-pronged unicorn.

But Cousin Hannah had not been persuaded by dreams and visions or far ripples of snow like surf. She had compensated for her lack of patience by her impatience which was so fine that it was like a virtue, just as if she had already seen into all the dark abysses of human nature, even those filled with the glowings of dim water jewels or treasure troves of thieves, and so she had had no use for further experience or knowledge, it would seem, cutting through great cables of iron as if they were silken threads, even those delicate threads binding us to reality like the cables of poor puppets dancing in the whirling storms of years.

She had been, in fact, a person of that swift, mercurial, resourceful temperament my mother had always admired, looking upon Cousin Hannah as if she were an emancipated extension of herself, a Captain Derring-Do who engaged in those adventures my mother only dreamed of through all the endless years—a being never slow to make up her brilliant mind, seeing all hazards before they had occurred and choosing the lesser dangers though they were also very great as fire and flood and falling stars, stars dragging other stars in their wake, and living by her inscrutable choices as if there had been no alternative, no road except the road she had taken, no ship except the ship in which she had sailed. She had collided with many icebergs, but she was no oriole or butterfly dashed to pieces by snow and wind. The iceberg had moved to allow her passage. There were always many dangers in her way, certainly, but she had survived so long as she had travelled. She was always travelling on distant roads—and where the road ended, crumbling into a great chasm or roaring sea of sand, she would go on, crossing great stone deserts and viewless abysses as if they were city streets—indeed, had always said that the dangers had been less than if she had crossed the traffic-crowded Boston streets where coachmen cracked their whips among the smoky stars and horses screamed and chauffeurs blew the horns of old Renaults —so that her journeys had utterly fascinated my mother, who surely would never have had the energy for such adventures even if her feet had been winged so that she could sail over sailing mountain peaks and go through dazzling clouds.

Cousin Hannah knew the Alpine and Himalayan abysses and Peruvian passes and great snow-peaked mountains of this sublunar world with intimacy as someone else might know the complexities of Boston society or the genealogies of Beacon Hill—as she might know, my mother thought now, the mountains of the moon and moon craters like eyes of dead water birds staring through burning clouds and lunar seas of dry winds, seas of echoes—so that my mother, though she had forgotten so recent an event until she saw Cousin Hannah with her cheeks burned to the color of old saddle leather by snows and winds, would suddenly be reminded of her poor husband, who was lost while walking between two frozen mountain peaks as the snow whirled before his face, as the snow clouds roared with ice, as he saw beneath him ten thousand pinnacles of snow and ice and the snow casting up surf and spirals of foam, and she would ask of one who was not likely to respond—Have you seen my husband?

She would want to send out a searching party, a rescue mission. Indeed, she would implore that Cousin Hannah should search for him the next time she travelled through the Alps—search for him where the great snow clouds roared and rolled like the elephants crossing the Alps with Hannibal, search for him where snows were older than any people in this world, where snows had not melted since the death of Charlemagne, search for him in dark valleys, search for him where Childe Roland had blown his horn before a dark tower and where no other sound had ever been heard—look for her husband in dark caves, look for him in narrow passes, look for him in great gulches hemmed in by walls of ice and snow, look for him under the snow, look for him in Swiss chalets as small as jewel boxes set in clouds, look for him in all those hidden inns where he might be sleeping with the inn-keeper's snow-breasted daughter or a beautiful bride, the moonlight on her cavernous face—for suddenly my mother would refuse to acknowledge that her dead husband never would return. Was he sailing? Was he lifting a beautiful lady's skirts in clouds and winds? Where was he philandering now, my mother would ask of Cousin Hannah, for both knew the faithlessness, the treachery of man? Was he racing dogs through snow clouds?

Great as Cousin Hannah's adventures were on the perilous road she took, she had always avoided, through her prescience of the most distant events, that road on which she would have been killed by brigands waiting in narrow passes or killed by a suddenly cracking glacier or a sudden snow fall loud as church bells or snow blindness blinding her eyes or the talons of a great golden mountain eagle swooping down through miles of clouds upon her turreted head which was reflected on clouds. In all the unenlightened countries, for not all could be reached by telegraphers with towers upon their heads, there were hired assassins waiting to kill her, doubtless to this day, my mother thought, taking consolation from the fact that the news could not possibly have reached them that Cousin Hannah was no more, that she was sleeping with her ancestors in a grey New England churchyard where many tombs were marked only with the sign of the codfish, her jeweled sword at her side and her great star sapphire upon her breast, her sapphire which Mr. Spitzer had pinned upon her old grey army coat which had seen so many campaigns in India and China, so many foreign and domestic wars for the emancipation of woman.

Though she was this gaunt maiden in New England—indeed, a daughter of the codfish aristocracy—yet disguised as an Arab king she had ridden against the great camel turbans and the great cloaks in those great deserts where the sands whistled like the memory of New England blizzards, and she had been disguised as a lazar ringing his bell in many holy cities, and she had heard the long cries of muezzins, and she had been in a palace of ten thousand singing winds—nay, in ten thousand singing palaces—and she had slept in all the tent cities of the East and had travelled with many caravans across the desert seas, and she had penetrated many Arab blockades, and she had deceived many desert sentinels with their eyes blinded by singing sands, and she had ridden horseback in Persia against the great Persian chessboard kings riding as slowly as if they moved across great chessboards, and she had slept among the fallen pillars of the ruins of Persepolis in the midst of the emptiness of the great plain—so that my mother, upon the occasion of this visit, had asked her if she had seen Darius the Great but had gotten only a negative reply from her—and she had slept in Isfahan, and she had slept in Shiraz, and she had travelled over the red hills of Moab and over the Dead Sea, and she had disappeared for six months inside Arabia Deserta where it was believed by the outside world that she was dead and where she had heard an archangel blowing a ram's horn three times—reminding her of lonely mountains where she had heard this sound—and she had slept in Babylon, Nineveh, Crete. Her white horse was named El-Burraq after the horse which Mohammed the Prophet had tethered at the Wailing Wall for a moment before they had taken the invisible road which ascended into heaven.

Yet never had she departed from this world—though great were her adventures, many of which were recorded in the old Boston newspapers by some old, dreaming newspaper reporter who had never left his desk and was not likely to do so until he was carried out feet first into a greater desert—and others of which were never recorded as she had gone to places where no newspaper reporter had ever gone. Once when she was travelling by white camel through the howling desert sands she had seen a caravan of lonely Riffs, men, women, and children on their way to the Town of the Third Market Day when suddenly they were attacked by an overwhelming number of Spanish soldiers equipped with modern American firearms—and instantly, wearing her Arab disguise like a great tent which shielded her from the desert sun, forgetting that she was a stockholder of American firearms, old blunderbuses of the Civil War which no one manufactured now, old cannon balls which had already exploded, forgetting what her own mission was as her proud heart could not endure injustice of any kind in this world or that one should triumph over another as the mountain peaks triumph over the shadowed valleys, she had ridden against the courtly Spanish cavalcades, driving them before her like chickens running in a barnyard before the shadow of the hawk or of the storm, and she must have killed many men that day as my mother tremblingly believed, many Spaniards who would have been surprised to know that the great Arab challenger wearing a hood with withered fringes like the top of an old surrey was a woman—as even the Arabs would have been surprised, for they had thought she was a phantom appearing out of the sand and had praised Allah when she was gone, disappearing into the howling sand storm which had apparently resurrected her—perhaps riding on to make war against great third-century khans dreaming under their bellowing satin tents—great sultans sleeping with their horses—though Cousin Hannah, of course, was inclined to minimize such adventures or not to speak of them at all.

She attributed no importance to such distant encounters, treating them as if they were all a part of the work of the day or of the night, the long night, treating them as less than something occurring in my mother's opium dreams, which doubtless she did not wish to encourage as she had come to overthrow the dream—and that was why she had lifted her glittering sword. She was dedicated to the overthrow of the dream and of the dreamer in all countries and upon the coasts of incense—and perhaps if she had succeeded in her own country, my mother thought then as now, would never have gone to those far places where her failures would not necessarily be known.

Though the ships she had taken might encounter furious storms at high seas where the great waves rose like mountains or might encounter pirate ships flying black flags with skulls and bones or furious men-of-war, strange Phoenician boats or English frigates or Spanish galleons bent on robbery or Charon's empty boat drifting on the midnight tide or a derelict New England schooner rising out of the billowing curtains of the fog and bearing down on men in life boats, snapping them apart like egg shells, though she might be attacked by Moroccan pirates returning from raids upon the sleeping coast of Spain with beautiful captive girls, yet she had always survived, for those ships which she had not taken were always those ships which had disappeared, leaving no survivors to tell that they were gone. She had gone by ship to Europe and more distant ports more than forty times in more than forty years—to ports which were never reached by any other ship or star—yet never taking two ships simultaneously as my mother did when she sailed in her dreams with the evening tide—sailing in one ship for the living, one for the dead—so that no matter what happened, she would always reach port—and many times might hear her ship whistling in the long and lonely night as it passed her passing ship. Doubtless it was in the ship for the dead that she had enjoyed many more voyages than she had taken, sailing in the six months' darkness.

It was in that ship that she would sometimes talk to the man on the lonely star watch, asking above the music of the bugling night, the waves roaring with thousands of lonely voices, perhaps the voices of all who had ever drowned, all who had ever died—Is it a star? Is it a spark? Where do the waves' motions take us? Is that a dolphin's shining back or island? Will the tide draw us shoreward, but who draws the shore, and do the hills and valleys move like waves, swelling and breaking into trees of foam, human faces? Watchman, where is the shore, and is there no shore, no shore of light or darkness? What are those fountains of light breaking upon the waves and the clouds, stars like fires burning upon the waters of the darkness—Arcturus, Andromeda, rainy Hyades? Is there no shore but the argosy of the moving stars, or are there stars like watchmen's lamps put out, or are they the eyes of a peacock? Is it winter-rimed Orion or the eye of a bird? What birds do you see, and are they drifting leeward like the stars?

CHAPTER 3 1

PERHAPS it was understandable if Mr. Spitzer would sometimes reply. For he indulged my mother's moods so long as they were not of reality, he being profoundly, ever and increasingly convinced that reality would kill her as it had killed her canary which she thought was flying over the waves—but if she was already dead, yet lived, she had proved that there was life after death, that she had escaped that which was not escaped by stars or by Mr. Spitzer in his dark cloak which had eclipsed the moon, the sun, the stars. Perhaps, too, though not usually expressing himself, he had secretly liked Cousin Hannah, who had openly disapproved of all those subtleties which were outside her realm—a realm which, however, Mr. Spitzer believed was by now enlarged as was his own—so he and my mother, though disagreeing as to many things—as to the weather about which they could never agree—whether it was raining or shining with the dulled light of a sunken star, whether it was a hurricane or a great calm never to be broken by wave or storm—as to the time, the hour, the place, the evening guest, whether he was or was not a denizen of this fallen world, this planet with its great water eye winking in the wind— had been bound by their mutual admiration not only of Peron who had gambled his life away but of this old cousin who was a type of adventurer making their own adventures seem forever unfulfilled. Indeed, she was the acme of forlorn romance.

Even after so many years, my mother and Mr. Spitzer would seem to hear the loud detonations of Cousin Hannah's rage, rage against man, her bombardment of this star as if it were the distant star.

The lace curtains billowed through the vast rooms, and the glass prisms shook with the memory of that wrath which would never spend itself. For unlike my mother, Cousin Hannah, though keeping her own mysteries in death as in life, had never been known for her tranquility, her evasiveness, her concealment of her impersonal emotions, her dissembling. She had always believed in being direct.

She had wanted to carry my mother away from this dark tower, to rescue her from opium dreams of the dead love, and so the valiant heart had fought her losing battle with shadows. She had won greater battles than this which she had lost, this which was not recorded in the long history of her suffrage campaigns, this more fearful than her long winter marches through heavy snows and storms of icicles as sharp as swords and howling winds, her desert treks through sand storms driving like glassy stars against her face, her journeys into forbidden Mecca or Medinah or Fez or sacred citadels of men. Yet though she had been poignant, cutting like a two-edged sword, never seeming to hold back dormant forces, never sleeping, never seemingly closing her eyes upon the memory of the body of love which requires the silence and the darkness for its fulfillment, the closing of eyelids, though she had not been one patiently to consider a problem of stellar magnitude still unwinding, not solved even now when, it would seem, she was safe and dead, plucked up into the bosom of Abraham where sleeps the dove, carried into darker storm clouds than my mother had ever known, Cousin Hannah had been perhaps right in that prophetic spirit which had seen all things at one swift glance as does the eagle from its mountain aerie or nest of clouds, perhaps nearer the chimerical truth than if she had lived, my mother now thought, to consider every precarious ramification, every branching and breaking of the spirit, human or unhuman. A great traveller in this life as perhaps in death, she had led a nomadic existence, finding no bivouac for a restless spirit, no resting place for the night, no oasis that was not a mirage with camel humps of sand—though true, she had once spent a night in a desert tomb—though for a practical reason, the fact that there was no other roof, no other shelter. She said that it was the tomb of a great desert beauty. She had brought my mother a mirror from a tomb, saying that it should reveal the transience of human life.

She had never married, for her life had been shadowed with grief which was mentioned whisperingly with hesitation even now by my mother and Mr. Spitzer, both of whom seemed to wish to bury the great secret of Cousin Hannah's life and so would seldom resurrect the memory which the great captain herself had seldom or never mentioned. They preferred to speak of her as they had known her, and seldom would they lift the veil upon that secret and even then would be only tentative in their approach as if the revelation should conceal the secret—they would skirt around it endlessly like the surf skirting a barren shore, remembering all else before they remembered the secret heart of the dead captain, the secret begetting the secret through eternity.

That great captain, she who was cuirassed by suffrage and whose shield, my mother said, was emblazoned with a cherub carrying a lightning bolt, would never have been capable of such evasiveness—for had she not bearded human lions in their dens in Persia and startled great shieks in their ivory beds and African kings under their purple plumes and negotiated great torrents of ice and snow and deserts of stone? Had. she not ridden against great turbaned Turks like the great sea shells looming through the thin ripple of surf and fog? Some were surely equipped with swords under the cutlass moon.

She had said that my mother was in love with no man on earth but with a fleeting shadow, the mere shadow of a man, and it was this shadow against whom Cousin Hannah, girding her loins with suffrage like that iron girdle worn by a great Crusader's wife whose husband was away in

Holy Wars, had battled with swords of ice and swords of fire, lightning flashes, storm clouds, rolling fire balls. She had said that my mother's love was dead, but she did not seem to know that death was necessary to my mother's love. For what was man but a shadow, my mother had asked then as now, a shadow driven to and fro by the wind, and when had she ever seen a man on earth?

Cousin Hannah, one not easily giving up, not easily discouraged, had spent all her life discouraging my mother's love of the dead man. Though Peron had so greatly admired the captain of a lost campaign, for he had always figured that she would lose the last battle as she had lost the first, his gratuitous suicide had elicited no comment and no recognition from her, and she had sent not one horseshoe of the red and white roses to the horse-player's grave in memory of the horse which had lost, not one great dice cube of the white roses marked with the red roses or two dice cubes in a lucky throw, seven and eleven, not one figurehead or great cartwheel of flowers or harp, not one servant wearing her livery, not one representative such as might be sent by an enemy power to a foreign state in a stage of truce, yet though after he was dead and buried under the autumn leaves and falling snow, she had ignored Joachim as if it were he who had died, he who was removed to some far realm which was not quite of this mundane world, he who had gone to the buried nations, he who also might never be seen again albeit he was her lawyer to whom she had certainly entrusted many legal and financial affairs. And it was he who would pay his last respects to that great captain, he who would write his elegy for her—a few mournful taps with his cane upon the sidewalk. No such consideration had she paid to him, he had been vividly reminded at the time of his brother's departure.

She had never so much as sent a card. She had never laid down her arms, her pistols and her swords. She had never flown a black flag from her roof to show that, as Mr. Spitzer believed, each one who lives is shrunken by another's death, even be it the death of a rival, even be it a lazar in a distant city, that she was withered by just that loss of memory and recognition which had been hers when Peron had greeted her. He had always asked her how the great battle went, whether she was winning or losing. A light had gone off, but she had acted as if a light had gone on. Perhaps she had thought that her realm of conquest was extended, for her furies had not diminished but had increased as she had furiously tried to climb the walls of forbidden cities of brides, those who were held in thralldom by a cruel bridegroom, their faces cold as snow, as snow on mountain rocks, lace skirts of snow wrapped around their feet, those who would never be awakened by the kiss of any living man or love.

She had paid Mr. Spitzer but one great compliment, one attention, the fact that she had ignored him through all the active years of her life although he had continued to make his punctual calls, always to her empty house, coming with important documents for her to sign, notices of stock transfers, notices of accrued interest, notices of bankruptcy, of vacant rental properties—doubtless knocking at her door when he knew she was absent—perhaps riding, far away through deserts of snow whirling into shapes of minarets and towers and riders on their horses, her white horse El-Burraq with its eyeballs of foam and fire, the great Arab charger which went by ship with her—so that he had timed his steps not as a matter of chance but of elegant strategy, the most careful design, a countermove to her ignoring him. By the shrouded windows, the closed shutters, the closed gates with their broken lanterns, the chimneys from which no smoke or spark emitted, the summer furniture left out all winter upon the snow-shrouded lawn under the white trees with their long white hair blowing in the wind, the tattered and faded striped awnings of the old summer pagodas like the tents of Arabs, the iridescent frozen fountains and the canvas shrouds wrapped around the nude marble statues, the old newspapers blowing upon the porches, the creakings of the rusted chains of swings when the wind blew through the long arcades, the ragged birds' nests big as human wigs upon the broken columns, last year's autumn leaves scurrying before him like an army in rout, by all these signs and testimonials it was evident that she was not at home, that she had pitched her tent in some far desert of ice or storm or that she was travelling in the Alps, lost among the snow-topped peaks which cast their reflections on the glacial clouds where might be a castle none should ever find, climbing those glacial mountains with her Alpine retriever, the old St. Bernard nosing at her tracks through unmelting snow where might be seen the whirling footprints of twelfth-century kings and queens or birds which had paused for a moment upon those peaks hundreds of years ago.

He called when he knew she was far out on the high seas drifting in an open boat upon the great waves of the storm without captain or sail or compass—though never did he breathe a prayer for her as he knew that she would always safely make port and knew that her head was still enclosed in an arch of bone under the great sky which was like a stone shell with only a few wandering seams of light and cracks through which there gleamed the distant stars—knew that he would surely see her again in this life—that she would ride her foaming horse through mountainous foam upon a distant shore—or if on windy battlements the great battle went against her, then she could always fly her skirt as a sign of her surrender—called always when he was sure she was engaged in some far siege of a sleeping desert city or was planning a new campaign, a new and furious assault upon the inscrutable powers—knocking at her door with his ivory-headed cane, knocking three times as on the door of an Asiatic tomb and hearing no response but the silence, for she did not even keep an orderly or winged boy to wait on her—tapping only when he believed that she was absent, when she was probably fighting against the shrouded Moorish kings in great deserts and the great Turkish lords with their heads adorned by radiant jewels like the sapphire stars flashing lights and with their jeweled swords uplifted above the mother-of-pearl flanks of horses plunging, rolling in a sea of foaming clouds.

Sometimes, hesitating for a few minutes after he had knocked, hearing only a hollow sound as of the wind blowing through an abandoned house or a lonely alpenhorn or velvet portieres shaking like dark clouds or great antlers of great elk heads shaking in a long, dark hallway—they were those Cousin Hannah had left in her last estate, and they had now migrated to my mother's house—he would be overcome by the weird feeling that he was not alone, that he was being observed by a pair of bright, dark eyes staring at him as through the latticed shutters in those mysterious Oriental cities where the secret women look out, where the women can see the men, but the men cannot always see the woman—a fact which, it would always seem to him, acted greatly to a man's disadvantage. For he might spend all his life without ever seeing a strange woman. Or he might imagine that his veiled wife was beautiful long after her beauty had ceased, when her veil concealed the visage of the naked skull—and doubtless this was why in the Oriental countries there was polygamy. For a man could not be sure what manner of woman he loved.

Sometimes, though with an understandable hesitation, he would knock again, fearful lest the door should suddenly open, for really, he did not want to see Cousin Hannah, one who had never been beautiful—and not even her worst enemy could have said that hers had been great beauty once—and it was merely a routine call when he would perhaps have passed through that neighborhood in any case. He would not have minded if there was no one at home, but he did object to being made to seem ridiculous by knocking upon the door of a house which contained an unanswering occupant. Surely, though harassed by many distractions, he could not have knocked upon the door of the wrong house. He would feel that he and most of Boston had been deceived, that Cousin Hannah had probably never left home and was watching him now, that she knew of all his ghostly visits, his long journeys through rain and sleet and hailstones and howling snow, that she had been secreted all along in this great house with its many chambers and had merely given out to reporters the news that she had gone to a distant country, riding against the Turks and great Berbers in kingdoms of the Islamites. He would tap lightly with his cane against a trembling window glass, hoping thus to startle her, to take her by surprise—but was himself startled by hearing the sudden flutter as of spectral footsteps in empty rooms or the whirring of a bird's wing against a window glass or dusty mirror which, long before Cousin Hannah's death, was draped by veils of black chiffon in memory of some earlier death he had forgotten. When asked whose, she never had replied. So that he would knock upon the door again though very softly.

Sometimes, listening with his ear at the door, he would hear the whinnying of a distant horse—though he was perhaps less startled than he should be, for he had always understood that the Arabs sleep with their horses. Yet he could not help being very much annoyed by this persistent oblivion to him, his failure to arouse her. Even his patience would be sorely tried in view of the long journey he himself had made so that, though he was relieved that there was perhaps no one at home, no one who heard his knock, yet he was also disappointed, most especially as he had brought these exceptionally important papers which she disregarded as if they were worthless as perhaps, he must admit now, they were—for what were earthly riches, great castles and lonely towers, even great railroads in the face of the emptiness of life? Staring with his great eye rounded at the great keyhole—he had always wondered why the keyhole should be so great that a butterfly could have flown through it—he would be overwhelmed by the increasing certainty that there was another great, rounded eye staring at him with equal astonishment, its iris streaked like a sunken rainbow, perhaps a rainbow under miles of water, or perhaps it was a star or a candle flame passing in a distant room. Hallo, hallo—he would call, literally banging against the door. But he had simply misplaced the phenomenon. It was a star passing in a cloud, a star passing outside the house, perhaps a distant head light. It was a bird twittering in a snowy bush.

Besides, if there was still some doubt persisting in his mind, he could always read some of the old newspapers which had collected on the porch—with the reservation that they were not always accurate, of course, that the newspaper reporters seemed to know not much more than he did, for they reported journeys which she had not taken, and she had taken many journeys which they had not known. Slightly tapping with his cane upon the broken flagstones and great stone urns, stamping his feet to keep him company in a lonely vigil as the snow whirled around him, he attributed his error to the low state of his own consciousness like fire burning under water, the torpor of his mind which omitted so many things but saw much which others did not see. Often he had seen the lunar rainbow when others had not seen it.

He would put through a slot in the door his calling card embossed with the butterfly which was his sign of resurrection and eternal life—so that she could never accuse him of having ignored her—so that she would know that he had come during her absence, a period sometimes so long that it had seemed an absence from this world. Sometimes he was windily shaken by the thought that it might be his own absence—he was this empty cocoon. He would have little or no hope that she would ever sign the stock transfers which he pushed through the slot—so would be very much surprised when, every now and then, they would be returned to the old State Street Bank and Trust bearing that large, rapid, flowing signature which the old bank clerk knew was, in spite of all life's mysteries, indubitably hers. But Mr. Spitzer, continually searching for lost heirs and heiresses, knew more about these strange families than most people did. He was not so sure as the old bank clerk was—particularly as he had sometimes mistaken Mr. Spitzen's signature, the microscopic handwriting which required a magnifying glass.

Perhaps after she had died—certainly before the house was torn down, demolished by the great wrecker—surely not even Mr. Spitzer being capable, he believed, of such great forgetfulness that he would stop at a house which was no more, an address which had disappeared as if by magic from this mundane world and could not be found in Boston or its suburbs—Mr. Spitzer had continued his visits for a brief period, knocking at her door with his ivory-headed cane which, like his high silk hat and aggrievedly punctual airs, assured him of his own existence—often dropping his calling card through the slot—forgetting that he had buried her who had never buried him—perhaps imagining that she continued in this life as he continued—that disguised as an Arab king with her head shrouded by long purple and gold with long purple and gold tassels streaking the wind, she was storming a tent city—or leading her veiled army through streets of broken colonnades where horses' hooves clattered against the ancient Roman stones of those desert cities exhumed by the long purple and gold drifts of the sand and soon to be covered again by the great sand storms which covered great kings but would not cover her—or she was once more in the phantasmal Alps with the snow blinding her face, the snow flurries blinding her eyes—climbing unclimbable mountain peaks.

Truly, she was sleeping in that grey New England churchyard, surely he well knew, he having been the only mourner for the simple reason that most people thought she had died years before she had died. She had outlived her fame by several years—there seeming nothing sadder to Mr. Spitzer than the insubstantiality of human praise—that yesterday's bright star should be the daylight firefly lost in light. That would never be his problem, of course—for he had no name, no fame to outlive, just as he had found out—that there would be no one to give a passing thought to him, no one to shed a tear like a pearl on the grass. Her great St. Bernard was sleeping at her feet with its Red Cross bottle between its paws so that, in the long and lonely nights, she might take a nip. Mr. Spitzer had surely seen to this life-saving provision. Frost was on the trees and butterfly bushes the day he buried her. The trees were veiled with snow and ice. Frost rimed the great eye of the moon. Her horse was rolling at her feet. Her horse was rolling in the flood. Her turret reached above the highest mountain peak. Perhaps her Alps had always been carried in her heart as was said of many great mountain-climbers.

Out of her last estate—not nearly so large as some people had thought—he had intended to erect, though in a land where there was no memorial art and where for many years even church bells in mourning for the dead or for marriage had been forbidden, where there had been no way to mourn this mortal passage of a dying soul, where only the great waves had gonged as the cordages of the throat had trembled, that great tomb of which the design still remained only in his amorphous mind, for he was still composing the epitaph about which he could not decide—though he had composed, at the time, her elegy, a few mournful taps or muffled drums to the accompaniment of the bursting of great storm clouds, great thunderheads rolling across a darkened sky like a flight of horses and shot with artillery lights of green and rose and silver and gold, shot with meteors buzzing like bees. His timid music could be played only when there was a great storm all but blotting it out. He had thought of so many desolate possibilities in memory of her he could not settle on one, for he was so evasive, forever and forever turning in his mind what the words should be, and sometimes he thought that instead of a great tomb carved with this fallen knight she should have a ship, perhaps a resurrected ship, one which had already keeled, one which had been at the bottom of the sea, or perhaps a church bell or a great town clock in memory of her or a bridge between two worlds or even a busy highway. For what instructions should he give to the great stone-cutter in memory of one who had a stony face forever clouded?

Here lies the great captain unhorsed, Mr. Spitzer thought. He had written many epitaphs but had crossed them out. Here lies that great Crusader who rode against the Saracens and the Greeks, the Romans and the English and the French. She raided the Etruscan towns. She invaded the cities of night. Brigands in foreign countries searched for her, but now they will never find her though they search through all the world. Here lies the greatest captain who fought against all nations and rescued many ladies from their dark towers and cruel lords but could not rescue herself. Here lies one who searched all her life for her dead love, a body covered by the snow. Here lies one who was pitiful. Here lies one who shared our common lot of mortal frailty and died of her life. She was not fallen in a foreign field. She died at home. She perished in a domestic war. She died in her own old tent bed set in a windy place with no aide-de-camp to see her go, none to offer her the jeweled cup, the jeweled sword. She was taken by a greater captain who was wearing a winding shroud. She has gone over to the Islamites. Here lies the wounded dove, its wings broken in the storm. The rose of Sharon is growing in a desert place. Here lies that great desert king. Death snatched away her beautiful bride. Here lies the dead love of the world.

Oh, the splendor of Mr. Spitzer's grief spending itself on nothing but the empty air! He feared that whenever one died, he should mourn for two, perhaps through sheer generosity. Perhaps he should mourn for one who had died, one who was immortal and could not die. Perhaps he should mourn for one who could not be born, one who had by-passed this world. So that, not knowing what to say, hesitant as usual to make up his mind, just as he could never decide upon the inscription for his brother's tombstone or even the name, whether it was his brother or J.S.—settling on the cognomen Spitzer in that case but never deciding which brother it was, and perhaps he never would decide, doubtless because of his great reluctance to face the ultimate truth—he had chosen a simple headstone carved only with her name—being not even sure of that, of course, for she must have changed her name at some time during her life—with neither the date of her birth nor of her death—since like many ladies she had been sensitive as to her age and had not told the date of her birth and since he had forgotten, after so many years, the date of her death and thus gave her, at least in his own memory, this extension of time— perhaps not yet acknowledging that she would not return as my mother dreamed.

Perhaps he could have looked up these dates in dusty registers of births and deaths, deaths and births—but he had preferred the charity of his inaccuracy toward one who, utterly negating him while he was still alive, would never have shown such compassion as he had acquired since his brother's death. Besides, in his legal capacity he had found that these records were not necessarily accurate or complete—for had he not found that the old clerk of the death rolls had made an inordinately great mistake, that he had listed Mr. Spitzer's name among the dead? Yet he lived—though he had been unable to convince many a desk clerk. Even insurance agents had argued with him that he was dead—whereas it was certainly to their advantage to prove that a man lived.

He smiled with ineffable sorrow to think that she had ignored him who had outlived her, that he had continued in much the same routine long after it would seem that her great adventure had ceased. She had thought that my mother's life was the imitation of death, that she wasted her precious time with these two brothers, both unreal no matter which one had died or if both had died when one had died—for Joachim, though he pretended to be so true, was weak as water, deceitful and wavering and blown about like foam, and Peron was equally deceitful even though, as it had seemed, he had never pretended to be true and had not pledged eternal love or even one shining moment or its dead image repeated in time. But the lack of a pretended faithfulness made him no more honest than a dishonest man, just as Joachim's air of honesty had not kept him from being low, a poor musician, a poor lawyer who did not know the difference between a victory and a defeat. It was six of one and half a dozen of the other. There was no great choice between them, for a choice should imply a difference in the ultimate results. It was Hobson's choice. It was a choice between death and death, not death and life, not death and love. She had predicted that, at that time which should require the proof of human experience, both would reject my mother, preferring the shadow. Though Peron should die, Joachim's life should not be worth a candle's flame in the headlong wind, not worth a star snuffed out by the great candle-snuffer. Both were equally insecure, as unsubstantial as flame and water. The flame evaporates the water. The water extinguishes the flame.

Cousin Hannah had scoffed at my mother's imaginary quests, her search for the external man—for was it flesh which made the man, and was it his weight, his measure, his girth, his enormous body? Should man be judged by the magnitude of his appearance, and could only the dead monster arouse my mother's awakening love? The less the body to the vision, the less perceived, the greater the force of spirit and the greater all these unleashed powers of night, furies like the wind howling, Cousin Hannah had said, shouting at the top of her voice—though perhaps, of course, my mother had only imagined this message—perhaps, as usual, she had been dreaming of that which was not, just as she had believed. The external man, there was no doubt, had been Cousin Hannah's foe, just as if he were an imbecile or some poor creature besmeared and bedaubed, gilded and enameled. Probably, she had sworn an oath against him, giving her gentleman's word of honor—just as some other lady might take a vow which should unite her to the object of her true love— or should he be absent from this world, should serve as a barrier between herself and any other love which wore a human face. Cousin Hannah had also objected, perhaps with unintelligible fervor, to phantoms of the air, those to whom she had wished to deal, as if they had been her immediate rivals, the death-blow, the finishing stroke, the coup de grace, those who, my mother believed, had always eluded her, as if by artifice eluding artifice. For they had not been physical presences, these old kings who already, to the sound of muffled drums, had passed away.

CHAPTER 32

Cousin Hannah, a lady who had forcefully expressed herself, a lady who had never drawn in the reins or paused to hear another person's nugatory opinion—perhaps because she had already known it, had already heard the faintest whispers of the dead in desert cities and music of distant flutes and harps—had fought against vanquished competitors when there were none except those of my mother's drugged dreams, such as a horseman riding through the window when the wind blew the long billowing curtains as in a desert storm, when a dead seagull was blown screaming through the great, many-turreted house which was only its reflections on clouds. For this consanguineous relative had been interested in her overwhelming suffrage battles for woman on every front, her conquests which could never have been satisfied by temporary victories or the overthrow of man in this world. Perhaps, in fact, the ultimate victory would have been the ultimate defeat.

She was certainly dedicated to a greater assault than the immediate moment could provide, her ambitions having been boundless, causing panic in my mother's soul, causing my mother to dissemble her feelings when she came, to simulate an emotion of indifference she did not really feel. Cousin Hannah, unlike my mother with her superfluity of bewildering pretenses, intending to bewilder other people but also bewildering her, was not one to drag her standards in the dust, not one who, even for a strategic purpose, in order to advance her cause at some far military outpost, would seem to declare an amnesty, a period of forgetfulness or of oblivion, of death-like sleep, it seemingly not being in her nature to propitiate, to reconcile opposing forces, to hold them in abeyance. She was not one to invite her enemy to a banquet, to ease his suspicions with goblets of wine before she dealt the final blow—whereas my mother drank both the glass and the wine. She must have drunk at least a dozen long-stemmed goblets. Cousin Hannah had preferred to take the offensive, to advance by open hostilities, brandishing her sword like a cane even when there was no one.

She had preferred the strident clash of arms, the pitched battle against man—perhaps, too, against woman—though how could she have been the misogynist, the woman hater, the foe of the weaker sex, of all that was frail in life? She had always described herself as the high-souled lover of woman, whom she had come to rescue from slavery to man worse than enchantment by an Eastern drug or spiritous liquor or witches' brew, and she had fought against all obstacles known and unknown, clouds and cloud-bursts, even those of the imagination. And could she be the enemy of beauty dreaming at her glass? Could her heart be capable of such ambivalences, splittings? Could she hate that which she loved? There was no doubt that she had given her life to the conquering of man, be he even the most powerful horseman, and yet she had been opposed to the frivolities of the so-called weaker sex—the great garden hats decked with billowing plumes, the billowing silks, the secretive veils, the atmosphere swooning with the seductive scent of narcotic flowers, the frilled parasols which were used by beautiful ladies as weapons of flirtation requiring as great a skill as fencing, perhaps a greater skill—as when the ladies suddenly lowered or twirled or raised their snow-white parasols or shadowed their already shadowed snow-white faces—had urged woman to use her parasol as her sword or her shield, her greatest weapon of offense or defense—had often urged woman to take off her great hoop skirts flounced with ribbons and lace, to show her little bird feet, to fly her skirts as her banners in her war against tyrannical man, the cruelest lord who was ever known, the greatest oppressor of beauty in all countries, to fly her skirts on tallest mountain peaks above the shadowed purple valleys. So that my mother, whenever Cousin Hannah came, had lifted her white umbrella, perhaps because the snowflakes were falling, whirling in the dim air lighted by singing candle flames singing and flying away, perhaps because she heard the whistling of the winter wind or many cuckoo clocks striking in a dark forest as those loud hoof beats broke upon the frozen clouds and shattered the trembling window panes, those lighted by the flickering stars.

My mother believed that Cousin Hannah had been the image of that past which never was, that future which might never be realized. She had been extemporal, sudden and abrupt, acting on the spur of the moment, impulsive, swift as a twinkling, a flash, a breath, brief and meteoric, hastening through this life as if it were a journey one should make with the utmost quickness and dispatch, as if one should not spin out the moment beyond the moment, temporize, gain time, sleep. She had always been hurried, keeping all her appointments except that one which she had missed. She had gone on many journeys that nobody knew, for she had an important message to bring. A long-limbed jockey riding a long-limbed horse, her steeple head lost in the clouds, she had galloped, vanished, faded in the darkening air, sometimes before my mother knew that she had come. She must have circled the world twice in windy afternoons or nights, seldom drawing her reins, seldom pausing, perhaps stopping only for a moment at my mother's house. Such a lady, my mother thought, should have been employed by the old Pony Express. She should have brought the message to Garcia. She was certainly the greatest courier of every storm. She was certainly the greatest weathervane. The barometer dropped when she came—it was colder than a sea of the icebergs calved by the great glacier moving through the dusk, colder than the Weddell Sea, colder than the lunar sea. She could have outridden all the jockeys of this world—and, long after the race was over, would have ridden on and on where there was no other rider, where there were only howling winter winds and shrouds of snowflakes and where her horse left its tracks in the snow. She was tall as a ship's mast.

She had been like all my mother had ever loved, at least in her imagination—an adventurer in far places, one who was often absent, one whose ways would never be entirely charted, not even by the greatest cosmographer of the lost stars. Her face had not been attractive, certainly, not even in my mother's dreaming eyes which saw transparencies as if they were real, not even now as she remembered her—fortunately for her as my mother could have endured no beautiful or potent rival, be she even a dead bride with her face covered by a veil of snowflakes—for Cousin Hannah had been this great challenger of Foreign Legions she had driven before her like the transparent leaves scurrying in the winter wind, like the whirling snowflakes, this grim-visaged defender of woman's unsullied honor, her beauty which should be as white as virginal snow, as cold as snow upon the frozen mountain peaks—and she had been one who, as she had lived by the sword, should have died by one sharp blow, a martyr to her cause, my mother still believed—that Cousin Hannah's should have been a hero's death and loud requiem and eternal repose in the deserts of snow or in the snow-topped mountains which she had often climbed and where she had pitched her tent of singing winds. But she had died in no foreign war, had not died while storming distant battlements or walking the edges of crumbling abysses. She had suffered for years from frostbite. She had died after many years of semi-invalidism— in her old age confessing to my mother that she no longer believed in the glory of these foreign conquests—that these great battles had been as nothing to her, had been as mere incidents in a busy life—she realized now when she was passing over to the realm of one who had overthrown great kings and had slain minotaurs—that the greatest heroes were not those who perished in the loud clash of arms where dogs and horses screamed or while storming against desert cities or great mountain towers. The greatest battles were fought in the domestic wars by those who had never left home. They were fought by man and woman. It was always an unequal battle, for woman reigned supreme. The man who had left home was a coward who should never be forgiven by her in her lonely grandeur. She had died while sleeping, perhaps while dreaming, there was little doubt in my mother's mind. A map of her military engagements in distant countries was pinned upon a bedroom wall— traceries of spiralling journeys through all the Middle East and lands not shown on any other map, journeys to cities no one had ever visited before and journeys of possible return, journeys into impregnable Asiatic fortresses guarded by great stone birds.

But of course, it was impossible to know how the great captain could have made this death-bed confession—since she had not answered her telephone though my mother had called for years, and it was many miles between my mother's sea-side house and the old Boston mansion between

two water towers with factory chimneys in the smoke-clouded background
and anvil sparks like stars flying through clouds and heavy traffic of old-
fashioned vehicles on all sides, and my mother had visited her only in a
dream when she was riding in her carriage driven by the dead black
coachman driving the black horses who wore black plumes and knew the
way as if they had gone that way many times before as was not the case.
My mother had taken to Cousin Hannah a bouquet of red roses. The
door had opened instantly before my mother knocked. There had been
none of those delays such as Mr. Spitzer had usually known when he had
visited the great captain before her fall into physical mortality and had
knocked three times and had waited in a windy, roofless vestibule stamping his feet in their great coachman's boots as the snow fell. A winged
hand had opened the door to my mother. When had this visit occurred,
Mr. Spitzer asked vaguely as if he were not himself? Perhaps a visit was
all the reality there was. This visit would have been so difficult to arrange
—particularly as both ladies were in their beds and perhaps entertained
only the ambient ghosts of all dead loves. One was dead, and one was
dying. He had been the only go-between, musically whispering as he had
thought what to say, what not to say. Cousin Hannah had certainly not
had long for this world—as she must have known when she had seen him
in his dark cape, the snow like ermine upon his collar. He certainly
hoped that my mother's visit had not occurred after she was dead.

Yet what clouds, what obstacles had there been in her path that she
should have fought so valiantly where there were no defenses, where all
was evanescent as a dream, where the walls might crumble at a lonely
trumpet's sound, the toppling towers fade as Boston faded into fog and
water from which it came? For my mother, though surrounded by many
walls, by many defenders, swordsmen and cupbearers and powdered and
peruked footmen, many defenses and imbroglios of being and sunken
cities with gleaming towers in clouds, had been defenseless when Cousin
Hannah came, striding back and forth as the candle flames shook and as
their reflections shook a few seconds or minutes later in distant mirrors
rippling with light, perhaps years later. My mother had been bed-ridden
then as now, veiled by many illusions and draperies of medieval lace,
cascades of white lace rippling from her snowy bosom to her feet as the
white umbrella floated over her floating swan bed in a dazzling cloud.
Sometimes she saw only a large foot. Sometimes it was the foot of a lady,
sometimes the foot of a horse, perhaps a winged horse. Sometimes she saw
only a gleaming sword lifted in the air. She surely knew the day that
Cousin Hannah died, for a riderless horse white as snow came through
the window, and the snow fell around my mother's bed. And the temperature dropped, and there were great icicles hanging from the ceiling,
and the prisms danced. For years afterward there was the mournful music
of Chinese flutes and lutes.

In the many years before Cousin Hannah's death, however, and they
were surely extensible years, years when she was still a visitor in this dark
house, she had never failed to emphasize, by her physical presence and by
the self-assured brilliance of her manner which caused the competitive

candle flames to dim, by her libertine and yet patrician airs, my mother's essential loneliness, the fact that she had been abandoned, that the mysterious bridegroom had left her. All her loves were imagination—the pharaohs, the captains she imagined in their swan boats with their long fluted wings drifting through clouds. All her loves had left her, and they had never been. No one, not even Cousin Hannah had ever touched my mother's cold heart, cold and hard as the mountain rock. No one had awakened the sleeping lady to life and love. There was no fairy prince such as my mother dreamed of, and there was no man, and there was no cold kiss like a snowflake falling through the dark air under the glassy sky.

What beautiful femme fatale was my mother to be this lone lady in an empty house, talking to shadows, to far ripples of foam upon the wind, visited so seldom by anyone except old Cousin Hannah who, though very busy in another sphere, though pushed upon far more than Mr. Spitzer by a thousand considerations demanding her immediate attention, a thousand important papers to sign, ten thousand, though often in the merciless glare of the limelight of publicity which was so very different from the light of a halo, though greatly agitated by her attacks of neuralgia, had remembered her, a creature of such fragility that she should never be forgotten, not in the desert sands gleaming like a lost star, not in the roaring of the heaviest surf or city traffic, be it in Boston or Cadiz or Rome, not even though Cousin Hannah, to visit her, might have come from picketing in a cold, sleet rain in front of a skirt factory in a dead New England town, forgetting that she owned most of the town and most of the skirts, or though she must hasten to start a street car strike in distant Ithaca, New York, challenging the conductor to a duel? She could not help being, as she was very ardent, very self-congratulatory, boasting of her battles on many frontiers—especially as she knew my mother's nature was ever a changeful and capricious thing, her attention wandering even when she was confronted by this great captain who, unlike my mother's other visitors, these hollow men, these advocates of lost causes, these men of straw, these things of naught, had existed when others had ceased to exist, when they were apparitions scattered by the wind, when they were less than poor street Arabs. For was not Cousin Hannah real, no poor apparition who had traversed the borderland between the dreamer and the dream, and did she not come from far, travelling toward the distance lighted by a firefly or desert lamp?

She had surely been instantaneous, spasmodic, explosive, attempting to take by main force that which might have been taken by peaceful means—if she had come with flutes and viols, with silken whispers. But that would have been to encourage the dreams of one who was always supine, one who believed that she was already dead. Cousin Hannah could only discourage such a fancy which was the pretense of death. For she had seen the valleys of dry bones, the skulls of the dead in foreign countries where autumnal legions fell. She had fought for freedom on every unknown front, particularly for freedom from man, who had never seduced her. She had not dragged through the meaningless days and nights, and it had seemed that she would never do so, as she was spurred by her necessities, loving action for its own sake, loving the loud crystal cannonades of war, bombardments of distant escarpments and lonely castles where no one seemed to be at home and great icebergs burning with inner celestial fires, never retreating except to approach again, perhaps by ambush, and it surely had seemed that she would never linger here like the sleepy myrmidons who did my mother's bidding, fetching and carrying for her, fanning her with feather fans, bearing great golden harps on their heads, harp strings played by windy seagulls, grand pianos with keyboards of surf played upon by foaming wind, that she would never linger like the half-frozen fountains in the ruined gardens, the stone faces, the stone helmets in the gardens of the dead. Surely, she would never linger here like the dead jockeys riding the dead horses, the mandarin polo players riding through clouds, the dead yachtsmen rigging the boom-sails of ships which had already gone down, keeling for the last time, the old sporting crowds billowing in the wind, making the sea's noise, the centaurs laying great golden eggs like moons upon the grass, the red roosters crowing in the eternal dusk.

Had she come from Outer Mongolia, the great Wall of China, the kingdom of Prester John, shores where there were the ewe-necked birds and antelopes with twisted ivory horns? Had she come from Manitoba, Hudson's Bay, Cape Reprieve, the Laurentian Shield of great rocks bearing mica glittering like gold and sapphires which turned to rubies, rubies which turned to sapphires, such metamorphic jewels as my mother wore on her long fingers gleaming like northern lights, the opalescent Far North of which she dreamed, imagining that it was she, this beautiful corpse sleeping in a bed of snow? Had this great traveller been lost among ten thousand singing islands of snow and ice and wind, and had she battled singing icebergs, pushing back an iceberg with her rusted pike as she stood at the prow of that rotted ship which never would return, for it would be engulfed by the great iceberg slowly moving through the dusk with wakes of snow and frozen foam? Yet surely she was not an opium dreamer, for she had visited all those places of which my mother dreamed, and she had even visited here. Had she found the Northwest Passage in the howling wind? Did she bring a message from a great king to a great khan, both long since dead?

For every soul must know finally its Northwest Passage, must find that which cannot be found, the crevice narrow as a thread suddenly opening into those great abysses filled with cities of frozen pinnacles and towers.

She had been very different from my mother certainly with her apparent submissiveness, her tinkling airs, her powder box mentality, her clouded looks, her faded silks and cobwebs of light and permanent iridescence, her neutrality which had permitted her to sleep through many years, not knowing how time passed or if it passed—though also, as my mother had thought then, Cousin Hannah had seemed, in some ways, in spite of her amazing vigor and resurgence, one who had been always time-worn, old, ancient, obsolete, almost extinct, almost out of time's way, not one who had ever known the spring-tides of life, the seed-times and the golden seasons, the mating seasons when like was joined to like, when they were interwoven and entangled. She had not known the golden-footed honey bees like stars zooming from flower to flower in the evening light. She had not known, it had seemed, the mating calls of the evening birds. She had not known the stately mating dance of the whooping cranes, white in the mist, the mating dance of the pink flamingoes who performed intricate floor patterns, circles and arcs, and then two by two departed with each other through fogs and mists.

My mother could not remember Cousin Hannah's vanished youth, that time when this great lady must have been inexperienced—she having been old within my mother's memory of her. Who could have imagined her as a bride, a young girl veiling her eyelids with dreams, trembling with the expectation of her lover, perhaps such a one as was not on this earth? Perhaps she could have been married to herself only when she was old. Perhaps only then could she have wedded man or woman. What lost romance could have been hers, in view of who she was or was not? Much must remain forever undefined. Who could have imagined her mate, though rumors spoke of an old suitor who had languished for years because she had abandoned him? She had left him at the church door with a white bouquet in his hands. It was said that after that he had subscribed heavily to the suffrage movement.

She had been the veteran of so many winter campaigns, desert marches through burning sands. She had lived through so many dangers—this strange, dark lady standing in a beam of sudden light, a lady with ravaged, burning eyes, a saber wound upon her cheek, a grizzled chin. Her nose had been, though prominent, only the shadow of a nose, a great promontory over which there fluttered the shadow of a bird.

She was never faint-hearted, never easily discouraged like that faint heart which never won fair lady. Rather, she had flourished upon renewed discouragements, almost with a kind of terrible zest as if each failure brought her closer to her triumph. When discouraged, she had only seemed to withdraw into oblivion. She had been very near when one had supposed that she was far away upon a dangerous errand in a dangerous mountain pass of overhanging cliffs and hurtling snows. She had been far away when one had supposed that she was near. She had consulted her armorers, her archers, her fusiliers. She had returned with new attempts—or perhaps her life had been one long siege, for her retreat had been a skillful withdrawal, not a coward's retreat, and she had always rallied new forces, storming this castle as the sea corrodes the shore of rocks, sunken porches. For her failures, though many, had not been absolute.

Surely, she had only seemed to fail to break up my mother's marriage, which was in all probability doomed from the start, it often seeming to my mother now that she had married only in order that she might say there was a man in the house, and yet her husband had left her, for she had married that great traveller who never would return, and sometimes she thought she had married merely in order to proclaim her independence, to defy Cousin Hannah, who had urged her independence of man, that she should arise, take horse, make war, join her troops, fly her skirt upon some lonely mountain top as that great flag which would be seen by all the nations of the world and would strike pity and fear in all men's hearts. At times she said that hers had been a formal wedding, that she had gone to church for the last time, that she was carried in a hearse. She had never returned to Boston. But she was very vague as to this, however, and might suddenly change her mind, her mind always wandering.

She was always so very vague as to who her husband was. She once said that she had been married on the tennis court, that wearing her flying veils and silks she had been married merely by passing a few balls or one great ball which was the winged moon flying above the clouds. She once said that she had been married on the clouded archery range, that with her face swathed in veils she had shot a golden arrow through a cloud. She had been married to a sail-boat which suddenly lifted its wings and sailed away. She had been married to a porpoise and a star. She had been married to an iceberg. She had been married to a church bell. She had been married to all the fading images of this world. Cousin Hannah, beating with her white umbrella upon the bridegroom, scream- ing like ten thousand demons in the cold midnight air, had tried to cause havoc, a riot, a howling mob such as might be found at a war or a race- track. She had tried to intrude, to carry my mother away as the robber bridegroom carries the swooning bride though pursued by mad relatives and furious cousins and weird huntsmen and barking dogs and mourners in their carriages and all the furies of the white-lipped universe. For these elopements were always resisted by heaven and earth, as if all nature should protest. There had been this great public embarrassment, the stars whining like old dogs who have lost their quarry. My mother, blushing behind her billowing wedding veils, feeling the wind whipping through her voluminous skirts, ten thousand acres of lace, had felt as if she were hypnotized, drawn by a magnetic force which came from no known place or star, as if she did not know, as there was such great confusion, what she was doing or who the bridegroom was, for she had never seen his face. She had fought against the empty air, the whistling wind. She had lost her pink silk slippers in the evening surf. Her feet were walking in a cloud of snow. Sometimes she said that, in the midst of this great struggle, her wedding gown had been torn to shreds by brambles and spikes of stars. Sometimes she said she had not been touched. She had been mar- ried to a phantom. Nature was dead, cold and dark. For weddings are funerals, and funerals are weddings. When one marries, a part of one must die. When one dies, one is forever married, married through separa- tion unto eternity. The great lover is always the absent one. He is one whom no one has ever known or loved.

Sometimes she thought that she had ignored this uninvited wedding guest—sometimes, that she had frozen her with her remoteness, her icy chill—or again, that she had given her a sidelong glance which might signify much or nothing. Perhaps, indeed, being of a fickle nature, forever irresolute, even at her wedding, she had intended to encourage her, as one might encourage, with almost complete security, those who have passed beyond all hope, those who never will return.

Yet Cousin Hannah, noted for her persistence when the cause was lost—perhaps only then had it seemed most attractive to her—had acknowledged no permanent failure though rebuffed in a way which might have humiliated and permanently discouraged a man. And if she had been a man, would she have been that pale cavalier who, with disheveled locks, with foaming mouth, is driven by the mare, the white mare he rides upon, turning whichever way the mare turns? Would she not have governed with the proud supremacy of one who has neither too much experience nor too little by which to guide the wild spirit, knowing when to relax his guidance, when to use a tight bit, short reins, sharp spurs? My mother had surely always thought so, admiring, in the midst of her drugged dreams, Cousin Hannah's swiftness, the way she had raced the whirlwind, the snow storm, the sudden avalanche, the falling cyclonic star, the slowly whirling snowflake mirrored on a glassy sea. She had never used the long rein, had never slowed her horse to pace with dying stars, or so it had seemed then. She would never have given herself up, my mother had believed, to weariness of spirit, the dullness of the senses, or that renewal of life which comes through unbroken sleep, a moment's metamorphic resurrection—and how could my mother have foreseen then that which was yet to be, that the great captain, old and crippled and broken by many wars against great pashas and dreaming shieks, would die in bed and not upon the lonely battlefield in a far country—that she would die in that obscurity in which she had not lived, for none should see her passage—that it was my mother who might still arise and die while travelling? Who could have known the mysterious denouement then? There had been nothing, for many years, to indicate that Cousin Hannah would ever retire from mortal conflict like that great conflict raging in her heart. Many times when all had seemed lost, she had sharpened her wits.

My mother had always wanted to die while travelling—as then she would never completely die—for every traveller dies merely by passing through a city, and none will know that landscape which he passes through in the long night. Death is that which is caused by our partial knowledge.

CHAPTER 33

✧

INDEED, one of the Boston newspapers, in memory of a lost social season, that which had never been, had once referred to my mother as a famous beauty of the past, the late Mrs. Catherine Cartwheel, nee Snowden, widow of Jock, the fashionable dog fancier, the fabulous yachtsman, the great mountain-climber who had disappeared when the mountains moved like waves—making this mistake doubtless for the simple reason that she had not been seen in Boston for so many years, and there were probably many persons who had never seen her riding to the hunt. In fact, when she was alive, and this had been the chief subject of her present despair, she had been ignored, and seldom had anyone attended her great garden parties in the whirling snow and boar hunts in shadowed gardens and yacht meets which were attended by great kings wrapped in canvas shrouds—that they might suddenly sail—so Mr. Spitzer had not told her she was mentioned now. For there was probably no good reason to arouse these slumbering resentments. This reference to her had seemed, of course, elegiac, as Mr. Spitzer had certainly considered, though with only a moment's chagrin as he had realized that superficial opinion had little to do with the course of events—for she was still entertaining Chinese mandarins and ambassadors to vanished courts and kings of vanished realms and great balloon ascensionists who long ago had descended to earth, dragging their shrouds and cords through gardens of lilies. He believed, after only a slight hesitation, that the mistake had not been deliberate—that doubtless it had been only the mistake of a printer's devil, the jumbling of the print—though one never knew, of course, how such misstatements occurred or what ghostly hand had guided the great printer's devil. Had he also jumbled the stars?

Mr. Spitzer, therefore, had thoughtfully, benevolently not corrected this crucial error—believing that he was not in the position to do so—believing that it was unimportant and possibly trivial, that there were many more important errors to rectify, as he had said, squinting with one eye at his brother's watch, trying to detect a moment's falsehood—that though my mother was believed to be dead—yet my mother lived, as he well knew, for she was an opium taker in love with her starry illusions—and he believed it best that she should not be disturbed, that these illusions should not be corrected, at least not by him. So he had allowed things to take their course, for they ultimately would, and some day this Boston newspaper, though noted for its errors, would probably be right, having merely mistaken the time—so that, until then, he should be grateful for a moment's grace, he presumed, and should keep his appointments and should be quick to depart. But he was slow to depart. He himself had read in the same newspaper that Mr. Peron Spitzer had been seen recently walking along Benevolent Street, peering into old doorways—looking for a particular address, no doubt, Mr. Spitzer had thought, wondering what on earth Peron should have been doing in that neighborhood. Mr. Spitzer, the very next evening, just when the lamp-lighters were lighting the lamps, had walked down the same street—his black cape whirling around him like the sobbing of the rain upon the river Styx. When there were such errors as these, who knew what to expect next? For years he had seen no carriages on the streets of Boston—and that evening he had seen a carriage. My mother should remember whatever memories she pleased—even her funeral, as he remembered his which had afforded no special pleasure to him, bringing him no special privilege, bringing him not even the wisdom of the dead, bringing him only this diffused sense of woe, this sorrow which seemed to have no source in his own life.

She should think—and the idea often fascinated her—that she had never been married. She should think that she had been married once to a stranger—that she had been married twice to the same stranger or twice to two strangers, her second husband being the mirror of her first or her first the mirror of her second—that she had been married several times to several strangers, as often as an erroneous clock struck. She would often say that she was the kind of woman who could love only the man she had never married, perhaps the man she had not known, had not seen. She would swear, of course, that she had never married Mr. Spitzer—and she never would, not while the stars shone in the glassy heavens. Her bridegroom had been a white camel veiled with lace in the fog. Her bridegroom had been a church steeple. The bride had been a door. The bridegroom had been a key. The bride had been a keyhole. The bridegroom had been the wind. The bride had been a flame. She had rejected, upon each occasion, Mr. Spitzer, this faithful friend with his omnivorous appetite for sorrow. For she would not listen to him—and besides, he was in no position, as he might say, to correct her, to modify her enthusiasms, to bring her back to reality, that which was unreal. As for Mr. Spitzer, though she seemed to remember that he had been at her wedding, thus reminding her of the spacious heart she had broken, the altogether different life she might have lived had she accepted his invitation to live in a secluded place and listen to his future music, that which had been as yet unwritten, Mr. Spitzer could never remember this wedding, being oblivious to it just as if it were something which had never happened, something which had transpired outside his field of consciousness and had not involved him—and thus he expressed, as she did not seem to recognize, his seething belligerence by his blank passivity, his attitude of indifference which had protected him as if it were a dark cloak.

When my mother was married, there seemed to have been a great many spirits in the air, some with garlands of bright, metallic flowers, a great many voices in the wind, glassy pebbles rolling on the shore. Spray and foam had frozen upon the trees, draping the trees with glittering webs, with weird, fantastic shapes. There were swords of fire, swords of ice. The sand dunes, as she remembered, were sheeted with ice and pale streaks of snow. There had been driving sleet, angular motions as the snow whirled in circles, iridescent breakers leaping toward the luminous sky, drowning the stars, and the dunes had shifted in the wind, and it was always another place. Yet my mother was still so vague, her mind clouded when she tried to reconstruct the fallible details of this wedding. For as she might often remark, her powers of ratiocination were not good—so many crystals dashing even now against her cheeks, and her eyes blinded by the snow. Sometimes she could not even remember herself. Sometimes she thought she had worn a long white nightgown and carried a bouquet of red roses, that she had been married to Death while she was sleeping —for she had seen her dim reflection in a mirror which was covered with the scum of aged ice and rimmed by frozen grass. Yet she might be wrong, of course, as to who the bridegroom was. She had seen many bats and owls, sometimes their images in dim mirrors pale as ice. Near-sighted bats flitting by on leathern wings, filling the air with their cries. Owls, great horned owls hooting above the lonely church steeples. She had seen many lengthening shadows, many fashionable carriages. She could remember, she could still hear the wild, ethereal wedding music, a vast overture which was never quite completed, an eternal prelude to nothing—many reverberations, many keys and strings and wandering echoes, many wandering flute notes, the withered harp strings played upon by nothing but the fingers of the invisible wind—but as to the unreality of the musician, that unreality made no conceivable difference to the strings of the harp which had moved and stirred with ineffable music in dim chambers. There had been echoes of echoes. The sere stars shook like autumn leaves. The waves moved and stood still. It was this entire creation which was this fiction.

She remembered the dead lute-player in the garden, his pear-shaped body, his long, twisted neck, his broken strings. Nobody knew how he had got there. He was this man who was this musical instrument. There had been a great many formal king penguins, a great many melancholy seals—though probably the bipolar illusion was created by memory. There had been a great many tinkling duchesses. Sometimes she had seen Mr. Spitzer in his high silk stovepipe hat, his long black cape, and sometimes she had seen only his enormous shadow moving across a sea of ice, moving like an eclipse. Sometimes she had seen the black coachman, his silver buttons, his white gloves—and sometimes, though hearing the coachman's cries to his horses, she had not seen him.

But of course, as Mr. Spitzer had frequently pointed out through all these years of perilous illusion, my mother's distended memory was always quite beautifully inaccurate—as if she knew that accuracy would have destroyed her—and while she lived, there must be these unexpected multiplications, these fusions of images—and also, he sometimes thought, with considerable hesitation, that they might perhaps continue when she was dead. So one might not know when she was gone. There would still be these dream fugues, these polyphonic compositions, these many sounds of many voices, whisperings, tinklings. What should she do with accuracy, and why should it confine her? Who was he to correct these surface impressions or differentiate between black and white, green and yellow and red? Who was he to say that a thing was different from what it seemed? How would he know? Suppose there was no escort from here to there, that each must go alone through darkness? Yet she imagined one, though there was no escort to accompany her where she was going. Besides, he did not think she was going anywhere. It was he who journeyed, going on a long route many miles outside his way, checking milestones or lamp-posts or steeples hung with bells or bridges, studying the velocity of wind over bridges, the tonnage of wind pressure against cables, ascertaining that sometimes twenty thousand tons of wind broke against a single string, for he was writing harp music which should be the exact imitation of the wind playing through the strings and cables of a bridge, trembling bridge, the bridge reflected upon water, and his music should be finished only with the dying wind, wind dying over the water, he who went to the post office day after day to inquire for a dead letter, to ask that they should trace a letter which he had mailed to himself many years ago and which had never been delivered though it was marked clearly with his return address, the address of the sender, an envelope containing a piece of blank paper, he who looked through every street, often for what, in the midst of his meticulous errand, he had forgotten. Or the house had moved. Perhaps it was in the lunar Apennines, he sometimes thought. Or he had reminded someone of his brother.

Mr. Spitzer, sighing ponderously, would try so desperately to explain my mother to himself, to understand her changing moods, for it had been and probably must always be his fate to spend his life with her, though she would always deny him in favor of the celestial years, those not of this shrinking star. He had come gradually to believe that her conscious states were probably like the unconscious states of other people—but that though she was enslaved by her drug habit which had robbed her of her sense of time, she was probably no more enslaved than others were by their predisposition toward illusion, and she was probably no more distant from reality than were the lamp-lighters going their lonely rounds or those who must punch time-clocks in great factories, those who must turn great wheels, little wheels. They, too, could live only while they dreamed. They, too, were never quite awake. So when she slipped into death, it would be as if she had slipped into that unconsciousness which was coexistent with the wild sea of eternity, or so he hoped, that the great change had already come. She was so nearly always unconscious—hers was a greater freedom, a greater aura of improbable possibility than if she had ever closed a door or written finis to a deathless dream as Mr. Spitzer's brother had surely done. And though she might seem aloof from the world, yet it was this very irrationality which bound her to the world and Mr. Spitzer who knew those paving stones which were clouds. He, therefore, even in spite of some acknowledged impatience on his part, must patiently indulge her mercurially changing moods, whether of mistaken memory or of the present moment—and besides, he was so often surprised, even to the point of incredulity, by her memory of those remote or recent events which had transpired outside his consciousness. He had tried, of course, to blot out his unconsciousness, fearing it as he feared death and vast seas of roaring voices, to live only in his conscious moments and by the ticking of his watch, never to join in the chorus of this dumb-show—to be unlike his brother, who had listened to the promptings of a dream jockey telling him where to put his money and thus ruining his life and involving Mr. Spitzer in such vicarious debts, those he could never hope to pay to creditors he did not know. They were apparently innumerable, so he was furtive, trying unsuccessfully to avoid talking with strangers.

My mother heard only the dialogues in a dream, those he could not always hear—and why should he object, especially as his mind was filled with the wind music after it had passed? Besides, as was well known, as he could not too often remind himself, she had no respect for logical sequences, none for the relation of cause to event, none for this web of causality, none for the correct order of time, none for the place, none for the person—confusing noon with purple midnight or the pale moon's setting with the moon's rising like a moth over the waves or life's ending with life's beginning or mountainous seas for mountains with foaming crests. How often Mr. Spitzer had heard her talking to a person who was not there—and though looking around him, turning his head from side to side, could not hear the answer which she heard—though apparently what the other person said was quite rational. It might be a very conventional conversation upon the weather, whether it was raining or shining or whether a moon shone upon the moon—or as when she said to open the door, as when the other person said that the door was already open —except that the door was closed, and she was talking to a human-sized blackbird. Mr. Spitzer would get up and open the door.

CHAPTER 34

SOMETIMES, her mind wandering and lost as if no time had passed, my mother thought she had been married in white, veiled in white from head to foot as would be conventional for one who was married for the first time, for one who was trembling on the threshold of conjugal life. Someone had carried her in his arms, for she had fainted, and she had never been aroused. Someone had carried her across a threshold, and she had not seen his face. Yet she had been married in black, as befitted one who should be married twice, and she had been married in church, a great cathedral domed by many-colored glass, with bewildered angels blowing bewildering traffic horns, cherubim riding on the backs of bottle-nosed dolphins, tapestry kings and queens among the long grey shadows —and it was during a funeral, but she did not know whose funeral it was, for she had not seen the corpse, the corpse at her wedding. But it must have been an important personage who had died, for the funeral was very regal—there were many halberdiers and torch-bearers, many faceless mourners, many shrouded relatives and many carriages with black curtains at the windows and great funeral wreaths and people weeping in the streets as if a mighty emperor had passed. My mother had inquired, and someone had told her that it was the king of France who had died. Someone else had told her that the king was a dog, that it was a dog who had worn the crown and diamond cross. Someone else had told her that there was neither a funeral nor a wedding—there was an auction sale, and this abandoned house was going under the auctioneer's hammer, for a great beauty had passed away, dying in her sleep. The black flags were certainly flying at half mast, and there were men carrying gilded Louis Quatorze chairs on their heads, men carrying rock crystal candelabra, men carrying empty picture frames.

Sometimes she had been married by a false preacher—sometimes by a false priest—sometimes, more often, though this was usually at ten o'clock in the morning, she had been married by a St. Bernard dog, an Alpine retriever who had come to her in a prophetic dream, saying that her husband would be lost, for he would fall between two frozen mountain peaks, and her marriage bed would be as cold as a bed of snow. He would probably be buried under an avalanche concealing some things while revealing others, or a glacier would move over him during the long night under the frozen stars. This dog had licked her with his tongue. This dog had given her the Viaticum, though whether the provisions for a journey or the last rites given to one when dying, she could not say. This dog had spoken in church Latin, my mother believed—though sometimes she thought it was Caesar's message to the Gauls, and she was probably in the purple-wreathed Pyrenees or at a ski resort covered by an avalanche of stars. For she was not sure, her eyes dazzled with light—and why should she be sure of anything, she with the ecstasy which came from her sense of the incompleteness of life, its evasiveness? Besides, Mr. Alexander Pope was holding her hand. Sometimes she said she had been married at home, there being no eye witness but the black coachman, now dead, though driving her down darkening streets. And what city was it, she would ask, and where was she? She believed it was no city. It was all cities, and it was the city of the dead.

Nothing had happened at all as she had said before, or everything had happened simultaneously like one image repeated in many mirrors. She had been married at midnight. She had been married at noon. Rousing herself from a long period of sleep, years or months or hours, she would be sure, at last, how it had happened, this marriage with space. She was quite sure that she must have been married while she was fast asleep, and she had never awakened. She had been married in her riding habit, carrying a purple fan which had turned into a sea shell. She had worn her archery veil. Many golden arrows had sought her heart. For she had been abducted, much against her will—or wishing to escape many misfortunes and immortal woes, had eloped with the robber bridegroom, and she could still remember, she could still hear the cries, the shrieks of her pursuers, some of whom must have carried rusted firearms or bows and arrows. She could still feel, even after so many years, the freezing winds upon her cheeks, the winds whipping through her long, wild hair, her eyeballs congealing. She could remember a leaden moon, for love had died when she was married. The sky was grey, filled with luminous mares'-tails, with horse-head clouds racing along the wind. Life was this one moment. The sea, seen through the fog, was the color of a dead pigeon's breast. Sometimes she said that she had seen the bridegroom, sometimes that she had never seen him. His face was veiled by whirling fog.

She said it had been a Gretna Green wedding, an elopement with the man she had not planned to marry, and she was pursued upon these wild New England roads by fifty wild long-haired Cossack horsemen, their wild horses pounding like the surf blows upon a barren shore, and she was pursued by furious, hairless, human-faced dogs and furies unnameable, screeching harpies, half woman and half bird, those who came to carry away the souls of the dead. Was Cousin Hannah the first horseman? Was she the second?

Was not marriage, as that great suffrage captain had always said, the death of a woman's soul, the sacrifice of her finest impulses, the wasting of her shining talents, for was it not an empty world? My mother, perhaps through disappointment, believed so, agreeing finally with Cousin Han-

nah's objections to the wedding which had come so near the funeral—
though it was not my mother, it was my unknown father who had died.
Perhaps the funeral came before the wedding. Cousin Hannah had reminded my mother once again that she had no husband, none but the
dead, no better half, no mate, no lover, no man, that she was spouseless as
the day she was born. She was bereft, robbed of her finest gifts and
powers. There were only these old, howling ghosts which were not even
the ghosts of the past. They were the ghosts of the future. My mother's
beauty was already fading. Time had already marked her. It had left its
little claw foot. Cousin Hannah had merely been more realistic than my
mother could afford to be, less capable, it had seemed, of self-deception
when she looked into her mirror—for had she ever fooled herself or led
herself astray? Where were all these contemporary admirers my mother
imagined—these elegantly powdered fops, these perfumed beaus, these
tragic clowns, these lounge lizards? There were none, Cousin Hannah
had triumphantly said, but in my mother's mournful imagination, that
which seemed so difficult to overwhelm. Yet who had died for love of her?
Men die of many reasons before they die of love, this cynical suffrage
captain had observed. What rivals were there now? What fencers sparring
with each other or with shadows, with mirror images? Cousin Hannah
had urged my mother, now before it was too late, to face the void reality
of her situation, to know that there was no one—that only woman was
capable of greatest love—that no matter which way she turned, which
road she took, she would never find the love of her desire—there being no
man who loved her, she had said, both before and after the various
debacles of my mother's life which had started with these ruins. Then
why imagine one, his eyes glittering in the wind?

No man had ever been so courageous or foolhardy or persistent as
my mother supposed. My mother, as a realist, would have done better
never to have given herself over to mortal man, according to those fierce
arguments which, though seeming to deny human nature, ranged over a
wild terrain like the regions of human mortality, no level plain but a
land of many levels and abysses, chasms and maelstroms and whirlwinds,
storm centers and seas of dead calm, many clouded promontories and
shoreless seas, thunderheads and wild steppes and sudden declivities,
terrible crags in unbelievable isolation girt around by blackest storms
and whirlpools, dead volcanoes and seas of fire, seas of ice, seas of glass,
valleys where the sunlight never shone, stairways cut out by erosion,
beetling cliffs, natural campaniles and leaning towers and bald domes,
pinnacles where no birds came, giant precipices and inaccessible shores
and seas of which no soundings had ever been made, of which none knew
the depth, submerged continents, rivers under the ground, footless places,
places where no one had ever heard a voice crying in the wind, where no
echoes were awakened, where were no echoes of echoes, where would
never be heard the sound of muffled drums, the sound of water falling,
falling from clouds, never a charivari for a lonely bride, never the peal
of church bells, never the drone of honey bees in buildings which were
great hives of stone, never the rattle of stars like autumn leaves, never

this sepulchral laughter, hollow and gruff, never the cracked bell, never the hullabaloo of the huntsmen, the screamings of the horses, the hoot of the great snow owl, the ululation of the dog, land where never would be heard the roar of the surf, the sound of a winding horn, the whistle of a night train, land of no insect cry, no wood-note. It was only this great captain who, though denying human nature, knew the unknown soundings of undiscovered seas—only she who knew this unknown land, she who seemed to have been this traveller through this land of desolation, land where no bird sang, where were no footsteps echoing through dim corridors, where should be no man, no woman, no answering voice.

Yet Cousin Hannah, no mere evanescence flitting fast away, had reiterated her proposals many times, inviting my mother to go away with her, to escape this life. It had seemed that nothing could discourage her in an ultimate sense—that even through continuous failure, she must continuously triumph with greater and greater fury, with tensions unrelieved. Cousin Hannah had been, indeed, like some old warrior who, frightened by the silence, by no answering response from a besieged city, must strengthen his assaults with additional cavalry troops, armored ships, lost flotillas resurrected from the deep, greater cannonades, balls of burning gold, flashings of fire, enraged strategies, just for the reason that there is no defense, no answering cannon ball. Perhaps silence would have taken the silent city. Perhaps all the doors and gates had been already opened to her, and there was not a man upon the ramparts, no watchman in his tower. This, she apparently had not known, her frenzies always pitifully increasing, just when there was no reason for struggle. Besides, my mother had endowed her with life, my mother had believed —allowing to her a completely separate, wild individuality, not really resisting one who rode roughshod over her dreams and would admit no defeat. For this old warrior had lived in the heart of conflict, even by the loud clash of arms, and the silence would have killed her as it had killed the sparrow. She had not been invited, but she had come in spite of my mother's desire—how often, making this old house echo with the sound of mighty hooves, echoes which had cracked the mirrors. For she had been this dauntless spirit, one who had built, it had seemed, unlike my mother, no castles in the air, one who had not lived by soporific dreams alone, one who had lived where there was a loud stampede of horses, the shrill whistle of meteors, or the whistle of the wind. She had seemed so strong—one who could always, by the merest gesture, have unhorsed the rider, unmanned the man, causing him to take alarum as she approached, causing him to disappear like a wraith in the storm. Many a poor foot soldier must have fled before her coming. Doubtless many a skull had cracked.

Cousin Hannah, however, had presented a bold front, even when there was no one. She had shown a courage which had seemed almost beyond necessity—for what man had there been to challenge her or ask her for her calling card, her credentials? The sentinels had slept at their posts. The footmen had looked the other way. Truly, there had been no defense, no unimpregnable fortress in this life—the furies had all been hers, and she had cried the loudest, perhaps because she knew the silence of the unanswering heart. My mother, perhaps the only one who saw her in many of her visits, had wished that she could meet a man of such puissance, such ascendancy and sway and almightiness as had galvanized this old cousin, making her seem almost metallic, making all mortal men seem, by comparison with her, creatures of pallid inanition, of little courage, mere old women ready to end in smoke and ashes. For they were null and void, and their fortifications so easily crumbled, and they were as ineffectual as the poorest gallows birds with their chains gibbering in the dark wind.

So Cousin Hannah had been curiously right, even when wrong—though my mother had not wished, naturally, to show her secret agreement with her—and was never more preoccupied, more dreamy, more flirtatious than when Cousin Hannah came, passing those barriers which were like air. My mother, determined not to be overwhelmed, had given herself over to the most romantic dreams, as she remembered now, to the most priceless nostalgias when, in the fading of the light, she was gradually aware of her visitor, the face which showed its haughty suffering, the burning eyes. My mother would say that she was not at home, that she had gone to Pisa to see the Leaning Tower, and she had been away for several years. She was living among the Bedouins. She was riding on a white camel across a desert of snow. Yet what man, as Cousin Hannah had stormily asked, was worth a woman's secret life? What man was worth a woman's imagination or memory or hope? Who was worth the candle's end, the dying flame, the darkened mirror, the funeral wreath upon the bedroom door? What man was worth this long debate, this raging war or state of protracted seige seeming so much like peace or sleep? What man should break a woman's heart unless it was already broken long, long ago by a force stronger than woman or than man, a centrifugal force which could not be resisted, even like that force which breaks the stars and sets the dead moon to wandering?

My mother could not have answered these baffling questions—even though, as she sometimes realized now, she might have asked them herself and perhaps only long after Cousin Hannah's death, that death which had not been by fire or sword. But then, as my mother had supposed, that great Crusader was not a man's woman, for she was never encumbered, my mother had believed, by trailing satin skirts and ropes of pearls and veils like snowflakes whirling in the air—and never was she a bride—and God forbid that she should have become that which she had despised with all her heart and all her muscular control, a man, be he even the slave of love. God forbid that she should be a man, this most marvelous creature, almost imperceptible and yet bright-eyed, a tall, thin, dark, handsome gentleman with black plumes on his black velvet hat, with aquiline, hooked nose in air, with pointed chin and perhaps a silver Renaissance beard powdered by the falling snow and perhaps a silver sword, such a man as my mother had used to imagine when Cousin Hannah strode across this mortal stage, my mother's bedroom, here where were the darkened mirrors, the dying candle flames, the vases of fresh flowers. Many passions had played on her dark, shadow-spotted, imperious face, yet though it had seemed passionless as something already remembered and forgotten and denied. Perhaps her great battle had been with herself, my mother had believed. For though Cousin Hannah had believed herself to be absolutely right, she had been nearly always wrong, at variance with life, and had always acted as if she were about to meet, even in this secluded place, her enemy, a timorous man, though perhaps he should be that man whom no one else should see. Or only my mother should see him, all others sleeping.

Cousin Hannah had been so piercing, witty, incisive, quick to express herself—my mother, in spite of her inclinations, and though she had taken enough drugs to put an entire army to sleep, could not help being greatly fascinated by this remarkable visitor, so different from the others who came and went and left their calling cards, for they were the dead. Though my mother's mind had necessarily wandered, then as now when she thought of this old cousin who now perhaps was wandering among the shades, yet my mother's attentions had been riveted by this unusual force, as if this one caller should prey upon the mind when all others were forgotten. Cousin Hannah had tried to infuriate her, to cause an outbreak, to cause a breach in my mother's fragile defenses, perhaps an eternal breach, a wound which would not heal. She had had no respect for the tranquil mind, the mournful heart, the dream of death. She had never attempted to master her riotous feelings, to subdue her unruly spirit, to curb or restrain wild horses of her desire, running away with the bit between their teeth. She had never submitted to another's will. She would have died rather than have done so. No one believed that she had ever slept.

She had always been, as my mother lovingly remembered her, trying to reconstruct a faded personality, a great wit, flashing back, making merry with a macabre retort, an apt paradox, a parable in unknown tongues which had left my mother nearly stunned as if by another spurious deception, and she had scintillated, emitting sparks like the undying dream. She had seemed to wear great silver scales. She had seemed to shine in her own light. She had been quick to move. She had not been heavy-footed, slow to move, calculating every movement in advance of her making it, living through the future as if it were already the uncertain past, nor was she elephantine like Mr. Spitzer, the elephant with the angelic wings, the failing memory. She had dazzled. There had been no lack of presence of mind, of acute perception diamond-sharp as to each fleeting moment, each phantasmagoric event which did not transpire in reality. Her denial of the dream was not her ignorance of the dream—for had she not over-heard the whispers of sleepers in tent cities shifting with the wind? There had been no lack of audacious elegance, for she had not been graceless, and she had not seemed out of all proportion, voluminous enough to contain two people, herself and another, a secret man, even should he be only a puppet, a mere pygmy upon a boundless horizon, or a butterfly sailing at midnight, a blind moth sailing down the light.

Nothing had agitated her so much as the sound of a cock crowing.

At the sound of a cock crowing, she had strutted, dancing a weird dance, giving off showers of metallic sparks, stretching her long neck as her cheeks twitched—doubtless because in certain Moroccan courtyards which she had visited, she had seen that the cock is great golden sultan, lord of the morning, lord of all he surveys, that even the hens wear black veils like the secret women in purdah, including those great beauties who never will be seen by their lords and masters. So as had been her message before, she had wished to take off these veils. God pity the lip-reader in all those countries where, Cousin Hannah had said, the women wear veils—and God pity the deaf and the mute in all those countries where the human face is not seen.

She had always worn around her belt numerous iron keys which had jangled, giving off dissonant music. By her splendid elan vital, forever spending itself, yet never spent, continually renewing—for should she not quicken the earth by her death, and should not the clouds give up their rain when she was dead?—by her amazing eclat and thunderous career, by her explosive notoriety which had always raised a hue and cry and brought her before the public gaze, she had shaken many people loose from their moorings, and she had struck fear into the hearts not only of many courageous men, perhaps also the hearts of many timid women, few being, it would seem, capable of rivalry with such a venturesome chasseur, mountain-climber, and chamois-hunter leaping from peak to peak. As to her own career, it was said that she was jealous of Mt. Blanc. She was jealous of the slumbering Jungfrau, the snow-topped peaks in clouds, jealous of the Eigar, the Moentsch, the Matterhorn, Monte Rosa, waiting for great snows to melt, hissing like foam, waiting for snow-peaked mountains to reach sea level. Nothing so adamantine as the Alp of wedlock, however, and nothing so undissolving as those great peaks of snow and stone, the great thunderheads forever in the clouds which were storm centers attracting lightning flashes and thunderbolts. Should mountains crumble at a breath, great avalanches fall upon the mountain-climber and his Alpine dog? Should snowflakes fall upon the face of the dead mountain-climber like a veil or a shroud?

My mother, having no object for her love, had viewed her as the object of her lost romance, wondering why no man had been this woman, why no woman had been this man, why poor old Cousin Hannah, an unmarried spinster, her energies as yet unspent, was always like a travel-ler between two worlds, why she would seem as strange, even while she lived, as Mr. Chandelier or a seven-branched crystal candelabra glittering in a far heaven, moving from star to star which lighted in the reflection of that passing flame, as strange as the golden cock crowing in the twi-light of my mother's opium dreams. That cock which, its feathers ruffling in the ebbing light, an Irish housemaid swore had also awakened her—and she had thought it was morning, and she had polished a mirror all night long, and she had never been convinced that the night was not the day. And finally, she had gone stark, staring mad. For my mother's dreams had become confused with this real apparition, and so my mother had often felt, when Cousin Hannah was still alive, that she should apologize to her profusely for the continuous mistake which she had made, confusing her with another, one she might never be. Cousin Hannah, though she had not taken drugs, though she had walked from room to room, had seemed just like someone who might have succumbed to this habit in order to exaggerate self-confidence or to compensate for early death or early sorrow. Yet there had been no death, my mother had believed, and there had been no sorrow. She believed that they were not the same. Death negated sorrow. Perhaps by the same token, sorrow negated death. Cousin Hannah had exceeded these human dimensions by many dazzling cubits, just as if her head had reached above the stars— man seeming a dwarf by comparison with her.

For what was man, a mere apparition in this empty house? Who knew? What was man, this poor amalgam crumbling at a touch? He seemed inanimate, and suddenly he moved, just as if a dead hand should suddenly move. What was man, this constant obliteration, this which was always in the process of ceasing to exist, of becoming no more, perishing, passing away like the wreath of the wandering foam, like the song of the dead bird? What was he but, at most, a nine days' wonder, short-lived and ephemeral and deciduous, a creature of changeableness, a creature of transience, a falling star, a meteor gone before we knew that it had passed? He was the broken sea shell. He was the dead cocoon. Who had organized this illusion? Who had placed order upon this old chaos which, as it seemed to decrease, was forever increasing, just like one of my mother's opium dreams? My mother could see the mirrors dancing, flying toward the ceiling. And that was why she had always yearned for clarification—a teacher of arithmetic who would teach her to add, subtract, multiply, divide, find an integer—and then, when she knew arithmetic, she would learn plane and solid geometry, my mother said—for if she knew geometry, she would know who the geometer was, whether that which began with a rational abstraction should end with an irrational dream. She would know whether he was sane or insane, this great illusionist who, with his golden-footed compass moving across a clouded sky, had designed these great concentric circles and eccentric circles and half moons and elliptical paths, these wandering orbs and diamond horseshoes, these relations and properties and measurements, enlargements, doublings, mirror images, figures in space, the spiders' webs singing like the candle flames. Nothing lived except through imagination, and nothing died except through imagination. My mother yearned that there should be one real person in the world.

But Cousin Hannah, unlike these hallucinations, had been no mere speck, dot, or mote evolving into life, no mere fragment or scintilla or powder or dust, no one toward whom one might remain indifferent as if she were only a button or a feather or an old song, a dead hand, an immaterial being of the air, a mere nothing, a piece of trash, an imperceptible gleaming of an eye in the darkness, perhaps my mother's eye which stared at my mother all night long. Cousin Hannah had surely been vivacious, even in the dimmest moments—a threat to weakness. My mother never would have believed it possible, even though centuries should pass, that Cousin Hannah's strength would fail, that she would give way, fall to pieces, crumble into dust, become an invalid in a darkened room. For fate should have had a better fate in store for her. Besides, she seemed to have passed beyond these considerations, to have circumvented them even during her life. Perhaps, of course, wishing to differentiate between herself and the fortunate many, my mother had attributed to her a quality of endurance which she, a horizontal invalid, did not possess—nothing enduring. She had wished to envy this perpendicular woman, proud and free, seeming to dilate the heavens by her grandeur. My mother could hear the stars rustling, falling like the autumn leaves—the cold winds blowing through empty corridors and lanes. There was always the slamming of a door—though whether someone was going or coming, she could not say. There were scurrying footsteps, perhaps of little mice in the wainscoting.

My mother had felt both very flirtatious and very guilty, trying to resist this man who was no man, for this man was surely not Cousin Hannah, and it was my mother's mind which wandered, just as when she talked now for hours to the white cranes crying in a saw-toothed cloud. For her imagination, as she knew only too well, had always played upon her such terrible tricks—those which should have driven another lady to distraction—surrounding her with as many imaginary lovers as if, though she was isolated, she was the center of attraction, the magnetic force. Was she not the magician, and should she fool herself by these evident deceptions—like a Houdini fooled by his own tricks?

Nothing, of course, had enraged old Cousin Hannah more than such untenable forms of rivalry, and they had caused her titubation, her staggering gait even when she was quite alive, still able to take care of herself. Nothing had enraged her more than, when there were no other rivals, her embittered knowledge of these dream loves which should have no counterpart in reality, no answering face. She had continued to try, as long as she had lived and was still able to travel back and forth, to overthrow these loves which were no loves and seemed, therefore, invulnerable—to overthrow these imaginary men, to rout them from the castle as if they were all thieves. She had never ceased to urge my mother to follow in her path, to take flight away from these vain, narcotic dreams immobilizing her. Her contempt for old Joachim had remained necessarily boundless, like her indifference. Through the passing years, she still had not recognized him. Or so my mother had certainly believed, though with some bewilderment. She had distrusted all men, categorically. All were opposed to her, this marvelous old maid who was prepared for a great conflict.

Cousin Hannah's needs had transcended merely mortal needs, my mother had believed—that this brave warrior had outdistanced ordinary life, that hers was a shining pinnacle beyond this horizontal plain. She had cared for no man in this world, for no man in the next, and not even for the idea of a man, it had appeared, nor had she ever ceased to express her various aversions upon the subject of man, puny man when, in that halcyon time of long ago, she had used to come to see my mother for a few fleeting moments which seemed, in inaccurate memory, like a few fleeting years, the extension of a dream. She had stood by an oblong mirror in my mother's bedroom.

Perhaps she had placed her faith quite mistakenly, my mother thought, in woman—for even this faith might seem now to have passed, long ago, into a realm of doubt, Cousin Hannah being dead, having now no identity, no face. She might be now a cloud, a bird, a tree in the wind. She had distrusted my mother because my mother was a woman, so very whimsical, quick to change her mind, guided only by her wandering emotions, losing her way through snow clouds, wandering lost like a snow goose in a snow storm, leaving no path upon the snow or the clouds, no trail of bridal lace upon the snow, going in all ways but the way which she intended, unable to focus her attention upon one object, unable to differentiate between the subjective and the objective worlds, the inner light and the outer darkness. She had distrusted my mother because my mother, even through her lack of faith, had placed her faith in Mr. Spitzer, at least in the dead, sorrowful half of him which, like the other side of the moon, was never turned toward this world. Cousin Hannah had never given up, though the years had passed, her belief that Joachim would cruelly disappoint my mother at the last, crucial moment, abandoning her to the furies and to the gods of revenge, even as Peron had done at the first when he had apparently committed suicide, taking a coward's way out—leaving Joachim to accept that vicarious responsibility which had always been the slow brother's sense of peculiar guilt and of inestimable loss.

CHAPTER 35

❧

WHAT a fine time they would have playing cards—poker or some such dangerous game—my mother and dear old Cousin Hannah, that lively partner who, as if she had stood behind my mother's shoulder, had foreseen my mother's every move and had out-witted every mistaken strategy. She had played a mean game of cards, my mother liked to remember and would triumphantly remind vacant-faced Mr. Spitzer, who could not tell a heart from a spade, of course, or a diamond from a club—unlike his brother, who had always had an ace in the hole—for what did Mr. Spitzer, this plaintive Joachim, know of cards or of the audacity of one who had played a devil-may-care, death-defying game, even when seeming to lose? He had been so cautious, scornful of any means by which he might have won a game even if he had been playing —and he had been too proud to compete, to risk winning or losing. As he would have expressed it, he had not entered the lists. Perhaps, however, it was his pride which gave him his knowledge of that which he did not know.

For Mr. Spitzer, of course, in his abysmal ignorance of cards, as he would sometimes tentatively remark, as if searching through vast chan-nels of memory, had always believed that Cousin Hannah was a card cheat—that she was not, as my mother seemed to think, a gentleman of honor—a trustworthy opponent who would recognize the rules—and in-deed, he had heard, he said, wild rumors to that effect many times. Though he had not mentioned such rumors in the earlier years, for they had reached him only recently, by devious paths, his being the dead hound's ear. He had always believed that she had cheated and that death would not increase her honesty. Death, he had no doubt, was itself a great deceiver. Life was filled with many illusions and deceits, and death was filled with greater illusions, greater deceits. No man was incorrupti-ble. He looked for no improvement on the other side.

My mother thought he was merely embittered by his brother's astro-nomical gambling losses which, though they were not Mr. Spitzer's, had also impoverished him, keeping him in a state of colossal bankruptcy for years—that he, therefore, nurtured this sense of private grief—or that he was embittered by his own sense of failure in music, just as he was jealous of anyone who was brighter than he was or swifter in the race. Though he was this great, disappointed lover, bearing his grudges as if they were those which would not die when he was in his grave, yet his admiration had never been completely and unqualifiedly given to any human being, living or dead, not even to himself, my mother believed, and she could agree with him at this point, for she was always of these cruelly divided opinions as to him, being reminded by his face that he was not his identical brother. If he had had a different face, she might have forgiven him for his continued existence upon this planet. He might have seemed less reproachful—and not this living reminder of himself. Naturally, he must have been quite jealous of old Cousin Hannah who was no more, and my mother very much doubted that his jealousy had died, that it had been removed by the fact that his opponent had been removed. His jealousy had increased. His jealousy had been fed by every new disappointment.

So if Cousin Hannah should deign now to come, descending from her high place above the stars, my mother said, Mr. Spitzer would surely have to go and spend his lonely evenings elsewhere, doubtless in a colder, starless climate, for there would not be room for both Cousin Hannah and him who occupied so great, so unconscionable a space, this corporeal, fat, soft-jowled, many-valved, sleepy-eyed gentleman who so often sighed and shook, shook and sighed, seeming to have no will power and not even, at all times, his own point of view, greatly though he insisted upon his own point of view, his unbiased integrity—for my mother would not want him to be here to remind old Cousin Hannah that he, perhaps just because of such indefiniteness, had survived her, that his forgetfulness had overcome him—he being, even in this life, amorphous—unlike Cousin Hannah with her dashing spirit, her cavalier airs, her irresistible strength which had caused many a man, even a British prime minister to quail, great Turks and Persians to tremble on their thrones. What a character this old cousin seemed, even now! She had cut quite a figure for herself, really, in this world—and she was still, my mother insisted, unforgettable even when she was forgotten. And why should she not visit here for a long winter season—here, where were so many vacant rooms, so many empty beds, the beds of great kings who had migrated to other beds, even like birds of passage, so many liveried servants to wait on her, so many gilded footmen to fetch and carry, so many grooms, so many gilded mirrors where she might see her face? She should sleep in a great, four-postered bed behind a closed canopy. And why should she not dream, imagining another life? There was certainly always room in this wide house for another weary traveller from the world of the dead—room for one who had crossed dark waters—room for Cousin Hannah, who should come with dancing nymphs, with troops of singing stars. And this cloud citadel should be hers. A light burned at the window against which the blind moth fluttered with jewels upon its wings.

So Mr. Spitzer should not set his foot here again. There was really no place for Mr. Spitzer. Peron would never have lingered here—and old Joachim, this evening guest, must quickly go—so that Cousin Hannah, now when she was dead, cold and petrified and rigid, now when she should have passed beyond the powers of insult, should not be confronted once again by this persistent obstacle, this vacant face which had always seemed to her unreal. From every sphere, Mr. Spitzer should be missing. He should be missing from time. He should be missing from timelessness. She had certainly not had the patience for an elegiac problem of greater or lesser magnitude—the mournful, wild howling—the idiotic stare of foolish grief. She had certainly struck terror into the hearts of those who were more courageous than Mr. Spitzer, he who was the timid of heart, the supine, the stupid, the slow, the myopic, he who had continued with his immemorial problems long after it was possible to do so, his evasions, his way of suddenly, it might be said, removing himself from the mortal scene or the immortal scene, of not being present just at that moment when he was needed most, when one word from him might have clarified the mystery, the surrounding cosmic darkness lighted by only that one star which, burning within, could never see the light. My mother was still so unreasonably proud of her.

How often my mother had been confronted by silence roaring like the ebony waves of the sea when she spoke to Mr. Spitzer, he who did not reply, for his mind was on some other star or starfish gleaming or broken starboard lantern to which there still clung minuscular lights at the edge of the billowing surf or jellyfish tide lighted by a streaming star. But Cousin Hannah had always answered her, sometimes achieving communication in spite of unbelievable distances—many miles between these two rival ladies—many streets, many houses, cupolas and spires and bridges—sometimes vast continents—great plains and endless horizons and mountain peaks shrouded by eternal snows—many moats, many castles—and no Western Union messengers—and no telephone, no humming telephone wires, no means of modern communication. For she, unlike my mother who was always in her swan boat, had not led an isolated, self-centered life, talking to grotesque shadows on a wall, sometimes the shadow of Mr. Spitzer's cape, the great Inverness slipping from his broad shoulders like the outline of an unknown land, a gentle declivity sloping from a cloud, the shadow of his high silk chimney hat nodding as he slept, a sudden glitter where there might be the reflection of a jewel or of his eye suddenly opening or of a flashing star, talking to dead men, poor creatures incomplete and helpless and unknown such as those he sheltered by his compassion, all the realizations having already taken place in such a way as to show that the realization had contained in itself the theory of all that was lacking, all those things which might never be in heaven or on earth. She would have ridden, if necessary to achieve her goal, against a heavenly host, the artillery of paradise, and many lost platoons—and nothing, no consideration of self-protection could have stopped her once she had made up her fearless mind. She would have ridden naked through the gale. She would have ridden through the storm of years. Never had she asked for shelter, never for the complete understanding of any other person, never for the halo of self-pity nor of impersonal pity like the lunar halo upon the cloud where was no moon, never for a many-winding sea shell to close around her the mother-of-pearl walls of protection against the outer world. She had taken refuge, it had seemed, in no feminine wiles, in no drugged moments outside of time such as the opium lady might indulge in, dreaming of the imaginary man, the great lover who would never depart though little men should falter and fail, for that dark captain of the light-footed brigade had lived by her all-consuming faith that there should be, if she should triumph, no man on earth, perhaps not even herself with her cap gleaming like that of the Crusader whose cap was covered with shells of mother-of-pearl to signify that he had made his great journey and had returned from Orient paradise. Perhaps there should be no man in heaven. My mother often wondered if she had ever succeeded in overwhelming every enemy—my mother seeing, so seldom in her life upon this alien star, a man, flesh and blood and bones, a man who did not crumble into clouds and waters, fire and neighing horses.

Indeed, whatever might be in doubt, Cousin Hannah's entire life and perhaps her death had been devoted to the suffrage movement upon all fronts known and unknown, domestic and foreign and undiscovered, the triumph of woman over man, even of beauty over strength, and thus she had been a public figure of considerable magnitude, one who had ridden horseback through many distant capitals already evacuated and was like a great stone horseman with a stone helmet. She had not met the problems of life with passivity. She had been the great pioneer in this original movement away from conventional boundaries, a person who had gone restlessly to far frontiers receding with her and who had watched all night by flickering desert camp fires and who had known the extremes of burning heat and Arctic cold. She had not been merely another old maid dreaming with her ivory-boned knitting needles, her balls of grey yarn, her purling of grey stitches by the unravelling surf, her empty looks, her continual looks at an alarm clock or a darkening sky as if the stars might be another alarm clock suddenly ringing. Such empty servitude was not for one who had combated demoniac hordes or empire-makers, one who had heard the white wolves howling in deserts of stone and snow, one who had seen the burning bush, the dried-out arroyos, one who had pitched her tents in strange lands from which no living man returns, not even should he be the most valiant, one whose life was geared to a celestial meaning beyond and above the petty affairs of time. For she had been this unconquerable, tumultuous suffrage captain, armored by her pride, carrying her emblazoned suffrage message to the far corners of the earth, even to the unpopulated countries, to countries where there was no man, where there was perhaps not even a male reindeer startled by her coming, running along the lower sky as the starlight shook above his head, his great antlers clashing like tree branches in the streaming wind, where there was perhaps not even an old bull walrus who should suddenly submerge at the approach of this old hunter with the glittering eye, the shining spear, the sword of ice. And man should be as secretive as woman.

She had wished to overthrow man, both as to the marital state of which ideally, as she had never been married or given to her true love, she knew nothing in actuality, and as to paternal domination, the regnancy of the past and of the future, and even though one's father should be dead, though he should be only some old ghost with hollow eyes and burning hair, a formless face, a dream retreating at cockcrow, a dream receding into nocturnal depths at the light of the wavering dawn, though he should be less than a breath, a flame in a doorway, a burned feather in the wind, a shadow on a wall, though he should be less than Cousin Hannah now was become. And yet she had been real, no mere chimera like the others, those who oscillated between two fixed points or states of mind, never escaping these limitations. For she had been flesh and blood and bone, one whom my mother had thought she had known as well as she knew herself who was not easily mystified. Cousin Hannah's life had been well known, not shrouded in mystery as was my mother's life when she remembered herself, these ladies like phantoms of the undying past, these many, beautiful, waxen ladies parading in a room of mirrors and phantoms, each but the partial portrait of the other so that each was incomplete. Cousin Hannah had been a continual center of public interest. She had lived in such a way that her life had seemingly included no such multiple mirror images and imaginary loves, yet though she had known the secrets of the living and of the dead, the secrets which husbands whispered to their dead wives, the secrets which wives whispered to their dead husbands. Domestic couples had whispered their secrets to her—usually the reasons for their separations. She had known why so many great Antarctic explorers had left home, why they had so often named after their undiscovered wives their discoveries of new continents, great glacial mountains of snow and ice and lakes of ice and mirroring chasms under the snow-packed sky indistinguishable from the firmament of earth—it was colder at home. It was colder where the sleeping lady slept with the snow falling on a lacy counterpane. Cousin Hannah had told my mother that there was nothing so cold as the heart of a woman who had never been awakened, never would awaken through centuries of snow and storms moving mountains. Who would have imagined when Cousin Hannah was at the pinnacle of her glory, looming above my mother as snow-peaked mountains loom above clouds and shadowed valleys, that she would come to the same end to which others came, that she was merely mortal and would not escape that fate which few or none escaped? Perhaps that old captain was already dying when my mother knew her. Most people go to bed for love, but such an active lady would never have gone to bed for love. She would have gone to bed only to die. My mother asked again and again where there was no one to hear her, for she was alone except for the talking swan boat—and Cousin Hannah came no more—who would have foreseen that she would die in bed, clutching in her withered hand like a claw a faded rose, that which she must have plucked from the dark air, for who had brought a rose to one who was already forgotten? My mother would forget that it was she who might have been the dream visitor bearing the rose in her hand.

For Cousin Hannah, this proud cousin on the male side, not on the distaff side, this impatient and mettlesome spirit, this old New England suffragette with the glittering eye, the pointed silver beard, the lifted sword, the jeweled saddle and spurs, the courage which gave no quarter to the coward and no understanding to the fragile of body or spirit and no compassion to the weak, had ridden against the omnipotent foe wherever he had presented himself, and she had been one whom no perilous adventure or long journey would have affrighted, one who would have ridden to the sable shores of Hades or even farther had that been her desire, perhaps even had there been no desire. Surely, if she was not frightened by a long journey, she would not be frightened by a short journey. Like a shooting star which probably knows not its destination when it starts and probably knows not the course of its singing journey and probably knows not where it will end, she would have overshot her mark. For she had been spontaneous ever and quick to go, not easily contained by a deathless dream or a dying dream. And why should my mother who was confined always to her bed not admire her—one so fiercely free, so untrammeled in this life, and never hedged about by the boundaries of either love or death, one who still might be riding in a desert place with her Mahound?

What cared that great captain for the memorial art which Mr. Spitzer practiced, his quavering harp strings reaching through clouds to catch the wind music where there was no wind? She had refused, while she was still alive, a stained glass window in memory of her—something which might be, my mother thought, the emperor and the unicorn or perhaps the lady and the blackamoor. She had believed in no image, neither the living nor the dead.

Only my mother and Mr. Spitzer perhaps now in all the living world remembered her, famous and grand and dead—but she was often mentioned by them, for so vivacious was my mother's continuing memory of her that, though the years should pass, sometimes leaving no trace, less than the wing motions of great gold-eyed white ptarmigans on snow clouds, Cousin Hannah should remain in mind, even like Queen Maud Mountains with her trailing cape of snow reaching five hundred miles, her glassy peaks, those over which no sea bird ever passed. Perhaps, indeed, the great lady, her eyes burning in the cold starlight, was more vivid in death than she had been in life—she having achieved emancipation, having escaped this wide-meshed net of years as a fish escapes from the fisherman's net or as the fisherman escapes from the boat.

Sometimes my mother spoke of her with such familiarity—one might suppose that she had seen her only yesterday, this persistent figure with the beetling eyebrows, the eyebrows like feathers upon which the snow had fallen—though of course, this was not possible, my mother knew, even when she was entertaining the lively dead. Yet how cordial she would be now if Cousin Hannah should accept her formal invitation, her announcement that she would be at home, receiving at three minutes after three until five minutes after three when she was expecting Madame DuBarry with her Persian hound. As cordial as my mother had not been before when she, having no other way of escape, had been perhaps perverse, unnecessarily evasive and diffident, unduly timid when confronted by this spectacular, self-confident friend who had crashed the gates and whom she had resisted as if she were a plague of fiery locusts, those who have no king. Mr. Spitzer had always fled before that great captain's coming as if she were the spectre of his doom, his own annihilation—so he must flee now before she came. Personally, he had always thought the fearful captain of the horse quite gloomy with her project to organize all ladies to rebel—for had they not already done so, creating this unbelievable havoc in men's lives, causing such great disorders that he never stepped on terra firma without assuming that it was terra incognita, that he never stepped before, tapping with his cane, he tested it to ascertain that it was no cloud?

Perhaps my mother would even understand Cousin Hannah's suffrage message now as she had not wished to understand it completely then, she having resisted her message as if she had been a messenger coming from the enemy camp, a messenger coming from afar, coming with evil tidings, as one who told her that she had lost the battle or that her love was dead, killed on a foreign battlefront, killed while guarding the ramparts, killed at some far frontier between life and death. Now she would greet her with no alloy of reserve or doubt—asking her to take off her great plumed hat, as she would never have done in the presence of a lady, for she did not believe in showing inequalities—to be seated, as she would never have done, for she had not had the time, and she had always remained standing as if ready to depart, perhaps at a bugle's ghostly cry, perhaps at a rooster's crow as the evening sky turned from grey to rose— asking her to remain here for a long winter or for many endless snow- bound winters when no postman could find the house under the snow banks or even its glittering towers—though when she was precariously alive and perhaps in full possession of her senses, she had had no faith, to be sure, in any after-life upon this planet or form of creation which should follow after this, none in the harpist plucking his own withered harp strings, being his own musical instrument under the flying stars, none in the rustle of faded silks upon a dusty floor, none in the echo of an echo, the whisper of astral bells through still, vacant rooms. Perhaps she had had no faith in this life, it was surely well to be reminded again, though her life had been crowded with dangers which had kept her actively alive, those of the vast suffrage movement raging on all fronts and some which were unknown as mirrors looking out on nothing or vistas seen from the other side of the dead moon.

She had had no time for courtly graces, the dance of the hours like garlanded barefoot nymphs in flowing draperies. She could never have taken her place in the pattern of a minuet, slow and graceful, a dance consisting of a shift from one foot to the other, a high step, an act of balancing between the right foot and the left when the weight was shifted from right to left and the left part of the body was drawn into the right. Nor could she have danced with another partner—never had she appeared in a ballroom, not even if it were crystal—she had escorted, it had seemed, no lady to the dance. She was not like Mr. Spitzer who, though always a portly gentleman, had been, in his youth, an excellent

dancer, taking every step with mincing precision, with calculated airs
which had aroused his twin's bewilderment. She was not like my mother
who had been, before she had gone to bed, the most marvelous dancer,
even her walk having been a slow, elaborate dance under the glassy
lights—confusing to persons with whom she had tried to carry on a polite
conversation. They had felt that she was easily distracted. She had always
seemed to give her attention to those who were not there. For she had
walked in circles and semicircles, describing various elegant patterns in
her most casual movements, measuring the distance from a blue brocade
divan to a gilt and ivory chair as if this distance were a complicated
problem in infinity or in eternity, as if, when she walked from room to
room, she walked between two stars which were not coexistent in space.
She could not move from room to room without her intricate choreogra-
phy and her musical attendant, a blind harpist harping in the fog—could
not walk down a long corridor without as many preparations as if she
were going on a long journey, though doubtless she was going only to a
distant drawing room. And she had frequently asked for her candle-
bearers and for her carriage, her bearskin hat, her robe of leopard skin,
her charcoal foot-warmer, her falconer's gloves embroidered with mystical messages from the living to the dead, or an amulet which should be
found at a far outpost. Or she had asked that the ice-breakers should go
ahead of her and clear a way, break the mirrors, break the ice. Whereas,
the suffrage veteran, casehardened and seared by many weathers, the
burning light of a star and desert cold and forever whirling snowflakes
and hurricanes, had been as courageous as Sherman marching to the sea
or as Napoleon at the gates of Moscow—obsessed by her desires to which
my mother was indifferent.

Cousin Hannah, unlike my mother who carried on long conversations with triple-crowned, heron-footed King Canute, he who, with all his
royal powers, could not command the waves to stand still, the tides to
cease, had had no time for small talk, the adventure of polite conversation, no time for talk of wind and weather and yesterday's cloud formations, the meditation upon the eye of the whirlwind, no time to indulge
herself with talk of old wounds which had closed or had never closed, old
love affairs which had ended or had never ended, no time for a cup of
perfumed tea made of the distilled essences of flowers or moment of
intimate and unexpected revelation, as when one confessed that one was
the opposite of what one seemed, that all one's life had been a living lie,
a monstrous joke which had baffled one from the beginning, leaving one
no peace—that one had always turned against one's self at every point,
that one had gone against one's grain and loved what one had denied.
That one had loved in secret what one had denied in public. For she
could not have been trapped—could not have been taken unaware,
thrown off her guard—could not have been persuaded, by any means
when she had still the power of making rational decisions, to confess that,
though she had been this old suffrage captain and rider through the
storm of years, one carrying a great suffrage banner with rippling golden

tassels, she had yearned for marriage, or she had loved a man. Or she had yearned for a homunculus, a little man, a mannikin, a dwarf whose head should not reach above the tops of meadow flowers, a gentleman's gentleman to wait on her. It would have seemed, at that date, quite impossible in the nature of things. She had had no time for domestic bliss. For the suffrage movement had been her true love, her awesome husband, the masculine dream of her life, the abundant resource of her strength. She had been married to no other husband, it was quite sure. She had been married, it had seemed, to the suffrage movement, even as if she were a bride, as if the suffrage movement were her husband, her lord and master who had carried her away—or she had been this great lord, scythe sword in hand, her head reaching among the stars, this mighty captain who had rescued so many fair ladies in distress, breaking their invisible chains. Hers had been this other way of life, my mother had certainly believed, admiring her that splendid unity of character which she herself had never achieved, she being, in spite of her great efforts to achieve unusual orientation, this fragmented ego, these fragmentations of partial selves, of splintered mirrors and partial images, vague and illusive thoughts seeming to have a being of their own, to act outside of her even when she was sleeping, phantoms crowding over her bed, often with whirrings, rustlings of audible sounds—so many selves, such as the look-out in the crow's-nest, the negress in the belfry, the human barometer moaning whenever the wind shifted, the lady in the phaeton, the figurehead in the foam, plowing the waves of the disturbed sea. For hers was, indeed, this buried life which had altered her.

But Cousin Hannah's life had not been haunted by Cousin Hannah's buried life—by a contingent existence, the inexpressible, a way of life she had not chosen or had abandoned, another life she might have led—she having followed seemingly only one course, grand but not simple, the way of suffrage which had stretched before her like the infinite steeplechase stretching between two leaning steeples in eternity, one at either end, both hung with church bells—she having never divided herself, as it had seemed, into opposing factions, warring camps, the battle raging in her own breasts, the battle of the right arm against the left—and no one could have believed that she would ever go another way from that which she had already gone, riding at the front. Doubtless she had had, unlike my mother, an external enemy, one who was physical, one who was not discarnate, a creature of clouds and foam, a spectre of a butterfly—so that she did not need to wage war with herself or declare a period of forgetfulness, a coward's peace with its duplicities, the sleep of infinite compromise. Nor was it necessary that she should control her spiritual agitations only by a greater battle—in order to forget herself. She had forgotten herself long ago, perhaps in the great battle of the white eunuchs with the black eunuchs. Ah, she had known a eunuch who had become a father, she had once told my mother—that it was most surprising what even a poor eunuch might be capable of—though he was a most pitiful fellow, indeed, and had been used by a great shiek to guard, in supposedly perfect safety, his love, black veiled love. And this poor eunuch, dying for love, had been strangled and left in a desert courtyard. The hens clucked over him.

Hers had been rather—to judge by the external appearances, and perhaps there were no other appearances, none that were not external unless to a blind man—that quality of hardy temper which had enabled her to meet the complex difficulties of the opposition with unflinching firmness, with undiminishing vigor even when her strength diminished, with dauntless and increasing spirit when her body faded, with heroic fortitude when she was faced with only gentleness and evasiveness, with that noble rigor of manner which was and perhaps is always the out-growth of the resistance against quavering timidity, even one's own—as doubtless she had feared that if she gave in to the tender emotion but once, she would give in forever, be forever lost, and those great battles might as well never have occurred, for she would be vanquished, even by the blow of a wandering snowflake like a lost mirror image wandering in time—and hers was also that contempt of physical hazard which came from the fact that, forgetting herself or the claims of her heart, her human heart, for she was not superhuman, she had encountered greater dangers than most men know, certainly greater dangers than most women know in this life. Surely, she had been without likeness upon the face of this gliding earth. Where had she not gone? Where had she not entered? She had crossed so many boundary lines which had been forbidden dur-ing her life, had passed through so many gates guarded by minotaurs and dragons and speaking birds—and why should she not now cross this, now when there were no signposts, no watchmen in the towers, now when there was no obstacle under the tented sky? Had she not crossed into Mesopotamia? Had she not crossed over into Transjordania and many an emirate? Did she not know Felix Arabia as many another lady might know her drawing room? At many a frontier between two lands of infin-itely reaching desolation, she had been met by bribers with golden coins seeking to induce her to turn back—and she had not been influenced by their suggestions—and she had not been discouraged by great, frozen mountain walls, by fathomless abysses, by bottomless pools. She had never given in to threats of death or bribery—it having been her intention never to do so until the last woman on earth had been rescued from the last man on earth, even should he be only a man in a dream. And her pride would have permitted no angelic compromise with the powers of darkness and of light. Never would she have been actually in two worlds at once. She had wished to rescue the slave, not only the economic slave but also the slave of love—to cause a harem revolt. Muezzins in lonely towers had wailed like traffic sirens at her approach. She had caused many a flutter in many a dovecote, my mother still proudly remembered as if the doves were fluttering in lightning flashes. White camels had screamed as if they had suddenly seen the ghost of an old love. She had caused many a shiek to turn white, white as the bones bleached by the desert sun.

Why should she not come now with the loud stampede of elephants?

And why should she not now visit my mother, my mother asked—spend her old age here where there was a gentleman's gentleman, his head a steaming silver teapot, to wait on her, to carry her tray, stand at arms until he heard the angelus murmuring through dim, crooked streets? Her visits to this sea-invaded New England house, unchanging throughout the years because it was always changing, even through changelessness— with its crazy porches and balconies and chimneys and widow walks lighted like amphibian stars and intricate mother-of-pearl circular stairways, great wentletraps reaching to mother-of-pearl clouds, helmeted snails in salt pools, rain-drenched gardens and broken shells and furry buds, dandelion heads thin as the deceptive Pleiades in earth-settled clouds, constant cry of surf, snow billowing like surf or like a lady's whispering skirts edged with lace, fireflies like fragments of dead souls flitting through the purple dusk, prows of old ships half buried under the snow-white dunes moving like the flood, old figureheads of wooden admirals and queens and caliphs breaking through ghostly waves—had been made while she was still alive and in command, an organizer of chaos and of Stygian night which knew no time and no harmony, when she was this great Khan of the suffrage movement sacrificing herself and her energy to the universal suffrage, the battle raging in heaven and on earth, when surely it had seemed that there had not been the slightest nuance of another thought which should be in opposition to her faith, that there had been no cloud, that she had entertained no shadow. And why should she have indulged in self-reproach? Yet the extremities of faith in anything might always beget, my mother knew, its opposite—as death might be the parent of love—or love might be the parent of death—and so my mother, through all the empty years, yearned for her as one might yearn for anyone who was no more, anyone who was less than water, less than fire, less than wind, anyone who was less than a thought, less than a dream repeating itself with only those variations which might be expected in the logic of an illogical, unexpected dream. If a thing was predictable, my mother at that moment ceased to believe in it. She suffered from claustrophobia even when she thought of the moon, the sun, the stars, the pathless places, places where her feet could not take her. The mere idea of certainty would have caused and, indeed, had often caused a panic in her mind—an entire change of scene, shift of wind, toppling mountains, toppling cloud-topped towers, minarets fading into the sun's gold, moon's gold—a change so complete that, though she accepted it without a breath or sigh, with that breathless wonder of one who was already dead, she was bewildered most by that relic which was most familiar to her, such as this bedroom. For she was always quite beautifully obtuse, even as a matter of her habit—taking an opposite view from that taken by other people, as Mr. Spitzer had more than once astringently accused her, with a decisiveness unlike his usual hesitant manner of acknowledging, at all times, two truths, neither of which should be true. And their day was her night. And their winter was her summer.

CHAPTER 36

✄

MR. SPITZER, though ordinarily polite to the point of painfulness—his brother would never have had such patience, it was sure—would arouse himself from his patent lethargy just long enough to make the accusation—brief, acrid, unassuming—a sudden spurt of bright energy which seemed to pass like something almost outside his dark, heavy consciousness, that which seemed always water-logged—perhaps as surprising to him as to my mother—to state the fact that she had never loved any living being—not even when, as it certainly appeared, he was dead, and he was in his grave. And the only miracle was this routine of daily continuing life—no less for him than for the evening stars among the bulrushes gleaming like rush lights, the floods creeping at the low stoop of his door, the whistling winds, the lean watch dog barking at a shadow, playing with a bone—for there was nothing but this repetition which was meaningless to him, utterly without validity, an imitation of life. And he was the counterfeit of himself—this face which passed for his face and yet was not his identical face—though others should recognize him and torment him by their mystified recognition, more mystifying to him than to them, certainly. For they were casual strangers who recalled those past events he did not know, those broken continuities which he was trying to understand. But who knew the hidden man, that man he might never be, neither himself nor his twin brother, perhaps that man who should have been born alone as he must die alone?

How often, when he stepped upon the solid ground, it was water running under his feet. It was the surf, the booming, buzzing, accursed tide, the nightmare ocean where all must change identities, sleeping under the salty waves. That was life, but he was also near his death, never more than a step away from it, perhaps not so far as a step. He was sure that he must hear, a minute after others heard them, the church bells ringing in a distant valley—or a train whistle at a lonely crossing. Each sound reached his dead ear always a minute late. He was always in danger of walking into the path of a hurtling vehicle. Fearful of bodies falling through space, he looked continually upward into an indefinite sky. Sometimes he heard only such dialogues as one might hear in a dream—or fitful conversations traced upon the enclosed air a decade

400

ago—the shrill whistle of silk—the friction of pebbles troubled by roaring surf—perhaps when, wrapped in his silent music, he had not thought he was listening, for his attention had wandered. He had thought he was listening to the music of the spheres, that which no one else had heard. And that was why he tried to be so accurate—because accuracy was impossible in this mistaken world—because there was always a discrepancy between an event and his consciousness of it, though by that discrepancy he lived—because every singer was singing a little off key, and every instrument was false.

His eyes were separated from his ears. His reactions were retarded—and thus both pitiful and ridiculous. He saw the traffic signals always a little late—heard the musician only when the music had ceased, when the almighty overture was no more though the music was never complete. So he lived at this second remove from reality, as he would sometimes hesitantly conclude, his flaccid lips trembling and wet with the evening dew, his milky eyes gleaming in the purple darkness—at this second remove from life, this second remove from death. And what more could happen to him? Yet he sometimes felt that, if he should do something he had inexplicably never done before, if there should pass through his mind, winging like a blackbird, an alien thought, one not familiar to him in some other life, if he should suddenly tap his foot upon the polished floor or move creakingly from side to side or dress in clothes other than these funeral clothes, the sombre black which he recalled he had worn ever since his brother's death, if he should forget to wear his wrist watch or carry his cane, then all the skies might fall upon his head, break like mirrors into a thousand splintered fragments, and he would be lost, irretrievably lost like all the others, and my mother would not know him, and he would not know himself, this familiar face so little altered by time, and there would be no world, not even this world of her imagination or of her mistaken memory. Thus he was conservative where she was radical. It seemed to him that she had never distinguished between imagination and memory, the thinnest line sometimes dividing them, a line thinner than the thinnest thread of starlight or moth spittle hanging in a cloud, weaving a moth pearl or swelling to a moon or a universe, perhaps an invisible line—that never like him, this responsible citizen of this world with the grave and erroneously punctual airs, had she been forced to make, as to imprecise matters, as was his task continually, precise judgments which should be important, larger than the immediate moment, larger than the past or future—abide by them perhaps when they had been wrong or when their consequences should be the opposite of his intention, when the greatest sorrow should be turned into this joke—perhaps a joke including sorrow—or correct the errors of illusions by errors even more imponderable, more mistaken than the errors he had corrected. She had accused him of absent-mindedness—and of leading after his brother's untimely death—he could never be certain of the hour—a double life, a life of moral duplicity, a life half in the shadow. If half in the shadow, was the other half in light? He had led a single life—knowing he was dead. Perhaps the mistake could never be corrected. There would be no way to change the flaw, the warping with which reality began.

My mother, and undoubtedly she was an incorrigible lover of the dead, just as Mr. Spitzer tremblingly knew, could be concerned not with Mr. Spitzer's insistently elegiac problems, however, not even at this late date when, if he had been truly and irrevocably dead, gone beyond recall, he should have been almost forgotten both by herself and by his superficial brother who had had no powers of memory or whose memory had been only in his own behalf, only for self-preservation, for keeping his own skin whole, as one might continue one's mode of fleeting existence from one's past into one's present life so that one should be unified by every moment and all of one piece and not broken—for she was concerned, now so many years after Cousin Hannah's amazing life and death, with that fearlessly adventuresome cousin's many problems of personal unity, burning like flame or like a lost star, seeming to press upon her now with an ever increasing insistence, demanding her undivided attention as if they were immediate and not already resolved, as if the last rooster had not already crowed over her, shedding its golden feathers through a cloud, as if she had not found herself in some other realm, perhaps that of the eternal darkness. Darkness was the greater part of life. Our star's light did not reach out far, did not illumine the entirety of space, was feeble as one firefly in the heavens of the universe tossing like a wild sea of milky light.

Or perhaps that great captain of reason had lost herself, sometimes my mother thought with almost equal certainty, always changing her mind just at the moment of crucial decision—for she was always very brilliant at building a road to a conclusion she would not reach, though step by step it had seemed inevitable. Her ways, in fact, were so very frenetic that, though outwardly trying to maintain his serenity and his unbaffled calm and his dignity as one who was beyond the flow of time like some old sea shell already pulverized by a thousand tides or some old boat dashed against a thousand lighthouse rocks, Mr. Spitzer would grow seethingly impatient in his heart, knowing that his salutary reasonings and his mild reproaches would be of no avail to bring her back to reason as if it were itself not another human fallacy, a lost project, most unreasonable—so that he would sigh, yawn, creak, tap with his cane upon the floor as highly polished as a mirror, consult his broken watch, hear a church bell like his cape tolling when the wind blew. What could he say to remind her of him? Had he not endured through great tempests and greater calms, those which would kill even the undying heart? Hers was undoubtedly the logic of madness, as he had many times pointed out, though with that genuine hesitation which showed his own precarious uncertainty, that of one who walked on clouded waters or clouds—for was he sure he wanted to correct this dream continuing beyond the limits of time, perhaps of space or mortal circumstance as if this one star had forever faded, disintegrated into stardust wandering without a central star or core or point of return, a spindle by which to wind the wandering threads of light? He almost admired her suddenly reaching some other end than that which she had consciously intended, taking some other road, that which he could not have predicted for the life of him or even if it had been his death, immediate death—without his sigh of memory— though looking back, he could see that this change had always been implicit and perhaps predictable, at least in unsafe retrospect. There was change even in a frozen world of frozen icebergs, frozen shrouds. He felt, great though he was and though occupying so great a body in space, that he was somehow withered, shrivelled, depleted. Cousin Hannah, unlike himself, was aggrandized by the pathos of distance. Death had not diminished her. She seemed to have added new dimensions and taken on new ways. She seemed like that dead tree which, only after it is dead, will break into a curiously fugitive, wraith-like mist of fading flowers, perhaps upon one single branch.

My mother, not easily defeated, not even by time's passage which should have defeated so many less courageous ladies, not even by stars whirling from the tree of heaven like the sulphurous autumn leaves whirling in a livid sky, by the fissures of rocks and the flowers in stones and the great chasms of which one could not see the depths, the leapings of long-roaring ebony waves where the black coachman was buried though he was bodiless now and though at times she saw his lantern eyes where fireflies glittered, the white manes of the running horses streaking the waves, would try to evoke the return of time and that proud suffrage captain who had been in grey New England a warring old maid urging ladies to arise and rebel and who had been in Araby a great desert king with whistling shrouds, golden tassels flying in the wind, the leader of the light-footed, moon-breasted brigade in a perfumed desert of veils and mists and shrouds under a sky where all the silver-lighted and rose-lighted heavens had melted together like one great rose trembling with auroral lights—would try to woo her back from somnolent death into this active life as she might woo her other imaginary lovers and loves, some who had abandoned her—now when, of course, there seemed no possibility or only the remotest possibility of the great lady's return before the heavens opened like lightning flashes in the heart of the trembling rose, now when if she passed, she passed in distance, and she was like lightning without mercurial flashes, thunder without sound of hooves striking on tinder clouds, clouds with no shadow of the great horseman with his silver-turreted head, clouds without a shadow fringing a star-flowered meadow, clouds without rain or snow or cloud-burst. Besides, even while she had had control of her intentions and desires, Cousin Hannah, engaged in so many conflicting struggles simultaneously in distant countries and windy palace skirmishes and battles of umbrellas and tents, going on so many perilous pilgrimages and foreign missions, pressed upon by a thousand or ten thousand engagements and suffrage battles for the imminent conquest and future subjection of man who was her enemy even when he did not know that she existed, could not have been persuaded to stay beyond her hour or half hour or quarter hour, the strikings of distraught, fantastic cuckoo clocks. It was impossible to know how she could have been engaged in so many activities without at some time contradicting herself, great military tactitian though she was, a lady continually consulting her archers. She had been hurried, imperiously urging flight, flight into Araby—for my mother's sequestered life had not been the most important life to her—there had been, as my mother still enviously remembered, her cheeks twitching with jealousy as she turned toward the shadow, so many other ladies to rescue from despotic, one-eyed ogres in darkened rooms, ladies as beautiful as my mother was and perhaps more beautiful and with as many darkened mirrors framed by gold, and perhaps some of them had escaped and gone away with her.

She did not answer her telephone—still disconnected. There would be only a confused, hen-like cackle of feminine voices or a buzzing in my mother's ears. Or a Boston florist answered, asking my mother if she wanted him to send a funeral wreath or bridal bouquet to her door, the ivory door opening upon the door.

Perhaps only my mother, with her forever wandering, inattentive mind, had resisted Cousin Hannah, that old bugler of the suffrage movement with her face dissolving into windy clouds—so why, though my mother waited for many years, should that great peregrine of romantic suffrage return to this darkened house washed upon by the sea rains and swells with its roofs crumbling into flowering tides, this old house with its air of perpetual mourning, its gardens of broken lilies in steaming fogs, its dim, unvisited rooms, shrouded furniture and half-strung harps and table set for the dead? She had not returned. She remained indifferent, never replying to my mother's cordial invitations which, though my mother thought of sending them by every imaginable messenger, by mourning dove, by winged Mercury and gods of storm, by any traveller going to Asia or Afrique, even by a eunuch clothed in satin draperies, one who never would leave home, she had probably not yet sent, having her qualities of evasiveness even now, her irrepressible moods, her desire to escape reality, just as she had never opened those letters she had inscrutably written to herself and had asked Mr. Spitzer to post, for they were illegible or written in wavy lines like the sea's surface in a calm or written in hieroglyphs she could not read, and she had evaded self-knowledge as if it were a funeral bell self-tolled above the darkened waters of a dream. She had always been afraid of the sad news she might read—the news that she herself was dead—that she had died in her sleep —perhaps with no eye witness but Mr. Spitzer who was certainly not an accurate judge of such unholy events—or that she lived, that her life was this form of death.

How often, dreaming that she was awake in the candle-lighted darkness, she heard the death of the wind, a pale, incorporeal body dying as she listened, as she watched the wavering candle flames. Often, she wept over the deaths of persons she had never known, never loved until they were no longer the citizens of this world. But which world was it? Perhaps, though she protested otherwise, though she was voluble in her protests, talkative as a magpie in a dark forest, she knew that the old suffrage captain could not be reached, at least not by the ordinary means of communication, that she had always had her secrecy, that she had changed beyond recognition and was not now the person she had been in this life or had never been, having existed only through my mother's dreams of her. She had passed beyond the farthest verge. She had plunged into that viewless abyss in which there is only the imitation of time and which swallows whole cities, roof-tops and towers, bridges and busy streets, broad thoroughfares and also those dark alleys so narrow and crooked that one must go by foot, neither by carriage nor by automobile.

Where was she now, my mother often asked—could Mr. Spitzer tell her, for had he not buried her with anthems, with pealing bells, thunder rolling down the darkening sky, hailstones as big as cannon balls, a cannonade which shook the earth? The earth was shaken from its foundations. Had not both earth and heaven mourned to see her passing? Had not the heavens divided, splitting apart? Had he not put the old suffrage captain away, hidden her from the face of man, the face of woman?

My mother, in her more rational moments, thought that Mr. Spitzer, though he seemed to be searching his failing memory which was wide-meshed enough to allow the passage of a boat or a star or a city, though he often refused or failed to distinguish these boundary lines, was being unnecessarily obtuse in his refusal to answer, for if he should maintain this silence, how should she reach Cousin Hannah now, in order to send her a gilt-edged invitation to winter here, to stop here in her passage—if he would not tell her the place, the present whereabouts of this old cousin whose place was never known? Where was the street, the house, the door, the door of a house which had been demolished long ago or moved brick by brick, column by column to some other star? Should she send a fleet messenger to a cloud, to all the waters of this world, to all the desert places, the stars, the crystal sands, the sighing winds? Should she send the wind to make its music of friction upon the sand? Should she send a slow messenger to overtake the swift—like that horse which stands still, waiting for its rival to come around the track? Old Joachim's blank-eyed indifference was a pose, an attitude adopted for a moment—he was envious of one who had escaped the purlieus of mortality long ago, one who had passed beyond the pearly gates, leaving him behind as this pedestrian in the great city of darkness and of moving light. His envy had never died, having outlived its subject or its object—he trembled at the thought of that returning spirit. Obviously, he wished to keep my mother in this remote isolation, her love being absent. He wished to have no rival in life or death. He was a man so competitive that, if there had been no other rival, if there had been no dead brother with his identical face, he would have been a rival to himself and still unsatisfied, indulging in his bleak feelings of eternal disappointment, of something forever missing in the nature of things. He was this obstacle, this darkness between my mother and her love, her dead love, it little mattering who that dead love might be, what face it wore—just as my mother had always known and as she would accuse him, perhaps when he had already turned away into the fog-streaked darkness, his cape billowing in the wind caused by his motion. He had departed, but she would always be confronted with his returning face, no matter if all else changed.

Though as to other matters, his ignorance might be quite complete —and therefore, as Mr. Spitzer privately considered, so might his knowledge be complete—for total ignorance was total knowledge—my mother thought old Joachim's uncooperative silence was not, as to this particular matter, his ignorance, his oblivion to one whose face was blurred by clouds and winds—for he could so easily have removed her doubts by telling her where Cousin Hannah was, whether above the stars or under the stars, what had become of her whose violence had known no bounds, whose passions death itself could surely never compose. For his own reasons which were not my mother's reasons, he was oblique beyond necessity, merely pretending not to know where now that great captain had gone, she who had been the queen of the strong-minded while dwelling on this earth, she who had objected to the song of even a male cicada in a star-lit cloud—and if he did not know, then who should know, my mother asked, and who should tell her the present address of one who had always travelled? If he did not have knowledge, who should have knowledge—if he could not locate her in heaven or on greater earth? Who besides he should know the unlimited space, the horizon never curving, void where there was no voice, where was only the answering silence? And should he not strike a flame in the tinderbox of his imagination, a flame burning like a star? My mother thought he should light the darkness.

Was it not he who had seen her last? Had she not gone over from the cross to the crescent? Had he not seen the atmosphere of an immortal illness, the changes of her mortal body before the last darkness fell? Had he not seen the dying body in the enclosed air, the dark air scarcely streaked by beams of the fading sunlight, the emaciated face, the shrivelled mummy features, the grey forelock, the hands like bird talons clutching at nothing? He had been the last caller there surely as he might be the last caller here. Wearing his mournful cape, he had gone to pay his last respects, to carry my mother's message to a dying love. He had sat by her bedside and murmured diffident, distant remarks not calculated to disturb her peace—he was the last eye witness, the last living person who had seen her, heard her. Had he not heard the death cry like the birth cry, the rattle in her throat? Had she not entered through that door of death which, though very narrow, is wide enough to admit the skies and the stars, constellations unknown to man, mountains and dark valleys? Or was it the door of life? Or were they one and the same, my mother asked? Had he not hung the funeral wreath, the purple and black ribbons upon the door? Upon what threshold had he left her? Had she ever said farewell to him, farewell to life? Where was she now? Which road had she taken? Was it the old Boston Post Road where the imaginary mail coach rumbled, clattering over cobblestones cast up by the sea? Was she riding all night long, riding through a blinding snow storm as white camels screamed under the seagulls screaming in the desert clouds? Perhaps she was in some great Crusaders' palace of ten thousand singing rooms lighted by candle flames.

What a wild, uninhibited existence had been hers! How important she had been and also aware of her importance to others—a reformer whose works had been done in public, and should not Boston have remembered this great horseman by an equestrian statue though Boston, a city not easily forgetting its past, a city not distinguishing between past and present or present and future, remembering every breath, every whisper, every dream as if it were indelible, remembering even the drunken whaler sleeping in a doorway, the dead fisherman sleeping in his scallop upon the tide, had apparently forgotten this great Crusader who had fought against the great turban-winders winding their turbans in clouds, the swan-breasted mandarins with snow upon their mouths, the mother-of-pearl pagodas of Peking and other cities upon a faint horizon, some not of this earth? She had driven a breach in the walls of Moscow. She had caused a sensation in St. Petersburg. All the czars of Russia had trembled at her approach. The court ladies had swooned. Had she not ridden from Minsk to Pinsk, pursued by wild-eyed Cossack horsemen who had admired her? Had she not wintered in Archangel, summered in a frozen clime? She had crossed Siberia many times by foot. She had come in through the Grand Central Station, sometimes with a whistling sound. She had crossed Brooklyn Bridge, Waterloo Bridge, the Bridge of Sighs, the Bridge of Lies. She had gone under all the bridges of the watery world in a black gondola flitting like a blackbird. She had visited many hanging gardens. What a great traveller she had been, crossing so many countries in the darkness when no one knew. And should she be restrained now, she who had known no master? Death had only extended her travels, enlarging her horizon which had never seemed limited by perspectives or intercepting mountain peaks or mirages or tents appearing in a distant haze. Had she not climbed the seventh crystal stairway, climbing above the lonely crags which lifted their heads above the clouds, the eagle's soaring flight, the eagle's shadow on a sea of leaden-colored clouds? Had she not gone to many buried cities and some which never were? She had gone to some which might never be. Had she not gone to Babylon, riding ten thousand nights and days, riding until she was suddenly old, until no one remembered the image of her vanished youth? Had she not entered many doors and visited the inner courts of many seraglios? Had not her way been lighted by Mr. Chandelier, the rock crystal branches lighting a dark sky, moving as she moved? Which door had she gone through, walking from room to room, down which arcade as the wind whistled?

Had she not crossed the shoreless sea of which there was no end, no foam of the in-coming tide, pale surf blown like this milky light against this darkened window where a low star burned? There was no surf-line. There were no beached barques, no flooded twilight piers, no winches of wherries creaking like the souls of the dead, no whispering shrouds, no cockleshells upon the tide, no creeping mollusks, no singing pebbles blown along the shore, no music of friction which was the music of creation, of creation's dissonance, no hunchback dunes moving in the wind, no beach grass or tree or bird, no long-limbed surf birds, lords of the purple dusk, seagulls flying through the roofless, wall-less house, no beacon lights. There was no sea. There was no sound of the sea roaring and booming, booming against rocks.

Had she not crossed this pathless desert, mesas of snow and ice, frozen salt lagoons like great, staring eyes, like mirrors in a darkened room? My mother thought so. She thought that Cousin Hannah had gone to the most distant places, streets where the sun was shining. She had gone from polestar to polestar. She had gone to streets where the sun never shone, where it was black as ebony or coal. She had gone from world to world with probably less care than Mr. Spitzer, infinitely cautious, his eyes milky as dandelion plumes enclosing sparks and staring in the evening light, his throat filled with pigeon cooings and whirrings as a phosphorous light crossed his face in the fog, might cross a familiar Boston street, talking always to himself, noting always that an old landmark had disappeared, perhaps miraculously in a city loving its dead, that the old horse fountain, clogged with the autumn leaves, was miraculously gone though he had seen it only yesterday, or another old house had been torn down, perhaps while his back was turned. So that he was really afraid to turn his back upon the world. There were now no hitching posts—certainly none for an old coachman wandering through this forever fading or faded world, driving imaginary horses. The sky was pearl grey streaked by mare's-tails. Mr. Spitzer walked, sighing as he remembered all those things which had disappeared, perhaps including himself.

But Cousin Hannah, who had known only passing scenes and who would never have noticed the absence of a street or a bridge or a tower or a town clock, had entertained no such cautions or reserves as guided old Joachim and horses' heads—and should she be conservative now who all her life had aggressively flaunted the conventions, rebelled against feminine politeness or timidity? She had needed no guide through mazes of this life or death or channels of overhanging rocks. Should death bring such great alterations as had already occurred? Was this justice to her? Surely, though she herself might be illusion now, cloud and whirlwind and flying desert dust or a wandering snowflake in a summer cloud, she had not been one to live by such hallucinatory beings or images as my mother entertained here in this dark house which she had not left for so many years that she had forgotten the time of her journey, continually shifting her journey in time, in space—changing the city as she changed her mind or according to the roaring of the surf like a city—so that perhaps it was only yesterday that she had lain down for a moment on her pale-blue silk divan with its golden lion hooves, asking that the curtains be drawn, that she should be awakened at three o'clock. And many years, some which had left no trace, had passed since then. She did not always know when her last journey was—perhaps it would be in the future—just as she did not know whether the house had grown larger, smaller.

Sometimes she thought the house had grown larger, large enough to include almost the entire population of the dead. Almost, almost. For there might always be a moth visiting another lighthouse or star. Sometimes she thought the house had grown smaller. There were many reasons for these shiftings.

So also she might change the time of Cousin Hannah's last journey, for who knew when or where it was? Had she not crossed Al Sirat, delicate as a human hair stretching between two towers, the bridge over the lake of infernal fires to Moslem Paradise—heaven where there should be no woman but only the dance of the black-eyed houris, feminine spirits who looked like women but were not women—where should be not even a grey hen laying the naked egg of reality in the long, whispering grass of a dream—where should be only the masculine domination, the golden cock crowing at dawn, shedding his feathers in the wind, feathers like golden flames lighting the world—heaven where, as my mother proudly thought, no woman should be allowed, not even should she be, after so many transmutations, this old suffrage captain, this sheeted rider, this desert king riding the white Arab horse—had she not stormed cloud citadels, gold-topped towers—frightened great, sensual pashas dreaming upon their beds of clouds, migratory clouds? Had she not triumphed over the golden cock pecking the golden seeds of the sun? Did not the night descend—sometimes suddenly, perhaps at dawn—was there not this shuttered dusk—this twilight like the atmosphere of perpetual grief, almost senseless?

Should my mother address her letter to Madame or Monsieur—to what street, what house, what city—for who should know her face, my mother wondered, her face in an inaccurate mirror of consciousness, mirror out of which a snow-white bird should fly, its long white wings drifting upon a cloud? Was she king of the living or queen of the dead? Not every lost chord could be resolved. There were wandering flute notes. Logic could not contain mystery. Time could not contain time. There were such stirrings, rustlings. Sometimes it was only a curtain blowing in the wind—or a shutter banging—or the many weathervanes creaking upon the many roofs, turning in all directions—or a chimney falling in a tidal storm—a cloud of wasps as the sea turned to fire. Sometimes it was only the cry of a foghorn coming from far out at sea. My mother heard so many things which others could not hear—not only a leaf falling on the other side of the world but that which would be more wonderful, establishing a connection between now and then, star and star, a leaf falling on another star. Indeed, sometimes she heard the stars falling like the leaves into this great abyss which was the memory of the dead. Yet who should see Cousin Hannah again as she had been in this life or recognize the old suffrage captain, the burning, ravaged eyes of that resurrected spirit who, it was known now, had been an apparition even in this life? For she had been an apparition of herself, now it seemed—her elongated shadow blowing on a wall webbed with candle light, her head like some great cliff reaching above a sea of weltering clouds. Sometimes one had seen only her hand, her mailed fist. Sometimes one had seen only her naked foot. She remained ambiguous as that which never was.

She had seemed perhaps less real than now when she was no more, no more of this cosmography or general description of the world, this anatomy of sorrow—now when one should only remember her, an image changing in the dusk. Was she become a man—bold as fire, puissant, invulnerable to any attack—or was she woman, a beautiful lady in that other sphere, her dark hair whirling across her eyes so that she could not see her love, perhaps as helpless as my mother dreaming of her dark love more beautiful than earth, the equine ravisher who carried her away, he with his foaming nostrils, his long white mane, his whirling hooves, his burning eyeballs like two moons, the woman with a horse's face? How had she not changed? All definitions failed and failed again—all sharp lines were lost, wavering and blurred, for she was darkened and obscured. Was it heaven, or was it earth, as insubstantial as my mother's dreams, my mother having already died, as she believed, she being herself this pale lady with the wild dishevelment of hair, the wandering thoughts like phantoms drifting down the wind, like the reflections of faces in mirrors where no faces stared? For if a woman should be in heaven, it should not be heaven long, my mother thought, proud of her omnipotence, her ghostly powers, proud as if it were herself and not that old suffragette who had invaded paradise, taking heaven by storm, in whirlwinds of these mutations erratic as a travesty of God—that heaven should soon be this hell, this hell of chance, this creation flowering out of death, its brother —that there should soon be this chaos raging like this earth of whistling winds, storm bells, barking dogs, gnashings and ravings, demons in every shadow. One should not know one's mother's face, one's father's face. The infant should be an old man crying in the storm, plucking at his beard.

CHAPTER 37

AND winged mirrors should drift toward the ceiling, then as now—or there should be these reversals, and the ceiling should be the clouded floor, fluid as water, the waters of a dream. The darkness should be filled with luminous eyes, dolphins riding the white-lipped waves, barking before the prow of the boat and not in the wake as usually occurred. Clocks should strike the inept hours, and there should be this loud discord, this music of wild dissonance crashing on all sides, sea shells moving through the darkness, this loud sea booming like darkness upon the shores of light—even as now, this mistaken earth which was perhaps its counter-earth, there being no limits between heaven and hell, nothing real except this mistaken dream which knew not its end. For if it ended, there would be no dream. But who was the dreamer? What face, what mask did he wear? Was he a domino or a man?

As to that heaven beyond these dimensions, there should be no harmony, no silent music like the music of the spheres, the planets wheeling in their courses, scattering pale foam, had not my mother always said when arguing with morose, abject Mr. Spitzer, that there should be no further organization, no orientation more than this which he had already experienced, that nothing should be simple there because nothing was simple here? Order, had she not always said, was a mad man's dream, the maddest dream of all, a suicidal plan omitting the irrational elements, the phaetons rounding the avenue, the stars blown out of their orbits, and how should we live except by accident, for were we not already dead, we who breathed and walked about, our breath like frozen plumes upon the winter air, our eyeballs cracking in the cold? Were we not living on borrowed time, being, even as my mother was, these pale phantoms of ourselves or others, and was not the sunlight only a hallucinated, pale, moon-washed moment, greater deception even than the darkness and the whirlwind? Mr. Spitzer, wishing to be agreeable, had made a false report as to what might be upon the other side. Peron had been right—and Joachim had been wrong. Mr. Spitzer had lied to her as he had lied to himself—though in every lie was a grain of horrible truth—and in every truth was a beautiful lie, that incipient lie which should some day be true, truer than truth, though she would be unconscious, and she would not know. For each face hid the grinning skull, the laughter of the dead.

Anomalies bloomed like a dark forest here, here where every phantom but one was cloaked in flesh. What body cloaked her spirit? Was my mother a tree or a bird? Every lover was a masked robber, robbing her of her pearls which did not diminish in their number.

Doubtless my mother believed in no definitive moment, no solution of the enigma, no separation of the falsehood from the truth, the illusion from the illusion of life—for how should they be separated? How should she know when she had crossed the invisible line of demarcation, all being imagination in this erroneous life? There should be only this extension of this moment, only this dream of time's demented passage, for there was no time. There was the illusion of time. There would be suddenly a whirling windmill. She would hear these voices roaring through the empty, echoing rooms, then as now. She would hear the grinding carriage wheels, the pebbles roaring on the beach. There would be the spray of surf upon her cheeks, the salt encrusting her hair as if she had grown old. She would see, as in a dimmed mirror, wavering shoreline and dwarfed hemlock trees, tops of snow upon their blackened branches, steepled human heads, heads hung with church bells, perhaps the black coachman, the diffused radiance of the carriage lamps in the fog, the partings in the curtains of fog. There would be the sheeted gleam of jellyfish, the thin rattle of naked trees, strummings of beach grasses, the dead seagulls blown upon the wind, the moon like a drunkard's blear eye. And so, being always under the pervasive influence of opium, both overstimulated and inactive, robbed of her active powers and of the isolation of her physiological tragedy, perhaps only half conscious, my mother would never know that she herself was no more, that Mr. Spitzer was no more, neither the living nor the dead, that she was living merely through these nocturnal dreams of escape, that she had also died through them, that she was supine, nearly inert, that she would probably never walk again or take a step in actuality, that she was, as she would so often say, this beautiful, bloated corpse which had never awakened to life, to love.

And why should she ever awaken to this knowledge? What was the knowledge of the void, the dark and empty places of which Mr. Spitzer sometimes spoke, his voice rustling through the darkness as his rusted throat strings quivered with the unaccustomed effort, and his tongue felt as if it were made of leather? How could there be an end, definite and clear, clear as if someone had said his last farewell, taken his departure? How should death be different from life, my mother asked—or recognizable when it came? Life had surely been, for her, this opium dream and never tangible—she thought it must have been this dream even before she had depended upon sedatives in order to ease that pain she had never felt, to assuage that weariness which had not been hers, even before she had retired. Death was this dream's immeasurable extension, varying from day to day like this common experience of light and shadow, this volatile landscape of mercury and wind, this seascape. For one had died before one had ever lived, or one had died while telling an immortal joke, that which had concealed great wisdom. One had laughed one's self to death. Death was a mountebank.

It was true, my mother was deceived, perhaps only self-deceived—thinking that there would be no immediate collapse, sudden and complete as if the wind had blown against a house of cards, no cessation other than her periods of temporary unconsciousness when, with her eyeballs staring, her lips foaming, her face darkening and contorted like the face of a drowning woman, her head roaring with old dreams, she enjoyed that uncertain omniscience of which she was so proud—for she could see many aspects, many sides to every question, shadows of shadows, refractions of refractions, splittings of splittings, invisible facets. Her opinions, indeed, even as to the simplest matters such as whether it was night or day, rain or shine, multi-colored rain or dark sunlight, were always divided. She was always aware of that half of the earth which is always in darkness—aware of the earth which, viewed from another celestial body, would seem like a dead moon. One could see the quarter earth, the half earth.

Perhaps, as Mr. Spitzer had more than once remarked, in consideration of his own private sorrow and anguish and self-doubt and rapturous desire for unity, for some single point of view which would be at all times constant and unchanging, guiding him with even greater precision than the lodestar, she did not really wish to make up her mind, to adopt a single point of view to which she would be constant, to adhere to it even when the world changed around her, sweeping like waves, a sea of dreams when apples changed to door knobs.

She had seen so many sudden and altering alterations, so many changes, here where nothing changed, where the same cobwebs hung from the stained ceilings, the same gargoyles laughed or wept, and there were these same interior fountains, a great many things changing which other people, doubtless the literal-minded, thought were standing still—movements which stars might observe, movements known to mirrored fireflies, to death's-head moths, to blown surf, to human dragonflies. For nothing really stood still. There should be, even when the great musician was no more existent, wrapped in the silent whirlpool, this music which my mother heard in a still house, this which shook the enamelled heavens and the earth like a dice box. There should be, when the dreamer was dead, the dream which had dreamed the dreamer and the wind and the waters, double moons, two moons riding in a cloud, two moons shining in my mother's bright eyes, these white-lipped waves running in a perpetual motion, this transforming sea which changed all bodies and knew no walls, no limitations.

How often, she heard wild sobbings in an empty house, echoing shells. She complained of the cold when the day was as hot as furnace fire. How often, she saw stars whirling around her as thick as snowflakes. She saw stars marked like dice. She saw sable snow whirling from the sky, snow blackened before it fell, black as soot from a factory chimney, even like that purity which was corrupted at its source, for the dreamer was dead, this whitening skull, sable snow like black plumes drifting from the burning cloud, like raven's feathers in the warped wind, snow black as the ace of spades, the night usurping the law of day. But who was the dreamer, still she asked, astonished that she was not the dreamer, as she might suppose—not the dreamer who had begotten her—that she was these variable dreams, ebbings, risings as when the wall-eyed dolphins came with their flowing curls? She would be so puzzled over these, almost to the point of an absolute distraction. She would be crazed by dreams she had not dreamed.

How many years since she had seen the sea which she could have seen at any time if she had ever allowed the shutters to be opened? How many years since she had walked in the sunlight, wearing a drooping garden hat and ribbons which were her racing colors and lace skirt, perhaps when the gardens were covered with the hoar frost, the icicles which did not melt? And there had been thin cracklings in the air which had been the color of the glassy starlight. She could scarcely remember the day. For the day was mortal, one mysterious sunbeam bisecting the darkness, but the night was immortal, specious as eternity, the invasion of space, all walls dissolving as if they were inaccurately mirroring fog, all familiar relationships changing, all familiar objects changing their shapes, raging like confusion in empty rooms, and there were these thresholds of hallucination, more doors than probably there had been in the day, doors opening, closing, soundless footsteps, these incalculable errors going on and on, repeating themselves as in a dream which could never be, though it was the same dream, twice the same, having its assertive qualities so much like the nightmare of this repetitive life, one would not know it was not life, its opposite. There would be the footman with the golden torch at the door. There would be the hat-tree in the hallway, place where seagulls perched. There would be the gilded-legged chairs in a dim drawing room.

Love might wear the face of death, the grinning skull, as death might wear the face of love, the beautiful lady, as we might be other than we seemed, as we might not know ourselves who stared at us, who caused this fear, or each person became his living opposite as man became woman with her heaving breasts, as woman became man, or two forms were blended into one which was amorphous, being neither, or one saw one's brother with one's sister's face, her flowing hair, the black hair hanging like a shroud, or one saw one's father wearing one's mother's clothes, her flowing silken draperies, one's father who gave birth to the dead child, the dead child crying in the darkness, or one saw that God was dog, an old dog barking at the barking surf, the wandering foam upon a scalloped shore, the sea which was lighted by mysterious candle flames, or one saw the white polar bear upon the ice floe in the whirling snows, or one wore another's head, staring into a frost-wreathed mirror, seeing that he was a stag, seeing these great antlers shaking the powdery starlight, for there should be these strange rearrangements of composites, these deranged elements, these velocities like wind, and there should be these somersaultings as when the ceiling was the mirroring floor, trees of enormous crystal growing with their roots in the clouded sky, their branches under the earth, or marble stairways should dissolve, running like moon-colored water under one's feet, or the sea should be the land, or the land should be the sea, the shoreline changing, and there should be the pink fog, the blue fog, the purple fog, the black fog, the black and white piano keys, or birds should speak with human voices. There should be no searchlight but the dream playing over the dark waters of the dream. There should be, then as now, no fixed star, no point of reference which did not move. There should be these moving shorelines. For the living were those who had already died, and the dead were the living— my mother scarcely distinguishing between life and death—all being that involuted intricacy through which she lived, even when she was no more, even when she was this beautiful corpse like the body of reality with its dark waters and sunken stars, its undiscovered shores. No one should escape. Yet where was that old suffrage captain who, this daughter of the codfish aristocracy, her silver helmet gleaming, her scimitar uplifted like a new moon, had disappeared beyond an opaque cloud, had passed beyond a far horizon? Where should she find my mother—or where should my mother find her, this creature of transience?

My mother, her mind drifting like a cloud, would try to locate her in places which could not be located, not even in the cosmography of a dream which should know no differences as between life and death, here and there. Yet my mother would think of sending her a message by the footless messengers or birds who could speak ecclesiastical Latin, perhaps by sea shells which had rolled on the floor of the Lost Atlantis. Was she under the earth—above the earth? My mother would complain of sudden agitations. She would complain of a star entering her foot. Sometimes of the buzzings of fiery bees—for there were these sensations, these disturbances which could be traced to no other source. She would suddenly half rise from her bed, her bed-clothes dragging around her like a crazy queen. Her eyes would be enlarged as her face turned purple, then black, and she would scream until someone answered her. Though there were often such disrelated phrases, she might not be speaking of Cousin Hannah.

Which road had she taken, my mother would ask again—did it wind, turning and turning upon itself, or run straight—and were there slate roofs, and were there golden domes and wooden steeples—or had she gone where there was no road? Who had seen her last—if not Mr. Spitzer, he who had visited the distant city—and where was she now— and why would old Joachim proclaim his ignorance which was suddenly unabashed—why could he not locate her? But he could only repeat, plucking at his dead ear, that she was dead. He had not seen her in the star-lit places. She had left no double. She had left no daughter. She had left no son. She had left no lover who would mourn for her, for perhaps, of course, she had been her own dark lover, he had always thought, her own ghost who had come to rest. Was she not already in her grave, her grave clothes wound around her, moldering and wet, her face veiled, clouded by obscurity so that no one should see her again on earth—not even when the black coachman came, and he was dead? She had gone to that place where was no individual, no consciousness, no memory, where was no color, no sound, where all these temporal stresses and strains were forgotten, and time should not exhume, as Mr. Spitzer tentatively remarked, that which time had buried, that which had no likeness, for there was no medal ever struck off in memory of her, the great general. But my mother did not think so, of course, for she could not admit this total extinction, not even of this great lady with her suffrage message—my mother having witnessed, even in her life, these many obliterations and this dark flood and the darkening sky. The cross had turned into the immortal rose—the rose had turned into a cross, a cross upon a crossroad, a wooden gibbet, a gibbet with creaking chains, and the hawk's wings darkened the sky. Her head was eaten by great birds. Great birds had plucked out her eyes. Death was madness. Madness ruled supreme. What was life?

There must be an image of that which had no image, that which was void and without form, for my mother could not face oblivion, her fear as of a great cloud, a shadow. She feared those periods of her oblivion when she did not know the months, the years—centuries collapsing like moments, turning into crystal dust on other planets. Perhaps there might be beyond all modes of being a being without mode, point beyond the ultimate point, that eternal point where all lines converge, both beginning and ending, where there is no distinction, no individual, no image, no ego, no shattered memory, no mirror of consciousness, as there might be also an unknown land—land of infinite greyness, stretching from naked pole to pole, perhaps always only a step away—land of no bush or tree or flower or bird, no signpost, no bony finger pointing through the fog, no road, no direction. Land where no human voice was ever heard, where no surf roared, where none should make reply. It was this land my mother feared, this step she would not take. And this was why, as she would say, she had remained horizontal, this horizontal invalid upon her mother-of-pearl boat bed—why she was not perpendicular like old Cousin Hannah, lifting her banners on the other shore.

Death had taken Cousin Hannah—though no one else could take her, a woman of such undying strength—her feebleness had seemed, at her last hour, a sham. Death had been, at last, her bridegroom, sometimes my mother thought when she thought of the fighting suffrage brigand, so proud in this mortal life that no mortal man could have possessed her, that perhaps not even an immortal could have possessed her, nor could she have been ruled, it had always seemed, by fickle woman, not even by my mother and the spidery coils of her feminine beauty, by silken fetters which, like those human relationships which had seemed so frail and easily broken, easily denied, turn to iron when we try to escape them. She had passed a thousand moving frontiers where there was no watchman but a dying star. Had she not gone to the court of the emperor worm? Was she not where each deceiver was, the gay or sad? Was she not under the steaming turf—gone where poker-faced Peron was—gone where were all the dead, skull-faced jockeys, furious as whirlwinds, the dead dice-throwers rattling old bones under dimmed street lamps, and their skulls were their dice cups? She was in the underworld, probably very different from this. She was in the night of clay. She was in the driven clouds of paradise, the tormented whirlwinds turning upon spindles.

For that great lady who had denied the love of man for woman or the love of woman for man or its natural consequences, she surely knew a great deal of that life and love and all those ambiguities my sad mother had missed. Even Mr. Spitzer thought so—that Cousin Hannah's life and horizons had been much greater than theirs, she having gone to places where they had not gone. Had she not startled great pashas dreaming in their mothers' wombs, great pashas playing with crescents and evolving from pearls in the womb of time? She had crept into a seraglio among a great shiek's wives, wearing a veil so that she would seem but a woman in this court where the great shiek ruled until one day when he had exhausted all his other loves he had pursued her, believing that he would see, beneath her veil, a beautiful face, for only beauty should conceal her face. Why should an ugly face not be revealed? A man should be forewarned as to what manner of woman he loved. Suddenly, as he pursued her through mirroring rooms under rock crystal chandeliers, she had lifted her veil—and he, seeing that great, gaunt, bearded face, had gone stark, staring mad. This was but one surprising experience. For still another time when she was invading a harem to organize the girls, a great shiek had lifted his burnoose—and Cousin Hannah had gallantly bowed —indeed, had apologized for her mistake—for the greatest shiek of the East was a beautiful lady with large liquid eyes—and there was not a rooster in the courtyard, not a male hound or horse. Cousin Hannah had fled.

She was buried, as Mr. Spitzer knew—he having been that mourner who had felt no grief, no grief but his lack of grief—and yet he was not self-congratulatory, considering that, by a curious quirk of circumstance, he had outlived her. My mother, not easily defeated, however, still thinking of a future card game even when Mr. Spitzer reminded her of the impossibility, would try to seduce the fragile creature to return, to come here once again, now when, according to all the odds or almost all, there was not the slightest chance, not even, as Mr. Spitzer sometimes remarked, a Chinaman's chance. Had not the riderless horse already come through the opalescent door or window, to signify that the great postilion was dead? The great rider had already fallen, helpless as a snowflake falling from a cloud when there was neither snow nor storm. The last conch trumpet had already blown, sounding like the first, thin trebles drifting on the air. The last sobbing requiem had already played, as Mr. Spitzer probably knew, for he, plucking his dead ear, heard the silence. Never again, though my mother should plot and plan, spreading her shining nets, setting her traps, would Cousin Hannah return, riding her high horse past the moving sundials, the frozen fountains, coming through all the changing seasons of life, urging suffrage before it was too late. Death had throttled her. Death perhaps had made her timid, my mother thought—and yet she had been bold, her eyes burning with that fixed intensity of one who has lost his reason for being intense, one whose last card long ago was played.

CHAPTER 38

∗⟨

AND about other characteristics and limitary features which had
singled Cousin Hannah out from the average individual and ascertainable way of life if there was such a way, my mother was indefinite, as
might be expected so many years after she had last seen that great captain
of extremes, one who had seemed never to reconcile herself with life—no
one knowing exactly what that year was, even to this plaintive moment
—and besides, my mother's mind was clouded, veiled by other dreams,
dreams perhaps of an immortal love whom time or snow should never
touch—just as Mr. Spitzer, being as one dead, was never noted for his
power of reconciling opposites or for his good judgment, his capacity to
remember these individual traits, and perhaps he had preferred the cold
and marble face, the unremembered face of an ideal love. Only with
greatest reluctance could he be prodded to remember the formidable
captain of the lost suffrage troops, and then only for awhile, remembering that she had forgotten him. He must be prodded and forced to
remember, for that matter, even the most important events, those of his
own restricted life which had its sharp limitations. Or perhaps—it was
always possible—as anybody knew who knew him—his abstractions,
seeming so like indifference, were caused by his enraptured thinking of
the beautiful music of the spheres, filling all space with its sound as of the
human will, music his dead brother heard but which Mr. Spitzer could
not hear, could only imagine in this silence, chords of the great sounding-
board of the rational cosmos vibrating through seven deathless eternities.
Or he heard, in this dreamland to which he had come, the vibrations of
the seven-stringed harp, each string bearing the music of soul and spirit
and astral body flying like a moth between two stars. Or there were polar
lights accompanied by strong sounds, whistling, hissing, crackling music
as of the wind.

My mother thought of the great traveller. As to Cousin Hannah, her
chief distinction, other than the movement to which, quite unnecessarily,
she had sacrificed her life, had been that she had travelled to the outermost reaches of space so that my mother envied her to this day, much as if
her journeys had not ceased, as if she were in clouds and whirlwinds. She
had always come with a whistling sound. My mother had used to greet

418

her by saying as the chandeliers shook, as the lights dimmed—Hello, traveller! And where do you come from now?

The lonely cause of suffrage had seemed to my mother to be quite unworthy of Cousin Hannah's adventuresome spirit in the far places, of course—and the unflagging efforts had seemed a great waste of time—for time would itself level all pinnacles and all powers, including that great rider—though it was not to be trusted, my mother's point of view, continually shifting, for all might have been quite different from her report and Cousin Hannah not so obdurate, not so courageous as she had seemed. Perhaps it was that great captain who was weak, my mother who was strong as if only the most delicate creature might endure. My mother had always managed—perhaps without wishing to do so, for she had almost no will power and could not concentrate unless on that which was not there—to distort even the most familiar reality, to turn aside the rushing stream or draw constellations into flights like birds, to see life in her own clouded way which was, of course, untrustworthy as to the great things and as to the little things, just as Mr. Spitzer plaintively knew, tapping with his cane upon the sidewalk—and had she ever trusted him or his masculine eminence, his higher wisdom which could overlook and dismiss accidents as mere episodes of no importance in the history of a long life or a short life? One who had followed her descriptions of anything would have found himself much confused, even in a city which he might know like his own sad, empty heart or loose flagstones. So it was not to be believed that Cousin Hannah had greeted my mother by remarking—Babylon is fallen. My mother undoubtedly misunderstood as to time, place, person—opium begetting so many changing phantoms. Perhaps it was the great gold-eyed chamois to whom she spoke when there was no other visitor. Perhaps it was an Alpine crystal-hunter who had cut great steps in ice. For my mother's mind must always have been wandering far and wide, travelling though she herself should remain this beautiful and unawakened corpse, the cold and frigid beauty of the past—this dead beauty who, spending her life in the aura of a lost romance, had never loved, had never been awakened by a mortal or god.

Surely, my mother had evaded, wherever possible, the direct renunciation of life—going by all other roads—and had preferred never the immediate moment of realization but an unearthly romance which should suffer no deterioration or change brought by harsh experience inasmuch as it was not subjected to these mortal laws of change and chance and these accidents like the great snow avalanches falling over the leaden roofs with the sound of church bells tolling for the lost crystal-hunter, and surely she had loved that love which never was, yet was more powerful than any love which should be realized in this mortal sphere, the heavenly bridegroom none should see, the lover never to be discovered on this clouded earth—never, unless he should come in death's guise, carrying her away. So that, though many years had passed, she would imagine that she was this great courtesan with a snow pompadour and snow birds in her hair and her memories of her undying conquests, innumerable triumphs, innumerable loves which had never been hers. For if there had not been one, then there must be many, my mother dreamed—many eleventh-century lords fighting for her hand, many great Conquistadors, sahibs in winding cloth of gold, black and white eunuchs making war.

How beautiful my mother had been as a young girl when, heavily veiled like that face too beautiful to be seen on earth, she had been herself a great traveller visiting many strange countries and distant cities not of those countries, or so she dreamed now, dreamed of her many fleeting loves, loves starting up from a single glance, flickering like flames, like stars spawned nowhere. Her head roaring with circular winds, dark whirlwinds and crystal visions multiplying, she dreamed of the great stone dogs, the stone huntsmen awakening into life, dreamed of fiery fishes upon a far horizon. She talked to dead men with burning eyes. She dreamed of Cousin Hannah who, in my mother's bedroom, had walked back and forth, rattling great iron keys, striking against a stone wall, striking against the empty air, or fighting a mirror with her jeweled sword as if no time had passed or dimmed this glass. But when had my mother last seen this great visitor? When in death's dateless night which knew no beginning and no end?

Yet though there was no time, though all were immortal, one was always missing as if there were time, for there was this loss. Oh, how happy, happy, happy my mother would have been, she still insisted and had explained long ago to old Cousin Hannah with her furies and rages of regret, if only the great gambler had lived, if only my mother could have enjoyed the company of this man of great wit but little brain—no legal knowledge in his head, no intellectual pretensions whatever, no desire to impress anyone with his solitary personality, no music of refrain in his heart—though yet if it had been Joachim who had thoughtlessly died, she would also have been, of course, quite regretful, at least in a transient moment perhaps forgotten now, she had admitted at the beginning before she had become accustomed to the fact of Joachim's precariously continued life and Peron's death uninterrupted by any stir of wind or wind upon another star, his death so complete and absolute that she could not imagine it. Sometimes she thought that only he lived. She had missed that gay brother in his bright cloak, but she might have missed old Joachim with his definitive regrets, which were already a matter of habit long before his brother's shocking death, much like his dressing himself each morning in the correct clothing of his despair, as if for a funeral, his whispering, his tolling like some old town clock forever out of time. At least, she had whisperingly admitted this sorrow to herself if not to any other person who now remembered it, the great suffrage captain being no more—the fact that, whichever one had lived, she would have missed the absent one, this sense of her ineffable sorrow being so necessary to her and to her continued happiness. Her eyes blinded by her own brilliance, she could scarcely distinguish at times between her happiness and her sorrow, for the absence of anyone was like his presence. So that Mr. Spitzer, though feeling himself obliterated, often wondered why she should miss anyone, here where the heron-footed twelfth-century kings might well be visitors, causing the candle flames to gutter or stars to brighten in a dying wind. But she was obtuse.

Explaining Peron's absence and that which might seem like his indifference—that which she had always known, even when he was alive—had he not been faithful through his absence and his prolonged neglect of her, she asked, and when had she last seen him? If he had shown her the slightest attention, if ever he had telephoned her or left his calling card upon a jasper mantel piece or marble cliff above the roaring waves or left a bouquet of withered flowers, if he had paid the slightest homage of recognition to her love, she might have questioned his feeble love. He had expressed his love by his silence, his distance. Death had surely given no voice to that which had not been expressed in life. His love had not been corrupted by its finding any form of vulnerable human expression. No vehicle or image had been great enough to express his love, that which had left him absolutely speechless, silent, withdrawn, remote. That which others thought was his hatred was his love, my mother believed, his love greater than his hatred. He had been frightened by her beauty and her power. He had absolutely ignored her, for if he had come near, he would have been vulnerable, unable to resist the magnetism of her attractions, as he must surely have understood. Should he who never entered a battle lose it? Petty men could love in petty ways, but this unexpressed love was as heavy as all the stars. This dead love which never was and never would be real was the one undying love.

So that my mother was bored by Mr. Spitzer's little attentions and dreamed of her escape long after it was possible. Should she never rise again, return to the world? Should she never again visit those beautiful cities of which she dreamed—the cloud-capped towers, shoulders of crumbling snow, hives of light where a lost queen buzzed? Long ago she might have fled, leaving no trace. Cousin Hannah had invited the opium lady to come with her to Egypt and the far places—not, as might be supposed, to view the mysteries of the desert and stone tablets under the desert sand and mummies with long, wild hair and gold coins upon their eyes and mysterious amulets giving their true, secret identity—but to show, when she appeared at that great captain's side, that one could join her movement for reasons other than being ugly and old, that one could be both beautiful and independent of man. And if my mother had accepted these insistent invitations—or numerous others which were offered to her, brought by the couriers of every storm—her life must surely have taken a different course—different, at least, to this extent—she would perhaps have done, in actuality, all she dreamed of now. She would certainly never have spent her life in bed, enjoying her memories of the triumphs she had never experienced, the challenges she had never accepted, not even though they were those of that old suffragette with the burning eyes.

My mother, if she had followed that urgent advice, that which was unasked for, that which was unwelcome, freely given as the wind, would have ridden in a balloon with four snow-white horses following a white bird through infinities of clouds. Or possibly she would have picketed Buckingham Palace in a furious snow storm or ridden on horseback through city streets with her suffrage message. She would have visited the land of the somnolent Kurds, coming with such stealth that none should see her. Hers would have been a nomadic life, for she would have been a wanderer under the nomadic stars. She would have slept in many silken tents hung with gold and silver camel bells. She would have found herself locked many times in castles moated by black lakes, but she would have been triumphant, managing her escape like the greatest escape artist. She would have deceived her jailers many times, passing in disguise so many times that they might think she was the turnkey.

Or perhaps she would have lived all her life in Italy where was, she believed, no necessity for her imagination, for every thought had already found its form of expression, and there was not this dreadful New England climate of the howling winter winds, the sand grains sharp as stars. There were jeweled daggers and poisoned cups. There were centaurs on the roofs. She would not have given herself up to these easeful dreams of a lost romance, a dead man playing a broken lute. She would not have ridden in her dreams in a funeral gondola black as a blackbird through the twisted canals of Venice as now, talking to someone whose face was masked, a dark gentleman she had never seen and would never see, and she would never have thought of those who were dead, the inverted reflections of doorways and faces, the oar bisecting the wing of the angel mirrored upon the flowing waters of the dream. Her life, instead of this escape from reality, would have been reality. Indeed, there was always some great cause which should exceed the dream and which should give meaning to life, my mother believed. No one should think of the shadowy substances as of a dream, the marble heads, the folded wings, the tenebrous shades, the whirling autumn leaves, the snowflake falling on the cold, dead face of love. Indeed, my mother dreamed so much of Italy—many travellers, seeing this shrouded house, said that the lady had gone to live in Italy—though others said that she was dead, and that was why the house was closed, why the windows were broken, why the centaur slept in the garden pillowed on stone, why the old barouches with their gold fringes flying rounded no more the sunken avenues, why the pillars leaned upon the wind, why the snows piled up upon the roofs, why the chimneys emitted no fire or smoke or cloud, why the jewel boxes glittered with dim jewels, why the mirrors remembered the faces of the dead.

Perhaps no one should think of that old New England suffragette, that great freebooter who had stormed so many fortified castles, donjons and walls and angle towers and palaces of singing winds, echoic voices. As my mother thought now of that great cavalier servente with her suffrage message which seemed the opposite of love. For all base metals were transmuted by time into finest gold like that which lighted the clouds, but darkness and whirlwind remained, and life's essential mystery was that which never would be solved, not even by death which should be the end of mystery. Not until Cousin Hannah was old and sick and dying, in fact, had my mother wondered as to that great lady's life in a personal sense, finding that, though illusions dissolved in the aqua fortis of memory, yet mystery increased, and other questions must be asked. Perhaps no human being could ever be entirely dismissed or understood. Life contained death as a cloud contained a passing star—but what was the cloud, and what was the star? Whom had Cousin Hannah loved if not the image of the dead? She had wept if a snowflake touched her rain-mottled hand. A tear had streaked her granite cheek. Many tears had made great rivulets. She had wept if she heard a skirt whirling, rustling in the wind though sometimes it was only the tide whispering upon a lonely shore or white wing lifting in the wind.

Yet at the time which had allowed no time for the memory of a dead love, no time for a precious nostalgia or a task never to be finished, a cause never to be realized, her public activities in behalf of suffrage had seemingly spoken for themselves, having been sufficient and unmysterious and unequivocal in their majesty, requiring no explanation or afterthought, so that my mother had always felt, when confronted by that great captain with her burning message, a sense of guilt as to her own retirement from the heart of conflict, her espousal of dreams, poor opium dreams which should not bear the test of reality, visions which should dissolve at a touch. She had felt guilty as to her entertaining of so many imaginary lovers and loves—and rather envious of one who had seemingly espoused the cause and quest of reality and was wedded to it and not to the dead heart, the stone face of an unawakened, unawakening love. Such mysteries were beyond her understanding, it had seemed, for she had seen all life in terms of her great cause and watched not the nuances or rose quiverings in dusk. She herself certainly was never occult, and the mysteries of the East had held no charms for her as for my mother sleeping through endless years in this dark house, doubtless because the great traveller through narrow passes and desert cities and cities in clouds had seen the East as one who stares with lidless eyes, eyes blinded by sand and snow, and knew that beauty faded like a spectre with her approach.

Her skin luminous as glass and seemingly composed of hard, angular grains, gritty as if it were made of particles burned by volcanic fires and terrible whirlwinds, she had been quite acute, shrewd and sharp—steep, abrupt as a sharp curve upon a cliff—to the eye, instantaneously brilliant —to the hearing, piercing and shrill—and she had been sharp-witted, dashing and wild and reckless, and she had been like a finely tempered blade, cold and nipping as the winter air, trenchant and incisive and keen, acutely poignant, fine-pointed and sharp-edged, never oblique, never obtuse. Such masculine virtues could not but have been admired by a sick lady, though my mother recognized now that she could not have competed with them, and so at the time they had not made nearly so vivid an impression as now they made in inaccurate memory, a widely netted seine catching only the biggest star or fish. Moths and butterflies escaped my mother's memory.

This great, dazzling visitor had seemed so sure of herself and her flaming cause, the fixedness of her limitless purpose, the noble clarity of her self-forgetful motives, her ways which could never be turned aside by whirlwinds, it seemed, or wandering snowflakes, avalanches falling like snow Niagaras in her path, roarings. Not even when trains were stopped, buried by snow, was she stopped, buried. Her light had burned. She had burned like a live coal. Snow buried many cities but did not bury her. Nights when all others were frozen in their tracks, she went on. She had despised frailty as if it were a reproach to her unless it was itself an aspect of her undying strength—for had she not sacrificed her life and all her personal interests to her grand idée fixe, the rescue of pale ladies held by one-eyed ogres greater than death itself or monstrous love? There had seemed no rivalry between Cousin Hannah and other hierarchies of buried self, that which needed no interpretation coming as an after-thought, no elegiac music like that remembered now, the memory of the memory of music.

Music had never filled for her the vast amplitude of space as for Mr. Spitzer writing now his nocturne in memory of her. She had heard the thinnest whisper, the faintest flute whisper in a glassy cloud or winding horn upon a distant mountain peak or a lady's skirt lifting in a vagrant wind, but she had not heard the thunder-clap, the cloud-burst, the cry of the sea bird in the storm rising to meet the cloud. Her will had cut away the non-essentials, and she had transfigured time.

She seemed never to have broken the tryst she had kept with her own imperious will, and she had seemed exceptionally sure of the follies of others, the divertissements, the pretensions, the foolish whims, the wasted graces, the wandering airs, such as my mother's opium dreams that she had found a stairway to heaven by means of which, continually ascending and descending, she could over-hear the decrees and whisperings of the dead, buzzings of stars like paper wasps in the wasp-colored starlight, gossip of dynasties which were no more on earth and perhaps had never been. Cousin Hannah must have believed that the dead were silent, that only the living whispered, sighed, breathed, moved. Her great battles had been with the living, it had seemed then. Her impersonal energies, quick to react, had apparently allowed to her no final rest. Her energies were like sparks starting of themselves. There were always sparks blowing in her path.

Unlike my mother who was cold and lonely and withdrawn, Cousin Hannah must have lived, though she was versatile, in only one dimension, that which could be measured in a single line, and my mother had pitied the great lady, naturally, at the same time envying her the stark elegance of her salvation. She had survived to old age simply by forti-tude, by putting aside all thoughts of self-protection such as might have killed another lady, by riding against great mountain peaks whirling like tormented seas of snow and light. Where were those great kings whom she had come to slay? She was like someone who was in perpetual motion, being never twice the same—and the word perpetual was that which had always frightened my mother, having a special significance for her, this jeweled corpse for whom all conflicts should have ended long ago. Or was it Cousin Hannah who had already perished in some great conflict, my mother who had lived, she had sometimes asked, wonderingly musing aloud upon the terrible fact that action was no necessary criterion or measure of life? And indeed, one sometimes sees, in dead things, action —in dead matter, a sudden revivification suggestive of life, as when the dead tree boughs move and break in the wind, or the dead eye suddenly moves, winks in the wind. Had not my mother often observed such phenomenon, the thrust of the dead swordsman, the cry of the dead seagull drifting on angelic wings above the snow storm, especially when a lapse of consciousness occurred, when she could no longer observe? There were these gleamings of far, sudden lights at empty windows, these irrational, mystical, four-faced doorways through which there stole, when no one else was looking, the mystery of the fact which had retained its mystery, the terror and the beauty, the wildness and the pang of human life, of those who brought the fog with them.

My mother had watched, with bewildered fascination, Cousin Hannah's regal airs, her wild grimaces which seemed almost beyond possibility, the raven feathers shadowing her cheeks, her paradoxical attitudes, so much like something my mother might have dreamed, scarcely more surprising than if Cousin Hannah had been the incarnation of Clovis or Cuthbert or Crispin or Charles the Mad or the Beloved or the Bold or some such old creature come to transient life in my mother's presence, one of the perennial dead, those who, though long hidden under the frozen ground, yet continue, bearing with every spring new flowers, sad as the memory of a preternatural spring. My mother had been naturally disappointed, sorry that her distinguished visitor was only, as usual, this sterile suffrage misanthrope who had never loved, this wild insurrectionist disrupting her dreams and causing other dreams to start, sorry that she was not a gentleman sans peur et sans reproche, that she was not the hero of a lost romance, that she was not even a mock hero, an imitation of the reality, that she was not a French chevalier who had travelled great distances or a Red Cross knight or Richard Coeur de Leon, that she was not the early French kings carrying their oriflammes or some old Rinaldo riding, through centuries of dreams, his bayard, his wonderful bay steed which had never grown old though he had grown old, sorry that she was not the Prince Charming to awaken this Sleeping Beauty, to awaken all the servants in the house and the birds in the garden and the life-sized chessmen, those who had slept a hundred years.

Her feelings of disappointment, however, were vague and short-lived, perhaps because someone had just announced a traveller from Spain, a viceroy or lamp-lighter, or a door had slammed in a distant part of the house. Someone was always coming, departing. For even then, so long ago, my dreaming mother, never quite sure of the reality of an external event, had been irresponsible as now, permitting herself that fitful inaccuracy which, in the ultimate sense beyond experience, as Mr. Spitzer had always timidly realized, might be more nearly accurate than truth itself would ever be, truth seeming only another precarious organization of the fleeting and mistaken dream. Did he who with his cape rustling timed his uncertain steps by tolling bells know better than she?

Church bells always ringing might some day be right. Did he know better than she the time, the place, the person? Did he so much as know whether he was a man or a butterfly, a lost psyche drifting down the wind? And most people, it had been Mr. Spitzer's unfortunate observation, were at some level disoriented, unaware of the existing situation with reference to such apparently clear matters as time, place, identity of persons, even themselves, and they imagined what was not. How often had my mother seen, perhaps because she wished to ignore the factor of time, the boat moon rising at dawn, one star burning to portside, the eye of a porpoise, the sun rising at twilight? How often, even here in her bedroom, had she been lost, wandering through labyrinthine streets in a foreign city of changing signs? My mother's bright eyes were blurred, cobwebbed by her predisposed illusions, by nightshade and bella donna, and she could hardly keep awake for more than an extensive minute at a time, her erroneous dreams seeming to her, for obvious reasons, more real than life, even when there came one whose head was turreted. Lunacy reigned supreme, infecting even those most sane. The very atmosphere seemed infected by my mother's dreams. And perhaps, of course, her dreams had seemed more real to other people, too, than life could be—there was always that impossibility, more real than anything which seemed merely possible—at least in this old house by the roaring waves, this loony bin.

CHAPTER 39

✧

It was ironical, but it was true—the great Bostonian lady, though she was in the avant-garde of the rational suffrage movement—though she had fought all her life to overthrow the distant pinnacles of romance, the ivory towers and minarets, had always become, in my mother's eyes, this person evoking a dead romance, even through the fact that it was never to be consummated in flesh or spirit or haunted fact, that it was like something already dead. She had seemed a person not quite of this modern world in which all romance had already been destroyed by telephones and Western Union messengers, for someone was always counting the minutes or the words, and there were always these interruptions causing so much havoc in my mother's life. One got the wrong party time and again. One was answered only by a tired servant. Or there were always these busy signals, buzzings like thousands of Libyan honey bees, my mother still complained, or the people were not at home, the telephones ringing in empty rooms or monstrous roosters crowing on a dark continent. There was the silence. There was the splashing of a star. Someone had gone from France to Hades, sailing in a darkened boat. So my mother had felt, then as now, as she had felt from the earliest times, even when she herself had been active and a great traveller, her isolation, her distance from life, and she had not been able to resist, in order to compensate for her many disappointments and for that sense of loss which had preceded disappointment, her wandering imagination. She said that her imagination was all there was.

Indeed, Cousin Freemount-Snowden, even when she was that great knight errant storming against this castle perilous with its dreaming towers reflected on clouds, its windows lighted with stars, coming with her petard and army of clouded girls, causing candle flames to dim in windy alleys shadowed by poplars, had seemed a person not of this material world and time, one not bound by mortal circumstance or thought, and so should she be subjected now to mortal law as if a dream should be real, as if it must go through its autumnal cycles and grow old and wither and die and fade like the stars fading at dawn? Should they fade with every morning of swimming wasp-colored light buzzing like the sea upon this shore of barren rock? Should she fade? Was she not herself the phantom, a creature of the immortal night, her great Coriolanian eyebrows bristling, her hair streaked with white, her great Roman nose casting its shadow and reaching like a granite cliff where there might perch a blackbird or shadow of a blackbird? She had fought against the dragons of despair flashing their great silver tails through miles of clouds, the seven-headed monsters wearing golden turret crowns, the flame-tongued ogres, the terrifying, red-eyed basilisks, the thousand doormen at the thousand doors. She had fought against the great turban-winders upon a lonely beach streaked with thin threads of foam like the waves. She had slain the minotaur sleeping in the drowned garden where were a few fishes glittering like sequins of golden light. Obviously, or she would not have visited my mother, coming as the undaunted aristocrat, assuming that she was always at home, attributing no importance at all to the subjective life my mother led. Cousin Hannah, and might God rest her soul, had been determined, indomitable in every way, never recreant from her great cause when she was still alive. She could never have turned back or lived again that life she had not led, not even in a dream. For her boots were in the stirrups, and her long-maned horse rolled in the flood, and she must ride, ride, ride to that victory which would be her own extinction.

Could she have been so easily deceived as my drugged mother was, imagining that she was indisposed or that she was elsewhere, that she had gone out with the black coachman, his eyes rolling like dice, to make a series of afternoon calls in the great world capitals or in one great city which was the fusion of them all or in harbor cities reflected upon the watery clouds? She really was enslaved, chained by invisible demons she could not escape, perhaps for the very simple reason that she imagined herself free. And perhaps, she had thought then, she was imagining this visit, even though it certainly seemed real, for she had heard many footsteps scurrying to and fro, distant doors slamming in the wind and sea shells closing their doors, horses crying on the other side of the world, a blind dog barking at a long-tailed comet. But if the visit was real, then the visitor was not, my mother sometimes thought, for there were such roarings in her head, such poundings, singings, whistlings in her ears, and her hands grew frosty, and a dank dew coated her brow, and she was benumbed by hallucinations. It was as if the perpendicular pronoun I had come to see my horizontal mother, there among the blowing shadows, and was dancing about or had suddenly divided into two, herself and her reflection in the darkening clouds. And was the old suffrage captain already dead, my mother would ask now—and was there a chink in her armor, a stain of blood caused by that wound which had just missed the heart? And who were the descendants of this lonely squire? Was she father to no one, mother to no one?

Had she fallen in some far field of snow blown by wind, perhaps upon a stone escarpment? Had a mountain goat seen her, her great foot in a cloud? Or was it my mother who had died while she was unconscious, wrapped in deepest sleep, and was only dreaming this amazing visitor, the shadow of a ghostly casque? Where had she come from? What was her message none might ever hear? Had her message changed in transit, just as a traveller changed during his travels, few men being at the end of their journeys that which they had been at the beginning? The dead were those who travelled fastest.

The personal pronoun I did not always mean, of course, the same being or thing to my mother. How often, eating an apple, had she said—I am eating myself? How often had she said—I am a cloud eating the moon—I am eating an hour-glass—I am eating a door knob? How often had she warned a hallucinatory or even a real visitor not to be seated in a golden fourteenth-century chair set upon a floor of clouds—for she was the chair, and she might crumble into the glittering stardust? She was the divan, the mirror, the lamp, the rug, all of which might suddenly move away in the evening light, leaving a bare room with plaster walls, something worse than an empty tenement, for even a tenement might have a picture on a wall. She was Brooklyn Bridge, dissolving when a rose petal fell on Brooklyn Bridge, dissolving at a single footstep. She was everybody and the rose petal, too, the cause of this dissolution which was this creation, and she was the street lamp beaming through the fog like one great pearl, a sarcophagus enclosing the moon's flame—much to Mr. Spitzer's envy. He had supposed he was the lamp-lighter and the flame, the city of trembling bridges. And if she was everybody and everything, how could she be she and live, for what was her personal identity among so many transshifting objects and flickering shadows, and how should she walk where the landscape moved like waves? Undoubtedly, she was many things to many people, so that there could never be, as she would lament again and again, pitying herself because nobody pitied the poor opium lady with her dreams begetting her dreams, her charmed personal memoirs, one for the living and one for the dead and one for a murdered archduke, beginning memento mori, something to awaken, as a token, all slumbering memories, raptures, loves, even those which were not her own, all lost movements, gestures, reachings of the hands through clouds, something to evoke her thoughts like a faint perfume lingering in the air when she was gone.

She was this great social hostess entertaining so many guests, one of the world's greatest ladies if not, indeed, the greatest, most sought after by her male adorers—and at the same time, she was this recluse with the stained cheek, hidden away in this dark, many-turreted house—never travelling, yet always travelling—for she was this great traveller, and the spokes of the wheels of her carriage were sleeping cherubim with folded wings, forever turning through seas of clouds flashing like star-jeweled moths under a glass sky. She was immured, and yet she was extra muros —beyond these walls forever—wearing her great garden hat and lace mantilla and great cascades of lace in a snow storm whirling at her feet, sometimes raising her white umbrella over her like a cloud, greeting an old friend from Newport or addressing, in a fugitive dream, her black coachman or the Chinese emperor or Czar Kolokol, king of the Kremlin bells, silent against the leaden sky. Often, she had been seen waving to herself in passing, or she had made banal remarks to the beautiful lady who, under her drooping ostrich plumes, nodded and smiled from the other carriage, seeming to recognize her, though this lady had lived and died in the twelfth century. She had died with a dagger driven through her heart. She had been murdered by a cruel rival. My mother knew, of course, the most intimate details, those hidden from history, much as if she had been present at the scene, knew when a heron flew over a chimney or when pebbles rolled on a distant shore. She had known several murdered archdukes in several centuries and many great khans who were sleeping in their satin beds and would not awaken again. Sometimes the clouds were pointed like cities of tents. What was time to my mother, and why should she have been concerned by finite duration, time when time should be no more, for did she not live through timelessness? Yet it was true that there was probably no one who spoke more learnedly of timetables, railway stations, shipping schedules, flight schedules, beginning with Icarus who flew too near the sun and lost his feathers, falling into that burning sea which was later known as Icarian and burned like the lost star. The sea was his tomb. Perhaps this was when the first starfish appeared, my mother said.

Speak not to my sleeping mother of the soul which was divided into only two parts—or of the reversals of polarities, the meetings of opposites, the imperial organization of chaos—but of that disorder which seemed itself innate, a greater mystery than life or death, the spirit messengers reciting revelations in the darkness, eyes burning like stars in the fog, sea birds with burning feathers drifting before their eyes, dolphins with shining curls upon the long wake of the waves, the swell of the sea which breaks upon the distant shore, the foam of sound caused by the breaking billows. This world sailed ever between two worlds. She knew when the Phoenicians were about to sail, when their fleet was expected in darkened Brooklyn or Boston Harbor. She knew when the seal boats were about to sail from their ice citadels in Labrador. She knew when to expect the Gloucester fishermen who had gone down a hundred years ago, wrapped in their torn sails. She knew the hour of the charioteers.

Whenever she passed through a phantasmagoric doorway, she had always found that there was yet another doorway she must pass through, that each room led to another room, that there were new visions, voices, clouded raptures, mirrors looking out on clouds or mirroring nothing. For my mother's soul was like a many-spiraling house with many rooms, many cubits adding to dazzling cubits, many stairways leading to many heavens, many galleries and crystal caves and boxes and dimensions of existence different from those of the merely understandable, comprehensible world, which was certainly beyond my mother's comprehension, being the central mystery—or if she had ever understood it, she would have lost all interest, subsiding into a new coma none should disturb, and her eyeballs would have been as cold, as hard as hailstones. So she could never seem to escape from this house which continually extended like the idea of infinity and was lighted by two moons, twelve moons. Or perhaps it continually diminished, indefinitely divisible, and space was the illusion in a frameless mirror.

But in any event my mother in her dreams, trailing clouds of deathless glory, leaving the scent of her face powder or of the flowers in her hands, moved from room to room, never finding a way out, the house seeming infinite, every room being but the partial reflection of every other. In every room, there was someone missing. There was something missing. There were dead splendors. The floors wavered like water. The walls seemed to move. In every room my mother was a different hostess, only partially present, surrounded by different guests, bevies including the Egyptians and the Florentines and numerous variable sahibs, and there was always another door leading to another room. Sometimes she embraced a reindeer. And no matter which room she was in, she thought of all the other rooms, those she had not yet visited, or the long corridors hung with mammoth crystal chandeliers. There were many drifting mirrors, many cascading stars, stars rushing like streams, tides of faceless memory, still breathings, train whistles like arriving tides, departing tides, the tides whistling like the Midnight Express, carriage wheels on pebbles leaving star streaks. Certainly, there was no one more volatile than she was in the midst of her vapors, surrounded always by those things which, like qualities of her thoughts, seemed so unsubstantial, fleeting, and transitory as a snowflake in summer. How often did she reach for the door knob which was the sleeping flower or bird?

Her imagination was ambient as air, as water, as cloud. Though staring at a wall, she saw all things, shadows of eyes, shadows of foam and surf and wind, those rainbow-colored balloon fishes trailing their negligee streamers over her head, perhaps those ribbons which would wrap around her, or great leviathans rolling, lifting like islands in the flood, submerging. This life was a scheme of mirages, even for those who lived. The dim silks stirred like waves. Many a boat had capsized on these waves, and many a sailor had gone down. The present moment was already freighted with the burden of the past, fusions of other moments, faces like old town clocks seen through a blowing mist, each clock striking a different deranged hour as she passed in a dream with the black coachman wound in his cloth of gold, for surely he was her prince of the East, and that was why life was so very complicated for my mother, who was simultaneously in many places at once, it sometimes seemed, why she also enjoyed that sense of being dead without which she could not have enjoyed this life or its extension. She saw, as if she were travelling, the purple roof-tops of pagodas sloping through clouds, the faces with Roman numerals, the void faces which told no time, no hour, those for whom the last hour had struck. She saw an idiot who had become a great philosopher, a philosopher who had become a great idiot. She saw one who was both an idiot and a philosopher. Of course, except for her most demented moments, however, my mother knew only too well that she was capable of producing fantasies, altering the appearances so that she should see what others did not see, such as the sandpipers running back and forth through the thin light of the evening surf, as she would always say, for she believed that they were invisible, the light waning like the neap tide upon the shore of darkness, or the stormy petrels flying, with swallow-like flutterings of their great wings, through the mirroring rooms which were walled by curtains of fog, seeming to penetrate these illusive walls as if by miracle, then flying out again. She heard their coarse cries and cries of lonely trumpeters. She must have spent the same winter in many places at once, in many grand ski hotels set upon the snow-crowned mountain peaks, or taken the waters at many spas at the same time as the snow darkened the air, under many white umbrellas strung with planetary pearls.

Yet my mother knew, even through all her variegated fantasy, her banishment from scenes which she had once enjoyed, perhaps only in her imagination, the great regattas at Cowes, unfurlings of sails which had already sailed into the eye of the wind, the horse races at Deauville where some horses were winged, Florentine plazas and the Champs Elysées after this life is over, multiple balloon races—how opium had poisoned all pleasures at their source, causing the great, swirling fog like winding walls of pearl, perhaps destroying or distorting even the rational cosmos, that which Mr. Spitzer most loved or claimed he loved, and causing ancient castles to be moved from one mountain top to another, their carved escarpments frowning above unfamiliar valleys and lunar lakes of echoes, and also causing the stars to move out of their stations, and she knew that she had deluded herself to a large extent, for there was nobody. There was not the master of all harbors to whom she often spoke. It always did seem too late for her to come back into the world. Indeed, she could not count the years, so many and simultaneous to this horizontal lady, her heart like wandering snowflakes, her eyes congealed. She could not even count her magic pearls, her runic dirges, her bishops walking by the absent sea which roared at the darkened windows.

My mother knew that she was helpless and bereft, even though she seemed so independent, this alienated and this jeweled corpse who should dazzle every stranger with her prismatic wit. Everything seemed to fail her, as she would often complain, but her mind, that which had deceived her. When her mind cracked like a crystal in the cold, she would certainly be gone, leaving no trace, not even a rose petal on a marble stairway or her glove on a rickety end table, not even her hat with its white plumes, not even a footprint in the marble dust, there where no one walked, no book turning its pages in the wind, its pages fluttering like the wings of a bird, no distilled image in a darkened mirror warped by waves, no image at all by which anyone should ever remember her, the opium lady, as she remembered, after so many implausible years leaving no trace, the great suffrage captain who had urged her to arise from her canopied bed, take arms against a sea of troubles, ride against great kings, make war against man who had held woman too long in his power. Masculine pinnacles must be leveled to the shadowed valleys. There must not be these great, overhanging crags, these sudden precipices, these fathomless opposites. Equalities, which had always been innate, even like those pertaining to the mind or spirit or its phenomena, must be verified. The veils of pretense must be stripped away from masculine pretense, even as from woman's heart—to show man for just what he was, a blushing coward who would leave woman to fend for herself, to fight against great mountain peaks.

It was not merely the void—it was the aching void my mother had tried to fill with her vast social life, the social whirlwinds turning on distant spindles, the numbers of the numberless dead crowding in empty rooms, the mewings of phantom seagulls by a phantom sea, the barkings of phantom dogs. It was the doorway leading to the doorway. It was the other room, the other soul. And how should my mother have self-knowledge, she being so many selves that she could never know them all? How could she compete? One might know a great deal of one's difficulties and seem to triumph over them, thinking that, through luminous self-knowledge, they had been destroyed, even like dragons slain by saints—and yet they would appear again in a different guise, a different form of being or non-being, or almost exactly the same as they had been before, repetitive as madness must almost always be. Perhaps the dragons would appear as saints, wearing their shining armor, or the saints would appear as dragons with their silver scales shining through the foggy dusk and their sequins like stars shining through clouds. As for my mother, she believed that her own sanity was simply this—she knew she was insane, quite mad, poor lady, and she had passed beyond the realm of hope. She knew it was an empty room.

In fact, as she would sometimes vivaciously insist, perhaps talking only to herself, perhaps talking to Mr. Spitzer when he was not really there—self-knowledge had never helped to allay her eternal illness, to calm her mind, to lull her torments, to still these waves rising like a sea in storm, these boomings, buzzings—but rather, self-knowledge, the knowledge of so many selves, had added to these wild waves of thoughts roaring upon all shores and upon the shores of Hades, the bony shores where all the drowned ships came, where the loud, white-capped breakers broke like the mournful weepings of the dead, where the dead seagulls whirled and cried forever above the turreted clouds like her lost love, disturbing my mother's sleep so that, at times, she was almost driven out of her mind, almost made witless, almost driven to cease taking drugs. Yet if she should ever give up these drugs, those which she had taken for her continued life on this star or another star—how often Mr. Spitzer had assented—should she even hear the secretive ocean crying or know so many of the ocean's unrevealed secrets, the secrets of the living and of the dead scarcely to be distinguished from each other?

And besides, as she would ask herself over and over again, crying out in the moth-pale dusk, pulling the gilded bellrope furiously for hours, so that the entire house was filled with the sound of gonging fog bells, boomings like the cries of the loud sea bitterns, and footsteps were running in all directions, which of many selves should she have knowledge of, and how should she know which self of selves was true, reigning supreme, herself or her rival Belshazzar, perhaps the last king of Babylon against whom she had raised her white frilled umbrella, and should she be able or willing, even if she knew, to give up all the beautiful false

selves for the sake of one who was true and, in all probability, quite dull
and void of thought, a dreamless idiot bereft of sense, an empty skull,
someone no one would really care to come to see or spend another hour
with, and even Cousin Hannah might evade like poison, a poisoned cup
or a sword drawn through a cloud? Though my mother might often
contradict herself, saying something very different from what she had said
before, yet she really preferred confusion to order, these interesting, illusive ambiguities, there was almost no doubt, and so there had never been
any way of really persuading her that she should prefer, instead of wandering stars and wandering Jews and false moons and clouded perimeters
and peacock feathers burning in clouds, a simple scientific truth or statement of true or false, a clear and unprejudiced vision of reality which
was by its very nature prejudiced.

It would be her argument, at this point, that everyone else was just
as drugged as she was, perhaps more so, others perhaps not knowing that
they were drugged, and also that there should be, to light this darkness if
she should arise from her bed and if they were disenchanted, no great
torch-bearers with streaming meteoric hair in the wind, with burning
lamp eyes shining through darkness, no clearers of this darkness, or everything would go out the window, sweeping back into the terrible sea from
which everything had come, and there would be no Lord Murdock Burdock Thrushmorton, he who was twittering like a cage of canaries, he
who was, as most rational persons might not care to understand, a
wooden leg stamping along old Gothic streets where the leaning spires
gleamed through the fog, a perfect English gentleman. Though sometimes he was striking like a dozen distraught city clocks. Sometimes he
was loudly ticking, and yet again, he would stop ticking, and there would
be a period of silence—and then all of a sudden, he would start ticking
again, striking all hours with a fine disregard for the time, striking thirteen bells far out at sea where no time was. He was really quite canary-
brained.

My mother, though wrapped in slumber, would make a special point
of greeting Burdock at all hours. Oh, come in, she would say when she
heard his heavy footsteps stamping through the foggy dusk. Did you
bring the fog with you, or is it the medicine? Is it God's drug? Oh, is it
you, Burdock? Dear Burdock, of course. You have come a long way. And
do go right on twittering, Burdock. These little things never bother me.
Twitter on, Burdock. Twitter on.

Or she thought that Mr. Res Tacamah had gone out of doors and
was sitting on the beach, sitting on a beach chair under a striped awning
in the midst of the enormous fog, though he was only, of course, the
porcelain drug bottle with very large ears, that drug bottle which contained the purple fog and the glowering genii, spirits of fire or air, sparks
upon a far horizon, gleamings of distant cities upon the moving waves,
stars, clocks, faces. And as for Mr. Res Tacamah, the author of so many
fantasies, they who were under his omniscient control were less mad than
they who were not, my mother believed, for the former did not act upon
their diverse principles—they only dreamed. Their madness had never

yet outreached itself, yet though it reached so far, reaching like great tentacles through the pale, veined mist—for where the sea sweeps up, must there not always be a shore, the temporary place where the sea meets with the land? Here, my mother believed, the sea had reached the shore. The dead had reached the living. Each was hypothetical to the other. The dream had reached the dream. Our faces were dashed against by the sea's spray, by the salt tears of the sea. The fog was where all walked who walked, and the nights were long. This was surely no place for those who worshiped the uninterrupted sunlight.

This was surely no place for those who worshiped health, for those whose countenances were honest, for those who avoided shadows and chimeras and great hermit crabs. This was a place for those who walked with their eyes hidden behind their hands, shielding their eyes from the wind, the dashing spray. This was a place where absent-mindedness might live, luxuriating in the sense of that eternity which might never be—except, of course, by an act of imagination. And yet whose act and whose imagination? The ordinary restrictions of life were not regarded here. For there were so many other absent-minded persons who might share my mother's state of mind, such as Lord Montrose of Montrose, he who knew nothing of himself, for he changed his personality whenever he changed his high silk mourner's hat, and he changed his hat quite often, and there was a gentleman who was just his wooden cane with the serpent's head, and there was a gentleman who had left his wooden head at the hairdresser's, and there was a skull grinning at a banquet table, he who had eaten himself, and nothing whatever was right with the world —and if it had been, then what a pity for the world, my mother would always think, trying to think what the world would be like if there had never been mistakes such as hers, if there had been no clouded margins of doubt, no errors of consciousness or of creation, if there had never been this erroneous creation, these wooden hands like traffic signs pointing through the fog, and the wind sighing through the trees, and the leaves falling fast, turning from brown to gold, and bubble worlds quivering and breaking in the wind. And was not God dreaming, too, dreaming these opium dreams, so who could be right if God was dreaming? Did not a moth dream, spinning its bubble world around itself? And if we did not close our eyes, dreaming the only light there was, should not Gabriel lose his plume, his bright feathers falling like the whirling snow in the surf? Should there be no angel of the evening, no angel of the morning, no angel unfurling its wing like the long white sail of a sloop? Should there be no dream—which was another way of saying—should there be no reality—for were they not commingled and perhaps the same?

CHAPTER 40

COUSIN HANNAH had passed over into the realm of the dream—or had she always been there—one with the cloud-topped citadels flashing their lights, the great Crusaders with mother-of-pearl shields, gauntlets of mail gleaming like fish fins in earth-settled clouds? Was her vizor up or down when she came with her bright eyes burning among the shadows? Or was hers a sepulchral armor from which the spirit had fled? Her voice, my mother remembered, had been remarkably vibrant, more like a man's than a woman's, a husky baritone, ranging between bass and tenor and partaking somewhat of the quality of both, sometimes seeming, at least in memory, as loud, as heavy as iron bells ringing in a leaden-colored northern sky, as loud as the wind blowing among the leaves burning like flames, causing constellations to fly like birds from windy branches, causing submarine memories to arise and unfamiliar landscapes to appear with marble statues staring out on clouds and bridges crossing nowhere and roads dissolving and stars shrinking to fireflies. Her voice had been a Gothic cathedral weight, an oratorio accompanied by many singing, whistling voices. She had spoken several foreign tongues with perfect fluency, switching from language to language with accustomed ease, with vast aplomb, employing the dead languages, the languages of the dead, the languages no living person had ever spoken or heard, my mother believed, still wondering why, as her message was plain, she should have spoken at all. Silence should have spoken for her. My mother had seen mountains higher than the highest Alps, frozen waterfalls with long cascades reaching from heaven to earth, steps no crystal hunter had ever climbed or carved, and endless stairways crossed by cloud after cloud, reaching above the topmost clouds, and the black sunlight, the spears of shining rain—as if the psychological mystery should remain long after its cause was gone. She had heard rollings, pealings of thunderous hooves in the distance beyond all hearing—all being then as it was now.

Indeed, the reverberations, like those of a psychological experience invading our dreams, or a dream invading our experience, had caused the cloud ceiling to shake, the baroque mirrors to crack and move upon the air, revealing the wild, contorted forms of things which were ordinarily familiar, even as this proud suffragette, with all her eccentricities about her, surely was, she being no dark stranger coming from afar such as now she seemed. She had beaten against my mother's frail defenses, for all was fair in love and war—screaming, raging, roaring, had ridden through windows and mirrors and clouds and stars, causing my mother's head nearly to split into two, so great was the impact of all these disoriented impressions whirling and fluttering about her—like turreted steeplechase riders leaping over her clouded bed all night long—though that great captain of extremes, that great rider before every storm, had come to still the chaos, had come not to create but to destroy the last romance on earth, like this my mother remembered now—along with many surprising things like sporadic growths in time, like sudden cloud-bursts, like sudden angels blowing ivory horns in clouds, like unexpected doors, like secret avenues and roads and sudden windings, windings within windings. My mother never had given up her belief that all of space could be wound, unwound like a bolt of silk. Never had she believed that it would not be possible to live in a vanished time.

My mother had not known then so many languages as she believed she knew now—and yet she had seemed to understand instantaneously, even without her knowledge, without the slightest conscious effort on her part, without betrayal of her profound ignorance, as one may sometimes seem to detect the words hidden in the muffled music of church bells or creaking of stars like old doors on rusted hinges in fading clouds or blowings of winds in lonely places, which was fourteenth-century Saracen or Spanish cavalier, which was seventeenth-century French, the language of the Nubian boy, of singing candle flames, of singing moths, the language of Volpone who died an imaginary death and then was never again recognized by his friends or his enemies, which was medieval mocking birds singing in a dark forest, which was Sanskrit from a holy text printed on a snowflake, which was ancient Eskimo hunter under the long-reaching northern light beams whistling like golden chords, which was the barkings of seals on crystal ice spars under the frozen clouds, which was the hieroglyphic language of the drowned Egyptian sailor in his great turban winding like waters and clouds, the language of the dead Finnish king with the long heron toes, third-century Chinese polo players storming over the roofs of Peking, which was Provençal, that language of the wandering Troubadour sobbing forever to his lost lady love, the snow upon her mountainous brow, which was Greek shepherd singing to his flock, which was spoken and which was never spoken. Cousin Hannah had surely known many languages of people in remote places, kings of sunken thrones—though her furies against archaeologists with pick and spade had always been, of course, intense, like her furies against believers in a future life or a past life or that past which should be the future when all stars should be one great star and endless horizon with no chasm or crevice between star and star.

And thus my mother, though she had never studied any language but the French of a Peacock Alley menu or the Latin of a clouded mountain tomb, being also very vague as to these, very easily distracted by buzzings in her ear, had acquired a splendid proficiency as to that which she did not know, she understanding, she believed, to this day all

languages, owls and nightingales and whirling dervishes, chantings of
Tibetan monks and cries of Chinese mandarins with great butterfly
sleeves rippling in the wind and screaming contests of Platan rails like
the human voice exerted to its utmost pitch and cries of tree locusts
lighting like stars in distant starlight, songs of the living and of the dead,
Greek and Persian, cries of the cock in a Moorish courtyard, songs of the
birds in windy gardens, songs of the silence more beautiful than any
sound she heard, and there were moods in which she could hear anything
she wished to hear, simply by turning her head, a leaf falling on the other
side of this planet, perhaps where no other leaf should ever fall, the
raspings of a window shutter blown monotonously in the wind in a
distant city, that which she perhaps had never visited. For a person of her
presumed illiteracy and lack of a formal education, that which should
have been given to one in her exalted social sphere and higher walks of
life—she knowing only tennis, as she still complained, as if it were she
who had driven the sun against the clouded net, stopping time—her
knowledge was magnificent, astounding her by its brilliance—for who
else had talked to so many water carriers in clouds, boatsmen of star
boats, a rider in the great Coffin of Stars passing with darkened lights
over this watery world like the herring fleet upon the dark waves where
silver fishes slept flashing their lights, and who else had talked to voices
buzzing like bees in Magellanic Clouds, so many pharaohs in swan boats
passing with the sentinel moon around the earth?

Who but that forlorn suffrage Troubadour with his streaming silver
curls could have taught my mother these dead languages and languages
of the immortal past, including many languages for which there was no
written or spoken word? Doubtless they were the true. How else should
the opium lady have learned anything more, for example, than a tourist's
French or Italian spoken by some old boatman singing like a nightingale
or cries of street Arabs among the windy horses or Boston Greek, and how
should she be this human Tower of Babel? Though she had travelled
widely in the years before her marriage to a phantom, she had always
required a skilled interpreter, no matter with whom she spoke, and his
message was so often blurred in transit, just as a thought is changed by
speech. Perhaps the most important thoughts were those which never
found expression. She must have learned these many tongues after her
travels were over—by watching, with fixed attention, the old creature's
asymmetric face and changing facial expressions in a darkened mirror,
the pride and fury of her eloquent gestures as she had urged that my
mother should ride against the king of the Medes—or else how could it
be that now, even after so many years of the great captain's absence, my
mother limpidly understood, as if no time had ever passed, the language
of bawling Alcibiades, that drunken war lord whose alcoholism was forever opposed, as she believed, to her opium dreams which were inflated
or small as a sand grain glittering in the fog, Alexander the Great, King
of Macedon, he who had discovered a new star at the edge of space, the
bird king whose head was turned backward upon his shoulders that he
might see where he had flown, the rabbit king with his ears above the

starlight, many who were kings before Christ and many who came afterward, Boethius, Balboa, Baldwin, Christolpho Colombo who had sailed to extend the boundaries of the known world, Canovas del Castillo, he who wore a mask and was not known to his love, Hugh Capet who had arisen from his watery grave, who came with his grave clothes wrapped around him and seaweed wound in his hair, ageless Dante, revolutionary Diderot, Harold Harefoot, any other visitor from the realm of the dead, that she listened for hours to Ahaseuris, the Wandering Jew or, as she preferred to think of him, the Everlasting Jew, that she listened for hours to Hebrew parables in palaces of red sandalwood or heard sandpipers? When she pulled a bellrope, there was a king. How else could she hear now, merely by turning her head or pulling a bellrope, the street cries of undiscovered desert cities, tinkling bells and many horns in faraway Cathay or Boston, a thousand voices speaking with each other all over the world? How else could she communicate now so easily with Darius the Magnificent, who so often answered the telephone when she called to the kitchen to ask why the service was so slow? Or perhaps she heard the sleepy voice of Potiphar.

My mother did not wish to imply, of course, that venturesome Cousin Hannah, a soul given over utterly to the establishment of justice on earth, had spoken only these foreign tongues, inasmuch as doubtless she had wished to be understood in a way to leave no gilded aura of doubt in my mother's wandering, dreaming mind which, brilliant as star flashes, was irresolute at the moment of decision as if she might always turn and go upon some other road. Cousin Hannah had also spoken the King's English, of course. Naturally, for she had been a member of one of the finest families of the Old Guard, a beacon of suffrage.

She had employed many a picturesque oath as might be expected of an old veteran of the cavalry suffering from increasing debilities as passion increased—my mother still hearing, as she recalled these phantasmal visits which might as well have been made by a fox-hunter as an army officer, such words as zounds, God's wounds, hounds, egad, by God, caitiff, craven, coward, defender of the faith, halloo, halloo, halloo, tallyho still ringing in her ears—and the wind howling among the cypress trees blown to the weird, pollarded shapes of animals, griffins and eagles with silver-lighted eyes. Or maybe she was awakened by a voice crying—Avaunt, villains, knaves, blackamoors, blackbirds, Boanerges—and it was only her own voice which she had heard in her sleep and which had awakened her. Sometimes she thought she was both the fox-hunter and the fox.

How, after so many inchoate years in which she had followed her own wavering inclinations like sunken stars, could she be expected to remember the sequences of those states of fact or being which had occurred without consecutiveness, not as an order of events in time, wave after superficial wave, not succeeding or following each other as a result of what had gone before—but the medley, the imbroglio, Pandemonium, Saturnalia of her deranged imagination, convention of sundials marking different hours, just as she recognized though holding herself superior to circumstance or place or person, whether dolphin or drowned king drag-ging his purple robe or net of stars in which he was caught? My mother had never been able to regulate rank and order as at a feast, to direct the order of processional as at a funeral. For things were so likely to turn topsy-turvy around her—and a step forward would be a step backward, and the king's valet would take precedence over the king, or the after-clap preceded the thunder, and the after-glow came before the sunset, and the echo came before the song, and the death came before the life, and the after-image came before the image in her brain, and the first star came at noon. And there were so many refractions, oblique passages from one medium of being into another, occultations as when a star crossed the moon, and counter-clockwise movements which were also out of time and illogical, filled with those moments which were unforeseen as if they had not been. There was apparently no more logic in retrospect than there was in the fleeting present tense. In fact, there was no total way of knowing what might have happened if one listened to my mother's irre-sponsible memories or her momentary impressions now of time which never was.

There had been quite a din, certainly, and the dark birds singing in the bushy trees—though my mother might have been unsure, at all times, of the import, English being, as it was the one language she really knew, the only foreign language to her, as she would frequently remark—and maybe Daniel Boone, wearing his coonskin hat, talking sign language, had just stridden across this mortal stage, and that would be quite normal. They enjoyed many silent conversations pertaining to his dis-coveries in the American wilderness and to the life of the oppossum which, when caught, feigns death, the sleep of death which is neither sleep nor death. When Boone came, there were also a great many mur-muring pigeons, though perhaps they were the ubiquitous pigeons of St. Mark's Square, for my mother could not easily tell as she subsided into sleep. She was struck by moon blindness, that inflammation generally affecting, as she knew, not the eyes of the rider but the eyes of the horse. She heard the angelus, the sweepings of angelic wings through golden clouds. As for Boone, she had always found him most open-minded, receptive to her ideas and impressions—and why not, for were they both not dwellers in this untamed wilderness? Or maybe, of course, there had been an emperor's riding party hunting the unicorn through silver glades, or someone had just sighted the fox. Or a fat lady riding a horse had taken a hawthorn hedge by slow motion leaving a wake of phosphorous.

There had always been, in fact, just such competition for my mother's attention, even when, long ago, she had entertained, perhaps before the memory of any living person, a living guest. Perhaps her greater distinction was that she had entertained balloonists who had not been sighted for years, horse heads in drifting clouds, lutenists who had known Mozart who had not known them, harpists harping on a sea of glass. For my mother, her head roaring with perpetual dreams, had been so easily turned aside and might so easily have been mistaken, hearing other voices, the church bells tolling in a distant valley, the snowslides over the city roofs, or whisperings as faint as the whisperings of leaves in the surf blown upon another glassy star, moths flying toward her mirror. Sometimes, with a serene unconcern for facts, as was well known—as Mr. Spitzer, believing himself to be non-competitive, had so frequently observed—she would introduce the living among the dead—assuming that, though a person was still among the living, sentient and breathing, his heart beating in his breast, his heart beating in his cheek, his forehead, he had already passed over to the other shore, whether of darkness or of light—had already furled his sail for the long anchorage—for it was not only as to herself that she made this great mistake. And after all, as Mr. Spitzer might patiently wonder, what anachronism could there possibly be in the realm of the dead? If one waited long enough, all things would be true, or so it had often seemed to him, pulling the jowl of his cheek, tapping his teeth with a toothpick which was a tiny diamond-headed gold walking stick, waiting all his life here to prove that he no longer lived, that he had died long ago.

Who else should know, when my mother was gone, the dead social season, the dead customs, the dead capital cities, the dead horses, the dead jockeys, the dead soil, the dead trees, the sterile and barren hills, those states which were as certain, as complete, as irrelievable as death, lacking all color, fire, glow, luster, tang, all sensation, all memory, more quiet than the most death-like time of the year, and yet returning as if there were no death? Almost all returned. And when my mother was gone, she with her tinkling airs like ice prisms breaking in sun-lit clouds filled with the haloes of absent moons, her vapors and romances and veiled looks, who should live in this closed, empty house, move through the still rooms, hear his echoing footsteps? What firefly should remember her? Who should meet a mandarin upon the stairway climbing through a many-pinnacled cloud? Who should meet a horseman in the hall or fording a dark stream, the horse neighing when he saw the spirits in the waters? A horse knew what the horseman did not know. Who should play tennis upon the ruined courts under the winged, flying moon passing over this cinder world? She was many selves, many beautiful, volatile Psyches wandering about—and she was lying in bed, propped up among satin pillows with space wound around her like a satin bolt, combing her hair in a psyche knot—and should she be stilled who greeted every friend as a stranger, every stranger as a friend or a cousin? Indeed, one of the reasons for her retirement from the world had been her habit of greeting every stranger as a friend or relative. Ah, Cousin Jack, she had used to say to any great prime minister she had never seen before—did you have a good crossing?—or turning her head when the wind blew—Cousin Wilbur, I thought you went down in the boat, that you sank beneath the waves, that you were lost in the great hurricane—so that she had gone to bed to save herself from further social embarrassments. Then she had begun to speak where there was no one. Perhaps Cousin Hannah's prowess, too, my mother thought, had not been physical, of or pertaining to the nature of this created existence, to the body as contrasted with the mind —perhaps all the vanished suffragette's most startling adventures had been in a realm not of this reality, for perhaps she had dreamed as my mother was dreaming, and who should know when the dream ended? Who should know when, where, why, how, to whom?

And why should my mother, though she stayed at home and was surrounded by her illusions like walls of glass and saw few visitors in reality, few who were flesh and blood and imaginative sentience, certainly few of the beau monde, envy any other globe-trotter, no matter how distinguished or stained by miraculous travels and adventures in foreign lands—unless, of course, it was herself she envied, herself who had escaped from her, this fatal beauty in a darkened bedroom, here with a dead rose in her hand, a darkened mirror and a rose, herself who wandered like a breath, a spirit, a shade, disembodied except for a dream, herself or many lost selves who wandered through the world, not only the known world but the unknown world which she knew so very well because no one knew the unknown? She did not know the known. Indeed, if one had no knowledge, should one not have freedom to imagine all the colors of the mind, even this perfect vitality, these dreams that came after one's death? And when they vanished, fading like spirits into the air, nothingness did not succeed. All things were merged into one another, were merged as a cloud, were lost, were indistinct—and life was that which, as it had had no beginning, should have no end, not even this death, my mother dreamed. I am dead—had not old Cousin Hannah always whispered, even when she was vitally alive, the beau ideal of suffrage, the flames burning in the empty eyeholes of her eyes? And had my mother been called upon to prove her dreams, that they were dead or that they lived or that they were inextricably confused, that they were real, my mother would have crumbled into crystal dust, the dust returning always to the dust as the stars fluttered downward into the convex pole of the heavens—though the dust was ever that which should reassemble into new and beautiful forms, so strangely like the old, even like an episode or summary which should be forever incomplete, for there should be a slight variation, a departure from the past, a change, a chance, a minuscular difference even without the necessity of death. Suffrage had required cloud-rack and storm, clouds like lace curtains blown in the wind. Suffrage had not required the eternal darkness unlighted by one star or spark.

There were angels in all the angles—non angli sei angeli—angels on all the irregular roofs. There were flying buttresses like angelic wings. My mother's mind was an iridescent jumble of all those thoughts she had not thought, all those dreams she had not dreamed but had lived through easeful death—and that was why she did not know what time, what place it was, why she would probably never know, yet though she knew. Nothing could be explained except in this way—ignotum per ignotius—the unknown by the still more unknown, the mystery turning on the mystery. Nor did she seem to wish to try to correct, in any genuine way, her errors—or imagine that there should be a golden mean between extremes, a sound mind in a sound body, a cure for nature's imperishable ills. Such an idea, if it had ever occurred to her, had been put away. It could not be said that she had lost her faith because of some great debacle or storm destroying at one blow the reality of simple days. She had had no faith to lose, so change had followed change, and chance had followed chance. Three o'clock had followed twelve o'clock. Aeons had transpired between the first bell of the clock striking twelve and the twelfth bell. There had usually been two or three other bells. There was always a person occupying the place of another. There was always a charmed substitute, a flight away from the heart of life into that realm where death itself was doubtful, a matter of definition and not of fact. Had not opium caused her somnolence—but what kind of explanation was this, returning upon itself as if the truth were mighty and would prevail? Had not her somnolence been the cause of her taking opium and various drugs, distillations, elixirs, essences, for had she not always been, even before her succumbing to this fatal drug habit by gradual degrees, the errant somnambulist, the sleep-walker who, walking in her sleep, would have walked out of a window in a cloud above the topless cliffs or walked into the roaring, silent sea of dreams where all should change? Perhaps she had done so—but who would ever know if that were true? Would the sheathbills have told? Would the ruddy turnstones have betrayed her secret? Would the stormy petrels have answered? Would the turreted sea shells have known, crawling along the beach where the waves roared and rolled? Would anyone have known if reality was missing? And had she not disappeared, as she would sometimes ask, crying out in an opium dream of many dimensions, many clouds—where was she now? Who would ever find that lost lady walking through silver-slippered rain as the winds blew, the winds whirling through her foaming skirts?

She imagined that she possessed ubiquity which caused her confusion, that which did possess her, twenty resemblances of herself appearing in twenty places as if she were that wild image reflected upon twenty crystal glasses—perhaps all in the same room—yet each being so possessed by her total soul and dreaming, rapturous mind that she could not tell which was her true self and which was her reflection upon a warped mirror or cloud or star, whether she was herself or a chimera blown upon the wind—for she was the heron's blue eye in the moon-lit cloud—and sometimes she thought she was riding on her own back, one image being mounted upon another in such a way that she did not know whether she was the horse or the rider, the carrier or the carried. A rider on a bicycle was to her one entity, the rider and the bicycle being as one consciousness, even as were the harpist and the harp. She could not imagine the pianist without the keyboard. The four horses drawing her carriage could not be unharnessed, nor could the coachman descend from his box in the altitudinous cloud, for horses and coach and coachman were one entity passing through the rolling fog—and if they should be disassembled, they should be like the psychological explanation of that mystery which could never be explained. There was no place, but there were all places dreaming together, flowing like water into each other. All was water. The water flowed over the mooned sand. The sentinels slept at the shifting border-lands. The doors opened before she knocked. Many years after she could travel no more, she heard the coachman's whip like the dark tree branches whirling, scraping in the wind as the great, toothed clouds scudded along the sky, the long-bodied coach dogs barking at the wheels, the turning wheels of spokes which were the sleeping seraphim. As between the figurehead and the greatest captain of the greatest boat, as to which knew more of waves and surf and storm, my mother believed that the figurehead knew more, the waters roaring at its mouth. For one thing, it always went first.

CHAPTER 41

So MY mother travelled toward distant cities, or they travelled toward her with finger minarets breaking through foam and cloud, mosaic emperors. For after death, she still experienced implausible sensation, and life was guided by the eyes, the ears, the senses every one, the conspiracy of the uncommon senses. There was no difference between life and death, she always would insist, or only an infinitesimal difference, perhaps only a hair's breadth or wandering spray of foam or sand grain, a difference which could never be resolved. Who should know a greater danger than hers? Did the dead know, or did the living know? Her spirit moved through all her body's winding channels, cried at all the doors and windows, the chinks of this corpse. Her spirit departed from the lady. Her spirit moved and lived outside of her, even now, going by many ways upon many errands, unnecessary errands in the void, and she did not know how many selves there were which came and went. Perhaps one of them would never return, she guessed. The one which did not return would be the immortal one. The immortal one would be the lost. Absence was not necessarily the same as death. Day after day, sometimes in the night, she would count her innumerable, heavy pearls, heavy as supernumerary planets in seas of clouds—when she had counted them all, as she would sometimes say, counting her pearls again, she would be lost. Sunt lacrimae rerum. But her tears were never for persons. To her, a human personality was a mere appearance, like a shadow upon the water.

Sometimes she had passed beyond her various conflicting points of view and was quite lost, lost to vision—therefore, all-seeing, seeing everything at a glance, even in a sudden flash as of lightning, all the torrential stars which blinded her with their unholy brilliance, the boat going like a moth before the flood cascading from heaven to earth. For to see all things would be to see nothing. One lost one's sense of perspective, one's sense of direction, going in two ways at once, perhaps returning on one's self. One lost one's magnetic sense, such as migratory birds are perhaps guided by, finding their way above the clouds when the earth and all familiar landmarks have disappeared.

How should my mother's interests not be divided and scattered, for was she not interested in everything, both in symmetry and asymmetry, asylum and freedom, the bright-eyed and the dull-eyed, the beau ideal and the unprepossessing, hard-featured, misshapen, ill-proportioned, crooked, distorted, cadaverous, gruesome, horrifying monster? Was she not interested in both those who were spotted and those who were unspotted, those who were beautiful and those who were disfigured, even as she was? And she would sometimes try to cover her blemishes with beauty spots, hoping thus not merely to conceal her imaginary blemishes but to heighten the ineffable beauty of her face by contrast. She looked like a domino. Quite often, her white face was covered with black patches among the blown shadows.

Perhaps, dreaming in her swan boat which navigated waters and clouds, she imagined she was walking through a blinding snow storm, that which made the world so unearthly white, and the tree branches white as snow, and she was naked except for her jewels, her pearls and diamond chandeliers, and yet she was not physically cold. The snow was warm as fire. The snow was streaked with opalescent blue and green and gold, burning with interior light like skin which shows the pulsing of the fire within. Surely, she had gone on foot—for one foot moved before the other foot—and she danced at the edge of the abyss—or, suddenly whirling, moved away from it and the clouded floor lighted by fire, by these reflections. There would be little doubt in her mind that, though she had not walked for so many years that she would sometimes ask where her feet were—as some other lady might ask for her gloves, her hat—yet she was walking, quite naked, through a world of snow, for she could see her footprints in the snow—the tiniest footprints imaginable. Perhaps they were the footprints of the drugged snow birds, ciphers by which she might find herself again when she was lost. Or they were the footprints of the snowy, long-limbed cranes who, with their wings folded around them, stepped for a moment on new peninsulas in the clouds. Or they were the footprints of the snow-white whetsaw owls, hooded birds as tiny as white robins in the snow, hooded birds with tiny, owlish, human faces, and they stared at her from a dark tree bough with a bony human hand like that of some old scarecrow. There were footprints everywhere, and she thought that they were hers. Perhaps they were the footprints in the snow banks, perhaps in the twinkling clouds not to be distinguished from the earth. Perhaps they were the footprints of the sharp-eyed, sharp-nosed, long-tailed weasels, the footprints of the secretive gophers who live under the earth in their honeycomb passages like cities of the dead and seldom emerge and are seldom or never seen like the spirits of the resurrected dead. Perhaps the gophers came out of their graves, too, just as my mother emerged, lifting her hood. They were the pocket gophers with large cheek pouches and bright, sharp rodent eyes. She saw the gopher citizens. They saw her, this beautiful lady wandering through snow and wind edged with pale medieval lace whispering like billows of surf upon a distant glassy shore, her hair whitening as the snow fell, the snowflakes falling around her as her eyelashes froze like the long eyelashes of many-faceted stars in winter clouds.

Perhaps she saw the footprints of the groundhogs who emerged on Candlemas Day to see if winter was over and, as they saw their shadows on eternal snow, returned to their hiding places under the ground. Perhaps she saw the footprints of the rabbits going down to the frozen brook, the rabbits wearing lace veils and silver petticoats, walking upright, going everywhere she went through the whirling snow winding around her like a shell. She saw their pink eyes in the dying light. Sometimes a great rabbit came and talked to her of Caesar's campaign and the War of the Roses, mad Antony's love or Helen of Troy.

For my somnolent mother did not move, was always in the same place, and thus no one really knew where she was. She spoke of a vast continent, a shoreless sea, a moving cloud which dazzled her. She spoke of voices which no one else ever heard—as of train whistles where no trains were, trembling harp strings, music of city bridges in yesterday's wind, doors slamming on another star, carriage wheels grinding on pebbles on other stars, nightmarish voices bringing with them the bodies of dead loves, silent loves which spoke to her. She spoke of echoes bouncing off a star, a mirror. She complained, raved, ranted, raged, whistled, shouted, great bells like tides gonging in her forehead, a comet entering her foot, a bee buzzing in her cheek, a night bird whistling in her ear, a starfish scraping a lost string or chord. She complained that she was lost inside her ear and could not get out. She was lost among these roarings like a great sea beating upon no known shore of darkness or of light. She was lost in this wilderness of whispers, echoes, winding sea shells.

The ear, my mother said, was that great continent no one had ever completely known or understood, and no one had ever completely explored, and Aristotle had said that the ear was the doorway to the soul. My mother was lost for years and years inside her ear, trying to find her way out, out of this vast continent where there were so many doors and porticoes and fallen columns, secret arcades and weird deserts of stone, so many vast, trembling lakes and mirrors and reflections of clouds, so many mirroring ballrooms and trembling chords and grand pianos played upon by waves of haunted sound, grand pianos upon ledges of stone, thousands and ten thousands of piano keys of black and white moving like the surf of consciousness in the long, sighing wind, so many wind harps and harp strings and lyre birds, coral reefs lapped by waves and undiscovered seas and starfish shoals, vistas of clouds and endless city roofs with chalk-white human faces, silvery marsh lands and cries of the lost reed birds stirring among the reeds inside the ear, cries of the white loons above the salt flats like sunken stars, train whistles and foghorns, awakening echoes and echoes of echoes, reverberations and tremblings and hollow, sepulchral voices, voices crying in marble tombs, voices without bodies and sounds without sense and dead sounds and old dogs barking at lonely tides or shadows and multiple insect buzzings, whirrings of papery wasp wings, songs of silent moths upon a silent flood, snorings and howlings and brayings, neighings of wild horses and brass winds, so many valleys of the moon and seas of echoes, crazy chimney pots and slate roofs, cracked bells and church steeples and muffled trumpets, dark porte-cocheres, spiraling sea shells, great mouthed conches moving in the whispering tide, dark rivers and innumerable stone steps and turnings and windings, paths never returning upon themselves even when they return, paths through this lost eternity, this madness which was this ear where she was lost. And who would not be confused if he was lost inside his amplified ear as she was?

There were many lost chords, wandering echoes, flute notes, many looms of trembling sound. There were a great many people talking in an empty chamber, talking to each other or to no one. There were some who talked to her. She awakened to the sound of ten thousand tiny silver door-bells ringing against the music of a dark tide. There were many scream-ing, human-sized sparrow hawks, their contorted apparitions in dim mir-rors, stars which had wandered off their courses, stars like candle flames singing in the wind.

She would scream and cry, though no one heard her—or rather, no one paid attention—Let me out of my ear! Let me out of my ear! My God, she cried—is there no silence? How did I get inside my ear in the first place? Where is the door?

Indeed, she was lost, walking up and down stairways inside her ear. There were so many winding paths and great stone walls like the walls of China, so many towers she could not count. There were many over-hanging rocks and wild, fantastic faces, stalagmites and stalactites and hollow, echoing rooms. She had come to a cul-de-sac. She had come to a great saddle rock. She had come to the great cliffs overhanging the silent purple sea, purple and clouded and undiscovered. So no wonder if she felt like Balboa discovering the Pacific Ocean, as she many times remarked—seeing far away one white sail. Perhaps, however, she had taken the night train to a distant city, and she was going to the first night of the opera in a perpetual first night. It was always possible. She was dining at the Ritz.

For some of her dreams were almost normal, a mere matter of rou-tine, it would always seem to those who knew her best and lived in her atmosphere in this old, amazing house where were so many invisible servants to wait on her, so many invisible spirits with audible voices. And who should ever wish to abandon and forsake human nature's propensity to dream? Who should wish to do so unless he should be the maddest man of all, a tornado of self-deceit? Who should wish to flee away from his dreams unless he should flee to death, another dream which should be perhaps the extension of this or very different? Who should escape this house? For sometimes it seemed that the house with its turrets and towers and porches moved in the night, moved to another place, and perhaps it was set down in a strange, dead city where no one had ever been before, and there were no voices in the streets, and yet my mother heard voices. Had she not known great miracles, even that this great, sea-blackened house should move in the night from place to place as the tide roared? Did not the furniture sometimes change—the mirrors hanging lopsided on the walls, the chairs moving in their places, the marble statues flying off their pedestals? Did not the windows look out upon a different sea or a different street? We all knew these changes in the night, and we should have grown as accustomed to them as to the sound of the wind. Had not my mother made walls to speak, oceans to freeze, nights to endure or not endure, mountains to dissolve into singing like the mountain brooks? Was she not like a drill sergeant commanding her thoughts, martialing her resources in ways which should have caused the amazement of vanquished Cousin Hannah? Then what should be so strange, so unaccustomed if, instead of moving the house, my mother should decide to go to New York by train and leave the house where it was, here by the black sea? Indeed, was there anything essentially wrong with her taking the night train from Boston to New York, sitting up all night, riding second class, watching the station lights which passed like dim stars, the muffled, hooded station-masters swinging their blurred lamps which were the stars? So that the heavens should be disarranged? Why should anyone think this journey odd? Should it even call for a comment? She travelled, but she never moved.

Yet why, she herself might ask, should this night train pass through the snow-crowned Alpine mountains where were these great shoulders of snow, the frozen pinnacles in starlight, the buried castles with lights flashing at their windows, the sunless valleys, and why should this night train pass through so many little cuckoo clock Swiss villages, all singing cuckoo, so many steaming mists rolling like snow combers—if she was only going, as she supposed, from Boston to New York, a familiar route which she knew so well, she could have predicted every station or every other station—and why should this night train, though the run was short, only a bobsled's run, pass through the unknowable reaches of the frozen great Gobi Desert where was no railway, no head light but a star, no engineer of consciousness, and why should all these beautiful horsemen be riding along with her, their black feathers flying in the wind, and knives between their teeth? And who were these courageous brigands following her? Were they following her or the nowhere train? And was one of these banditti, by any chance, the opium lady still would sometimes ask, old Cousin Hannah, an apostate from her great cause which had been the death of the world, one whose face my mother ought to recognize, even in a dream, or was my mother's only a fugitive dream of incarnation when the body had ceased, when stability was quite impossible? And why all these great trestles and busy streets and asphalt highways, these many iron bridges, the flashing neon lights, and why should this night train pass through so many cities where were no lights and where my mother had never visited before, where now she was? Why was everybody sleeping? Who were these sleeping sentinels? Who were these great feathered bipeds perched upon the chimneys?

Yet no matter where my mother went, no matter upon how many mysterious journeys, some of which were blurred as if they had not been, she would return just as she departed, so that her goings and comings seemed, rather than separate events in time and space, simultaneities, for hers were many coexistences, and thus her absence was not noticed by those in charge of her. Perhaps they also would not notice her absence from the world. Besides, she made so many self-contradictory remarks, gave so many impossible orders which they could not carry out

unless there should be greater havoc than even she imagined, as if Newfoundland should suddenly be New England or New England should be
Newfoundland with seals upon this coast and only a few old Tory refu-
gees with powdered perukes and crinolines who had come with the wild
geese and were waiting for Washington to fall. Others noticed only her
pallor, her low pulse, or a sudden rise of temperature. They were stupid,
or they were stupified by darkness and cold. In any event, though perhaps believing when they first came here that she could improve her ways
if only she would change her mind and get herself upon some other path,
perhaps new and untried, employ new tactics, new approaches to life,
they gradually and ultimately believed with Mr. Joachim Spitzer that the
antidote would be worse than the poison. The antidote would kill her as
the poison never had. The antidote would kill the triple moons, the
wandering sun gods with their golden feathers, their fetlocks washed by
waves.

Her wounds were, moreover, unlike those of her attendants, never
visible, and were quite beautifully concealed, and the alterations of her
moods would never really seem to alter her or leave the mark of time.
Another change was surely always possible. She could so easily be off on
some new flight or prospect. Was she going? Was she coming? Was she
staying? Was she within doors? Was she out of doors? She would return,
even from another world. She would manage somehow her intricate,
secret escape even when it seemed impossible. How should she guard her
bridges or lower, over the mystical doorway of this great castle, her port-
cullis, a grating of iron through which the light should still filter, showing a more extensive world, that which, though it should not be of this
world, though it should exist only by associations floating in a shadowed
atmosphere, yet should have its celestial and infernal regions, spirits
riding upon the gales, spirits who should never recognize a wall or a
closed door or an empty room? For her environment so rapidly shifted,
even while never changing—one could vaguely sense these changes, a
change of altitude or temperature, a sudden freeze or flurry of snow, an
iceberg breaking, burning like the interior of a star, a dark cloud passing
the face of the moon. Did she not cause the snow to fall in summer? Her
seasons were not necessarily of this world, and her glorious clocks kept no
time, it was always pointed out. Did she not control the luminosity of the
stars, the watt power? Did she not control the turning water wheels? Had
she not built great bridges, often with only a sigh?

Was she not mechanical, a great engineer, a great mathematical
genius who, if her mathematics had been accurate, should have succeeded
in the manufacturing industry in a way to elicit nothing but admiration?
Would not her own father have faded beside these brilliant gifts, these
cataclysmic moods which were like these many windlasses and engines
running by themselves? Did she not direct the winds, the unseasonal
gales, the great tornadoes which blew us all apart, and did not her
lighthouse send its beams over the dark waters? Did she not build great
cities of minarets and phaetons in lands which had been unpopulated,
where only the raven had spoken? The raven had flown with a golden

book between its hands. Were not the creatures of the beach her servants? Had she not made a man into a tortoise with stars upon his back? Had she not commanded the waves to rise or whistle or be still, and had they not obeyed at one time or another her commands? She believed that these were all her powers—she was not impotent and lonely though so far removed from life, and whirlwinds whistled with voices at her approach. She had caused the lories capsized at the low, glassy tide to right themselves when the tides came in, to ride upon the dream floods like every soul going down to its estuary. She had caused the drowned schooners to rise, spreading their white wings upon the waves. She had caused old figureheads to rise and plow the waves, the waters flowing over their eyes. She had raised the spectral dead and caused the dead to walk through snow and whirling foam, sunlight and shadow under the pale sky. Like furies of the avenging ghost, the same corpse returned forever and forever with the tide. She had illuminated the dark lands of shadows and shadow shapes.

At least, in our old house, most people would seem to agree with these miracles, for there were few people or none who remembered the outside world, the world where my mother was not and had not been for so many years that now it seemed as if her dreams were not the substitute for reality—they were the only reality there was. For it was true, as must be finally conceded, perhaps by everyone except herself—she could not walk. She only thought she walked, for she was this sleeping lady. She was forever stretched out like a clouded horizon. She was forever prone, and she only thought she was like one of the marble pillars upholding the roof of a tomb. All that could transpire had already transpired, surely, long ago. There would be little change. There would never be another sorrow. There would never be another love.

Pallida morte futura. One could see that she was pale, pale, pale as death under the lace canopy of the pale, clouded sky, for she had outdistanced herself so many times in tempting death, it would seem that one day, even from the point of view of Mr. Spitzer who believed himself to be the incorrigible optimist, she would not come back, and he would not find her again, and he would not come back, but she always came as if her journeys had not been far, not nearly so far as his. Perhaps she was the whirlpool, but she was also the still center at the heart of the whirlpool. She drew toward this center all bodies which could not resist the beauty of passivity. She was everywhere and nowhere. She was a star burning under water, a night flame burning in a glass. If one spoke, she did not hear, even if one announced his coming, even if one blew a trumpet opening the heavens, for she heard a silent voice. So great was this pressure she felt, like waves and mountains roaring over her head. There were stone lions roaring in this room.

Her hair was wildly streaming across her brightly shadowed eyes, and her mind was unhinged, an old door swinging in the wind, and her thoughts were dislocated, a cosmography like nothing known on earth, perhaps like nothing known in heaven, a complex pattern of dreams winding on dreams which none should untangle, even like the tangled skeins of the sorrows of her mind which she imagined as dwelling in her aching breasts and in her heavy limbs. How often had she not complained—nature was unknitting her? How often had she not complained —nature had been unkind to her, an immortal beauty none had ever loved? No mortal had lived long enough. She was restless, even though she rested. She wandered, even though she was still. She was fixated for years on the idea that she had swallowed the blue divan with the golden lion hooves and wings and triple golden crowns, so that she could not get through the door, wide though it was, wide enough to admit a long-haired star. Sometimes she said that the blue divan was rose, sometimes that it was mauve—though the color could be told by the color pulsing under her skin. She complained for years that she was the door through which she passed or could not pass.

Poor mother, dreaming her life away like this as if there were no other life! She should have been quite sad, for she had swallowed so many door knobs which should have been apples, and she had opened so many mystical doors of wisdom, and that was why she did not know where she was going at all times, why one step did not follow another step. She believed, however, that she would some day die, and then she would be happy, divinely happy, for then she would have found a key to the door. She would have found a keyhole, perhaps only a keyhole in a cloud. She would rave on and on like this, sometimes talking to a darkened mirror, a dying candle flame, a wandering fish with flashing fins. One could see that, with all her marvels around her, with all her legions of inexhaustible resources, yet she was, just as she complained, almost exhausted, that her imagination might perish before she perished, that she might suffer a rude awakening from this eternal sleep—and then who should she be, and where should she be? And who should ever find her? For what form would she have taken? Perhaps, though the prospect seemed impossible, there should be that future life which has no knowledge of the past continuing into the future. My mother always thought that if one should ever reach another planet, one should find that there were already upon that other planet a mirror, a rose, a door, a mystery.

For Mr. Joachim Spitzer was not tragic, she believed, though he suffered from the vast reaches of unrequited love as from the most delicate instances of that love which was not returned, that love which was itself illusion, less than the fabric of her dreams, and though he was this mourner for the impossible dead, and though her estimate of his tragedy had often sorrowed him, diminishing him in his own sad eyes, for he had supposed that it was in the magnitude of tragedy that he had excelled. Could she have acknowledged his tragedy which he had acknowledged, he would have been less sad, perhaps triumphant that she had finally recognized him as the unique individual he was. He would have known his identity. Rather, to her, even as he reluctantly knew, for she had taunted him with his inadequacy so many times and had reproached him for his continued life, he with his perpetually broken heart, broken if not yet pulverized by grief, not yet reduced to stardust, must seem slightly humorous, even ridiculous, as exaggerated sorrow must always seem when it has outlived itself or any true emotion or focal point, when there is no longer necessity of feeling what one feels, when there is nothing, no new impulse, no new disappointment to increase that sorrow and give to it the dignity of the present moment. He did his best to keep his sorrow alive. He was like a man who, having made one mistake, must make it again and again for the rest of his life—perhaps knocking forever at the wrong door—and thus making many other mistakes, each more comprehensive than the last—simply to show that he had not been wrong in the first place, that he deliberately did now what he once might have done without intention, perhaps in an unconscious moment or perhaps prompted by a prompter off stage or ghostly music falling from clouds. Mr. Spitzer seemed almost to be imitating himself, perhaps not too successfully as there were those imitations of which the original was never quite known. How be certain what that voice had said or when?

As to these interweaving twins, it seemed to my mother that the suicide Peron, though smiling when he should have wept, most remarkably smiling when he should have smiled, smiling at my mother's protracted grief for him and for his sudden end, his violent death for which there had been no preparation in her mind, had exceeded pale Joachim in his capacity for melancholy—for Peron had killed himself by jumping from the tallest building in a cloud as a star flashed, as a train whistled. My mother did not believe that happy people terminated their lives nor even their happiness, nor could she agree with Mr. Spitzer that they lived to grieve in memory of themselves. Really, she could be quite maddeningly reasonable at the most unexpected moments, surprising everybody by her brilliance, even herself with her opaque mind. Her acumen, especially several years after an event, was astonishing to her, eliciting many remarks and seldom her silence. Besides, sometimes the event had not yet taken place as there was no time, no perspective. There were only shifting sands in starlight and wind.

As to that brave corsair of suffrage who, oblivious to my mother's pleadings, came no more storming at these ivory gates, roaring through these empty rooms, there had been no tragedy in her life or in her death, which had been quite natural, my mother had supposed—there had been only a few tragic scandals blown upon the winds of sorrow but no core of fact, nothing which could be proved. There had been only a few whispering voices in clouds, voices like icicles breaking in wind, like whistling snow geese. And how translate what these voices uttered? My mother always would insist that Cousin Hannah's life, just like her own, had been largely imaginary, transient, unknown, unexplored, passing like a dream. She, too, had left no path where she had travelled. She, too, had disappeared in snow clouds and sand storms—though perhaps my mother had never really known her, had never seen her, for she had given her attention only to wandering shades and sparks of light or the great faces looming through fogs. Yet how inept that great pyramidal lady seemed now in retrospect, pitiful as is all strength which turns to weakness, and how should action differ from meditation? Perhaps my mother had never really known anyone, not even that old suffragette who, having no feminine defenses or offensives, unable to blush if she lost her skirt, unable to stagger or lean upon an escort's arm, unable to faint, unable to swoon away into unconsciousness or sleep for years even if she saw the greatest Moor or the great turban-winder unwinding his turban in the clouds over the city, unable to cry out for help, unable to do battle with a fan, a seductive look, a flirtatious wink, had gone to her grave in a forgotten year, perhaps long before my mother knew her. For how could she know what time or sorrow was, they being concepts of existence as alien to her as if she had lived outside of time and beyond sorrow, they being all she had ever denied? The years collapsed to a moment whenever my mother looked back. She could not tell whether a thing had been a star or a firefly. She was so irresponsible, not even Mr. Spitzer's corrective conscience assisting her. Perhaps that was why Cousin Hannah changed so much in that memory which gave no report of the living world.

And as for my mother, she had kept herself, at all costs, vastly amused, sacrificing her life to her amusements, just as she remarked when she thought of the infinite sorrows she had missed. Any criticism of my mother's life must take into account, she herself had always said and Mr. Spitzer agreed, this sorrowful fact, the lack of sorrow. The lack of sorrow was a sorrow, too. She had always used to think so when she had used to see old Cousin Hannah riding her white horse through a cloud—that the great captain had paid a price for her lack of sorrow and lack of human love, her isolation from the heart of life. She, too, had paid her toll for that which never was. Though always engaged in a great struggle like that of self-forgetfulness, perhaps she had not succeeded so well as my mother had succeeded. Perhaps Cousin Hannah had been more vulnerable to the arrows of chance than my mother had been.

Perhaps my mother had led what might not be considered, from the strictest, most unsympathetic point of view, a fearless and an honest life. She was like a person who, in a bare room, imagines many things, chairs and tables and draperies, swans, roses. An honest life would have been the realization of her vexed dreams; these tumultuous moments. She would have slain her tragic hero. She would have died a tragic death. She would have died young, even before she had acquired the sense of having lived through so many experiences which she, left in this isolation, had never known or had forgotten. Her friends and household servants, torch-bearers and footmen and handmaidens, would have covered her with a winding sheet and carried her high up into the mountains and buried her in a singing cave. Sometimes, of course, she thought they had already done so. For she heard the mournful song. She heard the sound of dripping waters, though probably this sound was only that of the waters dripping from the mouths of the animal gargoyles under the roofs. Perhaps she was sleeping in a tomb.

And meanwhile, how amusing life could be, with how many projects, how many quickly changing plans, how many expectations, stars shining at noon, golden vessels which covered over the terrible faces of the real, golden veils which covered over grief, maps of the unknown, ways to hide remorse and to deny passion, ways to escape this sense of one's estrangement. Cousin Hannah, my mother thought, might so easily have imitated her, instead of fighting those old suffrage battles which she was bound to lose. She should have eaten lotus flowers and ridden on the winged horses or in a long-winged sloop. She should have created for herself an antagonist greater than this life, and she should have given herself up to him, the monster of a dream. My mother lay awake, hearing all night long, though the bright sunlight was burning, the lonely train whistles in tides such as the sleepers hear at night, even in their sleep when they are assaulted by the sense of an ineffable distance, the sense of loneliness when each soul, though many, is yet one soul alone, and what happens to one must happen to all. She would ask—were there not many roads to the crown of her head? How far was the distance from her head to her feet, how much farther than Tibet, and where were her hands which had flown away? What actual hazards and difficulties innumerable could there be to her, unmoving, yet out-running pursuit, the self running ahead of the self, the self which had never assumed the permanency of the earth but lived only where there were these shadows of her in the immortal wind? She was swifter than her own mind, swifter than her mercurial thoughts. She was far, yet she was near. She was within, yet she was outside. She was life, yet she was also not life. She was everywhere at once because she was nowhere, diffused through starlight.

My mother watched the others come and go and disappear, though some, as if to prove that they had visited her, that all was not imagination in this life, would leave gold sequins like fishes gleaming on the watery floor where the tide had swept. Some would leave great golden lanterns gleaming through the dusk. She would see dim, startled faces in the mirrors wreathed by seaweed. There was a carpet of starfish under the blowing tide. An emperor's attendant left the emperor's white umbrella, billowing like a white bird in the wind, the emperor's white hat tall as a mountain peak covered with the star-strewn snow. My mother swore that she had been visited by a sacred elephant, for she saw a pair of elephant's ear-rings, probably those of the invisible elephant in the rolling fog. Once there were thirteen chandeliers left upon the beach. Once there was a horse's tail, an Abyssinian fly-swatter. There were all kinds of strange objects turning up in my mother's bedroom, things which seemed to turn up from nowhere, things which seemed to whirl around her like the dance of the dead years. All of a sudden, someone would stumble over an object which had not been there before. A divan would move. Or a chair would move when there was no one. There were fingerprints upon the doors, marks of lobster claws upon the mirrors, the gold and silver goblets. There were stains upon the tapestries of the chair backs which were woven with the portraits of beautiful ladies. There were indentations in the silken pillows where imaginary guests had rested their heads. There were wandering surf-lines, thin whisperings of silken foam in the wind, undulations of oargrass. It was almost as if this sea-blackened house were a booby trap, a place to ensnare the unwary, a place to delay him as in sinking sand. Once there was a purple feather fan which one of these imaginary guests had surely left, proving that, though there had been no one, his visit had been real, tangible, self-evident. There was no other explanation as to how this feather fan should have appeared in this place, everyone agreed with my mother, for no one remembered having seen it before. The evidence was so beseeching, even like that of the created world, that which most people seemed to have forgotten through their long isolation here in this old, hollow house of the many rooms which no one visited, the dim, shrouded parlors where no one stirred, so many that, it was often said, a man could have lived here for years without ever being discovered by anyone. He could even have enjoyed room service, an invisible servant to wait on him when he pulled the bellrope.

Perhaps, of course, this fan was one of those my mother had carried when walking through the still house, making a grand tour of the empty rooms, waiting restlessly for the fashionable guests who, though expected, did not arrive, those who snubbed her and ignored her constant invitations and beseechments because she was quite mad, poor lady, and never walked except in her dreams, because they feared that the wine, though brought by invisible servants, though beautifully served in crystal goblets, would be drugged with that nepenthe which should rob them of their personal sorrows, their corporeal senses, and their powers of reason, that she would put them to sleep, that their carriages would stand forever in the driveways under the ground, their skeleton grooms sleeping, their skeleton horses also sleeping, only dreaming that they moved as the storm clouds moved down the dark, tumultuous sky. Those who might have been fascinated by the idle prospect, those who had already been subdued by life, the luckless, the ill-fated, ill-starred, ill-omened—they were not those who had been invited, of course—though they were those who had stayed. But that was many years ago—before my mother, acknowledging, to all practical purposes and intents, her defeat in this social sphere, had gone to bed—and if this fantastic plumage was hers, she could not remember that it was hers, and it seemed only another proof that there had been a recent visitor, someone whose eyes were the moon and the sun, someone whose face was a flame of fire. Once there were rusted sleigh bells competing with a Chinese wind harp. Once there was a pair of riding gloves, fur-cuffed and silver-embroidered, someone must have left upon a table. Yet it was possible, of course, that my mother had left these gloves upon a table many years ago, though in a distant part of the house, perhaps when she came in from the imaginary hunt ball, that she herself was that emissary she believed had so recently visited here. Had she not used to carry, through the still house, a hooded falcon on her wrist? Had she not often gone to hawks and hounds, riding in windy drawing rooms?

Things had so seldom changed in actuality—except for the shifting sand dunes and amorphous differences according to the time of day or night or the season of the timeless year—except for my mother's fluctuating dreams of that time before she had retired from the world of the living—and these dreams continuing unabated with deceptive persuasiveness like an influence it would be futile to resist, an action in inaction. That which had never been, it was only that which was, for it had neither beginning nor end. The love which had never come into being was a greater love than love, and there was greater passion in restraint than in passion, greater being in non-being, greater torment in no torment than in torment.

Still other visitors might throw jeweled dice upon the floor, and others would scatter their calling cards scribbled over with illegible messages, polite invitations to repay their visits, comments as to ancient shipwrecks and storms and birds of passage, birds of omen, tergiversations, countermands and countermarches, veerings, shyings, doublings, wheelings, ebbings, regurgitations, reflex moments and mirrored images, marriages of opposite such as light and darkness, questions as to when my mother would return from her long journeys. When would she return— from where, from what far country—return from her Saracen conquests or her Chinese wars or her long winters in St. Petersburg—or had she lost la lutte finale? Should she come with a great calvacade, even like Captain Freemount-Snowden at her triumphant hour?

Forasmuch as my mother's life had been death, should not her death be life, so my mother would logically reason—still dreaming of an old romance, years after it was too late, years after it seemed that she should never awaken again unless, as Mr. Spitzer had often warned, she should awaken only to take one wild look around her and sink into her grave, never to return to life again? And she should suddenly alter, growing old over night, the years catching up with her who seemingly had avoided time, clinging to the illusions of her youth long after these illusions could be sustained? And she should no more envy the liberation of an old suffrage captain who, casting off these mortal fetters, trooping her suffrage colors of rose on white, red rose of her blood, had gone upon her last journey, that from which no traveller returns except in our dreams waxing and waning like the moon? Or by death were all made young and beautiful again? Or was death to be only, as Mr. Spitzer seemed to think it was, the forlorn extension of this life, another of the imperceptible moments of change such as he believed he had experienced—so many times, he had lost count of his many deaths, and no statistical record was possible? Yet unlike Cousin Hannah who was noble in her resolution, had he not always returned, as he would sometimes sorrowfully ask my mother, chagrined by her thin fantasies which denied to him his own miraculous recovery, the fact that he was resurrected, the fact that he was clothed with flesh, and his body was his body, and his was a soul with many sleeping eyes?

But my mother still, even after Cousin Hannah's death, must continue her rivalries, now when there was no living antagonist, no patriarchal suffrage captain urging her to arise and go forth, to be no more this sick lady in a darkened bedroom, dreaming that she was a beautiful consort sleeping at the jeweled feet of God, the mountain snow like pinnacles upon her breasts, the feathery snow upon her eyelids, the snow upon her mouth. Once she dreamed she was the unicorn. My mother had the subtle power of vanishing, even like the others who came and went—perhaps for hours which were years, years which were hours, hours which were not hours—there being no hour in the world of the dream. The boldest deeds might cease and flee. She could cause the self to rise and go forth, even to the forbidden places. She had gone to places where there was no North. She could go away, vanishing in an instant, and no one else could see her, and no one could know who or where she was—whether she was a dead emperor or a dog borne along on a marvelous bier through shining or dark streets. She could be many persons with many heads, limbs, arms. So that one should not know, when he addressed her, which person she was, for she was so fickle—she sometimes failed to recognize herself and the person to whom she spoke. One must take into consideration the surrounding atmosphere, the humidity or the freezing weather, as when there were showers of hailstones on the snow-blackened roofs. One could hear her talking to the great, roaring winds, the walls, the doors, the windows.

CHAPTER 42

✳

My mother rode in the carriage with the black coachman and the four alabaster horses through the sleeping house, passing through ever widening doors, passing mirrors and fountains as the horses' heads turned through clouds, passing grand pianos. One could sometimes hear her directing the coachman, saying to turn right, turn left, follow the winding road, watch for the road's edge, the clouded void, the lights of the city. One could sometimes hear her directing the wind. Again she would say—Watch out for the celestial traffic. Watch out for the swan boats. Oh, what a congestion here!

She journeyed by glass carriage from room to room of the dim house, passing with torch flames and golden birds reflected in mirrors, passing the tapestry landscapes of emperors and unicorns and sleeping ladies and mountain peaks of snow and sleeping dogs, passing under striped awnings with golden tassels blowing in the wind until she came to sleeping Boston which might well have been a city not of this world, or thus she dreamed through endless years, hearing the horses' hooves like velvet leaves falling on velvet clouds. Driven by the coachman with his head wound in a golden turban like a moon or like a blackamoor arising out of those dreams which knew neither death nor time nor love, for no dream dies except into another dream, the eight long-necked horses turning their white heads like foam through sun-streaked clouds, she came at fading sunset to the old, gaunt, high-steepled house which she recognized because of the water towers against the clouds and the stained glass windows trembling in the broken light, calling on Cousin Hannah when she and not the opium lady was bed-ridden, too old and fragile and unmotivated to move, to visit the opium lady in the sea-swept country house with its many pavilions under the unsinking stars, great argosies with their prows nosing through clouds white as fields of mountain asphodel. The distance could be transacted. My mother went by carriage long years after both the coachman and the lady were no more. For if Cousin Hannah could not come to see her, then it was she who must make this journey through the sleeping city by many meandering roads to see her great rescuer when it would have been dangerous for her attendants to have carried her even when she was sleeping in her bed. My mother made many reports of her farewell visit which had taken place when she was perpendicular and Cousin Hannah was horizontal, old and withered and almost mummified, almost beyond recognition, only the faded starlight in her eyes. Was my mother sure she had reached the right cousin? She might have been, my mother thought, an ancient pharaoh sleeping in a swan boat, perhaps in its nocturnal passage following the moon around the earth.

Though that visit could never have taken place in this life, for both ladies were bed-ridden as Mr. Spitzer knew and so frequently reminded himself even after so many years of his own precarious oblivion, and both were immobile, yet he was obscurely grateful to my mother for her fitful accuracy as to the changing traffic lights like fireflies under the glass-domed milky heavens, city lights gleaming like minor constellations in moon-streaked clouds, the way the sleeping horses, the sleeping coachman knew the roads and the jogs in the roads and the glistening milestones which marked no miles, bridges and sunken towers and gate posts carved with curious beasts and birds which Mr. Spitzer might himself have forgotten, though going that way so many times. Perhaps he was so victimized by routine itself that, consulting his planetary wrist watch which told the course of the minutes if not of his own steps through light and darkness, he did not notice many of those details which he took for granted, being unable to live by a continual surprise, unable to die by a continual surprise, and gearing himself at all times to the unexpected as if it were the expected, as if no new surprise could ever assault him who was always surprised and valued his dignity perhaps more than his life. Perhaps he had already taken his last step.

He was always very grateful that the opium lady's distraught observations of that distinguished suffrage captain's probable last days upon this earth coincided so nearly with his own in spite of many accidents and irrelevancies such as the time, the place, the person, perhaps also the city. Indeed, her farewell visit or visits called to his mind many exactitudes of evasive substances and qualities and essences and elixirs he might have patiently ignored, for he had been preoccupied at that time as usual by his quasi-legal interests such as his unflagging search for lost heirs to lost estates or castles and porches which were buried under the water and his studies of ancient population rolls, graveyard registers listing the names of the dead, birth registers, census reports from which one person was always missing no matter what time or place it was—it seeming to him that doubtless that person was himself, neither the living nor the dead, that he was always precariously absent—and he had been studying or composing, he was almost certain, epitaphs in dozens like bargains, saddest elegies for those who lived, Epithalamiums sadder still, dirges for the drowning or the drowned, odes for marriage or for death—and he had also been involved by an inherited project to resurrect all the sunken ships of the world, the barnacles growing on their sides, or those which were retrievable like stars brought up by the fisherman's clouded seine— ships sailing upon those waters which were greater than this world— though mindful that this world itself was, he had many times observed, a sunken star, a ship which had gone down with storm bells ringing and with all hands lost and wreckage floating on the waves at dawn. So much was submerged, perhaps forever. Water floated to the port-holes of his own eyes as he lurched toward starboard under unfamiliar stars, how often he had sighingly remarked. He was covered with barnacles. His ears gonged. Water flowed from his mouth. Should the lost locate the lost?

He had been making then as now a list of ships which had gone down and the approximate location in which they had disappeared both as to latitude and longitude though there were insurmountable difficulties, of course, in spite of his carrying his compass with the broken foot and two wrist watches and blank star map under the unfamiliar stars, the waters blowing in his path with musical uncertainty, for if he knew the longitude, then he did not know the latitude or vice versa, or perhaps the waters moved, his mind being not sufficiently comprehensive to retain all memory, all orient pearls winding fold after fold like clouds enclosing flames or stars, all winds and waters and birds of omen and stars of passage, all currents and countercurrents and that tide which seemed to move with him and his shifting meridian, his black cape soughing like a sail, one eye burning to starboard, one to larboard, all dates of sailings, dates of arrivals in unknown ports, the time also being mysterious upon the forever tolling waves which kept a different time from earth so that, not knowing this present hour, he would try to find out the time when the ship was last sighted sailing into purple sunlight or darkness and whirlwinds and clouds. This was not always possible, of course. The reports were not always to be trusted. Sometimes there were no eye witnesses.

He studied the lists of the lost ships, some which had disappeared many years ago, perhaps long before his birth, his sailing—some which were sunk in seas of calm, never heard from again through ten thousand whistling tempests—some which went down for reasons never known to man—beautiful sail-boats moving with stately motion like dancers across a ballroom floor under a glassy sky hung with lighted crystal chandeliers moving as the dancers moved—Racehorse, lost in the China Sea with a great mandarin aboard, a flaming gold butterfly flying out of his butterfly sleeve before the empearled waters rose to the clouded sky blotting out the stars—mail boats, vanished far out at sea, no message ever brought by migratory birds or marine angels blowing mother-of-pearl horns on foam-crested mountainous waves, white horses—white-winged schooners spinning like tops in watery abysses, passengers never heard from again on water or earth or in a sea of clouds—ships sailing into port with no one on board, the table set with plates of gold—Oceanus which sank with the evening star, rose not with the morning star though the captain gave good hope—ships colliding where it would seem no two ships could ever meet, for this was the eternal sea—ships which were never to find anchorage—Arcturus, found drifting under the northern clouds with all her lights on—fishing boats, sloops, shells foundering off a darkened shore—Ptarmigan, swallowed by the Arctic pack, her captain frozen in the snow like a shroud while writing his last log under the frozen nail-head stars holding down the coffin lid of the sky—though he would sail again—and doubtless would add another note to his log, even like Mr. Spitzer adding another note to his music when the iceberg melted—ships upon their maiden voyage vanishing into the frothing deep—Nautilus, turned upside down before she ever left harbor—Roman galleys sunk with Egyptian slaves chained to their oars—ships of Grecian saints sunk off Peiraeus with marble dolphins, marble boys—many old ferry boats capsized upon the dreaming flood over this subterranean world.

He was particularly fascinated by those ships which had left no wreckage, those which had disappeared without trace, leaving great doubt as to where they were—just as he was concerned by lists of passengers, though even more by ships which had not carried names of passengers or which had carried mysterious passengers, he often likening himself to that ship carrying that supernumerary passenger who, darkly hidden from him, was his soul. He was concerned by contraband cargoes and by the tonnages, keelings, sailings, figureheads. Some of his best friends were rope-makers, sail-makers. One he knew had strung his ship like a violin and played the strings with his bow in every storm of ten thousand whistling voices. He told Mr. Spitzer that it was his music he played. But Mr. Spitzer believed that this was an exaggeration, for he had never heard his music through ten thousand whistling voices in storm and whirlwind. He had sought for the elements of harmony, but this was chaos. He dreamed continually of the foundered ships and of the lost ships returning and of the lost stars beaching upon some distant shore of light or darkness, the lost passengers staring through mists and fogs, the glitter of fireflies when all dead souls should sail into port, when one should not be missing like the light of a faded star or firefly—but when would that time come, bringing with it the fullness of days? It would never come, he knew, at least not within his own life time. It would come only when he was dead, perhaps not even then—for he would not always remember himself, a firefly.

He was grateful meanwhile for my mother's dream life as if it were an achievement exceeding forlorn fact, happy that she had visited the distant city of minarets and pearls in order to say farewell to the resplendent suffrage captain whose life had passed in the storm of action and who, after great fame and the eclat of a thunderous career, was dying in a startlingly personal oblivion—happy that these two great ladies had arranged their hallucinatory meeting just before Cousin Hannah had set sail for the last time, doubtless with a stranger on deck, and none could say it was this great lady's maiden voyage, for she was like an old ship lurching through the storm of years, and her decks were blackened as were her chimneys.

My mother's farewell visit was only in the realm of imagination—and in what other realm could a farewell visit ever be, Mr. Spitzer asked—for was not farewell the one perpetual memory even when it had taken place? Farewell was a matter of opinion as to the time, the place, the person. Had he not spent all his life saying farewell to my mother—as she to him—and did they not lament those days which never were, nights which never were? Perhaps he could not say farewell to anyone because he had not bidden good-bye to his brother whose memory was now the only life to him—sustaining him through many weary hours—and surely, as he would often sighingly whisper, his brother had not said farewell to life. Should not eternal recurrence be the one law of life, and should not the great lamp-lighter going his rounds through darkened heavens light that lamp which had gone out and was himself shining through clouds?

My mother had passed through the rooms of mirrors reflecting mirrors as the carriage wheels turned on gleaming pebbles streaked with phosphorous, as the white-maned horses neighed. Perhaps she had passed under the midnight rainbow. Perhaps she had passed through the pearly gates and down the marble roads where the surf roared and through the snow clouds and the reflected flights of wild swans and through the sleeping city as the shafts of golden light beams struck the minarets and domes of great sultans. At any rate, the coachman following the sleeping marine horses had fetched her to Cousin Hannah's ivory door, perhaps after long journeys. She had descended by step-ladder and had dismissed the sleeping coachman, telling the sleeping horses to drive on, rounding the avenue lighted by the stars. She had entered the darkened house where Cousin Hannah, scarcely recognizable, lay stretched out like a clouded landscape no one else had ever visited, its vistas forever reaching toward frozen poles which were never visited by ice-breaker or migratory birds. As my mother's visit had not occurred in time or space, there was no way of questioning it, of subjecting it to the test of validity.

She had walked unescorted through the dim house. She had not even leaned on her cane. She had needed no one to show her the way. She had worn her great velvet hat with the billowing purple plumes, her trailing velvet skirts, her high buttoned boots which doubtless gave her ankles support. Perhaps they were magic boots. Perhaps they walked of themselves. She was now that visitor, that unverifiable phantom she dreamed. She had conversed with Cousin Hannah for a few enchanting minutes.

This much was understandable to Mr. Spitzer who went continually back and forth and who with all his uncertainties knew these roads between two dying ladies, the great sundials with their numbers blotted out by fog, the great hour-glasses gleaming through clouds, reversing themselves with drifts of sedimentary stars, the stardust on his eyelids as the wind sighed through his sails, as his heart-strings trembled, for someone was playing a violin, as his voice whispered with perhaps a slightly rasping note or a star whispered or a frog croaked, my mother dreaming this visit, just to the extent that, as it had transpired in a dream, he felt that the actuality could not compete, for how could he arrange that which was or would be real?

Of what necessity, he asked, to arrange a visit which she imagined had already taken place? And what was time to her? There would have been innumerable physical difficulties and hazards if he had tried to arrange the meeting of these two ladies—and should the mountain peaks meet the mountain peaks or move like waves in a storm or the stars shine at noon or churchyard owls flap their wings at a dying lady's bedside? If so, these things must happen of themselves. They needed not his intervention. Life was a dream, and death was another dream, as he had often observed, and even a dream was a dream, he having long ago accepted the fact that there were no paving stones but clouds, no earth which did not move like water running at his feet. He was more surprised by his own miracle than by anything—the fact that it was he who should go back and forth, still unrecognized. And besides, as one lady was so soon to leave this world, what difference would a few minutes make—what difference if the two ladies should only dream they met to say farewell, and why should they not have promised to meet again? So that he had listened with wandering sympathy to my mother's frequent reports upon this unusual visit which had taken place and would not have been surprised by the understandable errors she might have made, by failures of conformity as between the dream and the reality which was real except that it was missing. Seldom had he found a complete accord between one person's view of life and another person's view.

Yet he could not help being surprised by over-hearing Cousin Hannah's remarks upon the same visit, the same conversation—her saying to my mother who had stood in a beam of rosy light—Hello, traveller. Do you come from far, traveller? Cousin Hannah remembered my mother's purple feathers touched by light, her skirts trailing through miles of crystal dust, her walk like a mad rooster's dance, Mr. Spitzer had no doubt—that it was my mother who begged Cousin Hannah to arise, go with her, cast off these mortal chains.

But the old lady could dance no more, go no more, not even staggering, leaning on her cane as her cheek twitched, as her livid eye winked— the great career was drawing to a close when Mr. Spitzer came with his testamentary legal papers or his greetings which he brought as one who came from the living to the dying, as one who came from the dead to the dying, as one who came from the dead to the dead, he sometimes thought—or actually, from the living to the living. She was not yet dead. He was the ambassador from one world to another world although he doubtless never would know which ambassador he was, which world it was. These were not matters for him to ascertain. He travelled without authority and crossed into many countries where man had never been before, merely by his sighing—thus came to the house where he had knocked so many times before, getting no answer to his knocks though never yet discouraged—though now before he could knock upon the door once, twice, or thrice, the door had opened of itself or was opened, just as my mother said, by a winged hand which whirringly disappeared among the shadows of the long hallway lined with the heads of antlered moose with their great, mournful eyes staring at him almost reproachfully as if it were he who had slain them, he who was responsible for the death of all sensual life and love though quite the opposite was true, those great moose heads reflected in dim mirrors like the idea of immortality which has no separate existence, as he had thought, timidly searching through many secret rooms for the failing suffrage captain who should be in a distant part of the house which she had left long ago for Holy Wars and to which she had returned when she was worn out and broken and old, passing her later years among her souvenirs of battle against man and trophies of war much as some grand flirt might pass her twilight years among trophies of her imaginary conquests—silken fans, mirrors, portraits, perfume bottles, miniatures, gloves, dance programs, gowns worn upon some great occasion, locks of lovers' hair, bouquets of withered flowers sent to her by old beaus no one remembered now. Many a great huntress had done her stag-hunting only in drawing rooms. But here there was nothing feminine, nothing evasive. Here there were only such masculine trophies as the great stone helmets which had once reached above mountainous clouds, the great stone shields flashing with jewels, the great stone swords, the various signs of struggles which were seemingly long ago resolved. Her last years had been empty. She had lived in those last fleeting years as one whom time had outdistanced, one believed already dead by an ungrateful world, one passed over and forgotten, Mr. Spitzer must continually remind himself—though, alas, she had forgotten him who had wished to congratulate her upon her victory. She should have come back to Boston borne upon a catafalque. There should have been flags flying from the roofs. There should have been ship whistles blowing in all the harbors and ports of call throughout this world. There should have been lights burning at all the windows and reed torches burning at all the doors in memory of the unextinguished spark. There should have been crowds lining the streets to see this great captain passing. Perhaps she should have been a general now if there had been gratitude. She should have been promoted surely to a higher rank.

But she had outlived her fame, and no one remembered that war in which she had fought—so that doubtless, or thus it had seemed to Mr. Spitzer, she must have been dying at last of a broken heart—just as if she had not escaped throughout her entire life from subjection to human love or a divine love. Her public had been unusually fickle, it was true. Who remembered the loud glory of her days or the stealthy battles won at night when she approached the sleeping city, the darkened towers? Who remembered the call to battle, the sound of an ivory horn far away in glassy clouds? Who remembered the lightning flashes and the thunder rolling when she was victorious? She was forgotten by most of those she had rescued from darkened castles, from ghostly loves. Perhaps they had already passed over to the other shore. She had outlived those lovely ladies swooning when she came to carry them away from despotic husbands and lords—indeed, was like some old lover who had outlived her love. No longer was she that great captain of suffrage—or if so, she went where none could follow her or hear her bell tinkling in the storm. No longer was she the leader of those great armies riding thunderously into war, flying their silken petticoats as flags, nor were there camp-followers pitching their tents upon her trail as once in mountainous mists and valleys shadowed by clouds or great stone crags where she had been the head of many a military campaign upon the powers of darkness—but now there were no beautiful ladies who left home and husband to follow her. Though always by indirection, she had broken the hearts of many men. Her great Crusades were almost over, surely not just beginning, and she had not found the Holy Grail or any object of her quest. She was that Jason who had not found the golden fleece. No longer was she that beau sabreur of suffrage brandishing her sword—for the sheath had outlived the sword as doubtless, Mr. Spitzer had thought, the body had outlived the soul. Or the soul had outlived the body. There was but one great ogre left to slay here in this darkened house.

He almost thought once more that she was not at home. He almost thought that, with his usual accuracy, he had arrived too early or too late—for others were not so punctilious, so considerate as he was. Simply by being on time, he had missed many a person he had expected to meet—though in that case he had usually met with someone else. He had stumbled over old helmets and cuirasses and cannon balls. Or so he remembered now. He had gone from room to room seeing everywhere the signs of her militant enthusiasms, her great wars, and earlier wars such as the Peloponnesian Wars, the Siege of Rome by Hannibal, the Saracen wars, the Civil War, the Boer War, many Balkan wars—how many wars, so many that he had wondered where the man of the house could possibly be—medals, ribbons of honor, citations from various battle fronts, pictures of Custer's Last Stand, Sheridan's March, Paul Revere's ride to arouse the sleeping Minute Men, the Siege of Atlanta, the rout of horses, busts of army captains, Caesars wearing laurel wreaths, turbaned Turks, camel troops, swords which she had captured from furious or dreaming shieks, the burning of Carthage, the taking of Venice. Certainly in this great house which entombed so many military grandeurs he would not expect to meet a sleeping lady among the shadows in a darkened room, the starlight burning in her staring eyes, a snowflake melting on her sunken cheek, her hand as frail as an almost transparent leaf—but some old war lord toppling toward his doom, his marble horse crumbling under him, crumbling into clouds and waters. Doubtless most of these battle souvenirs, fire axes and swords and cannon balls, had been in this house before she had ever left Boston to pursue her great wars for the liberation of ladies from man in all countries. There were also many pictures of Cousin Hannah when she was at the peak of her glorious career upon this earth, when many men had trembled at the mere thought of her, when many women had swooned at her approach, had fainted, had fallen—for ladies had fainted then more easily than now— and now it was the man who fainted—Cousin Hannah with her bow and arrow—Cousin Hannah as the great bloomer girl who had taken off her voluminous skirts, one arm crossed before her bosom like Napoleon on the eve of a battle greater than Waterloo—greater inasmuch as the outcome never would be known, for it was raging on all fronts and in many bedrooms—Cousin Hannah challenging a street car with her umbrella— Cousin Hannah launching a balloon under which was written—I have launched a new world—Cousin Hannah riding on horseback at the head of her suffrage troops—Cousin Hannah wearing an old boater and striped shirt—Cousin Hannah launching a ship which was manned by ladies—Cousin Hannah leading the needle workers to strike albeit she was the owner of a mill—Cousin Hannah dressed as an Arab king, wearing a burnoose and long skirts. Mr. Spitzer certainly envied her the power, passion, energy of her life though believing that it had been directed into the narrow channels of a lost cause. For where had her great struggles reached?

He remembered that almost her last public activity had been that she had tried to organize a blacksmiths' union—when there had been almost no blacksmiths, for the horseless carriage had succeeded the horse. And suppose there had been only one blacksmith, one Vulcan of the forge left on all the earth—could she have even so much as have organized him, the anvil, the horseshoe, the flying spark? At the very last of her life she seemed to think that she had organized the pickets around an old town clock. They picketed the clock at every hour. So her life crumbled. All her years seemed only this dying moment, and all her journeys might have been a dream so like his own needless journeys back and forth. Time had never advanced for her, it seemed to him—and, indeed, in many hysterical and nervous persons he had observed that all of time is but the crystalization of one sad, wild moment. They go not beyond that time though time may pass.

There were also pictures of the Taj Mahal, great Crusaders' castles carved in rocks, those of ten thousand singing or echoic rooms, Mr. Spitzer had no doubt, hearing the wind blow through lonely avenues, many mosques and harem gardens and sacred pools, clouded mountain tombs and desert cities, tent caravans and cities of minarets rising through sand, two ragged mountain climbers climbing Mt. Everest through blinding snow and wind, or so the caption read, an old-fashioned barouche with its lean-ribbed horse rearing at the edge of a crumbling abyss, the driver's face blurred by a shadow, many mountain peaks.

Mr. Spitzer, searching through old newspapers, old documents, letters, testimonials, some with almost faded print—perhaps before and perhaps after Cousin Hannah's natural, unnatural death—was reminded of many mysteries of her career which he was able to put together like the pieces of a lost mosaic, though there were always and doubtless always would be a few pieces missing as from his own consciousness. There were many lacunae, many port-holes through which a spirit might escape. A man died not necessarily at the hour of his death. No one net could ever drag in all the stars, all the fishes, all the birds, moths, butterflies of this sublunar world. Forever would a lost psyche wander down the wind. Also, she had inadvertently assisted him in his gradually emerging knowledge by her death-bed statements which seemed to propose another life. He was reminded then and upon many other occasions of many anomalies like his slow music, many hidden chapters in this life, this death—perhaps that hers had always been, in spite of the publicity which could never quite be trusted since arising from an unreliable source, since brought to some old newspaper reporter by astral voices, by a great maharajah or storm courier before the age of the telegraph, a hidden existence which was the opposite of what had been supposed by the majority. For every being, Mr. Spitzer had observed, must contain its opposite as the heavens contain both moon and sun or as Mr. Spitzer contained his brother in the sunlight. So that she was perhaps not too different from himself in his oblivion. He had not known the hidden part.

Only the out-croppings had been seen, looming like great mountain peaks though always crowned by snow clouds piling up like other mountains or great snow birds. He was not sure that even these were visible. Vision failed him always at that crucial moment of his understanding. Surfaces mystified him almost as much as depths. How many times he had trembled at the edge of that great abyss lying in the path of every mortal traveller. Perhaps she had already been engulfed.

He remembered and perhaps had been reminded by her on her death bed that though she was Hannah in Boston, this virgin warrior who would seem to evoke no answering romance, not even one pale or dying or deathless spark, though here in Boston she had fought against man, she was Hamid in the East and was so known throughout the cities buried under the desert sand. In fact, she was Al Hamid. There her fame was that of mystery, only a great secret having permanence. Rumors like winds had whispered from tent city to tent city, perhaps were still whispering. Also, she had been known while travelling through mountains of snow as the Great Moor or Black Moor, though it was some time before Mr. Spitzer had understood the significance of this fact. Here her mystery was that she should be famous, for no man had ever really known her, a creature so mysterious that fame had only increased her mystery. It seemed to him that fame had blinded men to her and her essential beauty, that of deprivation, of absence of being. They had judged only by the externals which were certainly never very prepossessing, never in her favor. She was surely not the dove—she was the hawk. She was rapacious. She was fierce as the winter wind. No tender sentiment had ever been hers when she was alive. She had seen men beheaded without a wink of her eyes. And yet, oddly enough as he had discovered perhaps only after the unknown death of that great suffrage captain who had tried to destroy the last conventions of love and death which were perhaps equated in her mind, the one coming only with the other, and who had struck fear and trembling in all men's hearts and some women's hearts and who had ridden against great shieks in windy tents, there had always been, hidden somewhere in this world, a timid man who had loved her, Mr. Spitzer believed—though he could not say what man it was. But surely there had been some men attracted to one who had been so courageous in the face of every obstacle and mirrored obstacle, one who must surely now elicit an elegiac love for that which never was, one who should not go to her unknown grave without the farewell kiss of a leaf falling in the wind or a snowflake falling, fluttering through a cloud.

Rumors of lost loves which had once seemed apocryphal seemed real to him at that last hour as he approached the summing-up and his farewell. Farewell to the great mountain peaks, the shadowed valleys, farewell to this intrepid traveller who now must leave this life which in a sense she had never known, for each who dies must leave that life he did not know, did not dream, did not live. Much must be forever unexperienced and merely hypothetical, a premise never to be pursued. And that was always death, even in this life, for each who dies must die twice, it seemed to Mr. Spitzer with his nearly comprehensive sympathies, his great understanding which almost caused his heart to fail, his heart to cease to beat. Perhaps, indeed, his heart was more silent than her heart beating now. The tumult and the sorrow of her life once more returned, even as he watched. He had thought that perhaps she had never recognized the personal nature of her sorrow, but he had been wrong.

For possibly even she had found that she could not escape—and if so, what were the years? They might never have been, and she might never have engaged in her great battle. He had stood in the dim house of that great battering ram of suffrage, feeling that he had come to the inner citadel where mystery remained forever unsolved.

He had been reminded of many self-contradictions, many opposites, many hidden facets of Cousin Hannah's life, some he might never have known, some he might have forgotten, some which might be seen only in that light which comes before the everlasting darkness falls. Such light might be itself illusion like the crumbling years and time's passage from dawn to dusk. Time passed not the same from dusk to dawn, Mr. Spitzer knew, living now from night to day as he had once lived from day to night. Darkness fell around him even in the brightest sunlight ruddy as a fire. Now he began to attribute value and importance to all those things once mockingly dismissed, though perhaps by his brother. Suddenly, though doubtless Mr. Spitzer was egregiously mistaken as usual, he began to see that Cousin Hannah's life, instead of being a flight away from the heart of life as he had imagined, instead of being solitary as the ace of spades, was solitary as the ace of hearts, was one long act of love, perhaps a ghostly love but no less real because of being that. Perhaps it was a celestial love or the nearest one might come to the devastating perfection. He might previously have denied this—though now he was ready to understand, to concede the presence of much he might have thought was missing—perhaps a secret man, a shrouded lover more beautiful than any man on earth. She might never have been, as he had supposed, the lone player playing the lone hand. There might always have been a secret partner in her grief which he perhaps had never truly sensed until now —someone who shared her destiny, someone who had lost this game of life with her or played for higher stakes than others knew. Naturally, his own musings on the subject were not quite rational—for was she not irrational like all great lovers of all lost loves? He almost hoped so, being almost ready to believe that only the irrational saved us from the last death one died. But how could he judge the dying or the dead? His consciousness would not endure, perhaps had already faded. He would be unconscious at that moment when he ought to be able to judge, and thus he would never know the difference between right and left, good and evil, love and hate.

True, as he was reminded by a distant church bell striking above a subdued traffic buzzing like honey bees in distant meadows, she had long ago left the bridegroom waiting at the church door, carrying in his hands a bouquet of withered flowers, pale lilies streaking the light until the sky darkened—at least according to those old rumors still going the rounds, Mr. Spitzer had over-heard, though no one had ever seen the face of the bridegroom, and none knew who he was—and when the music had struck up, the organ music pealing from heaven to earth—Here comes the bride—there had been no bride. There had been distant thunder peals, Mr. Spitzer thought, and mountainous thunders rolling—and just at that moment, he heard a distant cloud-burst. Usually, of course, how often Cousin Hannah herself had pointed out, it was the other way—it was the gentleman who left the bride at the church door, he who abandoned her. But Cousin Hannah, that great original, had always gone by opposites. She had always stolen a march. She had lived by being the master of the unexpected, the unpredictable, the sudden turn or flight. There were some who whispered that the abandoned bridegroom had died quite early because of his grief. He had simply laid down and stretched out his feet and died, clutching in his hands those withered flowers as if the bride might come. He had never lived to see old age. There were others who whispered that he had lived to a grand old age and had never married, love's arrow striking him but once. For timid souls adventure but once and if they are disappointed, will never be disappointed again, Mr. Spitzer believed, that they needed no further invitation to withdraw from life—they withdrew at the first blow, perhaps before the first blow was struck—did he not remember his brother? Not twice would they be rebuffed and some not even once.

Perhaps there had never been a recognizably human love—Mr. Spitzer sorrowfully considering that possibility—and the unknown bridegroom had been relieved by Cousin Hannah's precipitous flight—though outwardly sorrowful, had secretly congratulated himself that he had escaped, particularly in view of the lady's subsequent career of thunder and lightning, her leading so many revolutionary forces, storming so many citadels to rescue so many veiled ladies and carry them away from their husbands and lovers and friends. Perhaps he had been very gay and had openly consoled himself. Perhaps he had not recognized his happiness. Mr. Spitzer really did not know, of course, and never had found out. Various researches through various newspapers and legal documents and old letters he read after Cousin Hannah's death had not told him who the bridegroom was or when he had died, whether old or young. And Mr. Spitzer was willing to let the past be veiled by its own mystery.

He did understand, however, that after the wedding which did not take place, Cousin Hannah had hyphenated her name and changed her signature, signing her name ever afterward C. H. Freemount-Snowden, doing so upon the advice of a Boston numerologist who was a great authority upon the mysteries of the East and desert cities buried under the sand though he had never been in the Orient and had lived all his life in East Boston and had seen Boston only at night for more than twenty years, emerging only at night with other old camel drivers and goatherds and tent-makers and card players and people who came out only at night under the flickering desert stars. There were more of these people than the census-taker had ever counted. They emerged when others were wrapped in the great cocoon of sleep. The city of night was very different from that of day, Mr. Spitzer knew, having lived most of his life at night though he had once been the creature of day. He had always preferred the creatures of night, the phantoms fleeing at dawn. Surely, however, that great suffrage captain with her burning idealism shining like a lost star had not been a divided personality like himself, Mr. Spitzer had believed—that she had suffered no great breakage or scattering of her powers, that there had been no feeling that she might have lived in some other way, died in some other way, that there had been no lingering aura of doubt as to her great battle for woman's freedom from love or the ghost of love or whisper of a ghostly skirt soft as the whisper of a snowflake in the dark air. But he had been wrong, as he knew now in retrospect, for his judgments had been very superficial at the time. This, of course, was before he had had to change his mind about so many things which he must have accepted as a matter of course—before the last stone had fallen into place under the dying stars. Mr. Spitzer knew now as a matter of undubious certainty that there had always been a few timid men camping on her clouded trail though perhaps none could follow her to her high, frozen altitudes. Also, he had ascertained that a great shiek had come to her aid, backing her because, as he had written to her, he considered himself the chief victim of the harem system, that it was he who was trapped, he who wished to escape from being hen-pecked. He had written that he was the scrawniest rooster throughout all the Moslem world. So he had sent her bags of gold upon his camel trains. Without doubt, too, many husbands must have been grateful to Cousin Hannah for leading their wives to follow this will-o'-the-wisp—and thus many husbands were released from bondage. Mr. Spitzer, always hopeful and hopeful most when he was discouraged most, would not have been surprised, therefore, to find a great love emerging at the last moment, a secret man in Cousin Hannah's life, perhaps the mysterious bridegroom or the caliph who said that he was in a cage. But he was surprised to find at the last moment a secret woman, a bride.

Were not all moments flying together now, all contradictions resolving themselves, and was not the body reunited to the soul by death? Was there not only one star, one body, Mr. Spitzer had asked himself as he tiptoed, guiding his body which was too adipose for his mentality which was as subtle as a moth? He must remind himself, too, to expect many surprising things of one who had not lived in the ordinary way and whose death would be no doubt extraordinary like every other death. She had always lived by contrarieties and by going against the grain of the accepted opinions. So he had been as usual very cautious, expecting many surprises when he came to Cousin Hannah's bedroom which was her death chamber upon this alien star. Where, he wondered, was the great tent-maker now? Where was her tent?

He had heard the wind blowing through canvas shrouds. He had heard the tinkling of a distant bell, perhaps a camel bell. Perhaps he had heard a muezzin's lonely cry in the great desert of this life. He had reminded himself that whatever he found or saw, he was to show no shock or surprise, no bewilderment.

Death was the great innovator, he knew, and capable of as many changes as life, perhaps more than life. He was determined not to lose his dignity. He was determined to express only the proper sentiments, to say only the correct words. He was to act as if all had been expected, even his own dream visit at this hour which might be beyond the last hour for both of them.

Yet he had been surprised to find the lady sleeping in a vast, high-ceilinged room hung with voluminous satin folds and shrouds like a great desert tent or pagoda. He might almost have been creeping under some great skirt or crinoline—large enough to conceal a city, its spires and towers and temple bells. The roof was like a clouded city over him. Perpetual starlight hung upon this place. In the blurred whiteness he could scarcely see his way. There was almost no color but white upon white in that great, lonely, shrouded room white as sand and snow and cloud. He had heard the music of the wind, many whistlings and sighings. He had come doubtless to the last encampment. He had stopped for a moment, looking around him, peering with myopic eyes already blinded by flying sand and glassy stars, trying to find his bearings, some familiar landmark in that place where he had never been before. He had been surprised to find her sleeping with her bare feet, long-toed and knotted, exposed to the pale light, her head covered by a white shroud, a white sheet wrapped around her like a winding shroud—for a while thinking that he had come too late, that her spirit had flown, that he was in her tomb—until remembering that in the East all things were the opposite from here. In the East all sleepers slept with their faces covered like Ahaseuris, their feet bare. These conventions were not the same in all countries under the sun and moon and stars. He must behave as if he had crossed a far frontier.

In the East one never wished a friend good-night without hastily adding—good-morning—to indicate that one hoped he would survive the incalculable dangers, the journeys of the night, the long night, the hazards encountered in the night—as he had remembered then and upon his few subsequent visits. When one said good-night, not to add good-morning would be a sign of enmity among the Arabs. So that he had always said, when leaving her—Good-night and good-morning.

Indeed, these were his last words to Cousin Hannah—doubtless before the everlasting night began. And might there be once more, Mr. Spitzer thought, the city, its golden towers and spires flashing as some old oboist played a few notes for the morning. Ah, yes—might there be resurrection and eternal life.

She had been startled when, hearing his velvet footfalls, she lifted her great hood and saw him as perhaps her last visitor—the light flashing in her cavernous eyes though her face did not change its rigid expression, for her features were frozen by pain or age into one great grimace as near to laughter as to sorrow, these emotions being perhaps no longer distinguishable and perhaps of no importance, all values changing. For perhaps happiness would be sorrow over there, or sorrow would be happiness, or they would be the same. How could Mr. Spitzer know? Surely, her eyes had flashed at that last hour with recognition of him, Mr. Spitzer, though there was certainly no way for him then or later to know whether she thought he was himself or his dead brother, he who had played his last spade. It was so near the end, and her reaction never would be known, she carrying to her grave what would always be, for Mr. Spitzer, a tantalizing enigma. Might it not always be asked which one had died? Oh, how he wished that she had told him the great secret!

Oh, how he wished that she had told him what spirit she saw gleaming beyond that great facial mystery which was perhaps his own, his double, perhaps his double in eternity like a light shining through a cloud! Doubtless it was too much to expect that she should be concerned with him. It is possible that death, like love, makes for drawing into a narrow house before the spirit flees or fails.

Yet by his faithfulness that he had returned until at last he had found her, dying and broken and old, her consciousness burning low, soon to depart this life, she should have known that he was Joachim, this old watcher of all dying stars, that it was he who came with messages of love or hope, he who had returned in spite of all those years in which she had ignored him, she being in this propensity not alone. Her profile seemed to him like that of some old patriarch—so rugged, long-nosed, sharp-chinned, with greater declivities, greater crags than he had remembered, greater caverns—and in fact, it had occurred to him that in any other place he might not have recognized her. If he had seen her on an alien star, he might have passed her by—or if he had met her in a desert or in a distant city where the traffic roared. He was by nature absentminded. He would not have known her in a snow fall or a rain storm, most particularly as his own eyes were almost blinded. For what was the individual to him who had lived beyond all petty concerns of mine and thine and here and there and then and now and had long ago seen the individual fading like a shadow when the light appears or like the light before the sweep of the advancing darkness? All things seemed tentative and nothing substantial as to this great gentleman. For this reason, the ideal immortality from his point of view would be that which would include the body—he would sooner let the spirit go if there must be a choice. He would sooner be like some great, many-doored, many-windowed, vacant, untenanted house waiting for the spirit to return, perhaps sensing that it had returned at some time when he did not know, perhaps when he was sleeping. Perhaps it was the lackey moth. So all his windows were broken, and all his doors were open to rain, wind, sun, great monsoons, and roaring or stealthy tides like whispers. He guarded not against the peregrine spirit crossing his threshold.

Though confused as to himself, yet surely there was no one so expert as he in conducting a dying soul on its last journey which he likened to a voyage—no one who had gone so far out with that dim sail under the eye moon shining through a cloud and yet had returned, no one who had enjoyed his own great experience or greater in that realm which lay between two worlds, one never to be visited except by the living, one never to be visited except by the dead voyager.

It was some time now before, in that vague whiteness of Cousin Hannah's death chamber which surely no man had ever visited before, for surely he was the first to penetrate that secret citadel as he was perhaps also the last, his mind roaring with old winds, old voices, old melodies which were never uttered on earth and of which he knew he must be careful, subjecting each to his close scrutiny, knowing his echoic heart which had so often betrayed him by impossible substitutes, old sea shell music whispering and old tides returning with old wreckage though they were never known to return as they had been, waves scraping a bone or conch upon a lonely strand, he noted patches of various muted colors as where a lizard might have sunned itself upon a rock, a white curtain blowing with long, slow undulations upon the desert wind, though perhaps this wind was only the wind of his delusive memory which had so often betrayed him. He had been too often seduced out of his wits. He had been too often blown athwart when there was no cause, when all was silence and stillness. Surely, too, all great climaxes were coming together now in this dim room, and there were many warring elements, many precipitations, many rain storms and hail storms and snow storms, snow falls, cloud-bursts, flashes of lightning scrawling across the clouds, illuminations of things unknowable, many snow-topped mountain peaks stretching in long chains as the air grew thinner and colder, many polarities reversing themselves. Perhaps the ice was melting now.

Perhaps she was slipping into outer darkness as the cordages broke and could not see as the dark waters rose that it was he who had come this long distance, he whom she had already believed to be of the darkness, he who was this great lamp-bearer with his lamp light dimly gleaming like that revealed by shifting sands, he who accompanied her as far as man might go into that other realm. Perhaps she was alone as must be every voyager in his frail boat, this body. Perhaps it was he who was in darkness, having only a blind man's memory of light just as his might be only a deaf man's memory of sound, a dead man's memory of life. Perhaps he was the blind lighthouse keeper, the blind engineer, the blind railway signalman at the crossing, the blind architect, the blind portrait painter, the deaf bell-ringer ringing these tides. The sorrowful idea had often occurred to him, contributing to his melancholy—he often likening himself even then to that star which, though brightly shining, sees not its own light. He was that butterfly which sought the shadows. He was that little gate-keeper who did not know which gates he kept. He was at the edge of darkness but did not know upon which side the darkness was. Perhaps the darkness enfolded him. Perhaps as she could not live forward into time, she lived backward—and the hour-glass of her heart was being reversed even like his, sands and stars moving in another way. He had seen these changes before.

Perhaps all moments were coming together now, fused in one great glassy retort, and there might be retrieved that love which time had lost, and there might be delivered that letter which was dropped into a slot thousands of years ago. And yet it seemed to him that there was no return, no return of the living or of the dead.

It was some time before, with his eyes blurred, he saw the crossed sabers like smoky light beams gleaming through northern clouds above her old army tent bed and recognized that this was no great beauty he had come to discover, no beauty hidden by that great mask of clay, that this was the living skeleton, that she was doubtless dying as an old soldier who had stormed the last barricade, an old captain of the horse, an old army general who had suffered greater wounds than this last wound she suffered, for it was the one which he believed would not be remembered by her. Nor would it be remembered on which side she had perished. So often at the last moment one changed one's mind. So often one died on neutral ground. He had been a little surprised, however, to see in this bare and windy place a dim-eyed marble Aphrodite where the white curtains blew, seeming to him like a jewel which had strayed out of its setting until it occurred to him that wherever there was a jewel, that was its setting and not to be questioned by him, certainly not then. He had said nothing for some time, daring not announce himself, not knowing how to make his presence known, it seeming to him that it would scarcely be appropriate to leave his calling card when both she and he were present. If there was a trumpeter who had gone before him, he had not heard the sound. He had not heard even his own footsteps tapping on marble or velvet. He had maintained his silence as she had stared with unbelieving grief at him, perhaps thinking he was an apparition—as he most certainly was not. He was not an imaginary visitor. He was almost certainly himself according to his definition of that changing moment, he was almost certain though she gave him no reassurance. He was reassured that he lived, particularly by contrast with one he had believed was soon to be leveled as dust to crystal dust, her breath rasping with a sound as of great chains, her eyes congealed by freezing clouds and winter winds though the clouds seemed to be coming from within, and there were sudden avalanches, snowflakes spiraling through a rift in the tented ceiling, and he could see the glacial formations as one who stared from within another's spirit.

He had been tactful as usual, however—just as she, even at that last moment which would have made no difference to her, was not tactful— for she did not greet him either then or later or call out his name in acknowledgment of her great mistake, in tribute to his triumph over her and shadowed valleys. Truly, her indifference had seemed boundless, not limited by life, this feeble spark.

He had sat by that rickety bedside, drawing out his black handkerchief with which to mop his face sweating cold dew as he smelled the ashes-of-roses, thinking—why did she leave him in the darkness? Why was she unable to concentrate upon that illumination he brought to her—tell him who he was on either side the great starry abyss? She had clutched at faded bed-clothes, turning and turning her head, crying out—seeming to be living in some moment of the remote past, her face frozen by unchanging grief, the snow upon her cheek, her mountainous brow. So that he could see the snow would never melt, for the great icebergs were forming like swans in clouds. Perhaps his great golden boat had sunk long before the birth of the world, and there was only this wreckage. He had shaken his black handkerchief in the air with a whistling sound like an old explorer's mournful flag—feeling that he should claim this great continent stretching now before him through infinite desolation of snow and ice and clouds, these unknown peninsulas. And why not? For was he not the great explorer of desolate mountain peaks looming through miles of clouds and frozen bays like eyes or sunken moons and shadowed valleys no one had ever crossed before albeit his only skiff was a butterfly in a storm cloud?

Perhaps he lived suddenly only because she would so soon be dead, no longer of this known world—there being no coordination and no ultimate harmony of all these lost effects and secret hours—and it was she who would finally escape, he had no doubt, and go where he could not. His feet were too big for the narrow passes, thin threads of light reaching among clouds. His heart beat low, and numbness saved him from the last surprise as he felt the sinking of a star through endless waters. So that he could not be all that he would have been to her when she was dying— could not declare himself to the silent ear, the closing eye, the staring eye. It had always been his great problem that he could not make himself known. She had always fought against the spirit of man, and yet had she escaped being a lady pale as the moon-spotted snow cloud—or if she had escaped before now, then had she escaped at this last hour beyond the last when she was emaciated and old, broken by life like someone his brother might have loved, and when she was facing greater enigmas than any she had ever known and when certainly she needed a man of strength and verity to protect her against these dashing elements, blizzards, whirlwinds, hailstones, great shrouds of snow blowing in her path? Did she not need a brave companion to conduct her through the everlasting darkness, never to abandon her until she had come to port, perhaps upon an alien star or this star which had been strange? Would that it could be Mr. Spitzer, but he was old and so very uncertain of himself and his faint thoughts which he could scarcely muster at the climax, he having passed long ago beyond the climax, he having lived into these dying years, minuscular years of this galaxy.

His reason failed him most when he needed it most, and she was wild, frightening him so that he was at a loss as to what to think, say, feel, how to conduct himself. Had he not loved always only a beautiful face? Perhaps his usual torpor overcame him. What should a man say when he came to bid good-bye to one who had believed that he was buried years ago though never by the falling snow, he believed, never by robin red-breast covering him with the autumn leaf, for no one but himself had seen his burial? His grief was so diffused through clouds, winds, waters that it was this grief which gave him sympathy, no doubt, for all living things, and identified him with all others—this which caused him to sympathize even with her. Would that the world could be young again, small as the cup of a flower, that stars could be like spores falling through clouds and not upon a barren place. Perhaps the starlight splattered his sleeve. Yet she did not see him.

She was like all flirtatious ladies—not faithful to one who had never been her love, or so it seemed to him—that as he had never loved her, she had not been constrained by faith in that which never was. He had been no other's love or image, but she had not known him, had not recognized him like an invisible presence in that room—or if so, had given no sign. He might have been a dark cloud through which there shone no star.

So that he would lose her as he found her—already lost. For how unstable that great lady was in all her ways, how foolish, vain, tempestuous, unpredictable—going in two ways at once, coming according to no known schedule or routine—taking all men by surprise and shattering their most precious certitudes, violating their cherished beliefs, in all ways acting not only against the human law but the divine law in every country, even when that law changed from border to border—flitting from war to war as someone else might flit from spa to spa under her great white umbrella, battling no one but swans—seen now, seen not again for years—sailing in the darkness or at dawn—seen first here, then there—sinking beneath the flood, then rising—forgotten, then remembered—believed dead, then reappearing just when the last memory of her had faded from men's hearts and minds or had burned so low that they had ignored the possibility of another return.

Astral voices or glass prisms shaking in wind in halls of mirrors had not always announced her coming. Flames burning low had not always announced her going. Seldom had she been at home. She had tented but for a night and then had moved on through deserts and clouded mountains.

Now he heard her labored breathing and knew that she was weak, perhaps unable to defend herself against the last assault of death which came not with loud armies but came like a thief in the night, came like silken whispers of faded skirts spangled with sequins, like snow or foam upon the wind, like old loves remembered and resurrected at this hour when all things were fading, came like a voice whispering in a sea shell— and so how fickle, how irresponsible this great lady was when she was dying—no different from others. And how should she be exalted at the hour when she was lowered? Hers was the same fate which others suffered. Even an old suffrage storm king was unreliable at heart, fickle in death as in love, it seemed to him—he could not count on her, for hers was this secretly feminine heart perhaps beating through all things even now, causing pulsings of clouds, shining of stars in distant heavens— sudden veering through desert sands, shiftings of clouds and winds, changings of roads in fog, mountainous cloud-bursts, snow storms breaking over the leaden roofs, Alpine and Andean peaks burning in the celestial fire of a ruby's heart. What mad dance was life, and what madder dance was death, this whirligig of leaves and stars?

Who escorted this lost lady now, he asked, there in that dim room where these great obstacles formed like whirling mountain peaks, like endless clouds streaked by rays of dim radiance—and where were all those gallant ladies who once had loved this dying king whose essential mystery, he felt, would never be completely revealed, for who should light the taper of this life when it was waning or had already waned? It seemed to him ironical that the great, bearded buccaneer of suffrage should be forgotten by those she had rescued from desert dungeons and mountain towers and valleys of dead kings, that no one blew the bugle now for her awakening, for that reveille which should be hers when heaven opened like a door, she being that ivory door—that door through which she walked, trailing her clouds of glory like the dead moon, huntress moon with her dogs—strange that it should be an old sentimentalist like himself returning after years of emptiness to find out the secret hiding place of this old captain of hearts and darts, the snow upon her forehead, upon her shrivelled cheeks, upon her colorless lips, upon her withered limbs like a last benediction to one who had mustered angels that they might fight against the sensual sprites ascending into Christian paradise beyond these fields of asphodel gleaming like thin veils of stars. But where was now her armor of virtue, and where was her lordly helmet, and where was the strength of this snow maiden seeming to fade as he watched? He saw between himself and nothingness the dissolution of this great mask of life, asking—should not death veil all ladies, both dark and fair, and should not all be as brides going to the bridegroom cold as mountain snow?

Where was the heart of the mystery, he asked, here where white curtains blew around him with their long sighings and where he had thought that he might find the heart of the rose or the mystery beyond the cherubim gleaming through clouds? Where was the reality beyond the apparition? Perhaps the secret casket contained a vapor and not a jewel. Perhaps it contained a cloud and not a moon. Perhaps there was no answer but the void calling to the void, the darkness to the darkness. Perhaps hers was the empty boat, the spent sail.

He did not wish to imply, of course, that there were not still a few Promethean sparks of life in her—sudden leapings, flamings when the light had gone, no doubt, out of his own pale eyes. Doubtless she could still get out of bed and serve and protect herself since she permitted no inequality, no servant in her house, neither black nor white, not even a chessman. No slave might wait on the great Abolitionist who had fought against confederacies and crazy blackamoors arising like chimney pots through clouds and eunuchs black and white and candle-bearers lighting the darkness and great white roosters with their red combs burning in clouds and the tented mandarins of Peking and muezzins with their lonely cries starting up flamingoes spiraling into burning clouds above moon minarets and crescents and jasper domes of desert cities with singing walls. Perhaps there were servants of whom he did not know, weary foot sergeants and orderlies, their voices whispering among the shrouds and cords. Perhaps there was some great monster of a perpetual servitude. She could walk by leaning upon her crutch with her old army coat thrown over her crippled body, no doubt when he was gone, though she was always in bed when he found her, when he came in his dark cloak to view the ruins of the years, what havoc time had wrought or what havoc time had not wrought, when he came to her whispering tent dilated by this dying music like a wind blowing between two stars. So that it was his dubious privilege to be present during her hallucinations, for she would cry out when Mr. Spitzer came—Oh, is there no pavilion to hide me from the storm? Shall I not be hidden from men's eyes?

CHAPTER 43

✥

Mr. Spitzer carried in his hand that high silk hat which was almost his only God, his black cape flowing like water from his shoulders, covering him and starfish on a lonely shore—and would that he could hide that great suffragette from the storm! But she was dying, and he was as one already dead, so he could not help her. He could not have helped her even if he had lived, if both he and she and most other people had been wrong. Besides, her own great problems eclipsed now his own like some great shadow passing a firefly moon or star. Life's eternity must be lived within life's brevity, it seemed to him with his sorrowful face blotted out by clouds. Sometimes she was fording a dark stream which grew into a river ever widening. Sometimes her foot was crossing an endless desert. Had he not witnessed such journeys many times before?

He could gather by her wild screamings that she did not know who she was, where she was, that she was fighting a great battle against many armies or a great horseman, that she was plunging through clouds or climbing mountains of screaming winds as wild horses screamed on waves, the snowflakes whirling in her face, that she was storming those great citadels of which the doors had never opened before and perhaps would not open now, not all doors opening at once, that she was living through all she had lived through and much that she had never lived through until now, much that was a new experience as he had thought, for there were these great snow banks piling into towering clouds and frozen mountains and many jeweled turrets moving in her path, frozen valleys forming at her frozen feet and crystal chasms cut with endless stairways as distant moon haloes appeared in glittering clouds, as some far dog barked at a rolling or falling star or firefly suddenly shining in a cloud, lighting the helm of a dark boat—so that all unwillingly, for he had no actual need of any further knowledge of the dream or the dream's extension in eternity of which this life was but a moment, this life having already faded like a dream untenable and uninhabitable, he had discovered many things which others had not known or had ignored or had interpreted incorrectly as to this great lady's former life and imminent death and many unimaginable details they had forgotten or had dismissed as unimportant or adventitious or trivial—that even this great lady wept if a wandering snowflake touched her hand as he had already observed but had not fully understood, that she was fragile as were all mortal things, quick to break, that she was given to wild dreams, visions, fantasies, presentiments, forebodings, fears of the unknown, fears of the untried and of the unexperienced and of the unknowable as of the known, fears of nightmares asserting themselves like living night, night which may never die though day must transact itself between the morning star and the evening star.

Endless day would kill us all, it seemed to him. Few could endure the absolute truth. Most must be self-deceived, perhaps by the very idea of time or memory or that ghostly love which never was and yet endured. Most must clothe the dream, the spirit and the cloud.

Though she still apparently did not recognize him and though he had certainly given up all hope that she ever would, yet she seemed to arouse herself from greater and greater lethargy whenever Mr. Spitzer came, almost as if his coming were a signal light to this great emir of suffrage or to a dead thought awakening after years of metamorphic sleep—for there were these sudden memories as of a buried self coming to life at last and never seen before, never known until the uncertain hour beyond the final hour which was the end of experience.

So that, as had happened so many times, often in instances beyond his autonomous recall or haphazard memory, Mr. Spitzer's grief was somewhat vexed and thwarted and turned aside by his not knowing exactly whom he was mourning for, and he was baffled utterly upon this occasion no less than upon others which had engaged his wandering attention which had never yet focused on one face. How often in his perambulations he had greeted the dead or buried the living, only to find that he had been mistaken. Perhaps it would be equally mistaken to greet the living and bury the dead. Though doubtless that time would come when he would not be mistaken, when he would know all he did not know, that time had not yet come. That time had not come when all people were dead—or all were living.

He did not know who was dying or where or when or how or why, even as he with his clouded sensibilities and his broken heart was not sure who he was, whether living or dead—though he was always mourning for one or the other—not sure where he stood or where he should cast his vote and probably never would find out. He believed, unlike his brother, that the dead cast no vote—and so Mr. Spitzer made no choice. He had not been inside a ballot box for years.

He believed that the confusion raging now in this great tented room was not his own which he necessarily felt and that his light was shining within, clear as the jewel burning like the one steady star—he was not torn by these interior storms greater than raging elements of the exterior storms as reason was uprooted like an old tree in the wind, as heavens were reversed. So that breathing softly with almost inaudible whispers, he had betrayed no astonishment, no attitude of questioning, for had he not been present at many other dream carousels, imponderable hallucinations, illusions, tricks of memory like these returning loves? All that she had rejected, it had returned—or almost all—all those passions she had

subdued, those loves she had denied, those loves which had not perished
in the storm. For this was the great climax, the acme or peak, the con-
summation of all those years in which, or so it had seemed to him then,
she had fled from life and love or any human image or any commitment
to a greater love, one which should exceed this life, be in death that
which it had not been in life.

He had heard many whisperings, had known when there were clouds
of eye witnesses, voices crying in the storm, snowflakes whirling in wheels
in distant heavens, the soft hiss of snow or fire or burning twig, the cry of
a bird, the desert sands howling in the starlight-colored air, glassy pebbles
rolling through clouds or clouds breaking upon a distant shore of light.
Perhaps, though usually inattentive because of so much demanding his
attention, he would have listened more closely if he had realized that
there had been a parallel to these wild dreams in reality, itself no doubt
another dream or dream within the dream like a box hidden in the great
arcanum. But he had been acclimatized to such wild ravings and visions
as these long before, through the peculiar and altogether undefined circumstances of his own tentative or vanished life, and had learned not to
ask for the flesh which clothed the dream, the body which accompanied
the spirit through its many bewildering peregrinations—knew only too
well the street lamps shining through the fogs where there were neither
street lamps nor fogs, the doors opening upon a void, the rooms without
floors or ceilings.

So having seen the crumblings of dreams and many cloud-bursts
lighting the world with deathless vision even as one died, he had not
understood the quality of the literal which gave this terror to her cryings
—or had only vaguely sensed, as he understood not then but in dubious
retrospect, that all she had said was true had been true somewhere somehow, that these were not merely restless flights of her imagination as she
battled, winked, twitched, screamed, scratched the empty air or clouds
with her long-fingered hands like claws, seeming to want to hold on to
something, seeming not to want to let go, seeming afraid, yet ecstatic, the
wind whistling through her grey stained sheets as if she might set sail at
any moment. She was like some old ship which might capsize in the
storm, having already done so. He had supposed that she was delirious, of
course—though the irrational might be the one immortality, the one
thing lasting forever, even like the last cry, the last vision in the dying
eyes, winking eyes, staring eyes. Perhaps this moment was the only moment. And yet it had seemed to him that an old suffrage captain of
nobility should have died in peace with reason on her side at the last
moment, for had she not fought all her life for greater and greater independence from the ways of men and gods and for that greater isolation
which was surely increasing now, he had hoped, that she would be subjected no more to every storm, that she would be no more in the heart of
the storm?

Death should bring everlasting peace, the reconciliation of all opposites, all warring factions, it had surely seemed then, that there should be
some final resolution. Yet perhaps he was wrong, of course, he knowing

little of these mysterious matters or what came afterward. Death was that which blew us all along—sometimes far off our course, no doubt, into these ever widening whirlpools—more often than not where we intended. Death was the wind whistling through these shrouds, the wind blowing these snowflakes, these glittering sands, the wind causing these dead chords to tremble, these dead voices to sing, whisper, shout upon the wind. There was no death but the dying wind. The wind was always starting up somewhere. Perhaps there were singing winds which never ceased—those great palaces of singing winds such as he had heard of, those of the great Crusaders. How might he know—except that he was this great musician voicing the music of the dead?

She had surprised him by the fury of her activities, though he could not but note her waning strength as she cried out against the lid of the tomb descending, the glittering stars she saw like nail heads through glassy clouds—and then cried, almost with the same rasping breath—Oh, is the lid raising, lowering? She cried when Mr. Spitzer came with his dark cloak flowing, his high silk hat in hand to pay that deference which any gentleman might pay to a lady—Oh, I am lost! I am saved! Who raises now the lid of the sky? Or who lowers it? Who sinks this coffin now under the waves? Where am I? Who am I? Am I myself or another heart, she asked, clutching at empty air as the wind whistled through her sheets. Oh, is that you, great lamp-lighter?

She could not decide whether the lid was lowering or raising, for this life might have been her death, the crumbling of the ruddy rose, the fading of the sunlight, someone dying every evening, something dying— or perhaps she came at this last hour to believe that death might be her life, her love, her whisper in the darkness, her gasp, sob, cry—or so it seemed to him who could surely have shared these moods if only she had known or heard the answer of his dead heart, his whisper in a distant cloud or the scraping of a starfish on a lonely shore.

He would say to her that, indeed, the lid lifted—for was he not present, showing that the dead lived?—and thus surely, by his return and continued existence he should demonstrate quite visibly that he had lived, that he had transacted the gulf between two worlds, and that he who said farewell to her would be the first to greet her over there, especially if she thought he was his brother. So his good-night was always followed by his good-morning.

The air had thickened with clouds of eyeless witnesses, and there had been many voices continuing through silence—and yet she had not seen him, heard him. She had not seen his face in the drifting cloud.

Having witnessed such dreams and visions before, having seen so many phantom boats like cockles in whirlpools, he should not have been surprised by anything, considering that nearly all were as familiar to him as the blue stone gleaming like a lighthouse on his finger as now this dying soul sailed to where his light would never reach. For should one pale firefly light the entirety of heaven and earth, rolling clouds and rolling waters and faded stars pale as jellyfish losing their colors on a distant shore? He had sat by her bedside, often consulting his watch with the broken crystal, reminding him of a jellyfish or of the thin-rayed sunlight in the cloud, keeping at all times the attitudes of dignity, remorse, patience which had always been his, to that extent that perhaps some people thought he was unfeeling—for someone must maintain spiritual equilibrium as this body plunged like a wild horse and crumbled and faded and this light went out. Not even the great lamp-bearer could light this darkness. Perhaps he was persuaded by his own memories of unexperienced life—not himself but all which was unhuman and unknown. As to himself, he long ago had learned that there is quiet in the heart of every storm, every whirlpool. What good would it do for him to lose his calm? Her calm, he hoped, was soon to be greater than his, increasing like the honeycomb which multiplies its cells of itself. Soon she would be where there is no sorrow, no sorrow in the winter wind, the dead heart. She would be where sorrow came not from within or from without. No beauty that was merely human after all had ever sufficed her. So like a palmer she had wandered through this world.

It seemed to him that at times in that dim chamber he could hear, plucking his dead ear, tapping with his gold-splashed, ivory-headed cane upon the parterred silver and ivory floor which was like that chessboard where no chessman ever moved, weird cymbal music, music of flutes in glassy clouds, or wind playing strings of hailstones like those strings of beads hung in mosques, and he could hear the tinklings of distant bells blown upon the wind, whirlings as of a lady's skirts, footsteps upon the whirling snow—for the old lady was dancing. She was dancing on a lonely mountain top. It did seem strange to him that her last life on earth should be this mad dance, dance of death, especially as hers had been, or so he had always supposed, the most austere existence imaginable, her cause so great that there had been little room for any other thought, certainly no room for the lute-player he seemed to hear plucking his lute now in a distant cloud where the snowflakes fell like stars or plumed pods—so that he was amazed perhaps unwillingly by the sudden assertion of these feminine frivolities to which he had been long accustomed by the opium lady's dreams and felt that perhaps the great suffragette was guilty of some great joke now when she should have been most serious and most sincere, least capable of deceit, that she was making a parody of life just when life was fading or had faded, just when the great mask of reality, unreality crumbled into clouds and waters and melting snows as the wild swans honked.

Vanity, however, was that which seemed to know no end as long as life endured—at least seemed to be that which took longest dying—in woman's heart as in man's heart, Mr. Spitzer sadly thought, and perhaps also in the heart of God dreaming the image of the dream, the stars burning like eyes in the peacock's tail, the stars in burning clouds—and doubtless there were halcyon clouds in unknown latitudes, winds blowing through lonely porches and colonnades, many reflected minarets, many hanging gardens—for all was vanity in this life and in this death, it seemed to him, like the old tree uprooted in the wind with its branches whirling, clashing, or like the white wing moving through the cloud, his own spirit sobbing like a wild sea bird, the skiff moon accompanying this world, the star upon the moving flood, so that even this old suffrage captain had not escaped the common frailty of vanity—vanity of silken skirts flounced by lace, great parasols fringed by gold, waters, winds, the auk's egg, the star in the clouded mirror, the mirroring cloud, the glass barouche, the moon in the cloud or in the water, whatever had veiled her and hidden her from men's eyes.

Perhaps all things were illusion, just as he had always told himself, this crying, this crumbling, this falling away, this vanishing, this revelation of that which was no more, and there was nothing given but this dream. Perhaps this dream was not given but earned. He had heard, as his own spirit fluttered, these whispering silken skirts like tides moving through clouds long after the death of the world—he surely was not mistaken—for there were many contradictions at the heart of all things human, many opposites which never would be resolved so long as there was life or death or one fading star—and should he be appalled by the feminine being reaching now through darkness and whirlwind and whirling snow as her hands clutched at nothing in the dark cloud, not even a starfish, as the snowflakes hissed like fire upon that ice-bearded face where one cold spark glowed in that cavernous eye staring at him through miles of clouds, staring without recognition? Her eye stared through a milky cloud growing at every moment more opaque.

He must remember that when nothing was possible, all things were made possible—things which might have surpassed imagination when there was a question of even the remotest possibility becoming familiar —as he should know best, remembering his dead brother. His brother had crossed the Rubicon of disembodiment long ago, and that had been a great shock—there was no shock so great as disembodiment, that which heightened sensitivity, Mr. Spitzer believed—that the disembodied suffered most from the sense of hearing and amplification of sound, that they could hear everything, every footstep, every singing shroud, every snowflake falling through a dark cloud, and even the whispers of moths in their sleep suddenly sounding with a thunderous roar. Ah, where was that silence which should have been Mr. Spitzer's now?

He had been witness to this great lady's screamings, babblings which had revealed so much of vanished life, that past which, as he had thought then, was not memory—but something almost spontaneously starting up outside of the scheme of time, whether future or past. So he had naively supposed—not wishing to recognize that one life might contain all— scarcely daring to ask—was it possible that she had always been this pale Don Juan beneath her mask, this gentleman so frail, changeable, uncertain, evasive that his might have been a lady's trembling heart and tendency to faint, fall, slip into a simulated unconsciousness where all might be permitted which was never permitted by consciousness? If she should sleep, should she not love? Perhaps she had always been more fragile than some of those great ladies she had tried to carry away from monstrous loves, mirrors, clouds, doors—perhaps he had always known though only now recognizing her, just when she was about to change beyond all future recognition.

She surely had mentioned, in the midst of her ravings, many things which were rational or were familiar to him—more often pertaining to the remote past than to the future—but this had seemed all right to Mr. Spitzer, who was happy that she could not contemplate the great abyss toward which she headed now, happy if she could be distracted or turned aside from contemplation of the void—it seeming to him far more appropriate to evoke some old Caesar among the horses or caliph in his bugling, whispering tent, fortune-teller, crystal-hunter, seer, Cupid wreathed with roses carrying an hour-glass in his hand at this last hour than to speak of tomorrow's weather or what might happen next year—who might win the next election, for example, or the next horse race at Churchill Downs when the track was muddy, the next yacht meet, things less believable than heaven or hell to one who died, for they were of this world. It would be tactless of him to speak of such possible matters as political campaigns and horse races, both of which flourished because of divisions of opinions, because all men were not of the same thoughts as to who the winner would be—and besides, the future was forever postponed, no one yet having ever lived through it, and the future was locked in every heart, dead heart. The future was that casket containing no jewel. Not even the sun shone. Not even the moon lighted the cloud. He was glad that, though she did not see him with his dark cloak and his face almost blotted out by the shadow of his perpetual eclipse—for if he was not the moon shadowed by the sun, then he was the sun shadowed by the moon—she saw the others, the centurions, the horses, the cities which were a night's encampment in desert sand—whatever might make her feel that there were more people over there than here—for she was about to join the vast majority, just as the Romans said of those who departed this life. A greater city than any on earth would be there. There were probably only a few people who thought like Mr. Spitzer that it was a smaller city.

To him, at least, it had seemed better that she should speak not of the future but of the problematical past, of cities buried under the desert sand and never exhumed or snow glittering like mica upon the golden roofs, even of a dream sultanate, of things made safe by their remoteness and by their inaccessibility, minarets and hanging gardens with centaurs walking through clouds, castles, mirroring pools—so that by his tactfulness and self-effacement he had encouraged this great suffrage captain to take another city now by storm and whirlwind and driving snow. Or so he had supposed. He had supposed that all would be over in a moment, that physiological death was actual death or that one would soon follow the other as the dolphin follows in the wake of the boat or as the tide brings a shell to shore. He had scarcely whispered, not wishing her to notice his presence now or be frightened by the knowledge that someone lived, breathed, whispered—for what difference would that make to her when she was dying, when she was wrapped in herself? He had preferred, even as through all his life, a state of everlasting peace or at least of truce, much as if he were already dead, and she had been right in so supposing—and if she saw him now, he was an apparition who had appeared out of the fog.

She was certainly in a battling mood. There were inscrutable forces coming to her assistance even now when she was frail as the almost transparent leaf pivoted by cyclic whirlwinds or driven over some great granite cliff. She plunged ten thousand miles. She sank from pole to pole. She rose at some far height. Perhaps she rose at some high pinnacle above the mortal storm, immortal storm.

Mr. Spitzer heard her ask as an old clock struck the hour—Watchman, what hour? Are my men picketing the old town clock? Are they the hooded thirteen apostles? Is that the black knight? Is that the Moor? Oh, have you seen my love, dead love? Did she lift her veil embroidered with the stars, and did you see her eyes shining through a cloud? Shall I see her?

Mr. Spitzer heard lute notes. He heard her when she seemed to be speaking to a blacksmith who was shoeing her wild horse with diamond sparks, its white mane drifting in great, rolling clouds, its eyeball glaring through a cloud. She asked—Am I the anvil? Am I the hammer? Am I the anvil which is struck or the hammer which strikes? Am I the flying spark? Am I the star? Am I the horseshoe? Am I the horseman or the horse?

Mr. Spitzer heard her say to the golden archer turning in windy heavens, pointing his arrow—Oh, archer! Is that the arrow which will reach my heart, dead heart? She said to the armorer—Oh, armorer! Is that the hole through which the arrow passed? Is that the helmet? She said to the cup-bearer—Is that nepenthe? Is that forgetfulness or remembrance, future or past? She said to the eunuch—Who comes now? Is that you, Blackamoor, winding, unwinding your turban, the turban moon in the cloud? Oh, Blackamoor, are you my only love? Is that the rooster crowing? Is that the nymph?

Much better that she should speak to the golden archer over the city and the blackamoor and the cup-bearer, lamp-bearer, better that she should speak to the great turban-winder winding, unwinding his turban in the cloud than to Mr. Spitzer watching by her bedside under the funneled stars in the smoky light, sometimes more nearly asleep than awake, for his vigils were long, and perhaps now his memory was short, fluttering, snuffed out, it being hard for him to remember what had happened only yesterday. Sometimes his memories of yesterday were like something which had happened to a stranger. He found it hard to remember down which streets he had walked, whether it was rain or shine, which corners he had turned or had not turned, or who had tapped him on the shoulder, what lazar demanding alms or what old dopester advising him as to the horses which had already run, the great beauties or the nags, what old gambler trying to make another touch, what old musician blowing a tinny traffic horn.

So that perhaps in this death-bed scene there was a greater security than in transitory life, though he did not know which aspect of Cousin Hannah was dying—would hate to think all were dying, facet after facet —so much of her life having always been hidden from him, no doubt, as from human eyes. Perhaps only the sand lizard had known her. She had spoken of many things which were in themselves no doubt believable—if history could be believed—the armies moving at night across a wave-streaked desert floor, the luxuries of imperial courts, garb and weapons of soldiers who never again would hear the trumpet sound, the screamings of stone horses above the roar of desert sands, the chargings of stone horsemen, contests in the great amphitheatres between Christians and lions, games and many other details of ancient government and life, roaring lions wearing crowns of gold, glass crosses, for they were Christian converts, the architecture of Eastern cities trembling like something under water, even like the hulls of the old ships with folded wings, paving stones of silver and gold lighted by frozen torches, the great pagodas moving through clouds at the edge of the world, the great stone boats among the leaping waves, gardens of beautiful odalisques no man had ever seen unless he died, their faces veiled by torpid moonlight, walls, palaces, towers, camel market places, sacred pools of ibis and swan and heron-footed king, all of which Mr. Spitzer could almost follow, though her remarks were punctuated by continuous cries, whistlings, whinings, whisperings as of a hidden chaos—and perhaps he could hear through all her cries the tinklings of camel bells, tent bells, wind bells, the winds sighing through desert shrouds and falling snowflakes. He had certainly always thought that she was nearer to Mt. Hecla, the iceberg burning with inner fire, than to the burning desert sand, the desert rose. His eyes were blinded as he watched. From tiny bits, broken mosaics, gleamings of stone traced by the lizard's path, pieces of glass gleaming through fog, he had to put together a complex pattern he was only beginning to understand. Was it a city or a mirage shining through clouds? Was it the future or the past?

Her dreams were certainly not omens of the future—no crystal-gazer being needed now to predict the uncertain run of fate like shoals of starfish or golden-wreathed lions' mouths or moon jellies brought upon a lonely tide after all movement had ceased in this world, nor would it be told by flights of fluttering swallows in the dim empearled chamber as before the death of some old king with rattling ivory bones, a smile upon his face as Mr. Spitzer thought—considering that she would never play another card, neither heart nor spade—never rescue another love, not even herself—so were her dreams of the past or of the perpetual present —or did they, most subjected to time, transpire outside of time—and did they have a being of their own as he imagined? Did they arise from some deeper necessity than time, time which was as thin, as superficial as a sheath of ice upon a brook where the tinkling water ran, this artifice a man might see beyond, knowing that it was he who was the creator of time and circumstance and memory and love? It seemed that she knew not of those limitations which others knew—almost as if her life might have its beginning now when it had its end. There was perhaps no coordination at this last hour between dying and dying—as if something escaped. Was her tide not free, obeying its own movements of rhythms and return, harnessed to no moon? Was her tide not coordinated with this dying tide—as if her highest tide, great breakers and rolling clouds, great thunderheads dashing upon this shore of rock, came but with the neap tide which others knew, the least of the lunar month, the lowest tide going out with that diminished or diminishing music Mr. Spitzer heard with his conch ear, the waves scarcely reaching to his ear like the foam whisper of city traffic? Besides, there was this lingering presentiment that she had died long before—perhaps long before him—for how did he know that the person dying now was one he had not seen since his forgotten youth and who had existed so largely by rumor? And how did she know him? Perhaps he had only her word for it as to who she was—only her uncertain testimonial as to all those adventures through which she had passed or might be passing now, it seemed to him, he always permitting the spokes of the wheel to extend as far as possible before they reached the clouded rim of doubt like some great jellyfish where he saw the shadow of a boat, the shadow of a sundial with its arm a flight of birds.

At times she seemed to be speaking, there in the blowing fog, to the Emperor Tiberius with his trailing purple robes. At times she seemed to be speaking to kings in fields of clouds as the luminous cloud ceiling lifted with fishes' fins, that which had once been the floor of the ocean becoming the ceiling, showing their long webbed toes upon a desert floor streaked with golden coins, their golden crowns like dented discs gleaming above this sea of shifting light. At times she spoke to whistling satin skirts or winding shrouds. It was hard for Mr. Spitzer to resist the impression that there were obscure beings besides himself in this room—many people he surely would not have expected to meet in this life or if he wandered forever through the wide realms of death. At times he was almost of the opinion that they were the same and indistinguishable. At other times there seemed a subtle difference—much as if man's beginning should not be his ending or his ending his beginning—as if there should always be these two centers of storm like two poles of being—as if there should be these mercurial differences flashing forever and these nuances and these incalculable moments like moons or suns—or else how should there be even the idea of progress, and how should one justify one's sorrows if one had experienced nothing, learned nothing—dying as if there had been no life, no love—as if nothing had happened to teach the wisdom of the heart—as if this life faded like a dream which would be succeeded by no other dream or memory or falsification of memory?

Mr. Spitzer surely had heard her saying many things which he must have heard before, perhaps in some other life, one he had not lived and yet remembered—that two parallel lines would not make a box, that there would be no box—that eight lines were required for a box in order to enclose something on four sides. Oh, that's a mere board, she said, a mere spar, an old piece of driftwood drifting on the tide. Mr. Spitzer could certainly agree to this, nodding his head as his torpor increased—

and after all, he might console himself with the thought that she had not asked for his agreement. She spoke of a keyhole so greatly magnified that a star passed through it. Mr. Spitzer had thought that only a spindled butterfly could pass—but then, he was used to shrinkings like his faded music. She spoke of a building so greatly magnified that it was endless, no doubt, as Mr. Spitzer knew, no vision encompassing all its roofs, minarets, domes, towers, sunken gardens, mosaics, porches, stepping stones, stairways.

She spoke of the great snow-horned Alps forming, rising in her heart, the frozen pinnacles, the crystal caskets through which she saw the stars, the frozen stairways rising through endless clouds, the bearded crystal-hunter climbing with his pick axe through mountainous rolling clouds and fields of streaked light, unfading starlight, vaporous clouds enfolding him and the crystal moon and the moon's reflection on a cloud, a cloud like a swollen eyelid through which the moon shone dull as lead. Or so Mr. Spitzer thought though perhaps, of course, he might have heard incorrectly. So many times he heard voices which others did not hear. Oh, the whole thing's full of fallacies, she suddenly exclaimed—you can't stretch it to that, or else the line will break. It's the merest silken thread, this cable. Why, it's a hair, dear heart, a hair of starlight reaching through a cloud and not a bridge, she said as if she were speaking to someone, though Mr. Spitzer could hardly believe that he heard what he heard, for his ears as usual deceived him, and all these wild remarks were like something he was dreaming, much as if he resurrected that past which never was—he awakening, sharply reminding himself that he had never trusted her adventures in the remote past when there still might have been a possibility of checking on them, perhaps ascertaining where she was, who she was, had never trusted her when there was surely greater reason for his trust than now when she was crumbling, fading into wind, snow, sand, shadow, starlight under the sunken moon with its crumbling porches, sunken towers, broken columns, drowned thresholds, drowned horses' heads, drowned dophins with their faces turned toward the sky. Why should he believe in her now when there was no proof? Why should he believe in the future when he could not believe in the present or past?

Yet he listened sympathetically, of course, being attuned by long experience with things chimerical and fading, so great was his capacity for understanding when the reason for his understanding failed and faded like the last drop of color drained from the sky, when he heard these shrill cries breaking through glassy clouds or heard only the dying chord forever trembling or a falling leaf in a forever whirling whirlwind or the faintest whisper ever to reach human ears, perhaps the thumping of a dead heart, dead bird.

It seemed to him that his understanding always came too late. It came only when it was too late to do anybody good, being like a gift freely given to one who could not express his appreciation, his gratitude for the bounty of memory or recognition.

Mr. Spitzer saw the over-all meaning of life only when life was over, perhaps not even then, for he heard this whistling, crying in his dead ear. She cried, sighed, whispered, screamed, shrieked, whistled though he could not always distinguish her voice among so many singing hailstones, singing stars, clashing rocks, whispering clouds, snow falls drifting like curtains in the dark air. She seemed to be lost in the storm increasing cell by cell. She was like a mad jockey riding in the steeplechase of years. She plunged, rose again, was visible for one moment before she disappeared, climbing in distant mountains with their shoulders starred by snow, snow upon their jeweled crowns, rising through distant snow clouds and cloudbursts as this cosmography was changed in the shiftings of clouds and stars and falling snow and phantasmal peaks and frozen cascades and still lagoons and waters roaring like the tears of the world. He did not know the person to whom she spoke, for he could hear her voice but not the answer, not even an echo crying when the silence increased like the snow upon the mountains.

If you lose footing now, she cried, then you fall ten thousand miles. You fall with falling stars. You fall with stars, waters, boats, snow, sands, swans, this falling world. Oh, where's my little boat I put upon the tide? Where's my figurehead? Oh, is that Ur of the Chaldees glittering there where the sand blows, lifts in the wind? Is that Nineveh, Crete, Babylon? She asked, perhaps after many hours when there was only the wind— Does the wind whistle through sand, through rising waves crested by the pale pearl of foam? Is that a sea shell? Is that a turret? Is that a stairway? Where's my helmet? Where's my rose? Is that the little gate-keeper in the grey light? How do you do?

Did she come to the great city beyond human experience, or was it a dream she dreamed long ago? Indeed, had she ever left Boston, Mr. Spitzer sometimes dreamily wondered—or if so, had she ever returned? She asked of the great crystal-gazer who had appeared out of the void and was staring through clouds—what did he see as he gazed into the crystal ball? Did he see an eye? Was it the eye of a bird or a woman? Was this her hand she saw, long-fingered and veined with light? Was this her finger reaching through a cloud, a door? Was that a minaret, dome, tower, wall, city, door, threshold? Was that a valley shadowed by an icy mountain peak? Was that a moving mountain or a cloud feathered with silver light? Being hysterical, she did not always know who she was, where she was—perhaps had never known—indeed, perhaps had been as mystified as Mr. Spitzer was. Should she not escape from reality, she asked, for had she not always escaped—when had reality bound her? She had always escaped from herself—at least until now—and should she not escape from herself when all things were dividing, crumbling into water, snow, cloud, when falling leaves were corpses like the falling stars? She seemed to be wandering through crystal desert sands and great marble mountains much as if her journey had not ended, as if it were beginning. If ever she had had a disciple, she was alone, none following her now. None knew where she went or even when. She spoke of mirages which this life had been, sand storms, hail storms, narrow threads widening into never-ending valleys, frozen rivers winding through clouds, crumbling roads at the edges of bottomless chasms through which the stars shone, the pebble which started the avalanche. The wind was singing in her dead ear. She spoke of the sand dunes rising to the mountains, the glassy clouds, the stars. She said that the shell enclosed this pearl world. Was she tossing in her little boat? Was that the great angel blowing his horn upon a lonely mountain top where the great pearly combers rolled, rising like mountains, ram's horn she heard winding through miles of clouds as the snow powdered the thinning air, and did she hear what she had always heard, these tinkling bells, camel bells, tent bells, snow bells falling in the wind at astral altitudes, wind bells falling from star to star, dying notes, silent footfalls, a snowflake falling in a cloud or a white feather drifting? Did she hear that which was never heard, see that which was never seen by man or woman on earth? Whom did she see now? Was that the great lamp-lighter coming now to light her way through worlds of darkness and desert sand? Was she the burning phoenix or the star? Then put out the light, she said. For she was hidden. She was hidden from human eyes. None should see the face of love and live. The light should not shine on her or reveal her hiding place, nesting place. Should she find in the light that which was not found in darkness and in whirlwind? Should she find love only after she found death? Life's problems did not decrease when the great paradox was yawning in her face.

Her mind wandered on and on as Mr. Spitzer, though trying to concentrate, trying to focus upon a distant halo, felt himself slipping into deeper sleep, doubtless because of his increasing sympathy for the great suffrage captain now when it was impossible to subject her forlorn adventures to the searchlight of consciousness, when the dream required no counterpart of truth or testimonial of any eye witness, ear witness, for death required no life or principle of contrast in order to be death, it had always seemed to him. As for himself, he was supernumerary, unnecessary, no matter where he was. Death said not what it intended, for its intentions were over along with all lack of realizations. Death required no image, no body of love, medusa or sea flower. Death required no spark, not one pale facet gleaming through a dark cloud, not one firefly lighting a wave. All that a man might experience—had he not said—was it not always here, locked in his own heart, both future and past? Was not she her own enigma, that intricate lock which would be opened by no locksmith, that crystal casket enclosing her on three sides, and who should tamper with the dead heart, and who should awaken the dead to life and love when the great mystery was over?

One eye closing, one eye gleaming, glaring through livid clouds and darkness and whirlwind, she stared at him as he heard her complaining of howling winds, freezing stars, great snow clouds thundering in the wide heavens, flashing diamond horseshoes, glare of a torch light in her eye, a burning reed. She asked—Oh, where's my court musician? Comes he not to the dying king? Comes he not with his great gold harp strings played by the flying seagulls, the seagulls flying among the strings, strings reaching from heaven to earth, and is that the starfish musician scraping

these ivory keys? Is that the harper? Who blows this great Triton's shell?
Where's my Arab, the gold-fringed top drifting over his eyes like the old-
fashioned surrey in which man rode as in a shell? Is that you, Abdullah?
Ah, is it the month of Ramadan? Is it Shiraz or the sandalwood and the
jewel and the incense of a dream, that great eye shining through a cloud?
Is that you, great horseman rising with a star through the clouds, and do
I hear your long-bodied dogs barking at your horse's feet, the snow falling
upon another falling star, or is it only the singing wind? Is that you, my
Chinese lord, great pagoda, great mandarin with a ladder of swans
perched upon his head, and do you move through the city? Where's my
great swan-breasted king who moved through waters and clouds with the
moving city? Where's he who never was? Does the snow fall on the roof?
Where's my love, my love in the mountains, my love in the desert, my
love under the earth and my love above the earth, my love on some other
star or this star, the jewel gleaming in his forehead? Or is it the third
eye? Is it the eighth day of the week, the thirteenth month of the year? Is
that you, great turban-winder winding your turban, unwinding your
turban through miles of clouds, great dancer in the infinite, and do you
come to strangle me so that I cannot cry out, and my voice is drowned?
Who pulled the bellrope? Is that the bellrope or the umbilical cord?
What are these muffled bells? Does the wind whistle through my sheets,
my shrouds? Where shall I tent this night, upon what star where the
moth tents, sleeping in its own bubbled light?

Half rising from her bed, she cried—Ah, Black Moor, beloved of
woman, you who made all hearts flutter and all women lift their veils!
You like the black rooster crowing in the white snow! Crow no more,
black rooster shaking prisms of blue and green and gold in clouds, for the
night descends like a curtain, and the night is long. Ah, black rooster
with his gold comb in the cloud, gold eye, purple eye! Did he crow over
me, flap his wings in some hallucinatory dawn? Ah, crow no more, black
rooster, she cried. It is different over there. In heaven it is different. In
heaven the black rooster lays the egg, and the white hen crows. The hen
crows, black rooster, she cried, and none shall stop her. It is she for whom
there is no dawn. Still half rising, still in this almost flying position, the
old suffrage captain pulled the flying bellrope in a dream, asking—What
are these bells, bells, bells ringing, ringing the bell-ringer, and who has
ever heard them, who but I? Are the mountains clanging like church
bells, old church bells the great Crusader heard when he returned from
distant lands, lands of his eternal sleep, the snow upon his mouth,
his eyes, the snow upon his helmet like a roof reaching into clouds? Is it
the clock in some old church steeple rising through snow? She cried
against the clanging of bells, mountains, waves, this earth like a bell
ringing in a dark cloud, ringing for her dead love—then fell back upon
her pillow, still crying.

Strange phantoms moved through clouds as this great suffrage captain was returned to her ancestors, even like some old king who gives up
one throne for another throne, lays down one crown for another crown,
increasing his principalities by death's limitless territory. So that this old

lawyer with his portfolio and rustling papers, his face among the light-checkered shadows moving in the wind, could only say—I see the king. But where is the queen, mad queen of this deathless romance? In fact, Mr. Spitzer, though he should have been prepared for any surprise or shock, was very much surprised by this old suffrage captain's crying out for her skirts—until remembering that, of course, she was as usual right in matters sartorial, that in ancient days both kings and queens wore skirts and that even unto this day in the Forbidden East, forbidden no doubt because of the peculiar custom, the men wore skirts, and the ladies wore trousers or bloomers. So that there was some doubt in his mind as to the identity of this phantom who was this Black Moor with black skirts whirling over mountains of snow, over finger minarets, over mountain pinnacles above black lakes reflecting stars—for this Black Moor who was woman's great love might be a man and not a woman as Mr. Spitzer might have supposed. He supposed that this Black Moor was in some ways related to the black coachman of the opium lady's dreams—Mr. Spitzer always finding that there were pawn figures moving not only from dream to dream of the dreamer but from dreamer to dreamer—and thus there was this incalculable factor contributing to the breakdown of the individual's life and integrity, it seemed to Mr. Spitzer—that no one could simply be himself. How often had he awakened dreaming his brother's dreams of shell games by the slowly moving, musical tide, horse heads running through clouds as if the inveterate gambler never would be cured, not even by death itself, that death on which, of course, he had taken his chance, though none had known whether he had won or lost?

Mr. Spitzer, his head drooping, nodding like a tired flower upon its stalk, for even a flower must sometimes sleep, heard many buzzings, cryings, heard this old suffrage captain crying for her Black Moor, her black-veiled gondolier with his oars breaking through black waves, waves of starlight—Where's my crystal casket, skull, box, jewel of consciousness, unconsciousness, ear, eye? Oh, love, thou art not living—but thou art not dead. If thou wert living or if thou wert dead, my problems would be simple. Must there be ever a compromise? Must I be involved in some great conspiracy with a maharajah? Where's my skirt which trailed through trailing clouds over these sands of time, she cried, and where's my love, dead love, dead heart, dead rose—and shall the living find her now? Is there no meeting place, place where two parallel lines meet? Where's my mirror, drifting through what cloud, cloud drifting over the dark, the sun-lit waters? Where is my hand reaching? Is this my hand I see drifting before me, or is it the wing of a bird, white bird fluted like fingers? Is this my foot, but what need have I now of feet, for where can my feet take me that my spirit cannot go? What are all these flagstones, blue, green, rose, gold shining through clouds? Is that my skirt like the bell ringing in the wind? Is it the clapper or the bell? Do the mountains ring, and does the sea answer, and is that a wave rising?

Mr. Spitzer thought she might still call upon her waning forces, still arise and get out of bed and walk like the cripple healed by some great, sudden miracle—for was she not capable of some new impulse or intuition which should defy all ghostly powers?—but she lay prone as an everlasting horizon, stretching out her withered limbs like those dim promontories which had never been explored by man and reached through endless clouds. She asked, babbling like an idiot—Is that the tent-maker? Is that the tent? Where does he set his tent, upon what star or cloud? Alas, what shell is this which covers me? Oh, I am buzzing like a bee hive filled with the buzzings of bees, she said, like a great stone hive. I am buzzing like an iceberg. Is that a wasp or a star? I am a tall building filled with lights. I am a blackened funnel belching smoke.

She complained that she was buzzing, buzzing, boiling inside. She heard star whistles, hurricane winds and bells, thunderings, roarings, poundings, earth ringing like a bell which filled the heavens with ringing. Was there no instrument to measure this pressure she felt inside of her—these inner cloud-bursts, flashings of stars, snow clouds thundering in distant heavens, stars falling, these burning crystal sands, mountains rising to the moon, the stars, clouds filled with eyes?

Oh, that's water running at my feet, she cried. There is a butterfly, its wings drifting down the wind. Its wings are folded. My sail is spent. Oh, the rope is frozen in my frozen hand. I am climbing mountains. Oh, shall I fall now as others fell? Shall I fall into the great abyss of which there is no floor, no ceiling? Shall I fall into love or death? Are both one? Then where's my love that disappeared, her hair like the white feathers drifting through snow, her gold eyes staring through a cloud? Are these two moons? Crystal-gazer, did you see her where the snow fell in the wind? Be careful now which way you turn, which step you take upon the snow falling into the clouds, the clouds falling into the snow when earth is this firmament, when this firmament is not this earth, she cried, half rising again in her bed, reaching. For many who sought for my true love were lost in the great avalanche of waves and snow. Ah, how many skiers were lost like the sail-boats. They were entombed by clouds and snows moving in the wind. Look not into the things that are to see the things that are not. Oh, you great crystal-hunter with crystal on your brow, you like Mr. Chandelier moving through clouds, did you see her, find her, find my sleeping love, my wild swan girl sleeping beyond the veil of snow? Oh, is it Bacchus and his crew of satyrs crowned by flowers, and are there dancing nymphs beyond this world, nymphs dancing with goats? Is this love, or is this death which veils me? Do I hear flutes, lutes, strings? Are those the music-makers or the dying wind?

Mr. Spitzer, having been present at the opium lady's many hallucinations—and, indeed, he was not sure that he had not confused them in memory with these—should perhaps not have been as surprised, as disturbed as he was by this old suffrage captain's confession of love, eternal love even when he could not be sure who was the lover and who was the loved, for all things were transitory, and it did seem that she in her last hour was making a parody or false image of life just when life was fading or had faded already so far as the limits of experience were concerned. So he had been silent in a room bugling with the memory of music. Perhaps she had always lived beyond experience—but who was he to say or draw a final curtain over the face of a dying lady? The light was already fading from her eyes. He could not say that he would have liked to have called her back to reality—for what was that? It had always disappointed her, and whatever disappointment she might feel now would be less than this. It had always been the void, the empty place of phantom stars, voices, winds. He could not be so presumptuous as to give advice when he had already failed or offer this final hope when there was no grain of hope, not even a sand grain. Should he say to her—It is not so difficult over there as it is over here? Should he say—You will find what you have lost? Should he say—Lo, I have returned—you have returned from your long journey through snow and starlight and wind? Such talk would certainly have been quite meaningless to her, one who, he had always understood, believed in no future life upon any other star or this doomed star. Her skepticism was greater than his. Had he not always tapped with his cane before he took a step—testing the pavement to see whether it was stone or cloud—at least for many years? Had he not always tapped at every lamp-post, feeling his way in the blurred light, being at all times uncertain of left or right or where he was, where he was not, where he might never be? Had he not knocked many times at the wrong door? And perhaps this sense of being lost, this early loss was what had drawn him to her in her dying hour, that which held him as he watched this dying soul depart and wondered who died, whether she died as she had lived or had not lived. Did she die as a stranger to herself? Did she know who she was?

He had surely heard these whispering skirts moving through seas of clouds, these silken whispers as of lifting or scudding sails, these delicate snowflakes blown like a lace scarf upon the wind—he surely was not mistaken—sensing that her opposite might be present in this veiled darkness, that even this great captain of the horse, though denying man, had lived and loved, the powdery starlight revealing now that rugged face like something carved out of rock as he heard her crying, crying with glassy cries in the winter wind like the hailstones falling through a cloud, the pebbles rolling and falling—for now all contradictions which had slumbered were increased, being like all things of this world and not of this world, all things human and unhuman, and should she be constant now, she who had never been constant before, and should she be predictable, she who had never been predictable, she who had kept no timetable but her own heart, she who had gone and come according to her whims, moods, sudden changes of spirit, violences like sudden whirlwinds, and should she be faithful, she who had never been faithful to any merely human life or love, she who had perhaps required a greater love than life could offer, a greater passion, a greater cause, she who would have felt restricted by marriage as if it were the grave, and should she be burdened by the ideal of truth when she was crumbling into lies, visions, dreams, phantoms blown upon the dusk of the world, inarticulate cryings, shoutings, whispers—and should she recognize those whom she had never recognized, acknowledge those whom she had ignored—and should he not long ago have been immured as one who was beyond surprise, one who had suffered the last great surprise which life might bear—one who had been baffled by so many great problems that he could hardly consider hers, he envying her that great transmutation which she doubtless suffered now beyond all consciousness—for who escaped this great crucible—so why should he now have felt, perhaps for many years, this slowly dawning astonishment as he recognized that she might be subject to sudden changes, veerings, reversals, somersaultings like Pierrot, opposites of her intentions, fits, starts—scaling unbelievable heights of roseate glory, no doubt, but falling away from her clouded pinnacle, falling like the evening star—changing her mind at that very moment demanding a decisive force, an unflagging attention or devotion, an unswerving integrity, a recruiting of her powers—and should he be appalled by that bright spirit reaching now through clouds and darkness and whirlwind as the withered claw hand reached at nothingness in the dark cloud, as the snowflake of this life hissed like fire, as the fire died in her staring eye? There would be only a few more flashings, gleamings.

Should she be unified now when she was falling apart like some old ship at its seams, some old ship with broken sides reeling in whirlwinds through which it had already passed, no captain on board? He had told himself, doubtless because of his maritime memories derived from a remote forefather, that not even the greatest calker could calk her now, that not even the greatest carpenter could mend her. If the Southern Cross should be missing from clouded heavens or if the Northern Cross should be missing, then who could return it? Who could return a lost star or the constellations flying like birds across this world? Water ran through her jagged holes and port-holes, and water covered the upper deck, the lower deck, and water soon would cover the forecastle, the long-haired crow's-nest. He had caught himself thinking of tonnage, keeling, listing, ships' bells in wind and storm, wondering whether the figurehead was the New England wife or great turbaned Moor plowing through waves, had caught himself wondering who the passenger was or whether there was a passenger or whether there were only a few old snow birds perched like ghosts upon the leaning mast. For she was going down. She was whirling in the whirlpool. Soon there would be only the wreckage, only a few old spars drifting upon the tide or some old barnacled tree branch brought up upon a distant shore where, of course, Mr. Spitzer would not be.

For he would be upon the other shore. He would not be over there. He would be over here.

He had kept telling himself that there was nothing new which should startle him, for he had been present in many storms, many whirlwinds blowing leaves, many monsoons of dying vision. He would not have been surprised by fishes like candle flames or eyes floating over his head, by great balloon fishes with negligee streamers streaming through the dusk—would not have been surprised by the celestial horse-headed peacocks crying in the windy gardens—or some great shah with his face shrouded—he having witnessed all of these things before, no doubt. She had certainly offended his dignity or his sense of the probable, however, by asking an invisible presence for a mirror now when even the greatest beauty should no longer stare into her glass, when she should be grateful for clouds and distortions and whirlwinds, when her face should soon be the skull naked as the skull moon in the cloud, when she should surely have veiled herself with secrecy like the cocooned women of the East whose lords do not see their loves.

And did man ever see his love or woman see her love? All earthly imagery was slowly dying. Yet would there not always be some firefly or spark or memory of human life? Would there not always be some house, door, sea shell with water running at its mouth, rose, cross, zooming bee? If this earth were totally abandoned, would not a bee zoom in a meadow of wild flowers or ambrosial water stream from a horse's foot or an old door creak on rusted hinges, a seagull perch upon a tapestry chair, a prism break in the wind, a leaf fall?

As if to confirm his prolonged suspicions that now she might be giving up her great cause as she gave up her ghost, this breath of life, that now at this last moment she might be reversing herself, going over to the other side, going over to the opposition, denying all for which she had ever lived, struggled, suffered, as if now she might be remembering that timid lady she had killed long ago in her own heart, that lady like fire burning under the pearl skin of the snow, like some great eye staring through clouds, she had cried—My mirror, oh, my frozen mirror now! Hand me my mirror. Mirror over which the long-limbed white bird flies as over frozen lakes, clouds, mountains! The snow, the snow falls on my mouth, my eyelids. Oh, I am falling now, slipping. Pebbles roar, breaking like glass. Am I falling into death? Am I falling into death or love, eternal love, or am I awakening? Is this the beginning or end, or was there ever only this one moment, moment when I lost her? Oh, where's my skirt, white skirt lifting in the wind? And was it not edged with flounces of lace, with veils of snow, with meadows of wild flowers? Were there not great cascades of satin reaching from heaven to earth? Was there not the white of edelweiss embroidered upon the hem? Were there not fields of asphodel thin as Pleiades through which we climbed like sailor birds?

A sail, a wing, she cried—a wing, a sail! A light, a light! I see a light upon the other shore. Is it the will-o'-the-wisp, and must I follow her who followed me? What firefly now before the dark helm of this dark earth boat? Who leads the voyager and the voyage?

The wave rises, falls, she sobbed, cried like the rising, falling wave as Mr. Spitzer listened with considerable astonishment, wondering whose death-bed scene he witnessed. He thought perhaps he was asleep.

For he seemed to be hearing things he could not possibly have heard if he had been awake, and many times it had occurred to him that perhaps he had never been fully awake throughout his entire life. He must also remember that he was perhaps not the best of all possible witnesses to death-bed scenes, for did he know whether he was alive or dead or who he was? Besides, he had a tendency to keep things alive after they were gone. So that he must leave at all times a wide margin for error or doubt and must be hesitant now in reconstructing this enigmatic memory of her last words and must also recognize that, as he had told himself at the time, she was not in her complete senses and perhaps not responsible for all she said, for all lives were flowing together as the walls between individuals were broken down, it seemed to him. Also, there were cells which could be defined as neither of life nor death but perhaps of both, being amorphous. What thin membrane was the skin to enclose the individual, whether of rose or star or candle flame. So no wonder if she should seem someone else at this last hour. And yet how strange that she should cry for her beautiful skirt of clouds and waters as he might cry for his skin, as he might wish that he were clothed.

Perhaps she had cried all her life like this, and he was only hearing her now like music previously ignored. Oh, where's my skirt which I took off so long ago in a snow storm which blinded me, confused me, he heard her crying as the silence increased, and shall I put on my skirt again like the surf booming against the great, jagged rocks reaching through clouds? And was there the snow billowing like lace through which I saw a falling star?

Oh, who will cover me and make me beautiful for my great lord who comes in darkness and in snow and whirlwind, the snow upon his mountainous brow, his great stone helmet plumed with the white feather of the bird, his breastplate flashing with jewels? And is there not a stairway, and is there not a door? Do I come again to that dark tower? Is that the winding horn? Shall I put on this body and this love?

Is that my love, my skirt moving through clouds, and are there not ribbons like rivers flowing through clouds, snow clouds?

Oh, is she in the shadowed valley or at the highest mountain peak, or do the mountains move as I watch now, or was this cosmography never of earth?

Oh, where's my love, my lost love, my skirt, my dead heart, my living rose—she cried and cried in darkness and in whirlwind—where's my skirt I lost so long ago, and who has found it? Where is it? Upon what mountain now, what stony lip reaching through clouds, what heights where none may climb?

Skiff moon, did you see her, my nymph, my lovely girl? Huntsman, where is she? Did the mountain goat see her, her gold eyes staring through the cloud, dark cloud—where shall I find her now, my rose, my heart, my dead heart, the snow upon her breasts, her limbs—and what are these great pinnacles rising now before me—or is that the mountain goat rising to a distant peak, staring at me through clouds, his gold eyes, his beard? Does he come to my bed? Do I die now and know not whether she died or lived? Who searches now for me through mountains and deserts and under the falling snow? Do dogs bark in distant mountains?

Death might be her life, her love, her whisper in the darkness, she whispered, for should love be extinguished by death?

CHAPTER 44

THERE had been some truth, not all being as moonbeams in this life. There was granite, and there was sunlight. The truth was less but greater than illusion, Mr. Spitzer knew throughout the after-years, slowly putting together these fragments, hints, suggestions until the shadow of the truth emerged if but for a fleeting moment. How odd it had seemed then when Cousin Hannah was dying that she should have spoken so much of skirts, laces, flounces, petticoats, for was she not that great bloomer girl who had been the enemy of fashion-mongers and who had spent all her life urging that ladies take off their skirts, that they relieve themselves from unnecessary encumbrances which dragged them down and weighted them and made it impossible that they should carry on successfully the battle against men? How odd that at the last, as one who was going over to her mysterious bridegroom, she should call for her skirt.

Over this chapter of her history Mr. Spitzer would certainly draw, as he might say, the veil—would never reveal to any possible future biographer that she had not been, as all had supposed, the great hero—or that if she had lived as a hero, she had perhaps not died as a hero, not even as a great heroine blowing her angelic trumpet or some old Triton's horn. But truth to tell, no one had inquired for years and years. She had already lived beyond all but the most feeble memory of her. Her fame was certainly tarnished, dimmed by time long before Mr. Spitzer ever knew her. No one had brought her a laurel wreath or medal or crown. She had already passed into oblivion.

The days of her loud fanfare were over long before she died, so that only he had heard her last remarks, her crying—Oh, where's my love, lost love? Where's my little snowdrop?

So that he, perhaps not understanding fully all that he understood in retrospect when his understanding would do him no possible good, had brought to this great suffrage captain a handful of white flowers, snowdrops delicate as a wraith of mist upon the mountains, and then had been surprised that her agony had increased when she saw the white flowers like snow melting in her hand, and that from that moment she had begun to fade. It was almost as if his own magic had done this, albeit it was a magic he was powerless to control, he often reminding himself of a musician whose baton had gotten loose from him and continued to dance, conducting music of clouds, waters, winds, avalanches. The last light had seemed to go out as if the sunlight faded from her living eye which had stared at him and was now this pale transparency like a hole in a dark cloud.

She had cried through dying years—Oh, my love, my love! My love blinded by the snow, the snow in the wind! Have you gone to find your skirt, and where did you leave it? Did I not warn you, beg you not to go, she cried, though little did I dream that you would not return, that I would search for you through all the after-years? Or else I would have gone with you, and we would not have returned.

There was no one to see your nakedness, she explained, your body white as that great peak booming into clouds. So why this sudden modesty? There was no moon, and there was no sun in those clouds pale as ashes over us. There was a false moon, and there was a false sun, and the planets were false. They were false as paper boats.

So Mr. Spitzer thought, hearing her, that perhaps, indeed, it was all a colossal jest—for certainly it seemed strange that a suffragette should die like this, crying for her love, dead love.

False modesty killed my love, she cried, and not I, not I, my love. There was no man in all those mountains. There was not the eye of a sparrow. There was not one star looking down. There were no watchers in the snow, the clouds. I could not see you or your shadow. You turned away so suddenly, she plaintively accused, took one step soft as the snow falling through the cloud, soft as the hiss of a snowdrop. You whispered— I must find my skirt. I must find my skirt, my love. Farewell, farewell, my love. And how could Cousin Hannah, battling for her life, influence her then or hold her back?

Did not great winds blow against me, Cousin Hannah asked—and what sail had I to reef and tack, haul, let out, draw in? What anchor to cast upon the moving rock? My eyes were blinded by the snow, the wind, by the great icicles driving sharp as swords against my bleeding heart—so that I staggered, wandered. My breath was a frozen plume. I could not see my breath.

Oh, lord, great lord, lord of the lost creation! Is that the iceberg, she shouted as if she were living through that moment now, as if an iceberg were charging like mad white horses with long white manes, as if she heard a ghostly boom shattering clouds—and who can blame me if I fall or fall not?

Did I let go with my hand which should have clung to yours, even through all eternity or for one moment? Was this true love or false, she asked as the wind howled. Was I false, and were you true? Was I true, and were you false, false as the snow glare, false as the heart of darkness and whirlwind? For false was my true love's heart. But who am I to accuse? If we cannot be true together, then let us be false together, she cried when she was dying.

Ah, my lovely bride, she whispered—and are you bearded by the hoar frost, and are you now as I was or as I am become? Why were you in love with the other side of the mountain range, you who were content with little things before, veils, hats, skirts, mirrors, you who loved cats' eyes, poodle dogs, ribbons?

Why were you suddenly so grand, you who loved only frivolities, flirtatious airs? Why, this great suffrage captain asked of someone who was not there, were you in love with those great snow-crowned mountain peaks where no castles were, where no great stone griffins looked down from the clouds, the clouded heights? No lights shone through the clouds, no lights at any window or door. Did I not ask for you at every castle gate? Did I not blow my trumpet in every lonely courtyard? Did I not arouse sleeping stable boys? Did I not howl in every wind? Did I not search for you through mountains of snow and deserts of snow and under crystal sand?

I pitched my tent in distant mountains. I slept in tombs. Ah, love. Let us put on our whispering skirts. Let us gaze into our mirrors now, she sighed, when life departs, when none can see us. Some secrecy should surely be the privilege of the dead. We have no horoscope, no future.

She asked when there was no sound but the rain running through an old water spout—Who knocks now at the ivory gates? Is that you, Black-amoor, or the water carrier with his tinkling bells, the muleteer? What goes into the making of a mirage? Is that my butterfly, my peacock? Have I not sought for the lost image through the dusk? Did I not drive a phaeton through a cloud? Did I not go before the wave?

Ah, had not Cousin Hannah inquired of white-winged birds and skiers in lonely mountains and skiing horses, chamois-hunters of the chamois leaping from peak to peak, mountain-climbers with their St. Bernards nosing through snow—Have you seen my love? Was not this Mt. Blanc always in my heart? Does she stare through gleaming prisms? White lady, where are you now?

So that Mr. Spitzer was very much confused. Much that he might have heard was then perhaps unintelligible to a man who, like himself, was guided by his reason even when reason failed and who heard the beating of the heart long after the heart had ceased to beat, for the dead heart was like a sea shell carrying its own roaring. Indeed, he would have preferred to eavesdrop upon the roaring of a lonely sea shell—and thus had heard many forlorn and beautiful things in his walks along the beaches. Perhaps it took a long time for such remarks to sink into his consciousness as through miles of clouds, a long time to realize that what he had over-heard had been something more than he had supposed, something less, that it had pertained not to the imaginary phantom or being blown along the dusk but was the confession of this great suffrage captain's personal love, dead love which had prompted her suffrage movement and battles against overwhelming odds. She, too, had loved and lost. What was unexpected about this?

She was this beau joueur of suffrage and its martyr, had he not always thought, and should he be surprised by this last logic of her life, by this ambivalence splitting her apart into the lover and the loved? Should he be surprised that even she should contain within her a seed of buried hope to move mountains and stars and cause great avalanches, heavy snow fall on the roofs? For all had begun, as he might say, with ghostly love—and all had ended no doubt with the same, that ghostly love which was the beginning of love like the love of the Troubadour for the dead love, false lady, love founded on death.

Yet great problems, great surprises had been in store at the end for this old lawyer who, long after things were over, must go on with them, much as he heard race-track music long after Peron's last horse race upon this star—though why should Mr. Spitzer have heard this undying music or the starter's winding horn—or were there two dream tracks, he asked, like heaven and hell?

Adventitious moments, trivial attitudes he had dismissed before, irrelevant intuitions which had never quite escaped from the crevices of his memory, all had somehow added up to mountains of the moon and that residue of mystery or love time could not kill, for it had never existed in time. Scandalous as this great lady's life had been and filled with many tremors, many shocks, it was the silent and unknown moment most disturbing to him, that moment in which he had seen her human heart and frailties allying her at her last hour to other ladies and perhaps to men.

Truly, if she was this woman's hero, yet she was impotent and powerless—for a moth's wing brushing against her cheek might have killed her—he knew when this great golden chanticleer of suffrage could crow no more, when there was only a rattle in her throat like pebbles washed by tides.

He knew then, with something like a forlorn certainty he had never previously experienced, why she had gone into the distant countries beyond the eyes of men, why she was always lost in clouds and snows and sands and whirlwinds, why she had fought those incalculable wars against great lords and kings shrouded by winding sheets, why she had travelled in the deserts of Persia where there grew no flowers, why she had climbed like a sleep-walker the mountains of snow crumbling at a step above the void where no star was. If she could not be trusted then, who should trust her now? Might not some dead impulse still start up or a flower bloom? Might there not be heard as in a distant cavern the beating of her dead heart? Might there not be heard the faint tide under sand, the faintest trickle?

As for cowardice in the face of great obstacles, that subject seemed to him as complex, as complicated as human love, not easily understood. She was known for bravery, for never wearing the white feather of cowardice, and yet she had accused herself of cowardice when she was dying in that lonely chamber where only he was eye witness, he seeing best with his eyes closed. She had acted as if she had been cashiered from every army and exiled from every land, driven beyond every border, known and unknown. She was a man without a country. She was that poor mollusk who had no sea shell, no mother-of-pearl mantle, Mr. Spitzer often thought, seeing this gaunt skeleton emerge through leaden-colored clouds like a forbidding coast. She had acted as if she had failed in her own esteem, as if she were not that great leader she had seemed, that valiant rescuer of dying ladies in windy towers, that noble Crusader armored by her pride, her tenacious courage, that dashing adventurer others had supposed she was, so many ladies and some unfortunate men having envied her the great exploits and deeds of prowess and deeds of courtesy for which she had been all but immortalized long years before her actual death which none knew, and none remembered what her deeds were. She herself had been forgotten, just as he who does not remember the whirlpool will not remember its center. Actual death could add scarcely a note to that which had already occurred.

So that Mr. Spitzer's addenda was scarcely needed now, it being his fate to come always at that gratuitous moment after the end, she having already passed into that tenebrous obscurity and moon-streaked fog where were only shifting forms like flowers turning into birds, birds turning into flowers, he would suppose, that death was this eternal transmutation and could not be localized. Who rung these changes? Images of lead were turned into finest gold. Yet for her there seemed a greater finality than perhaps for him, this watcher in the storm.

Had not the greatest heroes been prompted by secret cowardice, and was not this often the meaning of their lives, and had not Cousin Hannah said so, that this was why they rode away to war? They had been guilty of some fearful act of cowardice, and this had driven them to greater and greater battles and victories by no means conclusive, this inner knowledge that they had already failed, that though they might storm great mountains, climbing through monsoon weather to snow-topped citadels never reached by any mountain-climber, they had already lost some greater battle than history might record. Perhaps that battle might be the tiniest ever fought, one for which there was no battle music, no great hymnal. He had always thought that the burning moth was more heroic than the burning star, for the star burned because of its own nature, and the moth burned because of its desire. And yet he was not sure—perhaps the star burned because of its desire. He did not know, all things being relative. Surely, the great hero might be a quavering coward at heart, how often Mr. Spitzer had himself timidly observed, and the weakest creature might be the greatest hero. No hero so great as some tiny skiff going down in a great storm. No hero so great as the moth winging toward the star.

And thus he guarded against giving honor to the greatest captains and kings, those who had won great acclaim, those whom the world recognized and applauded. He guarded against giving them undue honor even when they were forgotten. He preferred to acknowledge those who had always been ignored, those to whom had been extended no accolade. After all, he had been ignored. Was he not himself in some degree heroic, knocking upon this door, bearding the sleeping lion in its den? Yet there were some who might say that he had waited until it was safe to come to this great anchorite of suffrage upon the rock reaching through miles of clouds, some who would give him no recognition for his previous efforts to find her out, to catch her in the shining toils of memory. For as to this great lady, was she not weak, frail, timid now, even like all those to whom she had objected with such savagery that it seemed the laughter of the storm? Perhaps she had been killed by her laughter, even like Mr. Spitzer's brother. Perhaps she had been killed by a tear.

He knew that there was no such thing as safety—not even for her—certainly none for him, this old lawyer going through her rustling papers when she was dead, doing his duty, winding up her affairs which should have wound up themselves had there been any justice on earth. He had seemed to hear a ghostly footstep. He had seemed to hear a snowflake falling in a dim abyss or a curled leaf blown, tossed about like a cradle upon the whirlwind of death. He had heard a closing door. Perhaps he had heard nothing except what he dreamed, of course, as when he heard the voices in the clouds or the roaring of the long-tongued surf.

He had proceeded with caution, as had always been his custom of never jumping to a quick conclusion, a false conclusion, for then he would have to retrace his steps if that was possible. He could not trust his memory. His judgment must proceed with circular motions, doubtless because he was a musician before he was a lawyer. The law had restricted him. He had searched through old desks inlaid with moon-washed mother-of-pearl in which he had supposed there would be secret drawers —as there were—and he had opened them and many secret boxes by secret keys of trembling silver and gold—many pigeon-holes, many archives where were records of these great marches through waterless regions and mountains of porphyry and sapphire mountains, marches over great table lands, her battles in polyandrous countries and polygamous countries, her battles where the illusion of monogamy pertained though every couple slept with a ghost, her great rides against patriarchs and shieks, husbands and lovers and sons, her battles in buried cities where were those palaces of sandstone and long-limbed white cranes walking with folded wings—had gone through many old, mildewed letters, papers which had rustled in his trembling hands, papers rustling at his feet as if he heavily plowed his way through neap tides under the trembling paper moon like a white sail or kite upon the wind, papers rustling on the floor like the wings of white birds, some written over in spidery hieroglyphs—whether to some mad Antony or withered Cleopatra, he could not say, though surely he was confronted by mysteries greater than the Sphinx, for he was confronted by the mystery of the sterile heart begetting the mystery—some letters crumbling into ashes and dust, some in language of the shrouded dead, unintelligible as the language of lip-readers in countries where the lips were never seen, where the eyes were never revealed, some in foreign tongues which he could not read and never would have translated, for they were those languages which could never be translated by the greatest translator, languages for which there were no words, and we had forgotten our origin—and of what avail when all things were translated, even like the cryings in the voiceless winds, the voices in rasping clouds, or the far barkings of moon-white dogs?—many which had read less like letters to a suffragette than like love letters to a great love, perhaps to a dead love or god. Was there no key to open the human heart, no locksmith to cast the mold for this key, silver or gold, to open this enigmatic lock? Perhaps this mystery was the key, he had told himself, and there was no key but the mystery. There was no orchestration to include every flute note, whisper.

Perhaps this great suffragette's life provided the only illumination ever given upon that darkness which was never reached by light, the long fingers of rosy light reaching through the clouds at dawn, never reaching her. Certainly, her death did not denigrate, did not strip bare as when the leaves were blown from a tree in the wind, did not decrease the mystery of her life but rather had increased it, even like his own, Mr. Spitzer had found, and was inclined to believe now that this truth was seminal, that all other lives were increased by this great mystery of death, that all who lived had already died. Perhaps a leaf had fallen in the wind a thousand years ago, or a star had fallen through a cloud. Perhaps a door had slammed in a distant city. Perhaps a snail had crept out of its shell in the sand. The tide had swept over a salt flat pale as marble under the dead moon, Mr. Spitzer had observed. Death happened in many ways, more ways than love, some which were quite subtle, some which were bold.

It often seemed to him that the only wisdom or understanding which was his had come after the great event, and it seemed to him that in all other lives this was the case, that all were at the misty borderline defining no known realms. He would have liked to have asked of every whispering sea shell upon a lonely beach—What was your past life, and what waves washed over you, and what messages do you bring from a dead love to a dead love? Indeed, he had once found an old sea shell written over with the mystical writing—For all dead loves and all remembered things. I have travelled through many seas. He would have liked to have asked of every falling leaf—Did you fall twice, perhaps once in a dream? Of every starfish—Is this your second coming? Of every whirlwind or shape of darkness—Is this your resurrection and eternal life, this passage? And of the dolphin dying, gasping upon the rock under the star dying at clouded dawn as the light dies in a lover's eyes—Is this as it was, ever will be? Is there only this dying moment? Must not the lover die of love?

Staring with enlarged myopic eyes—and oh, what difficulties of vision were ever his—Mr. Spitzer had read these old papers shaking in his shaking hands so that he felt like the wind-blown poplar lighted by fish lights, had read these old papyrus scrolls like faded lilies crumbling at a touch, perhaps had read each paper twice—and if at times with a more than natural hesitation, if at times the print was blurred as if he read by moonlight, by one moonbeam streaming through a dark cloud, had done so with no more difficulty than he might read his own signature years after he had signed his clef or the snail writing in the moon-empearled sands moving like clouds marked by waves when the moon had faded, signs of stars drifting through plumed clouds, messages left by waves of blackbirds flying on a windy day of dissonance like his musical notes when the wind blew around his dark cape, his cape ringing like a bell, leaf imprints on stone, snowflakes falling from a dark cloud and melting as they touched stone. Ah, how many shapes of snowflakes, cartwheels, earth-borne asters, stars, flowers, lace mantillas through which eyes stared.

Yet he could not help being almost perpetually surprised that so many people had written to this great suffrage captain as if it were she who held the key to the mysteries of the complex human heart growing in complexity, for was not her heart in darkness and in terrifying whirlwind, he had asked when she was dead, and what should she know of life and light and love, and what human being had ever touched her? There was no open sesame to these mysteries he felt. Was she not shrouded by the darkness, and had she ever been revealed, and had there been even a moment of illumination lighting every heart, the living or the dead or that which was both the living and the dead, that which was the shadowed heart? Her star had passed long ago. Darkness now was hers. Surely, no Judas cock would ever crow again at dawn, and never would there be another dawn, he had thought as the clouds settled over her. Sometimes that whirlwind was like a great cone, a great cone reversed, standing on its apex, a shape of darkness through which one saw no spark or transitory star passing like a first love or last love and not one firefly gleaming in a distant cloud. And what should this old maid ever know of love and all the ramifications of the human heart, unhuman heart? What desire had ever been hers or what ambition? What goad, spur, motive?

Never had any other great suffragette received so many confidences, heard so many secrets of so many lives—Mr. Spitzer was almost inclined to believe that she had never been a suffragette at all, that suffrage was her mask. People had simply misunderstood her. Stars had spoken. Leaves had whispered. Waters had roared with voices. Pebbles had declared that they were tombs, tombs of scimitar moths. Clouds had whispered, rustled, sobbed, and there were falling snowflakes singing in her ear, her ear winding like the conch. Sand grains had whistled on a lonely star, and tides had whispered like the skirts of that great desert king, and night birds had sung among the salt-starred leaves. So many people had whispered their confidences to her, pouring their secrets into her ear as into a great stone ear or chamber of echoes, as if it were she who knew most of love and death and marriage, things she had never experienced in this life so far as anyone had known. Yet perhaps her admirers were right. Perhaps he knew most of love who never loved, and he knew most of death who never died, Mr. Spitzer thought, and he knew most of marriage who never married, was never committed to one road which had its ending. For sometimes the happiness of married couples was so secretive, so remote that it was as if they had withdrawn from life. It was as if they were dead, locked in an everlasting embrace. Perhaps the greatest love did not find its form of expression, either human or divine —no rose, flame, brook, swan trumpeting down a cloud. For all would fail. The light would go out of all eyes.

CHAPTER 45

Mr. Spitzer, this old Joachim who, the light fading from his eyes, trembled at the thought of any kind of love whatever upon this barren earth no matter what love it was, had read by faded candle flame this almost faded print twinkling like birds' feet or star points in rolling and vacuous clouds under a sky faintly gleaming like the mother-of-pearl lining of a sea shell as he considered that she was diffused through waters, clouds, stars, that none could reach her now. Indeed, he marvelled, with considerable chagrin in view of his own faithfulness, that anyone had ever reached her, for certainly she had not answered to his knock when he had come with great, increasing punctilio and many messages year after year to the empty house. He had passed that way many times when he was lighting the lamps, brushing softly like the wings of a moth, and had often knocked, receiving no response but an echo or faint whispering or rustling as of a curtain blown upon the wind.

Yes, how many letters which had been delivered to this great wanderer, she who had wandered like some penitential palmer with sea shells on his hat to show that he had prayed in the Holy Land, this forever wandering spirit seldom seen by man, letters inquiring after lost loves and dead brides and wandering husbands, many parchments without a return address, many without a name, some which were blank, so many letters that if they had ever reached her throughout the years, they must have been delivered by blackamoors stepping out of clouds, eunuchs in turbans of winding gold, rose-breasted pigeons flying under the crescent moon, boat moon drifting unmoored in a cloud, winged boys, cavaliers serventes such as employed by Venetians, or in this harsh climate the old Boston mail coach doubtless still rumbling upon some distant, winding, frost-rutted country road, the ice veiling the horses' heads, all marked with her official stamp Answered. But what had she answered and to whom if there was neither street nor name nor road, and what was the meaning of the confessional if the individual was not known or if there was no individual now? Never had Mr. Spitzer known an individual who did not crumble into waters and clouds if he watched long enough. So also with this old suffrage captain. Probably the answers never would be known, and this was an uncertainty necessarily most disconcerting to one who, like Mr. Spitzer, had yearned for a final answer and certainty beyond all doubt and no further equivocation even if it had meant the death of love and who would have been happier, much happier if there had not been one bird song or if all stars had been one great star or all fireflies had been one firefly glittering in a distant cloud and who had expected that others should have a greater certainty than his and who was disappointed, left with these questions unanswered. She had surely never answered him—had, indeed, ignored his existence for years beyond his memory. She had ignored his inquiries, his knocks, his hesitant tappings upon the rain-splashed sidewalk or the cloud.

There were the questions going on and on, questions winding upon themselves with other questions, but there were not the answers which he was left to imagine when she was dead, questions which he was left to answer as best he could, often inadequately, piecing together lost remarks, gleamings, fragments, splinters of undying thoughts casting an unholy radiance, often finding no answer but another question or question mark, particularly when his mind was occupied with something else, perhaps remembering his silent music, dirge or Epithalamium no ear or conch had ever heard, often telling himself that it would be the utmost naivete to plead his ignorance and his innocence, to plead that he was taken unaware by mysteries never intended for human eyes or ears, that he was shocked as if he had stumbled upon some great secret, that he had come upon the great abyss or stepped upon a pulsing cloud where he had thought there was no pavement. For certainly he had never suffered the ultimate shock but once, and certainly no surprise was ever complete so long as one lived, and there should be nothing surprising to one who had seen whole cities dissolve, one who had been prepared by many hints, glints, gleamings for this eventuality, and yet he had been surprised by the almost total confirmation of his suspicions, surprised that this great lady should have been this old captain of hearts and darts, one who was a rider through the storm of years, yet knew no love, no answer of the heart. For if one knew all hearts, one should know none. Love's image was that which was never reached by love, Mr. Spitzer knew now. Should love be reached, then there would follow, no doubt, the revulsion to that which had attracted love, and there would follow the death of love. He had watched her crying for her clouded mirror, but he had been mistaken in supposing that she wished to see her reflection, for never had she reproduced herself by mirror image or the cry of the night bird of love among the reeds of the hidden heart or the far splashing of water, and all had been, as he was fond of saying, illusion in this life as in this death. All had been his own sad vision, and all had been his own sad music only the dead had heard, his silent music of ripple and response. There was a rift in his lute.

Yet who could escape this ambivalence which Mr. Spitzer saw now—life and death, lover and loved? Some cherub in a cloud had surely looked down on her, staring with enlarged eyes until the light faded from this world. She was not alone. She was accompanied by this image as Mr. Spitzer by the moon, horned moon in the cloud. And was she not now this sleeping beauty whom all ladies become, her head wrapped in veils and clouds and pillowed on stone, this lady sleeping under waters and clouds as the snowflakes fell upon her staring eyes, her eyelashes like the hairs of the stars, and was she not beautiful as all those ladies she had ever tried to rescue from cruel lords and dead loves and cable chains binding them to this world? Who could escape love, for was it not like fate, that pertaining to human beings as to all things mortal, to the leaf falling at a certain angle in the crooked wind, the pebble skittering in the brook, the whisper of a moth in a hurricane, a falling star? Well might she always have been, beyond all the illusions of life, Mr. Spitzer thought as the clouds settled over this granite face so harshly outlined, as the myriad clouds turned to stone, these frozen mountains and foldings of stone beyond nature's reach or empire, these frozen lakes no bird or sail had ever crossed, these great snow pinnacles like pointed stars reaching into clouds descending to earth, this desert rose, this lost Eros, this very pinnacle, this god of love, dead love, all that to which she had objected.

Mr. Spitzer could hardly believe his softly glowing but near-sighted eyes as the snow fell over the unrecognizable face of a dead bride or bridegroom, one lost in the stormy passage of this life, one who might never find a mate, he had thought as he heard the thunder of snow in distant mountains or over these roofs, and there was much that he would never betray to human eyes, not even his own. There was much that he had forgotten, for his memory was brief, brief as a raindrop splashing in a distant pool of water or the cry of a night bird in the whistling of the winter wind or a spark in a cloud, how often he had remarked, none knowing the transience of life so well as he who had lived to see all things passing, forever passing, and that was why sometimes he wept with his tears falling like great waterfalls over great stone cascades rising for a moment through clouds or why his voice was like a thousand moths whispering in faded snow storms under the faded stars in the grey light of dawn, why his voice whispered when there was no one to hear him. Life was but a bright moment, a moment of burning intensity, and that moment had faded. Life had been a long dying ever since—or a brief dying—he did not know which. His brother had said that the universe was something shaken out of a dice box—and that the great player might shake the dice again. Sometimes Mr. Spitzer would hear the dice rattling, the old bones dancing.

Never were there so many triangles, so many angles, courts, inner courts, intaglios, desert gardens, ghosts of love as Mr. Spitzer discovered now, coming upon this knowledge of this great suffragette's secret life when, to all intents and purposes, it was over, one with the universal cloud, the great mirage.

It seemed quite strange and even paradoxical that she should have been not only this suffragette, one more often on the wild steppes of Tartary or in the Atlas Mountains or in the mountains of the moon than at home, and also, for reasons never to be understood, this authority upon all the manifestations of love, tragic love, whichever Mr. Spitzer, this disappointed lover of woman, might imagine—indeed, that she might have understood, if ever he had written to her, if he could have put the speechless things into words, his own great problems of love involving the fading cosmos, that she might have answered, most particularly if she had not known him, if he had been a stranger. But what would she have answered if ever he had dropped his own inquiry into the slot, asking—Do I live, or am I dead? How strange that none had seemed to realize her lack of experience and her great guilt, that she had killed her love, that so many had written to one who was barren as those great shoulders of rock where grew no flower—for why should they have thought that she who knew most of bedrock knew most of wedlock, that she who had never married knew most of marriage and its eternal woes, disappointments, severances, that she who had never loved knew most of love, its failures as to the ideal love and its realization on earth—and why should they ever have thought that the blind see best, seeing only the memory of the cloud, that the deaf hear best, hear even the muted cry of the snowflake, that the dead heart lives longest, knows most? Why should they ever have thought that one who has never seen color knows most of color? Why should they have thought that she might understand their loves, strange loves most mystifying to them, that she might hear their unintelligible cries, sobs, whispers, raspings as of sea shells opening, closing their doors—and what had she answered to them who had asked the way of life of her? Had she answered from a cloud or from under the waves of the sea or from under the great stones settling over the graves? It was plain that she had answered—but what, Mr. Spitzer must ask again? What was this enigma like a key which would open no door?

She might almost have been running, particularly in the years when she was not at home, a bureau for advice to the lovelorn in all countries —for never were there so many beautiful postage stamps, some which would have surprised a philatelist, even an old stamp-collector like Mr. Spitzer—and some missives which had been written before the age of the postage stamp—or had been delivered by those cloud spectres—and never had he read of so many vanished bridegrooms, those who had vanished at the altar, perhaps before the marriage knot or noose was tied, before they were anchored to their dying loves, so many runaway brides who had jumped over cliffs, lovers who had broken woman's heart or man's heart, lovers who were not what they seemed and were like traitors in the enemy's camp, their faces shrouded, so many cruel husbands and lords— so that he could not help thinking that such letter-writing was certainly a curious secondary activity for one who was devoted to the prime cause of suffrage as to her spouse, as to her love, her only love, one who had sacrificed her life for freedom from the bonds to love, eternal love or the love which was but for a shining moment. She had surely led a double life, perhaps a triple life, perhaps a life which could not be figured in terms of numbers, it seemed to Mr. Spitzer even before he knew the cosmic magnitude of her deception—that she was no one in whom one should place his already shattered faith, a faith so weakened by so many blows, hammer blows, for none had ever yet seen this dead star. How so many should have placed their broken faith in this great father of suffrage was a mystery, almost an enchantment robbing men of their senses. She was that great betrayer of woman, woman with her whispering skirts, chaplets of pearls, veiled looks, women who were brides even when there were no loves or when there were only their imaginary loves. Surely as if she had been the greatest lover of all women, she had betrayed them all even as she had betrayed man's feeble spirit. How frail, how weak was nature in this room. She had led her followers astray though perhaps not by intention, perhaps because of the brutal winds, the roaring and singing rocks.

Yet who of her vast heterogeneous public—fortunately now no more or almost no more, for she had outlived them all, so none might ever know what Mr. Spitzer had discovered, and he himself might forget— would have suspected in her such vast deception as this he saw now, such ambivalence of motive and countermotive, action and reaction, impulse and memory, such blurrings of dead and deathless chords, such confusions as between love and death, death and love, such yearnings for the infinite reaches of space, she having never been the unitary person her followers had naively supposed when she was alive, she having been more confused, more bewildered than they who had followed this great bellwether through the storm clouds and doubtless had heard, even as they died, her tinkling bell, astral voice, bell like a small voice in every cloud, every storm?

Mr. Spitzer had surely heard bells ringing when Cousin Hannah died—bells in rustling clouds, movements as of skirts. She had heard a bell, a tinkling bell, a moving tide, perhaps a sea of doorbells, harebells in the wind where the scimitar moth moved. These auditory hallucinations had ushered in visual hallucinations, no doubt, or had been followed by them. They could be timed, at least in dubious retrospect depending on one's position in time or space. The one had come before the other—just as life seemed to return as it was departing, for life departed not suddenly all at once. She had seen a mountain goat white as the moon-white ewe rising upon a rising pinnacle in the moon glare above the endless expanse of snow, mountains and clouds, the mountain goat who had seen her love, mountains which moved perhaps as clouds stood still, and there were those great snow-crowned peaks moving through clouds, those crumblings into a void, the hiss of snow like the sea's foam at some far edge of the world. She had seen a mountain-climber in the flashings of crystal lights, perhaps an iceberg moving with stately motion like a wild swan beyond the curtain of the pearl-strung fog lighted by ice spars. She had heard the whisper of a snowflake spiraling in a cloud, a rasping star as if the wind scraped desert sand burning and cold, a voice she had always heard through gales and whirlwinds, it seemed, and had cried when she was dying—Is that my love whose delicate footsteps I must follow now?

Oh, love, must I follow you as I once followed the great snowy ptarmigan in the cloud? Oh, love under the huntress moon, have you found your skirt, your skirt billowing where the flowers grow, perhaps where I shall never step? Is it on the mountain slope or in the valley of the shadow? Is it on the other side of that great mountain peak looming like reproach, reproach to me who killed my love, my only love, for did I not let you go? Is that my love, and do the fireflies light her face with myriad constellations? Do they keep vigil now upon my glittering girl? What light is that in the dark valley, a window or star under the snow? Is it some mountain hut or old Crusader's castle emerging when the snow moves, covered again when the snow falls?

Does the light exist only by reflection, she asked where the darkness whirled, or memory? Put out the light, she said. So that Mr. Spitzer snuffed out a candle.

Sometimes, lost in raging whirlwinds, driven against by spears of ice, by furious clouds, by snows hissing like terrible fires, she herself seemed to be climbing mountains, even as she heaved, struggled, tugged with sheets, breathed with heavy breathing like the rasping winter wind outside the star-lit window and cried with the starlight shining in her dulled eyes—Oh, I am clinging to a narrow ledge. Oh, God help me. For each is the mariner soul, struggling far from any port. Save my body before you save my soul. For my soul is already lost. Or is my body lost? Shall body and soul be reft asunder now? Shall that happen which has already happened? Did I not fall, and shall I fall again, or was I always falling? Did I fall from ledge to ledge? Snow crumbles under me, and pebbles roar, and twigs break, and silken threads give, and mountains hiss like the waves of the sea. The sea roars in my ear, whorled ear. There is a voice which speaks through every silence. My love, my love, I hear your voice like a whisper in the storm. Is that the whirling leaf? Oh, body and soul land, to what do I cling, over what terrible darkness increasing now? What mountain-climber will ever find me where the snow falls like a shroud?

Break, cable, break—unfurl, sail, she cried, and let me go. Oh, let my ship plunge into the whirling vortex. Let my ship fall ten thousand miles, plunge like the wild horses upon the foam. For I cannot cling much longer to this great ledge, and the wind beats against my face, and this was a cloud where I set my foot, and this was not stone. This was not earth. This was not water. This was not air or starlight or wind. Upon the mountains there shall be no anchorage and none upon the waves of the sea and none upon the sands, for the sands move like the waves of the sea.

She had cried against the whistling winds, the blinding lights driving her against her will. She had spoken of some old ship with its shroud winding in the snow like an Arab traveller at some far edge of the desert world where the wind shrieked from star to star in endless monotone. She had complained of the winds shrieking through her shrouds, breaking her cords, the refraction increasing as the darkness increased, star glare and moon glare, white squalls and dark shadows, the cloud which was greater than all clouds, all clouds over her, the hailstones beating on icebergs, the great ice floes and spume and splinters reflecting darkness or light, the snow upon her winding sheet, the iceberg engulfing the boat of

the lost mariner, the great ice floes flashing lights almost as steady as
signal lights, the jewels in her crown flashing lights of unearthly stars
through clouds before the darkness settled like the darkness of the grave,
before the great ooze, the rainbow colors oozing from the mouth of the
dead, colors like the midnight rainbow arching the dark sky when she
was dead.

Yet had she ever died? For was she not a hooded rider on desert
sands, and was not hers that great saddle of stone with foaming headland
breaking through clouds, and was she not perhaps the greatest shiek or a
lady with her face veiled, secretive as the sea medusa no sunlight ever
reaches? Her name was hyphenated like her life, there was little doubt in
Mr. Spitzer's mind, very little doubt, she being one who had known
herself no more than a butterfly emerging from its cocoon or an eye
shining in the storm cloud, and so Mr. Spitzer certainly believed that it
was best that there should be an end to this crystal-gazing when the
future was no more than a dead dream, even as the past had been. And
yet he was not sure. Was it possible that she had been dead when she was
still alive, that she should live now when she was dead, he asked through
all the after-years, for he was always trying to establish balance? It seemed
scarcely possible even to him with his memorial grief keeping itself alive.
Her accounts were closed. There was little more to add. It seemed that
her great career was ended in darkness and in whirlwind even as it had
begun. He was very certain that now a veil, a final veil should be drawn
over the life of this old maid who had ridden through storms and whirlwinds and whose heart was the heart of darkness and mystery.

Ah, what glitter and aplomb and loud alarum had once been hers in
lands where there were few travellers. But was she not one now with
universal darkness, with Stygian night, with this long sleep of unawakening death? Better that none should know what Mr. Spitzer knew, that
none should know that love had prompted her because of her immortal
guilt—a virgin's blood staining the snow, so she had cried, or was it the
sunlight burning through a cloud, lighting far pinnacles, the sunlight
touching the snow with red and blue and green and gold like the shot
colors of bolts of multi-colored silk unfurling, gleaming through snow
clouds?

She said many times, not knowing that it was Mr. Spitzer who over-
heard her last remarks, not knowing that it was he who listened with his
discretion, his unbelieving air, he who encouraged no remorse of the
dead over the dead, he who believed that the dead should rest and that
they should suffer no more, for they had paid their passage through this
life and should come to their safe harbor now beyond these storms of life,
these storms of death—she cried that she had lost her love—her acolyte,
her beautiful girl with whom she had travelled through the snow-
pinnacled mountains upon some distant roof-top of the world.

So that Mr. Spitzer could not but wonder—What world? And what
were these two great ladies doing in these all but impenetrable mountains, he had vaguely, fitfully wondered, not sure at all times that he
heard what he heard—since there was so much competition for his atten-

tion, so much din and so many loud screamings and so many whispers and glassy flute notes—since it was difficult to follow such pale threads as these, difficult to give his attention to that which was no more, particularly when the clouds thickened like fleece in the shepherd's hand, and there were halos where there were no moons.

No disrespect was shown by Mr. Spitzer's attitude. Not even indifference was shown. Certainly, there was no greater sympathy than his for all who had seemed to live in one way and had lived in another way, perhaps its opposite, but his attention was diffused by his experience, both real and vicarious. Did he not live his brother's life? He had accustomed himself to snows and winds and clouds, waters and stars and fireflies, his own consciousness sporadic as a firefly in a cloud. Better that none should know, therefore, this death-bed scene which he had forgotten, the snow clouds forming when she died, snow clouds hissing like long-necked white birds of passage invisible but heard, heard like the wild geese flying over, cleaving the windy heaven at night, cleaving the dreams of the sleeper in his bed. For he, too, is ever in clouded passage.

So Mr. Spitzer had thought—and indeed, not through his oblivion but through his compassion which was an altogether different matter, had almost dismissed these death-bed remarks as irresponsible ravings, even like those of the wild birds of passage making inarticulate cries or the wild sea booming against jagged rocks and the clouds, great clouds piling up where no castles were and where no light gleamed at any window—for well he knew that at the last moment a totally or almost totally alien life might appear, that at the last moment many a being might change his mind as to what his life had been or would become, or might reveal a life which had been hidden underground before and which would arise to the surface perhaps only for a glittering moment as this person breathed his last or which would arise perhaps long after he was dead, wrapped in the shrouds of the Arab. Perhaps at the deepest depths there is no individual or image, neither bird nor fish nor flower. Thus at the depths of sleep no face is remembered. All things have flowed into all things. A man may die each night, sinking into the drowned depths of sleep. The deepest sleep is dreamless. Perhaps the image exists only as it arises toward the rippling surface, even as the dreams of the dreamer come into being and exist only as he arises toward the surface of his awakening. And as a man dies, as he slips from the intangible moorings of this life, he sinks into his dreams before he reaches dreamless sleep. He hears great buoys ringing as he goes. So that Mr. Spitzer had been inclined to dismiss such windy utterances, attributing them to that delirium in which any man with his failing senses should engage without anybody else's check upon imagination or memory, the judgment of no observer being required. For who should know whether or not after the last pulse beat there is another pulse beat like the color of blood returning to the grey cloud? Certainly, Mr. Spitzer was in no position to know of these transcendent evidences, perhaps because they were his life. And why should this old captain not see butterflies of imagination or memory or hear the trumpetings of angels upon distant cloud roofs or angels rolling away the stones of tombs, perhaps mere pebbles covering water holes, hear even her own crying long after she had passed? For this was surely her privilege. It was what Mr. Spitzer liked to call the prerogative of the dead. The dead earned something, surely—perhaps only this doubt.

Thus he doubted her. Perhaps this doubt was all there was. It was doubt of love, but perhaps it was also doubt of death. In view of so many hallucinations occurring at her last hour or long after the last clock bell had tolled, in view of so many shrill cries mingling with the sounds of the faint traffic horns in the distant city which had once roared and clanged but which seemed to have sailed upon a wave, perhaps when no one knew, sounds seeming to ebb like the thinnest memory of the outgoing tide, like the distant surf-line when the tide is almost still or frozen, when only the old trees lean tideward creaking like his own heart, Mr. Spitzer had naturally supposed that she spoke of some lost love of her imagination and never of actuality, never of flesh and blood, that this was this phantom wandering through clouds, the white breasts, the snow-white limbs of this veiled virgin with her face veiled by snow, white plumes like snow upon her brow, this beautiful lady appearing at the old suffrage captain's last hour or perhaps the hour after her last hour—for time was not time to those who died, and time touched not them, and they knew not these seasons of the year. Indeed, Mr. Spitzer had supposed that out of great loneliness such as might confront every dying man with his fear of the void of creation or his fear that something might be there, perhaps one sporadic light, this damosel with the long white veils had appeared to accompany the old Crusader upon another journey, to guide him through the infernal mountains of frozen furies and great snow-slides, snowslides which might hurtle at a step like suddenly awakening tides. And after this experience as watchman to the dying heart, Mr. Spitzer would surely say to any explorer returning in his ice-shrouded boat from his polar voyage to the magnetic North—Nothing so cold as Boston on a winter night. Nothing so cold as these great mountains rising from a lady's heart. Nothing so cold as the night that this star died, night that the great dray horses were frozen on the roads, night that this harbor was frozen like the frozen wharves, night that the coachman was frozen in his box, night that the sailor was frozen in his shroud.

So let be forgotten now that one memory by which she had lived, that feeble act of cowardice which had motivated her heroism, and let it be forgotten that she was possibly the greatest literalist Mr. Spitzer ever knew, that she had lived her great romance, that she had done what others only dreamed of doing. Let her be remembered for her noble acts, her many rescues and escapes, her self-forgetfulness, and all the speculative newspaper accounts of her. If there was a blot upon this great captain's escutcheon, a blot red as her blood upon the white snow, best that none should ever see her as she was or understand the monumental meaning of her last remarks or see what he had seen, hear what he had heard. Best that none should know that she had died with a sea shell at her feet and had talked to a ghost, perhaps to many ghosts.

Best that she who was already forgotten should be remembered for her public deeds, glories, honors, powers, the innumerable coal mine strikes she had helped to start, picket lines in which she had marched before grey mills, balloon ascensions into seas of roaring clouds where balloons were scraped by moons breaking into fire, launchings of suffrage ships like those great duchesses sailing at night from darkened ports, battles on foreign or domestic fronts, rides against great minarets and crescents and crescents trembling in water, desert marches and forays upon cities of tents moving like sails, clanging career, that there should be no publicity attending the last rites for her secret heart, that she should fade into veiled obscurity like the firefly fading into the glowing iceberg or some other star. The stars faded at dawn.

Mr. Spitzer resented the brevity of man's memory of this great public hero, forgotten now as some poor foot soldier or Foreign Legionnaire who had perished in burning desert sand or some old Crusader who was buried by a snowslide—but what image could he evoke when all was over, what effigy for her tomb which he was always planning in his amorphous mind and yet could never decide upon? It would be neither the anchor nor the heart. Granite should not give an image to that which was the cloud. As time could not contain her who had organized the pickets around the old town clocks, no image could approximate her memory. No clock could keep the time for her even though it was the time kept by the mooncomb, the jellyfish, the starfish gleaming on the timeless sand under the stars gleaming like starfish. Hers was not even the figurehead of the ship which had gone down. No sundial marked her hour. What image could restore the memory of this unknown love?

Would it be the mountain-climber with his moon-white dogs rolling at his feet though only the sea shell had roared at hers, the ski trooper shrouded in white poling into heaven or returning to snow-bound earth, the veiled eunuch with the black mist of a forgotten dream around his face where one unextinguished spark burned, life being that which takes longest dying even in a eunuch's heart, the beautiful girl who had been the desert rose or nymph or fawn, the mysterious shiek of some forbidden seraglio never reached by man, the rooster thief, the blacksmith, or this old New England war horse crowned with a wreath of flowers because, though she seemed ugly and old, hers was the victory? Was her trumpet made of melted spurs? Sometimes Mr. Spitzer thought that over her grave there should be, in memory of the fact that she had been a great travel-ler, perhaps only a milestone marked—Twelve Miles. It was odd, but he thought of her whenever he came to a milestone. He thought of her whenever a clock struck.

He did not know how she should be remembered when she was forgotten, yet though she had been this great firebrand of suffrage burn-ing bright as a bright star in the wind, something nearer to earth than most stars as are the stars when one has climbed a mountain top, no doubt, but certainly nothing had ever seemed stranger to Mr. Spitzer than that men should exert themselves to climb mountains perhaps for no purpose whatever but to reduce by an infinitesimal distance the distance between themselves and the stars, to bring the stars or heavenly bodies nearer to earth. Sometimes they risked their lives for this. Sometimes they perished in the roaring clouds, the avalanches, the mountains hurtling like the clouds, and mountaineers lost long ago stared out from behind great crystal walls.

This seemed to him a great, unholy effort when merely by reaching his pole he could bring down the stars as some old pigeon poler might pole the pigeons homeward through the evening clouds, pigeons of opalescent blue and green and rose and gold, pigeons many-colored as Joseph's coat, pigeons glowing like the glowing clouds, the fading and trembling clouds through which they travelled, returning like lost souls to the chimneys and roofs. Certainly, nothing made him sadder than that men of that civic pride and that sterility which built no stone monument to the living or the dead should chase pigeons from city streets and roofs and ledges, pigeons opalescently shining like souls, dead souls returning, souls who whispered over the slate roofs, for did not pigeons make water-logged Venice beautiful, more beautiful than beauty ever was when it was inanimate, casting their shadows on moon-colored paving stones and waters and clouds, roosting on angelic wings and on the reflections of wings on waves, roosting on the heads of gondoliers who carried the dead to their temporal resting place? Here in old Boston town pigeons roosted on clock hands and clock pendulums. Pigeons had stopped an old town clock. Perhaps they were his soul, the fragments of his spirit, for only the psychic life was important to him, especially when the physical life was gone, and he was but an old pigeon-roost himself and filled with pigeon murmurings and shining wings, whispers, voices, carrier pigeons seeking him out through clouds, some with billets doux from the dead to the dead, whirrings, memories forgotten and returning, almost all returning, there sometimes coming to him those pigeons none had ever seen on earth before or the pigeon with the Red Cross upon its snow-white breast, the Bleeding Heart, the snow-white turret. And if there sometimes came passenger pigeons now extinct though they had once darkened the heavens over this wilderness, roaring, clanging like church bells in clouds, making a twilight of sunlight, who was Mr. Spitzer, dreaming among the shadows, to question the moon, the stars, the waters, and the clouds, to ask how this could be, to be the skeptic of another's life? He was that toll-keeper who asked no questions, letting all things pass.

Nothing frightened him so much as man's loss of memory or the emptiness of that fame for which he himself had lived, writing his silent music passing into silence before it was recognized. Could he say that this great lady should be buried with lonely cannonades or pomp and ceremony at Arlington, the President mourning her passage, for she had died a hero's death in some forgotten year, perhaps according to the Anatolian calendar or perhaps in some forgotten Ramadan? When had she heard the winding horn? But she had been a coward trembling when a snow-drop melted, and he had composed that music to be played to the sound of thunder-claps and rain and the watery stars burning low near earth when earth unthawed itself, when flowers burned—and garlanded mules with caissons and riderless horses had not accompanied her to her last resting place, nor had there been mourners lining the streets and flags flying at half mast and black banners hanging from the roofs as would have been if he had had his way, if he could have carried out his ideas and intentions as well as her indomitable spirit had carried out hers, if he had been also the literalist, one who did whatever he dreamed, one not confused because he was become his brother. Perhaps she should have been buried in the Tomb of the Unknown Soldier lighted by a perpetual flame, for she was unknown, and no one knew in which battle she had fallen, guarding what windy ramparts. Perhaps hers should have been a desert tomb, a mountain tomb, or a tomb under water, a turret sinking beneath a wave. Should she not be claimed by the courtly French, claimed by the heathen Turks? Should she not be remembered by the Greeks and Medes, the Persians, the ivory kings rattling their bones? Should she not be greeted by great Romans in their cities of tents dissolving when the sand blew? Mr. Spitzer would have liked to have said to them—Here was the noblest Roman of them all. She knew her Carthage. She was covered by the desert sand. But there was no one to hear him. There was no one but Mr. Spitzer to mourn the passing of a dying soul, and she was buried in that grey New England churchyard, hearing only the sound of the water running through a rusted spout or the leaves falling, rustling over her grave, or a snowflake melting in a burning cloud as Mr. Spitzer came to his last understanding of her, knowing only when she was dead that she had lived and loved and lost. He thought of her in winter hurricanes and when he was pushing away the stars with his cane, when he was going upon his lonely paces, brushing with his sleeve against the deathless dust of a dead planet, tapping lamp-posts reverberating in a long row behind him, lighting lamps in a sleeping city where only he was awake or where perhaps there was only one other distant wayfarer, a figure blurred by the long-rolling sea fog, perhaps a toad with eyes like lamps.

Light revealed not what the darkness hid, and winter brought not to life that which the spring had killed. She lived perhaps only in his faded memory of her dead heart—and was he not dead who remembered her, who heard a faint thumping under the frozen earth, and what witness was the dead to the dead, what reliable witness, Mr. Spitzer asked with spindrift gleaming through a distant cloud or crescent moon falling as he spoke to no known listener? Surely, she had sinned against her own finest sense of honor or against the code of chivalry as might many another lady who had gone to fight great dragons showering golden seeds, great krakens curling around the helms of boats and dragging them to nether seas with veils of starlight, great minotaurs and Chinese lords and shahs of Araby and husbands whose wives abandoned them when they were sleeping, wives who slept with other loves as snowflakes fell upon their hair—and what other great lady had challenged icebergs, driving against them with her sword as they reared, rose, plunged, challenged her, bellowed, roared with crests of foam, with wakes of clouds, drove against her as if they knew where they were going, as if great glaciers could make up

their minds and announce their intentions and veer from their courses
as she veered from hers, veered like the wild swans flying through clouds,
the wild snow blowing in her face or falling from a mountain top, her
eyes burning like two stars or one star and its reflection in the icy glare
—but could she not be forgiven now, or could she not forgive herself? As
a matter of fact, Mr. Spitzer thought that though it might be that the
great things moved by law, perhaps the smallest things were indeterminate, that only they escaped this wheel of fortune or these sealed orders of
that fate under which man had sailed and which was determined long
ago and was inscrutable, that perhaps only some delicate rainbow-
colored butterfly gleaming through the mist or far ripple of water
streaked by moonlight or snowflake like a web of lace laid upon the
mouth of the dead could escape this universal cloud freezing now like
marble hills, that perhaps the tiniest perception might be free to wander
outside with freedom to move, change, alter its course as if it were a
thought thinking after the thinker was no more.

This was surely the case with himself. For was not this body like an
old coat hung upon a nail, and what connection had there ever been
between the body and the spirit, and had not the spirit flown? Body and
soul were divided even in this life, it seemed to him. Death was no more
than life had been. Had he not lost his butterfly, perhaps in aeons past?
Was he not an empty coat or shroud? So that he was curiously aware of
the most fugitive moments he might once have ignored, twigs breaking,
pebbles skittering upon a skirted shore, waves lapping or stilled in a
mournful moment under the tented sky, the tiniest whisper lost in silence
like the shout. And this was why he could never quite concentrate, why
he wandered to and fro.

From sources now forgotten, from last remarks and clouded hints
and twilight gleamings, doubtless from old love letters read by moonlight
or from gilded bees buzzing like comets in a snow storm or from traceries
of the gold dust upon his sleeve, upon his whirling cape, or from the
whisper of a sea shell or from her own roarings beating like the waves
upon the dead ear, thumpings of the dead heart, Mr. Spitzer had understood that greater threat which was reality and not her dreams, that all
this old suffrage captain spoke of had transpired as if it were a dream
which could not die, that all was real as if no moment died, as if no
momentum ceased, for suffrage had been caused by her dead love which
had been the main tenet of her faith, and this great impetus had stirred
her so that she could never rest, never cease. Perhaps he had always
known this. He had known at the beginning that which he had rejected
and to which he had returned at the end, though after circling many
problems which were never hers. One moment was all, and it was passing.
The mountain goat looked down on her, perhaps even like those great
ivory kings with golden planetary crowns, those great Crusaders who had
gone before her into mists and clouds, and the moon stared with that
blurred eye which knows not the difference between yesterday and today,
and a white bird lifted its archangelic wing when the wind blew, and
there were those constellations which had already fallen like showers of

sparks coldly glittering, seeds of dead stars like many things destroyed in consciousness before they are realized, yet shining in the darkening clouds as if they might suddenly burst into flame. No bellows could start up the dead stars or bring into life that which never was. There was only this dying moment, moment of transition between the now and then, between the here and there, the wind singing as she went with the snow winding around her like a winding sheet, the snowflakes blowing in her face as she became oblivion. Her image was lost. She was lost in narrow passes. She was lost in some great gulch beyond the imagination of man, surely beyond a woman's limited and temporal imagination and attribution of importance to petty details, for these mountains were surely not of earth, Mr. Spitzer had thought. For she was hemmed in by these great, glacial, frozen peaks forming when she died, a new horizon suddenly looming before the loss of consciousness, an old horizon returning, forming like the ice crystals upon her brow as the snow fell upon the city roofs and in the narrow defiles, as the snow hurtled through the clouds. These helmets crowned with snow looked down on her like the old gargoyles of castles seen through snow clouds where no traveller had ever stepped, gates where none had reined his horse.

Such dislocations Mr. Spitzer could surely understand, for he was old Joachim of the forgetful memory and the unsteady heart—and only yesterday he had stopped to drink at an old town pump surrounded by pigeon murmurs, only to be told today when he had returned that it had disappeared from earth twenty years or more ago, that it had disappeared with the age of the horse. In fact, perhaps it had disappeared with the crinoline. Perhaps it had been here in Colonial times—though Mr. Spitzer, of course, had not dared to ask which Colony it was. Earth wandered like the milky pod upon the wind. Nothing was certain.

Or so Mr. Spitzer thought, for it had been difficult to understand her ravings when she was dying, crying that her feet were wearing horseshoes, that she saw a sword in the wind. He had heard her screaming that she was not the rider—she was the horse. He had heard her crying that she was afraid of a great horned snow owl where no owl was.

Who searches now for me or sounds his winding horn—had she not cried and cried again—as I search for my love, my love in the mountains, my love in the shadowed valleys, my love upon the wave-streaked desert floor? Forgive me, love, that I did not follow you. I betrayed my love only by a moment. It was the blinding glare. Could I stay the moon? Do I pass with all things passing—but where is my dead love, the white breast, the snow upon her mouth, her eyes? Oh, is she in the shadowed valley or at the highest mountain peak, and where's her trailing skirt, or do the mountains move as I watch now with my dead eye in the storm cloud forever moving? Do they move like the waves of the sea, she cried, like the moon in the cloud, like the many-haloed moon upon the waves, upon the snow, the foaming snow like a sea of milk, the snow hissing in the cloud, the desert sand white as the unicorn? Does love escape love's vigilance? Could I follow love through twelve mirrors?

Forgive me, love, she whispered with a hollow whisper, that I died not before you. Forgive me that I lived when you were dead. The soul should go with the body. This world was my sepulchre. Forgive me that I moved, whispered, breathed, lived—wild horses screaming in windy gardens when I passed, peacocks clashing their windy tails in gardens of the mandarins, and the desert sentinel sleeping when I passed, seeking my dead love—but yet have I not come to where you were, where you were not, my lovely girl with your face veiled by snow in the wind, your eyes shining like two stars in distant clouds? Have I not returned where none returns, where none ever was? For time returns not to the dead hour, the dead heart.

Could I influence that which was magnetized by greater love than mine, she cried, and if I could not hold her back when I was strong, how can I hold her back when I am weak, when I am going with the outgoing tide hovering, rising with great billows streaked by the moon's passage, leaving faint eddies, ripples, pools upon a barren shore, the salt marsh glittering like the lost star where the firefly whirls? Does my skirt walk by itself, its great flounces lifting in the wind, its ribbons streaming in the streaming clouds?

Or is my skirt my sail—and do I veer, tack, whirl in the wind, and am I blown from pole to pole?

Were not all other loves the memory of this, she asked Mr. Spitzer though not knowing to whom she spoke, and do I die now, and shall I be as now she is, this ghost of my dead love wandering through deserts of sand and crystal mountains like these great refractions? Am I naked in these mountains of stone or black clouds—or shall I find my skirt to cover me, my skirt I lost?

Shall I find my skirt, my love, my love, my skirt where the snow falls and the wind blows, my love who died that she might find her skirt, her skirt that moved with whispers through the clouds and skirted the empearled horizon? Alas, what great windjammer is this blown upon my path? What bellows now is blowing this dead wood of my heart into flame, breaking my dead heart, blowing these cold sparks like the phoenix in the cloud or rose? Ah, traitor moon! she cried. You were fickle as woman. You waxed, and you waned. You went not in a steady course. You hid behind a cloud whenever I was looking for my girl, the snow upon her eyes, upon her eyelids.

I sought for her as I am seeking now, climbing naked through mountains of snow, climbing like the hidden moon through clouds. Oh, say. Are the dogs barking? What old dog nips now at the hunter's heels, or does the sea shell roar? Is that a whistle? My God! Is that a raindrop? Who is that dwarf, a turret on his head, a rose at his collar? It is the rose of consciousness.

Mr. Spitzer, from sources now forgotten, had gradually ascertained that this great protector of woman had let go her girl's hand, her dove-white fluted hand in a snow storm long ago as in another life, and what eternal troth was this so easily broken that it might just as well never have been made, he asked, he being himself this old romanticist at heart, one not easily acknowledging the death of love, one who might believe in love when the last romance had faded from the earth, one who might still hear a sob, a whisper, an eddying pool, a tiny footstep in a cloud, or who might at least hear his own whispers in a silent world? She had cried when she was dying with no one but Mr. Spitzer to over-hear—still not hearing him, not even when he perhaps whispered his name like some old musical motif running forever through memory—had cried with that self-centeredness and self-forgetfulness which might be understandable in those who are departing from this world, had cried that she had killed her love, or else her love, that love as pure as snow which had never yet touched earth, that love which had faded in a cloud, her love had killed her in the mountains and in the clouds and in the valleys shadowed by the horned moon or some great saddle cliff of rock over-looking that cosmography no man had ever seen on earth.

For truth to tell if now the truth must be told when the truth was losing its meaning or changing its meaning, if resurrection must occur just at that moment before the final burial, the interment of clouded memories and hopes and dreams, she had not gone alone upon her first journey as doubtless she must go alone upon her last journey, or so Mr. Spitzer had precariously thought, there being that point beyond which no living man could accompany her through lightning flashes illuminating snow clouds, the clouds drifting over her face and casting their shadows which drifted in the wind, and no trumpeter swan could accompany her though clouds bellowed, for he was extinct, and no attendants could look down on her through foam of lace, through miles of clouds piling up like the snow banks piling up above a firmament of lower stars.

Mr. Spitzer had heard her crying as she died, perhaps long after she was dead, for he could not trust his own sonorous consciousness of things transpiring so near the void, he being already extinct—Did I not let you go, my love, my mere snowdrop of a girl, for did not the furious winter gales blow me athwart like an old mast, an old cross-beam breaking upon the waves rising like the mountainous seas with foaming crests, seas where no bird of passage ever slept?

Did I not let you go in mountains more desolate than these rising now from my dead heart, and was this being that great hero men thought I was when I blew my trumpet outside the ivory gates and the walls of dead cities, cities lighted by no lamp? Why should men have admired me and women have trembled, blushing like lamps, hiding under their veils at my approach?

In every country where I was, I was believed to be a great lover in another country. Shall love be infinitely postponed? If infinitely postponed, then it is love.

She had asked for forgiveness when she was dying—so Mr. Spitzer remembered, but he could not be sure, nor could he be sure that one should trust the dying who were already of another world. Of whom should she ask forgiveness? He was sure that none should give penance to this love, this body and this spirit. Oh, God, she had whispered. Forgive the cloud which knows not what it whispers, the voice which knows not what it says, the sob which knows not what it utters, the silence which knows not what it hears. Forgive the lover who knows not when he loves. Perhaps only in memory I loved. Perhaps only in the future shall I love.

Forgive the falling leaf, the falling star, the downward motion of all things, even those which had gone upward. I aspired to greater heights than most, so I fell a greater distance. I fell from star to star. My life was one long act of falling.

Forgive the disintegration of creation which is creation as I cry—Oh, nightmare, were you my only love? Nightmare persisting when life is no more, why should I not love you? My heart is broken. If the star could not resist, shall the leaf resist the whirlwind created by the star? Forgive, too, the self-contradiction of life and death, for both were contained within us.

Forgive this breaking body as you forgive the star, the star whispering in the wind when the star is no more. Forgive the secret none can tell. None can tell and live.

Mr. Spitzer had whispered his name, surely, in the concealing dusk —only his last name then, of course, supposing that it would make little difference to her—daring not to say whether he was Peron who had died young or Joachim who was old, Peron who had loved only the old or Joachim who had loved only those who were forever young and beautiful, those whom age had not marked. For really, he did not know. And the night wind could not tell him. Chords wandered into alien music. His music was made almost entirely of lost chords. His music returned with more notes than he remembered—though this inaccuracy was that which he did not question, accepting the fact that music grows, winds upon itself, fades, expands, gathers momentum, sleeps while on the wing, pivots, rises, falls, ebbing, surging like the music which was never composed. He accepted the music of oceanic waves, music of sea shells, music of glassy crickets in chimneys, train whistles, street cries, cloud-bursts, whatever he heard and even that music never heard, that music never rising into sound, that music which was so like his own. She did not hear him whisper his name, nor did he hear it. He was outside her problem. But why should he have expected to enter as a counter in that life which he had never entered before—why should he enter now as even the sorriest pawn or knight or king or queen when all the chessmen were suddenly swept over-board as by the hand of an invisible player? He did not know who the invisible player was. Perhaps it was the storm. Besides, he was concerned by so many interests—such as his international register of butterflies, those lost long ago in storm, some before this world. And yet there were colored counties on their wings.

I lost my first disciple as I shall lose my last, for the mountains moved then as now in the shrill tempest never ceasing, Cousin Hannah cried, storm ringing like sea bells until my ear drums burst. There were flashings from the walls of crystal suddenly rearing up like wild seas of flames. Great precipices and promontories reached into clouds which seemed themselves the trembling mountains, pouncing, pawing. I fought with lions in clouds. My eyes were blinded by the snow flurries, the icicles like crystal daggers, the hurtling snow, the hooded snow, the ghost, the moon rolling in my path as if it had rolled out of its orbit like an eye rolling out of the skull of the dead. I could not find my way to follow you, my love. You were following some other love.

You were faithless to woman as you would have been to man. No allegiance had ever bound us, but you were the traitor, breaking that bond which never was. We were two lone women. There was no man.

The greatest man would have been but a puny girl if he had tried to hold you when you turned to go in the wind shrieking like the wind the night this world went down, dragging its sail. Stars quivered for long afterward. They are trembling now. Starlight broke like foam upon the doomed prow, upon the wooden helmsman. Stars are blind. Love, I was blinded by the snow storm. Never again did I see the human face. Never again did I hear the human voice.

I did not let go your hand. It was you who let go my hand in the snow storm where the snowflakes fell like the stars in the wind, where the unfurling snow shrouds shrieked above the mountains which crumbled as if they were not stone. They were foam and crumbling mist.

I thought all my life I had abandoned you, but it was you who abandoned me, I know now. I did not abandon you, and yet I suffered as if I did so, and I knocked on doors under the earth and in the clouds, and I cried on every mountain top—Oh, who has seen my love?

Black was my true love's heart though white was her skin, skin like the opalescence under which are burning fires. She was white as the snow upon the mountains, the ice citadels burning like the stars in clouds, the hurtling clouds.

So that my confusion knows no end, Cousin Hannah cried, for I am distracted by the shrill winds, the hurtling seas which fall through darkness, the great stones falling like the clouds—ah, all those precipitations never caused by love but caused by death which is the same, my love. Death opens the dead heart. Death caused these secrets and all these cryings in the night, long night. Death caused these clashings of rocks, screamings, cryings, whisperings, sorrows never to be revealed by dawn, by dawn's light upon the face of love, dead love. Death knows there is no love but the shrouded face.

Death is love, and love is death, have I not always said, and was not this the meaning of my message few but the dead or dying could understand, for few could hear these whispers?

I lost myself the night I lost you, my love, she cried, and I have been a wanderer ever since, wandering over the face of the earth, wandering through mountains and whistling sands and snow clouds, crying at many gates and in many desert courtyards and dark towers. Have I not whispered to the Bedouins in their windy tents, to the dreamers of ancient Samarkand, to the Persians, to the great shahs in castles of ivory bones where their lights burned low as life departed, to the mandarins in their snow-streaked gardens where only the white cranes heard, to the desert princes and mountain kings and storm kings, to the crown princes who had no crowns and no sceptres to lay down—that he who loves shall lose himself in love as in death—stay not this last of love, this first of love, and let this spirit sail upon the wind, for his breath is his sail—let his bright spirit go as I lost you, my love, my love of loves, and never would I see another dawn though the roseate light streaked the clouds, for dawn is not dawn unless it shines on the face of love, and my love has no face? My love is veiled. My love is mysterious.

So have I wandered from land to land, from the crescent to the cross, from the cross to the crescent more times than man can tell. Many crystal-hunters lost their lives seeking for my dead girl.

I played hide-and-seek with the moon in the cloud the night I lost you. For the moon hid behind the cloud as it is hiding now, and the snow settled over the sailor world. You had gone over the mountain top scarcely lighted by the light of the horned moon, and my tears froze like the hailstones in the clouds as I waited. You had gone to find your skirt on the other side of that white mountain peak which we had climbed to be above this world, and you came not again though I stood still. It was always so. I shouted over lonely mountains. I looked in deep ravines.

Surely, Mr. Spitzer had heard these ravings—and when he heard them no more with his listening ear, when her heart was stilled, had heard the roarings of the sea shell which had been in bed with this old Freemount-Snowden when she died, sea shell seeming suddenly to tremble with a roseate light, a long roar of waves departing, waves departing. This was certainly a strange way for her to die—with a sea shell roaring at her feet—like the memory of a wild sea—but there were stranger things to tell, things which he, Mr. Spitzer, would never divulge except in a secret moment long years after her death or after his own death when no living soul remembered her or journeys this great Crusader had taken through the waters of this life, this death—the empearled waters, Mr. Spitzer liked to think. Perhaps the jewel was the casket. Perhaps body and soul were one. She had surely taken her last journey now, sailing with the neap tide, sailing with the last tide which could not have drawn a sea shell or moth or fading star and yet drew her. How fragile at last was human life. It broke like glass.

He had heard the whisper of the·extinguished flame moving through a cloud. He had heard the cloud-burst, the snow hurtling over her watery grave. Only then and perhaps not then could the sorrow of her life be known, when it was ambiguous as her wild dreams which he had inadvertently over-heard when she had cried on her last bed, so that it was scarcely possible to distinguish between the truth and the dream, to tell where one ended and the other began, and perhaps they were always in some way conjoined as body with spirit, spirit with spirit, spirit with bird, he believed now when the great conflict was over, almost over, when it had nearly spent itself, when there was scarcely a memory of her but the snowflake falling through a cloud on a summer's day or perhaps wild diamond horseshoes flashing, glittering on a lonely shore where there were no horses with mother-of-pearl flanks, no bright manes of horses running, and the surf was clouded, the sea burning like a sunken star, almost like a pavement, and the heavens were without a star.

CHAPTER 46

Not only had Cousin Hannah been that great liberator of woman and not only had she been that Troubadour with her flaming message she had carried to the four corners of the earth, knocking on all gates, all hearts, even dead hearts as if they were paving stones—message that love should not be bound to mortal love—that love should flee with an immortal love—this valiant wanderer's life had included many secret chapters of mountain-climbing, as Mr. Spitzer now understood, that she was never bound to finite valleys, not even the valley of the shadow of death, for she had climbed so many formidable mountains and supernumerary peaks that if she had not been famous for her suffrage battles and duels and tournaments, her knightly jousts, perhaps with ghostly knights who long ago had fallen, perishing for love of the white queen or the black queen, she would have won her laurels and her spurs for the inexpressible and inaccessible mountains she had climbed, for the places where she had set her foot or pitched her tent hung with Moorish temple bells on golden cords, her tent cut with many windows, and she would have been famous for the mountains which were greater than mountains, for that great Matterhorn, Mt. Rosa, Mt. Blanc, Moensch, Wetterhorn like the undiscovered snow-peaked mountains rising Alp above Alp through consciousness when she died, rising from subterranean depths with crumbling castles burning with ember lights on their crumbling cliffs and snow hurtling through clouds like suddenly awakened furies, like roaring tides.

He had ascertained that throughout all the boreal regions of this world as throughout the Alps, throughout all the ranges of frozen mountain peaks and wastelands where there are flowers as secretive as snow on snow, the same flowers may be found, white on white, much like the flowers of consciousness in a dead or dying world or like the asphodel in fields of paradise, like the flowers hidden to man. Perhaps there was an astral flower growing at the North Pole or the South Pole or in a freezing cloud. An iceberg had seemed to move into the room when Cousin Hannah died, and the mirrors were rheumed with frost like her dead eyes, and candle flames were frozen into minor stars. It was colder than the Arctic Alps in a high gale when this soul breathed its last with only a sound like rasping cords, Mr. Spitzer had no doubt, though he was not there at the last moment, for he came before, or he came afterward. Never yet had he been present at a climax.

He had found in Cousin Hannah's house, long after her death, an alpenhorn which was twice the height which she had been and hung with a great silver bell to play the ranz des vaches and other melodies, perhaps call to a lost love, a dead love. So might no straggling sheep be lost where she was going now into the alpenglow, the reillumination of refracted sunlight burning like diamond lights upon those great snow-crowned peaks and roofs of snow which had already passed into the darkness ethereal and vast. Mr. Spitzer, acting as her executor, had appropriated this alpenhorn since it was not an object which she had mentioned in her will dated many years before her death and since there was no other claimant, no heiress or heir, or if there was one who might some day appear, Mr. Spitzer must wait for that person's appearance, and since he could not endure that it should go on auction to a stranger, especially as then Mr. Spitzer would have to buy it back for the estate, perhaps at a higher price, and perhaps, as he had told himself, if she had known that he had lived, he with his pigeon whispers and whirrings and blurred voices like sounds of tiny bells, she would have wanted it to be the property of the old musician who collected musical instruments even as an old boat collects barnacles, be it even the smuggler Charon's boat with a sea shell nailed to its mast—but what could an alpenhorn evoke here in level coastlands scarcely above the tide, what mountains rising to the moon, Mr. Spitzer asked? Or could the tide draw all things, even the meadows moving like the waves? It was enough if in such a land a man could keep his head above the water. Certainly, many ladies walked with their heads beneath the waves, moving as if through tidal waves which would never reach shore, for they were like statues upholding the rain-falling roofs.

A few notes from an alpenhorn blowing through clouds did not necessarily usher in the Alps, just as the lute did not necessarily usher in paradise—for all those lutes played by the angels of heaven were manufactured by the old lute-makers of earth painted like their lutes, and they were like the old horse-players—they were in their graves. He knew a great many of the old lute-makers just as he knew many lutes which he collected, along with old viols and harps, none which had been strung in paradise—and might some day collect old harpers plucking their own harp strings, following him through the rolling fogs.

Music arose from this chaos, it seemed to him in his old age, what-ever might be the end of music—that things divine were things secular, and so he valued, like aspects of a dying world, every corruscating pebble or spark shining through the iris-eyed fog where seagulls slept in the rotted hulls of old boats half logged by sand at the water's creeping edge, those which had disappeared in storms a hundred years ago but had returned, or sudden wings started up as he took his evening walks along this shore. And often, seeing the enormous shadow of his black cape on the soughing fog starred by stars, he would think how strange it is that ghosts have seldom or never appeared naked in men's dreams, that they were clothed by the clothing of a dream, be they sea shells or ladies or horses with flowing manes, stars, waters, clouds, pebbles, sparks—that there was nothing but this clothing, that there was nothing but this great mask of life and love, even of death. No sadder elegy than this—The great couturier has snipped his last thread. Mr. Spitzer would rather have written his own elegy. Surely, no one knew the limitations of music or of this life better than he, this old musician hearing, even in his disturbed sleep when he should have been wrapped in the silence of the profound, the raspings of sea shells, the neighings, coughings of horses moving through clouds, for what could be more impotent than that music which should not awaken the dead though the musician should wander forever through fogs and waters and rolling clouds, though he should compose, if not his elegy which was impossible so long as he lived, impossible to end, then his aubade for the evening star, morning star fading in the light, music which was made of the attritions of waves on stone and on his heart, dead heart which was the paving stone for the dreamer and the dream? What awakened him? For the dead awakened only to the dead and the dying to the dying. To awaken would be perhaps to lose the greater part of life.

So Mr. Spitzer believed that he had never yet awakened fully, never except from sleep to sleep, dream to dream. And yet his dying music had some power as if to suggest the dreamer when he had passed beyond the purlieus of mortality.

Mr. Spitzer, still in a mournful mood, for someone was always dying, had carried this alpenhorn embossed with mother-of-pearl, heavy as a tree branch, along the foggy beach when Cousin Hannah was no more, when doubtless she had climbed her last mountain, the hailstones like burning cinders dashing in her face, and he had blown a few wandering notes like some old ghost calling to his lost love as he had heard, above the ringing waves ringing like silver bells, the ringing, tolling of the silver sheep's bell which had once rung to the lost sheep, hearing also, as he did so, the cries of the grey loons in the grey fog and the bah, bahing of waves breaking upon this shore of stone and fog as thick as fleece streaked with the gold rays of the moonlight, waves coming to pasture like sheep with moony eyes beamed upon the waves of darkness, like many moons or like the souls of the dead as he had thought where the fog-bound phoenix fireflies lighted his uncertain and wavering path, thinking also that the sheperd was lost, lost like the Dog star in the rolling cloud, like the lost following the lost, but then quite unexpectedly as he was passing through an upland meadow like a fallen firmament starred with daisies in the fog, the fleecy fog, a ram had stepped out of the fog, and other sheep had followed Mr. Spitzer. And ever after that, he had been followed by men in the grey cities, by lost men although he was lost, and none more lost than he, this old musician blowing his horn in the clouds.

So from this old suffragette he had learned something, after all—she had brought him, by her dying, to reality—and she had taught him much, expanding his sympathies and his domain—as if only when she had died, he had lived, breathed, whispered—beginning to understand the meaning of all those ambiguities he might once have impatiently ignored, all those ambivalences he might once have attributed not to himself but to his brother's checkered career and butterfly life among the shadows—knowing now the power of a dead beauty, a dead love, a vanquished life, and that sterility which begets, even like death, Mr. Spitzer said, all beautiful things of this creation, the image of all dead loves. For who had ever known the present moment? The sense of the immediate was freighted with the past—and if it were not, then what would be the present but an empty room, a closed door, the hull of an old boat stripped bare of its shrouds, a withered rose, a dead love? For who had ever seen the living beauty, beauty stripped bare of all pretenses and all illusions, beauty revealed as beauty was—and were not all beautiful things the ghosts of themselves in this transmuting life, even like mirror images returning the reflections of that which had already faded, even like dreams, memories fading into air, perhaps as one awakened from sleep to sleep, even like voices faded in distant thunder clouds, whirrings, whispers already faded into music no one had heard? The weight of the unspoken music was that which Mr. Spitzer knew. The cloud upon the face of beauty was beauty itself. So never would he lift the cloud. The clouds had settled over her. If he knew not her omega, then how did he know her alpha? For she was already old, obsolete as some old coin which had gone out of circulation long before the age of Hugh De Capet, Mr. Spitzer thought, perhaps long before he knew her.

Cousin Hannah had surely been, though forgotten by mountain-climbers now, though remembered in no stud book of mountain-climbing which was probably less inclusive than the stud books listing the great stallions, sires and mares, though listed not among those who had lost their lives, those who had conquered great pinnacles of all known mountains and some which were unknown to man, though remembered not by any mountain tomb or cloud citadel, though no coin had been struck off in her memory, neither gold nor silver nor lead nor stone, not even though bearing the image of some great turbaned Turk or paladin, some old helmeted Crusader who had perished, if not on his outward journey to the Holy Land, then on his journey of return which was a longer journey, or some old Roman emperor who had minted too many coins, though remembered by no winged horse's head or harp, by no commemorative image but Mr. Spitzer's fading laurel leaf or breath of mountain mist or snowdrops or Alpine holy grass he had brought to cover her coffin when she was dead, the great mountain-climber who had conquered snow-crowned summits and frozen pinnacles, the great trail-blazer blazing like a rising star, falling star, perhaps the greatest mountain-climber unknown to history, surely the greatest ever known among ladies. Yet seldom or never had she spoken of her mountain-climbing exploits and expeditions until she was dying. For that of which she should have been proud, she was ashamed, Mr. Spitzer believed—and, indeed, had noted that many famous people valued not so much their world-shaking fame and splendors of posterity as one moment of oblivion. It was oblivion from which they had fled, and yet it was oblivion toward which they fled as if they feared that which they loved, loved that which they feared. Oblivion was ever at the heart of fame.

Certainly, as Mr. Spitzer must concede, there were many men who might say that she who had tried to take every lady's lily-white hand and lead her troops toward freedom under the silken banner of suffrage had been a charlatan, a mere poseur, a mountebank, the sorriest adventurer seeking only to mislead, to bewilder, to shock, to destroy their loves, to create chaos—but they forgot her motive which had been her love, and they forgot her secret cowardice seeming to Mr. Spitzer more heroic than greatest heroism was. Perhaps they would have loved her if they had known her weeping when a snowflake fell upon her mottled hand cold as the skin of a frog—if they had known that her granite was but a façade, and she was weaker than woman was, and she had crumbled now most surely into waters and clouds, darkness, whirlwind, snow, snow water. She was like a man whom woman had destroyed, a woman who was abandoned by her love, or an old house where no lover ever came and where the door banged in the wind. She was like all great lovers who have been set to wandering, crying at all gates, knocking on the doors of all dead hearts, crying for their loves, lost loves. She was like a dead planet wandering. Perhaps she had returned to mountains or wandered ever with the dead moon, that moon which, though dead, was the ensign of deathless love throughout history and in all countries under the stars and in countries where the stars had faded, countries where there were no stars or where the stars had fallen, Mr. Spitzer thought, most especially in frosty nights when the clouds creaked and moved in the windy heavens like the great stones rolling away from graves or in nights when he heard the winds creaking, croaking like the croakings of frogs which gave voice to that which was never spoken by woman or man. This was the music written by no man, Mr. Spitzer believed, listening with his dead ear as some old hound lifted its ear. Or was it the ferret? Was it before the day of the dog? Music lay under the silence, above the silence. This life was but the thinnest surface. He heard the thinnest whisper, a papery star falling or sand grain which whispered—I am thine only love. I am thine only love, my dear of dears. Because of me there grew this great pearl enclosing shadows and many windings and warped depths and opalescent flames.

She had been so light that she had had scarcely any way to lift herself from earth or to find her way through heavy winds and clouds, so delicate then when she was dying that she should have increased her body by ballast, that she should have eaten hour-glasses and goblets and door knobs and apples of Hesperides like the opium lady dreaming among the shadows or should have eaten sand grains and pebbles and barnacles like the light-winged cranes who do so in order to navigate a true course, flying in a long-tailed Y shape through windy heavens, flying like a Chinaman's cue, and who will close around a tired bird or a bird blown off his course, upholding him with the air current caused by the undulating flight of their oar wings, and who will go back for a lost leader drifting through clouds. She had been the boldest mountain-climber ever known among members of the weaker sex, there was little doubt, scaling Alps exceeding Alps, perhaps the mountains of illusion—the snow falling on her jagged forehead even when she burned, so that winter had come like a courtier in her wake, and the snow had covered her dead heart, bleeding heart under the pale sun streaking the clouds, and the air had darkened, and the clouds had frozen as Mr. Spitzer watched, and the snows had melted not. One bold in her sense of adventure which had not understood the courage of timid things, not even Mr. Spitzer's heart, or so he had always supposed, she had given, she had said when she was dying, when the last ember burned low for the last time, a long leash to love, harnessing not the dead moon in the cloud—such freedom as had never been given to her, bound to suffrage as to life, letting her love go. Her love had gone on strange adventures and missions. And yet had she not been the greatest coward, ignoble and not noble, Mr. Spitzer asked, so great a coward that all heroes were eclipsed by this persistent love? This love went on when there was neither subject nor object.

If she had been all that she had seemed to be, if her motives had been transparent and crystal clear, there would have been little point in Mr. Spitzer's musical post-mortem and inquiries as to the meaning of the secret heart which was not his heart—but there were great secrets and intrigues and fateful amours perhaps misleading him when she was dead, when she whispered no more her lute music in scraping winter winds and freezing clouds, when he must inquire in many streets, ask of many strangers in the fog-bound darkness scarcely lighted by a star, perhaps in those nights when he was stalled in the fog or when he, pushing ahead of him with his cane, unsteady as if there were waves in his path, moved uncertainly for fear of colliding with some old tramp like a derelict schooner with tattered sails reeling through the wind-tattered fog, appearing perhaps many years after its disappearance—Have you seen my lady—or my lord? Did you ever know her, one who lived in memory of a dead love? Do you remember her whom all have forgotten except myself, and I am no more? This is not a man you see. This is but the shadow of a man. Did you ever see her?

People must have thought that Mr. Spitzer was quite mad, asking these questions in the rolling darkness like an obsessed census-taker who might count the same persons over and over again, yet find that there was always one missing like a supernumerary star or spark or glow-worm. There was always one missing no matter how often he counted and no matter if the total increased so that he had gained many, for yet he had lost one who was incalculable. And yet he had found, though oblivion was hers, for she was covered by the eternal snow, that snow melting not but increasing like that oblivion decreasing not with time's illusive passage, for time passes not, and only man passes, one who had said that he remembered this great suffrage captain, one who knew her when she was the leader of the moon-breasted flock flying through windy heavens, one who had said that she was beautiful, an old steeple-headed steeplejack or steeple jill who, tall as a church steeple, had lurched out of the billowing fog one night when Mr. Spitzer, the wind blowing through his cape, his black cape dragging him from starboard to larboard so that he staggered, reeled, lurched, or went miles off his course which he had left uncharted so that he might gain new orientations through disorientation unmeasurable and might make no error as to latitude, longitude, unable to gain a mile unless he lost a mile or returned perhaps upon himself or was blown into whirling vortices like whirlpools of alien memory never ceasing, rippling for years after he was gone, his mast broken, was plowing his uneven way where strange lights like crackling stars broke under his feet and who had answered Mr. Spitzer's questions, as the wind whistled through Mr. Spitzer's shrouds almost drowning his voice, by these replies —I fell the night she fell. I was fallen the night she was fallen. When was the night? I fell when stars fell from the clouds, and there were falling paving stones, falling snows, great avalanches over the roofs, and there were amputated stars, whistlings, winds, gales, and white-winged schooners driven from pole to pole, and there were ladies scudding under white umbrellas. I am amputated, oh, my lord.

Ah, I am dead, dear sire, dead as the heart buried under the earth, dead as all dead things, dead as the balloonist shrouded in the garden, dead as the eunuch among the purple shadows, dead as the great harbormaster, Mr. Spitzer heard this old steeplejack saying, almost like the muffled echo of his thoughts as his cape belled around him, casting its shadow upon the glassy sands. There is a negress in the belfry. She is ringing—oh, she is ringing. Ah, I am no more, my lady or my lord. I exist, and yet I exist not, for my existence is my death just like yours. I live because I am dead. I am dead as the census-taker, dead as the watchman, the brick-layer, the surveyor with his plummet line. I am dead because I live, breathe, whisper. I love because I love not. I love not because I love. I am filled with self-contradictions like heart murmurs. I love because I have died, for all who have died have loved, and all who have loved have died. All who have loved have drowned, for they were not upheld by love or by stone angels arising into the foundationless clouds. Love sank with them. Some were drowned in the graveyard. Some were drowned in the city. Some were drowned in their beds. Some were killed by a rain drop, some by a sand grain. Some were killed by a snowflake. Some were killed by an avalanche. Some went down with the herring fleet, the herring like silver leaves. Some were killed by a pigeon's wing. I whisper because I am silent. I am silent because I cry. I cry because I depart. I depart because I stay. I am filled with murmurs, whirrings, bells, voices.

Look closer, sir. It is the clock face, the clock which tells no time, no hour in a timeless world of dreams, memories, altering chances. Time is the cloud which crosses this face. My machinery is clogged by leaves, wings. My minute hand pursues not my hour hand. My tall jockey pursues not my short jockey. My numerals are faded. Eternity was but a moment. The great steeplechase is over. What mad bell-ringer rings these bells like earth and heaven ringing? Pigeons ring these bells. There are only these flocks of pigeons flying across the face of the moon, dead moon, for it is the city of the dead where now you walk. Are you awake or asleep? What hour in the night and in the city?

And truly Mr. Spitzer had heard pigeon murmurs and cryings of cranes in the opalescent fog by the sea which was the color of a dead pigeon's breast, and he had heard cricket whistles of distant traffic and ivory horns in the fog where were suddenly lighted windows. He had heard bells, music of trembling bridges, footfalls. It almost might seem as if he were caught in one of the opium lady's dreams, much like the fly in the spider's web, but this was not the case, for it was not the opium lady but that great patriarchal suffrage captain who by her dying of which he had been the watchman as of a dying star had given a new meaning to life and love so that now his experience increased, and much that he had never understood before, he had come to understand, including his own life and death.

All was not over so long as there was one card out, one card, whether it was heart or spade. That factor of mystery made all things possible.

Much had seemed at that time like the acme of madness, perhaps some substitute for life, perhaps some substitute for death, perhaps a tragic love or act of renunciation which had been proposed by one who was dying, Mr. Spitzer had believed, understanding that before the great fiction of death there might be many imaginary sparks starting up either like a new life or aspects of life not previously revealed—it often seeming to him that if he had had no brother before, he would have had his twin at his last hour—perhaps to light the way for him.

She had cried as Mr. Spitzer remembered long years afterward—Ah, bright star of my love, find your way to the lightless star. Find your way to one who has neither wings nor light. For I am dying now, and mountains resurrect themselves before the last great cataclysm when mountains sink like tiny sails, and my love goes down.

CHAPTER 47

✂

THE quality of the literal gave meaning to these last of last remarks before there faded all color and light and sound, it seemed to meditative Mr. Spitzer, he who had listened to the roarings of the sea shell and also even to the whispers of the silent heart. Ah, the mountains moved, Cousin Hannah had said when she was dying. That was what happened. That was it. The mountains are her tomb. She is on the pinnacle. She is in the valley. Her blood stains the snow, and white is my true love, white as snow in wind and cloud where there is no moon, no nymph. Ah, could we have had a child, red as her blood, white as the snow, red as the rose on the snow—then would I not live now, and would she not live now? Would not our image have been in one body different from ourselves? Could I have been a woman, could I have been a man, this great battle never would have taken place. And yet have I not lived and loved, lived in memory of this dead love like something beating in my breast? Shall she live when I am dead, and shall we never meet, my love, love of loves? Is it all over, or does it begin? Do I hear the bugle crying reveille or taps?

So that after all, even like himself, Mr. Spitzer thought, she had deferred her life to the next life. He did not know, with his thoughts moving slowly as a largo over the waves, what he could have done for her, dying as one who had always been a stranger to him and who, by her failure to recognize that he lived, had already exiled him to the next world—except that he had wished her well, of course, and he had whispered as he had always whispered when he came to her bedroom like a great silk-shrouded tent—Good-night and good-morning—simply to imply that she would live beyond the night enfolding her as if it were the night of love which makes no distinction between the living and the dead, the past and the present, the lover and the loved.

For in the night, are not all loved, perhaps only by their dead loves returning? In the night, does one not hear the roaring of wings, surgings of waves, voices never heard by day? Mr. Spitzer heard his brother's laughter rippling all day long. His brother whispered in his conch ear. His brother's music of discord interfered with his music of total harmony or his silence.

And for that matter, if it was Mr. Spitzer who saw her off, he who saw the rippling of her shroud, he who heard the singing of her cord, he who said good-night—good-night, sweet prince—good-night, my lady— God rest you merry, gentlemen—he could be fairly sure that on some other star, perhaps not too different from this, his brother would say good-morning as this star faded and as the cock crowed and as the noises of the morning began.

The fact that Mr. Spitzer was this twin was not always a great inconvenience though it was always disparaging to him, perhaps in some ways he did not know. On the other hand, there perhaps were certain inscrutable gains. He could at least count on his brother to be a Welcoming Committee of One on the other side of this great void when this great suffrage captain lifted her shroud from her skull face like the moon fading at dawn, one faint light like a lost star burning in the empty port-hole of her eye before that light went out, the light fading into the glassy light.

Peron, unlike old Joachim, would not be repelled by age or ugliness which had all but stopped Mr. Spitzer's beating heart as it was this paradoxically living twin who had idealized deathless beauty and ageless snow and purity of the deathless heart renewing itself, yet had lived to see that even the moon had grown imperceptibly older during his brief span of his own life time, and milky stars had lost weight, casting their surf lights upon the earth much as distant lighthouses might light the tides with wavering spokes, and there was a patina of age like moon-washed gold upon the day's trembling clouds, and his eyesight grew dim as if he walked forever through blowing sands, shrieking winds. The winds were distracting to him, drawing him into whirlpools like some old caterpillar going to his doom. His skin was spotted by reflected moons. The wind contracted the iris of his eye, causing his vision to shrink. At any moment he might walk out of his skin as out of an old cloak. So that his day had become increasingly his night, but when was his day? His night was not his day, for night knew no boundaries. The pristine vision had faded, perhaps before he had ever opened his blurred infant eyes, perhaps when the first pearl-winged butterfly had sailed in the first dusky light, and doubtless this life was his darkness. He found it increasingly difficult to focus his vision, to tell the difference between near and far.

To his brother he owed much, far more than the promissory notes he was always meeting out of his own pocket, the bogus checks he was always making good, the fraternal charities to which his brother had subscribed in his memory, the old debts his brother had contracted in his brother's name, leaving Mr. Spitzer to pay, he owing far more, it seemed to him, than the inestimable debt he paid out of his own torn pockets spilling showers of golden coins, spilling more golden coins than he had known were his upon the wave-eroded sands streaked by the lines of the waves and flutterings of shadows of blackbirds like his musical score before the sand was swept by the chargings of the musical white-maned waves, wild white horses rising through clouded surf with crowns of flowers upon their heads—for his brother, by his dying, by his establishing, as Mr. Spitzer hoped, a colony under no flag, perhaps upon the other shore, a community not of this world as now it was but of this world as once it was—yesterday, yesterday, Mr. Spitzer sighed with long tremolos sweeping through his cape, starting old harp strings and withered beach grasses to rattle, whisper, sigh, and oar grasses to undulate scarcely above the water's edge where fishes slept like stars or where perhaps slept some small Moses in his mollusk boat, even like the pearl in its oyster shell under the oyster-colored cloud—or of this world as it might become tomorrow when Joachim was no more, when he was where his brother was—tomorrow, day after tomorrow—had robbed death of much of its power and of its brightest jewel which should have been its certainty, Mr. Spitzer believed, and night of its remorseless terror, terror like the winds of passage blowing some old bald-headed schooner from coast to coast, ripping its shrouds, and had made death seem, after all, as Mr. Spitzer sighingly remarked, slightly ridiculous, something like a private folly, hidden but not acknowledged, a love affair one carried on but did not legalize by marriage or any true-lover's knot or bond, a night's visit with some old prostitute whose face one would never see at dawn, so one might never know with whom he slept, whether she was beautiful or ugly in the light of dawn, for one would have left before the dawn, before the clouds lifted from that dead face, had not his brother said when he was on his way to another race-track or rattling, for a new throw, the bones in the ivory cup? His brother was always innovating. Yet mere innovation would not suffice, of course, life forever repeating itself as the rain recalls the rain and the star recalls the star.

This tendency of an image to repeat an image, perhaps with variations, was something to be considered, weighed, taken into account. And for that matter, the brother recalled the brother. So how could death be terrible when, after Mr. Spitzer's death, perhaps taking place only by proxy, he might hear his brother's laughter like an absolute obsession shaking him and rippling the stars or the cough of an old, purblind, rattle-boned horse rising through thinning surf under a falling star or even his own cough in the wind, the wind scraping, sighing around him as he walked the forever curving shoreline with one foot in the creeping surf, one in the creeping sand, no cable string to guide him, trying forever to reconcile two worlds or to understand what they might have in common, some common denominator pertaining to both equivalent sides of an ideal equation as if they were equal though this was not the case, of course, there being always some factor missing, a leaf missing on one side or a star on the other side, a planet missing or a plume missing or a pod missing in the wind, perhaps a paving stone missing or a lamp missing or a foam-crowned dolphin missing upon the foaming flood, the flood of time, of timelessness? And which side was this where a leaf fell before a star fell, where one followed the other to its grave? Who could measure this incalculable quantity and leave no remainder like a drift of crystal sand seen through a smudged glass under a thin trickle of stars gleaming through clouds like smoke? Or was it possible that there was only one shore, that where Mr. Spitzer was—always the distant, always the other shore so that there was always someone lost, perhaps himself, for perhaps he had already sailed in the creeping tide, the tide rising up to the port-holes? Perhaps, indeed, as he sighingly considered, it was himself who, though he had waved farewell to one who thought he was already dead, would greet, with his black handkerchief waving like a pirate's flag, that old suffragette when she arrived upon the other shore, her sails tattered, no watchman in the crow's-nest grown over with the long sea grasses strung with tiny barnacles, tiny boats. Sometimes he wondered, perhaps with indistinct whispers scarcely audible to him—did he really know, after all, which brother he was, for had he not lived on both sides, died on both sides, or was this death not of the past but of the future? And if in especially confusing moments of blurred chords and melting keys he did not know his own identity albeit he was like the great census-taker counting all, all moons of imagination or memory, all moons of yester-day, tomorrow, if he had stolen death as if it were the brightest jewel imaginable eclipsing this life and petty woes, then how could he ever know who anyone else was or plummet soundless depths?

Ah, what image was there of his love which had no image? It was not rose or bird or star, for all would not suffice though he should encompass all, and there was always one soul missing though he added to his count, though he should keep count as his brother had kept a tally sheet of the horses, not only those great race horses which ran through pounding starlight-colored surf but those which never ran in any race, were entered but never called, were called but never entered, pawing but never run-ning when the starter blew his winding horn, one lost soul never to be recorded on Mr. Spitzer's many-written palimpsest or tally sheet though he should keep count of rose, bird, star, horse, barnacle, cloud, sleeping pebble, hurtling or winged rock, every phase of the moon spilling its inexhaustible beauty in the cloud, waning, yet waxing again, waning, every blow of wandering still-born surf, every birth veil left upon the sand, every snow-crowned spruce tree in the silent whirlpool forever whirling, every steeple, all images of this fog-bound world where ships were banked in the fog, all memories returning as if they were his through which he had lived, moved, gathered weight, this flesh so enor-mous that it was his mother-of-pearl tomb where perhaps only one low light burned like the sunken star, yet though he was dead and not of this superficial world, world of deceptive surfaces, drifting clouds, illusions compounding illusions, facets gathering facets, and doubtless though he kept conscientious record, adding, altering, effacing when he recognized that he had been wrong, when he had made a mistaken or double entry, seldom effacing for fear he should efface himself, yet there would be no entry in his log of all the voyages he had taken like circumambient air or water or moon in the cloud or voyaging watchmen with vaporous torches circling around this circling world, all the whirlpools, currents, counter-currents, undertows, trade winds, birds of passage, long-necked sea-birds screaming in this transmogrifying flight, equatorial passages dividing no halves where nothing moved, where were ships like glassy flotillas of butterflies pinned upon a silken wave, circles not of this world and horse

latitudes none had explored, polar ice floes, voyages to stellar poles, spi-
rallings of foam, movements of fleecy clouds over water, shoals of thinning ship-wrecked stars on some far reef like city lights, city lights going
off and on as in the opium lady's dreams.

For no matter how inclusive he tried to be, there was a factor missing, something beyond the encompassing of all. Among all things possible, there was the rejected possibility. And perhaps the rejected possibility was all there was. Perhaps it had always been eccentric and lonely.
Perhaps, the idea had occurred to him as the one explanation possible to
contain all polarities and none, he was forever voyaging. Thus he was
forgetful, simply by his act of trying to remember, to forget no pigeon in
his walks. Once, coming upon a dead pigeon, he had burst into tears.
Perhaps he was forever between two shores as between two worlds, each
ephemeral, each receding from the other until there would be but a
narrow strand where the encroaching waters swept, whirling at his feet as
now, his black cape sweeping, singing his only dirge as he clutched his
high silk chimney hat in blows of flame-like wind and surf. For the waters
recognized no hedge or wall, sweeping over old meadows already marked
by corrugating tide and orchards straggling in the wind with golden
apples hung upon their boughs like moons and crooked fences and old
towns with leaning steeples and sagging doors where the old sailors
walked in their dripping shrouds, where the old spouters spouted like the
whales they once had caught and the fish eyes gleamed like candle flames
in darkened mirrors marked by wavering water lines, so that he was in a
perpetual fountain no matter where he walked with his blurred whisperings and swore to God he would not have been surprised if he had found
stone horses arising before him or wreathed cherubim sporting in his
lunar tide or old Tritons blowing their ivory horns from which the
waters poured, rising through his waves, or waves sweeping old pillars
crumbling or old helmets piled up upon his towering floods or satyrs like
fawns in his wake playing harps upon the pearly breakers or moon-eyed
dolphins playing upon the keyboards of the moving foam at some far
horizon or confiding centaurs walking through the narrow inlets of his
bay as he heard forever blowing, whirling, splashing around him these
waters like his music which broke through every wave, every cloud, rippled, fell, whispered, sobbed in lonely piazzas like the voices of all dead
loves, drowned loves where only the marble horses watched, pawing in
the rain-logged clouds, or there were only old many-mouthed gargoyles
under the slate roofs with waters streaming from their mouths. Yet who
wrote this music or composed these waterfalls, these clouds through
which the sun shone like a dead eye under a swollen lid? He was draped
by a fountain like an iridescent shroud or cradle of the moth or was like a
boat sleeping in a pearl, it seemed to him, a great boat in a small pearl, a
small boat in a great pearl shrouding its sail, or he was water-logged like
some old ship sinking even in his sleep as if its cargo were weighted with
iron bells seeking the magnetic floor of a sunken star or perhaps, of
course, like this old ship of the world which had sunk because of its
ballast long before it ever sailed, some ship with its cargo of all souls, all

lost souls which had gone down, all but his own sinking to the ocean's floor, sinking with the carriage and the carriage horses, fishes flying like the many-fluttering blackbirds as his sleep lay upon him, wave upon wave to a watery firmament where stars were drowned or where were the old sail-boats with their sails dragging upon the floods, no boatsmen in those boats. Perhaps all who lived were drowned. At times the moon in a cloud seemed like only an iris gleaming upon the wing of a moth. Perhaps this world was the Lost Atlantis with bells ringing under water like the umbrellas billowing in the pearl-strung fog when the moon was diminished to a pearl, this sunken continent for which we mourned, not knowing that we were what we mourned, that we were on the ocean's floor. If all were lost, how could one be lost? And when should he arise, he asked, in what glassily mirroring dawn, or should he never arise to that surface which was the death of love, this dead image in the dawn, the dawn light like medusas stinging his lidless eyes? He was swollen by many waters. Ah, he reminded himself of a pregnant woman swollen with many waters where no child was but the dead self, the self which heard no heartbeat. To his indifferent brother, he owed much—the thinly superficial world he might never know again, he having died, he having drowned, he being submerged, wrapped in the enfolding waters of sleep, winged barnacles growing on his bellropes, oceans and clouds rolling over him, under him. Or did he arise as he awakened to the surface where he was not and where love faded like an image fading in sleep, lost in light as stars are lost in light, lost like the far barking of a cosmic dog pursuing a leaf, lost in vaultless heavens like an echo of which there was no source but an echo fading, lost like one snowflake which was lost at the beginning of time or before time began, a star-shaped snowflake burning in a roseate cloud? Then surely he would find his love when the light faded, when the last light faded from his eyes, and waters rippled over him with long sighings, sobbings. Waters flowed over old flagstones indiscriminately leading nowhere, old milestones marking no miles, porphyry lamps, porches, grand pianos, harps, bridges, white-winged angelic schooners lifting their white wings as they sailed upon the tides obliterating the old fences, the old hedges, the old graves. So might that old suffrage captain find her love where the waves arose like snow-crowned mountains rising to the clouded moon, the drowned marine stars, the waves sweeping over this marginal shore as over his bars of music marked by clefs, old sea shells drifting upon a moorless tide like the minarets and domes of cities. Ah, there was none to anchor her.

What could he do for that old bloomer girl when she was dead—what elegy could he write or in what way commemorate that which surpassed not only his memory but his intuitional life? His life depended not upon his memory. He had sought for answers and had found only questions. He had asked of every dead heart and had found only whispers, sobbings for other loves. Who was he to restore that which was so plainly forgotten? He might wear a white rose in memory of her, doubtless a white rose which he had always worn along with a wraith-like spray of maidenhair as one who was not yet initiated into life, it seemed to him, and might die before he had experienced life. He might lift his hat from which flew an armada of white peacock butterflies often astonishing him as they flew past his eyes. For how many souls could he lose, and were they the same souls, or were they different souls gliding past him, or did he lose the same souls many times? He might fly his mournful flag. He might tap with his cane, thinking of the white lady veiled by white, the black night, thinking of the immortal loves as if they were mortal, too. For the immortal should exist only through mortality. Only mortality should endure. And had she not missed mortality, by-passing it like a comet which never reached this earth, yet lighting these trembling windows with its passing light? Some might think it was the light of an old train passing these windows—but it was a comet casting its pale gold upon the sleeper's eyes, Mr. Spitzer knew. He might throw old sea shells back into the dwarfed tide or that tide which was the magnitude of all tides flowing together now—say to some old sea shell whispering as he whispered, the music of the sea whispering, the wind bugling through his cape—Depart, depart, be utterly pulverized, leave no memento mori of her where the pearly combers roll, where the mountains rise with billowings and peaks and bellowings to the moon with its white horn, the clouded star—sail on, sail on until thou hast reached some other shore or art lost, thy sail going down in dust and foam. Be as finest sediment. Drift from pole to pole. Let the hour-glass be reversed. Or let the constellations fly like birds. Be utterly of water and cloud, thine image lost as the boatman in his barque when it is covered by the flood. But though acting often only through his somnolence and inactivity, his patient waiting, Mr. Spitzer could do nothing so foolish as to throw upon the tide that which the tide swept over in its own due time as over the dead cities, as over the towers and cupolas and spires and mother-of-pearl turrets and roofs, mosaic emperors, as over the skulls of the dead where the fireflies gleamed and were reflected on the flood like the last gleams of consciousness, where the thin waves advanced with long ripples, eddies, retardations. Doubtless to a small creature this minor flood might seem like inundation, though only rippling at Mr. Spitzer's feet. He had scarcely known what to do for her. He had scarcely known what to do for her or some old steeplejack knocked off a steeple by a pigeon's glistening wing, some old anchorite never anchored, or mountains sailing like the schooners through rippling clouds, lifting their white sails, had known how neither to shrink nor to expand, neither to furl nor to unfurl, neither to remember nor to forget, neither to stay nor to depart. He had not known whether to say good-bye or good-morning.

It was all he could do, obviously, to navigate himself by his windy cape, his flying scarf with its long silk fringes, his cane like his oar with which he cut away the tangled holy grass, and many times he had been lost, so many times that it seemed to him he was perpetually lost, yet though it was only through such loss that he could ever hope to redeem and find himself, so like himself and his dead heart that he would recognize him, perhaps at the moment of his own unimaginable death, and as a matter of fact Mr. Spitzer had perhaps passed beyond that necessity,

being where his dead brother was. Mr. Spitzer had forgotten at what hour
his necessity had ceased, all clocks tolling together with inaccurate accuracy in distant clouds, and after that had been no time. So much had
happened since then, sometimes outside his consciousness when he was
lost like the glass-backed fly between the cloud banks and the cloud
banks, the stars over him, under him. He had forgotten when he had
found that never could he drop anchor in a quiet harbor, that the old
planks were swept over by long-tongued waves, that the wharf sailed as
this world sailed during the night, for waters crept over the low portals of
his house and through his low door and through the broken window
lighted by a storm lamp casting finny lights like showers of sequins and
over his bed, the iron cot, and over the golden cradle strung by harp
strings quivering as with a celestial infant's cries, and he awakened ever
in the heart of creation's storm, not knowing how long he had slept or if
he had awakened in the dying light of dawn, the fog so heavy that this
was his nocturne, his elegy. He would not live to hear its conclusion. So
how should he judge another's life or death or know duration of one
moment of time, especially if there was timelessness in the heart of time
even as there was death in the heart of life, if time was but a human
artifice like moons and suns and stars, it seemed to him with his black
cape eclipsing moons, semi-moons, quarter moons? For his were subterranean memories seldom coming to the surface of life, all images being
blurred and all forms flowing into each other like fishes turning into
flowers, flowers turning into keyholes, flowers turning into birds, all
walls being permeable as sands through which the waters flowed, sands
like the thinnest shell of earth over the waves, and that great suffragette
had lived no doubt at windy altitudes, heights from which there dropped
no plummet line to reach this falling star, those great Alpine ranges she
had said were rising from her heart, rising above the meadows of wild
flowers where old knights had left their chalices, rising above a cloudline
where none might ever see her face or know who she was. There were no
bees buzzing in that snow storm.

Death was this shrouded mystery, it seemed to him, this veil of
gossamer which none should lift for fear of tearing the veil, so none
should ever know—Was she the bridegroom? Was she the bride? Or had
she passed to where no lover ever was, where no image ever was repeated
in the waters or in the clouds, where not even Mr. Spitzer could find her,
he being lost, wandering without purpose? If he knew not where or who
he was, how should he know her? It was no realm of purpose where he
lived. Disorientation seemed his fate perhaps more beautiful than purpose which had been finite. Sometimes, perhaps because of the heavy fog,
he seemed to be walking simultaneously on many roads. Obviously, she
had fooled her followers in many ways during her tempestuous life—so
why not in her death which wrote no finis to her great event, Mr. Spitzer
asked with the salt of the sea upon his mouth as he heard the sighing
cordages of a distant boat, the distant shrouds unfurling, rippling beyond
the sailor moon? The moon sank beneath the wave, sank with the long-
necked white bird. Perhaps death had come at the moment of creation.
Perhaps there had been no time between the love and the death. And by

extension, perhaps there had been no time between the death and the love. Ah, how Mr. Spitzer dreamed of these simultaneities like great climaxes coming together, roaring to the clouds, simultaneities of time with time, of love with love! He dreamed that all watering places should be one watering place. Sometimes he even dreamed that his death would be his brother's death, and this possibility astonished him, filling him with awe, and he was filled with forlorn misgivings such as of one who had already lived beyond his death, perhaps upon a narrow margin, a crumbling ledge. Yet was not his death impossible? He asked of sun and moon and stars—when should he be gone, leaving no memory of him, no residue, not even this blowing dust?

The wind had blown, and the white rose had withered, and the old stars had grown smaller and thinner and warped, floating like sand grains in the hour-glass of the trembling heavens, and there had been scarcely a ripple when this great captain sank in clouded depths, scarcely a crest of foam dissolving as the great breakers swept over her, pounding like long-maned wild horses, dragging her down from her high pinnacle of foam or snow or star, for she was like a drowner whom none could reach, one reached by no wavering lighthouse beam, and there was no Savior upon these waters, no fisherman in his boat, none netting moons and suns and stars and golden guineas sinking beneath the waves, none to bring her in as the fisherman brings the fish, and this great Crusader shell had sunk beneath the rising waves, the waves hissing, falling like cascades. She went down with none to uphold her, much like one who was drowned in love, a faceless being floating on the waves at dawn, staring with lidless eyes at the dark clouds, one abandoned by her lover when she went down, Mr. Spitzer thought. Drowning and love were ever the same, the waters of creation rising, falling. All who died, it had always seemed to him, died of love even when there was no lover, none to rescue them, and she was locked in love's embrace. Death was her love. Death was that dark lover who drew her down, and when should she arise upon the wave arising to the cloud? When should she unfurl her sail? Had she not died before, perhaps long ago as she was dying now?

Mr. Spitzer, remembering his twin brother, had ever held that death is not unique, not solitary, not that which comes but once in life and leaves no sign. Death left the white rose, the white bird, the clouded star. Death was ever this dying love. If it were not dying, it would not be love but would be death complete and absolute, for transience was this beauty breaking like foam upon a star or breaking like foam upon the figurehead, upon the prow, upon the oar. Death was this dipping sail upon a far horizon, this dragging sail. Death was this moment of rapture forever prolonged. Only the mourner lived longer than love, lived only to mourn, to reproach, to sorrow, even like Mr. Spitzer mourning for his love, yet well knowing that there would be none to mourn for him, none to write his music when he was no more. Death existed in dying memory.

So he could write no music which would cease, no silence which would not whisper. The sea roared when she departed. The salt water swept over old trees leaning tideward, old porches crumbling into moon-colored sand, broken pillars. The tide skirted this barren shore when she was gone, rippled, broke with great billows blown by wind upon the thin-lipped rock, the narrow shelf. The planetary wheel turned through foam and mist, casting great surf like starlight upon the face of the sleeper. The ruts deepened in old roads which had once been but thinnest lines through clouds, roads no traveller had ever travelled and where none travelled now, where there were only shadows blown by whistling wind. Old lamp-lighters lifted once more their dimming lights, and there were blurred harbor lights like lights under water, and there were lights like nets reaching through clouded heavens as Mr. Spitzer watched, wondering what fisherman in his dark boat was seining the stars with those nets so widely meshed that some stars escaped, even like butterflies lifting their white sails in the grey fog.

The music of the sea whispered to dead sea shells as Mr. Spitzer whispered, wondering who the great composer was if it was not himself with his dead heart, thinking that there was music written never to be played, music written to be contained in no score or box or coffin of sound, music for which there was no vehicle or instrument, no sounding board, no flying kite to explore the void, no trembling string, no harness bell, no carriage, music so intricate that many notes should fly away like blackbirds from windy boughs and many tones were lost and many chords were blurred and many keys were melted, silver keys melting with lead and gold, music so complex and complicated that not even the greatest instrumentalist could catch all its nuances like dissembling clouds, like starlight scraping on sand or the pumice stone of his heart so light that it was made almost entirely of cavities, music like music heard under water, music which should include, if it were complete as no music ever was—for if music was complete, then it was not music, not even the dirge—papery stars whispering in timelessness and autumn leaves almost transparent blown upon the winds of heaven forever down all streets like particles of Mr. Spitzer's psyche, body and soul, music which should include doors slamming and whirling multiform snowflakes, snowflakes like roses, cartwheels, moths, stars, snowflakes at the water's rippling edge, plaintive music of fiddler crabs, music of leaping fire, music of smoke fog, neighing horses winged like wild swans, music of chimneys and phaeton sea shells and wentletraps like winding stairways reaching from heaven lighted by fish fins to earth, music of time moving through space and catching all music, time moving as music moved and returning on itself, yet not returning, music of long-departed tides, tides coming not again or coming when Mr. Spitzer was no more, music of wind blowing through Mr. Spitzer's black, rippling cloak like a great skirt blowing as he walked in dying music of the dying tide, music which should include the silent whirlpool, music which should include the music of the silence, the dead heart. Music should include the lost musician with the withered string and the unuttered word. Perhaps Mr. Spitzer had sought for those analogies which never were. Perhaps there was music for which there was no rooster's crow. There was music for which there was no hen's cackle. There was music for which there was no rooster cackling and there was no hen crowing. Perhaps beyond the wildest tempests of sound breaking like discord on his ears which were attuned to silence as to love, beyond the crying winds and whirling rooster weathervanes and palpitations of dying stars, beyond the loudly pounding sea bells, there was that music which none had heard, even like Mr. Spitzer's music which none had played, music of the lost creation, music of things unutterable, silence sinking into silence, beauties never born or dying before their birth which was itself a kind of death, faces which were forever veiled as by the clouds. He heard the singing of a dead Troubadour who had died for the love of a lady never awakening from her enchanted sleep. He heard the pluckings of a lute in a singing whirl-pool or in a cloud. He heard the tinklings of a grand piano with its keyboard breaking like surf upon some other star, perhaps that star where human never was.

He saw the mountains rising into clouds, the clouds descending as when this great suffrage captain died, he still pondering upon the mar-riage of the waters with the clouds, the clouds with the stars, the snow-flakes with the waters, he still thinking—Even the greatest king is but an ebony snowflake falling, melting upon these waves. Had Mr. Spitzer not heard snowflakes whisper with human voices, a snowflake whispering in the dark wind as it fell—I am the king—a snowflake sighing as it fell with long spiralings between the clouds and the waves—I am the clown in the peaked hood—I am the queen—I am that great shah of Persia who perished ten thousand moons ago, loons ago—was slain by my love—I am the Ethiope—I am the skull-faced coachman albeit the fat-bellied—the Atlas moth containing its spirit in the cloud—the phoenix burning—the horse, the centaur, one head of the centaur, the rose fading upon these waters—the king with many crowns, crowns of rippling gold? Perhaps when this great lady died upon her old tent bed so rickety in the wind, camping as but for a single night, and never would she have died if she had not pitched her tent, if she had not stayed her journey, she was wedded to her true love and found her body and her spirit, her husband or her wife, and the wound of creation was healed, and the great abyss was closed, and there was that harmony such as had never been on earth—but Mr. Spitzer, sadly doffing his black hat with its black mourn-er's band which reminded him of the head-gear of an alderman, doubted that she had ever found her love, that image which had already faded like a star fading at dawn, doubted that the grave should contain one who had been ambiguous and never easily defined in spirit or in body or in soul, in divisible dreams or indivisible death. For he was the alderman of no ward, lawyer of no court, neither higher nor lower court, court paved not with flagstones of silver or gold as the light shifted, representative of no client, viceroy of no territory, king of no realm, emperor of no crown. He knew not which streets he walked, which windy corners he turned. Often he found himself an attendant at funerals of people he had only heard of or had never known. He came after the coffin lid was closed. Or if he came when it was still open, he was afraid to look at the corpse.

Little must have been different after her death from what it had been before, it seemed to him as he viewed in dubious retrospect these lost events and these fragments. The mysteries continued, being unabated by this end. Ah, sand grain scraped by starlight, thou art my love, Mr. Spitzer whispered with his face streaked by salt tears. Red is the sunlight upon the cloud, cloud burning with bees like meteors, bees which never pollinated flowers, bees of which the feet never touched earth's meadows or buzzed around apples like planets hung on windy boughs. A golden arrow circles around this earth, and my love rides an arrow whistling in the wind, or she is the music of the rain pounding upon the horse's ivory head, or she is the cloud. Should the arcanum of the grave contain, he asked, that which never was or might never be— even the uncreated creation, the love not loved, the whisper not whispered, the sigh not heard, the vision not seen? Should it include the road not taken or the road taken?

The waters of the grave arose to sea level and to water-laden clouds as he watched with the rainbow-colored iris of his eye expanding, reflecting upon the waters and the clouds. The clouds arose to snow-topped mountains and to moons or sank to them. He did not know what these movements were. He did not know whether he was inside or outside. There were moon halos where there were no moons, fireflies where there were no fireflies skimming over the ashen waves and falling like the disintegrations of a star. It seemed that she should come to no end which could be realized. Frustration endured longer than love and agony longer than peace.

It seemed more likely to him that she still must wander to and fro over the face of the earth and knock on many gates, cry at many doors, rein her horse in many gardens of human-sized lilies above the fleecy clouds and standing pools where there were croaking bull frogs and under the moon-drenched clouds through which there scarcely shone a moon, that never would her quest be over. For perhaps her quest was her love, her only begotten love for which there was no image but the child of her spirit or the quest through windy roads, snow embankments falling into the great abyss which was creation, engulfing valleys and golden horns and golden mosques and domes so that they were invisible as phantom flowers under the snow. The snow buzzed like the stars, the dial stars. He knew, for he was also the seeker after a dead love which moved, lived, breathed, sighed in every wind of passage, caused the rippling of lost chords more fearful than unearthly silence, broke like music on Mr. Spitzer's elegiac ear roaring like a great conch, whispering with departed or departing music, forever departing music, making him feel guilty that he lived—for was he not already dead? What more could he experience in life, what more of torment and sterility? If he had lived to twice his age, if he had doubled his brother moment for moment, hour for hour, heartbeat for heartbeat, he would have known no more than he knew now. If he had lived to half his age, he would have known as much. Perhaps there were those who by-passed this earth. Perhaps earth was too weak, too feeble a star to magnetize all. Perhaps beyond this life there was not that which had not already been, and he was wrong to suppose that the dead might find themselves, for surely he was lost, unable to locate the position of a flying star or a sand grain in the wind yet though he carried a broken compass. For was he not this wanderer on both sides, whether he was himself or his brother singing in a cloud—and when should he find that love which was an image which had faded, yet never fading, whole and complete, an image which should include the years of his death as if they were experience? And should not this experience be the finest?

The single were the lonely, it seemed to him, considering his own essential loneliness nothing had ever touched upon—and how should they who had never wedded go down in time which was itself this limitation—how should they be joined, begetting a lost image of themselves? He had always supposed that one must be wedded before one is bedded, though his brother had supposed otherwise—that one might be wedded but not bedded, bedded but not wedded. Perhaps marriage preceded, heralded death—or perhaps death preceded marriage, Mr. Spitzer sometimes thought, being at all times divided—that after one's death, one married his true love who had rejected him in life or whom he had rejected. For actually, in being rejected, the forlorn idea had but recently occurred to him, there was an element of rejecting, yet though it might be secretive—so the mantle of the sorrowful lover concealed much, not only that his lady had disappointed him, no doubt, by her coldness and indifference, but that his love for her could never rival his greater love for that disappointment which had made of him this wanderer and which had set him singing in this void where the stars also sang. The stars were as disappointed as he was. The wicks burned low. The wedding music struck up just before one's death, the extinction of that flame which had already burned out, or else one would never have married. One married only when there was no other road. Marriage was no by-road or path. Or so it surely seemed to him. So that when one married, one died, returning to the universal music or to silence so profound that it might never have been broken by a sound. Thus Mr. Spitzer, though great was his capacity for love as for disappointment, had remained single in his age as in his vanished youth, fearful to commit himself lest he or love should die, forever hesitant, forever equivocal, marrying not for the same reason that he, unlike his brother who would have bet on anything, even the direction of a rain drop falling in a vagrant wind, the splashing of a rain drop, whether it would fall on a windowsill or a pavement, the flutter of a leaf, or the falling of a long-haired star glimmering like the medusa under the wave, would never have gambled upon the dice or the horses, never have taken a chance, for marriage was that great lottery in which one took what one found, not what one chose, lost what one gained, and he had been perhaps fearful that at the very moment of marriage or perhaps after only a shining moment passing before he knew that it had come and gone, passing like a bright light blinding his eyes, for the eyes of love are always blind and robbed of judgment, even the most beautiful lady would turn into an old snaggle-toothed hag or nag, even like some old horse who had been ringed by the great horse-ringer ringing also sun and moon and stars, old horse showing its true colors in a rain storm, beauty fading as the clouds burst, her colors fading from her skin, the snow whiteness and glowing moon barnacles turning to black, the water running like a brook from her foot, the water running from her mouth, the golden mane and tail turning to bedraggled grey as of the thorn, so he would see she was no racer though she had gone so fast—long before the wedding music had ceased, for it was the funeral music which had begun, and they were the same and indistinguishable as the blurred strings in the star-blurred light. What inept musician was this who could not touch with his bow unless he touched two strings, Mr. Spitzer asked, his voice quavering? So that this fear of beauty was this fear of age, and thus he had never been united with his love, preferring that she should remain forever young and beautiful as one who knew no time, perhaps no space enfolding others like a dream. Perhaps, he realized now, there were no conditions or circumstances under which he might ever have married, even if she had accepted his suit or if it was he who had died, the opium lady who had turned her face toward the shadow, preferring the dead love, the reflected light, the muted voice, or voices distorted upon the billowing fog, whispers never to be understood. Perhaps, indeed, he could have married her only under some condition not conditioned, circumstance not circumstanced, state which was absolutely beyond all time, change, love, image—when there should be neither himself nor his brother in whose memory Mr. Spitzer lived, though often thinking that his memory had exceeded the bewildering object remembered, for his life was protracted beyond necessity. As for himself, he had totally or almost totally forgotten many specific moments of his own life and was hard put to recall what had happened or had never happened at any given or not given time, so confused was he by factors incalculably beyond his experience or, for that matter, his brother's experience which had been brief. He must remind himself that it was not he with his love of purity of motive, even of love undiluted by the shadow of death, his love of the unbiased act, his love of the clarity of the jewel not flawed, not clouded from within or from without but burning with steady radiance like a bright star, not he with his fear of the unexpected or unpredictable or paradoxical, not Mr. Spitzer but his brother who had loved only the old, thinking that the old would be suddenly beautiful and young when she was dead, that the years would fall away from her, and thus his brother had feared the old who might deceive him by the withered body like a veil covering that beauty which should be too beautiful for human eyes to endure. Just as Mr. Spitzer had feared that beauty who might grow suddenly old. His brother had died young, but had he ever married?

Perhaps death might be, Mr. Spitzer had sometimes thought in an idle moment reminding him of possibilities beyond this life, not merely the reversing of poles but the perfection of a celestial harmony excluding every discord, the final prelude to the marriage of body with soul, love with love, especially as to himself who had vanished except for his approximate image lingering like reproach, for only on the other side of life would he be united to his love when all the stars were singing together, when there should be no wanderer outside and no disorientation and nothing lost, when all which had been lost should be found or all which had been found should be lost. Then would the great census-taker count all, no doubt, all swans which had faded in the clouds, all winged barnacles, all glow-worms which had gone out, all sailing boats which had gone down, all roses blasted by the storm, all night owls hooting no more, and then would the old lamp-lighter tapping in the darkness light all lamps, including his own. His flue was blackened. His light had gone out in milky darkness.

Yet perhaps, as Mr. Spitzer sadly acknowledged, he had been wrong in assuming that harmony which was ultimate and which he had never known, had never experienced in all his wanderings as the wind whistled through his cape above the mother-of-pearl domes where the waters rolled, there being always a discordant note, something that was never in the score, music no angel knew, not even be it the angel of omniscience, for doubtless there was no angel who knew everything, its eye like the great purple partridge eye in the cloud or like the lake of the moon or the eye of the wind, the needle eye, an old foghorn blowing G-sharp upon its own with many tremolos as oceans roared, casting up surf as indiscriminate as consciousness after transmutation, a voice crying in the darkness or in the light, train whistles, whistles of stars arriving in windy stations, stars departing, some with head lights almost bearing down on him, an old dog barking at phosphorescent shingles strewn upon the evening beach shrunken to a moon's crescent or clumps of sea-weed turning from golden lights to grey or sea shells losing their muted colors in the wave-warped sand even as those who die must cease to breathe or a star fading at dawn which, though revealing many things, concealed forever the face of love, the sounds of a withdrawing tide, rising tide like palpitations scarcely heard in the throbbing of the fog, heartbeats under the water-logged earth, still breathings. Perhaps the solution would always exclude too much, too many possibilities, Mr. Spitzer thought, anguished because he could not realize all the possibilities of any moment, past or present or future. For if he could have known them all, he might have lived in many ways now unknown to him. Eternity would be that moment extending its rays in space but not moving forward, and all things would be possible, it seemed to him, merely by walking from light to darkness, darkness to corruscating light, the dust of a dead planet splattered like gold upon his sleeve, his eyes glittering like pin-point flames enclosed by cobwebs. Perhaps this was as it was, and he should ask for nothing more.

He with his portfolio stuffed with old torts and leases and mortgages placed upon those properties which were no more of earth, perhaps had never been of earth, citadels which could not be located and were perhaps under water, houses with flooded rooms, no divans but boats, floors which were warped mirrors, chandeliers reversed, grand pianos with their ebony and ivory keys swept by waves, porous castles which had crumbled into clouds, sunken violins, painted lutes, stone harps strung so wide that windy seagulls could pass through the strings and never touch them, chessboards of onyx and ivory and ebony and pavements moving under the waters sweeping, sweeping over the many-turreted chessmen of silver and gold, kings and queens and pawns, turrets of towering gold which had once tipped the clouds, deeds to imaginary wealth, cases involving usufruct of property, theft of a hat and a coat, theft of an old ivory-headed cane touched with the moon's tarnished gold spiralings and an old portfolio embossed with his signature in peeling gold, a candlestick, a mirror, a cloud, lawsuits which had never come to court and would never be called to court, never called by the great bailiff's horn, for no doubt all the litigants were dead though he was their representative, one who got no greater fee than a coin exhumed by the movement of sand, perhaps a sand dollar like the sun shining through a cloud, he with the false promissory notes to old chalk-faced bookies signed by his brother's name, many with Mr. Spitzer's music written upon the margins or upon the other side as upon his celluloid cuff with the diamond cuff links burning like two minuscular stars, for he was always practicing his small economies, perhaps because of his great expenditures, the fact that he paid out more than he earned, he with so many papers stuffed in his voluminous coat pockets or in the crown of his mournful hat or in the lining of his almost transparent, wind-silvered cape that he walked with a vague, rustling, papery sound in the silvered, papery sound of the cobweb-shrouded wind and was always shedding scraps of curled paper in his wake so that not even God knew how many masterpieces he had lost, how many papers torn, perhaps some papers which were blank or covered only with the writings of the starfish, the spider, the bird's enameled foot shaped like the star, the chrysalis of the moth, how many partial elegies going on and on, many papers scratched over with his vague musical notations like sudden runs of empearled water at his feet, whispers of foam like insect spittle upon the currents of the silent wind, it seemed to him, or falling leaves falling with a circular pattern in the windless air, for he was always trying to translate, even with his blind eye and his deaf ear, these notes into a component music, always trying to compose, in a manner of speaking, the sudden fierce blows of the archaic, echoic wind blowing him athwart, perhaps miles off his chartless course, there being no map to imagined destination which he had not realized until he had passed it, the rising and falling of waves where under a paper moon there rode a paper boat rudderless and anchorless as he was, there being no anchor to stay the dead heart, the heart like a wind-blown paper kite cut off its glassy string and wandering, the unexpected trillings of many-eyed water birds with long eyelashes staring through reflecting reeds of memory above still pools scarcely rippling as he passed or echoes of ethereal ship whistles in clouded marshes of sunken moons and sunken flowers, sunken boats, ship whistles of those ships which long ago went down, sinking perhaps in calm, sinking when there was perhaps no storm, even as one might suddenly die who had suffered no ill health or blow or accident, no gradual withdrawal of his powers, no slow diminishment of his consciousness, no evil fate but the quick cessation of his heart, whistles of trains over darkening waters, trains which ran no more on earth, their passengers staring no more through milky windows streaked by starlight like wreaths of foam, tremblings of lighthouse beams to guide the wanderer moth or boat, lighthouse beams sent by the blind lighthouse keeper, he who would never see the light, lily-colored light beams like long fingers reaching through darkness where was the dark boat, a long-winged sloop which was never to be reached by the light streaming through the portholes in waters and clouds, movements of fading stars and ringings of alarum clocks in fading tides, movements of starfish at the water's foaming edge, the water creeping and casting up spray like that mother-of-pearl sarcophagus which was the death of earth and every certainty, even as earth was this watery grave, this casket containing the most precious jewel, its lights dimmed as it returned to waters and clouds, must give up his habit of trying to describe and locate, trying to categorize, distinguish, codify, understand by definition if not by fact, separate the impressions from the senses, the nadir from the zenith, the way up from the way down, the mountains from the valley, the pinnacle from the cloud, separate the moon from the dawn, the moon from the noon, the stars from the blurred daylight of a dream which could not be defined, for it was like the interior of a star, must cease to sift, alter, refine, qualify, must use no more his intelligence in that situation requiring not his intelligence or his approval or his affirmation, give up his assumption that all things which existed should be tangible, that there were none intangible, no colors or sounds which were not material and not of this body and of this spirit which was this body even as this body was this spirit, that even his thoughts were made of finest particles, fragments blowing like the glassy sand grains in the mirroring wind, those winding around no spindle or star of light or darkness, those falling upon no place unless it should be, he knew now, his imagination. And what was imagination but the body with muted colors, patches of gold or silver light, a being as yet unbegotten, never to be, yet fading as he watched with the salt tears streaming from his livid eyes, his skin like an enormous drum, his skin streaked by the passing of the moon from behind the cloud or a track of foam or a firefly, perhaps a comet made of fireflies? Sometimes it seemed to him as if his navel were a star in the clouds, or perhaps the stars were buttons on a coat bursting its seams, and his belly rolled like the swollen sea of burning lights, or else he knew not his boundary lines or where he ended or began, and it was true that his feet might be frozen as his hands sweated, that ice might form upon one patch while sunlight burned upon the other even as ice covered the moon as a star burned, that the rain had drummed at his right side when it had never touched his left, or clouds had broken at his feet when his face was in the burning sunlight almost invisible, for he was always half in the shadow, and he had heard a screaming sea bird with one ear as he heard a locomotive whistle with the other, and many images had broken upon his consciousness in some tomorrow where he was not, or else he experienced the ravages of that memory which was separated from his life or his life which was separated from his death, and he was confused by all those glimmering impressions he had never experienced or known. Sometimes he reminded himself of that fat-bellied black coachman who, driving along an old New England sea road which crumbled under the horses' hooves and carriage wheels, gleaming from lights within as if he had eaten fireflies or coals of burning fire, mistook a firefly for the moon and followed a firefly into a sea burning like the moon, burning like a sea of fireflies streaked by shadows.

Certainty that there was unity as between life and death had never been, Mr. Spitzer believed, his brother's thought, his brother having been the master of illusion and sleight-of-hand and sounds coming from no source and colors immaterial and essences not of this earth and substances not of this body and having seemed to be, even when he lived, many beings besides himself, beings existing simultaneously and not this long-drawn sequence which Mr. Spitzer knew, so that now the far whirrings of a windmill of which the arms were seagulls, splashings of a rainbow-colored water bird in a rain cloud, creakings of some old, rusted ferris wheel turning in the wind or music of some old, creaking carousel could make Mr. Spitzer nervous as if all the horses were suddenly running loose, increasing his agitation almost to a breaking point, especially as the rain dropped on him, and he was agonized by attributing consciousness to everything, to things inanimate or to sudden sunsets dripping through a funnel in a dark cloud and splashing the sea with drops of fading gold, to sudden water spouts upon a far horizon or rainbows like crumpled silks lying along the fog-bound ground under the ashen-colored sky burning but with few beacon lights like the eyes of the dead, to old palings with rusted nail heads slapped by the encroaching waves, the waves billowing over old fences zigzaggedly crawling up the snow-white hill starred by starfish, the hill arising to the mountain, the mountain arising to the star, luminous pebbles rolling at the edge of the dark flood, creakings of old windlasses and weathervanes and cable chains, creakings of old tree boughs breaking into flower like phantom foam, the rainbow-colored rain drops dripping from the shrouds of the old boats beached like coveys of ghosts upon the bone-white sand or balls of glittering light leaping from cross-beam to cross-beam like the lights of corpo santo seen in flooded marsh lands or graveyards as he passed with his dark cloak soughing in the wind, the sudden lights of planets burning in his enormous shadow as the lights burned low upon this shore of consciousness, seeming like inaccurate constellations to light his way. Perhaps there was no fisherman but memory which faded, and not even Mr. Spitzer could remember all. Perhaps the meshes of reality were woven wide so that many escaped definition in life or death, wide as the places between the stars, and there were cities where there were no stars so that not even the most solitary heart could contain or comprehend all that was possible even like all that was impossible, for one was like that journeyer who went from star to star, one which was fading and one which might never be, and the only star was the journeyer. He was the journeyer between two worlds, both of which were non-existent. Surely the gates were wide enough to admit the passage of a moth with the moon spots upon its glimmering wings or sleeping dragonfly upon a silken thread drifting in starlight or tented butterfly or eye boat or spirit or something almost not material, almost not conscious, a snowflake falling not upon any land or water or any other star or cloud, a snowflake forever falling. A white moon sank into a white wave, and yet the wave reached not the moon. Perhaps those who had not been married before their death would not be married after death, even like that impoverished suffrage captain who rode upon a distant mountain peak moving like a wave and came not to any rest, being forever this rider through the storm. She might search only for herself and not her opposite, for all that she had lost in life, for stars never uttered, for visions never seen, for whispers never heard, confessions never told.

And had she found the body of her love, Mr. Spitzer sometimes wondered—had she found all that was feminine in life, in death—the clouds upon the clouds, the waters, and the rose, the moon like a white bird, the lace mantilla like the snow upon the rock, the blood upon the snow? Had she found, like the poor mollusk, its ivory shell, its helmet, its sword? Who was, indeed, her love now when she was no more—what image hidden by the snow, the cloud? It always would mystify Mr. Spitzer that there was this ambivalence when she died—as if, after all, he might never know her, especially as he suffered from his own divided opinions and diffused sensibilities. There were so many facets to consider. Certainly, she contributed even now to his increasing uncertainty—though he was of a mind to forgive her and to extend his compassion for this act of her oblivion to him even as, in these later years, perhaps more years than he remembered, for perhaps there was no time, he had come to be grateful, in an odd manner, to his foolish brother for the fortunate error of his suicide which had aroused, in many ways, Mr. Spitzer's consciousness and at the same time had plunged him into deeper depths than most living men have known and which had not been the end of wisdom but the beginning of wisdom. For if his brother had not been superficial, Mr. Spitzer would not have been profound. Or so he thought, though recognizing that he himself was increasingly capable of folly.

Surely every lady must be shrouded, veiled even as by the clouds and the waters. Surely none should go in nakedness, clothed not with the body and with the soul. The great couturier who clothed the world with the clouds and the sea with its waters and the night with its darkness must clothe this lady, this bella donna. Upon her mantle he must stitch the stars and the suns and the moons, upon the rippling hem, Mr. Spitzer thought, forgetting that the great couturier was dead, that he was no more who clothed the mountains with the snow and the storm with its pinnacles and the valleys with the shadows and the clouds with their diadems and the clouds with the clouds and the night with its stars. The lapidarian was become the jewel he had cut and polished, and the mosaicist was the dim pattern outlined in mosaic flagstones washed with the moon's spiralling gold where Mr. Spitzer walked, fearful lest he should

step upon a flagstone of suddenly awakening consciousness or sudden
fountains, for there were eyes gleaming in the fog, and the enamellist was
enamelled by powdery dust blowing in cold starlight, and the glazier had
fallen into the great crucible, and his nose was glass casting this shadow
upon the wind, and illusion was the world, each man being clothed but
by a dream, even as Mr. Spitzer wore not his body and his cloak, it
seemed to him, for his was the body of the dead. He was transparent.
Sometimes it seemed to him, viewing great paradox, that this great captain's skirt itself might have been her love. Perhaps her love was her skirt
hiding her great wound, her disappointment, her bleeding heart.

Perhaps after all she had loved nothing but that skirt for which her
love had died, as he remembered, long ago, chasing her skirt as if it were
a Holy Grail gleaming through a cloud or the ghostly sword Excalibur or
the golden fleece, the web upon the island orchard bough toward which
Jason's argosy sailed upon the rippling waters streaked by the path of the
voyager moon with bird-eyed galaxies in its wake streaming upon snow-
white wings fluted like great stairways. Her love had died in freezing
mountains, freezing clouds forming like opalescent icebergs around her.
Her love had gone down among the snow pinnacles. She was buried in
the white mountains. Snow and ice were her tomb. Her love had disappeared under the great snow fall, the curtain of snow falling like ropes of
pearls or blowing like the sail of a derelict ship under the iceberg moon.
The moon cast its aura upon the waters and the clouds. So when this
great suffrage storm king died after long voyagings and many storms and
clouds, Mr. Spitzer, scarcely daring to trust himself or his own fading
perceptions in the Stygian darkness unlighted by a star, had allowed to
her, as he was a gentleman of the old school and one who was ever
deferential, ever chivalrous, one who had ever said that ladies should go
first, that ultimate mystery or all those mysteries which should be hers
and every lady's right or privilege, be she even an old corsair hacked by
many wounds, some old brigand of the dead heart, the dead love, and he
had scarcely dared to look upon her old, shrivelled, claw-marked, rain-
spotted face spotted like the rain frog as she passed into this metamorphic
somnolence, this long sleep of years, for fear it should be beautiful in the
remote future or in retrospect albeit it was his dead brother who had
loved the ugly and old and time-worn and shrunken and who had seen
beauty where beauty was not, where others would be repelled—even as
he had seen life after death, life where was no life, disparaging this life
for that which was unknown to him as some other toss of the rattling dice
or turning of the starry wheel through starless heavens void and without
shape upon the waters of the darkness—as Mr. Spitzer must always constantly remind himself, for in his old age he was likely to forget, drifting
toward the shadow, forget that it was he who had clung to life as tena-
ciously as an almost transparent thistle to an old coat or a starfish bird
foot to the whirling hem of his cloak, a starfish dragging like a star over
the waters—and he who had loved a beautiful face, a sparkling eye, a
timeless beauty, he who should have watched, for perhaps the ghost of
beauty had appeared as she died, the years dropping away like clouds

lifting. Perhaps the last vanity had been hers. Perhaps the clouds had lowered like a veil. He did not know, for more than life or death he feared change, change of any kind. This was surely not a gambler's mentality. For he never knew how the dice fell—could not read the spots, the dancing spots—even as he could not read the score of faded music or resolve those chords which had already passed into the silence.

Perhaps at the last moment she suddenly believed in all she had denied, perhaps with her last rasping breath—or in one cell burning like a flame—so that it was and would ever be a question in Mr. Spitzer's mind which was like an echo chamber too beautiful and vast—should one be held accountable for one's entire life or for one moment of unforeseen and unforeseeable transmutation, perhaps a change taking place beyond all consciousness or memory or desire? Should one moment of inestimable madness dethrone that king who had ruled all his life with reason, he who had been an emperor of many realms and had concatenated every thought with every thought, forming a chain or series as with certain unicellular organisms? Or should the reasonable suddenly go mad, tottering like an old queen among the shadows, the screaming sea birds who knew not what empire it was? Should an old warrior die under the flag of peace? Should one go over to one's enemy? Should the reprobate be pure as snow, his limbs washed by snow water, or should the pure of heart be suddenly black as the ace of spades? Death should be private, beyond the realm of the intruder, it seemed to him. Or was this great change implicit like a secret logic underlying all the phantasms of life and death, and had it been revealed, and was it his only shock to know that he had always known it, yet had closed his eyes? He had been afraid of ugliness. He had been afraid to look upon that dying suffragette for fear he might see that changing face, that suddenly brightening eye, that beauty returning but for one moment before beauty crumbled into dust and ashes unlighted by a star or nettle or medusa. For should the old grow young even as the young grew old? Perhaps there was no end. Night begot perhaps only the night.

Perhaps she died as a beautiful lady crying for her feather fan, her skirt, her mirror rimed with frost, a dead eye like Joachim's eye staring through the fog—Mr. Spitzer did not know, having dismissed so much, he still maintained, as her delirium, being accustomed to so many hallucinations coming and going, so many images which could not be understood by reason, some which could not even be understood by madness, so many shadows of things unearthly upon the shadowed fog. And that was why even to this day or night the utmost caution must be his and why, no matter what egregious mistakes he might make, he would be ultimately right as to his grief which, he feared, though greatly he tried to include all things, even those which were disparaged, was more comprehensive than his love. Or perhaps, of course, he could love only the dead, those not awakening from their deep sleep or awakening only to fall into their sleep again, perhaps after only a brief sigh, perhaps still sighing.

No doubt he had written some of his elegies too soon, writing almost

as automatically as the sandpipers running back and forth in the creeping surf as their twinkling footsteps were swept over by the long-roaring,
musical waves of the sea, as their sentences which were punctuated by
scraping starfish or moon barnacles burning with lights within like fallen
moons were effaced by waves and sands, waves creeping over the holes of
the nestless birds—but in time his elegies would be the only memorial to
those who had passed out of existence or were about to pass—and who
then would question this lost sequence of events or whether he had
written his plaintive shell music before or after they had gone over into
the silence? He was like one who had built before he was born the house
in which he would live and die. Who then would accuse him of a certain
mournful prematurity, as it were, in expressing his grief—an eagerness, an
excess, a rushing forth to meet his delaying fate, his fate which had not
met him? Grief could never be expressed at the wrong time. Grief could
come neither too early nor too late. It was his calling card, perhaps that
which was blank.

He had laid over this faceless lady a skirt, thinking that, whatever
else betided, she had found her skirt, and he could not be wrong no
matter if he was wrong, for there was none to deny him, none to refute
his statement, and customs varied in different countries depending on
what tollgates one had passed, and surely a lady should be skirted when
she went to her death, and surely the dead had always been skirted in
earlier times, skirted by their shrouds. In the East where she was going
now, all men were skirted like castles of pearls by waters, under the full
and swollen moon or half moon or crescent moon. Surely they were
crowned with crowns of gold. In the East where men wore skirts, how
much easier for a man to dream that he was a woman, even as he might
dream in death that he was pregnant, carrying in his womb the
foetus, the mirror and the rose. Death was the Orient whether it was
heaven or earth, and she was ever the creature of paradox made more so
now, it seemed to him, shedding his tears which fell like pearls through
windy heavens, his tears splashing around him like watery worlds. He
asked himself many times who she was and what signified this skirt laid
over the body of a dead love—and really, he was still at some loss to
understand what the answers might be. For there was no cosmetician
necessary to those who wore the final veil, their beauty being hidden,
never revealed to human eyes, and just as none had shrived this body or
marked the hour of her death or the boundary line between the living
and the dead, as not even he could have timed the slow withdrawal of her
spirit, he had turned away for fear there should be, even after so many
years, a sudden spark or star shining through rolling fog like her returning spirit or that which had never faded and had moved not as the clouds
drifted over her. They were like lace drifting over rock. He did not know,
as a matter of fact, the hour of his own death—enjoying as to that
certainty only the most dubious retrospect and often mistaking the hour
—so that his was, indeed, this after-life—for he lived after his death as he
lived before his death—and perhaps like himself she lived beyond the
narrow line of consciousness, much like that music which was never writ-

ten or music spilling into silence before it was heard—so none should know when she had gone, and none should know where she had gone. The dead lived with their unfinished business. Infinite frustration was theirs. The line between the living and the dead was doubtless no greater, perhaps even less than that between the living and the living. Perhaps she still must wander, crying at many gates, knocking at many doors, arousing many watchmen in their dark towers, forever crying for the image of her love who had gone before her into the darkness.

Her love had gone before her death, so might not her death go before her love—for what was time at this last hour when the hours were never again to be marked by the dial stars? And if the pendulum moved again, cleaving through windy heavens like the wing of some great bird casting its shadow on the glassy sand, it moved only in a dream, Mr. Spitzer thought—he often consulting his broken watch like a moon jelly gleaming on his wrist, a watch with no numbers to the hours. Or sometimes he read the moon jelly in the moving sand or the faceless sundial, sometimes the star foot in the salt marsh, sometimes the periwinkle under the glider wave, sometimes the kingfisher's eerie cry, wondering what time it was. But time could not tell him the time. To ask of time the time was like asking of the thief—Where is the jewel you stole? Nor could one ask of timelessness.

Spitzer, though often searching his mind, did not know whether she was

Long after her last hour, perhaps long after his last hour, Mr. the Crusader upon some distant quest in search of a great rajah's jewel —a crown jewel which should be plucked from a crown of gold—or the Crusader's sleeping wife bound by a girdle of iron locked by an iron key, waiting for her love to return, not knowing that her love was dead—and what should be worse than that there should be one spark of life which glittered like the lost star? Would it not have been better if he had never disturbed this sleeping lady, never awakened her? Or was this as it was, and was she never deflowered, and did she only dream of one cold spark? Should the living child be born from the dead mother locked in her casket of iron? There were many keys, iron and gold and lead, keys of ivory, keys of glass, but none to fit this rusted lock. And there were port-holes through which the spirit could not pass. Doubtless there were keyholes which swallowed keys. There was no master key. Better that her cruel lord should never have plowed this stony land, fold upon fold, peak upon peak, land of no bird or tree or flower, no lake or eye of the moon, land like that desert and those mountains which he travelled now. Better that he should never have planted his seed before he travelled so far from home. He opened all closed doors but one, the door he had closed. Perhaps he had thought that it was the door of a tomb. Perhaps, leaving that silence he could not endure, he had thought that no bee buzzed within, that there was no honey in this great stone hive reaching into clouds where were no stars, that no light glowed within or without. No bird splashed upon the rain-flooded porches. Perhaps he had thought that there was no flood to uphold the bottle-nosed dolphin following the boat star through dim transparencies. So he had gone to Holy Lands.

Perhaps he had thought there was no hyacinth into which the bees were sucked, no aperture through which a city of minarets or domes or a white butterfly could pass, folding or unfolding its wings powdered as with glittering stardust, no butterfly born from this spindle star. No many-turreted seagull cried in empty rooms, and no lamp glowed at the darkened windows. There was no estuary upon which a nautilus could pass, going down to the sea to which all sea shells should return. No horse with its mother-of-pearl flanks rolling in great breakers of foam slept with her. No dog barked at a falling star. The night's darkness knew neither stars nor eyes. He rescued all ladies but one he had imprisoned, leaving her to rot.

Mr. Spitzer, her attorney closing her last estate before the old house was torn down to make room for the new traffic—and oh, how he hated these urban changes caused by the population growth or slow or sudden diminishment, these sudden shifts which sometimes found him walking down streets which were no more, reading signposts which had vanished in the fog, knocking at doors where were no listeners—unless the dead heart heard the muffled beating of his heart—or a heart moved under a loose flagstone—or the flagstone was, indeed, the heart—had been as surprised by unexpected, hitherto concealed aspects of Cousin Hannah's life as if he had found an iron helmet where the cherubim nested in the long-tongued grass—but far away from her—far, too far from home—perhaps upon a windy mountain slope starred by snow—perhaps where her great lord had fallen—or surprised as if like some old tree stump in a dark forest she had been the nesting place of butterflies, of old cocoons like velvet purses filled with ethereal coins. The old suffragette's unceasing duplicity was such as to startle even him among the shadows closing an empty house, sealing off room after room as if he sealed the chambers of the winding sea shell, wishing that the house could sink beneath the earth or that there was earth or that earth was sinking sand—far better this than that the house should be wrecked or that all should pass out of sight, that there should be only old palings like the flotsam returned by the waves, the helmsmen who were the boats, the old crates, boxes, dragging sails, that there should never be excavation in future time to tell the history of the dolphin and the rose, the sunken moon, the tree, the Alp, the star, the cloud, and images which never were. Far better that they should sink than that they should be lost, scattered, wrecked, the shipwreck rising through the waves at dawn under the shipwrecked stars burning low upon a distant coast, the stars fading as the light increased. The stars were blurred as if shining under water. Better that they should exist submerged than that they should exist at the surface where all were lost.

CHAPTER 48

PERHAPS Mr. Spitzer was the last of many messengers in the world of the dead, coming too late. Perhaps he was the first. Nonetheless he must perform the duties of his office, there in that old house which rustled with dim opalescence of wings like a pigeoncote, whispers only he could hear, his ear roaring, for he was in his own employment and doubtless would have practiced law if there had been no court of gold and silver flagstones, moonstones burning with fires within, or if every possible musical litigation had been settled, if there was neither theme nor counter-theme nor counter-counter-theme, no living counterpart, not a musical chessman moving through the tide, not a glassy cricket's cry in a stone chimney, if there was not a whisper under the rotting eaves, not the silence splashing into the silence like a pebble in a whirlpool, if every argument had been solved, if love cried not to love when life is over, if silence cried not to silence, if not a star had creaked and if not a pebble had rolled, if not a snowflake fell into a dark abyss, if every quarrel had been finished like an echo no longer reproducing itself. And far worse if the echo was inaccurate, being not the music of its source, or if the source was forgotten. How often he had noted black notes which were missing from his score, leaving him with a sense of ineffable vacancy like octaves heard in sleep but forgotten when he awakened, yet haunting him with their lost meaning until he could say—Ah, I almost see the meaning of this lost music—just when the meaning faded like the music. Perhaps the greatest music was that which had no meaning. And sometimes an engraver had added a black spot to his scale to confuse future musicians in that great day when his music should be heard, for they should play that which had been intended as a punctuation mark and not a sound. He feared that upon that day all the notes should be those which had been added by the great engraver, that his own music of sudden trebles, trills, and cryings had disappeared. But who should play that note below the threshold of sound—or winging far above?

There were so many papers still to go through, some not marked— old calling cards, some which were blank, bearing no name, neither his signature nor his clef, and scraps of paper like shining tinsel which Mr. Spitzer had left, no doubt, long ago when he had called at what he had supposed to be an empty house—or which had been left by the long-whiskered pack rat in the trembling starlight, for certainly he had taken something away—and so many boxes, trunks to open in the attic under the funneled stars in a dark cloud burning into a thin haze of smoke and casting pale gleamings upon the broken star-shaped skylight through which the rain poured and the snowflakes fell and, in the basement, properties to dispose of, some not worth carting away—the reindeer heads in a long, dark hallway staring into gold-framed oval mirrors like those in clouds, antlers which had shaken star beams, those great antlers like tree branches at the edge of a world of snow, tree branches which should suddenly rush away as in a roaring wind, those great antlers where should have been the faces of beautiful ladies, mirror images which had dissolved when the candle flames burned low like the low line of the stars in the fog—so many trophies of suffrage journeys and wars which were intended to release those in death's realm, those imprisoned by their cruel husbands and lords, those sleeping with their loves or not sleeping with their loves—for both should come to the same approximate end—and forty keys with which to open forty trunks she had brought back from suffrage journeys and voyages through star wrack and foam, keys which she had kept in bed with her that none might find her hiding place, nesting place—for even the wounded must seek a nesting place— keys which had jangled around her when she died—making a weird music like that of an inevitable event, jangling when she turned—among them all, no master key—and Mr. Spitzer's numb fingers, though those of an old musician whose errors were of greater beauty than the perfections of others—reminding him that a great violinist whose wrist shakes with palsy as his bow touches the strings is still greater than the mediocre violinist whose wrist shakes not—had fumbled as if he were asleep as he experimented with various keys, various locks—and wished that there had been a locksmith to open all locks, to turn all keys at once, even to open floodgates.

But there was no locksmith to betray this hermetical secret, and there might be one box more than forty boxes, and perhaps what was required was an arrowsmith to make that arrow which should reach this heart, dead heart, Mr. Spitzer thought, smiling sadly in the darkness where there was no one to see his face. Surely he could not see it unless in a mirror lined with the moon's rain-washed gold—and only then one enlarged, shining eye which might not be his, for his face was blotted out by the moving shadows. For the lights had gone out, perhaps with the last thunder storm flashing green and rose and gold, perhaps not so much gold as the gold emotion, that which was the mere feeling of gold lighting the dark clouds. The moon was fading as the dawn approached. What sadder than the moonlight where there was no moon, no other orb? What sadder than that the moon should forever fade, that the moon should rise not again lighting the twilight? This seemed a greater loss to Mr. Spitzer than that there should be no sun lighting the blurred dawn. Or what could be sadder than to be born after the moon set and to die before the moon arose, and thus one would never know the moon or would know the moon only as one knew the unknown before one knew the known and would know the unknown after one knew not the known? There was moonlight touching his cape, his fringed shawl, the fringes of his ecstasy, his hand which was a starfish, but he had not trusted moonlight or any star, he having brushed against the dust of alien planets as against lantern flowers when he was crossing distant meadows. Perhaps he had carried pollen from a dead star to a dead star, but he was in the darkness. So he had had to light matches to find his way through wavering darkness, and he was amazed by his preternatural courage—he had always been afraid to light matches, afraid that he might set himself on fire, afraid of sudden burning, crackling, hissing, for he was like dried wood and highly inflammable and afraid of sudden incandescence, afraid of burning, afraid that if he burned, then he would extinguish himself, go out like a spark under a wave—indeed, had preferred the watery places and the clouds like wet cloths wrapped around the moon, the clouds shrouding that dead face—and it was he who had groped his way through darkness as through light, through light as through darkness, scarcely able to tell the difference between them, for perhaps there was no distinction—whereas his brother, careless of Mr. Spitzer's fear, had burned like the brightest star burning in the wind, had burned like the thistle stars hanging low in clouds, had burned like a tree breaking into fire as if a star had touched the tinder of this earth, had burned like a tree of fireflies, had burned like a fallen star, had burned at the water's rippling edge—was always lighting matches, even in the pale sunlight— no light being enough for him—had burned like the dark spruce tree breaking into fire in a thunder storm, giving off thousands of sparks— had burned like bees in sunlight—and no doubt had gone through the door of the sun as Mr. Spitzer had gone through the door of the moon, the moon in the cloud, the moon in the water. Did the pearl know it was the pearl, or did the moon know it was the moon winding its nacreous walls around the sleeping flame, winding around the winding pearl which enclosed the fisherman sleeping in his long-sailed sloop, the wing of a white bird? Who should enjoy complete self-consciousness unless he should be dead, and would it then be possible, for did not one die into all things even as one loved, and so was death possible as that which was complete and final and absolute? It was Mr. Spitzer who had always groped, stumbling against the obvious as if it were the shadow, blinded by the light.

It was Peron, bright Peron who had lighted match after match and had left a sulphurous trail of burned-out or burning matches in his wake, no matter where he went—lighting his matches where were blowing draperies—much as if, long before his apparent suicide, he had tempted fate in many ways of which he was unconscious even at his brightest moments—showing, as Mr. Spitzer could feel with the match spark burning in his waxen hand, that he was capable of killing himself though perhaps by accident—perhaps because of a sudden gust of wind blowing out the stars—whereas, if Mr. Spitzer should ever kill himself, it would be by slow, deliberate intention, the most exquisite, and after he had consulted his broken watch and patterns of sand-blurred sandpipers like spots running upon a windy shore and after he had considered every impossible possibility, after he had looked forward to an impossible future and backward upon an impossible past. He was always posting, trotting, gaiting, cantering, pacing, racking, running, single-footing, slowing his music to a walk so that he would be prepared for all eventualities. Whatever happened, there had been a certain forethought in the most unexpected event so that it would be impossible to happen unless he had somehow lived through it before or had a premonition which had warned him, much like the effect preceding the cause, even like the whisper preceding the voice or the sob preceding the whisper—or perhaps like music out of place, the transposition of a phrase, music transposed to a dark shore, that of the rolling silence where no crying was—perhaps this shore—and he felt this now no matter where he went or what he was doing, that nothing could take him totally by surprise. All things which happened happened twice to him, had he not always said?—as his death would happen twice—perhaps also his love. Or perhaps his love would be that one continuum not broken by death's void, being that of which no distinction of content or image could be stated except by reference to something else. Often he reminded himself of a traveller who had passed through a city in the night before he knew that he had passed it—and by that time he was looking forward to it again—perhaps to be passed once again in darkness. Perhaps his love would come not only before but after his death. Perhaps this was already so, he having already died. Perhaps he lived through things happening as through things happening not, the lost possibilities which were never realized, perhaps not even sensed—and yet what more potent than the impotent lost? He felt this whenever a leaf fell in the wind or did not fall, when an icicle broke or did not break, when a snowflake melted or did not melt, when a pebble rolled before the dark tide fringed by light, when someone coughed in a dark street or did not cough, when bridge music quivered like the harp, when he heard his own musical coughing in the darkness awakening him from his dreams —for even his coughing was arranged in a pattern of music shaking him from head to foot—in fact, under all possible circumstances and some which were impossible. He felt this if he heard a whisper or no whisper, if a bell rang or did not ring, if a cloud burst or did not burst, casting dim radiance upon the shadow.

He felt all these little deaths which were like love—or little chances such as his brother might have taken, chances that one lived when one was dead—awakened only when asleep—chances that one's day life was less than the night, the night's darkness. And when should one take the grand chance—or was there no such chance, as Mr. Spitzer sorrowfully asked? He felt this slow dawning as to his own extinction, that it was something always being prepared for, much like something which had already taken place but was only by slow degrees consciously recognized —perhaps with many altering impressions, many qualifications, hesitations, dubieties increasing almost like another love or a large body of doubt—and perhaps this was another reality—as if, though one had lived with one's love for years, it was many years before one recognized that long ago his love had died—or that she had betrayed him, loving some other love, an image so like his own, yet stealing in to take his place—or he himself had died as his love did not recognize—or both had died and yet lived on in memory, each assuming that the other was the ghost—or perhaps both recognizing that they were the ghosts, the ghosts of their old loves, that even the leaves falling and the stars twittering were ghostly as were all things, the frog's croak, the splashing of the water, the flame's whisper, the cricket's cry, that all were secondary because of this dead love—and thus that through all these years, he had lived as with a stranger, gradually acquiring an intimacy amounting almost to insight —that perhaps there was a greater knowledge than one enjoyed of one's love, that love so early fading, so brief in time that it might almost be said to be timeless though casting its light of gold upon this darkness— that perhaps one knew the stranger in the end better than one knew one's love, dead love not awakening. And so one was loyal to this mistaken love as Mr. Spitzer was, allowing his compassion to extend through all the hazards of disappointment as if there were no other way, no other star but this dark hedgerow star fading before the empearled dawn.

Perhaps, as he saw the butterfly spark burning in his hand, lighting his brother's rainbow-streaked eye where but a moment before he had seen his own eye in a dark mirror, it seemed to point the way which Peron had gone, taking all the charm of life with him. So that Mr. Spitzer felt suddenly as if he were rehearsing for the grand exit—out, out of this life—if only he could find the exit of that old, high-shouldered house which was between two shadowy ivy-covered water towers and which, it had seemed to him in the darkness, was made of perhaps nothing but windows and doors, doors and windows of old houses which were already demolished—and yet where was the exit? The exit could not be the entrance, surely. Surely he had passed beyond the threshold. He had just arrived, and now must he go—depart, depart? Ah, but his heart was dead. Could he not penetrate to the dim interior—and, like Stanley, find his Livingston somewhere in this nocturnal jungle of strange beasts and birds and flowers? And would not Livingston say—Mr. Spitzer, I presume?

He·had known how to get into the house—so why could he not know, by the same token like a magical amulet, how to get out of the house—for was there not even a club-shaped keyhole as in euchre, a hole in a star, a broken window, a window or door which was not barred, or a crack under a warped door such as that through which the starlight seeped or the bat went out with its umbrella wings flattened as if it followed the light, a transom, a glass flue, a chimney blowing sparks, a crevice of some kind, an abyss? Did the house expand—or was it shrinking? Was it small as a pea pod? Or must the hour-glass of his heart be ever reversed, and must he live twice, and if so, must he die twice, perhaps once in non-retentive memory? Must the poles be reversed?

Who had blown this bellows raising this cold spark, this cold spark blowing to ashen-colored heavens where crawled the beetle stars as through crystal dust? And were there differences now, slight but inestimable, between what was and what had been before—or was that missing which was perhaps the infinitely small, infinitely divisible—perhaps a sand grain missing—with its pearl star which was its winding sarcophagus —perhaps a fluttering star missing—perhaps himself omitted from that seepage of sands and stars drifting downward through the bands of clouds, through clouds of eye witnesses like migratory birds or desert caravans under old fringes? He had navigated himself blindly into mirrors as into clouds, distinguishing not between glass and clouds, windows and doors, clouds and glass, doors and windows, and he had come upon sealed rooms he had not known existed in the light, perhaps rooms like mirrors opening into mirrors, doors leading into doors, just as there were many stairways leading to stairways, perhaps always the same stairway, the same old wentletrap catching little shells, bell barnacles, goose barnacles, boats—though they were in a long dry dock—and there were many obstacles, many divans which seemed to drift before him as he passed through great doors and little doors, many doors opening, closing, perhaps far away from him.

He had hoped, when he passed with his blurred light before a trembling window scarcely gilded by the remnant light of the waning moon, the sickle moon like a golden feather slowly wafting through a many-layered cloud as he paced back and forth as slowly as if he walked under miles of water, that some old watchman passing in the street outside his window—casting his coffin shadow upon the glass or cloud as Mr. Spitzer could see—the coffin shadow with one star faintly burning—or shadow like some old door over which there hung a fan light to light the wanderer home—albeit a door which would never open to anybody's knocking, tapping, scratching—or perhaps it was a window light—a light in a widow walk by a dead sea—a light like the wingless female glow-worm burning for the winged male who had no light—or a pilot lamp with one light forever burning, perhaps the pilot star when there was no pilot, for his ship had gone down—had hoped that the old watchman going his lonely way through jumbled streets would not think there was a thief in this old house which had seldom been entered when anyone was alive— house which had been empty for so many years that Mr. Spitzer's light might, of course, attract attention from the watchman in the street or some distant wayfarer muffled under his great fringed tapestry shawl as he passed upon a darkening road to places where there were perhaps no stars, no nebulae flung like glittering dust upon the dark clouds—and yet there had been no tangible treasure which would justify entrance and theft—for all had already been taken away—and Mr. Spitzer, acting in his self-appointed legal office, was but this unemployed lawyer who had come to make a last account tentative as all things must be, to sum up all which had been missing, all which had never been, to open old boxes, close old doors leaning upon their rusted hinges in rain and snow, doors of the old mollusks or tents like the tents of Arabs or old cocoons, rattle old dice cups like withered flowers, pods without dice, lock that which he could not open, open that which he could not close—and thus was very busy—certainly no man ever being so busy as he with his precarious leisure which knew no end since his retirement—he sometimes reminding himself of a flag signalman upon an oval where no horses ran like the long-haired golden planets running through the clouds, flashing their diamond hooves or their reflections like other worlds—he sometimes reminding himself of a customs officer at an empty port, no ships coming past his lighthouse casting its pale star beam although he counted contraband luggage, sheeted clouds unfurling like bolts of silk rippling to the moon upon the moving waters rippling at the hem, dim jewels in empty caskets, jewels which had lain long in the sea, those which were already diffused—for here was surely no jewel, no jewel dimly burning unless it was the water-freighted jewel of consciousness burning but one moment before it went out or burning but one moment after it went out.

There seemed no particular significance as to the sequence of these events, whether the flame burned before or after death—death existing as a matter of definition and not of fact—as if, indeed, the sequence existed not in relation to time but was that existing forever in space like that impossible coherence of past with future, future with past which was perhaps the secret locked in every heart like a logic surpassing man's imagination which was finite. Man could not see his own end, for he passed beyond his end. To Mr. Spitzer, at least, with his mind forever divided among possibilities, some mutually self-negating, blotting out others, it had seemed no less miraculous that consciousness should come before death than that it should come after death, casting light ripples upon the waters and the clouds like the star fading before the light of dawn, the light fading into the light, the light fading into the sea burning like the sunken star which was this world. Or perhaps it was a marsh light burning in the distance in the rolling fog. Should there be one star shining all day long as all night long, one star never fading through all the vicissitudes of life and death, the drifting clouds, the shadows? Then one would be dead in that unholy light which faded not, for life was the shadow crossing the light—and could there be life without the shadow, even the shadow of death? Consciousness was ever that which was sporadic, fluttering, not constant even in this life, just as sustained attention was impossible, for if one listened to one note long enough, or so it seemed to Mr. Spitzer, then that note would be two notes or one and its echo, trills, virtuoso prolongations into unearthly music, music of passage from here to there, now to then, and it was no doubt impossible that there should be, unless one was dead, total concentration upon one point—perhaps not even then—consciousness fading, flickering, going out. Should consciousness record the aspects of its fading or know when consciousness faded for the last time—and thus how could there be an emotional suffering of death, a connection between life and death, a bridge between two worlds, a looking forward to total extinction—a way of knowing, on the other side, when this life had gone out?

Perhaps there was only the bridge, no star at either end—there was only the passage over that bridge which was not there, just as there was not even its reflection of gossamer cable strings like cobwebs upon the darkening waters, the clouds through which there shone no stars. Perhaps only the observer knew when life had faded—and perhaps not even he was sure, a voice sometimes speaking out from among the shadows, the voice perhaps of one long dead. How could there be correspondence between what one was and was not, one's own undefinable identity which one would find unchanged and unchanging on the other side, especially if one had not found it on this side—if one suffered transmutations unknown to him, if one knew not what he had been or would become, if one knew not who he was or even when he was? Or was it always now, here? So soon, so soon this light would fade—was already fading as the light of dawn crept on stealthy footsteps out of the ambush of darkness, as moonlight trembled with departure upon the windows and the clouds, as the sound of traffic hooted in distance and as the flame faded, fluttered in Mr. Spitzer's hand—for as the light advanced, the stars were going out. All but one star was going out, this star with its dulled glow. To Mr. Spitzer it seemed at times that the stars, the great stars shining in the clouds and winds were egocentric, drawing all things unto themselves—ah, so vainglorious, he sighed—as if the vast spaces stretching from star to star were created solely for them, that they might cast their dying light—the old stars being, of course, small and warped as windy plumes of dandelions streaking clouds enclosing insect sparks, the banked constellations fading, he must have remarked at some point before, for they had lost their light, and they had withered like the old men—whereas it was not for these stars that space was created even with its many holes like those which swallowed up the stars—holes in ice swallowing the sled, the dogs, the ship with ice upon its shrouds—for these stars were created for space, and the abyss was the creation. The creation was not the stars. The mother of creation was this great abyss swallowing moons, suns, stars, city lights, cities, long-haired water lilies fringed by golden ripples under dying moons, Orion flying as if it were a bird. The creation was this void where the stars went out like city lamps.

Perhaps, however, in spite of all the arguments weighing so heavily upon one side—ah, which side?—Mr. Spitzer not knowing, he ever likening himself to an old bookkeeper keeping books in a dream, entering figures in the wrong column, yet still expecting to strike a balance, perhaps some day by merest chance of such insufficiency as to be subjected not to proof—so that Mr. Spitzer would burst into copious tears whenever he heard that an old bookkeeper or even a young bookkeeper had died—perhaps because of a correct entry—possibly a figure more or less, perhaps caused by pigeon scratchings on his page—or in a cloud—there was a balance, a communication between life and death not generally understood, certainly not by those who were the living, for they were dead—though the dead might favor Mr. Spitzer's extended hypothesis that they lived, breathed, uttered words, whispered, shrilly cried among the shadows—even answered Mr. Spitzer's inscrutable silence with their unutterable music of beginning and ending like splashings in windy pools—for perhaps only Mr. Spitzer with his capacious mind knew those intuitions coming after death like those which faded before death, casting their faint rays in clouds. When had life been? Were there but two terminal points with no winding road between, no journey between here and there in this world as Mr. Spitzer sometimes thought, and was one always at the beginning, ending? Was there no straight road? Was there no crooked crab walk where the sea reached its pale tongues of light through sands falling below sea level? Indeed, though his brother had gone before him, Mr. Spitzer felt that it was he himself who had gone—particularly when he heard a golden-footed honey bee buzzing inside him like the memory of light gilding the darkness of a grave or of a great stone hive or Arab's desert mosque half buried in crystal sand or when he heard his brother's whistle like an old train forever whistling on another star which, no matter how far away it seemed, was this star fading where the sandpipers ran like moon spots in the ebbing tide before the great breakers billowed, bellowing, howling like mad church bells. Perfectly or almost perfectly mad, for no one had died, and yet something had died perhaps long ago though faintly sobbing like the ending memory of unending, unremembered life and light and darkness.

Was he who was the lamp-lighter also he who put out the light, Mr. Spitzer wondered, or were they two different men—as if the evening of life and the morning were not one, much as the evening star and the morning star were believed for centuries by erroneous astronomers in their dark towers to be two stars although they were one? They were one although shining at different times, the morning and the evening, and in different spaces. Sometimes the morning star was seen shining low above the Western horizon like a lantern or glass phaeton a few hours after dawn, its light so dim that it might almost seem not to shine as it faded into the blurred light, sank through cloud banks into that sea where no light would ever shine unless it was the light shining within, going out. Mr. Spitzer's brother had died in the morning of his life—as Mr. Spitzer had lived until the evening, the night—or was it Mr. Spitzer who had died with the morning star fading into the distance of windy heavens, seeming more like a wasp or glass-backed fly than a star? Was it he who never again would see the morning star—he who had said good-night—disappearing with the first sweepings of plaintive light, dawn light omitting him—would never say, through aeons of darkness, good-morning? Yet he practiced to say good-morning, good-morning as the wind blew, whistling through his cape, was always saying good-morning now—good-morning—for never again would he say good-morning—good-morning on the other side, the other shore of light. For he had already said good-night—good-night, sweet prince and lady—good-night—and when should he say good-morning, good-morning in the burning of light where was no night, no darkness, no shadow? For he had not survived the darkness. He had gone down in darkness and in whirlwind. His star had fallen, never again to rise. Surely he dwelled among the shadows. And yet he was always whispering his greetings, whispering to any passing stranger in the billowing fog or where there was no one, no star, no long-haired star with blind eyes, not even a foot, an arm, a bone, a shell, not even some poor derelict pillowed upon the darkening flood billowing like silent music under which there whispered neither star nor fish nor bird nor leaf, none to answer him, for this life was a long rehearsal of music for the silence, that which could surely not answer or reproach, that which could surely not answer Mr. Spitzer's cryings, singings. Or were he and his brother one and the same as he sometimes dreamed—though recognizing that this might be his own extinction—one and the same shining in the morning, evening, pricking through clouds with star rays which trembled, turning like the wavering spokes of a wheel through light as through darkness, the spokes being sometimes the light, sometimes the darkness? Perhaps it was not the municipal watchman who passed down the long street of the lights going out but the old lamplighter with his trembling ladder of dreams reaching to the trembling stars soft as the breasts of pigeons whispering in star-streaked clouds, pigeons through which there shone the stars as through chinks in slate-colored roofs—or perhaps it was the ferryman who ferried the souls of the dead—or poled the pigeons home through wind-blown clouds—all but one dead soul—and the slow realization of this through all his torpid senses filled Mr. Spitzer with seething resentment, the realization striking him all at once from fore to aft so that his starboard keeled to leeward and he was suddenly very angry, perhaps beyond the justification given by the occult cause, perhaps reacting beyond the apparent motive, his mind buzzing like a sea of wasps, perhaps when his own light had already gone out, was put out by the great candle-snuffer who moved among the waning stars, the stars no longer shining like the daylight star in the almost perpetual fog banks winding like mourning bands around this world—for who had taken his place—and was he not himself the lamplighter and the light, the ladder and the star—in this sad dawn which was this dusk—or had he not always thought so—that it was he who moved upon those lonely rounds where living man had never gone before and none would follow him, he who knew the smallest orb like the eye of the water bird as he knew the largest circle or whirlpool, whirlpool whirling to a far horizon, he who knew rhombs, circles, semicircles, boxes, boxes within boxes, parallelograms, octagons, octahedrons, ellipses, eclipses of light by darkness, darkness by light, darkness by darkness, the forms of a divine nature, he who had plummeted the depths, the golden dust of planets falling upon his butterfly sleeve, his regal cape like that of some old king in the whirling darkness splattered by a trail of stars like torches burning under water, like port-holes, like submarine lights, like submerged marigolds, his periscope scarcely appearing above the waves, the starlight like a veil hanging from his hat brim, the fingers of his starfish gloves, the starlight on his shirt front, the ivory head of his cane like a small skull touched with golden light, curls of foam, his pointed shoes which stepped on waters and clouds, clouds and waters, no marble pavement but waters and clouds, his flying, almost transparent shawl embroidered with the golden S which was like a sleeping snail or a small pharaoh in his tomb or boat or ripple of the horned moon upon the many-haloed waves at dawn or the boat moon going down or his clef shining among the darkening clouds, the flying stars, the constellations

scattering like wild swans blown far off their courses by winds? He saw
the constellations flying, losing their glittering feathers which fell in slow
spirals like starlighted snowflakes in the darkening air of dawn, snowflakes which were the memories of melted stars and melted not, contrary
to what most people supposed, the great stars fading though the small
stars faded not but glittered in the pale sunlight of this dead dream as if
there would always be some sediment in the bottom of a bottomless hour-
glass, some memory dying not, memory of light in night or night in light
like the marsh star sinking as he watched with dying eyes. So that he had
felt envy as if someone were taking something away from him—though
what, he did not know—as if someone else might be the musician crying
upon the windy porches, the boatman going down, the lamp-lighter passing upon a distant road or where there was no road, no road winding
between the faded stars, no harp, no bridge, no wind plucking the
strings, no passage between here and there. And how dare another take
his place, Mr. Spitzer had wondered—feeling almost as bewildered as if
he were outside, yet inside. Where was he, he asked again, and who was
he who watched no star lighting the distance, none but in his memory?
And yet perhaps he shone in his own light, much like the star which,
blinded by its brilliance, sees not its own light—he remembering that
under the lighthouse it is darkest, even though the lighthouse seems a
star against which migratory orioles will dash, having mistaken the lighthouse for the star. Even Mr. Spitzer might have done so.

Ah, how, with the star obliterating him, he envied those who knew,
if not what they were or who they were, at least what their professions
were—he sometimes feeling an almost absolute certainty that he was not
the practitioner of Blackstone as he supposed, not the lawyer with his
claims and torts and cases in chancery, bankruptcy suits, last wills and
testaments and signatures to witness, documents to sign, some he had not
had time to peruse, notary's seals to affix to papers, some which were
blank, some which were old love letters he might have mistaken for legal
notes, both great and little seals, waxen and leaden and silver and golden
seals splashing over every page as if to give the mystery of authority to
that which had mystified him—for certainly his eyes could not read the
faded print, just as he could not understand the laws of every country or
the laws beyond the frontiers of this life, frontiers guarded by brigands
and thieves, or laws of undiscovered countries such as that to which the
old suffragette had sailed—perhaps this country where he was—and
could not even understand, for that matter, the laws of his own secret
borough made almost public by its immensity reaching on and on—far
beyond the pavement—for he had passed beyond where the pavement
ends—he sometimes feeling that he was certainly not the silent musician
whispering like the music of that plucked guitar string which is the
unheard music of this waning planet turning through milky space, its
music rippling upon the waves, each whisper reverberating for hours,
years like music in the silent halls, music perhaps only the dead should
hear—that his was darkness pin-pricked by no light or sound, no snow-

flake lighting this dead star—that he was certainly not, as he had supposed, the light-giver moving through darkness though the phoenix stars
should gleam through seas of clouds, casting many tiaras and towers,
casting their lights like diamond horseshoes or island universes shining
upon the waters which arose, rolled, ebbed, changed their changing conformation like the unpredictable tides of time—indeed, cast up great
Himalayas and shadowed valleys—that though he had never placed a bet
or vote on life or death, had never rattled dice, had never turned a card
and knew not these denominations, these dancing spots, neither spade
nor heart nor diamond nor club, had never or rarely sailed beyond
himself no matter how far the point, he was perhaps the gambler who
heard the rattling stars, the inadvertent gambler, not he who had lost—
for had he not taken, in an odd way, his chance on life—had he not
lived, perhaps in windy distance beyond his crying, sighing—or if he had
died, had he not also won perhaps greater stakes than known on earth?
Had he not lived almost apart from himself, the shadow and not the
sentinel, not the star? And yet he was the star, the light, the shadow
crossing the light. If he had died at one pole, had he not lived at the
other pole where were these thinning stars?

And when was this dread henbane of human life or life beyond the
human? Perhaps he was the stowaway who had hidden in the hold of that
ship which had gone down long, long ago. And none had known there
had been this secret passenger who was sleeping when he went down,
sinking through miles of water, he having already sunken in his sleep.
The captain had not known that in this hold there was this king wound
in winding cloth of silver and gold under the winding moon, the moon
casting its faint rays of lights on waters and clouds. This king had not
known when fishes like flowers or candle flames shadowed his face and
sunken mirrors reflecting drowned moons and stars, when barnacles grew
over the bellropes, when angel-eyed dolphins arose to the surface following a dying star. No captain had ever known the names of all his passengers. Surely Mr. Spitzer had not known, perhaps had not even attempted
to know. Perhaps he was the portmanteau personality carrying another
soul within his soul, as star in shadow of a box—perhaps a music box,
perhaps a coffin—or had he lost his soul, his little man, his miniature? It
seemed perhaps better to maintain uncertainty than certainty—to be, in
the midst of raging war, a small neutral country—to live as in a small
tent—to live beyond victory or defeat, irregardless of what might be the
fate of stars. It seemed better not to know that which was unknowable.
For surely if he had lost, his attitude was still that of some old gambler
who, though he had lost, congratulated himself on his winnings—as if
only by losing life did one win life, eternal life, perhaps only for a
moment more—but if always for a moment more, then never ending,
ending not even with the last throw. And Mr. Spitzer's brother had surely
never seemed so gay, so bright, so cavalier as when he had lost—many
observers having mistaken his attitude, no doubt, for triumph, for never
was he so flamboyant as when his horse had lost, as it was then that his
smile would seem to light the dark heavens brooding like the mother of
storms. He sorrowed when he won. His face was chalk white, his sorrow

covering his happiness. Perhaps the ever ending was, of course, the never ending, Mr. Spitzer thought. The appearances were deceiving, certainly in his case—so that he had come to distrust superficial impressions, knowing that they were so often false and that his attitude of well being was not necessarily founded upon the truth as insubstantial as water and sand. Though wrapped in his great coat like a turtle drawn inside his shell, he was surely not this fine gentleman he seemed in others' eyes. For he had won or lost, had lost through never winning or had won through never losing—yet though he would never have given or taken odds—unlike his brother who would have placed his bet on racing sea shells if there had been no windy carousels of horses or meets of yachts bugling in the wind. For if all was chance, then why take a chance?

Mr. Spitzer had lost a silver button from his coat—perhaps long ago, though he had not noticed this loss until recently and that still another silver button was hanging like the moon from a thread—or like a dragonfly from a cable—or like a star—had lost a silver button rolling in the tide, rolling where the surf advanced, rolling on that thin strand where moonstones burned like embers at the water's edge, where heart shells and bishop's mitres sang before the flood—and was afraid that the fine suit he wore was like the undertaker's suit which has no back—even like the clothing of a dream—was afraid to turn, was like the moon which turns but one side to earth though circling earth with passenger birds or unanchored stars. For psychologically he was this old bindlestiff who wore a backless suit, a crownless hat, and paper shoes. His clothes were rags, tatters, scraps of his dead psyches like faded rainbows, scraps of shadow and light like those of some old domino checkered by the shadows or tramp or scarecrow in the ebbing tide. Few would ever see him as he was. His apparition frightened him. He was the wind nipping at his heels in the blowing fog. He was his mirror image, the shadow of his dark cape through which there shone a star, for his cape was torn and full of holes, and it was threadbare—perhaps there were only holes as if the Arctic ice had melted and there were flowers growing at the North Pole, flowers like stars. Perhaps he had passed through a keyhole. Perhaps he was translated. He was the dog barking at the Dog star in the cloud. He was the wave at his feet, the surf breaking like the star whether of darkness or of light. And what did he know as to these fixed and immutable boundary lines, he would always ask, between life and death, death and life—for if he could move forward to tomorrow, crossing these boundary lines of which he did not know, tomorrow seeming no less problematical than the past, that past through which he had not lived, could he not cross from death to life, for could he not, by the same token, move backward to yesterday when perhaps he had died—say that yesterday or day before some other yesterday he had died, whispering, breathing his last with a rasping note, his voice fading into silence where no voice was ever heard, yet had lived to remember his muted death, his plucked heart-strings like the lute in the whirlpool, ebony whirlpool, its strings plucked by invisible fingers of winds, so he had perished but moved through darkness and light—or lived by moving not, by standing still as the boundary lines moved in the rushing, ebbing tide?

CHAPTER 49

✄

WHEN should there be his incorruptible dreams like the unmelting snow, the myth of his psyche never dying although horned mountains flanked with moon-white snow moved in his path and the snows melted like the stars molting their feathers, it seemed to Mr. Spitzer? There were human landscapes as there were geographical landscapes, perhaps not conforming. Sometimes a whole continent might be lost even as there were islands sunken under the waves. A whole continent with all its peninsulas and inlets might be carried away as by the wings of birds. A world might be lost like a lace handkerchief gleaming through a cloud or like the white rose on his coat lapel or like the barnacle before the rolling surf. There were great watersheds of rolling waves from star to star, skiers skiing like sails before the wind, the wind blowing a monsoon of stardust. There were mountain peaks dividing the paths of rain drops in which burned cores of inner fires. There were roaring streams, great avalanches of snow and light which Mr. Spitzer saw or heard. Seldom did he see and hear at once. When he heard, his eyes were closed. The waves pounded over him. They sounded like hooves pounding bells. He heard the waves under him. They drummed like some old drummer drumming taps. It was never reveille in this windy world.

He should have been oriented, and yet he was disoriented by his great experience of living when he was dead, waking only when he was sleeping, sleeping in a watery grave or in an ice hole, the strangest things occurring to him, baffling him because, no matter who or where he was, it was always this one great star like a floor of embers still glowing with burning lights or the eyes of birds, this star which seemed the remainder of many stars honed away, this sediment greater than all other stars had been or would become though they conspired, a denizen of heaven which had floated loose, floating like a celestial door from a cloud or like a rafter on a wave, this where the strangest things occurred like the muffled beating of his heart in the silence, this which was like mountains of moon-colored glass or splinters of the moon or valleys of shadow or a level plain reaching on and on, rippling where he stepped, sea level of his being and many hidden depths, many whirlpools still whirling though he long ago had passed, many delusive surfaces, this where was only the shadow of his unspoken music, perhaps only one grace note, an oblong and not a circle, this where he sometimes mistook his own great shadow for my mother's coach with one light burning within like a star or the eye of a bird or his rippling shadow for the human-sized blackbird he had seen upon a doorstep of a vanished house with blackened chimneys blowing sparks where the sea crawled with its long fingers gleaming with riparian jewels and reaching like a gambler's long-wristed hand toward golden coins or their reflections upon the fog, showers of sequins, a butterfly pirouetting in a cloud, butterfly which had seemed one butterfly but was always two butterflies conjoining over the suddenly shining wave, one with its image, a folded sail coming out from behind a sail upon a far horizon as the moon moved, blackbird pale as smoke through which the glassy fireflies glittered like all lost stars diminished by this magnitude made of minorities, or perhaps it was not one great blackbird with its reproductive shadow gleaming beyond the clouded pin-point stars, each like a separate world, but a globe or house of blackbirds like that which had slept all winter long beneath a frozen brook until the ice melted with a crackling, buzzing sound.

With stillness this freezing had begun, perhaps in a summer's day, the frost flowers forming upon the grass and the clouds. Ice had begun like formations of mother-of-pearl in the roof clouds over this world and the clouds under this world. Ice had turned the rivers into roads. Ice had frozen over the shrouds of beached boats and over the dog that had barked at the fading star and over the huntsman and over the bayed stag with its tree-top antlers and over the night wind blowing like a star. Ice had formed like mirrors in the frozen gale blowing other gales. Skaters were frozen upon frozen brooks. Ice had frozen so hard that it was like the roof of a tomb over this world, even like time containing all time. Ice had grown old, formation over formation, snow pack over snow pack, unmelting snowflake over unmelting snowflake, star over star, and flames were frozen. Ice had caught the frozen moon, the boat, the sea through which there shone the frozen moon. Ice had bearded the cheeks of beautiful ladies so that they were like ancient patriarchs. Beautiful ladies were the fathers of this world. Ice splinters had shone like lamps in the clouds, the clouds within and the clouds without, the clouds like crystal mirrors in this room, and chimney smoke was frozen. Ice had formed over the high-wheeled fringe-topped surrey lumbering under Alpha and the long-necked horses flying under Omega and the coachman's hat from which the waters had run and the blurred canary lights to starboard, larboard.

Ice had formed over Arcturus, over the Great Ram with its long horn, over the many-stringed Lyre with its strings like hailstones falling from heaven to earth, the Huntsman with his glittering belt, the Dog star, the Little Goat, the Wild Swan, the polar stars and the sub-polar stars, over the gosling stars in their nests and the old stars flying like arrows, over almost all the stars and the thin nebulae of the stars like souls not born, perhaps never to be born. Ice had frozen so hard that it was like a dome or like the shell of an egg. Ice had frozen so hard that it was like another star, one never of this world, one which should misguide mariners on other stars. Ice was packed as hard as ivory, an ivory ball. Ice was frozen into shapes of frozen roofs over the winding rivers and the seas and the lakes, ice piled up like weird spires and minarets and bell towers and bells under the ice-shrouded moon, the frozen eye, ice piled up as thick as phantoms in the frozen clouds turning like many-sided diamonds, Romans, Goths, Apostles, the twelve Apostles in their long white robes and the thirteenth Apostle, huntsmen, beautiful ladies, dogs, water frozen to ice so hard that the hooves of great horses had pounded on it as if it were a bell shaking heaven and earth, and cart wheels had left their tracks upon the rutted roads of ice over water, webs of water, ice doming this world, frozen waters where dreamers walked as if on solid ground paving the way from star to star, frozen waters where fishes slept, water where Mr. Spitzer had walked without wetting his feet, tapping with his cane as his great shadow passed, and ice had closed around the boatman and the many-sailed boat, the boat with so many sails that it sank because of its sails, the captain and the crew, eyes of great horned owls staring through veils of ice, and ice had frozen the wine goblets so that the wine retained the shapes of goblets when the glass was broken, and ice had frozen the wine dark sea, and the beds of the sleepers were shrouded with curtains of ice and snow, and the white cat was frozen upon the roof-tops, and ice had transfixed the archer with the arrow in his breast, he who, when the ice melted, would pull the gold-tipped arrow from his heart and leap into the chase as the hounds barked and the cat miaowed. Ice had frozen the sea to lunar stillness. Ice had formed like marble over the salt sea as over the clouds, and dolphins could not rise through frozen billows to the frozen clouds. Perhaps in all the world there was only one coal burning.

Icebergs were melting with a crackling, buzzing sound as if the sea gave up its dead, the sea buzzing with choral bees, a sound heard in meadows of wild flowers, pristine flowers never seen now on bee-belted earth, never seen in these clouded purlieus where earth itself might be a globe missing like a lamp missing down a dark street or road, winged flowers fading into migratory clouds, vocal flowers like trumpets, and this precipitation of wave over pounding wave was vast as if all the diamond stars disintegrated into crystal dust blown by wind as all shell cities of pagodas and minarets and mother-of-pearl domes were flooded from pole to pole of this unknown planet, from snowy cap to snowy cap, and earth seemed like a meadow sunken under miles of moon-colored water, perhaps small as a gnat or fly's back from some other star, a single firefly like a small meteorite, that terra firma which should not be found by the eye of the bird, and the farmer plowed with his bony skeleton horse beneath the refulgent wave which was like a mandarin's fringed umbrella over him, umbrella hung with golden temple bells, silver bells under the saffron sky burning like water marigolds, umbrella of silver, umbrella of gold, umbrella of purple clouds, pagoda umbrella of the falling rain, the rain falling in his eyes, his empty eyeholes where fishes gleamed like flames, and there were old schooners with their white shrouds gleaming like wings of snow which had momentarily settled on water, gleaming among drowned orchard boughs where hung those many moons retaining the amorphous shapes of the moon which had been washed away, nymph moon. Water flowed over the old sheep pastures where the sheep had bahed like the waves and over star-rutted roads lost in a haze of clouds and over the horns of many-clouded mountains with shoulders of snow, the zigzag fences climbing the climbing waves, the crumbling chimneys of extinct volcanoes, the eyes of birds, the lights in windows as Mr. Spitzer watched, and there was water flowing to his mouth, his first mouth and his second mouth, his eyes as if he were in this great crucible or trembling hour-glass. Perhaps the glass had cracked with a shivering sound as of prism music, the glass of heaven cracking from pole to pole as the stars fell like splinters, like fragments of themselves who were ever the fragments, and yet what form retained the shape of the dream or of the dreamer or his impression upon a dark, a shining cloud? Was there nothing infrangible? Was he the hour-glass or its trembling shadow, and did the shadow keep the same hour, or was it timelessness he saw streaming past him?

It seemed as if he were disintegrating into many images, phantoms blown by storm far beyond his knowledge—and if so many, if he had informed all things with his dying spirit, his spirit dying into brilliance or darkness, then how could he die or be extinct? He knew not what his frayed edges were or where he was, he occupying so vast a space that he was lost as if smoke or cloud arose from him to blot out the flame of his mind. He faded into light and shadow, shadow and light, darkness and bellwethering whirlwind, whirlwind without seed or orbit or path or road. He died through everything which lived, lived through everything which died, died through everything, and thus he lived in this dream which crumbled into this unfounded dream. He died at his zenith because he was at his nadir, died at his nadir because he was at his zenith. He lived through dying, crying, and silence. He died at the first breath. He died perhaps at the last because he had died at the first. He died at his unknown meridian. Perhaps he had not breathed and had not died. Perhaps his memories were embalmed. He died because of a road not taken or a branching road, a road branching into two roads or four roads, a many-forking road like Mr. Chandelier with his bright or fading lights blown by windy clouds, clouds streaked with the ray lights of Aurora Borealis and Aurora Australis from pole to pole, lights like the cage of a bird, because of music rustling through windy tree-tops or the wind bugling through brittle branches or branches falling from the weight of snow, because of the silence like a river flowing under him, river where he was shadowed. He died through walking a crooked path or a curving path, for there was no straight path in nature from point to point for journeyers in this void and few returning not upon themselves whom they had left in clouds and few who had ever truly left themselves. He died through standing still when others moved as in winds of passage or the plumed comet's slowly gliding path over these waves of sparkles, but what stood still? Not even he stood still where the waves crawled like the roof-tops and city lights. He died through sickness, died through health which had killed the immortal invalid, most perfect health, died through happiness which should have saved him, died through sorrow, sorrow by which he lived, died by not dying, died by living, lived by dying, so what were these distinctions to him, this old lawyer who had been the golden advocate of reversals, the pleader of lost causes, causes perhaps irretrievably lost, causes which were perhaps never popular in any public sense but of which he had been an unsolicited and unelected representative, a minority representing a majority, a hidden majority like those sleeping in the churchyard, causes which perhaps were never exactly stated even by him who with his fatal ambiguities had tried to reverse last judgments in every court paved with broken moonstones where the waters ran, perhaps only with thinnest trickles until the waves arose, this old musician who had tried to go against the tide flowing forward, writing his music like a tide to flow backward to awaken dead ears, dead eyes? He had not even awakened himself, there was little doubt, so how should he awaken another? Doubtless of him it might be accused that he had put many to sleep. He had rocked them on the waves. His was this barcarolle heard not by the singer. His music fell like a sickle feather on many-reflecting water, like his golden clef, his serpentine S reversed fading before he knew that it was gone through trembling clouds and palpitations of doubt, through troughs between two waves in the astral storm, through darkly warped or mirroring waters and clouds as thick as fleece where perhaps one light shone pale as a fire under snow, a spot of light gleaming when the firefly was gone, a lighthouse glowing under the incandescent waves, a letter missing from the boat alphabet of the stars. Alas, what sorrows were there in this empty world. It was like a box which was larger than one knew, especially when the lid blew off. The lid blew off in wind and soughing rain. Perhaps there had never been a lid. The box was smaller than one knew. Such was Mr. Spitzer's elasticity—he did not know what this world was—whether Ursa Major or Ursa Minor or a sand grain, a rolling spark, the thin wash of a wave. Perhaps it was a rain drop falling from the wing of the great archangel Uriel, or it was Mr. Spitzer's tear drop.

His tears were falling like the golden rain, like one who turned into his tears, his tears with their core of being, the spawn of his tears, his tears enclosing suns, moons, boats, flowers, butterflies, roads, his seed tears falling from another planet, his tears falling from the many stars and from the firmament of the clouds, the rain splashing at his feet, or were these ropes of fireflies, ropes of stars through which he stared? Were these ropes of snow blown in all ways? Were these ropes of pearls burning with inner fires? Were these phoenix lights, Mr. Spitzer asked, and not the stars lighting this dark world, the roofs and the spaces between the roofs, the spaces between the stars, the slate roofs of little, huddled towns? Ah, should he build a world from a tear, that repeating all sorrows, shadows, fires, clouds, waters, starfish, distant thunder-claps, or almost all? But why should any man weep if the heavens wept for him? If all were mourning, should he not be joyous as one who knew there was no death, that death was an illusion no less than life had been? He knew there was no death because there was no life. He wept only because none mourned for him, this old mourner with his shadow crossing his flame, his rainy whispers, the shadow of his cape, the starfish on his sleeve, the starfish where his hand had been, the barnacle like a great stone of growth upon his cheek. Sometimes it shone like the moon which gave the only light. His eyelids were swollen, heavy-lidded with weeping. Why should his tears fall like the rain splashing at his burning feet, the rain splashing with all these argosy lights of gold, swarming lights where the darkness gathered like the fireflies around a rope, an umbilical cord, a bellrope, or like the moths around the branches of an old tree trembling in the moth-colored surf as if with winged flowers in the crepuscular lights making a night of day? It was twilight where he was even in the burning dawn. This world was building itself, so he wept not for him but for all others as the clouds crossed his vacuous face with sequin lights, his baffled eyes. To weep for himself would seem an excess since he was already dead or dying to this world, this world dying. He wept for others who wept not for him. Some stones were hot, hot as live coals. Some stones were cold. Some hearts were beating when others were silent, for never all could beat at once. If all could beat at once, then he who was dead would be the one person living. Such loneliness would then be his that it was almost like his loneliness now. There was a time differential forever between the lover and the loved, Mr. Spitzer thought, for had he not missed love, that beloved face? Some clouds were dark when others glittered like mica, for seldom did all clouds conspire to be one and the same color and conformation and shape—and if they did, they would not be clouds. Seldom was there a perfect coherence where the clouds were driven by wind, great and small holes showing between the clouds and the clouds, the clouds which were heavy with the great rain or with the little rain, that cloud which contained a single drop, tear drop, the clouds without rain, the clouds of uncertainty, the clouds of regret, the clouds which were not the clouds, the clouds suffering these mortal shifts and changes which Mr. Spitzer suffered, too, in his own inimitable way with his short, rasping breath or his long breath blowing from star to star and his irregular pulse at times scarcely to be discovered and his wildly fluttering and startled and palpitating heart, that way unique to him so that his body seemed not his body though, in fact, it was his body which was like an old, many-chimneyed tenement lurching in the sea of the city, city where all were drowned or city which floated like a reef for but a moment above a wave, an old house so vast that it might contain many secret rooms and rooms within rooms and stairways and a golden coach and four, a swan, a dolphin, a rose, and sandpipers running like candle flames before the surf, an old house seeming empty with its many windows boarded up or broken though sometimes one saw a flickering light as if there were a secret inhabitant, as if his spirit like a tramp had taken refuge where the mirrors swam. Someone was at home—but who was he, Mr. Spitzer asked? Could his intelligence tell him who was this tramp, for had not his spirit departed before the storm arose? Who was this passenger? Surely he knew not.

So Mr. Spitzer had become this obsessed beagle and watchman in many streets, passing with his smoky light, casting his light on many broken windows of many empty houses where no one was seemingly at home, pulling many doorbells until there were many frozen doorbells ringing like an answer to his music, his howling in the winter wind, barking, crying until his voice was hoarse or scarcely rose above a fluted whisper, scarcely stirred a cloud—Halloo, halloo! Is there anybody at home? Is thy light shining, or hast thy spirit departed upon the evening wind?

Doubtless he had made a loud nuisance of himself, for there were many who had complained in a silent world, and he had suffered many unusual adventures, many misfortunes which were his fortunes, many fortunes which were his misfortunes, had gone through many reverses, had stumbled upon many living persons believed to be dead or dead persons believed to be living, had found all but himself whom he would probably never find though he searched through all of time. Never would he come face to face with him. There was always some discrepancy. His calendar was perhaps never that of earth, even of a vanished moment, and therein lay his problem—though it was that bringing him closest to reality—being unreal.

Wheezing asthmatically, perhaps even musically, for even his staccato notes were musical as breaking icicles, each spindle containing butterflies, and his sighing was legato, an unbroken swell, suffering from a head cold caused by an iceberg with its floating spars like jewels of light, stars buzzing like bees trapped in the rays of that great hive which was the sun, hearing many sounds which others did not hear, he was like an old clock always winding himself up when he was running down, always going into his eclipses and retirements, always sequestered and yet exposed, coming out of a partial eclipse only to go into a total eclipse, a greater and greater shadow, a greater somnolence. Sometimes he could scarcely hear his ticking, whirring. Sometimes it seemed as if the old clock had stopped. And yet he wound the old clock again as a dying man might wind a clock or make an appointment for tomorrow upon some windy street corner of quicksilver light and shadow. So Mr. Spitzer had done. He had wound a clock to awaken him when he was no more. He had waited for a dead man, doubtless many times missing his appointment though Mr. Spitzer had been faithful as to an old love. Perhaps to an unknown love he had been faithful. He had scarcely known the hour, the hour hand or the minute hand racing the hour hand, the great jockey or the little jockey, but he had been exquisite before the roaring chaos of no hour, of all hours racing together, and he had kept that certain calm of one who knows the music is already done. The race is already finished, perhaps long before it began. And what comes afterward is but a sigh or a cry or a loose pebble rolling by a glassy sea. How should he wish to know the result? He had tried to include all possibilities and even the rejected possibilities, the way taken and the way not taken, the life he might have lived, the death he had died, all that had happened, all that had not happened, and much that was impossible. So why should he be blamed for this impossible extension of time beyond its wildest dream or blamed for its failure, its crumbling, the star crumbling like the transitory snowflake? In the crumbling of time he found perhaps his only refuge, many things being revealed which had long been concealed—as others faded into a perpetual fog like heavy cloud banks rolling over him, under him, clouds through which there shone no star. Not even this star shone with a steady light.

So that his precision seemed an act of grace for which there was no justification and doubtless no necessity, mortal or immortal, no way of stating who he was, for he might be another, and if he had existed only by proxy, by some marvelous substitution taking place without his knowledge or desire or will, almost by magical sleight-of-hand, if it was not he who felt these enchanted mysteries and remembered the dead as he remembered the living or perhaps had forgotten both and made no distinctions because none or few were to be made in the fog which was the crumbling of light into darkness, none which should not some day disappear as if the little orb went into the great orb or the great orb into the little orb, this was surely better than nothing to him, and should he question his continued existence or subject himself to that great searchlight of consciousness which pointed out the real, unreal, drew a line between the light and the shadow, even a wavering line? The searchlight made the light it lived by. The light lighted only the light and never the darkness, for when the darkness was lighted, it was not the darkness but was the light. The shadow made the darkness. He lived between the golden spokes of light. He lived between the spokes of darkness. He moved through moving light and shadow—blotting himself out in either way—being at all times partly negated as if he were partly absent—or had already passed into another world—though nothing would have frightened him perhaps so much as that light shining where no darkness was. There was nothing he feared so much as the light of the sun. He was grateful for fluctuations, for soughing waves and winds, for changes passing into changes, and for the slow blurring of his senses. Who could afford to look directly at life? For life was itself this indirection, going not by a straight road. It seemed that by the shadow and mist and drizzle and fog he lived and not by the light, the light passing. He lived in that period in which it would seem that he was dead—as one who hibernated for a long period in the darkness—but in the incandescence of light when it seemed that he lived, he was dead, and so the greatest brilliance was delusive. The shadow increased, and this was his paradox, that he lived by that which seemed his death. The shadow was immortal. Sometimes it seemed that he was the shadow and not the man. Grey days he chose and long sighings and curtains of rain through which one scarcely saw the lowering stars, the stars coming down upon the waters, settling there perhaps but for a moment in erratic flight, perhaps forever as the waters rose to the clouds, as long-winged sail-boats were foundered with burning lights upon a reef which was a milky thread. It was a thread like that winding from his spool. Perhaps it came from the eye of a bird in the cloud.

It seemed to him that he might know all passages except his own which was forever tentative because noted by him. It seemed that he might know or think he knew the exact date of the death of an individual—be it even some old suffragette dying in her sleep or dying at the moment she awakened from this troubled sleep of life—this long sleep of love, for sleep had been her love—or he might miss death by an hour—or move it by a day, a year or two—forward or backward—still be accurate even in his greatest inaccuracy since few lived through changeful eternity, few unless it was Mr. Spitzer himself in his dying moment, his forever dying moment, that which he scarcely knew, perhaps moving that approximate moment as if it were a king or a queen upon a chessboard where the waves swept over all and moved even those not moving— though none had ever known the hour of the withdrawal of consciousness into unconsciousness, and the slayer of all hearts might never be, it seemed to Mr. Spitzer with his beating heart, the slayer of his own, might never know his own passage to another world or even this world—as surely none had ever known, though he sought through all of time which was not time, the date of the death of those vast mythological beings which were like psychological entities crumbling even while they lived, the griffin with its wings of gold, the centaur, the bishop and monk crabs walking upright in the surf with their glittering mitres and vestments, the worm who never turned, the phoenix burning like stars or jewels in the waters and the clouds, the mermaid giving milk to her young, as none knew the date of the sinking of the galleon stars, for they were always sinking, rising, sinking. Perhaps the individual was like those beings which never were and thus could never truly disappear, sometimes Mr. Spitzer dreamed though knowing he was wrong. Perhaps these mysteries were always going on—so that he was never sure which side of life or death it was—as if he were a man who stood at both ends of a bridge or as if he stood on both sides of a great gulf and saw that he was missing, missing from the clouded heavens, missing from the universe of stars and the small constellations which had no place, missing where he was.

He knew not whether he was himself or an image contained within an image like a boatman in a boat or an image without, a ripple, a stir, a silent whirlpool, a boat rising or a boat sinking or that which was forever passing, a dream dying before the individual died or a dream awakening when he was gone—a memory fading like a ray of light upon the water or never fading, burning like a dim jewel. None knew what the individual was, he being many countries, many times, many dimensions, one of whom no unitary statement could be made, of whom none would know the finality, whom none would sum up, he being all those whispers he had ever heard or had not heard, those clouds reflecting tall buildings through which he had passed as if there were no walls, the rustle of musical sound, a sigh, a cry, a quiver. He had passed through city lights as through shadows. He had translated his passion for immortality into mortality, making of this earth his heaven—for had he not missed earth as some might miss heaven, an island in the flood? Perhaps there was something irreducible, and that which was gone was never gone. Not knowing who or what the individual was, whether himself or another,

how often he thought of the last individual fading from this earth, knowing that there was no one to answer his sigh or cry, that never again
would come the mating season, that which perhaps had never been but in
a dream, and never again would the winds blow for him, and there
would be only the answering silence—for did not the last individual
know when he was the last, and did he not die in silence as the clouds
lowered? Or did he cry? Perhaps perfect silence was the perfection of love.
Did he see his image in the dusk, Mr. Spitzer asked where there was no
one to hear him? Rarely had there been known in the annals of time the
date of the death of the last member of an entire species—perhaps only
once, in fact, and that was when the last passenger pigeon winged its way
to another world, the place where all good pigeons go when they die as
Mr. Spitzer sometimes murmured in his weeping walks under the driz-
zling clouds, weeping his opalescent tears almost like tears of joy as he
sometimes thought he heard the almighty tumult of wings of passenger
pigeons roaring like the wild sea over him, blotting out the sun and
moon, but he dreamed. And he was wrong. None returned. Only he
returned. And even that was doubtful.

Whenever he thought of the death of an individual, he wept for the
death of the last passenger pigeon known to earth—Martha, who expired
September 14, at one o'clock in the afternoon just as the clock was tolling
one, 1918, A.D., at the Cincinnati zoo—dying peacefully, dying of dying,
dying as the leaf falls, dying as the rain gleams in sunlight, dying as the
snow clouds gather—and so her passage should scarcely have been noted,
but he had noted it in a war-torn world. He had written down this date
upon his shirt cuff. All others of her kind had been shot down by great
guns, trapped by nets like the fishes of the sea, clubbed, killed simply
because they were the many, the beautiful, the excessive who had made a
wilderness of this life and who had stained the heavens with serpentine
rose and blue and gold and who had been like great rivers rushing over
head, like thunderous seas, like mother-of-pearl pavements trembling in
the clouds, their wings shadowing all faces. They had made a music like
the sea where no sea was. They had swept like a tide over this sunken
continent. They were once more numerous than people in America, and
sometimes even now Mr. Spitzer with his memorial heart might seem
to hear the music of cleavage as the passenger pigeons winged over him in
the long night of his sleeping, but he was wrong, and Martha had been
the last, and her obituary was written in the timeless clouds like Mr.
Spitzer's music. The white of the cloud was her tomb and the gold of the
sunlight and the rose tips of wings which would gleam no more to eyes
gleaming on earth, eyes gleaming through iridescence of fog. Indeed, her
death had seemed a doubling like his own, for she had been, so far as
anyone knew, the last of the last, the last of all passenger pigeons who
had roared like the sea through the clouded heavens, and never again
would she be seen where the clouds gathered, and the key had been lost.
The great key-maker had thrown away the key, the key of silver, the key
of gold. No one knew the key to the starry universe in the milky cloud.
No one knew the keyhole. No one knew the door. The great candle-

snuffer had snuffed out this flame. This earth was also passing as the wheel turned, and there were many never returning, perhaps only seeming to return. Was this ever the way it was? So that Mr. Spitzer, feeling himself doubled by this grief, had been this solitary mourner for her as for a lost love. Having heard that she was still alive though faring poorly like one who knew his widowed heart, his heart widowed from himself, he had gone to call on her—but had arrived too late. She was already dead, so Mr. Spitzer had been writing ever since his epitaph for her, had been trying to capture her music. She had departed as upon the wings of evenings after many evenings, many moons of life. She had departed as through the glimmering of a star. She had gone as through a rain drop. She had gone as through a bubble of light. He had come with his white rose gleaming through the rain, but Martha had died before he came, and surely all the stars of heaven must have gone out in requiem for her, and surely many had not returned. They had not returned in the flashings of quicksilver lights or in the darkest days, the darkest nights, surely he knew best of all, for he had been this watcher of the innumerable stars.

She was embalmed and put upon a train to be sent to Washington, the nation's capital claiming her who was more precious when she was dead than millions of passenger pigeons had been when they were alive and carrying a continent upon their wings. Poor Martha was relegated to the baggage car, only an old night porter riding with her, and he was black as midnight and Mr. Spitzer's dreams of eternal life which never could be justified as life itself could not be justified. The old night porter had whispered in the night, had whispered like the rustlings of clouds, like the billowing of leaves. In the long night passing he had whispered, doubtless with pigeon murmurs. Perhaps he had heard the whirrings of his pigeon heart. He was black as the ace of spades, that card of chance which was the world. How precious then was life, this fleeting moment, and all things illegal as the dreamer and the dream of this continuing life, as all who were destroyed by politicians and lawyers and the great powers, as dead souls whom Mr. Spitzer remembered when he felt himself emptied of life. Should not man some day be where the last passenger pigeon was? Should not the slayer be the slain? So he mourned for her as for himself and clouds shining no more on earth or as he mourned for a stranger he had never known. It had seemed as if this night would never pass.

Mr. Spitzer, sitting up all night with his vast purple eyes enlarged by grief and pressed against a window glass as he stared at the dark and starless sky, the sky without stars even when there were no clouds, had ridden among the sleeping passengers through an empty countryside, noting that all along the way there were no twinkling station lights such as there had been when he came, and the stars were flown, and there were no lights to show where the next station was or if there might be such a station, perhaps some little way-station never noted before and shining with one feeble light like a lily shining through the fog, and there were no lights in any town and perhaps no town, and he had heard no sound but the long hooting of a night train trailing its cloud of purple smoke

with flying sparks, and at dawn he had seen no one, not a moving cart
wheel, not a person in any town of the grey slate pigeon roofs and purple
roofs and trembling spires and shadows of spires such as those over which
the pigeons must have passed, clanging like bells far out at sea. There
were more shadows of spires than there had ever been spires. This old
pigeon mourner had almost thought that the dawn would never come,
dripping as with the great painter's oily colors upon a canvas sky. He had
almost thought that he was alone in an empty world. If there were no
pigeons, could there be people or pigeon people or the pigeon-colored
dawn, rose and blue and silver and gold mottled like the pigeon's wing,
the twilight of this hour which was Mr. Spitzer's dawn? He had lost all
sense of the hour.

Perhaps it was just as well, for he had waited for hours for a jitney in
Washington, and now it occurred to him that he would have done better
if he had waited for a jinrikisha or a small jockey or a butterfly. It would
have been better if this had been some other capital. Finally, he had
hailed an old, high-wheeled checkered cab, a horseless car which, like a
first cousin to a surrey, should have been the first of its kind but was
probably the last. Its wheels had buckled. Its engine had sputtered, blowing a cloud of steam like a Turkish bath. Its windshield was broken. Its
head lights were bashed in like an insect's blind eyes. It had reeled from
side to side, street to street as if the driver were drunk or half asleep,
though if half asleep this did not signify that he was half awake. He had
not asked Mr. Spitzer's destination—and Mr. Spitzer had not told him—
so secretive was he by nature—and after all, it was before public buildings were open. So they had driven aimlessly where there was no other
traffic streaming or so little that they had not noticed it. They might have
driven through the wings of several archangels. Mr. Spitzer had shaken,
rattled, crying all the way until the cab-driver had asked—Oh, have you
lost your love? Mr. Spitzer, not wishing to arouse suspicion, had answered—I am about to lose her. He had gone around and around the
town, several times passing Lincoln's Monument—and once, in an absent-
minded moment, must have asked—Where's Grant's Tomb? Where's
Cleopatra's Needle? But if so, the cab-driver had not heard him. By and
by, he had got out, only some time afterward realizing that he had
forgotten to pay his coin, a Roman head—the cab-driver merely staring
at him with a long, glassy stare—had walked through the blurred clouds
and the rain, passing many lamps—the lights were just going on with
flutterings. He had felt that the flag of this nation and perhaps of all
nations should have been flying at half mast, for who should ever see a
passenger pigeon again pricking through clouds of rose and gold? For her
he had shed a pearly tear. He had shed two pearly tears, noting that his
tears splashed upward from the sidewalk. Surely, any ornithologist who
looked at him must have known what had occurred, must have sensed his
loss. He had lost his feathers. He had lost his bird. His bird had been
plucked. He had been nearly knocked down by a Chinese mandarin like
a moving pagoda hung with gold and silver bells while crossing a rain-
flooded street with the passenger moon. Ah, what muted tinklings he had

heard. They were like prisms of a lamp greater than anyone had ever seen. Perhaps he was always where the moon was, always in passage, never in one place, was neither the many nor the one, or was not so much an entity as a light shining upon all or a fitful light sometimes seen, sometimes disappearing through miles of clouds though his was this darkness gathering fold after fold like the clouds or a velvety landscape, this darkness lighting not him though the light streamed from his eye. He passed through banks of fireflies as through darkness and knew not what it was. Perhaps far away he spotted the light of earth, but he was not sure. So he forgave his deviousness. Finally, after much wandering and many false attempts, many knockings of his dead heart, many knockings upon many doors, doors of empty buildings, doors of roofless lofts, doors of tenements from which the inhabitants had moved away, doors of darkened embassies, no doubt, and he might even have knocked against the Capitol dome and lamp-posts veiled by fog and many darkened chimneys, perhaps against many surrey tops and many great crinolines sweeping the grass and many great balloons sweeping the clouds, many horses, he had come to the Washington Museum—where he had wished to pay his last respects, leave his black-bordered calling card as at the grave of a poet since he had missed his love when he was alive, and he had missed the beauty, the power, the tumult of every present moment—and had urged the old caretaker shuffling in his walks that a mirror be placed before her that she might be illuded, that she might see another pigeon in eternity, her image mirrored in a gold-rimmed heaven, a bird in a cloud, the light streaming from her breast, that she might not know she was alone as he was alone.

This old caretaker—wearing a grey dressing robe of faded flower patterns and a bellrope tied around his middle and carpet slippers with pointed toes and a white peaked night-cap—and this surely seemed a strange costume for a man to wear in a museum—but he was sweeping with his bramble broom, sweeping away feathers and sands and shells— doubted that she should be deceived as Mr. Spitzer was deceived. It was this incapacity to be deceived which caused extinction, the old caretaker had announced. Truly, she had lived through many mirages, refractions of light beams, drifting clouds, pools which seemed to disappear though for a moment gleaming, shadows of leaves, roof-tops drifting on clouds, shadows of clouds upon faces or cloud faces, and should she not recognize them now? As for himself, did he not face the end with perfect equanimity, and had he not sought his refuge in this refuge for wild life, this place where all had already ended? Seldom and perhaps never did he see a living man. He believed that Martha had died without belief in any future life though pigeons favor churches and statues. She had surely died without benefit of clergy and without confessing her pigeon peccadilloes, her small pigeon sins like drops of silver and gold and rustlings in clouds, for there were none, no progeny from her, not so much as a pigeon cherub. She had never sinned. Her little, rheumy eye had looked out with amazing clarity upon the clouded void as she had breathed her last, breathing so softly that her last breath was not heard, not even by sleepers in their graves or other passenger pigeons. She had known how a star dies. She had known that the starlight lighted not her path. Nothing would there be of her. She had gone back into the great, asymmetrical, and inarticulate chaos which left no writing on the moon, none upon the star, her shadow upon no cloud, no stone.

Her soul was not so much as a bubble of light, it seemed to this old caretaker who whispered, hissed, spoke through a bubble. Why, she was less than her least feather now. Why, this old passenger pigeon, though she had died as one passenger pigeon who was all the passenger pigeons who had ever been and much less and much more and would not be again, had no soul, the old caretaker said, and was never painted by the great portrait-painter—was surely not worth Mr. Spitzer's tear. It would be better if she had wept for him or for the old caretaker passing now. He doubted that ever again in time and space would there be a passenger pigeon winging over this winging world, or if there still was one dwelling somewhere in a leafy covert hidden from man, one whom man had not seen, one who hid under the clouds and under the snows or under the leaves, he still was only one—not two, the old caretaker said—for Martha was no more, and Mark was no more—and well, it took two to make a bargain—and she would never come again in heaven or on earth. Two passenger pigeons would be two more than there were. One there had been, and one was gone, for one was too many in the world. Even one was more than there was now passing over clouded brooks and meadows of archaic flowers. I doubt not that the flowers sang like birds in those days, the old caretaker said. Dear sir, dear sir. You ask too little, and you ask too much. She is but one, and she was gone at one o'clock— or to be precise, as few persons know—it was three minutes after one when she departed, giving up her little ghost—three trinitarian minutes. Father, Mother, Son. There was none for her on earth. You come too late. You should have come when your grief was premature, come when she was still alive and winging. You should have come when there were so many passenger pigeons that they sounded like church bells tolling over the earth as if some one had pulled the bellrope of the heavens and the earth. She is melted like the snowflake in this burning star. She is melted in the fiery furnace of man's disbelief. A star fell when she fell. This star went out. To find her now, you will have to turn time back—and that is impossible—or so many years forward that you will not be when she is seen, and I doubt that she will be seen by living man. You will be, Mr. Spitzer—but how could this old caretaker have known, have spoken his name?—where she is now. Never will you catch up with her. For if not in one way, then in another way you die, and she is gone before you. It could be noted of a dying species that when the great winter of death set in, and that winter was long, very long, there was no way to revive them, even when they were two—no way to multiply them. The great bellows-blower could blow no spark. If they became four, they receded to two again, and when one mate died, one was only one. Or if one gave birth, then think how sad was that last birth—almost as sad as the last death or the last breath. If one gave birth to two, yet both died, or only one survived. These dying species multiplied not like the fishes of the sea and the birds of the air and the sands and the stars. They seemed to know they were the last. They seemed to know that to start when all seemed ended would be a hopeless task. They had tried by many mother-of-pearl windings, and they had failed though their failure was egregious like all failures. And they suggested, the old caretaker said, that quality of life which is unique—a solitary episode—never to come again though one should set his decoy and whistle all the way from here to Labrador, whistle from star to star. For they were not easily deceived, even by living artifice—and besides, should they wish to come back if they could consciously decide upon threnodies of return? Should they wish to come back to that which they knew was extinct? They returned not with one rattle of the dice. Their fate was probably very much tied up with that of earth—these climactic conditions, the burning rocks, the clouds, the pressure of waters—they passed like man through fiery furnaces and waterfalls. I doubt that these passenger pigeons will come again even upon some other star, not even watery Venus or stars never seen on earth. What did you expect—the dove of God like that which flew up through Mary's skirts whispering like foam, the pigeon-colored clouds?

But Mr. Spitzer had demurred—Oh, no, no, no, no. What good did Mark ever do—or for all the good he did, for all the pigeons like the many stars, the stars which died with her and died when our star died, what difference now? There is no Mark, and there is no God. Let there be female and female, for female and female created He them, and only the female endures—like the wild sea, the sea upon all shores and even the shores of the dead. Every Martha must have her Mary like that snow-white pigeon with the red-rose breast who used to come to her through miles of clouds, the clouds streaming light where she was. Let there be a mirror shining in a cloud.

But he was refused, was threatened with eviction if he persisted— and besides, it was closing time. Did he want to be locked in with the old caretaker—or locked out, the old caretaker asked with a rasping sound? He wanted to be locked out, naturally, and had gone buzzing, bumbling through the purple rain, the midnight clouds.

He would have presented his indictment to the Senate on account of what America had done to passenger pigeons once as thick as stars in the clouds and had done to Indians in their lonely tepees and yet might do to the whooping crane and the lute bird trembling from heaven to earth and the wild flamingo and the seagull and the swan and the groundhog and the chirruping tree toads and the stars, the chirruping stars, but would have been put out of court, would have been accused of anarchy, of sedition against the state, of making a public nuisance of himself, of arousing protests of the nameless dead, of giving a voice to all those beauties which never should have been expressed, not even by his passenger pigeon music, his music like a fountain spilling through a cloud, would have been threatened with the Federal pen if he continued as this old pigeon lobbyist and advocate for lost causes and self-elected representative of passenger pigeons who voted not and lamenter with his true bills and bills of rights and his whispers and his coos and his rustling clouds, for none would have believed him, this old lawyer with the rose on his coat collar and the rain on his sleeve and the pigeon droppings on his hat brim and his opalescent cheeks shadowed as with multiple pigeon wings of silver and gold and his murmurs and his sighings and his ivory-headed cane, the pigeons rustling in his throat, the pigeons fluttering in his stomach as he had walked rustling through the rain with his pigeon walk. None would have believed in beauty passing like a scythe. So he had returned to Boston, the Great Hub. He had returned at midnight by many roads. Perhaps he had taken a road leading away from the center. Perhaps he was always in the rip tide, a place of two tides meeting like music and silence. He heard his distant breathing as he heard his silent heart beating under a dark wave, a wave rising to the moon. He saw the clouds with lighted port-holes. His sobbing seemed to come from a greater and greater distance and might be translated into the sobbing of a wave or a steeple bell tolling in the storm or the whisper of a sail upon the other side of the vanished moon, for all he knew, or at the other end of time, surely never in this place or space occupied by this body. Perhaps a bell had tolled at the other end of time, both at the beginning and the end. He heard a bell tolling far inland, far beyond his hearing. Ghostly wings were brushing past his face.

He was all but deafened by interior noise, roaring tides, sounds as of waterfalls where none were, cries, sobs, whispers. He was melancholy as a lip-reader seeking the shadows where the moon should light no face, for he was tired of reading lips which moved or only seemed to move as the moonlight moved, only seemed to move like the lips of marble statues shadowed by waters and clouds, and he was like a blind man staggering where the shadows whispered and increased. A stranger whispered in the darkness—Does a blind man blush in the darkness of the everlasting night, and does the night know shame? The night knows boldness where all are masked as by the night, the night without stars, and darkness winds around the face of the moon as the great turban-winder winds his clouds. So he who would not rob by day will rob by night. He who knew not his love in the dawn will know his love in the night, night where all faces are hidden, night of the dead men returning, or none has ever died. A blind man offered to lead him through a dark city, saying—This sudden darkness over the city, that through which you grope as one suddenly blind, is an advantage to me, for I am the best guide through the night who never knew the light, even the momentary light, and eternal darkness is mine. In a great fog suddenly descending, trust only the blind. He heard the leaves blowing in windy gutters where no leaves had ever blown before, voices crying where none had ever cried, whispers where none had whispered, foam breaking as flies specked mirrors, mirrors cracking in clouds, clouds breaking over him even in days of calm, for was he not dead? And yet perhaps he had not escaped the tempest when the body was like the spirit blown by storm, for he was not the creator of his dreams, not one who dwelled above the storm—he was the created, and he was spinning vertiginously, spinning like a top under the spinning star.

Perhaps he was the center of the great storm blowing around him, through him, blowing through many apertures, blowing shadows on clouds and glass which shivered like the light, the night. He was surely flooded in his hold. His cargo was flooded—cargoes of stained satins like the seas around him, clouded gauze, moons and suns like dinner plates lighted by candle flames shining on drowned mirrors. He had lost his sleeping passenger, a beautiful lady who had slept through the rising and the falling waves, sleeping until she was old, so old that none should recognize her, for few had ever seen her beautiful face which was hidden among the shadows even like his face. He had lost flotillas of butterflies breaking from his back but never before him and chambered nautiluses singing in the tide and sea-horses who had ridden with him. He liked sea-horses because in that realm the father carried the young, swollen like the bean pod in a rain-flooded garden, and the mother was the father sea-horse. He had forgotten to batten his hatches before the coming storm. He had forgotten to shrive himself, had forgotten to close his ears, his eyes, his senses five which now seemed fused as if they were more than five, all things being blurred. He had certainly forgotten to reef his sail, to drop anchor in a quiet bay beyond the storms of time. Water flowed through all his openings and over his tired sail, sail which he should have released if he had remembered, and so he would have righted himself, going against the storm, but now he was blown in all ways, and never would he find the covert side. There was no shore but that forever receding. What bays, what harbors had he made and what dim coastlines by which he should be found, and what city was his? There was no leeward wind. The storm diminished not when there came the calm. Perhaps he was the heart of the storm, and even his calm was the storm. He saw between the interstices of black wings the starlight trembling over him and many shrouded shapes coming out of pearl-hung fog and mist like the dead who lived in that secret city hidden in every city and who came out only at night. They lived but to die again as the dawn streaked the clouds with such pale rays that they might have been the light of a false dawn or dawn so near the twilight that they were one.

He was frightened by funereal steeple bells ringing just at that moment when he lived, perhaps for the first time, perhaps for the last time. Perhaps he had never lived before, lived only through his dying. He heard his living dirge. Surely some sound should be heard over the water, some sound as of a tolling bell. He heard earth mourning like a mournful bell which should be heard from star to star. Great bells of silver, bells of gold were falling upon the bell-ringers now, for they were caught like babes among the ropes even as the fisherman was caught in his net, his net going down, he being caught as if he were the great haddock for whom he had fished, and every bell was like a coffin swept by waves, for music's birth was music's death, dying as it was expressed, dying because it was ever approximate and not actual, and none should live to hear its completion or the last echo dying. So Mr. Spitzer was frightened when he heard bells ringing as if all music or almost all should be heard at once before it faded into that silence where nothing was, where was not even his deluded memory bringing these mistaken impressions of life, that through which he had not lived. Where was that silence? A great city was enclosed inside a pebble. A trumpeter was crying outside a small door, so Mr. Spitzer heard. He was frightened by his own great shadow or his shadow diminishing upon the waters and the clouds, frightened by the long roar of ice under the burning stars, lakes of fire, time moving through timelessness as timelessness had moved through time, rumbling plank bridges laid over nothingness or bridges swept by crescent waves, thin gossamer gleamings like lace gloves in the fog, thin traffic whistles scarcely heard or dolphins barking in lonely streets, sunken lighthouses with wavering arms of light, sudden flurries of sound, frightened that he had lived through all those forbidden moments he had tried to postpone or almost all, all perhaps but one, one he might never know, and those experiences he had tried to evade by many turns, many twists, many winding roads, many corners, even his death which had been an artifice like his life, for there were no facts but groundless illusions in this many-shrouded fog, and the phantoms were the facts, the stones crumbling into clouds and the clouds into waters. Should a dead man see winged umbrellas moving through the fog? He swore that if he had been the creator and not the created, he would have gotten no further than flowers and beasts and birds, would have written music for the dolphins beyond the threshold of his hearing, would surely never have attained to man and man's consciousness or these divisions into life and death. And perhaps he had never done so. He would have closed all eyelids before the eyelids had opened—or left the eyes without lids, without fringes to shadow them. He might have attained to mother but never to father in this world and never to this criticism of life where he saw the fireflies eaten by the birds. What world was this, he often asked as if he looked through the skin of a many-winding pearl enclosing him and all flames and shadows. He walked through a city where the waves arose, blurring a maze of angles, the waters rising to the door-steps, above the door-steps, so one must know his watermanship here in this watery world and be his steersman through narrow channels or wide seas. He walked with the stilt birds, saw them like ladders reaching into clouds as the old lamp-lighter passed with his pilot flame, heard his footsteps breaking through floods of faded music, heard the whirlings of ghostly skirts upon a lonely shore—but it was all a persistent dream, this vanished life, and nothing was real to Mr. Spitzer with his dark cloak covering his eyes, not even his own consciousness where the dark waves whirled and the stars went out, not even his unconsciousness where no image could be defined so that he endured when he was gone as into another world. Yet where was that world? It was always this star which was that other world, this to which he had come or from which he had never departed, it seemed to Mr. Spitzer with the water rising to his eyes or a black sail shadowing his cheeks, this where he heard the old postman buzzing like a bumble bee

dropping his message from star to star as from the living to the dead or
the dead to the living, dropping those letters which were never written,
never sent, were addressed to no name, signed by no name, and yet
arrived in Cupid's mail box.

Ah, all bee-hive cities were flooded as were the sunken islands of this
earth and coffins of flame enclosing secret stars, bells of silver, bells of
gold in seas of ringing bells, bells of the sea ringing earth, bells ringing
the bell-ringers in lonely towers, crowns of ivory under the waves, crowns
of silver where the waves leaped and roared like lions with golden
wreathed mouths, crowns of gold, many-eyed wings of snow-white
peacocks clashing their windy tails with atonal music in gardens of snow,
gardens under the earth, comets crumbling into fireflies in drowned
gardens and lights on sunken porches and swollen insect lights in sunken
roads, honeycomb lights of skyscrapers bisected by drifting clouds and
snow-crowned, many-headed mountain tops like sleeping kings and
queens and drifting white umbrellas and black umbrellas bellowing like
church bells and the life-sized chessmen who had walked on squares of
black and gold as if this life had been designed by reason and not by
love, dead love, but who now walked through the thin, angelic surf with
snow-breasted seagulls towering, sleeping on their heads where the floods
arose and even the thin lights of the clouded constellations like pin-heads
holding the pin-cushion clouds and a thin thread of starlight drifting
from a needle's eye and the eyes of the drowned birds immense as pools of
starlight ruffled by wind and the cobwebbed, thin lights of the Pleiades
flying like birds, now when icebergs of old dreams were melting, now
when waters covered this earth from pole to hidden pole, this clouded
earth, now when there were only these dim flames burning under the
veiled waters of the dream, for the waters flooded all dead hearts, the
desert places and the castles of dry bones, the black eunuch and the
white, the white eunuch who became the father and the black eunuch
who became the mother of himself swollen like the full moon with many
waters, the moon which was water-logged, the black rooster and the
white, the black coachman in his pearl-lined grave and the lady sleeping
in her coach where the waves of the sea glided over her and places where
no man had ever been, seraglios where was no dreaming shiek and where
great loves were lived without woman or man, and there was scarcely a
visible reef or thinnest bridge of light above the waves, and perhaps there
had never been, for one who escaped his love did not escape his death, his
death which was his love, and one who had resisted the star might not
resist the snowflake, and one who had resisted the strongest lodestone or
magnetic star might be drawn by the weakest as the star might be drawn
by the moth with its feebly pulsing wings or the moon by the wave or Mr.
Spitzer by the image of the dead, dead whom he had never known in life
and whom he would never know in death, dead who were capable of
greater virtuosity than his, dead who were capable of loving, sobbing,
sighing, crying. They cried like the children of the earth. Why was it said
that God created us? We were created by the dragonfly dropping upon its
silken cable line. We were created by the images of the uncreated crea-

tion. We were created by a falling star singing as it fell. We were created by a shadow moving where the shadow increased.

Mr. Spitzer well remembered that once he, like an old shipwreck riding on the storm in this shipwrecked world, his masts broken, his shrouds torn by all the gales through which he had passed and by many mirroring storms which might have been real and by many storms through which he had not passed, had only seemed to pass—so that he was like a phantom, a mere phantom of himself—passing like a shadow blown by wind—and would not have been surprised to see himself in the fog—for he was aged by many moons, moons through which he had not lived—his chimneys crumbling and his forecastle missing and his figure-head drowned and his sides caved in, his many battered stovepipes missing, his hull broken from fore to aft and paying out more water than the seas contained and grown over with such curious barnacles as built the reefs of heaven glimmering through the star-lit rain and draperies of feathery sea moss drifting around him like some old ship marooned in a watery grave, no watchman in his tower and the seaweeds and sea shells upon the brim of his hat as if he, too, had been to Holy Lands and was returning, for none returned from voyages he had taken, and none should live twice the same life or even once this life—and perhaps he had never sailed, had only thought he sailed with the wind blowing through his shrouds and all his larboard lights missing and all his starboard lights broken, perhaps washed up as shattered glass of lamps upon a distant shore where the sheeted glow-worms shone like a secondary firmament as black clouds rolled—by which it might be known that he had gone down—the water flooding all his decks and castles and the water pouring from his hat brim as if he were a living fountain or a man made musical, no lights burning at the port-holes of his eyes, no passenger aboard, no log of stars which would ever tell him the place of his sinking—had met one night with an old sailor reeling in the fog—indeed, as so often happened when Mr. Spitzer was absent-minded or when someone else did not see him or his wavering shadow which provided so great an obstacle, had nearly collided with this wayfarer shadowed on the fog, at least as it seemed now, even though Mr. Spitzer had heard an old foghorn blowing as if to usher in by an auditory illusion the night-mare of this life and whole cities of dubieties like phantoms blown upon the wind, phantoms of leaves, phantoms of stars, suns, moons, phantoms of phantoms—and this old sailor, probably having noticed the outline of Mr. Spitzer's dark cape soughing in the wind or blow-ing inside out so that the blackness was whiteness or mother-of-pearl buttons or half moons gleaming through the heaviness of the curdled fog or phantoms of jewels sparking on his cuffs or fireflies sparking in his eyes as shining pebbles rolled at his feet where the fog lifted in wisps and scarves and cities cried, cried with almost human cries, had told him above the whistle of the singing wind or under the whistle of the singing wind, had told him singing like a singing cricket that his ship had gone down in a great storm far out at sea, the waves as tall as chimneys, that all the others had perished, that only he had survived and was washed up upon this pebbly shore where the glow-worm's furry light was the only light which he might have mistaken for a star crawling along the earth and where was no light gleaming far out at sea, no eye in the flood, no iris of vision—and Mr. Spitzer had said, reeling between the storm and the storm as between his death and his death, between the coming and the departing storm which almost seemed like one long storm and greatest storm when it was calm, between his death which had been and his death which was yet to be, his death which he remembered and his death which he would forget as he would forget even a cricket's chirrup in the winter grass or a spotted bull frog's spotted cry or a whisper under a stone—Congratulations, dear sir. But should I congratulate you, or should you congratulate me? Should we not be condoled, for which of us lives? Should I not rather offer my condolences than my congratulations? I am that man who was always on his way to a wedding and came to a funeral, the funeral of himself and all dead days. I should congratulate you if the long journey were over. Are you the shadow, and am I the light, perhaps only one pale spot of light? Are you the light, Mr. Spitzer asked, and am I the shadow, or are we both the shadows? For the shadow crossed Mr. Spitzer's face and blotted out his eye even as he spoke, and his voice seemed to come from a longer and longer distance. Which of us is in eclipse? Is this the eternal eclipse, or is every eclipse temporal as I dreamed, he asked with a sonorous cry which turned into a whisper, perhaps some time afterward. You drown in your own drowning, burn in your own burning like that one spark which never will go out though under seas of darkness. Or say you survived the storm, dear sir, and are life's castaway—you sink in the calm. Greatest shipwreck is this, Mr. Spitzer had explained, to sink when there is no storm, for no sadder survivor may there be than this, dear sir, whom now you see or whom I see.

For by now he could scarcely see his dove-white hand in the fog, the milky stone upon his finger like a reefed moon or eye, could scarcely see the long-haired star in the glowing water or the drifting canopy clouds with their fringes of golden lights, certainly could not see the face of a stranger who had drifted past him. We both may be mistaken, Mr. Spitzer had whisperingly intoned as the clouds rustled over him, for he was mindful of many instances when he had been wrong, when he had carried on long musical dialogues where there was no one or when his dialogue had degenerated into a monologue which was equally dubious if he himself was gone, if no spindle provided this web of his thought. It is possible that you are not there—I only thought I heard your music, departing music—and I am gone. The fog moved, or I was moved, or I stood still when you moved. It is possible, all too possible that I am not here—neither there nor here. And often I have asked myself, if I am not on this side of life where I am, how shall I be on the other side of the watery abyss where I am not, and how shall I perceive there what was not perceived here? It is possible that we are illusions in the light-streaked fog. Better to have died when all other persons died than to be the one person living on, Mr. Spitzer had explained, perhaps talking only to himself—as sad as to be the one person dying when all others live and prosper and make love. Ah, but the ship of this world has gone down with all the sea birds screaming and the roofs under the waves and all hands lost, and all have gone down in this long night of love which is this death, and none will survive, and not even you will survive, and I will not survive. I died yesterday—or if day before yesterday or day before some other yesterday, what subliminal difference now—or if I die tomorrow? Perhaps by such uncertainties all live who live and all die who die. What calendar keeps the sea of the months flowing into the months, Mr. Spitzer asked, or are there only moments there, or are there only years, or is there only timelessness piling up like the slow pilings of waves of which none has ever seen the surface? Not even from highest pinnacles does one see it. Upon what sundial under the sea are notched these hours of the light which comes through wavering foam and many-shadowed water? I speak through all the waters of this world, for I am drowned, my love.

My love, I have gone down. My love, the cable line is broken, and I have lost my star, star which never was. My love, I have lost my prow. Both fore and aft are gone. I have lost my figurehead who walks upon another shore with her curls of foam streaming in the wind, the starlight in her eyes, but she plows breast-high through waves of moths. She lives, and I am dead. I live, and she is dead. For never could we co-ordinate this life with this death—there was always this discrepancy or an image running between even like the thought of the dead or the fused thought of the living and the dead like the sandpiper in the surf. He is one golden ball of flame. My sail drifts over the waves, Mr. Spitzer had mournfully whispered, perhaps like some old magician whose sail had taken on a life and meaning of its own, for he could not control his thoughts. My face stares through waves of moonlight crossed by the nocturnal butterfly, and never will I see the dawn when the moon closes its eye and the stars go out. When did I see it but in a dream, this mistaken dream of life? What part had I in this creation? I had no part, but to have no part is to have a part. I belched smoke. I burned in my own burning like the star in its own light. I was a chimney. I was a fountain. Your sunlight is my moonlight, for the sunlight comes to me only through the tempera of the moonlight, and I am like a woman enceinte, an eye within an eye. The waves roll at my feet. This surf is like a wing. The next wave will take you as it took this watery world and all the sleepers in their beds locked in the arms of love, ghostly love, dead love who cried, sighed, sobbed, whispered, whispered but a little while, whispered to the silent ear, the unlistening heart, and none shall know himself when the light of dawn streams like a silver river through a cloud, dark cloud, or like a river pouring from the mouth of the heavenly centaur. None shall know the cricket singing. Behold, my hand is a starfish in a grave. I branch into many branches and give the only light, Mr. Spitzer had whispered in the dove-pale greyness of the dove-pale sea ringed by a ring of light, whispered perhaps only to himself or to a sea singing like a sea of crickets, a sea of crickets chirruping. So also sang the cricket stars in glowing chimney clouds.

These were surely more beautiful music than was ever played by a young musician or by an old musician, staggering and blind, plucking his strings with his starfish in the court of a dying emperor or some old queen hidden under her canopy in the pearl-colored light, striking Mr. Spitzer with the sad, weird, wild music of those strings which, warped by the waves of the sea and many winds, were touched but once by the lover as love died, touched but once in life, touched but once in dying, perhaps not even once, touched like a barren woman by love, touched never to sing or sob again to the dead ear, music which should be like all that was solitary in life or death, all that was not mated, all that was unique, lone, never to come again, music which was to be like that love which was never to be repeated or the face of love which was never to be seen again or perhaps was seen not once or that death which was never to be died twice, death to be died but once, once in this life, music which was like the opening or closing of a door, music flowing in two ways at once, music never to be repeated and heard twice though it went on and on when the musician was dead, music never to be heard like the snowflake whispering on the wave, music never to be heard like the waters circling around the hoof of a horse, music never to return when the music was no more, when the silence was complete, for out of the complete silence no music ever grew, and there must be always a thread of music, even a faded thread of music running through silence if music was not to die from shore to shore, music moving when it was not heard, music moving but once in space and perhaps never returning, surely never returning to its point of origin since the point of origin had moved, music crying on all shores, music dying, music ebbing, music returning with such altera-tions that it might seem a different music to another consciousness or the same music, music which was never heard by consciousness, music fading into silence which was heavy with all the music which had ever faded into silence where no music was. This was surely, though he had never intended it, for no one could have intended it, that approximate music which Mr. Spitzer tentatively wrote—and what was sadder as he asked than to be the unwilling composer of the music which could be heard but once, perhaps not even once, perhaps never by him, elegiac music coming when his heart should beat no more like an unsteady hammer hammer-ing in his breast, a golden hammer hammering on glass until the glass should be as soft as a cloud, a cloud dissolving into slow ripples of rain, music coming when music should not pulse through him and silence and be the rhythm of his salt blood? For who composed his thoughts of the music dashing against an old lighthouse far out upon a finger of rock? And why should he hear this music when he was dead if he had not heard it when he was alive? This music wrote itself. It was written by the tide, washed out by the tide. Surely, there was no more difficult music than this for which there were no notes. Why, these notes were like the spots which had flown off some old gambler's cards and circled in the clouds and disappeared, circling never upon themselves, all being blotted out except for one spot, one spot of light or darkness at which Mr. Spitzer stared because it stared at him like the moon staring at the moon where no moon was or ever would be. And yet it seemed he heard this music more than once, heard it twice as he receded or advanced, heard this music of a ghostly world gathering music to itself, and so it frightened him like music washing upon all shores and shore where he was not, music where no music was but his mistaken memory, memory returning not his music but the music of some other consciousness, just as he was frightened by the gossipings of whirling weathercocks in cloudless, windless days, days faintly gleaming as the day star through the sunlight of his dead dreams when the sky was streaked like the iris of some great eye watching him, eye like a jewel where surely there was no eye of his omniscience. For his was but the finest splinter of partial vision lighted by a partial thought as seas of darkness rolled. So that he had learned to distrust himself, and whom could he trust? In whom could he place even one small grain of his faith? Who would not finally disappoint him, perhaps in ways he would never know and could not explain? He had prided himself on his passive exterior, his torpor, his slowness of response, the way a stimulus might travel miles to reach the knowledge of his heart, his latitude and longitude forever changing, that clouded surface so immense that a pin-prick of pain might be translated into pleasure before it reached his ebbing consciousness so slow to withdraw as death into life or night into light—but underneath he knew that he was quite responsive and tremblingly sensitive to many subtleties like quicksilver fading into clouds and celestial nuances not observable by others and quick to take offense—quick to quarrel in spite of his slow ways and his meandering thoughts—and with whom?

He quarreled like some old lover with his love who long ago had died or who perhaps had never been or who was yet to die. He quarreled with old palings the waves washed upon a shore where he had never been or with his shadow or with marauding starfish in an oyster bed or a door slamming in a rain cloud or the night wind blowing over distant reaches or a road not taken or a road many-branching like a chandelier or a sailboat which had gone down—quarreled with turret sea shells racing him upon a lonely shore—quarreled with old phaetons and dead passengers wrapped in their shrouds under the waves and seagulls sleeping like snow on mountain towers—quarreled with pebbles singing, crying in the wind—quarreled with old tree branches breaking into flame as they were lighted by a tinder star which was not there—quarreled with the extinguished stars and sudden flashing of light upon the waves—quarreled with his own heartbeat seemingly beating no more and with the muted colors of the ashen sky almost as pale by day as by night—quarreled with the phoenix burning of this star—quarreled with the groundhog—quarreled with a firefly all day long although it was invisible as the light lost in the light, the invisible firefly seeming as great as the invisible star. Often he could be heard talking to himself. He could be heard scolding a tree toad. He could be heard quarreling with an owl or a firefly under a paling or a crab under a wave. He could be heard quarreling with a burning thorn. Turning his head from side to side, he could be seen stepping through the slow slanting of the rain under almost perpetual clouds patterned like the mackerel's back or piled up into mountainous cumuli where no mountain-climber would ever climb or build his castle perilous lighted with many lights, a few gold wraiths of light of remembered moons upon his mourning cloak or the light breaking at his feet, flashing like a sudden star as he moved his cane with the slow movement of an oar.

How many times he might have spoken to someone who was not there—even to a man who thought he was a praying mantis in the fog, one who reached antennae through infinities of starlight and who if he moved would cause the crumbling of the stars—a praying mantis singing —perhaps when he himself was not there in the starlight-colored fog where he was this shadow or this flame burning, this flame ignited in the midst of rippling water, it seemed in that memory which, though very comprehensive and desirous of omitting nothing, not even one winged sand grain flying to another star or the breaking of a glassy twig in a cloud or the falling of a velvet leaf like the softest footprint never touching the cloud of the ground, not one rain drop with a flame burning within, had omitted so much, perhaps the whole content of mortal life, of certain death, of death which should be the end, his memory being that which receded more than it advanced, that memory which travelled slow as a starfish climbing mountains of snow, mountains moving like waves, that memory which was never accurate but which, as he slowly recognized, might have failed him completely if it had been accurate as that one track of actuality which none had taken as none had experienced the total consciousness of death beyond which there should be no thought or only this fugitive thought—for what should he remember of yesterday, today, tomorrow, all flowing the same for him through countless years like music which knew no objective time, none but the pulsing of his blood as salt as his tears or as a sea of his tears drowning him, the suddenly wild flutter of his heart, and what did he know of this immediacy coming to him like something already distilled through his dead consciousness or through many blurred visions casting mock halos upon the waters and the clouds, starlight filtered through the eyes of the blind before it reached him, music heard by the dead ear when his heart seemingly hammered no more or sounded far away with a faintly drumming sound? Were his two hearts, the living and the living, the living and the dead, how often he had asked of sea shells whispering, confessing to him the seas through which they had passed, the beds in which they had slept and many strange ports of call or lights burning on distant shores, lights never reached, the loves they had loved before consciousness began, the deaths they had died as flotillas of butterflies shadowed his moon-lit face though they had come from some far port?

His was not so great a division, it seemed to him, so great an ambivalence that his should be two hearts and two separate nervous systems increasing his discord though he had sought for harmony, two engines of his despair, two sail-boats, one going, one coming over the rimmed horizon, two trains which passed each other in the night with but a lonely signal whistle like that which went from clouded star to clouded star, two trails of purple smoke with burning eyes, two universes like reefs as thin as threads drifting above the clouds, one forever inexhaustible, one sinking under waves, for his was but one heart, so small a heart that it seemed to be lost under that great weight he carried, lost under folds of endless clouds with their fringes drifting, lost under enormous mountains crowned with light and starred with the almost transparent stars, under desert sands reaching endlessly like a sea, under the plaintive whisper of a wave never reaching the land.

There were years in which he could not hear a door slamming though the wind blew an old door back and forth on rusted hinges like those which hinged him, years in which he could not hear the tinklings of harness bells, could not hear the music trembling like the silent leaf upon the wind, could not hear the laughter of dolphins riding the wake of the silent flood. There were years in which he could not hear his beating heart or the rain falling like the blood of the stars. There were years in which he seemed to live in a world of sleep-walkers, of lip-readers lost in a fog, their faces blotted out so that they could not read the gestures of the heart, the silent heart. He was lost like a firefly in the midst of day, lost like handfuls of fireflies. The greater his orientation, the greater his disorientation seemed, so that the greatest sense of order brought him to the greatest chaos. So how should he find his bearings now? The star was lost no less than a firefly, the glowing ember, the star's heart. He had thought he was sailing toward stars, and he was sailing toward an intermittent firefly, a firefly gleaming low in the fog, a firefly who was the watchman. All of life's light was but this fitful gleaming.

And so, not knowing who he was, he always would insist, he being most mystified of all who were mystified—for even when he was almost sure who he was, the greater certainty brought the greater mystery—he had learned to distrust the most peculiar vivacity of his thoughts as if they had had their origin in someone else and should have faded long ago, wandering impressions for which there was no living counterpart, no image blowing down the dusk, no image of the living or of the dead, music for which there was no listener, love for which there was no response, no mate, night for which there was no light and light for which there was no light, knowing that for him there was no stone which was not a cloud, no cloud which was not a cloud, nothing which he could cling to, no anchorage, no faith, no faith beyond this present life, no death beyond this death, that there was no true friend to whom he could turn and none who might not disappoint him with a sudden falsity, yet though his false friend was true and seldom disappointed him by his failure of falsehood. It seemed that he who had played the role of falsehood so long had made of that role the truth, perhaps that one truth which never would completely fail him—and he who had been true had disappeared so long ago that he was false and treacherous—so this was

Mr. Spitzer's eternal paradox by which he lived and perhaps died—to trust only the false as he would often say, turning and turning his head as he whispered to himself or a shadow rippling in his path.

For why, as he might often ask himself, should he trust the truth which had already failed him if the false would never fail or trust constancy if only inconstancy was constant, almost constant, trust a stone if it crumbled like a cloud? There was no key opening suddenly all doors. He had found that there was no enduring foundation stone to this creation, no stone more substantial than the cloud fringed by light and shadow, the cloud drifting. The fog lying low near earth concealed the firefly and the star. The fog blotted out what the day did not reveal. Dawn was seldom more than another aspect of watery greyness scarcely touched by rays of light, seeming an extension of twilight palpable with all those mysteries which never would be revealed and perhaps had always been concealed from the eyes of man. The fog concealed the barnacle, the rose, the wing, the star, the sun shining pale as the moon behind the cloud, and obliterated the obvious differences between the living and the dead, between the bird and the star, between the star and the tree, between one place and another place, one man and another man, making of every man the inorganic phantom of himself, this spectre speaking to this spectre when the world itself seemed like the repetition of the world and all lost things, those which perhaps had always been lost. And if they had always been lost, could they ever be found—should not Mr. Spitzer rather be lost with them like an old piece of driftwood at the edge of the phantom tide? So he had come to ask himself in days when there was no other voice. The fog made even his voice seem strange as something almost unrecognizable and scarcely remembered by him, voice for which there should be no monument, no tomb, no image, not even the flowing of water. Why should he suppose his musical murmur should remember him when he was gone? He was forgotten now, so should he be remembered then? Perhaps there had never been actuality. Perhaps this world was the spectre of the spectre, the dream of the dream. The bird of the past would never catch up with the bird of the future. There was no mortice work between his future and his past, surely it seemed to him. Who ever again would see him in the haze of the sunlight, see him with this white rose he wore in his buttonhole, this starfish on the surf of his hem, the moonlight in his dead eyes? Who would see him as he had been in life? None would see him. And that was why increasingly, beginning with an initial experience he had forgotten or one which was quite recent but which he had also forgotten, his forgetfulness veiling his forgetfulness, his oblivion hiding behind his oblivion, he placed his precarious faith increasingly in the vision of the blind man groping through the sunlight of his dead days as if it were the fog which had suddenly descended over the city, baffling to all except himself with the fog spirals wreathing his hat, groping through the fog as if it were the sunlight he would never see, not even when the light returned veining the fog with lights of delusive gold, scattering showers of sequins like stars, the deaf man who answered when he could not hear or see in the blinding pall of the fog, could not read the lips or the signs made by the hands, signs of passage, traffic, yesterday, tomorrow, the way backward or the way forward in the timeless world of the deaf, that in which there was no sound reaching the ear, perhaps not even the memory of sound. Perhaps the golden hammer, the silver hammer had never knocked upon the door of the ear. Perhaps the deaf had never heard or had forgotten sound soft as a moth's wing beating upon a cloud, soft as a whisper never heard.

Perhaps they heard by reverberations, or perhaps some heard only imaginary sounds, such sounds as one might hear in sleeping, such sounds as Mr. Spitzer heard when he heard not. The waking lives of the deaf were like the life he led in his unwakeful dream.

They knew not time, this human abstraction, this division of time into compartments or sub-compartments of yesterday, today, tomorrow, hour, minute, second. They knew no more of time than a sea shell knows of a town clock, particularly when the dial numbers are faded and the bells are broken. They knew but the level or uneven plain of space winding through opal clouds, clouds like great obstacles, the clouds never lifting for the deaf, for they could see but through a refracting medium, and they were partially blind like all men. The deaf heard not, or they heard with their eyes. The deaf dreamed of reading the lips of many-mouthed gargoyles from which the waters fell. They walked through blurred space as if it were time, time of which they dreamed, dreamed these warpings of old tree branches making signs upon a lonely road, signs to them, dreamed these waves which sobbed, sobbed like the silent musician through silence, dreamed these footprints of birds which had already gone, the silent language of the hieroglyphic stars speaking their mysteries of flight, return. Their signs were the signs of this moment, this moment only, and it was fleeting like the gesture of the body, the hand waving farewell. Their heaven was a great circle their hands described, and their earth was a small circle, and their God was a plummet line dropping from heaven to earth. Their yesterday was a pointing backward over the shoulder, and this was also the sign for death. This was also the sign for that which was gone. But who was gone, as Mr. Spitzer often asked—what did the sign mean? It might mean that a bird had flown, perhaps that a pearl-mantled tern had departed from a fog-shrouded rock where he had thought there was a lighthouse. It might mean that a train had departed with never a whistle cutting the fog and never a head light like a pilot star. It might mean that a comet had passed. It might mean that all our yesterdays were dead. Perhaps someone had died. Perhaps it was a beautiful lady veiled by the fog, perhaps an old crone bent to earth. Perhaps it was a man or a child. Perhaps it was always a child who died. Each sign had many and indeterminate meanings, some which might never be translated into speech or sound. There was no time but going through space, moving forward, backward, the hand winging like a bird through the air or fluttering like a fish through a wave, forever darkening wave as Mr. Spitzer thought.

So no wonder if he trusted all persons who had lost a sense or the five senses or the six senses or all their senses and one more than there had ever been or the blurred drum of all their senses, trusted all those persons who had died or had departed, for they were nearest to him who had lost so much, had doubtless lost far more than he had gained. He trusted those who had lost their conch ears, their jellyfish eyes, their clouded skins, those for whom the body had already failed. They drew him nearest to the city. His loves were the blind train conductor, the blind signalman signalling to the blind man, the deaf musician, the deaf conductor of the mute orchestra, the blind portrait painter or he who painted portraits only in water changing its conformation as he painted, perhaps when a bird flew over head, the blind lighthouse keeper with his light shining both by day and by night, seeming a sunken star, star and its ripple, the crippled dancer dancing in the wind, the mute swan singing not even when it died, all who were disparaged and despised. By them he was magnetized. He was drawn even more toward those who had forgotten their origins or their identities or who perhaps had never known who they were or who lived only by their untenable dreams, all those who were dispossessed and wandering through the storm of years as he was. They drew him nearest to the city.

They were all his loves because he could not love or could love only by indirection, a long road, all his life because he could not live, not even should he live twice, not even should his be two lives, a long road and a short, all his deaths because he could not die, he being this fusion of all, or so it seemed to him in endless nights as his cheeks quivered, as his eyes glittered, as he felt the blood stream through his many-branching veins. He was dead, surely, and yet he lived. He lived, and he was dead, dead even to his own memory of remote or recent events. Scarcely could he remember yesterday. He had returned. He had never departed. He had always been in the midst of the traffic flow. He had always been at the busiest artery. He had always been where the streets crossed, or he had been in a long avenue where there was no crossing. The winds turned to candle flames as they whistled past him. He trusted all persons suffering some fatal defect, all who were blind as he was, yet saw, perhaps only by their own light as the firefly saw, as the star saw, all who were deaf as he was, yet heard the beating of the silent heart. He trusted the halo where there was no vision. He trusted the blind guide and that ear which heard only its own roaring. He trusted the sea shell when there was no other voice but this like the whisper of his dead soul. Buoys in lonely harbors played Mozart for him or played the uncreated works of some greater composer, one who was lost, one whom the world had not recognized though his music was that swelling the sails of the beached boats, slamming doors, blowing the flame leaves in gutters through all eternity.

What cenotaph was there for him, what empty tomb erected in honor of a person who was buried elsewhere, perhaps in a distant country, perhaps in a country he had never visited? Perhaps it was a country visited by no man, no woman. He trusted his false friend who was true, true as the city with its ding and dong and many thronging temple bells and sudden throngs of traffic crossing silver streams, sounds like buzzing bees, city with its head turbaned by many-winding mother-of-pearl clouds and its many doors and many windows or squares of light and dark and many shafts of light streaming between tall towers and shoulders of stone or snow, great jewels flashing through clouds, streets, roads, bridges, shadows of shadows, shadows of many umbrellas moving through the soughing of the rain or the fine slant of the rain, city of many-mouthed gargoyles, city of many cul-de-sacs and streets leading nowhere and crumbling abysses beyond which there should dwell only the stars not colonized by him, perhaps as small as pin-points shining through the clouds, perhaps as small as his buttons and cuff links, city of many lace balconies, fire hydrants, lamp-posts, chimney pots, city where sometimes Mr. Spitzer walked in the midst of the thickening traffic in the thickness of the clouds amazed by rustles of sound whispering through him like all dead souls returning, sounds like the flight of passenger pigeons streaming in undulations like waves upon the wind when the moon was like a passenger pigeon's eye shining through the dense medium of a cloud and the porphyry clouds were traced with only the memory of gold, thinning gold. The clouds were striated with lines of gold like some great sea shell or dome under which he walked, perhaps like the shell of some great egg, cracking shell, a rainy light splashing before his eyes as the wind whispered, blowing through him, blowing through many echo chambers and distant clouds. The powder of fading gold fell upon his eyelids. Some clouds broke not. The wind whispered, honked, whistled, sighed.

He heard the rustles of light beams, their music seldom human ears had heard in its entirety or even its approximate entirety. He heard the whistles of stars at either pole and a door opening so softly that he only seemed to hear. There were whispers lost in a long roar. A light went out so softly that he only seemed to see. He could not be sure when the light went out. Perhaps he heard it, did not see it. How often, his mind abstracted by many problems, surely by many which were not his own, by many which he had assumed as if they were a mantle of his being when he had no being, nothing to hide, no being to conceal, he found that he had wandered far off his orbit or his accustomed route, perhaps following that one instinct which had not died when all else died, following that unknown instinct, whatever it was, wherever it was, sometimes disappearing for years and then appearing again like the most feeble flame, that he was walking through the rain of the city where the rain of the city drummed upon the dark or golden porches and roofs, roofs over roofs, roofs supported by no foundations or pillars, the rain falling in cascades with mists rising from the pools, the rain falling on many-branched golden chandeliers moving through dim streets of the piled-up fog, crowns of hats and hat brims and surrey tops and umbrella tops whirling with rain drops like planetary music giving off showers of sparks no astronomer had charted as they were adventitious like all beauties and many twilight zones and webbed lights and reflections of lamps where there were no lamps and skylights like chinks in igneous clouds and the bald dome mirroring the drifts of the clouds and streamers of light, perhaps with one patch of opalescence, one square of mother-of-pearl shining through clouds, walking through seas of darkness or light, light which trembled where he stepped pigeon-toed upon the rain-splashed walks under the rain-splashed stars or the stars blotted out by the rain and the clouds and the cloud-bursts flashing like stars, a fat man stepping softly as if he were not sure of terra firma, waddling and pouter-breasted and almost breathless, almost breathless because of an unaccustomed effort of steering himself or being steered by wind, his soft hand trembling as he tapped with his cane, his cane tapping upon the stone which might be the cloud, his cane tapping almost in spite of him as the wind blew through old porches and towers and many avenues, turning his head from side to side, whispering with gentle murmurs almost none could hear, walking with crowds, crowds which seemed sometimes oblivious to him as he was perhaps sometimes oblivious to them. For never yet had his oblivion met with their oblivion—much as if a loving pair, separated by years, perhaps by some great quarrel, should try to forget each other and the death of love—and should succeed only by one forgetting when the other remembered, one remembering when the other forgot, both never forgetting at the same time—for then, or so it seemed to Mr. Spitzer with the music of the lost spheres trembling through him like organ music, both would be dead. Perhaps it would be by mutual agreement. Each would know when the other ceased. No messenger needed ever cross from one to the other. Or it might be that one would not know. Perhaps time healed all wounds, or perhaps there was no time. Perhaps there was no time in that realm of love which having died could never die. It seemed as if when love lived, it died—but having died, it lived and could not die—at least according to Mr. Spitzer's somewhat obtuse vision, for he had seen the other side of the tapestry, and this was the most he could say as to the immortality of love.

His eyes blinked when he saw an unaccustomed light. His cheeks turned purple as he heard the thumping, thumping, thumping of his heart, dead heart, dead heart in the city. It seemed as if the remnant rain was ever where he was, the rain drops whirring where he walked like a living windmill. The rain drops scattered from his hat brim. The rain drops rolled off his back. The rain drops glistened on his rain shawl feathered with shadows, its glittering fringes like flames reflected in pools. He heard the shoutings of voices, sudden screams when the traffic whistles were amplified to fill the clouds with roarings or when the traffic signals changed, seeming to him like wings. Perhaps he walked with the stream of the traffic, perhaps against it in the falling of the rain, the rain falling sometimes upward, splashing with golden drops to reach the falling stars, the stars falling like rain with its mist. Perhaps the stars fell upward. Perhaps they fell like golden apples toward the moon. Perhaps the moon fell in shards. Perhaps the heavens were reversed. He did not know. He argued with a traffic policeman for hours before he discovered that the traffic policeman was wooden. He fluttered where the church bells rang, ringing between the hours as if they were the hours, for every minute was the end of someone's hour or year. And who could compute these statistics?

He was caught among the bellropes, the billowing shrouds. He walked over great stone eyes of sleepers walking through mist and drizzle and thinning fog. He perched upon the ledges of great stone mouths. He slept upon stone shoulders or upon the wings of an angel, perhaps an angel in undulatory flight. Perhaps an angel ferried him with pigeons through the clouds. Perhaps he rode upon some great pendulum swinging through windy heavens, pendulum where the pigeons rode, or so he dreamed, dreamed that he rode upon the hour hand, rode upon the minute hand although there was no hour, no minute, for time had passed long ago, and this was not time which was passing. Perhaps he crossed the face of some old town clock or sundial mistaking him for twilight. The sundial knew no time but the shadow, and many a lovers' tryst had been lost. No one could run a train by the hour of the sundial or root the ponies home. He rode upon the masts of ships, some which had already gone down. He perched upon a great stone helmet. Surely, he cooed and whispered among the pigeons all day long. Their wings were the color of the sea streaked with a dying flame. Sometimes the sea seemed like one great pigeon caught in a moony light. Pigeon wings went out over the city like tides through clouds, sometimes with long roarings and sometimes with a muted sound scarcely to be remembered as the many colors of their wings faded into the trembling clouds losing their colors like sea shells upon the shore or like the city with its trembling lights. The shadows of their wings had left purple blotches upon his face, the fireflies shining through his skin, making a night of day so that he seemed to himself to be the blurring of all who were lost, all lost souls, all lost heavens of the firefly stars, and did not know who he was as he always would lament, sometimes with so soft a rainy murmur that he could not hear, and yet why should he know if all were lost, if there was one who was not lost, and should he not rather mourn for him who was found with the fireflies shining through his eyes? His own flame must surely long ago have gone out. He had burned in the midst of water. He walked through the webbed sunlight of dead days, the sun shining pale as the moon beyond the cloud. He was always walking in public parks. He was a habitue of park benches. He was a lover of fountains. He talked only to strangers. People said that he was a public nuisance, and doubtless they would have liked to have seen his light put out, not glimmering like this lost moon by day, not shining in his path when it shone in theirs. They scarcely looked at him twice or at his watery gleam as of one star shining where there were no stars or his broken gleam like two stars upon the waves. Perhaps he did not look at them or saw them only as shadows moving through fogs scarcely rayed with light. Perhaps he stared through a pigeon's clouded eye.

He was this old fan-tail fanning his tail, whirring in the music of the lingering rain or the rain starting again, each rain drop burning with opalescence, he with his pigeon murmurs, heart murmurs murmuring through him and clouded heavens, his fluted silver and gold and oily green and blue and rose streaking the waters and the clouds and the sky burning with many colors like stained glass windows or the pigeon's wing, the pigeon's neck sunset trembling in pearl-colored clouds so that he asked when there was no one else to hear him—then where was he if he should see a rainbow never seen before or should see, long years after this was possible, a pigeon, a pigeon in the rain, perhaps a passenger pigeon such as never seen now on earth, its neck as tall as a church steeple as church bells gonged, gonged with the memory of all the dead, its white breast quivering like a cloud with many hearts, and was he dead, or did he live where these wings fluttered? Was it this world or another world or this world as it once was, and was a firefly his architect? The firefly lighted its light before the world began, so should the firefly turn out its light after the world ended? He was walking through the rain, perhaps with all dead souls, all dead souls returning, perhaps where time was blotted out with all its tenses, future and present and past and conditional future, conditional past, all things which were and had been and were to be—all like passenger pigeons passing, blotting out the sun, blotting out the moon as if they were a sea of clouds under them, over them. He heard their wings over him. And how should he define himself or know his limits? His tears fell, splashing upon the sidewalks. His tears drummed upon black umbrellas raising like swords, like other birds of passage.

Many hurricanes were known to him though doubtless not known to watchers of weather, those who kept record of cloud conformations, burstings of floodgates, rising floods, floods pounding over sea walls, tonnages of waves like tons of rose petals dropping on lonely shores, changes of the wind, antique rain drops.

Sometimes his head ached—black spots dancing before his eyes as if the spots had flown off the cards—all spades, no doubt, and no hearts—all clubs and no diamonds—or spades, hearts, clubs, diamonds, all spots but one spot of which he could not see the outlines as the shadow increased, whirling in his path. He was crazy as a pigeon playing poker. And how should he, an old musician who had never known card spots and not even candle flames and nothing which was voiceless, who had known only the spots of his music flying everywhere and so seldom settling on him, perching for a moment like birds on windy branches, enjoy or be perplexed by these card memories as if he were an old card player or think that the sun was a spot on a card or that the moon was a spot on a card he played by a firefly's light, perhaps that one spot of light beaming on his face? His brother could never have accepted an ineluctable reality such as Mr. Spitzer feared. His brother had thought that there was something he could do to change things, to make for greater hope or greater hopelessness. It was that hopelessness which Mr. Spitzer felt, that by which he lived though so feeble that he knew he was expiring. Who, he might often ask with whispers seldom heard, had shuffled these cards in reality, placed his days and nights in sequences other than they were so that his moon shone only when others saw the sun, and the moon shone through all his days? Who had made of him this juggler trying to keep up two worlds? Or was there no other way, no way but this, and did he only dream some other way, imagine that the approximate life he had not lived was real while this was unreal, that in some other life he might have met and known and recognized his love so like himself that his love might have recognized him, there being scarcely a moment of discrepancy between them? They were born together. He envied the moth who settled upon the flower—the settled moth, the sailing moth or great water flower. He envied all things conjoining or even the illusion of conjoining as when he saw his image sailing over water. Sometimes he felt as if his whole life had been led by a false hypothesis, so when should he be true, true as his dead brother was? Or was it only Mr. Spitzer who was true, and had he taken his brother's place, and did his brother live? The answer to his question would have signified little or nothing, not altering his experience in the least degree or doing so in ways which were unrecognizable, for he did not know which brother he was, and this was the crux of his mystery. Perhaps the mystery would never be revealed. Was it Mr. Spitzer who was dead, perhaps living only by that dream which moved and stirred through a dead man's thoughts? He did not know. Perhaps he had never known. If he could say, he would know that he was speaking the opposite of truth the moment he heard the words or even the ripple of water or the wind sighing through the sails of a boat. Perhaps mute gestures should have told him more than music told.

Perhaps he was one, and perhaps he was the other, or perhaps he was the third who was the shuttle dream dreaming through him, moving, fading. His small presentiments made him shake with a vast fear, the effects being always greater than the unknown cause, the effects growing incalculably like the horizon he pursued. He staggered through the windless days as if he heard the singing wind. He reeled from side to side, back and forth, lost a mile when he gained two miles and when he went only one mile lost a mile as if he had not moved or had moved only an inch, an inestimable inch forward or backward, or lost two miles, and thus his progress was very slow, slow as the rasping of his breathing upon his vocal cords, and sometimes though he travelled straight forward he found that he had described a circle or many circles or semicircles, many orbs, and sometimes it seemed as if he could walk only a wavering surf-line, the foam of the starlight upon his face, and sometimes it seemed as if, returning upon himself as a bee in the planetary girdle buzzed like his consciousness, he saw all things twice, even those which he had not noticed or which he had forgotten, even those which had not been visible to him in his first journey. Perhaps his was always the second journey. Perhaps there had never been a first, even the first being elegiac with awakening memories, forgotten thoughts like the last. Starfish raced with him. Even when racing with a sea shell slow and torpid as he was, he came in second, never first in this great steeplechase where, as he would always say, the turf meets the surf. Sandpipers ran before him. He raced with an old carousel horse running loose in a rain-swept garden. He raced with an old sulky driver, the fringes of his sulky burning like blowing flames before his skull face as he passed him twice upon a winding road or a road going forever straight forward. His head roaring with old dreams, his eyes blurred by singing winds, the winds singing through him, sometimes he felt as if he had been hit by a many-branched chandelier swinging through a wide arc of the heavens, swinging with all its lights lighting this dead world and this dead face, it seeming to him that though in the wide reaches of space there had been no other obstacle, yet it had collided with him who could not move unless he brushed against a firefly or a moth or a star or a rose, all images passing as if with him, through him.

It seemed as if all his problems were doubled by his doubts, his creative doubts, mirrored doubts accompanying him in lonely ways or even through vast crowds—and never was he so lonely as in those crowds which knew him not or thought he was not there looming like some great obstacle—for they passed through him as through a cloud—and yet did he not think, feel, dream, ponder, weigh, consider, question, reply, and did he not feel dim whirlwinds sometimes stirring through him and perhaps greater hurricanes than man had ever known singing through him as the wind blew the stars out of their way, and did not his many-chambered heart roar with the memory of a sea of unknown origin, and did not his great arteries branching like tree branches carry his quicksilver blood into many veins branching into capillaries thin as threads or hairs of starlight, his fingertips stinging as with sea nettles, and was he not the living lighthouse at that one moment when he saw his light, moment when he was dying, and were not his lights burning in all his cells or almost all, even those previously darkened, burning perhaps by reflection like that star which had already gone out and yet shone on, and did not he see his light as he saw the darkness like a shadow passing over the crumbling moon, the moon diminishing to a thread or a spot, the darkness increasing as the skies were divided into day and night and pole and pole, the upper empyrean, the lower empyrean, the darkness sweeping like surf until there was perhaps only one ray of light, his own light shining, shining from him, and did not he see between the darkness and the darkness his cheek flushed red with his blood, his rose lip pendulous in the rain, his sparkling eye staring at him through the darkness lighted by one wandering flame or the fog enclosing him and winding around him like some great wall of mother-of-pearl or Venus shell? So did the child return to his mother. Was he rising from the sea, or was he sinking? Scarcely a light shone, and even that might be only the memory of light or light filtered through another consciousness, perhaps of one long dead. All objects seemed to double in this pervasive fog so that he scarcely knew which was the tree and which was the shadow, which was the city and which was the shadow, which was the man and which was the bird, it seeming as if his confusions had added another dimension to his life, his death—and how often he had nearly collided with himself though this would seem impossible. It would seem impossible that self should meet with self in the wide reaches of space, all of space winding between them, perhaps all of time or perhaps but one feeble moment, a sigh, a cry, a whisper fading over the waters of the dream. These waters reflected all images, all which were passing, all which were not previously visible, but did they keep none, or were the reflections real? Were only the unreal things real and the mirrored prow of the boat more real than the boat? So he must often have thought, trying to set sail upon a reflection, trying to board the shadow of the boat upon the waters although perhaps it was his reflection who did so and passed into the mirrored port lights. The shadow of his cape moved over the mirrored stars, the stars upon the warped waves. And how many blows there were which were not felt, winds not noticed by him, hammerings, cryings scarcely realized, whistlings in distance, his torpor seeming to increase, his sensitivity having never yet approximated all his thoughts which seemed like that calm which was greater than the storm no matter how great the storm was and even if it should seem to have no periphery or rim. If even the ragged remnant of a storm should cause a bird to fall fluttering from the heavens, that storm was great enough. Perhaps each storm had many centers. Sometimes he dreamed, of course, that he was not one but two or two so intricately involved that they were one or almost one so that his fate was another's fate, he being bound to another throughout eternity and by such intricate weavings and inner weavings that he would scarcely know which one he was. He was almost like that weaver who had spun out, had woven himself into his tapestry, weaving his body threads of silver and gold, visible and invisible threads, and then was amazed to find himself in another landscape—though doubtless he flattered himself if he thought he was the weaver of his dreams, illusions, presentiments, eyes staring through clouds when his eyes were void.

CHAPTER 50

❧

EVERYTHING seemed off key and out of course, how often Mr. Spitzer had lamented as the wind whirred around his cape, this universe tacking like the wild white snow bird away from central fires of jewels gleaming through clouds and relationships which were never to be found, never to be found by the snow bird or if found were never to be proved and codified and made certain as a map to the traveller who was yet to come, for they were forever shifting, veering in that wind which came from no known source, sleeping upon the wing or drifting like a slow curve of zodiacs where the snowflakes whirled big as cartwheels through which the moon shone or drifting like the long-looping sail of the boat which was never anchored to unanchored earth, and if he would orient himself as he approached the final chaos of oblivion or as it approached him upon silent footsteps moving through the fogs and cloud-lines like the surf upon some other star, he must find his way by present disorientations through vanished multiplicities of mirrors which had never lost their image as they drifted through the fog and vanished moons in all their phases from nymph to full moon and phases between their phases like the moons where no moons were and phases never noticed before and never quite asserting themselves and locked moons with tangled horns and vanished stars who had followed an old bellwether to his grave in this abyss of tinsel stars and those which were the trembling mirages piling up like mountainous waves of the sea or like snow-crowned pinnacles under low clouds or like castles upon the rocks with their light pricking through clouds, castles disappearing when the clouds disappeared, it seemed to Mr. Spitzer with all images doubling before his eyes so that when he entered clouded rooms, one room so like the other that they might be always the same room with only those discrepancies which might be noted, perhaps the fact that he was not himself, that he had changed imperceptibly from point to point, perhaps the fact that he had not changed and was ever the same man, the same in his end as in his beginning, perhaps that a candle flame had gone out or had been lighted in his absence, perhaps that there was a rose withering in a vase where there had been no rose before or a chair out of place or one door more than there had ever been or prisms breaking mirrors which should have looked upon eternity if they had not looked on time, he was often at a loss when he saw two golden chairs in the clouds to know in which chair to sit, for one chair might be only the dream, and one might be real, and one might collapse if he touched it. One might suddenly fly away with many tinkling bells. One might disappear like the Water Carrier or Cassiopeia's Golden Chair or the Crib or the Virgin or the Hair of Berenice in the clouds at dawn. One might be only the shadowed part of life. He dared not touch upon the strings of the constellation Lyre for fear he might touch only upon the imaginary strings, might be only the imaginary bird caught among the strings and causing these musical drops, splashings, whirlpools extending to a far horizon. Oh, could God be so cruel, unkind, thoughtless, forgetful as to make of man a lyre without strings, a trumpet without a throat, a piano without a keyboard, or dice without markings? Or was there only the dream, and had nothing ever been real?

Was there a doctor without patients, one so ultimately successful or such a great failure that he had no patients, not even himself, and could there be a lawyer without a brief, a dog without a bark? How careful of nature this fat man was, lightly stepping, seeming to himself sometimes entirely made of waters and clouds, things which had not yet taken shape or form or which had already dissolved like snowflakes on a summer's day streaked with fire. He knew he might dissolve into mists and clouds. Should a demoniac butterfly appear in the midst of the furnace fire when he was gone? Should there be a sign of him who had made no sign when he was alive? His breath was his spirit, and softly he breathed, never with rasping, and softly he sighed, whispered. He was frightened of loud noises. He was frightened of causing disturbances. What if his breath should start an avalanche or a waterfall? One might not be, and he had gained much amorphous flesh clouded like the atmosphere. He must pause for a moment before each door before he knocked, be sure it did not open on the void, be sure that he was himself and not the hallucination—was thus a man continually checking, rechecking, altering his impressions which altered of themselves, making little notes to mark his journeys back and forth and his many experiments, and because he took so much for granted, it might seem that he took nothing for granted. Because of great faith in this which was his after-life, his life after death, this which he was living now—for when had he lived before his death?—it might seem that he had little faith, that he lived but for a moment when there might be a sudden, sporadic glitter in the fog or that he lived by that dream which might be this extension beyond his death, dream dreamed by another dreamer. Caution was thus his only musical note. None so wild as he who was smiling when he sighed, who loved when he loved not, when he was incapable of love or commitment to any human form, his wildness exceeding his caution perhaps by only one shade, his marble-colored eyes staring at the faces of the dead.

Perhaps among dreamers he was the one person who dreamed not, the one person who knew the void of reality as it is given without dreams or substances or material conformations or roads or bridges between the islands of consciousness rising through the floods of unconsciousness—was one who had never lived by dreams himself and so must live by the dreams of others, die by the dreams of others. So all dreamers and all dreams were secondary to him, much like associations starting associations far, far away as in some other sphere. From whom had he learned? It might be assumed naturally, since he spent most time with her, since seldom did he miss a visit punctually by his broken watch or by the shadow on a moondial in a flooded garden, that he had learned most from the beautiful opium lady wearing her tower of hats as she chattered madly to him who was seated in a golden chair which creaked among the shadows where the whirlpools formed, chattering perhaps to him when he had already gone, when never again would he leave his calling card where the calling cards were piled up as if he had come many times when he had not come, as if he had come with the sails of schooners which had rounded the Golden Horn to reach her bedside, as if he had come with the octagons and the orbs of vanished moons—but it was not from her that he had learned that this sensorium fails, not from any calendar she kept that he had learned the date of his death when blackbirds whistled in a distant road or night suddenly descended like his cape blowing before his eyes or she saw the human-sized blackbird at the door and said—Oh, come in, blackbird. Come in, Blackamoor. Dear, dear, dear, dear, oh, my dear, my dear, my dearest love. To her he might always return, body and soul and spirit crying in the wind, for she waited for him as for his dead self whom she had loved or thought she loved, and she had always lived by such indirections and evasions that she would never know when he was gone or that she had entertained, among her evening guests, this living man whose heart perhaps had failed or still might fail. If it failed, he surely would come tomorrow evening as before with singing flames and whirling pools and constellations of fireflies, his heart trembling in his cheek, for his was this migratory heart—had he not already shown in ways to her satisfaction if not to convince himself?—or after this life was over, he might meet her on some other star—perhaps the first way-station after this, perhaps before one changed for that great central station where all loves and all stars would be one, one star forever reaching. Thus Mr. Spitzer seemed to agree that when life was over, it would begin for him, perhaps upon that star where the living love was united with the dead love and where there were no opposites, no differences, no differentiations, for why admit that nothing more could happen, that he could do nothing, that there was no way-station beyond this station and no other star but this which was fugitive and all but unrealized and unrealizable, so often blotted out by the heavy rollings of fogs and the changes in the winds, that he was this star derailed like some old train in the grass with the long grass growing up over his eyes and perhaps no rails and perhaps no wheels and no passengers, no engine, no spark? He was the nowhere train going nowhere as he heard a distant whistle. He had seen how one may be two or one may be many, many even in his dying, but what he feared most was doubtless not that one should be two—he feared that one should be one, both the dream and the reality, that one should not outlive the other, that they should be so involved that there was no division and no other road and no distance and no abyss of stars roaring between them or passing in one long blur like station lights, and thus one died as one, died with his unuttered thoughts and his unrealized loves and his unfinished business, his hope without foundation stone, died wholly who had lived partially, who had lived not as the star but as the day's firefly lost in the sunlight streaked with the dead iris.

No—not from the invalid lady flourishing on the enchantment of nightshade had he learned most as it might seem, for she had lived so totally by imagination that she had made nights of all her days but never had made days of her days and never had asked for proofs which could not be given by him or her, had lived by disassociations and mistakes of senses and sunken impressions and imaginary dawns streaking the cockscomb clouds, had heard a golden rooster crowing whenever a key turned in a rusted lock or clocks ding-donged the dissident hours or bees sang bright hosannas in the winter air darkening with clouds of blue gentians at many levels although her dawn might be only the tail feathers of a day already gone or might be only a sequin shining in a darkened mirror or this dead eye which stared at her, had kept no chart of time's dimensions or of the shadow growing on her cheek, had known no age or death, and had failed to distinguish between life and death or had taken one as the aspect of the other, had taken this life as death and death as life or had slept from death to death, had slept through silent whirlpools and storms tearing the heavens apart from pole to pole or breaking mirrors into these pale fragments of themselves pulverized like the dead stars, ground to an almost illimitable dust, and who could ever have foreseen that he might outlive her who mourned for him, might live to mourn for her as for himself, most especially as it seemed that she had outlived him and his image upon another shore? And if this image died upon this shore, then would not the other also die, perhaps only a moment later, so that only within the frame of this mortality could he know immortality or one more dubious moment, he not outliving himself although she might dream otherwise and make her plans to meet him on some other shore and although he might even encourage her hallucinations and seem to give to them the semblance of the body? Perhaps he did so in ways he did not intend. It was not all a matter of his will and consciousness. For he was contained by his skin, his many-colored skin patched with the silver and gold of a dying light. Beyond himself he would not live. His brother, too, would not live—and what of all other images—the lighthouse dolphin flashing its dying colors upon the rocks and the clouds in that trembling sunset never to be followed by the dawn, the slow wash of waves, phantasmal mountain peaks like sails of argosies going down, the ripples dying into distances, and even the moon like the paper nautilus and the sun and the stars, all things passing as Mr. Spitzer passed with his sighing, sobbing, all passing with him who was already of the silence? Could yesterday be restored, and who had ever known it in its entirety, the whispers lost under the silence, the voices not noticed then? Whatever he might feel, he must feel now—and whatever he might see, must see now with his conch ears each hearing a different music, a mote which struck upon him as if one mote of the sun should endure through the heart of night or shine through moonlight—must hear the musical landscape, must hear the musical landscape unfolding into hills and valleys and moving pinnacles crowned with snow with his eye, dead eye, bright eye, answer, sob, reproach, come with his muted sighing and his stopped heart—for life had its end, how well he knew, knew who had perhaps already passed its end and who lived but for that moment in which he recognized this unequivocal truth, that he should be no more on either shore. There was no harbor, bay, inlet which should not be touched upon by this death, none which should be secure, no stream of swift current or slow, no watershed, no waterfall flashing through clouds, falling from cloud to cloud like a stairway, not even a brook with thinning pebbles which clashed like cymbals in this thin music of water, worn thin by attrition, no hole where a starfish slept or butterfly was sequestered like this mourning cloak, not even the bed of a dried-up stream from which this music of water had departed showing the bare bones although the pebbles clashed and rolled as if with the memory of water. There was no other star. There was no garden where the white peacocks screamed in a snow storm on any other star than this, so far as Mr. Spitzer knew. As senses failed—one by one if not suddenly—if not at one blow—would he not fail, slumber, never awaken, sleep the last sleep, die the last death possible to him or perhaps the first? Perhaps the first was the last, he knew now with his eyelids shadowing his cheeks and his eyelashes streaking the clouds like these thin rays of gold which came from the light no doubt shining within. There was only this moment heavily weighted with his dead self, that old cargo which had been too great for the boat, leaking boat, the water flowing through all its port-holes. There was no twin star to this, moment for moment, leaf falling for leaf falling, sand grain for sand grain blowing in the wind, balance for balance, number for number, shining for shining, shadow for shadow, ebbing of tide for ebbing of tide, or star where the ebbing of the tide to the thinnest trickle of foam should be the rising of this tide, or star where this tide ebbing should be followed by the tide rising. They were one and yet were never known, being as mysterious as if they were the many.

One might think that this star had never been organic with its threads wrapped around a spindle which shuttled among the singing strings and wove this garment which was itself and the star like the long-haired medusa under the water and the bird, the petals of the rose, the arcades of the roofless porch, the crumbling columns, the wind among the leaves, the doors opening, the doors closing, the door of truth which was covered with a golden disc and was never opened by man. Perhaps it was never opened by woman or bird. Perhaps it was the keyhole star, and no eye stared on either side, and no key had ever turned. Surely there were lagoons never visited by man. Surely there were no two stars shadowed alike by the ambient surrey top with its fringes drifting in the blue midnight air, and perhaps the poles themselves had flown, and he only dreamed this polar night where all things were kept, only dreamed returning stars.

To him, indeed, if not to my mother sleeping upon her lace pillow, this life was the only one, fugitive and unrealized, scarcely understood before it was gone, a glitter only in memory, a light already extinguished, and thus his caution had increased with the years, just as many assumptions once taken for certain had become uncertain, and many premises had been abandoned, and many changes prepared for greater changes, for by many small changes he saw what greater change would be, and many confusions prepared for greater confusions, and he knew that even the longest life, the life of a star noted for its longevity or an empire enduring a thousand years, was brief as a snowflake melting in the burning air, and even a polar night must have its end when fireflies slumber like the swarming stars never to be picked out by the astronomer's clouded glass, stars never to be seen by the blind astronomer when he turned his dreaming telescope toward the empty heavens. Or perhaps he confused the star with the firefly planetoid shifting, glittering, never to be seen in those heavens opening like a lidless box, never to be seen like a pilot light gleaming upon the undiscovered shores of waters and clouds and not even on Mr. Spitzer's clouded shirt front, never to be recorded on any map at some far borderline where reality should cease, for a flying sand grain might grow to be a star even as had that sand grain which flew into Mr. Spitzer's eye and begot this pearl with the light burning within.

Yet this life was brief, especially when viewed in retrospect. It was a moment's fading luminosity, Mr. Spitzer had lived long enough to know now as he approached his end, his end which had perhaps transpired at the beginning, as he always would lament, his voice so small that it was lost in the wind, the amplifying wind. To know this fact so awesome that it almost stopped his breath, that it almost strangled him or caused his heart to gong and his chalk-white face to flush with the rose of his blood like the rose upon the veined clouds or on the waters spotted with the moon's dying gold, his eye to burn—to know that all that happened happened only once—perhaps not even once as the waters rushed at his feet—to know that the long voyage was over before it began or that he had voyaged by standing still, for there was neither starboard nor larboard—what pathos, power, and beauty this gave to fleeting life, life never returning to its origin, life which gonged its own dirges like the wind blowing through his shrouds or lifting folded wings—life which had been like discord in a silent room, like silent thunder, like seagulls playing grand pianos in a silent flood—to know that never twice, perhaps not even once could one pass the barrier reefs of heaven, passing through clouds and channels of overhanging rocks to these thinning shoals where burned these false signal lights luring him out of his depths—to know that there was nothing twice the same, that the door closing was not the door opening, that the door opening was not the door closing, or that the door opening once was not the door opening again, that the way up was not the way down, that great clouds reassembled not themselves, and great mountains dissolved like the smallest clouds spilling their uncertain fountains of rain, and many pages of the book of life had been transparent. Perhaps he had drifted far beyond the margins and was lost in sheeted clouds. He was like some old ship reeling in the wind without masts or sails or rudder, following the eye of the wind which was itself like one far light upon the water.

Perhaps he was not of this margin, canon, text. Perhaps he was the apocryphal firefly shining far beyond the edge of this world and its shadow, the firefly seeming the star, the indicator of the star where no star was, the shoreline where was no shoreline beyond this light or darkness edged by moving sand and foam. Or else every step took him to another shoreline. Were there not places which were neither of the water nor of the land, neither of the land-locked water nor of the water-locked land, neither one nor the other, places which could not be defined? Were there not places so ambiguous that they shared the characteristics of both? Surely, many an old sailor plowing the waves with his white sail had been engulfed, and many an old farmer voyaging upon the star-flowering meadows which seemed to churn as if with foam or old, skull-faced surrey-driver tacking with his lean-boned horse in the tacking wind had gone down, being suddenly swallowed up by that earth which swallows the horse and the rider and the carriage and blackened carriage lamp, no light burning to starboard, larboard, and many an old mariner chartlessly drifting over the body of his sleeping wife, over her hills of snows and valleys of shadow and snow-crowned pinnacles and still lagoons, lost like the white emmet in the snow storm, aimlessly drifting like the butterfly over sand or over mirrors of illusion had gone down, even like the child who seeks his mother and finds her, finds her in a sudden avalanche of moon and sun and stars. He finds her where all are lost. Many a man had disappeared, as Mr. Spitzer knew. As for himself, he was merely the dream of the dream or the reflection of the reflection as were the Big Dipper and the Little Dipper, the sand like a thin shell laid over the water in which a flame burned under a sky like translucent dragonfly wings through which the light shone, the turreted sea shell and the sea shell smooth as the egg of the bird, the sea shell thin as paper worn thin by waters and sands and wind's abrasions, the sheeted jellyfish over which the star moved, the sail upon the sand and the white wing of the bird in the white fog and its fluted pinions like stairways to heaven and its burning eyes, bird wound around by the shell of the fog, bird unborn, bird never to break through the shell of night, and he was nothing of himself when these reflections passed, and there would be no image of him in a spurious creation where the waves rolled to thinning filaments and the stars faded upon a chalk-white shore. Who should remember his shadow billowing or diminishing or the gold and silver lights pricking through him or burning like candle flames or burning in his eyes or the casket of his lighthouse sleeping on his finger when he was gone, the writings on his cloak, the writings of mutes for the ears of the dead, its hemline of silver or gold wandering upon the surf and the sand but never of one world? He was not the book of life, not even the book of death with the mother-of-pearl bindings like the wings of mollusks worn so thin that none should know where consciousness slept as water flowed into water both to write and to efface the messages from the living to the dead or the dead to the living or the living to the living—was but a moment's passage, was a handkerchief dropped from the hand of God, a shimmering web or net or seine, a winged island mooring upon the flood, a light upon the finger of God, a light upon the water, a light going out, a shadow increasing—was not the Holy Writ but was the mere flyleaf stuck between two passages or testaments, the Old and the New, was stuck between the patriarch and the cloud or water bird, between the opening and the closing, was like a film laid over every eye and a web laid over every face, a mere whisper, a sob where was no word, was stuck between the millstone above him and the millstone below him, was like the feathered millet seed drifting between the zenith stone trembling over him and the nadir stone trembling under him where these thin waters flowed, was ground to this fine dust, was almost parchmentized, was almost pulverized, was caught between the penumbra and the penumbra, between the snow and the rose, the light and the light, darkness and darkness, star and star, world and world, a sheet so thin that illuminations of silver and gold shone through him like candle flames at the sea's edge casting their elongated shadows or fire medusas big as cart wheels burning almost upon the surface of the water which was this minor firmament or like the stars pricking through the clouds, the language of the stars passing like the eyes of birds through lights of silver and gold, the nesting stars and the stars over the stars and the stars under the stars, the dolphin sleeping on the papery rock as it cast its rainbow upon the cloud, the long-maned horse with its flying mane through which the star shone, its hooves which gave off sparks, cups of silver and cups of gold and prisms and spots of gold and rainbows streaking these dead eyes, the shrouded rider through whom the firefly shone like the lighthouse beyond this world or the light of the fisherman's boat like the star upon the waves or fleets of nautiluses turning their sails, and yet there would be no writing when he was held like the obliterating light against the obliterating light, light without shadow, no minaret which had written him spiral after spiral and chamber after chamber and song after song and wave after wave as he had written no minaret, no vehicle of lonely music, no word, sign, mark, image in the silent flood, and there would be no star of this world in memory of him, none to mark his passage, no rose, mouth, door, flagstone, peacock in his garden, tower, dome, stairway, no water-mark, no signature, no name, and not even his little lamp-lighter firefly shining through the mother-of-pearl dusk. There would be not even the moth small as a fingernail which had moored upon the margins of the book and had not moved when the pages turned enormous as sails of windmills casting lights and shadows. His little firefly was his key of gold, his clasp upon his mantle, the light upon the sand. His little firefly was the light he read by. His little firefly was the soul of the dead. Perhaps his little firefly was all there was.

Had he not always said so, even when thousands of lights pricked through him and his heart roared and he heard ten thousand doors opening, closing, slamming in the wind? So he was cautious beyond necessity, knowing that he had already passed like the shadows trembling over the sand, the cloud as fine-grained as the sand blowing in his eyes, his many eyes, and he advanced but uncertainly, step by step. He walked like that murmurous tide which, as it is coming in, is also somewhat uncertainly going out, turning upon itself, being of many invisible movements and many which were inaudible, subsiding in order to rise, rising, trembling to fall in long cascades with its long-fringed shadows or lights of dying gold, advancing to retreat, there being a movement of retreat within each movement of progress, a counter-movement accompanying every movement, a movement of uncertainty, of hesitation, of retardation never to be clocked, and he walked with a lonely ripple as he whispered, perhaps outside a stranger's door. He advanced as he retreated and knocked upon the silence of every heart, he being of the silence although he cried, cried like an old town crier where no town was. There were always these double movements, he knowing not who passed over him with his shadow like the great huntsman passing at the far zenith of the glassy sky with his dogs leashed by sidereal fires and his stars like flying tassels of gold, gold lights upon the sea, the sand, the sea burning to fire, the sleeping marsh land, doors opening, closing when the great huntsman passed, passed over him, water dripping when the great water carrier passed, and sometimes he heard the dogs barking like the tide nipping at his heels. Sometimes the quail which had slumbered in the long grasses arose before him like a tide or like a tide subsided, even like his heart into the silence. If he took eight steps forward, then he must retrace his steps by six in order to see where he had been even although that place had moved and whispered in its passing upon this shore of broken hourglasses where was no hour or faceless mirrors which had drifted out of silent rooms, rooms without walls, and many an old boat which had been moored upon a river bed from which the waters had departed would be wafted as by a stream of light or by a word. Many would depart. This life was extended perhaps only one mournful moment longer than he lived, many pebbles rolling in the dried-up streams shining with light, and he might hear the tremblings of a single lute string in a cloud, and this ghostly after-thought like a presentiment of future life where there was none clouded every mirror and darkened every light. And yet some might live in the night who had not lived in the light, he sometimes dreamed, or there might be those gleaming cells which knew not death or life or these definitions, knew not whether they lived or were dead, for perhaps no messages had ever arrived, and they were like the scarlet pimpernels folding at the first approach of rain or like sea urchins who knew not whether they lived or were dead or were sleeping—or if they knew, we knew not that they knew, and they knew not that we knew not that they knew not. Perhaps all human beings were also mystified, even as Mr. Spitzer was. It seemed he heard the barking dogs in clouds or the tremblings of jangled lute strings long after he was dead or when the light shone no more in the eyes of birds or men.

Perhaps the light shone in the eyes of women when there was no man. Ah, he remembered that tall, staggy woman walking with a long slope and many sparks and many orbs shining through clouds and many janglings as of tree-top antlers played upon by wind as the starlight streamed like a river over her head, and he remembered how she had struggled in the flood. She had drowned in her bed. For those who drowned not in the sea are drowned on the shore. From an old suffragette captain tossing on her bed he had learned much, from her whose name was hyphenated, perhaps at that very time she had lost her love, from her for whom the hyphen was more important than the two names it joined, joined as man and wife, as starlight and star, for the hyphen was all, from her who long ago had paused in a broken melody and would not take up her music in this life. Perhaps she would take up her music in this death. She had died before he knew, before he had come with his arrangements by which to deceive the chaos, before he had placed her with her head pointing North and her feet pointing South that she might sleep according to the turning of the earth on its imaginary axis or the flights of birds, birds going North or South with rustlings as the window curtains blew in a still room and the snow fell. So solitary her life had been. How could death be different or provide any great change for her? Her mind had died before her heart had died. Her heart had followed after her mind, little doubt. She should have passed over the borderline without paying a toll—as one who had passed many times before, as one who had gone and had not returned, as one who had already paid that small coin which was the sun shining through a cloud. For surely life had been this darkness for her. So he had written this nocturne.

Perhaps his sympathies always would be with those who had missed their loves, with those who had missed their loves on lightless street corners or clouded mountain peaks, with ladies who had lost their skirts —surely not with those who had not lost their skirts as some might say, as that great lady might have hoarsely cried in self-contradiction when she was struggling with a sheet or riding her bed as if it were a boat with white chargers—before she was capsized, before she drifted sheetless, anchorless—and his sympathies were with musicians who had lost their harps, bridge-menders who had lost their bridges and tonnages of tiny bells in the gathering fog, cargoes of sunken spires, spires under the water, great warriors who had won every battle but the last which must be fought in bed even like the first which they had also lost—great lawyers who had lost their clients for whom they had drawn up testaments and wills leaving their properties which were never theirs to leave, perhaps to unknown husbands, wives, sons, daughters, loves such as he had sometimes turned up in his lonely walks like sea shells left by the tide or mushrooms growing under rotted logs or mushrooms starring the shadows or white narcissus flowers gleaming upon the grass where God had dropped His handkerchief—Mr. Spitzer having come upon some remarkable instances of the non-existent leaving their non-existent properties to the non-existent whom he had traced for years through clouds before he had found out that they were not real or lived only in dreams like the breathings of dying stars—it seldom being his fate to deal with that which was real in life, and he could remember no such instance which would have startled him as if it were unreal, unreal by contrast with the environment and, therefore, alone—and perhaps he had not chosen these dying people—and yet perhaps he was drawn by such extended cases although he had not chosen them, was magnetized by such dreamers seemingly choosing him to be their executor of last effects and vanished castles with their lights shining suddenly through clouds and mountain peaks hooded by clouds and snows and bridges over viewless abysses and lunar lakes, places never visited by man—places forever clouded like masks masking masks—and his sympathies were freely given to all who had suffered some great disaster—to those great maritime insurance brokers whose ships had all gone down in a single whirlwind spiralling from pole to pole for a hundred years, fire insurance agents whose houses all had burned by the sea burning like the dead eye, great doctors who had lost their patients, gamblers who had lost their dice, racers who had lost their horses, handicappers who could not tell the outcome of a race in prospect or in retrospect, musicians whose works would never be played although the music which passed into oblivion as when the snow fell on the roof or the rain flooded old porches was more beautiful than any which should be heard, and Palestrina should not be more beautiful than the spotted tree frog, shrivelled and small, sleeping in a tree hollow. For he would awaken. But Palestrina awakened not.